Cynthia Roberts ... Glamorgan, and ... Porthcawl on the ... which provides the setting for her novels. She has been a teacher and a journalist, and is the author of four previous novels.

The Fox-Red Hills

Cynthia S. Roberts

HEADLINE

First published in 1991
by HEADLINE BOOK PUBLISHING PLC

First published in paperback in 1992
by HEADLINE BOOK PUBLISHING PLC

10 9 8 7 6 5 4 3 2 1

ISBN 0 7472 3783 2

Printed and bound in Great Britain by
HarperCollins Manufacturing, Glasgow

HEADLINE BOOK PUBLISHING PLC
Headline House
79 Great Titchfield Street
London W1P 7FN

To my sister and brother-in-law
Joyce and William (Bert) Haigh,
this book is lovingly dedicated.

Chapter One

As Rice Havard's mare breasted the hillside that sheltered Great House, the autumn mist was already closing about them. It dropped lightly as a veil, and as silently, its moisture deadening the horse's hoofbeats and the thin, wild cry of the windhover which rode the hilltop air.

There was a fierceness in that cry, a sad forsaken quality he recognised, for he heard its echo within himself. The hunter returning home: weary, triumphant, blood lust sated. Havard's mouth twisted wryly as he took a hand from the rein to scourge the dampness from his springing black hair and his lashes. He would as soon not be returning home. There was nothing to beckon him with Rhianon dead.

He turned the mare abruptly upon the narrow track edged with the skeletons of ferns, their brittle bones cracking beneath her hooves. No, he would not return yet awhile . . . Could not! This land was his. These rounded hills and fertile valleys, the streams and cataracts, the greenness and mists, were in his keeping. With them he had inherited the scattered farms and cottages, the great estate, the people themselves, their burdens and demands, their very labour and flesh. Yet this brought no comfort. He was a rich man, but poorer than the least of those mean wretches condemned for life to some squalid hovel or to pauperdom.

He had been a proud man, powerful in his arrogance. He had thought himself armoured against hurt, protected by custom and birthright. Yet how bitterly had he been

1

humbled by grief. All that sweet loving gone to waste, warm flesh stilled.

'Rhianon!' The cry broke within him, and he knew by the mare's startled nervousness that he called her name aloud. The word came back to him, blurred by the hills and mist, a whispered mockery. He was filled with rage and despair.

He sought no victim save himself as, with a quick surging of resolve, he set the mare to gallop. Wild and terrified, frenzied as he, she answered to his mood. Her hooves flew recklessly over grass and fern, heather and thorn. She cleared ditches and streams, barred gates and dry-stone walls, lungs burning, heart pounding at her ribs. Higher and higher, wilder and wilder, until her heart burst within her breast and, with a cry, she fell to earth. Beyond the broken stone wall, Rice Havard opened his eyes wide, but saw only darkness. Blindness or death, he wondered, or the mist filling his eyes, damp as if the air itself wept. His lips curved into a smile. They would be the only tears shed. He felt a terrible coldness settle upon him, as though all that was warm and living within him flowed into the earth beneath and was already part of it. He knew no fear. No pain. Only a calmness, the satisfied weariness of a hunter returning at the last to his home.

Within the servants' hall of Great House, the household staff uneasily awaited his return. Few liked him, for he was a surly man, in spite of all his youth and handsome looks, and given to swift and unpredictable rages. He bought their obedience, but not their respect, since times were lean, and work, even labouring upon the farms and roads, hard to come by. Only those who had known him before the mistress's death in childbirth pitied him and held him in affection for what he had once been. There were but two whom he trusted and who, in turn, kept him in respect: the old manservant, Prys, and the housekeeper, Mrs Eynon.

Her title was a courtesy, for she had no family and no home, save Great House. She had been a foundling child, living upon her wits and what she could beg or forage, until, one day, despair and hunger had driven her to Great House.

Rice Havard's grandmother, glancing from the window of her room, had remarked with pity the pauper child's malnourished frame, the bare flesh of her feet bloodied by stone and briar. The child, believing herself unseen, had carefully smoothed her ragged dress, then practised a hesitant curtsey. Sophia Havard had ordered that she be brought within. She had given her work and, later, a name, Jane Eynon.

There had been children to watch grow, to tend, and, sadly, some to watch die, even Rice Havard's wife, who was scarcely more than a child herself. The Havards were all of Jane Eynon's family, and her devotion to them as natural as if linked by ties of blood. Yet, of them all, Rice had been her darling, her love. Reckless, handsome, charming, she had tended him as her own, neither indulging him nor sparing disfavour, yet understanding, and forgiving all. Of all who ever knew him, she was the one who loved him for what he was, not for what she would have him be.

Jane Eynon, coming now to take her privileged place at the fireside in the servants' hall, felt strangely, unaccountably depressed. None would have known it, for the years had taught her to hide her deeper feelings under that mask of expressionlessness which is the hallmark of the archetypal servant of others. If it gave her a reputation for hardness and lack of emotion among her peers, it did not worry her. She cared more for the services she rendered to the Havard family than the good opinion of others. Yet if the newer, younger servants sometimes mocked her, in secret, for her obstinate loyalty to those who, like Rice Havard, seemed undeserving of it, then they did so with feelings of awkwardness and shame. It was they who felt demeaned by her devotion, and their guilt made them like her no better. Yet there was not one amongst them, throughout the years, who had claim to cavil at her

3

injustice, or was rebuked without cause. As Sophia Havard had done from their first meeting, they respected her for her integrity and recognised in her some goodness perhaps lacking in themselves. So it was that they afforded her a grudging respect and she became arbiter of all their squabbles and imagined ills, and often, in her presence, they aspired to being kinder and more charitable than they might otherwise have been.

Not, however, today. The cook, a florid, raw-boned woman with a surly manner towards the kitchen staff, was banging lids and utensils petulantly, and scolding all within her hearing. The scullery and kitchen maids scurried about like timid, frightened shrews, inventing work to keep them occupied and out of range of her restless hands, for she was not above handing out a well-aimed clout at any whose sloth offended.

"Tis no wonder I grow vexed and irritable!' she exclaimed to no-one in particular, 'when meals are prepared, then left to rot, uneaten! It is a wicked waste of good victuals and effort!'

A passing scullery maid mumbled swift agreement. 'The master is a sore trial!' she persisted vehemently. 'Upon my oath, I have never seen his like! There is no depending upon him – no, not from one day to the next! He comes and goes like a flittermouse or a moth.'

'And is as partial to the bright lights!' agreed a young footman, anxious to ingratiate himself with the cook, who was apt to reward her favourites. 'From all I gather, he is more concerned with gaming and whoring than with his farms and tenants.'

'As you should be, sir, with your duties!' Rice's major-domo, Prys, had come unnoticed into the hall, casting a troubled glance towards Jane Eynon at the fireside before continuing his tirade. 'If you have no work, and nothing to do save belittle your betters, you were better employed elsewhere, at another's expense! It can be arranged!'

The footman flushed at the rebuke and mumbled apology before self-consciously hurrying without, gaze cast down

4

that none might see his humiliation. The other servants, mindful of Prys's supreme authority, scurried about even more nervously, and the cook sniffed and proceeded, less boisterously, with her labours.

Hywel Prys, splendid in his liveried uniform, moved quietly to stand beside Jane Eynon, who gave him a barely perceptible nod of gratitude for his intervention.

'I am afeared for him, Mr Prys,' she said, 'for his troubled mind. There is no knowing what might befall him. The fog and . . .' She left the words unspoken.

'If he has stopped at some inn, ma'am, with friends, might he not forget how that time passes, if the company is congenial? He has little to amuse him here.'

She sighed, flexing her fingers with their gnarled joints, and then let her hands fall helplessly to her sides. 'No, you are right,' she allowed quietly. 'There is little to draw him home, save . . .' She glanced cautiously towards the cook who, despite seeming occupied, was listening intently. 'You think there is truth in the rumours that there are other women? Gambling debts?' she continued, so quietly that only Prys could hear her. 'I fear that he wines too freely, for I have seen him barely able to sit astride his mare, and helped from the saddle by a groom.'

'And if he spends his time thus, is it a wonder?' asked Prys in the same quiet tone. 'It is forgetfulness he seeks, not drunkenness, and the one is but the means to the other.'

'Yet it will lead to his downfall . . . kill him at the end. I fear for him, Mr Prys.' Her eyes were bleak with hurt. 'I fear for him with all my soul!'

Prys, who had served as many generations of Havards as she, put a reassuring hand upon her shoulder, clasping it firmly, as if his strength might flow into her, and she glanced up at his face, thanking him wordlessly. Aware that the noise and activity in the room had somehow diminished, he looked up and, seeing that all eyes were watching him, pretended to be absorbed in brushing at his already immaculate gold-braided cuff. When he spoke, it was to

5

address the cook with chilling authority, his tone brooking no argument.

'You will do what is required to keep Mr Havard's meal palatable, Mrs Hodges, for it is his time and his wishes which provide your livelihood; indeed, the livelihood of every one of us. Should you consider the victuals spoilt and inedible, you will prepare more, with neither ill-grace nor argument.'

'Indeed, Mr Prys,' she declared aggrievedly, 'I am well aware of my duties.' Her gaze faltered, and fell.

'Then it would serve more purpose if you were about them, ma'am!' he said. 'Meanwhile, since you are all so naturally concerned for the master's safety, I shall send out some of the stable lads and grooms with lanterns to light his way homewards. I do not doubt that he will do full justice to the meal you have so lovingly prepared.'

The abruptness of his tone was neither lost upon the housekeeper nor servants and they set to work chastened, if unrepentant, eyes sedulously averted.

'Have no fear,' he said to Jane Eynon in passing. 'We will find him and bring him home.' Alive or dead. The words sprang naturally to both their minds, although unspoken. His thin, cadaverous face beneath the sparse white hair was filled with warm concern. 'Have no fear,' he repeated, thinking even as he formed the words how ludicrous and unhelpful they sounded. Jane Eynon watched him go, grateful for his ready kindness. He was a good dependable man, she thought, and no woman on earth could ask for a better. None but she. Her lips twisted wrily. So many times he had begged her to wed him, pleading that he would be grateful for company in his declining years and would not ask for love, or even deep affection, simply to be with her would be enough. He was a man of loyalty and character. Why, then, was all her love for Rice Havard, whose weakness drove him to drunkenness and wild excesses of mood, and whose vices were best not dwelt upon in her mind? She knew the answer. The Havards were her flesh and blood, as if born. Rice was the son she never had: feckless, indulgent, sav... others.

She had made her choice, and Prys kn... she rested her hands upon the curved rail o... pulled herself resolutely to her feet. There was her bones as persistent as the ache of sadness in he... but she drew herself tall and straight – a handsome, up... woman, impressive despite her age and the frailty of her bones.

With the deepening of darkness, the candles were lit at Great House and set upon torchères, while the wax tapers upon the chained chandeliers in the main hall sent flickering rainbow-coloured light over the prisms and strung facets of crystal glass. Yet Rice Havard did not return. The grooms and stable lads who had been sent to search for him and light his way returned baffled and drenched with mist, yet secretly unconcerned. Rice Havard was, like as not, imbibing at some tavern or gin den, or more actively engaged at some whorehouse or cottage where the man was absent. Such diversions were only to be expected and part of the life of a gentleman of leisure or, indeed, any man who was red-blooded and did not lack for pence. It was their opinion that Prys thought likewise, but was intent upon humouring the housekeeper. Indeed, he was as much of an old woman as she, and Havard would give them little thanks for it should he be meandering homewards 'in his cups' and able to speak at all! No, it were best to leave a man be, whatever hi-jinks he courted, or incur his justified wrath.

By midnight, Prys himself had become concerned that some accident might have befallen his master. Whatever the repercussions, he would command a search party of all of the servants available and, if that proved fruitless, call upon the services of the tenants of farmhouse and cottage. It worried him that the grooms and stable-boys had followed every inch of the known tracks over the low mountains and hillsides and found nothing. The master would

himself by spending the night with some
of the streets, however befuddled by drink he
became. He was too wily and openly as circumspect as
society and convention demanded, whatever his secret
vices. No, his absence boded ill. Prys was convinced of it.
Should he be proved mistaken, then explanation and apology should suffice upon the morrow. If Havard ranted and
raved at his interference, then it would be but a brief storm
and would soon pass over. He would sooner offend his
master than Jane Eynon, and that was a fact which invited
no argument.

The cobbled courtyard without Great House grew noisy
and crowded with all who could be swiftly gathered from
household, stable and estate. Summoned by word of ostlers
and grooms, men came mounted or on foot, armed with
lanterns, ropes, staves and grappling hooks, or simply
carrying billhooks and hedging and ditching tools; anything
to hand which might serve them in their search.

Prys was to ride out at the head of a small group of
horsemen, and gave clear instruction about summoning aid
should Rice Havard be found, whether alive or dead. A
single shot would suffice to call upon the aid of others.
Havard's doctor had been alerted and would ride with Prys
and, with them, two grooms and a pair of sturdy shire
horses supporting a makeshift carrier of hide, mounted
upon two stout poles, such as was used for coffin bearing
for the cottagers. If there were labourers among them who
felt uneasy at its presence, then none spoke of it. They
were a taciturn people, made superstitious by isolation and
custom, and kept their own counsel.

The bailiffs gave grim warning of the hazards to be faced.
They should keep only to the known paths, for fear of
marshland and bog, or disused bell-mines and quarries
overgrown with brambles and scrub. They must be constantly alert to gullies and streams and those iron-jawed
traps primed against animals and men.

The searchers listened in silence, faces grave and strained
in the lantern light, then rode out upon their way.

The clatter of hooves upon the cobblestones, the footsteps of the running men, their calls, and the dancing lantern lights drew a child to the huge window set above the yard. He was but ten or eleven years of age, and his face showed pale in the guttering light of the candle he held within the chamberstick. There was terror and confusion in his eyes, but curiosity too, and a fleeting excitement at witnessing so rare and unexpected a chase. Rice Havard's son, awakened from sleep, stretched high upon his bare toes, voluminous nightgown twitched awry as he strove to take in every detail of this unprecedented scene, seeking to imprint it indelibly in his memory. He glanced briefly towards the carved half-tester bed where his brother, Mostyn, lay drenched in sleep, fair hair outspread upon his pillow, thumb in mouth for comfort, curled fingers concealing his nose. Then Carne Havard's attention returned to the glorious disorder without. No, he would never forget the vivid pace and bustle of it all, seen through a gauze of mist that softened and diffused the chaos of lantern beams, lending it the gentle unreality of a dream. The horses' hoofbeats, blurred and diminished by distance, the muffled cries of the men, the jostling, swelling joyousness that surged from below surged as triumphantly within him, and he wanted to be there in their midst, or better yet, at their head as leader.

'One day . . .' he sighed and turned away. One day, the lands and all upon them would be his to command, and he would ride out valiantly when need arose to protect his estate and the horses, and the beasts of the field, and his own people . . . and Mostyn. His brother was scarcely more than an infant, and shy and timid as a girl, fearful of his father's swift rages. Carne knew that his father hated the child, but he knew not why, although he had thought about it long and hard, to no purpose. In Rice Havard's presence, Mostyn stammered and wept and once had grown pale and trembled upon the edge of a swoon until his nurse had been called upon to 'Take this brat away, clear of my sight! He will never make the shadow of a man! His foppishness and girlish ways offend me!' The nurse, as all the other servants, had unprotestingly done as she was bid and was careful that he did not again stray uninvited across his father's path. Mostyn had been but one and twenty months in age, and Carne had thereafter shielded him from the worst of Rice Havard's wrath and his drunken excesses. It grieved him that the two of them were so distanced when he knew, without doubt, that despite his father's changed ways, the old bond of pride and loving still tied him to his elder son.

There was little Carne recalled of his mother, for she had been dead these six years and more, but his remembrance was of a gentle sweetness enfolding him and the warmth of soft flesh and a strange ethereal beauty which, try as he might, he could never recapture in his mind. When Mostyn had come to the house there had been nothing but a thin helpless cry, a wailing, as if a small animal was caught in a trap. It had been a harsh stormy night with a restless keening wind so that, when that single, anguished cry had rung out, Carne could not be certain that it was not an echo of the tempest without the house. He had started fearfully from his bed and run blindly into the passageway outside, stumbling upon his nightgown in his clumsy haste, anxious only to seek the shelter of his mother's room, although it was forbidden. He had battered upon the closed door with his fists, breath sobbing in his throat, hearing his nursemaid's shrill cries behind him. It was Rice Havard who had come swiftly out, shutting the door, barring it with his outstretched arms, then gathering Carne to him, rocking them both in an agony of grief. Carne had been frightened to see that his father wept soundlessly and he knew that some unspeakable horror had come to them although he could not give it name. His father had surrendered him to his nurse's arms, and she had carried him away, bewildered, and resisting fiercely, wanting to be at his father's side. Had his father crept to his bedside that night as Carne lay asleep? He thought it was so, but could not be sure. Yet the words whispered came to him now with painful clarity, 'She is gone. I hate and curse myself,

10

and him, for what we have done.' Carne had struggled to open his eyes but his eyelids were forced down with the heaviness of shed tears and weariness. 'We shall have only each other now. We must try to make it enough.' The hand that had lain uselessly upon the coverlet was lifted and he heard the opening and closing of the door.

Carne was older now and knew that, although he had tried as hard as he was able, it had not been enough. He hoped that Papa did not blame him for it. In spite of all, Carne loved him dearly and was sure that one day, save for Mama's returning, everything would be as it was of old. He crept to Mostyn's bedside, his bare feet making no sound save where one faulty floorboard creaked a sharp protest, and stood looking down at him in the light of the taper flame. His brother's face was bland with sleep, the flesh rounded and pink as a babe's, eyelids blue-veined over the closed eyes. With a hurried glance at the door which led to the nurse's bedroom, and hearing nothing but the gentle noises of sleep, Carne stealthily crept outside, closing the door gently behind him.

There were subdued voices in the great hall beneath and he moved silently to the staircase, peering through the balustrade to the stone-flagged floor beneath. He saw Mrs Eynon with one of the older manservants, the man's feet awkwardly splayed, his hands crippled by some disease of the bones. There were others, too, whom he could not properly distinguish, for the candlelight from the chandelier and the chambersticks they held cast pools of light which served to intensify the shadows about them.

The great wooden door to the hall was swung open noisily upon its hinges, grating and scraping, setting his teeth on edge. Strangely, awkwardly, the men entered with Prys at their head, clutching his lantern still, while others unknown laid some heavy, obscene burden upon the stones.

With a cry that was torn from his throat, Carne half ran, half stumbled down the wide staircase, unaware of his chamberstick clattering to the hall below, and the candle spilling its flame and wax. Pain tore rawly at his chest as

11

he flung himself upon the makeshift bed of skins, and upon Rice Havard. Then Prys gently lifted him away as the circle of pale, anonymous faces closed in on him, fearful as hollowed skulls, to dissolve in his tears and disappear.

Jane Eynon, seeing the child's face and that of his father, so alike in their dark stillness, blur into one, felt a sadness greater than any she had ever known. With a weariness that all but broke her spirit, she gave orders that Rice Havard be set upon his bed and clean linen and clothing brought, for none must minister to him but she, who had tended his flesh from the day of his birth. She owed him that, and it was owed to her. None argued her right. Then, when all was finished, she took herself to give comfort to his sons.

Chapter Two

The clear bright crispness of an autumn morn brought no comfort to the few within Great House who held Rice Havard in affection. The atmosphere in the servants' hall and, indeed, throughout the whole of Great House, was one of shocked disbelief. Rice Havard had lived but two and thirty years. A brief, tempestuous reign. Yet he had died as he had lived, wildly, recklessly, fearing no man, and welcoming death. He might well have chosen it as an epitaph.

For those in Great House and beyond, life went on. The mist that had fallen with the coldness of evening shimmered and rose soon after sunrise, leaving the air refreshed. Carne Havard, watching its last vestiges from the high window over the courtyard, was aware of a sadness, an emptiness within. Yesterday he had watched the servants ride out, proudly elated by the jostling, thronging excitement of the scene. He had not wondered whither they rode, and why: to hunt a marauding fox perhaps, or some convict, or highwayman. If the thoughts had entered his mind, then they had faded and disappeared, swiftly dissolving as the mist on the fox-red hills beyond. He would not dwell upon what they had found, that strangely cold flesh, robbed of all life and vitality. The tears burned his eyes, and he knuckled them away with his closed fists. Was this what life was then? Wanting to ride out at the head of the chase, to own the land and the people; to be a man without, a child within? He walked hesitantly to the bed where Mostyn slept, his slumber deep and innocent of hurt. Perhaps what

13

Papa felt was nothing more than that, a deep sleep from which he would awaken elsewhere. He wanted him here, to take him into his arms and tell him that it would all pass, as quietly and unnoticed as the mist, and that the hills and all that he loved would stay for ever the same.

Mostyn stirred, struck out a fist in his sleep, and Carne heard him snuffle and watched him blink his eyes. He was scarcely six years old; an infant, no more. Yet, when Carne had been carried in Prys's arms to his bed, sick with loss and caring, Mostyn had awakened and come to stand beside his bed, eyes filled with fear. It had been hard to find the words to tell him of Papa's death. Mostyn had listened, face gravely intent, then he had smiled and clapped his hands, unable to hide the pleasure it brought him, dancing for the sheer joy of deliverance.

'He is but a child, Master Carne,' Prys had cautioned gently. 'Do not think ill of him. He does not understand.'

Mostyn had come to Carne's bedside to look at him. 'I am glad that it was not you, Carne,' he said earnestly. 'I would cry for you.'

Perhaps it was meant to bring Carne comfort. He knew that Mostyn *did* understand. It was that which grieved him most of all.

The servants of Great House went about their appointed duties with little enthusiasm, conscious perhaps that there was none, now, in true authority over them. Master Carne, although the heir and natural inheritor of the estates and lordship of Penavon, was scarcely of an age to undertake the responsibilities of a squire. That he would do so eventually was never in doubt, but how the property would be administered until he came of age was open to speculation, and speculate they did, without shame or restraint.

It was only to Hywel Prys, when they found themselves alone in a passageway where they could not be overheard, that Jane confided the true depth of her own anxiety. 'I do not know what will happen to any of us, should another

14

come to take Rice Havard's place,' she said dully. 'If there is some relation or guardian appointed . . .' She left the sentence unfinished.

'I cannot believe that we would be dismissed, Jane, my dear.' He was punctilious about affording her the respect of being addressed as Mrs Eynon before others, but now they were alone as friends, and his anxiety was all for her distress. 'We have been here so long, and served the family well. I am sure that they will beg us stay, for there is none who could arrange life at Great House better.'

'No,' her voice was bleak, 'we have been here too long, and are too old and set in our ways to take instruction from others.'

'But you would not desert Carne, for he has need of your guidance and, more, your love? I saw how, earlier, he clung to you so fiercely for comfort. He has had too little love, and that poor infant, Mostyn, less, I fear.' He shook his head ruefully. 'Rice Havard was a good man scarred by circumstance.'

She was swift to his defence. 'He loved Carne, of that I am certain, and would wish him naught but good. He would not willingly deliver him to any who would not care for him, and for the estate . . .'

'And young Mostyn?'

'Carne will protect his future, you may depend upon it. I do not think Rice disliked the child, but could not bear the full burden of Rhianon's death alone.'

'It is only a weak man, Jane, who would unload his grief and hatred upon a child.'

'One cannot love to order, Hywel!' The rebuke was sharp, angry. 'We are flesh and blood and human, not saints.'

'No, we cannot love to order, Jane.' There was regret and acceptance in his voice, and she felt a stirring of pity that she could not be what he asked. 'And if we are dismissed, Jane? What then?'

'The mistress, Sophia Havard, left me that small cottage near the mill, where her old nurse was tended until her

15

death, and a small annuity. I will survive well enough. And you?'

'I have spent little enough of what I have earned and my needs are few, save for those things which coins cannot purchase.'

He smiled wrily. 'Yes, I, too, will manage to survive.' He studied her carefully as he asked, 'Will you not pine for the children and, perhaps, sometimes, your work, and those who . . . have worked beside you these many years?'

'No, I will not have to pine for Carne and Mostyn, Hywel, for wherever I am, I will watch over them, and they may come to me at any time of day or night, for aid or comfort, for as long as I shall live, and they have need of me.'

'Yes, they will be glad of that.'

'As for losing my friends, should I be forced to leave Great House, then I hope that you, who matter most of all, will be there beside me at the last.' She put a warm affectionate hand upon his shoulder. 'The cottage will shelter two as comfortably as one, my old friend, although I fancy it were better if we were wed.'

He stared at her incredulously, his expression so comical that she could not but laugh aloud, then, remembering the occasion that had wrought her promise, her laughter was swiftly stilled.

'I am not sure,' he said haltingly, 'if I heard aright . . . and that you will accept my hand . . . or offer me yours in marriage? I grow confused with age, I confess, and my hearing sometimes plays me false . . . one of the harsh penalties of growing old!'

'You are a fine figure of a man, Hywel Prys,' she said crisply. If her memory returned inevitably to the dead man whom she had so recently tended, then she gave no outward sign. 'You will do, Hywel. You will do very well.'

'And you, my dear, are all on earth I would ask for,' he said simply.

She drew herself erect, and smiled at him. 'Then it is understood?'

'Yes, it is understood.'

They made to go their separate ways, before she asked impulsively, 'You know I have no parentage, none to vouch for me?'

'There is no need,' he said with quiet dignity. 'I cherish you for what you are. Like you, I have seen too many claiming to be high bred, who have damned themselves, and the past, with their living. We are what we have made of life, Jane, not what life and blood have made of us.'

'You are a good man, Hywel,' she said.

'And is it enough?'

'It is enough.'

Satisfied, he went upon his way.

Jane, watching Prys go, was painfully aware that he had not asked her what would befall were they to remain at Great House, serving the Havards as of old. She determinedly turned her mind to preparation for the funeral, banishing all other thought. She would have need of both tact and firmness.

Cook and her kitchen and scullery maids were abrupt and ill-tempered with the responsibility of preparing the funeral meats. There would be many august guests; noblemen and landed gentry needing refreshment, since they would travel great distances by carriage and the roads were rough and treacherous. Some must needs stay overnight, fearing to travel in darkness, and there would be rooms to prepare with all that it entailed, and meals to plan and order served. The yeomen and lesser functionaries, too, must be victualled, some, no doubt arriving fatigued upon horseback, others on foot. Then the details of the funeral ceremony itself, the church service, conveyances, and the coffin bearers to be instructed, the funeral coach made ready. Such feasting would bear more relationship to a celebration than a wake. Yet, beyond the grief, was there not cause for celebration? With Rice himself she should rejoice that he was freed of all worldly care, and knew the bright promise of eternity. She prayed that it was so, for

17

he had suffered long, and was deserving of that. Oh, but Rice Havard had been a stubborn child, arrogant, and with a wild streak of recklessness which even Rhianon had been unable, powerless, to tame. Carne was so like him in features and colouring that, with her failing memory, it was sometimes hard not to confuse the two. Despite what Hywel claimed, the inheritance of blood *did* matter. Like the characteristics of the flesh, it flowed through all, sometimes seeming hidden or lost, only to emerge with startling fierceness as time passed, and in another generation. A hidden river, flowing underground, only to emerge with renewed power and vigour. She could only pray that the wildness and self-destruction in Rice would not be handed down to Carne and Mostyn. She was an old woman, and it would break her heart. After them, she would care for no other Havard men; they would be the last she would look upon.

The living of the vicar of Penavon, the Reverend Penry Vaughan, afforded him scant pleasure for the people were generally vulgar and impoverished and he had not the experience nor, indeed, the desire to deal with them. Like many such incumbents, his living was in the gift of a member of his own family. Rice Havard's father was his benefactor and Penry Vaughan an inferior scion of the same illustrious family. Like many another receiving charity from a kinsman, however ungrudgingly given, he received it with resentment and ill grace. Demanding humility in others, he lacked it in himself, and burned with a corroding bitterness which made him singularly unfitted for the task he chose. Indeed, he frequently reminded any who was rash enough to listen that his ministry was not chosen by him, but thrust upon him. Perhaps it was not surprising that there were those among his long-suffering flock who might have said the same about him. Penry Vaughan was assuredly an inefficient and unloving shepherd of his sheep.

His arrival at Great House upon the death of his young kinsman, Rice, was less welcome than it might have been, although Prys, and then Jane Eynon, greeted him with traditional courtesy.

'And how is young Carne responding to his father's unfortunate demise?' His pale eyes were disinterested, dismissive of her as a mere servant. 'It is to be hoped he is taking it like a man.'

'No, sir. He is taking it like a child, as one would expect.'

He searched her face for any sign of insolence but, finding none, declared loudly, 'Then he must learn to control and fortify himself, Mrs Eynon. It will be expected of him in his new life. It would be a mistake to pamper the boy and encourage weakness.'

'You wish to see him, sir? To talk with him?'

'Talk?' He seemed genuinely perplexed. 'Why ever should that be necessary? Has he not a tutor and his lessons to occupy him?'

'I thought, sir, as a clergyman and kinsman, your sympathy might lend him comfort.'

His glance warned that it had been a gross impertinence on her part. His voice was as coolly dismissive. 'I am sure, Mrs Eynon, that you have plenty to occupy you . . . affairs of a domestic nature, which you were employed to undertake.'

'Indeed, sir, my duties are as well defined and pressing as your own.'

'Then you have my permission to leave and be about them. You may abandon all else to me. I am a member of this bereaved family, as I need not remind you, and need no instruction.'

'If what I have said offended you, sir . . .'

'You are not in a position, ma'am, to offend me, save by overreaching yourself. I fear that Rice Havard's defects in character made him a lax, over-indulgent master.'

'He will be much missed by me, sir, and others,' she said truthfully, 'for what he strove to be. I beg you will excuse me.'

He watched her leave, his eyes coldly appraising, before he mounted the staircase to the chamber where Rice Havard lay. Vaughan's lean, austere body, angular and fleshless, was a true reflection of the man himself, she thought. He was lacking in all grace and sympathy, a sour defeated man, ill-equipped to be a priest, for he lacked common humanity.

Chapter Three

The funeral eve had been cold and comfortless. In a clear sky, the stars glittered as abrasively as the hoar frost which, by dawn, had settled hard upon the grass. Carne Havard, in his bedroom above the courtyard, tried to peer out at the first cold streaks of daylight. The window pane was crusted with a shimmering rime and his thumbnail, gouging its crispness, sent down a shower of powdered ice. His breath upon the glass cleared a tiny hole, its edges thinning as gently as a mist from the earth.

The landscape without was as bleak as he and the faded colours of bracken and scrub upon the hills beyond brought him no pleasure. He had always thought of the hills as his own; his special, secret place, remote and swift-changing as the sky beyond. Now, with Papa dead, they were truly his. He owned them. Yet, did he? Some long-buried memory struggled to surface, something strange and disturbing. Shadowy, elusive, it pricked at the edges of his mind . . . Yes, he recalled it now . . . Papa upon his chest-nut hunter, and he in the saddle before him. He must have been young, for Papa's arm encircled him very tightly, and he had spoken the words which Carne had not quite understood.

'These mountains are mine, Carne. I love them, for they are all that is home to me. I claim to own and possess them, but no man can do that. It is they which own and possess *me*. Do not let them trap you as they have trapped me. You must learn to run wild and free.'

Carne had smiled and nodded his understanding, lest his

21

father think him childishly stupid, but the only picture in his mind was of a fox he had once seen, coloured like the mountain ferns, and running, running; beautiful from tapering snout to streaming tail. The next, and only, time he had seen it, it hung, torn and savaged, from the huntsman's hand, its blood smeared upon his childhood flesh.

'Oh, Papa, Papa!' he wept, while Mostyn stirred uneasily in his bed. Suddenly Carne hated him, and Great House, and the wild red hills, and the dead fox, and all that reminded him of what could never come again.

The house servants below had been busy long before sunrise, and would very likely be labouring still when the sun went down. There was an uneasy quietness within the house, the sounds of daily toil and chatter muted. It was strange, Jane Eynon thought, that there was a tangible atmosphere accompanying death, a quietness like no other she knew. People spoke in hushed whispers, a reverence in their tone, as if they might rudely awaken the one who would stir no more.

'And there shall be no more death, neither sorrow, nor crying, neither shall there be any more pain: for the former things are passed away!' The biblical words sprang, unbidden, to her mind. 'Passed away', so gentle a phrase for the violence of death. She dressed herself slowly, feeling that age and tiredness within her bones that she resolutely hid from others.

Penry Vaughan had granted Rice a resting place beside his wife and the generations of Havards who had gone before. Yet he had known as certainly as she that his cousin had wilfully abandoned life. It was true that none could prove it other than accident. Had Vaughan been prompted then by pity, or the need to keep inviolate the family name? And did it matter? No, all that mattered was that God should comfort him in the shelter of His arms, as she had held him so fiercely to soothe his childish ills.

'Dear God!' she begged, sinking to her knees beside her iron-framed bed. 'If he died by his own hand, do not let him linger for ever in darkness. It would be too cruel. Let him be joined again with Rhianon, whom he loved. Look kindly on his sins. I am a simple woman, without learning, and cannot properly read nor write but I have learnt that you are a just God and merciful. Be merciful to him.'

She rose awkwardly to her feet, clutching the bed frame as support, then fastidiously smoothed down the pin-tucked bodice of her black dress and fastened the chatelaine more securely about her waist. Reassured that no stray wisp of grey hair escaped the confines of her house-bonnet, she opened the door of her room and, with back severely erect, walked out into the passageway, and the day.

Carne's small clothes and his funeral garments had been placed neatly upon the wooden butler stand beside his bed. She had made sure that they were immaculately laundered and pressed, as befitted a young gentleman and the next squire of Penavon.

Carne came quietly to present himself for inspection and she studied him long and hard, saying finally, with proud satisfaction, 'Yes, you will do well enough. You will not disgrace us, I think.'

He hesitated, his expression grave and undecided, before blurting, 'Would you be good enough to see that Mostyn is dressed fittingly, Mrs Eynon, if you please, else he will wear anything gaudy which takes his eye.'

She strove to hide a smile, lest she offend him, saying carefully, 'Do you think it wise that he should attend the funeral, Master Carne?'

'Yes. He must ride with me, ma'am. I am firm upon it. It is our place, for we are nearest kin. It is perhaps all he will recall of our father, and it is better that he should not forget.'

'You will take someone with you then, to sit beside him in the carriage, lest he grow tired and fractious, and have your own tutor beside you?' she asked in concern.

'No, ma'am. I will have none beside us in the coach, save you and Mr Prys.' He stood stiffly, uncompromising in his fine clothes, a child in the garments of awkward

23

manhood. She nodded, for her throat was too constricted with pride in him to speak. She would have loved dearly to gather him to her and wipe away his hurt, but knew the time was long past. 'You will tell Mr Prys?' he asked.

'Yes,' she said at last, 'I will tell him.'

'What is to become of us, Mrs Eynon, Mostyn and me? I do not think I am ready yet to take Papa's place.'

'I do not rightly know, Master Carne.' He deserved her honesty. 'Mr Prys bade me tell you that when you return from . . . when we return, there will be a meeting with Mr Walters, the attorney-at-law. You will be required to attend. I can tell you no more than that.'

'Will you and Mr Prys be there?'

'No. We will not be invited, for we are servants, Master Carne, and it is a place for family alone.'

'Papa's cousin . . . Mr Vaughan. Will he be there?'

'Yes, I dare vouchsafe, for he is your kin.'

'I do not like him, Mrs Eynon.' Carne's voice was shrill, uneasy, to her ears. 'He treats me with contempt and has no affection for my father or for me. When he is near, he makes me stupid and tongue-tied, for that is what he believes me to be.'

'Then you must not give him that satisfaction.' Her reply was crisp.

'I cannot seem to help it, ma'am.' The admission was torn from him.

'Then you must remember that Great House is yours. You are squire of Penavon, and owner of its lands and all else. You must remember it and be proud although never less than caring, you understand?'

'I understand.' He hesitated before urging fiercely, 'You will never go away from Great House, Mrs Eynon, unless, like Papa, some accident befalls you? You will not willingly leave us . . . Mostyn and me?'

'Whatever comes, I will stay near enough to help you.'

'Have I your promise upon it, ma'am?'

'You have my promise.' She stretched out a hand and gently touched his dark hair. He came close to her for a

24

moment, burying his face in her dress, arms clasped tight about her, as if afraid to let her go. Then, suddenly, he was gone without a word.

Carne was seated in the Havard coach, with its liveried coachman and postillions, the family crest in gold upon its doors. Prys, splendid in his uniform, was seated rigidly beside him and, upon the leather opposite, Mrs Eynon was with Mostyn. Mostyn's legs were pushed out straight and his fair hair was curled and ringletted like a girl's, his soft underlip thrust into a mutinous pout because Jane's hand held him firm, impotent to peer without.

All along the mile or so of highway to the church, the respectfully silent crowds stood lining the narrow highway, the labourers in their best Sunday clothes, hats doffed and held against their chests, heads bowed low. Some wore armbands of mourning crepe and, from old custom, many dropped to their knees to recite aloud The Lord's Prayer as the cortège passed by. The women, who were few in number, wore dark clothes and bonnets, some with heavy falls of crepe, legacy perhaps of some earlier family bereavement. There were infants cocooned in shawls, with others pulling at their mothers' skirts, clapping and shouting aloud in glee to see the beplumed horses pass by. It was an event and an adventure; an occasion to remember without sadness through the years, for none in that crowd truly mourned him, although they paid him homage.

The funeral coach had come to a halt without the lychgate to the churchyard and the family coach drew up behind it, with Mostyn noisy and over-excited. Mrs Eynon had to catch him roughly by the shoulder and jerk him to obedience. Her bonnet had been pulled roughly askew, and her usually serene face was hot and flushed.

'You are like a river eel, Master Mostyn!' she exclaimed in exasperation, 'all wriggling nonsense.'

'Mostyn!' Carne's voice was low, but held such fierce warning that his brother was immediately stilled. 'Whether you are six, or six and thirty, it makes no matter,' he

25

declared. 'You will behave, and give Papa's funeral the dignity it is owed. You understand?'

Mostyn fidgeted and sniffed, lips jutting petulantly, but he nodded.

'Then remember it, for if you do not, and bring shame upon us all, I shall box your ears until they ring!'

'I shall be good, Carne,' said Mostyn after considering awhile, 'but I would sooner ride home in the glass coach, that all may see me pass. Those horses have feathers on their heads.'

Above Mostyn's head, Jane Eynon's gaze met Prys's, bright with ill-suppressed amusement as she pleaded with him silently not to speak harshly to the child. He nodded, as if she had spoken aloud, and descended from the carriage first, so that, with the postillion, he might more easily assist them down.

Carne, holding himself straight and tall, looking to neither right nor left, followed behind the estate workers who bore the draped coffin within the church. They walked slowly, moving with care, for the burden of the dead man and the heavy, richly carved oak of his casket made them wary of the uneven flagstones of the pathway. Once, one of them at the coffin's head stumbled awkwardly and all but fell to his knees.

Penry Vaughan greeted them stiffly at the church door, his lean cadaverous face drawn into a mask of piousness. 'I do not think, Prys, that it will be necessary for you to accompany my cousin to the family pew. Carne is not needful of a servant's support. He is old enough to practise self-reliance.'

'Mr Prys, sir, is here at my behest, because I count him a friend.' Carne's voice was courteous but firm. 'I will be proud to have him beside me.'

The clergyman looked discomfitted, but made no further demur since the boy was plainly set upon it, yet his expression grew even more remote and chilly as he moved forward to greet the rest of the mourners. The gravedigger, an ancient with curved spine and a face ravaged by some disease of the skin, held out his gleaming spade to tempt their coppers. Prys handed a pouch of small coins to Carne and the boy heard them clatter sharply upon the metal before the old man muttered thanks, and stooped with awkward haste to pocket them.

With Jane and Mostyn beside them, they made their way to the Havard pew, the vast and echoing emptiness of the church, with its vaulted roof and rich stained-glass windows, awing even Mostyn into silence. The pew itself was canopied and deeply carved, with tasselled cushions of red silk and tapestried kneelers bearing the family crest. For a time, Carne concentrated his gaze on the garlands and swags of delicately wrought flowers, fruit and cherubs until Mostyn declared with piercing truth that the carved children wore no breeches! When Carne finally looked towards the draped coffin there was tightness in his throat and his eyes pricked with tears so fiercely that it was as if a needle had been thrust within. The coffin blurred and faded; the tapers shone with sudden points of starry light. The stained-glass colours of the arched windows merged into falling petals, then into rainbows of shimmering brightness. Yet Carne's tears did not fall but trembled behind his lashes. Jane Eynon, seeing his brave struggle to keep them unshed, felt her own eyes burn with hurt. She watched him deliberately widening his eyes and biting hard upon his lip to compose himself. She looked away, lest her pity shame him.

Oh, but it was a cold service, Prys thought, and dry for lack of tears. The Reverend Penry Vaughan was a man without warmth or human charity. He had greeted the nobility and landed gentry as equals, affording them the benefit of his unctuous civility. Those of lower rank or achievement were addressed with reserve or condescension according to his estimate of their influence and worth. No, Penry Vaughan was less a man of God than of Mammon, Prys thought. He would be of scant comfort to those poor, needy souls who called for him in sorrow, or in dying.

'In my father's house are many mansions . . .'

Despite himself, Prys could not prevent a dry smile. 'Yes, mansions there would be aplenty, for those at ease in drawing rooms and library. But for the poor and serving classes? No doubt, the Reverend Penry Vaughan would banish them for the sake of tidiness to hovel or stable loft where they might labour usefully still. Blessed are the meek, for they early learn their appointed place!' And Rice Havard's place? Prys, glancing towards the coffin, then at the set tearless face of the child beside him, could only pray that God would be a merciful and loving father, to the living as to the dead.

Without, at the graveside, Prys stood watchfully at Carne's side, fearful that the formality and strain would bring the child low. Should Carne falter, then he would be at his side to lift him and carry him to the waiting carriage where his grief might decently be hid. Yet Carne did not falter nor weep overmuch, his body rigid and unyielding as the winged figure in stone which marked the mausoleum of the Havard dead.

Prys would have turned the boy aside from entering the tomb but Penry Vaughan had already taken firm hold of Carne's arm and was urging him within. Prys followed swiftly, undeterred by the clergyman's command that he remain without. As the coffin was laid within the sarcophagus prepared for it, and the great stone lid closed upon it, Carne swayed, his eyes and small fists screwed tight, as if he could bear no more. Then Prys was at his elbow, brushing the priest roughly aside in his concern and leading the child into the cool fresh air.

Jane had let fall Mostyn's hand and would have rushed to comfort Carne but Prys shook his head in warning. Distressed, she rounded unfairly upon Mostyn who was absorbed in wiping the damp earth from his shoe-buckles with his fine linen handkerchief. Jane jerked him to his feet more roughly than he deserved and his surprised cry drew the stares of all about them.

It was while they were thus distracted that the unknown

woman ran from the edges of the pauper crowd, dishevelled and filthily clad, eyes strangely wild. She stumbled towards Carne, with none seeking to detain her, for every man's instinctive reaction was to recoil. Even Prys found himself rooted to the earth, repelled, unable to make mind or limbs respond. She raised her hand and a glint of metal showed briefly, trapped in the light. The terror in Prys's throat was released in a cry as he ran to halt her, knowing, even as he found strength to move, that he was too late. The woman had already hurled the object away from her and was grovelling at Carne's feet, weeping, crying aloud, wiping at his boots with her disordered hair, kissing the ground where he stood. The collection of coins she had thrown clattered noisily within the open mausoleum, striking the steps clearly as they fell and finally coming to rest upon the stone floor of Rice Havard's tomb.

'I give you back their silver, Rice Havard! I need no payment.' She had risen to her feet, unmindful of Prys's restraining hand. She looked about her, wild-eyed, unseeing, face tortured with such pain that all about were shamed and stilled. 'I loved him! I loved Rice Havard. How many of you can say the same?' There was contempt and scorn in her voice as she looked defiantly about her.

'I loved him.' Carne's voice was barely audible, his face composed and unafraid. 'I thank you, ma'am, for coming freely. It was a kind act.'

None spoke as labourers rushed forward to secure the woman and lead her roughly away, spent and unresisting. A small, dark-haired child of some seven or eight years of age ran forward and angrily fought her way to the woman's side, scattering all with her flailing fists, daring any to approach the woman who stood bewildered now and fearful of what she had done. The girl led her gently away, her eyes first meeting Carne's, and filled with hostility and fierce arrogance.

When they were within the carriage, Carne turned to Jane Eynon, demanding, 'The woman, Mrs Eynon . . . the one beside the grave . . . she said she loved Papa?'

29

Jane glanced at Prys before replying carefully, 'There are few in Penavon who would not . . . recognise or know of their squire, Master Carne.'

'Will she be coming to the house then? Returning with the others?'

'No . . . I fear she is but some poor woman, deranged by some misfortune . . . a pauper, perhaps, and lunatic,' her voice faltered and died away in awkward silence.

'And the girl?'

'A pauper too. I have seen the child before. When I visit the poorhouse.'

'Then I beg you will take them both some coins and funeral meats, and see that they come to no harm. I would not have them punished for keeping Papa's memory.'

Jane looked again at Prys, helplessly. 'It shall be done as you ask, Master Carne.'

Chapter Four

Great House, despite the tragedy of the death which drew the visiting mourners to it, was a scene of quite incongruous liveliness and speculation. The main thread of whispered conversation returned again and again to the scandalous presence of the pauper woman who had grovelled at Carne Havard's feet, declaring her passion for his dead father.

Jane Eynon, supervising the dispensing of victuals and refreshment to those who must soon be upon their journeying, found her ire rising, although she tried to remain expressionless. 'They are like birds of prey,' she thought disgustedly, 'crowded over a newly dead corpse and tearing at flesh and vein, each determined to feast upon some choicer morsel than the rest. For all their preening and strutting, that is what they undoubtedly are: carrion; scavengers of the dead!' She moved between the crowded hall and dining rooms, unobtrusive, anonymous, but missing nothing. At an almost imperceptible signal from her, glasses were refreshed, victuals offered, trays replenished. Every need was anticipated and met, even before it became apparent to any other. She glanced about her anxiously for sight of Carne and saw that he was engaged in conversation with an elderly dowager who was regarding him with ferocious concentration through her raised lorgnettes. Prys, who was standing near Carne, ostensibly superintending the smooth functioning of the affair, looked up, and nodded his assurance. Satisfied, Jane took up surveillance elsewhere. Prys would ensure that the boy was not grieved by ill-considered gossip or maliciousness. The events of the day had given him hurt enough, God knows!

Of the woman who had so publicly claimed to love him, Jane knew nothing save that she was a pauper-woman, fallen like many another upon evil times. Yet she had shown the courage to return the few pence paid to her by the guardians of the poorhouse, although she would rue their lack and, doubtless, the punishment merited by her crime. She was a woman of spirit, such as Rice Havard might have admired, and she might even have shown beauty once, as well as fire. Yet he had loved no woman save Rhianon; a gentlewoman honed and smoothly polished by convention and birth. Such was the way of the world, and men. The rich and the poor were separated by insuperable barriers of birth, speech and class, which could not be breeched or surmounted. It was an immutable fact of life, and best accepted first as last.

As for that child who had rushed to the crazed woman's defence, physically routing all who would have laid hands upon the pathetic creature, Jane feared that her reward at the poorhouse would be measured in blows and deprivation. Whatever befell, she would do as Master Carne ordered and take them whatever sweetmeats and *bonnes bouches* could be spared. Also some coins to replace those so extravagantly thrown away. Thirty pieces of silver, the thought came, unbidden and painful, to Jane's mind. How much had Rice paid her for his betrayal of her? Would it have sobered him that, at his ending, she, in turn, had not betrayed him, but publicly humiliated herself? Jane felt old and tired, filled with confusion. Tomorrow, come what may, she would go to the poorhouse, where she was well known and made welcome. The pauper girl she would watch over sedulously and, if occasion presented itself, bring her into the kitchens of Great House, that her future might be kinder than the present. It was what the child's courage deserved.

With a start she recalled herself guiltily. Those mourners who had travelled but short distances would be returning directly to their houses, taking leave of those who must remain to be given bed and board. There was much to organise and, more immediately, the visiting flunkeys, well victualled in kitchen and scullery, must be sent to attend upon the departing carriages and their demanding occupants. Jane Eynon, always the archetypal servant, calm and seemingly devoid of intrusive emotions of her own, set about her manifold tasks. Master Mostyn, she reflected, amused, had managed to wheedle those funeral meats he so coveted, knowing that no servants would dare to challenge their betters.

He had railed and wept upon his banishment to the nursery until some smuggled dainties from cook had swiftly restored his humour, and his rage and tantrums were soon forgot. But Carne would suffer within, and none must know of his hurt.

When Carne, too, had returned wearily to his bed and the last of the guests and their servants had departed to their bedchambers, the house seemed to have grown unnaturally silent and chill, despite the lighted tapers and the huge fires of logs, their crackling and glowing sparks diminished, falling to grey ash. Jane, watching the last of the silver cleared, and the platters being carried to the scullery, stood for a moment reflecting upon the dying embers of the fire and the day. She pressed her aching head for coolness against the white marble of the chimneypiece, believing herself alone and unobserved. She felt unutterably weary and drained of emotion and Prys, entering unseen, was grieved by the defeated drooping of her shoulders and the deep lines of sorrow upon her face.

'Jane?'

She turned, startled, the habit of long training immediately making her stand erect.

'It has been a long day,' he said gently, 'and one without respite from work or care. A joyless day.'

She nodded, saying dispiritedly, 'I would as soon tomorrow were over too, that we might know what the future holds.'

'It will hold no lessening of my affection for you, my

33

dear, whatever else befalls,' he promised quietly. 'I will always be here.' He hesitated before adding, 'Or wherever life may lead.'

'Yes, Hywel, and I am glad for that comfort. I know that you will be a rock and a refuge to me, as you have been to Master Carne and me this . . . this endless day.'

'It will pass,' he said gruffly, 'as all else.'

'Yes, it will pass as all else,' she repeated. 'Happiness and sorrow, pain and loving, even life itself, Hywel. Yet it will leave its mark upon all; a scar to remind us.'

On the morrow, it was with understandable relief that Jane Eynon finally saw the last of the carriages depart, luggage safely stored upon the box, its occupants lavishly provided with victuals, wine and ale for refreshment upon the road. Then, with a sigh of gratitude that naught had gone amiss, she slowly returned to the house and her duties. Already preparation for luncheon must begin, for the attorney-at-law, Mr Randall Walters, was expected, and he dined lavishly.

After a meal not memorable for the congeniality of the diners, for their minds were overburdened with thoughts of the reading of the will to follow, it was Penry Vaughan who first arose, with a meaningful glance at his pocket watch and a murmured comment about the time he could not spare. With some reluctance, the attorney abandoned the port for the less salubrious refreshment of the library and Jane reflected that seldom could there have been a more ill-matched duo than the clergyman and the man of law. They differed in every particular. The Reverend Penry Vaughan was lean, ascetic, the very incarnation of rectitude; as spotlessly severe in dress as in habits. Mr Walters was grossly overweight, indeed, excessively gross in every respect, yet, curiously, he was the more appealing of the pair. There was a warmth and humour in him which Penry Vaughan lacked. Walters was self-indulgent, certainly, but tolerant of the foibles of others.

Carne had been summoned to accompany the two gentlemen into the library for the reading of the will; an ordeal from which Mostyn had mercifully been exempted. To his cousin's annoyance, Carne had insisted that Prys be beside him to lend him support and, despite remonstration from Penry Vaughan, he would not be swayed. The clergyman's anger and sarcasm only served to make the boy more adamant and, since the attorney made no objection, Prys was sent for and allowed to accompany the boy. The episode had increased Penry Vaughan's irritation and, by the tightened line of his mouth and jaw and the rigidity of his stance, Jane feared that it boded ill for Master Carne.

When the attorney-at-law was ensconced behind the large partner's desk of the library, and the Reverend Penry Vaughan and Carne seated before him, with Prys standing alongside the boy's chair, the preamble and will reading began.

Prys was afraid that after the strain of Rice Havard's death and the fierce toll taken of Carne emotionally by the interment, the exposition of the will might be too cruel a reminder of his loss. Yet the boy sat upright and dignified, thin face intent, his narrow shoulders carefully erect under his elegant coat. The Reverend Penry Vaughan seemed unusually animated, as if infused with a strange nervous excitement which he was unable to quell. No doubt he was expecting some small bequest from his dead cousin, thought Prys. Such greed and cupidity were not fitting in a man of the cloth. Not fitting at all!

There was a great deal of tedious and convoluted legal mumbo-jumbo to be sat through, including numerous modest bequests to servants and staff, including Jane Eynon and Prys himself. Master Carne, he observed, seemed to be drooping with tiredness; emotionally spent, and no doubt as bored and confused with the dry pedantry of the legal phrases as he.

Then, suddenly, Prys was alert, sensing in the attorney's changed manner a curious reluctance to continue. Several times he stumbled over words, voice thin with nervousness. He halted altogether on one occasion, plump cherubic face so moist with beads of sweat that he was forced to wipe them away with his pocket handkerchief. No sooner had he done so than they returned to glisten more fiercely at hairline and lips.

Master Carne, too, seemed to have stiffened and grown apprehensive, determining in the attorney's awkward embarrassment some incipient threat. Penry Vaughan alone remained untroubled, indeed, abnormally expansive and self-possessed. Prys tried in vain to make sense of what was being expatiated but the words were simply a jumble of unrecognised words and phrases, obscure and meaningless. He damned himself for being so dull and slow-witted, ashamed of his ignorance, and aware that Master Carne fared no better at comprehending either the words or the gist of it. Then, suddenly, Mr Walters laid aside the legal documents, polishing his eye-glasses assiduously, regarding them minutely, as if the words he sought might, by some miracle, have become engraved upon their lenses. 'So, Carne, my dear boy . . .' he was explaining avuncularly, his plump face shining with heat and embarrassment, '. . . the crux of the matter is . . . well, to put it baldly, there is very little money surviving, and no prospect at all of retaining Great House.' As the silence grew oppressive, he rushed in awkwardly to blurt, 'I fear that your father's . . . ill-considered investments and extravagant life style have rendered you all but penniless.' He arose clumsily from the desk and came to stand beside Carne, corpulent, uneasy, his face ugly with real concern.

'I do not understand, Mr Walters.' Carne's voice was thin, childishly bewildered. 'How can that be, sir? There are the farms and properties, the land.'

Penry Vaughan's cold tones made incisive reply. 'It is perfectly simple. Your father was a profligate, sir, a common gambler. He wagered away the roof over your head, your inheritance. There is no way around it.'

'I do not believe you, sir!' The denial was harsh and instinctive.

'You are impertinent, boy!' Vaughan's voice was

controlled, quietly expressionless. 'I speak none other than the truth, as the attorney-at-law has testified.'

'The boy is clearly distraught, sir,' Walters protested, 'and it is no wonder, for he is but a child, and has lately lost his father and all that is of comfort and value to him. He is in need of friendship and compassion, not vituperation!'

'He is of an age to understand and accept facts as they are!' returned Vaughan brusquely. 'It does him no service to cloak his father's betrayal and dissolute ways in pretty euphemisms. He did not make "ill-considered investments" as you testify; he squandered his substance upon gaming and whoring. Let us be clear about it.'

Prys, shocked, and cruelly conscious of Carne's distress, was angry enough to interrupt with, 'I think, sir, that Master Carne had best be taken to his room, if you will allow it. These past days . . .'

'No. I will not allow it. Nor will I be dictated to by a common steward, a menial in my . . . in the boy's house, or while it briefly remains in his keeping!'

'I will take him nonetheless.' Prys faced the clergyman calmly, refusing to yield or drop his gaze from Vaughan's. There was no concealing Vaughan's fury; his gaunt face was suffused with choler, the sinews of his neck engorged and standing proud of flesh, even the small veins of his eyes were reddened.

'It seems, sir, that you have not understood. I have been appointed Carne's legal guardian.' With difficulty, Vaughan controlled his voice. 'He will do as I instruct and you will remove yourself from this room, and from this house. Your services are no longer required.'

'I think, sir, that you are being unduly harsh,' the attorney interjected reasonably. 'We are all affected by the tragedy of events. When we are . . . shocked, not thinking clearly . . . we are apt to behave out of character, make ill-considered judgements. I am sure that Prys has only the boy's best interests at heart . . .' He broke off helplessly.

'His opinion, as yours, sir, is of no relevance or concern to me. Your part in this affair is ended. You may take your leave. The child is in my care, under my jurisdiction. There is no more to be said.'

Carne, pale-faced and trembling, was looking desperately from one to the other, swaying upon his feet with exhaustion and bewilderment. Prys, disregarding the clergyman's cold fury, ran to his support, lifting the boy effortlessly into his arms. He would have carried him without, but the door was barred by Vaughan. Walters had come to stand beside Prys, his plump rubicund face alarmed as he laid a restraining hand upon the servant's arm, cautioning quietly, 'You had best do as Mr Vaughan says, Prys. It would not serve to raise a hand to him, for I fancy that is what he intends. Provocation would be no defence in law, although, God knows he has offered enough. Do not, I beg of you, give him that satisfaction, else Carne will be punished as surely as you.'

Prys hesitated, then nodded. 'If you will bring him a chair, sir, that I might set him down.'

Walters reached at once for one of the chairs before the desk and carried it to where Prys and Vaughan stood regarding each other with open hostility.

'It will do no good to treat the boy as a milksop!' Vaughan's voice was scathing. 'He must learn to face up to life! There will be disappointment in plenty ahead of him. He would do well to be prepared.'

Walters thrust him aside with contempt as he set down the chair, declaring icily, 'Carne is eleven years old. I know of few who have met such grief in so short a space of time, or who have borne it with more fortitude.'

As Prys turned away to settle the boy, Walters said deliberately beneath his breath so that Carne would not overhear, 'It seems to me, sir, that his present misfortune will be as nothing beside his future with you. You are a man without kindness, devoid of all pity and understanding but I warn you that I shall keep watch upon him – and you.'

'I have no fear, sir, of your foolish blustering or idle threats!' said Vaughan dismissively. 'You will stand aside that I may speak to my charge.'

The attorney's plump-fleshed face grew flushed with indignation and he blinked rapidly behind his lenses, but he stood aside.

'Now, sir,' Vaughan addressed Carne, who, face ashen, skin bathed with moisture, was sitting upright upon the chair, held firmly by Prys's supportive arm. 'You had best stand upon your own two feet, as God intended. You are not some namby-pamby girl to be cossetted and made foolish. Stand up, I say!'

Carne struggled with difficulty to his feet, bravely spurning the attorney's kindly proffered arm and facing Penry Vaughan. He closed his eyes briefly, swayed, then vomited copiously over Vaughan's elegant brocade waistcoat. That gentleman made no demur as Prys wordlessly lifted Carne and carried him out into the clear air, the attorney having prudently held wide the door of the library. He exchanged a swift, triumphant glance with the old servant as Prys bore the child gently away. Then, returning to the clergyman, Walters declared, 'I beg you will excuse me, sir; my duties are sore pressing.' He gathered his papers importantly from the desk top, adding, 'You were right, sir. The boy should not be made to look foolish.' He smiled irrepressibly. 'As you say, it was clearly God's will that he be made to stand upon his own two feet. We can but give praise that the Almighty moves in mysterious ways.' His bow to Vaughan was courtesy itself.

Chapter Five

The shock and disbelief which swept through Great House at the revelation that Rice Havard had gambled away his fortune was no less fierce than at his death, for no-one, from the greatest to the least, was untouched by the tragedy. Jane's immediate protectiveness was for Carne, and she consoled him as best she could, but her heart ached, too, for those servants in her charge who would be reduced to paupery. There were some, frail and near-impotent now, who had grown old in the Havards' service. They could look to neither shelter nor work, for who would employ them? There were others, like Megan, the conscientious little scullery maid, barely thirteen years old, and sole breadwinner for a widow and her young brood, whose future would be bleak indeed without her meagre wages and those few morsels scavenged from the kitchens of Great House.

Despite Jane's outraged tears at Prys's unfair dismissal, and her entreaties that he stay at Great House to lend her support, Prys would not be swayed. He quitted Vaughan's service upon the instant, piling his few possessions upon a handcart from the stables to seek lodgings in Penavon village.

'I can do nothing for Master Carne. My staying would merely serve to set his cousin more firmly against him and he would bear the full brunt of Mr Vaughan's malice,' Prys argued with conviction. 'It is better that I go for, if I stay, I could not promise to keep my hands from that . . . devil's throat, and devil he be, for all he is a clergyman!'

'You will take care, Hywel, tell me how you fare?' Jane begged anxiously.

'You may depend upon it, as you may depend that we will be wed as soon as we are able, if that is your wish.'

'Yes. That is my wish.' Her voice was firm, her gaze steadfast, although her eyes were soft with tears. 'It is all in life I have to sustain me, Hywel. That, and my affection for Carne and Mostyn. When you return, I shall be waiting and ready.'

His leave-taking of the servants was subdued and seemingly emotionless for he was a man not given to words. Yet Megan, the scullery maid, and others had wept openly, and the cook who had battled dourly against his authority set a large, raw-boned hand to his shoulders, saying, 'You are an honest man, Mr Prys, and a fair one. None can dispute it . . . no more that you are a man of spirit.' Her voice grew rough-edged with awkwardness. 'You will be missed. Sadly missed . . . There is not one among us who does not wish you well.'

Jane had watched Prys leave, dressed unfamiliarly in the one good suit of clothing he possessed. Despite his fine figure and bearing, his hands upon the handles of the cart were the hands of an old man, liver-marked and gaunt of flesh. Yet she had never felt more pride in him, nor deeper affection.

Upon his bed Prys had set his beloved uniform, frogged with gold braiding, well tended, immaculate. Jane lifted the sleeve and held it to her cheek tenderly, as if his warm presence lingered within it still and would give her courage to face what must come.

One week after the reading of Rice Havard's will, Penry Vaughan summoned the household staff and servants of Great House to attend him in the main hall. He announced that the house was to be closed and they must needs remove themselves and their possessions within three days. At the murmur of disquiet and bewilderment which greeted the news he held up a hand, as gauntly forbidding as he. 'There

41

will be no exceptions on account of sickness or age, no recompense,' he declared. 'I will not take upon myself responsibility for the sins and omissions of one now dead. There must be no argument; no recriminations. The matter is ended.'

Jane, distraught at the prospect of so soon losing Carne and Mostyn and at her inability to ease the despair of those forced into homelessness, thanked God for Prys's stability. She could depend upon him. He was the one fixed and shining light in a world suddenly grown dark.

Yet when he had driven her out upon the makeshift cart drawn by an ancient mule, first sight of the isolated cottage cast her down again. It had lain empty and neglected for so long that its windows were filthy and broken, birds had nested in the torn holes of the roof and the door swung drunkenly open, sagging upon rusted hinges. Jane's cry of anguish released all the pent-up fury within her.

'It is a ruin, Prys! A wreck! Scarce worth the bother of owning! We had best turn the waggon and go!'

'Now, my dear, do not take on so!' he rebuked. 'It is true that it is in sad need of repair but it is well built of thick stone and its roof is of the same good slate as Great House itself.' He put an arm protectively about her shoulders and kissed her cheek. 'Adjust your bonnet and I shall tether the mule to that hazel tree and lift you down. It would be too easy a victory for Penry Vaughan, should we return abject and homeless.'

'You are right, Hywel.' She set her bonnet straight, the chin beneath it firm with purpose. 'It was but the shock of a moment, I confess, and my petulance and weakness shame me.'

'No, my love, you are as liable to sorrow and to hurt as the rest. But I swear, Jane, I will work for you and protect you as long as there is breath within me and strength within my arms.'

'And I, my dear, shall aid and comfort you, putting you above all others in my heart, for you are deserving of the deepest, most loving, commitment.'

42

When he had set her upon the rough track, she lifted a hand to trace with tenderness the deep hollows of his face and the gaunt cheekbones, seeing with remorse the tiredness of his grey eyes and the deep-set shadows.

'You said loving commitment, Jane? I have never been sure that it was love which prompted your acceptance of me, nor that I am deserving of it, nor should expect it, for I am the most ordinary of men.' His eyes were intent upon her face, hesitant, but not openly pleading.

'Why, Hywel,' she said. 'I did not think it fitting to say the words aloud, for I have said them to no other.' She touched his arm. 'I shall say them now without shame or false modesty: I love you, Hywel Prys. I thought, my dear, that you knew.'

'But how, Jane, if you have not uttered the words?'

'As I know that you love me, my dear, in every look and word and action, for they speak clearly, and to me alone.'

He lifted her into his arms, she laughing and protesting like a hesitant girl as he carried her over the stone threshold to set her down in the dark interior of the cottage, which reeked of staleness and disuse.

'It is a beautiful place, Hywel, and I shall make it into a home to be proud of,' she said delightedly.

'Not beautiful, my love,' he declared, 'but not beyond redemption, I swear.'

Jane's eyes grew bright with affection and unshed tears as she said with honesty, 'With you beside me, Hywel, it will be very heaven on earth.'

Their return journey to Great House was made lively by Jane's excited plans and her instructions to Prys as to what was to be purchased upon the morrow for cleaning and scouring of the cottage.

'I shall pay Megan to help me scrub and sweep every inch of the place,' she declared resolutely. 'It will be a favour to me and a kindness to her, for she will be glad of the few coppers it will bring.'

'And I will hire a willing carpenter and a slater to make it dry and secure.' He hesitated, biting his lip, hands fidgeting

43

upon the reins, before asking abruptly, 'You will not be afeared to stay here alone, Jane?'

'Alone? How should I be alone?' she demanded, genuinely puzzled.

'We are not wed, Jane, and you must leave Great House within the week. It is best that I remain at the inn.'

'Indeed you will not, Hywel Prys! Let those who are vicious-tongued and evil-minded do their worst! If their lives are so empty that only such venomous tittle-tattle will fill them, then they have my pity! No. You will stay where you belong, with me!'

Prys could not help but admire her spirit, yet he remained uncertain about the wisdom of it. For the moment, he was so filled with pleasure at her avowal of her need for him that he was content to let the matter lie.

Jane's leaving-taking of her friends, the servants, at Great House was painful beyond even her cruellest expectations, for she had no life and no friends other than Prys beyond its walls. Her eyes burned raw with tears and she felt a sick emptiness as she gathered together her few possessions upon the bed, securing them into neat cloth-wrapped bundles. Mrs Hodges, who was to remain until the morrow, lingered uncertainly at Jane's side, reluctant to take final farewell. Her plump hands were clenching and unclenching, face flushed and made puffy with tears.

'An ending and a beginning,' Jane said quietly, and Mrs Hodges nodded solemnly, unspeaking. Her gaze, with Jane's, rested upon the stripped ugliness of the iron-framed bed. Suddenly, she hugged Jane to her, clumsy with embarrassment at so painfully revealing her distress, and was gone.

When Prys arrived with the mule and cart Carne stood, white-faced and rigid, with an arm laid protectively about Mostyn's shoulders, watching as Jane's bundles were lifted on to the boards of the cart. Jane walked over to them set-faced, fighting to hold back her tears, and took Carne into her arms. He stayed dry-eyed, body stiff and unyielding, as Jane said, 'I will keep my promise to you, my dear. I will stay near you. You have but to call upon me, and I will come.'

'No!' His dismissal was angry, born of rage and sorrow at her abandoning him. 'Mostyn will have *me*! I shall take care of him!'

Mostyn ran to her, burrowing his head into her skirts, arms clasped tightly about her. He was crying so desperately that, seeing his small body wracked with sobs, Prys climbed down from the cart to comfort him. But he would not be comforted and, evading Prys's grasp, ran wildly indoors, violent in his grief.

Jane made to go after him but Prys took her arm and whispered reassurance as he helped her up on the cart. Carne had spoken no word, but stood watching the cart until it was out of sight, not raising a hand in answer to Jane's anxious wave and farewells. Then, face wrenched by grief, he walked within.

Prys's hand closed comfortingly over Jane's but her throat was too constricted with tears to make a sound. There was a weight of sorrow within her chest, hard and enduring as a stone, crushing her with its violence.

'Weep, my dear,' Prys said, ''tis better so.' Yet there were no more tears to shed.

Carne tried to comfort Mostyn but Mostyn turned upon him in a frenzy of anguish, kicking out at him and beating his fists hard against his brother's chest before weeping quietened him. The face he raised to Carne was tragic in its bewilderment and raked Carne with pity.

'She has left because of me,' Mostyn said wretchedly, 'because I am wicked, and she hates me . . . like Papa!'

'No, Mostyn! She has left because Cousin Penry has sent her away. It is none of your doing.'

Still Mostyn was not convinced, and asked, 'You will not go away and leave me, Carne? You will stay with me always?' Mostyn gripped Carne's arm so fiercely that he felt the bones of Mostyn's fingers bruising his flesh.

'No, Mostyn. I will not leave.' Carne's voice was low with hurt. 'I will look after you always.'

'And you will like me, Carne? You will not hate me like Papa . . . even if I am wicked?'

'No. I will not hate you. Now, wipe your eyes,' he commanded gruffly, 'for it is childish and stupid to cry.'

Mostyn sniffed and blinked, then obediently rubbed his eyes hard with his clenched fists. Carne was filled with love for him, and irritation, and fierce protectiveness. Mostyn was all that was left of Mama and Papa; Carne's blood, his inheritance. They belonged together, and no-one and nothing must ever come between them.

Chapter Six

Carne, seeing the familiar coach from Great House and the coachman in Havard livery, felt a swift upsurge of joy, believing Penry Vaughan had relented and allowed their old servants to remain. Yet the coachman was no-one he knew and his cousin's coldly inflexible voice bade him, 'Step inside without delay!'

The coachman fastened Carne's and Mostyn's baggage beneath the retaining net atop the coach and, setting his tricorne straight, made his way back to his perch upon the box. He took up the reins and stirred the horses into life. We believe the rich to be inviolate and protected from all hurt, he thought wryly. Yet that child within the coach has nothing. He has lost all; home, family, possessions.

Carne, pale-faced, sat staring at the black leather upholstery of the empty seat beside Penry Vaughan. His head was held stiffly erect lest tears should fall. It would be the cruellest of indignities if his cousin saw him weep like a girl. He blinked and forced his eyelids wide, then took out his silk handkerchief and blew his nose hard, surreptitiously raising the handkerchief to his lashes before returning it to his sleeve.

There was a fierce noise and commotion without and the carriage shook and swayed before coming to a halt with such a violent jerk that Mostyn was pitched bodily to the floor, his anguished cries adding to the confusion. Vaughan impatiently leaned over and tugged Mostyn awkwardly to his feet, commanding furiously, 'Stop that infernal snivelling! Stop it at once, I say, else I shall give you something worth snivelling about!'

Mostyn, who had been wriggling and yelling in bewilderment, was temporarily shocked into silence as the clergyman savagely thrust the boy into Carne's hands before pushing his head through the window of the coach and demanding irascibly, 'Probert! What is the meaning of this? Explain yourself.'

'They are driving out the paupers from the poorhouse, sir, and forcing them to the parish boundaries.'

'Well, it is no affair of mine! Drive on, I say!'

'I cannot, sir, for the confusion and uproar. The highway is full of them and I fear some might fall beneath the horses' hooves or the wheels of the carriage.'

'Drive on! They will scatter soon enough when danger threatens. They care too much for their useless hides to linger!'

Probert flushed, then removed his tricorne. Fidgeting with it hesitantly, but still holding his ground, he declared stolidly, 'I think, sir, they are helping a young woman.' He glanced meaningfully towards Carne and Mostyn. 'She is . . . heavy with child and cannot be moved from the path of the coach.'

'Then turn the horses wherever you are able and return by the longer way!' Vaughan instructed tartly.

'Would you have me stop at the physician's house, sir, and summon his help? It is upon our route.'

'I have already given you instructions, sir! If you choose to ignore them, or feel unable to carry them out, then I shall take the reins myself.' His voice was harsh and inflexible. 'If you wish to leave my service, Probert, you have but to walk away.'

Probert replaced his tricorne, saying almost inaudibly, 'I will do as you instruct, sir, and beg you will forgive my foolishness.'

Despite the handsomeness of Probert's face and figure and the proud uniform, he looked shamed and diminished as he walked back to take the reins from the hands of a

48

villager into whose care he had delivered them. The noise and cries from without seemed to have intensified, the voices grown strident and menacing as Penry Vaughan anxiously raised his silver-topped cane to urge the coachman to be away. Probert could not find space enough to turn the coach, for every way was barred by the seething mass of people converging remorselessly upon it. Anguished, he leapt down from the box to command the villager at the bridle, since his voice could not be heard above the frenzied clamour of the crowd. Instantly, he was caught up in the surging, chanting throng, powerless at first to break through the sweating, jostling barrier of flesh which imprisoned him. Then, dishevelled, and his heart thumping with fear, he was miraculously at the door of the coach, screaming to those within not to venture out. Panic-stricken, he somehow turned and thrust and clawed his way back to his seat, fearful that if the horses bolted, the disorderly mass of men, women and children would be crushed beneath their flailing hooves. His tricorne had disappeared and his livery was torn but he paid it no heed, half pulling, half dragging the man at the reins up on to the box beside him. He could make no sense of the chaos all about him, for paupers, villagers, and those men with staves, employed to drive the outcasts away, were all one.

Within the coach, Carne held Mostyn close to his chest, cradling his brother to him as thuds and blows descended upon the bodywork of the coach. It swayed perilously upon its springs. There was a fierce crack of wood upon glass and a window shattered, showering glass upon the two cowering boys huddled together, arms entwined, unable even to cry out in their shock and terror.

Already a brawny hand was upon the door of the coach and Penry Vaughan, distraught and crouched in a corner, had not the will to beat the man off with his stick. Skin ashen and clammy with sweat and fear, his only thought was of the humiliating indignities he might suffer at the hands of so barbarous a mob.

When it seemed to Probert that, despite all his fears for

49

the crowd, he must urge the horses on, or those within might be set upon and killed, there was the swift crack of a pistol shot . . . and another. The crowd halted, terrified and confused, and in the strange silence the horses reared and plunged and would have bolted had not Probert and his helper strained every nerve and sinew to wrestle them under control. It would be hard to judge, he thought wrily, whether it was the horses or their handlers who trembled and sweated most.

The crowd now seemed more subdued, bewildered rather than angry, as they shuffled restlessly, awaiting explanation or orders. The voice which penetrated the coach was authoritative and commanding, with no hint of unease. 'Those who dwell in this village . . . I bid you return to your homes. There has been enough disorder and bloodshed.'

There was a confused murmuring and a spluttered oath of defiance from one more mutinous than the rest, who, finding no support, foundered into silence. Then, slowly, the cottagers dispersed.

'You, sirs,' said the same voice. 'You who are authorised to escort the paupers to the boundaries. I order you to dismount and lay down your staves. These are not villains or prisoners whom you berate and crush with your blows. They have committed no sin, no violence or treason. Their only crime is poverty. These are men like you, with wives and children like your own . . . not cattle to be driven before you like beasts, with sticks and curses. Allow them to go in peace, with quietness and dignity. They are deserving of that!'

As the men began to dismount, silent and shamefaced, and threw down their staves, another voice cried out, 'What ... my wife, sir? Her time is near and she can walk no more. If I leave her now, then how will she fare? How will she live with a babe to succour and none to take care of her? Yet, if I stay . . .' his voice trembled and broke and all the crowd felt his despair and helplessness.

'She shall be taken into the church and you may rest with her. She shall not be moved until the child is safely

50

delivered. You have my word upon it.'

There was murmured assent from the pauper as well as from the few villagers who had not dispersed but remained to help them. Then it was to those who had been empowered to remove the paupers that the man next spoke. 'Is there one among you who would take issue? Or would forcibly remove this man or his wife from this sanctuary? I ask him to speak now, that he may be named and stand up before you all.' There was a long awkward silence, but none spoke. 'Then I bid you go in peace, offering what help and friendship you may, one to the other.'

There was the sound of shuffling feet upon the cobblestones and the gentle clatter of hooves as the horses were led away, and curt incisive instructions from the unknown man who had calmed and dispersed the crowd.

Penry Vaughan who, upon hearing the shots, had rejoiced that the militia or yeomanry had been called upon to quell the disturbance, had by now grown restive. His pallor and fear abated, self-confidence returned, and he arose from his seat and peered through the broken glass of the window, crying, 'Probert! What in God's name holds us up now? Drive on, man! There is no impediment.'

Probert, who had climbed down from the box with the countryman beside him, declared quietly, 'They are removing the pauper woman, sir. She who . . .'

'Yes! Yes! I am aware of her condition! But who has shown the impertinence and rashness to order her within the church? It is infamous! A blasphemy.'

'It was I, sir.' The young man who stood beside the coach was some four and twenty years of age, fair haired, fresh faced, yet, despite his youth, there was an air of firm authority about him. He was dressed, Carne saw, in the clothes of a gentleman, but carelessly, without distinction, as though he had taken the nearest garments to hand, knowing that, matched or ill-assorted, they would hang upon him awkwardly.

'Morrish!' Vaughan's tone was icily dismissive. 'As a mere curate in this parish, sir, you have over-reached yourself. Such matters are beyond your province! You have neither title nor authority for such action! I am deeply angered. Yes, that is not too strong a word, sir, angered that you have created so extreme a precedent. Such matters should be referred to me!'

Morrish surveyed him in silence for a moment, a smile twitching at the corners of his mouth as he replied good-naturedly, 'I fear, sir, the time and circumstances were barely convenient.'

'You are impertinent, sir!' Vaughan flushed, declaring tight-lipped, 'Your actions were ill-advised. The church is no place for paupers, or women about to be delivered of child!'

'Is it not, sir?' Morrish's face was expressionless. 'You will forgive me that I had in mind another such journey, another such child . . .'

The gentle rebuke seemed to lay raw Penry Vaughan's dislike as he vowed with ill-suppressed anger, 'I shall lay the arrogance of your behaviour and actions before the bishop, sir, do not doubt it! I reiterate, I am your superior. You are responsible to me, and me alone!'

Morrish said courteously, his voice firm, 'You do well to remind me, Mr Vaughan, of whom I serve, I fear it is too easily forgot.'

For some reason which Carne could not fathom, this calm acknowledgement seemed to inflame his cousin the more and Vaughan declared testily, after gazing at Morrish with evident antipathy, 'You will see that the pauper woman and her spouse are removed as soon as you are decently able! Then you will explain yourself to me, sir, as soon as they are set beyond the boundaries of this parish. Only then will they no longer be a charge upon the poor rate.'

'Certainly, sir. I shall report to you as you ask,' agreed Morrish, bowing politely. 'Although, then, they will no longer be your parishioners and in your pastoral care as they are now. You will wish to speak to them perhaps?'

'My sole concern, sir, is to see these children, my young

kinsmen, safely within my own walls. They are my legal wards and I bear full responsibility for them,' Vaughan said coldly. 'My only fear has been for their safety. As for your problem with the woman in her labour, then you must deal with it as you think fit. You have brought this dilemma upon yourself, sir!'

'No dilemma,' Morrish was calmly unruffled, 'for Jane Eynon has agreed to stay with the unfortunate woman and a midwife has already been called to attend the birth. When all is over, she and her husband and babe will be taken to Hywel Prys's cottage for rest and comfort, until they are fitted for work hereabouts or upon the way.'

'You know Jane, sir? And Hywel Prys?' Carne cried out, excitement making him so far forget his manners as to interrupt the young man.

'Indeed.' Morrish gravely raised the silk hat which sat awkwardly atop his dishevelled fair hair. 'You have the pleasure of their acquaintance?'

'Yes, sir,' declared Carne with equal gravity. 'They are friends of mine and Mostyn's, this long time. Good friends both.'

There was an audible exclamation of disapproval from Vaughan but Morrish continued as if he had not heard.

'Then you are fortunate, sir, as are all who have reason to value their kindness.'

Carne nodded. 'I shall be grateful, sir, Mr Morrish,' he amended, 'if you will tell them that Carne and Mostyn Havard send their kindest remembrance.'

'It shall be done,' promised Morrish, smiling, and offering Carne his long, bony hand through the shattered window of the coach. 'Here is my hand upon it.'

'You have detained us long enough with your foolish inconsequences, sir,' said Vaughan stiffly. 'Pray withdraw your hand that we may be upon our way. We will waste no more words in idle chatter.'

He called out to Probert who had been standing uncertainly beside the coach with the farm labourer who had steadied the horses. 'Return to the box, Probert! We will

53

be upon our way. We have tarried enough!'

'Sir . . .' Probert came to stand awkwardly beside Morrish, embarrassed and inarticulate in the face of Vaughan's irritation.

'Well, man? What is it now?' demanded his employer.

'I thought, sir, you might choose to have a word with Tom Hallowes, who labours casually upon the farms hereabouts.'

Vaughan regarded him stonily.

'He has helped me freely, sir, and willingly, to calm the horses. For if they had bolted, then many would have been trampled underfoot and your own life, sir, hazarded.'

'Very well. Send him to me! I will speak with him.'

The labourer came reluctantly and stood, ill-at-ease, before the window frame.

'If you will call at my house tomorrow,' declared Penry Vaughan, 'I shall leave some coins for you with my man-servant. You may come to the kitchen door.'

Hallowes looked at him intently, then said quietly, without rebuke or arrogance, 'I would take no payment, sir, for helping another. It is my reward that the young gentlemen are safe. Thanks serve well enough in return.'

Vaughan, reminded of his manners by a palpable inferior, remained obstinately silent, although inwardly seething.

'Then *I* thank you, sir . . . for Mostyn and me.' Carne's voice rose clear and was filled with genuine warmth.

'My privilege, Master Havard, sir.' Hallowes' weathered face broke into a creased smile as Probert returned to his perch upon the box.

Peter Morrish raised his silk hat in acknowledgement to Vaughan, but his smile was for Carne as he turned to Hallowes at his side, shaking the old fellow's gnarled hand and declaring loudly, 'It is a rare privilege to be in the presence of a true gentleman, sir. I shall long cherish it!'

He was savagely aware of how little he could do for the dispossessed paupers, although he had striven hard to find work and shelter for those men who were able-bodied and fitted to labour upon the isolated farms, or at breaking stone for the highways. It was the aged and impotent among them which led him to despair, and the women nursing their babes, or infants clinging helpless and bewildered at their skirts. The men would fend for themselves, labouring casually wherever work might be found, and bedding down in barn, stable, ditch or sty. Yet the sick and crippled could not long hope to survive.

The return of the flotsam and jetsam from the wars, the vagrancy of those no longer able to find labour in the towns, the high taxes, the high prices and scarcity of food caused by successive bad harvests affected all. The farmers, unable to buy fodder or grain, let their land lie fallow; animals were slaughtered, labourers dismissed. Those in tied cottages were turned adrift. Entire families took to the roads and byways, hungry, seeking food and shelter, with little hope of finding it. None save the rich could employ them and servants and labourers could be hired for a pittance, grateful for shelter and their meagre keep. Women, widowed or abandoned, would sell themselves into whorehouses or the gin dens and children were bartered into prostitution or the slavery of chimneys or factories, with none to raise a voice.

'Dear God!' Peter Morrish thought, and it was a cry of rage from his soul, 'I can do so little! I am helpless! I do not know where I might begin.' He watched the sad, disordered procession of pauper-vagrants struggle along the highway, bearing their bundles, the few treasured possessions of kinder days, wrapped in cloths or Bristol brown paper. They wore the drab grey uniform of pauperdom, their clothing poor and ill-fitting, the children bare-footed and carried upon the shoulders of others, or dragging wearily upon the dusty way. Some of the men had removed their wooden-soled clogs and carried them beneath their arms or set them atop their bundles to save wear. For some reason, this final humiliation affected him more than all else: that they retained dignity and self-respect enough to preserve what little they possessed lest they find work upon the harsh journey to where they were born and must return.

Wearied in flesh and spirit, he walked with them to the borders of the parish of Penavon.

Upon the outskirts of the village, the quiet procession halted. They could hear confusion and fracas ahead and one of those in authority mounted his horse and rode forward to see what occurred. Morrish, frightened and concerned, ran hard behind the mount. The scene which confronted him was strange indeed. A woman in pauper grey homespun was firmly locked into the wooden pillory beside the stock and whipping post. The skirt of her long gown had ridden high above her bare ankles which were clamped, rigidly outstretched, within the bars. She could neither move nor rest her aching limbs, for she was forced cruelly upright, her wrists thrust forcibly through holes in a second board at a level with her breast. Her skin was blue-tinged with cold, and she shivered from some ague or exhaustion, teeth chattering, saliva and runnels from her eyes and nose making a rawness upon her chin. Whether she wept from weariness and hunger, or because her degradation was witnessed by others of her kind, Peter Morrish did not know, but he was filled with a murderous hate and disgust for those who would inflict such misery upon another.

Already a pauper woman was at her side, filling the chained cup from a phial of water within her bundle and holding it to the prisoner's lips. It spilled from the corners of her mouth and another woman ran forward with a rag to wipe her lips, cradling the poor wretch's head, soothing her matted hair. Morrish did not know if she recognised her helpers or knew even that they were there, so wild-eyed and feverish she seemed, and near to madness. The pauper who had offered her the water had taken off her shawl, a grubby tattered thing, and wrapped it round the exposed flesh of the woman's legs for warmth and decency when Peter Morrish ran forward, divesting himself of the one good jacket he owned and setting it about the victim's shoulders. He had not, at first, noticed the child asleep in the long grass alongside the pillory, barefooted, as all the others, and dressed in a ragged, cut-down dress that had once been a woman's. In the noise and confusion, she awakened with a start and a cry of bewilderment and fear, kneeling before the woman and clutching her hand protectively through the hole driven through the board. From the grubby dampness of her clothing and the smears of earth and tears upon her fierce pinched face she must have lain beside her, unwilling to leave her. He could not guess how long the pair had remained there but the old woman's dress was stained with urine at the skirt and the stench of excreta and vomit lay heavily about. Morrish found himself tearing impotently at the boards which restrained her, fingernails scrabbling upon the unyielding wood, until pain and reason sobered him. The other men had run to her aid, trying furiously to free her, but to no avail for the boards were padlocked and secured with iron chains.

There was a tension and resentment in the air which spoke of ill-suppressed violence and Morrish feared that, incensed and desperate as they were, the paupers might rebel and turn upon the men who escorted them, seeing them as the whipping boys of authority. After anguished moments, there was a shout from the crowd of women and children upon the verge as a farm waggon, pulled by a sturdy shire, came into view and halted at a cry from the man at the reins. He was a handsome man, dressed in the fashion of a yeoman, and had a boy of some ten years settled beside him upon the cart. Without hesitation, the farmer clambered down, bidding his son to take to the reins, then, searching intently among the empty sacks and barrels upon the boards of the waggon, he brought out both a hatchet and saw. Discarding his coat, he set to labour, brawny arms bare and muscled 'neath his rolled shirt sleeves. He worked competently and with care, begging the woman to halt him should she be afeared or feel discomfort of pain. However, all the while he worked, she spoke not a word and Morrish, watching with anxious desperation, wondered if the horror of it all had robbed her of all power of speech. Beside him, the little dark-haired girl, teeth gnawing anxiously at her lips, stood rigid with pain and apprehension.

When finally the woman was freed, a murmuring, then a cheer, arose from those gathered about, who had forgotten their own plight in another's more immediate need. The poor creature, released, was at first unable to stand, her ankles and wrists rubbed to rawness by the harshness of wood. The child was alternately overjoyed and despairing, weeping from relief and trying to take hold of the woman's soiled skirts, begging to be acknowledged. Yet the woman's stare was vacant, without recognition. Then, when it seemed that she had scarce had time to gain her strength, with a cry more animal than human, she was running wildly, awkwardly, across the highway and thence to the open fields and hills beyond. The child she had abandoned would have followed her but weakness and grief made her stumble and she was held fast in the strong arms of the farmer. Her small fists beat upon his chest and she railed at him in frustration and rage, giving herself pain as she struggled and kicked out at him. Then, as swiftly as her anger had come, it ebbed away, and she lay sobbing and unresisting in his encircling arms.

'The child,' Peter Morrish demanded of a pauper woman anxiously, 'is the daughter of the one who has fled?'

'I cannot say, sir. It seems the poor creature was unbalanced by the death of . . .' she hesitated awkwardly, 'of the one she loved. The child took pity upon her and tended her as best she could.'

'And the punishment? What sin had she committed? Who ordered such violence?'

'As to who ordered it, then I believe it to be the guardian of the poorhouse, for she was first shamed before us and set upon a stool awhile, then beaten and set into the pillory. We were brought to view her, sir, but none would revile her, or throw a stone.'

Morrish nodded, unable to take voice for a time, unless it betray him. 'And her sin, ma'am?' he repeated quietly.

'Her sin, sir, was that she threw some burial coins into

58

a gentleman's grave . . . and that she claimed to have loved him.'

'Yes. I have heard of it,' Morrish admitted soberly, 'but it seems so venial an offence to have deserved such an ending.'

The woman looked at him intently, mouth twisting wrily as she said, 'The crime, sir, for a pauper lies not in loving but whom you love . . . and in confessing it. It demeans those who, if they neither hear nor see us, can believe that we do not exist.'

He could not deny it but seeing by his grief-stricken face the pain within him, she put a hand gently on to his arm, saying, 'There are such as you who offer what help they can.'

'It is so little, and useless.' He shook his head helplessly.

'No, sir,' her voice was firm. 'It gives us strength and hope, you understand? Without it there would be nothing.'

She walked quietly away to join the small procession waiting for her at the village's edge. Morrish would have gone after her, the words of comfort already forming in his mind, but the farmer stood in his path with the child in his arms, barring the way.

'It seems you have lost your coat, sir,' he ventured.

Morrish glanced towards the paupers and the horsemen beyond. 'It is a small loss, and one swiftly forgotten.'

'Yes, it may be put right.' The farmer looked down at the sleeping child within his arms. 'It seems, though, that I have gained a daughter. I will not let her be set upon the road for she has travelled a harsh way too soon, I fear.' He sighed, 'I wish I might make room for them all.'

'Yes, but you have made a start,' Morrish broke off awkwardly. 'Your wife, sir, she will not grieve that there is another mouth to feed? I know that times are hard upon the land.'

'No.' The man's voice was certain. 'She would grieve the more if the child were abandoned. We lost a daughter in infancy.' He settled the child more securely in his arms. 'As for feeding an extra mouth, we will manage well enough if we each take a little less, for the child is as frail-boned as a wren.'

'But with the courage of a lion, and a devotion which humbles.'

The farmer nodded, 'Yes, a brave little maid and true. We will see that she comes to no harm.'

Morrish walked with him to the cart and the boy, seeing the sleeping child, and aware of all that had passed, said no word but smiled at his father and took up the reins that she be not disturbed.

Morrish watched them go, then went to rejoin the paupers upon the boundary. A child had found a good home this day, and there would be others. He had to believe it.

Chapter Seven

Jethro Hartrey, seated upon the rough farm cart, looked
down with awkward tenderness at the sleeping pauper child
within his arms. She was a poor malnourished creature,
lean as a skinned rabbit, and with no pretensions to beauty,
saving the large, strangely coloured eyes, fringed with
lashes dark as the tangled hair. Apart from her frailty, her
eyes were the only things Jethro would have remembered
about her, for she was as grubby, ill-clothed and pinched
as all the others of her kind. Yet she had touched some
chord of pity and recognition within him. She cried out in
her sleep, a lost frightened sound, like the whimpering of
some small animal, and his brawny, hard-muscled arms
tightened protectively about her.

He turned to his son at the reins of the sturdy farmhorse
which pulled the cart to say, 'It was thoughtful of you to
set my coat about her, Charles, my lad, for I fear she is a
puny, helpless thing, ill-dressed for the weather.'

The boy, copper-haired and sturdy, nodded, only the
flush of sudden colour under his skin revealing his pleasure
at such praise. 'We will not be long now upon the track,
sir, and there will be a warm fire and, as like as not, good
mutton broth to comfort her. We have had a good day and
return with the cart emptied. It will please Mama, I have
no doubt.' He turned his attention to the rough, ill-used
track as the horse stumbled.

'But will the bringing of an unknown child?' Jethro
Hartrey muttered to himself. 'Times are harsh, and perhaps
it is not the right time.'

The boy flicked at the reins, biting at his underlip, staring thoughtfully ahead. 'There is only one right time, Papa,' he said, 'when help is needed. That is what Mama will say.'

His father removed a broad hand from the sleeping child to place it briefly upon the boy's shoulder, his face warm with pride. 'You are right, my son. I could have done no other than bring her home. Yet I fear she will be of little use about the farm, or even as servant within the house.' He shook his head ruefully. 'She is naught but skin and bone; half starved, I'll wager, and from the bruises upon what poor flesh she has made, beaten as well as neglected.'

'Perhaps, Papa, she was punished for looking after the old woman?'

'Perhaps.'

'Then we must be kind to her, Father, for she was that and more to the pauper,' Charles insisted earnestly, 'never leaving that poor woman but staying close for comfort, even though hungry and cold and in the dark, with none to help.'

'Yes.' Jethro's voice was low.

'I believe she is a good girl, Papa, and brave to face the darkness and the blows. I will be pleased to care for her as she deserves.'

Jethro was so moved and grateful for his son's understanding that he was quite unable to tell him so, lest his voice betray him, so he merely nodded and turned aside as if it were of no importance.

'If you are grieved or troubled about Mama, sir, I pray that you give it no more thought,' Charles said hesitantly. 'She always gives more kindness to the runt of the litter, feeling the weakest and feeblest to be most in need of loving care. You will see, sir, that I am right. It is her way. I have observed it.'

'You are a great comfort to me, Charles.' Jethro smiled at his son's quick look of surprise. 'You are sensible beyond your years.'

'I am almost twelve, sir. Many of my age are at work in the woollen mills or in the ironworks and bell mines, but

62

I am grateful to be of use to you upon the farm, sir.'

The cart wheel wedged in the depths of an old rut, jolted, and shook the occupants of the waggon. The empty barrels bumped and rolled amidst the sacks behind as they rattled their way noisily through the gates of the small farm, scattering hens and ducks in a squawking protesting blur of feathers and noise.

The farmhouse was a simple longhouse with outbuildings scattered about. Barns, byres and stables were of the same rough-hewn local stone which perfectly reflected the colours of fern, stones and soil upon the surrounding hills.

The woman who hurried out from the farmhouse doorway was young and pretty. With curls of richest copper colour escaping her lace-trimmed house-bonnet, her complexion had an equal vividness. There was a vitality about her, a joyousness in life as if, like the curls which tumbled about her face, she was filled with a restless energy which could neither be confined nor dimmed. Her shoes clattered over the cobbles as she sped towards the cart, impatiently clutching at her skirt to raise it clear of the compacted dirt and inevitable chicken droppings.

'Such a day I have had of it . . . and you, Jethro, have you fared well?' she was chattering breathlessly as she ran out, only to halt with a hand upon the bridle of the farmhorse, stroking its pink and whiskered nose. 'Heavens preserve us! Is that a child you have in your arms, Jethro?'

'Yes, Sara, my love,' he said, 'a pauper, with neither kith nor kin to bless her!'

'But where did you find her?'

'We came upon her in the village, my dear, being driven away before the horsemen to forage upon the road as best she could.'

'Dear Lord!' She tentatively circled the cart, coming to rest beside Jethro, looking down at the sleeping child and seeing a skinny, frail-boned infant, hair coarsely matted, face streaked with dirt and tears. When she raised Jethro's coat she saw with pity that the dress it wore was filthy and torn, the limbs beneath so thin that she could have clasped

63

them within her curled palm. 'Oh, dear Lord!' she repeated helplessly. 'What possessed you to bring her here to me?'

It was Charles who answered, leaping down from the cart to stand beside her, earnest face flushed. 'Because I said you would not turn her away, Mama!' Her son's eyes met hers in quiet pleading. 'She befriended a poor old woman, clamped in the pillory, and Papa was so angry that he halted the cart and splintered the wood with blows from our hatchet to free her.'

Sara's eyes were incredulous and amused as she demanded of her husband, voice purposely sharp, 'But did you not bring the old woman to me too? Is she hidden beneath the sacks? Why did you not bring me the rest of them, pray? Then I might have moved myself into the hen-house that they might take over completely.'

Charles, not knowing if she spoke in anger or in jest, fidgeted uncomfortably for a time, scuffling his feet upon the cobblestones and staring down at them, before looking up. 'They beat her, Mama,' he said, 'but she would not leave the old woman, always lying beside her at night. I think she would have stayed with her until one, or both, had died. You cannot turn her away! It would be too cruel!' His voice shook as impassioned tears sprang to his eyes and he knuckled them away fiercely, fearing them a weakness.

'Oh, my dear,' said Sara remorsefully, hugging him close, 'it was a jest, a stupid jest. I could not send her away, as you well know, for I cannot reject any abandoned creature, and I fear she has suffered rejection and hurt by too many. No, she may stay, and welcome. Now, there is an end to it!'

The child in Jethro's arms stirred and awoke with a cry and a start, eyes anguished. Her arms tightened about his neck as she burrowed her head against his chest, like some bewildered small animal seeking escape.

'Here, Jethro,' Sara ordered, 'give her to me, for it is a child you hold, not some pig in a sack or a stook of corn.'

Jethro delivered her into his wife's outstretched arms and the child looked at her intently, eyes wide with fear, shrinking away in the expectation of some blow or curse. Regardless of the girl's filthy verminous state and the stench of dried sweat and the heavier smell of other stale odours upon clothing and flesh, Sara held her close, soothing her, crooning to her gently, as if she were a babe in arms. She thought that she had never seen so pathetically ill-used a creature, nor eyes so wide with terror. Yet they were, without doubt, the most beautiful and remarkable eyes she had ever encountered, the more so for being set about with dark, bruised shadows. They were the clearest, deepest violet-blue, fringed by thick black lashes.

'Why!' exclaimed Sara involuntarily, 'you have the most beautiful eyes I have ever seen in all my life!'

The child looked at her, bewildered.

'I think, Jethro, that she does not understand, is perhaps not able to hear,' said Sara, chilled.

'No, Mama,' said Charles quietly. 'It is not that. I heard her speak to the old woman and answer the others. It is because no-one has ever spoken kindly to her before.'

'Yes,' said Jethro, matter-of-factly, 'it will be that, no doubt. I had best be putting the horse into the field to graze awhile.' He turned abruptly away, but not before Sara had glimpsed the softness of tears behind his lashes.

'I will come with you, Papa,' offered Charles, helping Jethro to unload the sacks and casks, then carrying them to the barn.

Once within the farmhouse, Sara set the child down gently upon the flagstoned floor and watched as she stood there awkwardly, hesitant in her filth-grimed clothing, gazing about her with swift, jerky little movements of her head like some timid, inquisitive bird, always alerted to danger.

It was a long high-ceilinged room with hams and faggots of dried herbs suspended from the smoke-darkened beams. The hams were crusted with saltpetre and their outer skins seemed as hardened and brown with smoking as the beams themselves. There was a vast inglenook fireplace with wooden settles beside it, the roaring fire crackling with burning logs and, about it, coopered pails with iron bands, bearing rolled cobbles of peat mixed with gorse or dried fern as fuel. The furnishings were of sturdy country style, solid and well crafted to withstand vigorous daily use. Like the yeoman and farm labourers it served, it was shabby, comfortable and unpretentious and, if lacking in refinement, then its simplicity was kinder to the discerning eye.

The pauper child's eyes, although wide with wonder and dwelling briefly upon the huge oaken dresser, softly aglow with pewter plates and tankards, and the enormous scrubbed table set with plates, cutlery, crocks, loaves of bread and jugs of ale, returned inevitably to the fire, and the iron pot suspended from a jack above its heat. It was bubbling and steaming fiercely, the aroma of mutton, vegetables and herb stock so tantalising that, despite all her efforts to quell it, saliva actually ran from the corners of the child's mouth and her stomach grumbled more loudly than the boiling broth.

'You shall eat your fill of it later,' Sara promised kindly, 'and sit alongside the fire until your flesh is warmed through, but first we must make you clean and pretty, for we shall all enjoy our victuals the more for that.' She took the child's grimy hand. Although she did not speak, she followed Sara docilely enough, having decided to trust her.

In the small scullery, with the child seated upon an enormous wheel-backed chair and her filthy clothing in a heap upon the floor, Sara poured cold water into the wooden tub she used for soaking the family's washing. Then she returned with a kettle of hot water which had been resting upon a hob before the fire. Testing the water with her elbow and, finding it comfortably warm yet not so hot that it might rawly scald the skin, she lifted the child into the tub to wash her with a rag of rough flannel and a ball of lye and tallow. At first the child recoiled with frightened squeals and cries, fists gripped so tight upon the washtub's wooden sides that her knuckles showed white as bone. Her eyes were closed as fiercely and she trembled, teeth chattering as with an ague. Then, finding no harm had

66

come to her, she exploratively opened one eye, and then the other, enjoying the rasp of cloth upon her flesh, seeing with delighted incredulity the skin turning from grey to mottled pink. She made no demur, even when Sara rubbed her tangled hair with the fatty bar of woodash until it lay plastered to her skull and squeaked clean, only to be rinsed with an infusion of herb-rosemary poured from an earthen pitcher. Then, her scrubbed-clean face grew etched in resignation as she suffered Sara to rub her hair dry and, with less tolerance and not a few winces and involuntary cries, to drag a bone comb through its burrs and tangles.

When all was completed, Sara lifted her out of the tub, and wrapped her warmly in a cloth of coarse linen-weave before abrasively rubbing her dry. The child's pitifully thin body was disfigured with dark bruises, and with earlier ones fading to yellow and brown, and Sara could feel the frailness of bone and the fleshless ribs standing proud of the stretched skin.

Sara had beside her a nightgown of her own, pintucked, voluminous of sleeves and skirt. Without thought or hesitation, she cut it with her dressmaking shears into tolerable shape, scything off the too-long hem, slashing the sleeves, until a clean, modestly functional garment resulted, part dress, part nightgown. Then, commanding the child to hold her arms high above her head, she slipped the clothing on. The child's smile was wide and appreciative with delight and Sara's almost rivalled it as she regarded the pretty dark-haired infant. She was, Sara thought, like an angel, lacking only wings in her gown of pristine white, face glowing pinkly from heat and joy, deep violet eyes sparkling with joy of warmth and ownership.

'Tomorrow,' Sara promised, 'I will go at once to the haberdasher's and buy some pretty sprigged cotton and muslin to make you new gowns and aprons, we will ride out upon the farm waggon to purchase stockings and shoes at the cordwainer's. Would you like that?'

The child nodded shyly.

'Come now, let us be seated at the table, for the menfolk

67

of the family are hungry, and we must not delay.'

Sara sat her upon a chair pulled up to the table, with the child's back turned to the fire to keep her warm in her thin gown. Jethro and Charles, having washed at the well in the yard, came to take their places, Charles beside her, Jethro at the table's head. When all three were settled comfortably, Sara came to stand briefly at the head of the board before filling the soup bowls. Seeing her new-found family with hands clasped in prayer and their eyes closed, the pauper child obediently followed suit.

'Dear Lord. We thank Thee that Thou hast this day given us of Thy food and bounty, and the added blessing of a new child.'

Jethro opened his eyes wide to ask gently, 'What is your name, my love; your given name?'

'I think, sir, I am called . . . pauper Anne,' she said.

Charles ventured quietly, 'But we should give her a new name, Mama, for she is no longer a pauper.'

'Then you must name her, Charles. What shall it be?'

Charles thought, lips clenched, brow furrowed in concentration.

'Well, Mama . . . if she is truly ours, and I am called Charles Jethro after Papa, could we not call her after you . . . yet giving her the name she always had, for she might otherwise find it strange, and grieve her loss. Can we call her Saranne?'

'Yes,' said Sara, stooping to affectionately ruffle her son's copper hair. 'It is a pretty name, suitable for a pretty little girl. It will serve your sister well.'

Chapter Eight

Saranne had cried aloud in her sleep, moving restlessly, pursued by unknown terrors in some dark and alien place. She had awakened with a scream of fear which had brought Sara running to her bed. She had tried to comfort the child, cradling her close and smoothing the damp hair which clung to her face but Saranne was not to be pacified, trembling and weeping the more, calling aloud for Marged, her friend. Finally, her nightmares spent, she had lain quiescent in Sara's arms until she had fallen into an exhausted sleep.

Jethro, tenderly protective of the child, grieved at the horrors Saranne must have endured, and that they haunted her so violently still. He had witnessed her courage and did not know if even the love and pity they felt for Saranne could ease her hurt.

'It is Marged she called for . . . the pauper woman within the stocks,' he said helplessly to Sara. 'We are strangers to her, and all is strange and new.'

Seeing his confusion and his fear that the child might reject their home and love, Sara replied compassionately, 'It is not the old life she weeps for, Jethro, but all that is familiar; all she has known in her brief living. The horror of it makes her cry and yet she clings to it, as she clings to Marged, because it is all her remembrance.'

He nodded, unspeaking, as she promised earnestly, 'In time she will forget, and become our own.'

'But I cannot bear to see her so sad and afeared, Sara. I will go tomorrow and search for the woman.'

'No! She would think you were come to persecute her, to capture and take her back! Let me go. I know the ways upon the mountain, every inch of the track, for I have tramped them from childhood. I will take her warm clothing, whatever victuals and comforts can be spared.'

He made to protest but Sara was firm upon it declaring, 'Think no more upon it, my dear. It is the best way for all. If she does not wish to see the child, or has fled beyond reach, it were better that Saranne be spared the hurt of it. She has borne sorrow and rejection enough.'

At daybreak upon the morrow, Sara surrendered Saranne into Charles's keeping, cautioning him to watch over her well, for all was new to her. 'Show her the beasts in the byre and stable,' she instructed, 'and the kittens in the barn. You may teach her to scatter feed for the hens, collect eggs, and to make herself useful about the farm.'

'Will you be long gone, Mama?'

'As long as it takes,' Sara scolded him briskly, then relenting, added, 'but when I return, if Papa be willing, you shall harness the waggon and drive us into Penavon village. I have a mind to buy a dress and warm coat for Saranne.'

Saranne stared at her, wide-eyed and solemn, then a flush had coloured her face and she ran to Sara and threw her arms fiercely about her, burying her face in Sara's skirt. She had spoken no word of pleasure or gratitude but Sara, with memory of the child's frail body within her arms, and the nightmare tears, had looked up and seen her son's eyes alight with honest pleasure. It was reward enough. The smiles exchanged between them were filled with affectionate understanding. She prayed silently that Saranne might one day feel as secure as Charles and as free to love openly.

With a basket upon her arm and a clean sack filled with clothing in her grasp, Sara left Holly Grove Farm. Tom Hallowes, their old farm labourer, knew the truth of her mission and begged to walk with her upon the way but she refused. Instead he told her, 'Jethro need have no fear for your safety, Sara. There is no violence in Marged Howell, no madness.'

'You know of her, Tom?'

'As many another, and had cause to be grateful for her kindness. But, in adversity, it is all too soon forgot. She is a good woman, and lies and rumour cannot alter it.'

Sara stared at him in perplexity.

'She is a *dyn hysbys* . . . a conjuror!' he said abruptly. 'One born with the power to heal, as her father before her. They hold it as a God-given gift and will take no payment save what is freely offered in coin and kind.'

'A wise woman?' Sara asked, startled. 'This Marged is a wise woman?'

'And, as such, persecuted and hounded by those who do not understand, fearing it to be witchcraft. Yet it is a force for good, for healing.' He paused before saying with conviction. 'Those who possess it are to be pitied for it comes unbidden, as with second sight, and they cannot be free of it. It sets them apart from all others. They are born to suffering like Marged Howell.'

Sara went on her way, troubled, feeling an ache of pity for the poor, tormented creature, yet fear too of what she might find. Still, there was a question to be asked, and answered honestly, for its shadow lay upon them all. She feared that, in her despair and weakness, Marged might have stumbled into some quarry or into one of the many streams which surfaced from the rock beneath. She was, she believed, as likely to come upon Marged Howell's dead body as the wise woman herself. Sara had wandered far and the weight of the basket and sack wearied her, yet she would not give up her search. Resting and stopping from time to time to stretch her cramped limbs, she called out Marged's name, but had almost despaired of catching sight of her.

When Marged crept hesitantly from her cave, standing awkward and fearful at first, she and Sara stared at each other without hostility, each unwilling to make a move which might alarm the other. She accepted Sara's offerings with dignity and told of how, publicly shamed, and driven close to madness by Rice Havard's death and the punishment she had endured, she had fled by instinct, without thought or volition, running blindly she knew not where. Like some trapped animal which, when released, is at first frozen of mind and limb, then will flee, even into the path of its pursuers. She had come at the end to the only place she knew. Marged was, Sara realised with pity, a young woman of barely her own age, although suffering and deprivation had set a mark upon her. Yet there was a refinement in her speech and manner and a delicacy of feature which, like Marged's intelligence, could not be hid by the filthy raggedness of her clothing. Her dark hair hung matted and her face bore traces of dirt and old tears. Yet once she had been beautiful and, but for her gauntness and the defeat and exhaustion which bore her down, she might seem so yet.

They talked hesitantly at first then with growing sympathy and trust but still there remained a reserve between them, things unspoken.

'The child . . .' Sara blurted at last, 'the little girl . . . We have taken her into our house.'

Marged became so still that she might have been lifeless. When she spoke, her voice was flat, drained of emotion. 'Yes. It is better so.'

'She has been crying out for you, calling your name. Will you not come to her and set her mind at ease?' Sara grasped Marged's arm, urging impulsively, 'There is a stone barn within the farm, with a hayloft above where you might live. It is dry and warm, and there you will be safe.'

Marged studied her, then shook her head regretfully.

'No. I am safe nowhere and would bring violence upon you and her. You are not deserving of that. If you will care for her, make her a home?'

Sara nodded, seeing the glint of tears in Marged's eyes and the trembling of her lips painfully stilled. Pity made her brusque, although she cursed the clumsiness of her words even as they were spoken. 'She is your child? Rice Havard's daughter?'

'No. She is not Rice Havard's child. I wish to God that she were.' There was such a violence of sorrow in the denial that Sara felt Marged's grief within herself. 'She came from Golden Grove . . . Anne, I mean.' Marged fought to control her voice. 'Farmed out as a helper to an old woman, now dead. Then she was brought to the poorhouse at Penavon.'

'And you grew to love her?'

'I grew to love her.' There was a depth of longing in the quiet words.

'I will bring her to you,' Sara promised. 'It will set her mind at rest, and yours.'

'That would be a kindness. I could offer her nothing, for I own nothing, am nothing. I would not have her live as I, persecuted, homeless, of less account than a beast of the field. You have been kinder to me and to the child than any other I have known. I thank you for that and beg that you do me one further kindness, if you will, although I have no right to ask it.'

Sara nodded, waiting expectantly.

'There is a young priest, he who helped the paupers, Morrish by name.'

'You would have me deliver him a message?'

'Please. Will you bid him come search for me, as soon as he is able. He is a good man, and will not refuse.'

'I will see that it is done.'

It was Jethro who took Saranne to see Marged, urging her along the overgrown mountain tracks, carrying her upon his broad shoulders when she grew too tired to walk more.

For all he was a strong and, sometimes, taciturn man, he had been so moved by the joyousness of their reunion that when he tried to tell Sara of it afterwards, he was scarce able to summon the words, and Sara had taken his huge, work-grained hand in hers and held it to her cheek. 'When we came within sight of the farm,' Jethro began, 'Saranne riding high upon my shoulders, she bent and laid

73

her lips to my cheek and after she had kissed me, said, "I am so glad that Marged is safe, Papa. I loved her. She was kind to me and to all who were sad or sick. I am tired, and glad to be coming home." '

It was also Jethro who went to Peter Morrish and begged him to visit Marged. He could not rightly believe that the clergyman would go, for he was a man of the cloth and the church looked harshly upon healers and conjurors, believing them to promote superstition and cant. Yet Morrish had gone, walking the long way from the village and back again to the poorhouse, as Marged Howell had asked. None knew what passed between them, nor why she had sent for him. Whatever the burden she carried, it could only have been made lighter for the sharing of it with another who was slow to condemn and swift to forgive.

Chapter Nine

Penry Vaughan was not in the best of humours. The coach journey from Great House to the vicarage with his two young kinsmen had cruelly unnerved him. The draught from the broken window was invasive and chill and scarcely less of an irritant than Peter Morrish's gross impertinence in allowing a pregnant woman into his church. It was shaming and intolerable.

'I fear, sir,' ventured Probert hesitantly as he helped Penry Vaughan to alight, 'that the coach has suffered damage.'

'I am neither blind nor deprived of my basic intelligence,' declared Vaughan abrasively. 'It will cost me a pretty penny!' he thought dispiritedly, forgetting in his pique that the Havard carriages and bloodstock which now graced his stables had cost him nothing at all.

'Come along, Carne!' he chided brusquely. 'I have not all day to waste!'

Carne lingered awkwardly beside the step of the coach.

'What is it, boy? Hurry up, do!' Vaughan commanded irascibly.

'It is Mostyn, sir . . .'

'Mostyn? What ails him? Is he asleep?'

'No, sir . . .'

Mostyn appeared in the open doorway of the coach, 'I want to go home, Carne . . . I do not like it here.' His childish voice rose into a wail.

Penry Vaughan, stumping his way irritably to the house across the cobbled yard, halted, then turned abruptly. 'You

75

have as little choice in the matter as I!' he declared. 'Beggars cannot be choosers!'

Probert, glancing behind him to confirm that Vaughan had disappeared within, lifted Mostyn down with a smile, swinging him joyfully about, so that he cried out in joyous laughter, all else forgot. Then, when he was safely set down upon the cobblestones, Mostyn said, 'I like you, Probert. Will you not take me home to Great House?'

'I cannot do that, Master Mostyn.'

Carne took Mostyn's hand and drew him towards the house. '*This* is our home, Mostyn,' he rebuked, but his eyes as they met the coachman's were so bleak that Probert all but lifted them back within.

Carne was delivering Mostyn into the care of his cousin's housekeeper, Mrs Groves, a thin, acidulated spinster with a shoe-button mouth and a high-ridged nose. Fiercely defensive of his sibling, Carne was gripping Mostyn's hand tight, his stance challenging, head held high and with all the arrogance of his father, Rice Havard. Mrs Groves felt an immediate antipathy towards him.

Carne, seeing the resentment upon the housekeeper's face, shuffled his feet, worry for Mostyn making him glower ill naturedly.

'Take Master Mostyn to his room,' the housekeeper instructed a maidservant who had emerged silently from a passageway. 'See that he is bathed and his clothes changed. Now, Master Carne, if you will follow me,' she commanded abruptly. 'I will show you to your room.'

Carne, obediently trailing the severe, rigid-backed figure in black calico, thought fleetingly of Jane's warmth of heart and understanding, and felt such a weight of grief for what was lost and ended that his foot stumbled upon the stair. His room was austerely furnished and smaller than the one he had shared with Mostyn at Great House. Yet he was grateful that here, at least, was a place he could be alone.

'I hope, Master Carne, that it meets with your satisfaction. No doubt you have been used to greater luxury and more elegant surroundings at Great House, but one must settle where one may.'

There was no mistaking the spiteful satisfaction in her tone. Awkwardness made him sound stiff and condescending, 'You have worked well for me . . . my comfort.' He faltered under her unwavering stare, the words dying in his throat.

'I have not *worked* for you,' she corrected. 'That is the duty of the lower servants, as you must certainly be aware. This room was prepared upon the instructions of my employer, Mr Vaughan. I am accountable to him, no other.'

'Then I am grateful, ma'am, to him,' said Carne quietly. He was so absurdly young and stiff-necked with awkwardness that, for a moment, she felt a stirring of shame at her brusqueness, seeing in his conduct the grace lacking in her. Perversely, she could not unbend towards him, feeling that she had been deliberately set in the wrong.

'A maidservant will be here directly to attend to your fire,' she declared. 'You will see that your garments have been unpacked and arranged for you within the clothing press. There is a hip-bath ready placed in the corner beside your night table. Mr Vaughan has but one manservant, but if you require him to . . . supervise your ablutions, I will arrange it.'

'No, ma'am,' he said firmly, 'I thank you, but I am no longer an infant like Mostyn who requires another's aid. I shall be pleased to care for myself.'

She regarded him stonily, lips set in disapproval. Fearing that his abrupt denial had offended her, Carne sought to make amends.

'My life has changed, ma'am,' he admitted earnestly, 'but it is for people, not places, I most grieve. My . . .' He hesitated. 'Those I took as example would wish it so.'

As if he had not spoken, she declared curtly; 'There is water in the jug upon your bed-table, and a ball of lye and tallow set upon a saucer. You will need to make yourself presentable and change your clothing for you are expected to dine with Mr Vaughan upon the hour of six.'

'Alone?' The word, high-pitched and querulous, escaped him involuntarily. 'There will be no guests, ma'am?' he asked more steadily.

'None!' She swept out imperiously, her house-shoes ringing upon the bare boards and her chatelaine jingling at her waist.

That boy is arrogant and self-assured, she thought, a sullen, unlikeable creature. Yet she was grudgingly aware that Carne was possessed too of spirit and determination, and not easy to cast down. If it came to a battle for dominance, as it surely would, between Carne Havard and his cousin, then she would wager that it would be the boy who must yield. Vaughan had the advantage of age and experience and it would trouble him not a whit to see his young kinsman not only dependent upon him but humbled.

Carne, listening to the diminishing sound of Mrs Groves' departure, wished childishly that instead of Penry Vaughan's guardianship, he could be surrendered into Mr Prys's care. There had been times upon the coach, holding Mostyn's trembling body to his own flesh, when sickness had burned in his throat, raw and sour-tasting. Yet, he thought despairingly, he would have relived it uncomplainingly a hundred times over rather than face the meal which lay ahead, with his cousin, the vicar, as reluctant host.

He gravely inspected his new-found kingdom and its furnishings, touching, probing and peering into all. Then he washed his face and body at the little corner washstand, and from the drawer beneath took out the silver-backed brushes and handglass which Jane had packed for him. Then he brushed his hair so forcibly that stinging burned his eyes and he could persuade himself that the hurt was of his own making.

When reaching for his small-clothes and his stockings within the bachelor chest, he came upon the pigskin pouch containing his childhood treasures, long neglected and forgot, and poured them upon the cover of his bed. A dark fossil with the imprint of a fern, the empty brown and white snail shell, a fragment of a crystal prism filled with rainbow light. He would have returned them to the pouch but his fingers chanced upon something small and square shaped, stitched lightly into a fold of soft leather. It took him a long time to unpick the fine stitching which secured it, for his hands were too eager, and the small pocket-knife he owned too clumsy to easily open them.

Inside were two perfectly matched miniatures upon ivory, barely two inches square, and set into delicately wrought frames of ormolu. The faces which looked back at him were sensitively captured by the artist's brush, young, and filled with vitality, the mouths curved and gentle, as if they shared some precious secret knowledge, undisclosed to all others. Mama and Papa, when they were very young, and as he now barely remembered them. Jane kept them for me, Carne thought, believing they were mine by right and that none could truly know and appreciate their worth save me. He would not part with them, but keep them close always. A talisman. A reminder, not only of those who had given him life but of Jane Eynon's devotion. Although he was only a child, he knew what penalty her loving gesture might have demanded of her: imprisonment, public whipping, transportation even. He wrapped the miniatures carefully in the fold of leather and put them within the pocket of his coat. Jane Eynon had not stolen them. It was Penry Vaughan who was the real thief, taking Papa's carriage and horses and other fine things unhindered and declaring them his own. Well, he would not have the miniatures and none should know of their existence, not even Mostyn.

When the maidservant came to tell him that his cousin awaited him in the drawing room below, for dinner was soon to be served, Carne was unafraid. If Jane, and perhaps Prys too, loved him so much and would risk all for his sake, he must not betray them by lacking courage.

The meal proved formal and stilted, with Penry Vaughan seated, glowering, at one end of the vast dining table of gleaming mahogany and Carne balanced uncomfortably upon a matching armchair at the opposite end. It seemed to the boy that there must be an acre of highly polished wood separating them, since the 'D' ended table had been needlessly extended with extra leaves, allowing four vacant chairs to be placed upon each side. Despite the wall sconces, the glittering silver candelabra upon the table, the pristine napery and crystal, the effect was gloomy and uninviting. Frugality had caused Penry Vaughan to forbid the lighting of every taper, a habit which he declared to be grossly excessive and vulgar, decreeing that one in every three would perfectly well suffice. Consequently, he and Carne dined in such timid candlelight that they were barely visible, one to the other, and hardly cognisant of what was being served and eaten. The food was, in any event, meagre and tasteless, and Carne's appetite poor by reason of fatigue and the misery of leaving Great House. Fortunately, the shadows cast hampered Vaughan's restlessly disapproving scrutiny. However, upon hearing Carne's quiet refusal of boiled mutton and capers, he declared icily, 'I fear the victuals are not entirely to your taste, cousin?'

'No, sir,' Carne replied quickly, 'they are splendid. I fear it is my appetite which is at fault.'

'Indeed?' Vaughan's voice was expressionless. 'Perhaps your palate has become over-refined and our humble offerings are not tempting enough. I am aware that you have been richly indulged, for that was ever my cousin Rice's way. He was extravagant and wasteful in every particular. Do you not agree, sir?'

Carne remained silent, uncertain how best to reply.

'Well, sir, I await an answer.'

'My father was generous, sir . . . as you say.'

'Not generous, Carne! A spendthrift and wastrel. If you cannot yet distinguish between generosity and profligacy, it will be my duty and obligation to teach you. You may begin with a lesson in politeness.'

He motioned the manservant at the serving table to return the plate of lamb to Carne.

'No, sir.' Carne's voice was childishly high-pitched, but

firm. 'I beg you will excuse me, for I have dined sufficiently, and well.'

The manservant, hovering awkwardly at his elbow was unwilling to force it upon the boy since, in the flickering of the candle flame, he appeared so pale and wretchedly ill-at-ease. The servant turned to go, but Penry Vaughan's inflexible voice halted him.

'Serve him, Davies . . . a substantial portion, if you please. We cannot allow our young guest, Master Havard, to judge us lacking in hospitality or purpose.'

Reluctantly, and with a glance of gentle apology, Davies set a piece of the glistening, boiled mutton, congealing unappetisingly in its own fat, upon Carne's plate.

'Now, sir, you will proceed to eat it, every last morsel,' ordered Vaughan evenly, 'since, if you do not, you will have it served to you for every meal until you acquiesce.' He poured himself a generous glass of wine, replacing the bottle on the silver coaster before him. Then, holding the glass aloft in the candlelight to judge its colour, he ostentatiously drank in its fragrance and bouquet. Carne had neither moved nor spoken.

'Come, sir,' declared Vaughan convivially, 'eat up your victuals if you wish to redeem yourself for your bad manners! It is a slight upon your host and the meanest discourtesy to do otherwise. Your obstinacy and uncivil behaviour do you no credit. There are many who would be grateful for such honest fare, and deem it a luxury!'

'Indeed, sir . . . then I bid you make a gift of it to any deserving pauper upon the way, for their need is greater than mine, as we have seen today.'

'You insolent young puppy!' Vaughan leapt to his feet, catching his wine glass with the lace frill of his cuff and upsetting the wine upon the polished wood. So intense was his fury that, for a moment, Carne thought he would rush to his side and strike him a blow. Instead, Vaughan controlled himself with an effort, clinging to the table edge, grim faced, as if he sought to still both his hands and his temper.

'Return to your room, Carne!' Vaughan appeared to have

regained his composure, save for the merest tremor in his voice. 'It is plain to me that you have long been denied the company of gentlemen and have forgotten, or perhaps never learnt, the decencies of civilised behaviour. You have been too long in the company of clods and oafs, menials without intelligence or breeding.'

Carne was aware of the manservant, Davies, stiffening resentfully as he replaced the salver upon the serving board, although he did not speak.

'Return to your room,' Vaughan repeated coldly, 'and reflect upon your obstinacy and ingratitude . . . and confess all with penitence in your prayers.'

'Yes, sir.' Carne's tone was deceptively submissive. 'I will do as you say, and seek forgiveness. I do not doubt God's understanding.'

There was a noisy clatter of salvers and lids at the side table which all but drowned out Vaughan's reply, but he paused to repeat, 'I said, sir, that those victuals upon your plate will be served to you again at your breakfast, and at every meal thereafter, until you deign to eat them. Mrs Groves will instruct the servants that you will receive neither food nor drink until you comply. You understand?'

'I understand, sir.' Carne walked slowly to stand beside him. 'I am beholden to you for offering to me and Mostyn the blessing of your house and board, and thank you, cousin, for your hospitality.' Then he bowed courteously and, with thin shoulders erect, walked quietly from the room.

The next morning, with Mostyn at his side, he re-entered the dining room and Davies hesitantly set down the cold mutton before him, viscous now, and with fat congealed about it. Without a word, Carne took up his knife and fork and ate it, every last shred, although the sickness in his throat all but choked him. He had, in the darkness of his room, thought bitterly and hard upon what Jane Eynon would have bade him do. Her words had come to him as clearly as if she stood guardian beside him: 'Defer always in the small things which are of no account, then you may

82

gather strength and purpose to hold firm upon those things that matter.'

'I am glad, sir, that your first lesson has been learned and taken to heart.' Vaughan's voice from the doorway was deliberately mocking.

Carne merely inclined his head, but said nothing.

'I trust, cousin, that you are more appreciative of your good fortune in being taken into the home of a kinsman and that, in future, you will prove more amenable, less intractable.'

'I believe, sir,' declared Carne quietly, 'that my father would willingly have done the same for you.'

'Cousin Penry, sir,' Mostyn's voice was shrill and insistent.

'Yes, boy?' He turned irritably.

'I like it here. It is a nice house and I am not frightened here, as before. My father shouted and made me afraid.'

Penry Vaughan's smile was wide and unfeigned for Mostyn, the betrayer, that gentle sycophant.

Carne, fighting down the sudden rush of gall to his throat, arose and bowed to his cousin and to Mostyn, the false. His punishment had been bitter to swallow, yet, now, it seemed of no account, as Jane had predicted. To Mostyn he spoke no word of rebuke, then or after. He knew you could not punish another for speaking the truth.

Chapter Ten

Jane was happily ensconced upon the perch of the hired mule and cart, with Prys at its reins, when, without warning, the paupers were driven forcibly from the poorhouse. Megan, the scullery maid from Great House, who had been chattering excitedly from the sack-covered floor of the cart, grew suddenly silent. The fury and noise of the horsemen and the panic-stricken flight of the victims terrified the mule into bolting. It reared and plunged wildly, eyes rolling, and all but hurled the occupants of the cart to the roadside in its fury to escape the screams and confusion surrounding it. When Prys finally wrenched control, the cart came to rest awkwardly beside a ditch, the mule trembling and sweating in a lather of fear, with those clinging to the reins and cart scarcely less terrified.

Prys, white-faced, and burning in every muscle and sinew, made certain that Jane and Megan had escaped with no bones broken, then turned his attention to soothing and steadying the mule. Megan and Jane, who had been flung into the body of the cart by the savagery of the jolting, were huddled together, unable to believe that their ordeal was ended. Suddenly finding voice, Megan began to gulp and cry noisily and Jane, barely able to move for stiffness and bruising, nonetheless stirred herself to comfort the girl. It was while they were thus commiserating, not yet aware of the miracle of their escape, that Peter Morrish begged their aid for the pauper woman. For all that he was still shocked and barely able to respond for trembling and exhaustion, Prys set out at once to seek a midwife or doctor to attend the birth. Megan protested that she would willingly stay, for she had seen the birthing of her own kin, but a meaningful glance from Jane to Prys settled the matter.

'You would be a godsend beside me, Megan,' Prys declared earnestly, 'and would save my old legs. Besides, the mule is cantankerous enough to bolt and leave me stranded else.'

So Megan climbed obediently upon the perch beside him as Jane walked beside the pauper, John Bessant, as he carried his young wife, Ruth, heavy with child, into the refuge of the church.

Jane was growing increasingly anxious and afraid as she awaited Prys's return with a physician. Her ears were alerted for the sounds of a carriage upon the cobbles without, for she was not naive enough to suppose that he would accompany Prys upon the rough-hewn cart. She leaned over and wiped the sweat from Ruth's face with a rag she had torn from the skirt of her own petticoat, its strips entangled upon the stone floor beside her. The vestry of the church was tiny and cramped, a cold place, made hazardous by an excess of heavy cupboards, wooden benches and chairs piled in disarray, a table, and a clutter of garments and impedimenta necessary to such a place. There was but poor light from the single small window set high in the thickness of the stone wall, and Ruth lay upon a bed of thin straw which John Bessant had begged from an ostler at a stables nearby. Jane had sent him, in desperation, upon the errand, and others, necessary and invented, for his agitation and remorse were pitiful to see and causing Ruth more distress than her own plight. She had little enough strength to endure the birth, and less to assist it, and that should not be squandered on giving comfort to others.

Seeing how cruelly John Bessant's remorse and fear for Ruth were debilitating her, Jane sent him upon yet another anxious search for more straw for bedding and for good clean sacking. He obeyed with evident reluctance, his boot soles dragging dispiritedly upon the stone flagged floor. Even as she took off her shawl to place around Ruth's shoulders, she heard him hesitate and turn back, his footstep brisk and aggressive. He tore aside the vestry curtain upon its brass rings to exclaim despairingly, 'I cannot pay the doctor, Mistress Prys! We have neither money nor possessions of our own, nor hope of labour hereabouts. As soon as Ruth is recovered, we will be set upon the road!'

'There is a physician nearby who attends the sick from kindness,' Jane lied, hoping not to perjure herself too damningly, since she was in God's house. 'His fee is modest enough to allow the poorest to make recompense, in pence or kind . . . and that over many weeks, if need be.'

'But I tell you, I have nothing!' His voice rose in agitation and rage at his own impotence as he sent his fist crashing in frustration into his palm, as if he would punish his own flesh as Ruth's.

'Hush!' Jane rebuked, hustling him swiftly into the main body of the church and pulling the curtain roughly behind them. 'I have not asked for payment, nor would I seek it! I offer my help as a friend, and do not doubt that Ruth and you would do the same for any other in the same plight, were you able! Since it troubles your pride so much, then you may repay me with your labour when you return with Ruth and the child to my house. Until then, make yourself useful here. Fetch straw or water, summon a midwife or wise woman from among the cottagers. Take yourself to the altar and pray most earnestly for the safety of those you love. Do anything save whine and reject the help that people offer you from simple kindness, not counting it a debt.' The words had been harsher and more lacerating than she had intended, yet they stirred him into action and she could not regret them.

'I am sorry, Mistress Eynon,' he mumbled low, in apology. 'I have always been a man who has made his own way, scorning none, beholden to none. I have nothing left save my pride, and it blinds me to the goodness of others. I cannot bear to see Ruth with neither dignity nor hope.' She saw the shine of tears behind his lashes. 'I beg you will not judge me too harshly for my rudeness.' He walked abruptly away, and she hurried after him to put a gentle hand upon his shoulder wordlessly. He simply nodded without turning, that she might not see his face.

Jane returned to kneel beside Ruth, feeling anew the sickness and fear she had kept hidden from John Bessant. Ruth's face was bathed in sweat. Her skin, although reddened, was strangely cold and clammy to the touch and Jane continued her patient wiping away of the moisture and fevered heat. Yet, even as she soaked the rags from the ewer of water which she had, in desperation, taken from the font beside the church door, the beads of sweat oozed afresh, to glisten and fall unchecked. The rags dried upon Ruth's burning skin, stiffened with sweat and crusted salt, her clothing clinging, sodden and restricting, about her swollen body. Jane, grateful for the chatelaine chained at her waist, loosed the small scissors and slashed ruthlessly at Ruth's coarse gown, tearing it fiercely from hem to neck, then ripping through the ragged bodice beneath . . . Ruth seemed scarcely aware of Jane's presence, her whole body trembling as with some violent ague, before convulsions racked her, leaving her so pitifully weakened and exhausted that she could neither speak nor open her eyes.

Jane covered the poor naked flesh with the two black cloaks which hung upon the vestry wall, knowing that fierce though the pains of birth might be, Ruth suffered some deeper, more radical ill. She found herself praying helplessly and, unable to relieve the fury of hurt which racked Ruth's flesh with pain, its violence so acute that Jane's hand, gripped within hers, grew numbed of feeling.

It was a nightmare such as Jane had never known, and would remember always in the darkest times. The fever which had burned upon Ruth's skin now gave way to a coldness, the flesh clammy and supernaturally pale. There was a veined blueness at her lips and nostrils and, so still had she become that Jane, fearing her dead, bent low towards Ruth's mouth, unable, even then, to find sign of breath and life. She had never before been anything but a spectator at a birth, watching others, observing, storing it unthinkingly within her mind. Now, alone, she did by instinct and memory what needed to be done. When the tremors began anew, she bathed, comforted, helped, unaware of the bloodiness of birth, only its necessity.

Doggedly, determinedly, she held the child's limp body, slippery and wet, within her own hands, cradling it tenderly, wiping the closed, viscous lids, nostrils and mouth with the clean, soft rags set aside. Then, knowing that the child was dead, she cut the umbilical cord and tied it, her fingers shaking and clumsy in her hurt.

It was then that the mule and cart came. John Bessant took his daughter from her and Jane surrendered her unresisting. Then, quietly, without fuss, Megan and her mother were ministering to Ruth. Gently taking the babe from John Bessant, the two women ushered them all quietly without, closing the curtains to the vestry with a finality which brought tears of realisation to Jane's eyes. Enfolded in Prys's strong arms, she wept with pity and helplessness and for the babe that was lost.

Dry-eyed, John Bessant walked outside into the street, returning from the cart as Prys had bidden him, bearing the drawer of the small chest which Prys and she had been taking to the carpenter's shop for repair.

'A cradle and a coffin . . .' Jane said.

Chapter Eleven

Prys had gone unbidden to search for the young curate, that he might comfort Ruth and give blessing for the repose of the soul of the dead child. Was a stillborn babe deemed to have lived? Had a separate existence? Prys did not know, his most violent concern was for that grief-stricken couple within the church.

There had been no sighting of Peter Morrish at his cottage, nor upon the byways, and it was Tom Hallowes who confided, shaking his head regretfully, 'I fear you will not find him, sir, for I last saw him walking with the paupers upon their way.'

'You are sure of this?'

'Quite sure. I watched him leave. He will not be back yet awhile.'

'Then I must await his return. The child will need burial and I would rather it were given with love and pity. A pauper is counted of little enough worth in life, and less in death!'

'Yes. That is a fact.'

'Yet a newborn infant is surely deserving of dignity in death!' Prys's voice rose impassionedly. 'It is human flesh, and blameless.'

'If we were all afforded the dignity we deserved,' said Hallowes quietly, 'I fear few of us would be fitted to lie beside it. We must trust God's mercy and judgement are kinder than our own.'

'Amen to that,' said Prys fervently, stirring the mule into grudging movement.

Jane sat dry-eyed and stiffly erect within a pew before the altar, awaiting Prys's return with the young clergyman. She had a yearning to rest her face against the coolness of the wood, and to weep, yet the grief remained, hard and unyielding as a stone, constricting her throat and chest.

Tender-hearted Megan had come quietly to sit beside her, banished by her mother from Ruth's side. Megan had been helpless to stem her tears for pitying that stillborn babe, and Jane found herself once more comforter to another's hurt.

'It was kind of your mother to come to Ruth's aid,' Jane ventured when sympathy, then firmness, had dried the girl's tears.

''Twas all I could think of,' Megan confessed, 'for none would help us, and Mr Prys was close to despair.'

'But the doctor, Megan. Would he not come?'

'No, ma'am,' she hesitated. 'We did not rightly see him, for the housekeeper turned us away, declaring that he did not treat paupers. She would have slammed shut the door, but Mr Prys had forced his foot within to hold it wide.'

'And then?' Jane demanded.

'She screamed out, ma'am, and a groom came running from the stables and held a pitchfork to Mr Prys's throat. He warned him to be gone at once, else he would pierce him through and likely set the hounds to feed upon his miserable hide and mine. Should we dare return, it would be a blunderbuss and not a hayfork we would face.' Megan's voice was bleak with remembered shame. 'There was no call to treat us so, nor to shout insults after us, for we had done no harm to any. I shouted back that Mr Prys was an honest man, a gentleman, and that the groom was naught but a drunken, useless clod, less than the muck from his own stables. But Mr Prys bade me hold my tongue, although he said it kindly. We fared no better at Dr Tobin's and the midwife would not budge unless she was paid there and then, in full, but Mr Prys could not raise the money. My mother came, without need of second bidding.'

There was pride on Megan's thin face and Jane smiled

and hugged the girl impulsively. Prys would never speak of the scorn and humiliation he had endured, Jane felt sure. He was a proud, private man but his hurt would have been for Ruth and John Bessant.

Recognising the familiar rattle and creak of Prys's cart, she hurried without the church to greet him. His face was unusually grave as he dismounted then drew her quietly aside to where they could not be overheard.

'Mr Morrish has left Penavon to march with the paupers,' he said. 'Do you think, Jane, that I should ride out for Penry Vaughan? It is the child and Ruth I think of. I have little hope of his value, or, indeed, of his coming.'

'No! Ruth was firm upon it. She will have him at no price. She thought him arrogant and contemptuous of those in the poorhouse. I fear that to insist upon it would be more than she can bear.'

He stared at her in silence before blurting out clumsily, 'There is something I must tell you, confess. I would have kept it hid, but it is burning within me.'

'What is it, Hywel?' her voice rose anxiously. 'There is something serious amiss? Master Carne or Mostyn?'

'No, my dear, there is naught amiss, save that I felt compelled to do something,' he faltered, 'something rash, and for which you might blame me.' His fine, strong-boned face was drawn with concern, his eyes troubled. 'The money I saved, Jane, from my work at Great House . . . it was to be a crutch and support for times ahead, when we have need of it. I have spent it, Jane, every last farthing!'

'Then I am sure it was not done without thought and good reason,' she said carefully after a while, hoping that her voice did not betray her apprehension. 'What is it, Hywel, that you have purchased so urgently and with such recklessness?'

'A coffin for the child and a plot within the churchyard walls. I have ordered the coffin carriage to bear the little one, and hired two horses.'

She stared at him in silence for so long that he grew afraid that his rashness had angered her, but she threw her arms about him impetuously, kissed him hard, declaring, her eyes bright with unshed tears, 'Oh, my dear man . . . my dear man! How proud I am of you!'

He gently disengaged her arms from about his neck, unable to hide his surprise and pleasure, but confessing awkwardly, 'I lied, Jane, without shame or remorse, for I could not see the child buried in an unmarked grave without the churchyard.'

She did not speak but he felt the comforting pressure of her fingers upon his own.

'The undertaker . . . I believe he knew, Jane, for he asked me if the infant had lived. It seems there is some difficulty about a grave plot else, and Penry Vaughan must be called upon to make ruling. I said, Yes, the child had lived. He demanded to know the parents' names, and if they were paupers, and I said. . .' Prys hesitated uncertainly. 'I said, No. They are soon to leave this parish for another place where work awaits my daughter, Ruth, and her husband, John. Our granddaughter would be in our care and lie beside us at the end, for I purchased the two plots abutting the child's. I have spent nigh on every penny I had saved, Jane, and cannot regret it, unless it has caused you hurt.'

'You did right, my dear, and I would lie as whole-heartedly, even were it to damn my eternal soul!' she declared with feeling. 'As for the money, 'tis well spent, for who can put a price upon peace of mind for Ruth and John, or upon such a warm and generous spirit as your own? It is worth those poor coins you have spent, a thousand times over.'

Jane pleaded to stay beside Ruth Bessant in order to minister to her needs throughout the night but Megan's mother, the Widow Griffin, was firm that Jane should return to the cottage with Prys.

'John and I will remain watchful beside her,' she declared, 'for 'tis plain that you have driven yourself beyond all endurance and are in need of comfort and rest as much as she.'

Jane protested but her pallor and exhaustion were plain, and John Bessant added his earnest persuasion with the assurance that Ruth would be well tended until her return upon the morrow.

When John and Mrs Griffin were occupied at Ruth's side, Jane carefully emptied her purse of all its coins, firmly rehearsing Megan in what she must bring from the village: candles, a tinder box, victuals, milk and ale, the cheapest wooden platters, spoons and bowls, all that was needed until the morrow, when Jane would return with clothing and food from the cottage. She watched Megan and Prys ride out upon the mule and cart then she stood indecisively before taking the pathway which skirted the church. It was certainty and comfort she sought, the strength to return within. Yet the only certainty lay in that tide of cold, grey stone that spilled about her. Anonymous. Claiming all that was past.

When Megan and Prys had returned with their purchases and Jane, Megan, John Bessant and Mrs Griffin were unpacking them and setting them to rights, Prys told John what he had done for their child. He told him quietly, unemotionally, and, when he had finished, John Bessant took Prys's hand firmly in his own, saying warmly, 'You have earned the right of kinship, Mr Prys, for you and Mrs Eynon have done more for us and the babe than any others upon this earth, and I thank you for it with all my heart. We will never meet your like again, of that I am sure.' His voice faltered and grew low, then he raised his head and looked resolutely into Prys's eyes, promising, 'We will not forget the kindness you have all shown to strangers, paupers . . . nor will we ever forget you. I swear, by all I hold most dear, that the good you have wrought will pass, through me, to others in need. You have restored in me the certainty that there are honest, compassionate people in a world grown hostile and cold.'

Penry Vaughan gazed through the windows of his study across the well-ordered lawns and shrubbery to the fern-clad hills beyond. The morning was mild, with that golden mellowness of light which comes with no other season but autumn, and Vaughan himself felt as mellow and at ease.

Carne had submitted to his authority, recognised his guardianship. It was a small enough victory but a beginning at least. The boy was in sad need of discipline and sound moral training. He had been too long alternately neglected and indulged, and without firm handling would show the same arrogance and profligacy as Rice Havard himself. Vaughan prided himself that he was not a vindictive man nor lacking in understanding. He would allow Carne and Mostyn to ride beside him in the open carriage as he paid his duty calls throughout the parish. Well dressed and obedient, they would serve to mark his charity in offering them a home, and raise him in the esteem of other gentle-folk such as he, for, dispossessed or not, near-penniless or not, the Havards were the undisputed squires of Penavon, and none could doubt their superiority.

With Carne and Mostyn beside him and Probert at the reins, Vaughan was driven out in the open carriage, comfortably aware that his sartorial elegance, and that of his young cousins, equalled that of their conveyance. He rewarded the shuffling self-conscious deference of his labouring parishioners with a brisk nod as he passed by, bidding Carne and Mostyn to do the same. To those less humble, Vaughan inclined his head and fingered the brim of his high silk hat, and to those his equal in birth, he raised it high with the added courtesy of a gracious bow. The ultimate accolade.

Probert's instructions were to first halt at Peter Morrish's cottage within Penavon village, but to Vaughan's annoyance his curate was not within. He was undoubtedly to be found at the church, Vaughan decided, and giving solace to the intruders and ingrates within. Burning with rancour, Vaughan returned to the carriage and, with lips compressed, ordered Probert to halt the carriage without the church for he had urgent business within. So severe had

94

been his mien that Mostyn's wriggling and chattering had ceased, and Carne had withdrawn more despairingly within himself, his thoughts upon his father's burial and his own isolation and loss.

'You will remain within the carriage, talking to no-one, and on no account venture upon the highway,' Vaughan commanded. 'It is understood?'

'Yes, sir. It is understood.'

Scarcely had he entered when there was a rattling and jolting of cart wheels upon the uneven cobblestones and the jangle and clatter of harness and hoof which heralded the arrival of a cart. Carne, glancing through the window of the coach, saw with incredulous delight that it was Prys and Jane upon a waggon, cluttered untidily with all manner of things, as fascinatingly haphazard to view as a tinker's hoard. With childish enthusiasm, Carne threw open the door of the coach and descended with impatient haste, flinging his arms impulsively about Jane as she stood, surprised, upon the highway before hugging him affectionately in return.

'Oh, Master Carne, my dear, my dear!' she exclaimed rapturously when she could take breath. Then, turning to Prys who had climbed down beside her, she said, unable to quell her excitement, 'Hywel! Look who has come to see us. Carne has been driven here specially. Is it not a treat to see him so well, and so elegant, my dear?' She turned again to Carne, hugging with renewed vigour, demanding, 'You have been allowed to visit alone?'

'No, Jane,' he broke off suddenly, face bleak with the realisation of what he had done. 'My cousin Mr Vaughan, is within.'

Prys, tight-lipped and pale with apprehension, exchanged a swift glance of warning with Jane and ran within. Carne, despite Jane's entreaties that he climb back into the coach before more hurt was done, and Probert's impassioned pleas from the box, refused to be deterred. Shaking himself free of Jane's restraining hand, he darted towards the open door of the church and she, forced into terrified action, followed despairingly at his heels.

The sight which greeted them was so bizarre and unexpected that Jane and Carne halted in disbelief. Penry Vaughan must have drawn aside the curtain to the vestry with such violence that it lay abandoned upon the stone-paved floor, rings and broken wooden pole beside it. Widow Griffin was half carrying, half supporting Ruth, whose face was pale as the pauper's shift she still wore, eyes wide with terror and incomprehension.

Their few poor chattels had been hurled into the church and lay scattered and broken all about. Penry Vaughan, trembling and all but incoherent with rage, was kicking wildly at the straw which had served as Ruth's and Widow Griffin's bed, sending it flying in a storm of chaff. Then, oblivious to all but the murderous hate within him, he raised an arm and sent the few remaining victuals and crocks upon the vestry table smashing noisily to the floor.

Prys, who had arrived moments before Jane and Carne, stood for an instant within the church, appalled by the noise and fury of Vaughan's violence. He was raging and screaming like one possessed, face contorted into a swollen mask, engorged, barely human.

His eyes seemed to fasten briefly upon Carne, although it was clear to Prys that they did so without recognition, or even sight. But Carne, rigid with terror, had surrendered briefly to Jane's comforting arms, face buried against her bodice to shut out the obscenity of his cousin's fury.

The man was insane, Prys thought, for Vaughan was laying about him now indiscriminately, sending everything and anything before him hurtling to destruction without reason or pause. Yet, still, Prys was unable to move, limbs made powerless by horror and disbelief. He did not know from whence in the body of the church John Bessant suddenly came but he did so with an anger as frightening as Vaughan's own. Pushing roughly past Ruth and Mistress Griffin as though he had not seen them, eyes wild with despair too long suppressed, he picked up the broken rod from the paving stone and raised it high.

Jane did not know what murderous blow might have

fallen upon Vaughan's skull had not Prys yelled aloud, then run to him, wrenching it fiercely from his grasp. Already one blow had been aimed, but passion and Prys's startled cry had swerved it awry so that it had fallen harmlessly, but with splintering force, upon the table edge, shaking John Bessant's every bone with its fierceness.

Vaughan, alerted by the crack of wood against wood, seemed to come abruptly to his senses, gazing about him at first with bewilderment at the chaos he had wrought. Then he rubbed a hand across his mouth, reaching within his coat for a silk handkerchief, dabbing it fastidiously upon his lips to wipe the saliva away. Seeing the broken rod in Prys's hands, and the two terrified women hunched within a pew, he hesitated, afraid perhaps that Prys would strike him a blow. Yet Prys threw it from him contemptuously to place a restraining hand upon John Bessant's arm and lead him away.

'You will leave this church!' Vaughan had believed himself under control but his voice rose nervously high. 'You have no business here. If you return, you will suffer for it!' To his chagrin, no-one spoke.

John Bessant lifted his wife gently from the pew and carried her to the door and out to Prys's waiting cart. Prys had taken Mistress Griffin's arm and made to follow when Vaughan's enraged voice cried peevishly, 'Clear this filth and mess, I say.'

'It was of your making,' said Prys stolidly. 'You clean it!'

Shaking with rage, Vaughan called after him. 'This is a sanctuary, the house of God. You had best reflect upon it.'

'No, sir. It is you who should reflect.' Prys's tone was serene, unruffled.

Vaughan, determined to vent his spleen, called out to Carne, 'Come here, sir, this instant! I command it!'

Carne left Jane's side and walked slowly to face him.

'You deliberately defied me! Did I not tell you to stay within the coach? Answer me, sir! I demand answer.'

'Yes, Cousin Penry.'

A stinging blow across his cheek sent him reeling against a pew and he clutched it for support, standing there, dry-eyed, a red weal disfiguring his cheek. Jane would have run to him, but Prys's warning look halted her and she knew he feared for Carne's safety should she interfere.

'Get back to the coach,' Vaughan ordered. 'I will deal with you in private.'

Carne raised his head and looked at him dispassionately, then with something akin to pity, 'It is wrong,' he said clearly, 'to use your strength against those in need like the paupers. It is a coward's way, and my father would not have behaved so.'

'Get out!' cried Vaughan. 'Get out, I say, before I start upon you in earnest!'

Carne, passing beside Jane, saw her tearful face made ugly with concern for him. He touched her arm gently, 'I am young now,' he said, 'and weak . . . but it will not always be so.'

Unlike Vaughan, she recognised beneath the threat the sad, despairing cry of a child, lost and afraid, and Carne's defiance gave her no comfort.

Chapter Twelve

It was a subdued little company which set out upon the mule and cart for Hillbrook Cottage. The late autumn day was dappled with pale sunlight, but it lacked real warmth. A soft breeze stirred the grass and rustled the last stubborn leaves upon the trees, so that they trembled and loosed their hold, drifting, gentle and weightless as dry, curled feathers. On the sycamore, the winged seeds still hung in dark, rounded clusters, like birds perched in the bare branches of a dead tree. When they took flight, it was with slow grace, spiralling, riding the soft wind as though reluctant to return to earth.

John Bessant sat hunched, face buried in his hands, not speaking, his mind intent upon the murder he had so nearly wrought. If Prys had not snatched the rod from his hands, his journey might have been to a cell and the gallows, and what would have become of Ruth? He began to shake and tremble, his flesh cold beneath the threadbare fabric of his pauper's coat. Jane, glancing at him with concern, saw that the silent tears were dropping from his cheeks and chin, squeezed through the clasped fingers of his thin hands.

'You are cold, my dear,' she said gently. 'We will soon be home and beside a warm fire. Then I will make you a warmed ale and a good hot meal.'

He nodded wordlessly, drying his eyes upon his palms, turning his head away that Ruth might not see the traces of tears upon his face.

'The breeze has still a raw nip to it . . . and the dust kicked up by the mule's hooves make a grit for the eyes,' said Mistress Griffin. 'It plagues me often,' she confessed, although all knew that she owned neither mule nor cart.

Jane said, 'There is food aplenty in the cottage; loaves and buttermilk, and mutton and herbs for a stew. We shall soon enough put flesh upon your bones, Ruth . . . and you, Mrs Griffin, shall stay and break bread with us. I insist upon it, and Hywel will drive you home upon the cart. The children will be safe enough in your Megan's care. She is a good and sensible girl.' Dear Life! thought Jane, I am babbling like a fool, afraid of silence and bereft of sense. Yet the question within us dies unspoken: who will give strength to our spirit? Who will help us?

In the carriage, Carne, seated opposite Mostyn, felt sickness churn in his stomach and the moistness of sweat upon his palms, the hollow of his neck, and his upper lip. His clothing clung to him damply, as if he had grown uncomfortably hot beside a blazing fire, and his mouth felt as dry and arid. He would not look at Penry Vaughan, he thought, but stare ahead as if nothing untoward had occurred and he had no reason to feel afraid. Yet he could not erase the violence of the scene he had witnessed from his mind, nor forget the sight of his cousin's face, grotesque, twisted in rage. Perhaps, Carne thought, if he concentrated hard enough upon the black leather of the seat beside Mostyn, he might go blind, then he might never see Vaughan's face again.

'Carne.' Mostyn had wriggled from his seat and was standing anxiously beside him, gripping his brother's hand in his own small fist, lurching and stumbling with the swaying of the carriage. 'Are you cross with me, Carne?' His voice was high with anxiety.

'No. Go back to your seat, Mostyn.' The words came awkwardly, for his tongue seemed swollen. 'I am not cross with you, I promise . . . It is none of your doing.'

'Return to your seat at once, Mostyn!' Penry Vaughan's voice was cold. 'You are behaving childishly. I will not countenance it. If you persist, I shall be forced to punish you!'

The rebuke was for Mostyn, but his gaze was upon Carne. Mostyn climbed disconsolately back into his place, murmuring bleakly, 'I called out to Jane, but she did not answer nor come to me.'

Vaughan's face had become suffused with ugly colour, his lips tight, but he remained silent. Mostyn, bewildered and frightened, had retired into his misery, unwilling even to look at Carne, for he seemed so remote and strange, as if they no longer belonged. A small tear escaped and trickled to Mostyn's mouth and he tasted the salt of it but made no sound.

None spoke within the carriage. The clopping of hooves, the jangle of harness, and even the rhythmic snorting and breathing of the horses seemed too loud and painful to be borne. Then, with the grinding of the carriage wheels upon the cobblestones of the yard, Penry Vaughan took up his silver-knobbed cane, adjusted his silk hat, and descended without haste.

Mostyn, upon climbing apprehensively from the carriage, was dispatched at once to the small schoolroom prepared for his studies and ordered to occupy himself usefully. Carne was sent to his room with the injunction to remain there until Penry Vaughan saw fit to deal with him. Carne sat quietly, awaiting his displeasure, sickness burning in his throat at the prospect of the punishment he knew he must endure. He would have taken the miniatures of his Mama and Papa from their pigskin pouch but he did not, for he knew it would but add to his cousin's rage and dislike. Instead, he held within his palm the pretty snail shell, creamily circled with brown, and fragile and delicate as a bird's egg, which he had brought from Great House. When Penry Vaughan entered, his face was a mask of sternness and he bore a hazel switch, cruelly thin and supple.

'Stand up, Carne!' he instructed. 'Do not slouch and cower like a guttersnipe or yard boy; you are a gentleman, and should face your punishment as such.'

'Yes, sir,' Carne rose apprehensively to his feet, his eyes

drawn involuntarily towards the switch although he tried to glance away.

Vaughan sent it whipping experimentally into an arc, the sound of it stinging swiftly through the air. 'I had thought of thrashing you . . . which is what you deserve,' he said, mouth pursed fastidiously, 'but I have decided upon a course of leniency, although it is against my conviction and better judgement.'

Carne, in his relief, felt his fist tighten upon the snail shell, crushing it, feeling the sharp fragments cut into his palm.

'Since you behave as stupidly as a girl,' said Vaughan contemptuously, 'we had best punish you as one. For you are clearly not man enough to withstand a beating.'

He intends to dress me as a girl, Carne thought in horror, and parade me before all. I will not stand for it! I will not be so humiliated!

'Well?' demanded Vaughan. 'Have you nothing to say, sir?'

Carne fidgeted uncomfortably, considering in his mind the time to best strike out and flee.

'No? I trust the full insolence and gravity of your behaviour render you silent. You do well to reflect upon it.'

Carne felt a cold fury rising that Penry Vaughan, who had behaved with such frenzied madness within the church, should call into question his own behaviour. It was unfair, wickedly unfair.

'Lift your arms, boy,' commanded Vaughan. 'Place them with hands above your shoulders, elbows to your sides.'

Bewildered, Carne obeyed as Vaughan threaded the hazel switch behind Carne's back, closing the boy's fists upon it.

'That is the way they teach girls patience and deportment, sir. You will remain standing so for one hour, during which time you may reflect upon your insolence to me before others not of our class in society. Such rudeness before inferiors is intolerable. Unforgivable. Mrs Groves will come here directly and see that you do not renege upon your punishment. You may not lower your arms, nor be seated, until the hour is past. Then you will devise a full confession of your sins and make apology by writing them upon the slate she will bring. I bid you good-night, cousin. You will not expect to dine tonight, for you are worthy of neither company nor food.'

Carne stood until his arms ached and his shoulders and elbows grew numbed of feeling. All was pain beyond endurance but he did endure and Mrs Groves had no criticism of him to offer to Penry Vaughan.

'He is a stubborn, determined boy,' she declared, 'arrogant by nature. It grieves me to say it, sir, but there was the trace of a smile upon his face, even though he had suffered a full hour of punishment.'

Vaughan, if he were disturbed at all, showed no sign of it, remarking that, 'It takes time, Mrs Groves, to break a rebellious animal and make it docile.'

Carne, sitting at his desk, with pain in every nerve and muscle, scrupulously wrote a list of his sins upon his slate leaving out his name, putting in its stead that of Penry Vaughan, ready to erase it at an instant. Stupidity. Ignorance. Rage. Bigotry. Insolence. Cruelty. The list grew and filled both sides of his slate as he scornfully catalogued Penry Vaughan's sins. He had only one regret, and that was for the crushing of his snail shell . . . well, two regrets in all. The other, that it had not been Penry Vaughan!

Upon the funeral eve, the burial carriage arrived at Hillbrook, bearing the tiny coffin of wood. Jane begged the undertaker set it before the fire upon two funeral stools, across which a draped wooden board was already waiting. When Peter Morrish came there was a watch service within the cottage with the four within keeping vigil over the tiny corpse throughout the night. The service by candlelight was simple, as befitted a child, and tears were shed for the waste of it and the cruelty of a life snuffed out as heedlessly as a candle flame before it was even begun. Peter Morrish spoke eloquently of the innocence of the infant and its deliverance from suffering and hurt and, when he had left, they resumed their quiet vigil around the dead child.

Upon morning, they had slept little and grieved long. As the funeral cart returned and bore the small coffin from sight and to the church, Jane saw upon the doorstep the evidence of kindness from people unknown; a few small offerings of fruit, eggs, meat and butter, spared with difficulty by those who would most feel its loss, a heap of copper coins and a sixpence.

Later, within the church, those few who attended placed silver upon the cloth-covered dish as recompense to the clergyman for his services. However, it was Peter Morrish who secretly placed a gold half sovereign upon the plate and, as secretly, handed the offerings to John Bessant, begging that he accept.

At the graveside the commital to earth was gentle and brief and Ruth, tearless, for all her tears had been long shed, thought that it was no more than the planting of a small and delicate flower, too fragile to survive the winds of circumstance.

After the service, John Bessant climbed upon the cart given to him and Ruth by Peter Morrish, their meagre possessions all around them.

'We will return,' he said, 'for I shall make it my pledge and duty to do so. Then I shall try as best I can to repay the real love we have known here.'

'Believe that we shall not forget you,' Prys said, gripping John's hand hard and clasping him to him briefly. Then he kissed Ruth's cold cheek, saying quietly, 'Until we meet again, my dear, in kinder times.'

With John and Ruth Bessant's leaving, Jane felt a real sadness of loss. Her mind kept dwelling uneasily upon the scene of violence within the church and Carne's part in it. His spirited defiance of his cousin had made her proud, yet she could not doubt that the punishment exacted for his contempt must have been hard to bear. There had been so much change of late that she often felt confused and uncertain. Yet, of one thing she was sure, that in Hywel Prys she had found a man of strength and compassion above the ordinary. In less than a week the final banns for the wedding would be called, and then no-one and nothing, save death itself, could separate them.

She sighed, and Prys took a hand from the reins to settle his fingers comfortingly over hers, believing it was their errand which disturbed her. They were bound for the carpenter's shop to commission him to replace the drawer of her chest. Since the dead babe had so tragically been laid within it, Jane had no heart to use it more. So absorbed in her thoughts was she that it was with a start she realised that the cart was rattling upon the uneven cobblestones and Prys was warning her to make ready, for they were entering the village.

With the mule safely tethered to an iron ring set into the wall of the carpenter's shop, Prys helped Jane to dismount. Sensitive to her mood and her reluctance to enter, Prys had asked kindly, 'Why do you not choose yourself a wedding bonnet at the milliner's, my love? I do not doubt that it would lift your spirits. I will deal with all else.'

Jane was of a mind to refuse, protesting that the repairs to the cottage, and the babe's funeral, had caused expense enough. Then, aware of Prys's concerned face, she felt shame at her meanness of spirit and purse. He was worthy of better. She would go to her wedding proudly, allowing it the dignity and importance it deserved.

She entered the milliner's hesitantly, glimpsing through the open doorway the women hunched over their labours in the humid, vapour-ridden air. One old woman, with a clenched fist of a face, was painstakingly shaping damp straw into a bonnet upon a wooden block, its crude shape a replica of her own pale skull beneath the sparse hair. Another sat stitching at a bonnet brim as if her very life depended upon it, as, perhaps, it did. Her fingers were raw-fleshed, for the straw was coarse and the needle's path unpredictable, but she neither slowed nor ceased her stitching. At the fireside, another ancient, bent almost double by some rigid deformity of the spine, was replacing a kettle upon the chain above the glowing coals, her hands so palsied that the spilt water danced upon the fire bars and hearth, then flew off in hissing globules. She glanced up and, seeing Jane, hobbled awkwardly towards her, giving a smile and word of greeting which she courteously returned.

Upon an impulse, Jane chose, not a serviceable bonnet in sober black straw, but a pretty confection of softest lavender with flowers and veiling which she wore triumphantly without the shop. If the milliner had thought it a vastly unsuitable choice for an elderly spinster, then she had not remarked upon it, for it was upon such vagaries that her livelihood depended.

But Prys was clearly delighted. 'My dear,' he said gently. 'You look as elegant and stylish as any lady in the land. I'll warrant that every woman in Penavon, whether matron or maid, will demand an identical new bonnet. Yet none could wear it with such grace and distinction.'

Jane smiled, her doubts dispersing before such absurd flattery. 'Perhaps I should be grateful, Hywel, that all your drab geese are swans,' she said, laughing despite herself as she took his proffered arm to be assisted on to the mule cart.

'Not so, my love,' he declared, bowing gallantly when she was safely settled, then climbing up to seat himself beside her. 'You alone are my swan . . . serene, unruffled, however troubled the waters.'

Despite the amusement which wrinkled the corners of his eyes and tugged his lips into a smile, there was a seriousness in his tone which belied his easy banter. Jane stretched out a hand to touch his, briefly, upon the reins.

'Well, my swan?' he asked indulgently. 'Where would you have me sail?'

She hesitated, then said firmly, 'To Penavon vicarage that I might see Carne and Mostyn.'

He shook his head despairingly, voice grown curt. 'I will not see you hurt and humiliated further by Penry Vaughan. He declared us to be unfit company and has the legal right to forbid us access. I beg you will reconsider.'

'No, Hywel!' There was anguish in her refusal. 'I must see Carne, else he will fear I have forsaken him.'

'You will be turned away like a common beggar. You will be insulted and made small before the child himself.'

'I should be smaller in his eyes, Hywel, and my own, if I did not try to show my caring,' she reasoned quietly. 'As petty and mean-minded as Penry Vaughan himself. As for being turned away like a common beggar, then I will beg and plead like one if need be, and feel no shame, as I plead now with you to do as I ask.'

'I do not agree with it, Jane,' he said stiffly. 'It is rash and will achieve naught save to inflame Vaughan and fuel his dislike for Carne. Yet, if you are so firmly set upon it, I will drive you there.'

He manoeuvred the mule skilfully between the broad pillars of the vicarage gateway and into the cobbled yard at the rear of the house. The cart jolted and rattled so perilously upon the irregular stones that Jane was forced to put a hand to her new bonnet lest it take flight. However, the mule's unmelodious chorus of disgruntled honks so echoed her own resentment that she could not restrain her laughter. Soon Prys was laughing too, to the contempt of a disdainful manservant who had been sent to investigate the uproar, and the bewilderment of a stable-lad who plainly thought them deranged.

Before Prys had opportunity to explain their errand, there was the distinctive sound of a coach approaching upon the carriageway, then swinging into the yard to halt beside them. There was no mistaking the Havard crest emblazoned upon its side, nor the four fine wheelers and leaders which drew it, nor the familiar livery upon the coachman, Probert, as he leapt agilely from the box.

Before their startled eyes, the Reverend Penry Vaughan had wrenched open the door of the coach, flinging it back furiously upon its hinges and descending unaided. The manservant who had been hovering uselessly in the doorway attempted to move forward to make explanation but

107

Vaughan pushed him unceremoniously aside, bidding him, 'Hold your tongue, man!' Then, white with rage, he turned to harangue the luckless stable boy, still fumbling inexpertly with the uncoupling of the horses, nervousness making him clumsy. The task surrendered to a groom, he tried to render himself invisible by fleeing behind the coach, there to crouch snivelling.

Jane almost wished herself the same escape. She could scarcely bring herself to look at Vaughan, so distorted was his face with anger and spite that it was barely recognisable. His speech was almost unintelligible, spluttering, protesting, his words spilling as fiercely from his lips as the saliva from the corners of his mouth. Once again, Jane relived the frenzy of his hatred within the church. The fear she felt then for Ruth and John was now all for Carne and she bitterly regretted that she had not heeded Prys's well-meant advice.

Almost as if she conjured him from the air by thinking of him, Carne leapt from the open doorway of the coach, disdaining the steps, to fling his arms about her waist, crying breathlessly, 'Jane! Oh, Jane! You have come for me! I thought I was forgotten.' He buried his head against her skirt and her hand stole protectively to his head to smooth the familiar dark hair. Immediately, though, Vaughan had torn him free, shaking him impatiently by the shoulders and exclaiming, 'Control yourself, boy! You behave like a street urchin, a guttersnipe! You have neither self-control nor manners! You disgrace yourself, and me!' He motioned to the manservant standing impotently in the doorway to the house. 'Escort Master Carne within,' he commanded. 'I will deal with him in the library. See that he awaits me there.'

As the servant made to hustle Carne away, Mostyn suddenly appeared in the coach doorway, face bloodless, eyes wide with apprehension beneath the cluster of pale curls. His soft underlip quivered with uncertainty as he strove to rub the bewilderment from his eyes. Prys had moved towards the coach and held out his arms encouragingly to swing him down in safety but the child ignored him, as he ignored Jane, terrified gaze fixed upon Penry Vaughan. Mostyn felt the old pain and sickness constricting his throat, the bitterness of rejection. He had somehow made his cousin angry, as he had made Papa despise him, and he did not know why. Carne, seeing the bewildered terror in Mostyn's eyes, hesitated in the doorway, poised to wrench himself from the servant's grasp should Mostyn cry out to him. Mostyn looked to Jane despairingly, torn between the familiar shelter of her arms and his cousin. Finally, it was to Penry Vaughan that he ran, clutching his cousin's hand, crying out hysterically, 'Send them away, Cousin Penry! Send them away!'

'Hush, child,' said Penry Vaughan. 'Do not disturb yourself. I will see that you come to no harm.'

Mostyn's hand tightened fiercely upon his cousin's fingers as Carne exclaimed, voice raw with distress, 'Shame upon you, Mostyn! Jane and Mr Prys have shown you nothing but kindness. You know full well they would die rather than cause you harm. Apologise, this instant!' His voice rose warningly. 'This instant, I say!'

Mostyn hesitated and looked up into Penry Vaughan's face, seeking some sign as to what he must do, then he stared hard at Carne, saying defiantly, 'They do not belong. They are servants, not people. Servants do not visit gentlemen. That is true, is it not, Cousin Penry?'

Penry Vaughan acknowledged by the merest inclination of his head that this was so.

'Besides,' declared Mostyn, made reckless by approval, 'they have driven here like paupers, gypsies. I know, for I saw some once, upon a cart. It is low and commonplace to travel upon a cart.'

'Hell and damnation!' Carne's shrill oath reverberated around the yard. 'The devil take you, Mostyn, for the arrogant, spiteful little wretch you are! I will have no truck with you! I will not call you brother!' He was hurried away before any could make reply, but Vaughan's lips were tightly compressed as he delivered Mostyn into the care of the housekeeper, who had come, unnoticed, to shepherd him within.

'Do not let them come here again, Cousin Penry!' Mostyn cried. 'They make you angry, and Carne hates me. Send them away!' he begged, weeping, and was gathered reassuringly into Mrs Groves' arms and borne within.

'You have heard the child,' stated Vaughan with malicious satisfaction. 'There is no more to be said, save that my kinsmen are *my* wards, in *my* care.'

As Jane made to protest, Prys placed a restraining hand upon her shoulder and drew her gently towards him, shaking his head in warning, although his eyes were as saddened as her own.

'Should you contemplate returning, then I shall be forced to inform my fellow justices. The penalties will be severe, you may depend upon it! You will trespass no more upon my property, and time!' said Vaughan dismissively. 'Should I hear that you have attempted to waylay my wards, or lure them to your house, or, indeed, to attempt any contact with them, I give you my word that you will long regret it. Now, go!'

Without another word he strode purposefully into the house, face set, shoulders high, and there was no mistaking his extreme satisfaction.

Silently, Prys lifted Jane upon the cart, tears of humiliation burning her cheeks as if they fell upon open wounds. Probert held the mule steady and shrugged helplessly as Prys silently took the reins, and the cart clattered awkwardly over the cobblestones of the vicarage yard and on to the highway.

'You said no good would come of it, Hywel, and you were right.' Jane's words, thickened with tears, were slurred and almost inaudible.

'No,' said Prys, grieved and repentant, 'I was wrong, my love. You showed Carne that you cared, that he was not forgot.'

She nodded, and tried to smile, but her face 'neath the brave new bonnet was defeated and old, as if she wore it for the burial of one loved. The void which lay before her now seemed deeper, and as barren, as the grave.

Carne's punishment was swift, and, Penry Vaughan dared to believe, salutary. Mrs Groves was instructed to ensure that his mouth was symbolically washed out with soft soap to cleanse it from those oaths so blasphemously uttered. Thereafter, he would be confined to his room to reflect upon his sins and to pray, most earnestly, for forgiveness. Moreover, he must eat alone, since his conversation and attitude made him unfit for civilised Christian company. He would, he was instructed, be expected to learn the names of the twelve tribes of Israel by rote, and be tested, most stringently, upon them. First, he must deliver a written essay upon the subject of 'The evils of Insolence, Indolence and Pride'.

'I trust I have made myself clear, sir?' Vaughan's expression was coldly supercilious, his fingers rubbing at his palms fastidiously, as if attempting to rid them of something unclean. 'Well, Cousin?'

'Yes, sir. You have made yourself clear.'

'Then it is to be hoped that your essay will be equally lucid, and your repentance transparently plain.' He permitted himself a dry smile of self-congratulation. 'When you feel that you are worthy of rejoining the more erudite and responsible of the human race, you may ring for Mrs Groves, and I will then consider your apology.'

But Carne did not ring for Mrs Groves and, after three days in isolation, Penry Vaughan was forced to return to the boy's room, claiming that his magnanimity now allowed him to consider the episode closed. Carne's sins had been acknowledged, if not expiated, and no more would be said upon the matter. Carne, who had enjoyed his brief respite from Vaughan's abrasiveness, meekly allowed himself to return to the household. It would not do, he reasoned, to show his cousin how much he had valued his privacy. His new-found deviousness did not shame him a whit, for he employed it only to counter Vaughan's own. It amused him to know that it was a skirmish in the battle which Vaughan had lost, although believing it to be won.

Later, in Mostyn's bedroom, Carne upbraided Mostyn most fiercely for his arrogance and the rudeness and insensitivity he had shown to Jane and Prys. Mostyn stared at him, wide eyes brimming with tears, lip trembling, a picture of innocent rejection, like a pup punished unfairly for something of which he was not even aware. He plunged his hand into the pocket of his coat and tentatively brought out three sweetmeats, wrapped carefully within his silken handkerchief, declaring with sincerity, 'I did not eat them, Carne. I saved them for you, every one, although they are my favourites. I cried that you were shut away, Carne, really cried . . .' The tears were flowing freely now, and he buried his head against Carne's frilled shirt front, small fists gripping so tightly at Carne's waist that he could hardly breathe. 'You will forgive me, Carne? Say you will forgive me. I did not mean to be bad. I swear it! I swear it!' Mostyn's raised face was streaked with tears which quivered upon the tips of his pale lashes. With his pretty, pouting lips and the soft curves of his flushed cheeks under the soft halo of his corn-gold hair, he had the look of a pleading, repentant cherub. Yet Carne could not be wholly convinced. 'Please, Carne . . . do not hate me. Be my brother again.'

Carne nodded. 'It is all right, Mostyn. I do not hate you. I promise. But you must promise me something too.'

'Anything, Carne. Anything!'

'That you will never again, knowingly, cause hurt to Mr Prys and Mrs Eynon . . . or any other deserving our respect.'

'But I did not *know*, Carne, that what I said was wrong and hurtful.'

If Carne thought he glimpsed a slyness in Mostyn's eyes and a small knowledgeable smile, they were so swiftly gone that they might have been imagined.

'Will you not eat the sweetmeats, Carne?' Mostyn coaxed, as distraction.

'We will share them,' promised Carne, 'for that is what friends and brothers should do with all they own, whether treats or sorrows. It binds them close.'

Mostyn had lost interest and was waiting anxiously for Carne to apportion the sweetmeats. The tears were dried upon his face and it now bore an expression of cupidity. It was strange, Carne thought, that even when his brother wept, his stricken face did not grow ugly and debased with grief. It remained exquisitely unchanged by emotion. No, that was not true; it was even enhanced. It was an observation he did not care to reflect upon. He scrupulously divided the sweetmeats and gave half to Mostyn.

'I have eaten mine, Carne.' The voice was plaintive. 'I think I cried so much that I have grown hungry. I could not eat when you were shut within your room, and cried so hard that I was sick, and Nurse had to let me lie abed until I was recovered.'

Carne divided his remaining sweetmeat and gave Mostyn the larger portion. Mostyn, satisfied, took it without demur and ate it greedily, promising himself that he would eat the one he had secreted 'neath his pillow, then charm the cook, Mrs Craddock, into baking him more. She could never resist his pretty ways and the payment for a swift, spontaneous kiss.

'I'm glad that we are friends again,' said Mostyn, embracing Carne, then giving him his wide ingenuous smile. 'I love you, Carne, best of all people in the whole world, and will love you until I die. When you were punished by Cousin Penry, I wished it had been me. I thought of you, and cried all the time, Carne, without stopping. Did you think of me?'

'Yes, Mostyn. Yes.' His brother was a lovable, unreliable rogue, Carne thought ruefully. He possessed that secret of charming others into submission, grateful for their privilege in serving him. Yet I love him, he acknowledged silently, because he is my flesh and blood, and I am bound to him.

'What are you thinking about, Carne?' Mostyn was bored, demanding attention.

'That we might be allowed to visit the stables and feed the horses.'

'Yes,' exclaimed Mostyn, clapping his hands delightedly. 'I will go, Carne, and ask Cousin Penry. He will not refuse me.'

Carne nodded. His mind had not been upon the horses but the puzzle of how Mostyn, when gravely at fault, could somehow make those he had wronged appear guilty and churlish, a prey to remorse. One day he might understand. Now it was enough to know that Jane and Prys had come openly to see him. He had Mostyn, and Mr Morrish too. He was not alone.

Chapter Thirteen

At Holly Grove Farm, Sara Hartrey, with Saranne seated beside her upon a three-legged stool, paused from her butter making at the wooden barrel-churn. Her back ached, and she straightened with an effort, groaning involuntarily and pushing some damply escaping tendrils of copper-red hair beneath the brim of her muslin house-bonnet.

'You are tired, Mama,' ventured Saranne. 'Shall I turn the handle, that you may rest awhile?'

Sara smiled and bent impulsively to hug the child, whose arms slipped gently around her mother's neck in return. 'I fear, my love, that it needs more strength than you possess,' she cautioned, then, seeing the bitter disappointment cloud Saranne's face, she added, smiling, 'but yes, of course you may help. I confess that I am all but exhausted. Come, I will show you how it is done.'

She placed Saranne's thin hands upon the handle of the churn, suspended upon its heavy wooden stand, and set it turning in a steady rhythmic motion. Then she released her hands that the child might continue unaided.

'See, Mama, I can turn it. I am able . . .' Saranne's face was scarlet with effort and clenched as furiously as her small fists with determination. Her deep, violet-coloured eyes were alight with pride at her achievement as she demanded breathlessly, 'I am a help, Mama? Truly? You are not sorry that Papa and Charles found me and brought me to you?'

'No, my love.' Sara rose from the stool where she had rested briefly. 'I do not believe that it was by accident they found you, for we had been searching for you all of our lives.'

'For *any* little girl, Mama?' The churn's motion had grown slower, less insistent. 'You wanted a little girl to help upon the farm and be a friend to Charles? To have one from the poorhouse?' The churn had ceased to revolve and there was a stillness in the small taut body that spoke of despair and the fear of rejection.

'No, Saranne,' Sara chose her words carefully. 'We wanted a little girl of our very own, to be a part of our family for always. Not a servant or dairymaid or someone to work upon the farm. We wanted you, and none other. That is why Papa brought you home upon the waggon, for he knew, the first time he saw you, as did Charles and I, that it was you we had searched for this long time.' She gathered Saranne to her, and the child buried her face against her mother's apron-covered skirt as Sara stroked her dark hair.

'I wish, Mama . . .' Saranne's voice was muffled, face hidden. 'I wish that I had been yours born, like Charles.'

Sara said quietly, lifting Saranne's small pointed chin and looking steadfastly into the child's eyes, 'Oh, but you are, my love, for I love you as dearly as I love him. You must never think otherwise. You have crept into my heart and have your own warm place, safe and secure, where none other can reach. We cannot be separated for, if we were, I would lose a part of myself, my flesh and my blood.' They looked at each other silently for a while before Saranne took Sara's hand and kissed the palm, then laid it against her cheek.

'I am glad you found me, Mama,' she said, 'for you were a long time coming, and when Papa found me on The Green, I was afraid. I did not think you would want me. I was dirty and ugly and even Marged ran away and left me. I thought it was because I was hard to like.'

The tightness in Sara's throat seemed to be choking her but she said with deliberate lightness, so as not to betray her pity, 'But, Saranne, my dear, you are beautiful! You are truly the most beautiful little girl I know and you will grow to be a lovely woman. With such pretty dark hair and violet eyes you will make all others look pale and insipid, and I shall be as proud of you then as I am of you now. But come, we have work to do and must apply ourselves to it without such feminine prattle or we shall be churning until dark!'

Saranne began to turn the butter-barrel with such vigour and fervour that Sara had to beg her, laughingly, to cease before the cask flew out through the window of the dairy and the butter grow so hard they would need to cut it free with an axe! She took over the task, bidding Saranne listen hard for the splatter and plop which told her that the butter was ready and leaving the side of the churn.

'Fetch me the water bucket,' Sara commanded when the butter was firm, 'and be careful not to stumble and spill it, nor drop it upon your foot, for it is heavy.' She watched Saranne carefully lift the heavy wooden pail and carry it towards her, small arms rigid, jaw clenched with effort. Then Sara took it from her and threw water inside the churn, draining off the residue of the milk through a wooden tap at the base and in to a crock, to feed the pigs. She ladled the butter into a wooden dairy tub with rope handles, set it upon a low shelf of cool slate and began to pound, squeeze and knead the oily mixture furiously to expel the moisture remaining. Then, with a butter pat, she set some into a small wooden bowl that Saranne might make her very own block. Saranne worked as energetically and devotedly as she, determined that there should never be as fine a sample as her own. Her face grew flushed with heat, her small hands so cased with butter that they slithered and slipped alarmingly, and once the butter itself seemed set to fly off and land upon the stone-flagged floor. When, finally, Sara approved it as 'the very best butter I have ever seen in all my born days', Saranne relaxed and, at her mother's insistence, washed her hands at the water-pail provided for the purpose, and dried them upon a bleached flour sack.

117

'There . . .' said Sara with satisfaction when the salt had been added, 'now it is all done, save to put it into the earthenware jars for the winter months. We have worked well together, Saranne, and when all is finished we will return to the house and have a mug of shot to sustain us. Take a saucer to the shelf where the fresh milk lies and skim the cream off it, then place it in the jug beside. Afterwards, you may take some of the buttermilk to feed the farm kittens in the barn.' Sara stood in the doorway and watched her daughter's careful progress across the cobbled yard. Saranne's newly acquired clogs were clattering joyously and her face was radiant as she bore her offering with stiffly outstretched arms, fearful of spilling a single drop.

Sara smilingly returned to the coolness of the dairy with its deep stone walls and shelves of stone and slate, no less pristine and shining now than when Jethro had been able to afford the services of a dairymaid to keep them fiercely scrubbed clean. Jethro had come to stand behind her, unnoticed, and slipped his arms affectionately about her slim waist, touching his lips to the soft nape of her neck beneath the muslin house-bonnet. Then he firmly removed the bonnet and dropped it upon a shelf, combing her rich copper hair free with his fingers and saying quietly, his broad ingenuous face gentle with affection, 'There! That is how I always picture you in my mind when we are apart: a glowing lovely girl, bright as sunlight and chestnut falls, or the deep heart of a fire. That is what you are to us, Sara, the heart and warmth of our home.' His deepset blue eyes were so grave, and his words so strangely unexpected, that she felt an unaccountable fear, a coldness, as if a shadow had blocked out the light of the sun. Jethro saw her shiver and said remorsefully, 'It is cold here, Sara, and you have been working too long and hard without a shawl to cover your thin gown.' He looked with concern at the evidence of her labours, begging her, 'Go within the house now, my dear. I will scour the churn and refill the pails with water from the well, and do whatever else must be done.' He hesitated, then confessed ruefully, 'I did not expect that it would come to this, my love; that you should labour as hard as I upon the farm, then in the farmhouse too. The harvests have been so poor, and the weather beyond enduring. It grieves me sorely that I must let land lie fallow for want of the price of seed, and dismiss good men who have been labouring selflessly for many a long year. The taxes cripple me and no farmer is safe while rich men, who know nothing of the soil and its needs, may freely buy as many holdings as their greed demands, and let others work them!'

'You have heard some rumour, Jethro?' Her voice was sharp with anxiety. 'You have reason to believe that Holly Grove is at risk?'

He shook his head but she could not wholly believe him, for he did not meet her eyes, pretending an absorption with the crocks of butter spread with their layers of sparkling salt. 'I have heard that Huw Thomas of Hill View has sold,' he confessed reluctantly. 'He was forced to it by hunger and want, and now the family is dispossessed, set upon the road.'

'Dear Lord!' she exclaimed. 'Is it possible? What will become of them, Jethro? There are young children, and one of them sickly with some aggravation of the lungs. You have news of them?'

'None,' he lied, unwilling to burden her. Jethro knew that Thomas, beside himself with grief and rage, had loaded his family and few possessions upon a donkey cart and delivered the pittance he had received for his farm into his wife's care, bidding her tell no-one but to use it well. Then, promising that he would follow upon the road when his work was done, he set them upon the long journey to her mother's small cott. He had returned to the house and shot the few animals remaining, then turned his gun upon the man who had dispossessed him. Afterwards, Thomas had hanged himself from the beam of his empty barn. Jethro knew, for he had found him, and would bear the scars of it to the grave.

Sara, seeing his distress but not understanding, asked

119

helplessly, 'You will not let Holly Grove go, Jethro? It has been all of your life.'

'No.' His voice was low, uncertain. 'I will not let it go, I promise, not while there is life in my body and strength to work.'

Charles had come to stand in the doorway, copper head raised enquiringly, eyes blinking as they became gradually accustomed to the shadowy darkness. Sara could not tell how long he had been standing there, nor how much of their conversation he had heard.

'Well, my dear,' she said, 'now I have two strong farmers about me.' She drew Charles and then Jethro into the crescent of her embracing arms, asking, 'Was it your father or me you wished to see, my dear?'

'There is a pedlar without, Mama, with a tray of ribbons, toys and lace. I thought it would be a pleasure to Saranne if she had a coin to spend upon some trinket of her own, if there is a half-penny to spare.'

Sara glanced at Jethro, then said resolutely, 'Yes, of course, and it is a kindness that you think of it, my love.'

'I have been considering, Mama . . .'

'Yes, my dear?' She hid a smile, for his earnest face was so like Jethro's, although his colouring was her own.

'I think we should give Saranne a birthday.' He squirmed under her scrutiny, awkward and embarrassed.

'Then it shall be this very day!' declared Sara, delighted by his thoughtfulness. 'I shall fetch a half-penny this very instant from my goat jug upon the dresser and you shall have a half-penny for yourself.' She hugged him affectionately as, pleased but too grown up to show it, he cast Jethro a glance of patient resignation and wriggled free.

Jethro, in an effort to shake off the black depression which bore him down, managed a smile which did not reach his eyes and declared heartily, 'And I will add a penny for each of you, for you and Saranne have worked harder this day than many a grown labourer, and are deserving of recompense. You may take charge of your wages, my son.' He dug into the pocket of his work-stained breeches and delivered the two pence into Charles's palm, closing the boy's fist upon them, then smiling freely at the boy's glowing, stammering gratitude as, with a whoop of irrepressible high spirits, he ran triumphantly into the yard.

The pedlar brought with him more than pretty gifts and trinkets, long denied those who lived lives of unremitting toil upon the isolated farms. He brought news of the world beyond and a brief gaiety to the tedium of everyday living. There was romance in such men, or mystery, for their lives were not encompassed by four bleak walls, but the freedom of the open road.

Today, however, the pedlar walked with difficulty, his feet swollen and bruised by the sharpness of loose stones upon the byways. There was an air of neglect and tiredness about him as he leaned heavily upon the gate of the farm, trying, perhaps, to raise energy enough to enter within.

He raised his head at the sound of clogs clattering upon the cobbles, a ready smile springing, from long practice, to his lips. Saranne, leaving the barn, and clutching her precious pence, inspected the contents of his cluttered tray and the gew-gaws and baubles fastened upon his person, singing and clapping delightedly as he played her a tune upon his paper concertina. Charles and she cavorted and capered so ridiculously that Sara was obliged, with tears of laughter in her eyes, to beg them to stop before she did herself some grave injury. Their purchases chosen and changed a dozen times and more, the pair were finally satisfied and the pedlar pocketed their pennies, raising his eyebrows in mute questioning at Sara as Saranne chose a tiny looking-glass which cost a half-penny more than the pence she owned. Sara nodded, almost imperceptibly, and the enchanting object changed hands.

'Today is to be Saranne's birthday,' Charles explained gravely to their visitor who, forthwith, gave her a string of glass beads to match the colour of her eyes.

'Violets and dew,' he said, his extravagant bow hampered by his tray and the concertina. 'Oh, but you will be a true beauty, my sweeting . . . and men will swarm about you, like butterflies, drawn by the promise of your lips.'

'Were they as honeyed as yours!' declared Jethro, returned to humour by the pedlar's nonsense. 'I have no doubt she would make our fortune!'

The pedlar joined in the good-natured laughter, then he turned to Charles and said, more seriously, 'You will achieve all you set out to do. Do not doubt it. You will have riches, yet be denied that which is yours by right.'

Sara saw Jethro stiffen, and the frown return to his brow. 'And Saranne?' she asked, to divert the pedlar from adding more hurt. 'Will she be rich?'

The pedlar hesitated, then said obscurely, 'Sunshine and rain. Poverty and riches. She will achieve what she most desires but the loss will be to others and run deep for generations.' It was as if he had spoken involuntarily, and immediately wished the words unuttered. He looked anguished and ill-at-ease, then his face settled into the familiar deep lines of a smile as he said, in answer to Sara's plea that he come within for refreshment, 'It will be an honour and a privilege to enter so warm and loving a home and to break bread with you, for I have been offered little upon the way and times are hard. You have heard of the tragedy at Hill View?'

Jethro's warning glance halted the pedlar's flow as he broke in quickly, 'Yes, we have heard that misfortune forced the family to seek a new home.'

Sara gathered the children who were exclaiming excitedly over their purchases and shepherded them within, declaring that she had need of their help to prepare a special birthday tea.

'It is a bad business,' murmured Jethro despondently, adding quietly, 'but there is nothing to be gained by inflicting grief upon them, for it must come soon enough.'

'Yes.' The pedlar's tone was grave. 'The country is in a turmoil and many are dying of disease and hunger. I have not seen such poverty and fear in all my wanderings. It will end in bloodshed, I do not doubt. The farmers and their labourers are dispossessed like that poor wretch yonder, driven by desperation to murder and to take his own life.'

Jethro sighed, 'There will be many more who will turn and fight. I do not doubt that I will stand beside them.'

The pedlar said compassionately, 'The land is neglected and animals die for lack of food. Little is grown and, when it is, the yield is poor, with none to harvest it.'

'It is true that, denied labour and the money to hire it, much of my own soil lies fallow and useless,' said Jethro, 'yet I cannot hedge and ditch it unaided, or even afford time enough to feed and replenish the earth.' He thudded a huge fist angrily into his palm, face bleak with frustration, declaring, 'I see no end to it! Men starve for lack of bread and my land for lack of care. Yet I, who might save both, must stand uselessly by. It is a cruel vicious circle which cannot be broken and I swear I do not know the answer to it all. I harvest scarcely enough to feed my own and the few beasts remaining in the fields.'

'Then it is kind, sir, that you invite me to your table,' said the pedlar quietly and with sincerity. 'None other has offered me so much as a crust upon the way and I am aware that it grieved them, for the people hereabouts were ever generous in their hospitality, and proud to be so.'

'I am a blundering fool to have spoken as I did,' admitted Jethro remorsefully, 'and my words clumsy and ill-considered. I beg that you will take no offence, my friend.' He put his hand upon the pedlar's ragged sleeve to guide him within the house. 'You will always be welcome to share our board, in good times and bad.'

'I thank you for that, sir,' said the pedlar, 'for I know you do not speak the words idly. A word of warning . . .'

Jethro halted, face intent.

'There have been bitter riots in many parts where I have made my way. In Carmarthen the people grew incensed that food was to be sold to others while they starve. A vessel was raided and the cargo stolen. The militia was called in to halt them, but they would not be denied. Elsewhere fury erupts over the tollgate charges and the enclosure of lands. Frustration grows by the hour. The mood is angry and explosive, and the yeomanry alerted. It will end in bloodshed if the absentee landlords swallow up the farms of those such as your neighbour at Hill View simply to swell their estates. The buyers they send to haggle are shrewd and ruthless, knowing when beasts are slaughtered for lack of grain, and the owners all but destitute. I met one such craven hireling driving a cart upon the highway but yesterday, and felt little urge for his company. He bade me climb aboard to lighten my load, but although my feet were raw from walking and my bones sore, I would not.' He spat viciously upon the cobblestones of the yard to show his disgust. ' "I would sooner sup with the devil!" I said.'

'That was a brave self-denial,' approved Jethro, smiling, 'and you may sup now with angels as a reward.'

'No. It was naught but a futile heroic gesture,' admitted the pedlar, 'and I know that full well, yet it were all I could do.'

As they entered the house, the pedlar observed, 'I see, sir, that you have planted a holly bush beside the door to ward off evil.'

'Indeed,' agreed Jethro, 'although it was not I, but my great-grandfather who did so. It is grown high as a tree, and as sturdy. There is a whole grove of them sprung up nearby and it is whence the name of the place derives.'

'I pray, sir, that it will prove protection enough,' said the pedlar gravely. 'Yes, I pray that most earnestly.'

Chapter Fourteen

Long after the pedlar had departed, and Saranne and Charles were safely abed and asleep, Sara, who had been stirring life into the embers of the log fire, asked Jethro anxiously, 'Do you think there was truth in it? What the pedlar man foretold of Charles and Saranne?'

'Nothing but moonshine, my love,' he reassured, 'with as little substance as his dreams and talk, and as swiftly passing. Think no more upon it.'

'Oh, Jethro,' she reached up impulsively and kissed his cheek. 'You are such a warm comfort to me, my dear. You are a man of honesty and good commonsense. A rock and a refuge.'

His broad rubicund face was suffused with pleasure as he said quietly but with an undercurrent of deep emotion, 'I hope I may always be that to you, Sara, for as long as ever you have need of me.'

She looked at him intently, perturbed by some strangeness in his tone, and would have asked him what grieved him so. Perhaps his thoughts, with hers, had been turned to their own dead child, the girl who had survived but three brief weeks in that sad, cold winter. Eira they had called her, for in the old language it meant 'snow'. As fleetingly and as gently as snow she had come into their lives, and was as swiftly gone. Oh, but the bleakness and chill had remained as if a splinter of ice had been thrust deep in her heart.

'Saranne had a good birthday,' Jethro said. 'It touched me that she bought only the little hand-glass for herself and spent the rest of her coins upon gifts for you and me.' His hand closed over the cheap clay pipe within the pocket of his breeches. 'She has a kind and loving nature, Sara, and that is her greatest gift.'

'Yes, my dear.' Sara laid an affectionate hand upon his shoulder. 'We have lost a child, but God has seen fit to entrust us with another.'

'No!' he exclaimed, wrenching himself free of her grasp. 'I brought Saranne of my own free will. None other was involved!' His face was ugly with resentment and hurt. 'You speak as though one child replaced the other. It is not true! . . . and I will not accept the solace of a lie. Eira is dead, and Saranne is herself, no other. If that is cruel, then life is cruel, and we can only face it upon its own terms. But I will not endure my loss meekly, Sara. By God, I will not! Not this, nor any other!'

The vehemence of his outburst shocked and bewildered her and she was frightened to see the glint of tears upon his lashes before he turned angrily upon his heel and strode without and into the yard.

I should have gone after him, Sara thought, tried to reason with him and gentle away whatever ailed him. All these years since Eira's death, when she had thought him resigned to grief, content within his life, had rage been festering within him, an unhealed wound, deep, close to suppuration? Was it that, or some unspoken fear, which plagued him? The plight of Huw Thomas of Hill View? The pedlar's coming? The death of Ruth Bessant's child reviving old pain? Or Saranne's bitter past? She did not know. She only knew that it was best to let him be.

The wedding between Jane Eynon and Hywel Prys took place quietly, as befitted two elderly ex-servants lacking in family. Yet there was a joyful simplicity in the service which touched a response in those few who came. Peter Morrish brought Jethro Hartrey to stand as supporter to Prys and Sara was in quiet attendance upon Jane. Mrs Griffin and Megan wept and smiled, then smiled and wept, most engagingly, and Ann Hodges, that outwardly abrasive but gentle-hearted cook crept into a pew at the rear of the church unobserved. Alone, now, and dispossessed, she had taken lodgings in the village as cold and comfortless as those at the inn. Yet, from her dwindling savings, she had bought as a wedding token a pretty fairing of a bride and groom standing before a church with a beaming parson beside them.

Jane and Prys, kissed and congratulated by all, bade farewell to their friends and made to climb into the proudly decorated mule-cart. Then Tom Hallowes crept from the shelter of a yew tree to present them with an iron horse-shoe for good luck and, as unexpectedly, to take over the reins. Peter Morrish, smiling at Jane's bewilderment, led them to a carriage hired from the inn and Jethro drove them, not to Hillbrook Cottage, but to Holly Grove Farm for their wedding feast. Ann Hodges had used all her old skills to bake and decorate a wedding cake, as fine as any Jane had ever set eyes upon, and, with Sara's help, as many delectable dishes as could safely be set down upon the board. It was an occasion, once more, for joyful tears and laughter, and Saranne, shy at first, took Prys's hand and soon had crept, with more confidence, upon his knee to nestle contentedly against him. For a moment, Jane's thoughts turned towards Carne, and Peter Morrish, seeing the tug of hurt at her mouth, said gently, 'I will find a way to unite you with Carne and Mostyn, Mrs Prys, I promise.'

'That, sir, would be my dearest joy,' she answered simply.

By the early afternoon, when the festivities were reluctantly ended, Ann Hodges had found both home and occupation. She was to cook and care for Peter Morrish as housekeeper and maid-of-all-work for the promised security of a roof and board, asking no further repayment. Jane and Prys declared this news to be the finest wedding gift of all.

Later, when they were alone, Jane told her new husband about a different kind of gift.

'There is a confession I must make to you, Hywel, and no other.'

'There is need neither to confess nor make explanation, Jane, for anything in the past,' he chided gently.

''Tis a cheerful confession, Hywel,' she explained, smiling broadly. 'It is that I do not come to you empty-handed, but with a dowry of my own.' She unfastened the high neckline of her gown, her fingers first exploring the low nape of her neck, then undoing something. She held in her hands, for his approval, a necklace of gold and onyx, opaque, iridescent, exquisite in its artistry. He could only stare at it in stupefaction, too bewildered even to ask how she came by it. 'It was willed to me by Sophia Havard and I have told no other alive, Hywel, lest it arouse envy and mistrust. I have concealed it always, but now, my dear, I hope it may offer us security against poverty and the ills of age, should need arise.'

'No, we will manage well enough, Jane.' He added awkwardly, 'It is better returned to those who will cherish it most, and wear it as you have worn it, with real love, and value for the giver, not merely the gift.'

She smiled at him, grateful for his warmth of understanding, as he fastened the clasp, then settled a kiss upon her nape.

As Jane lay that night in Prys's arms in their box-bed beside the fire of the cottage, she said truthfully, 'It has been the best day in all of my life, Hywel. I did not believe that such joy and happiness existed. I shall keep the memory of it always.'

'I am glad, my dear,' Prys said, 'for your happiness is all I have need of in this world, and the privilege to journey beside you.'

Penry Vaughan had informed Carne brusquely that there were certain matters to be discussed; matters which would certainly affect his present and his future. Carne's eager questioning had been answered with the curt admonition, 'Present yourself at my library immediately after breakfast.

128

It is ill-mannered, sir, to discuss family matters where others may overhear!'

So Carne lingered a while without the library, hesitant of knocking. Finally, he forced himself to rap upon the door and to enter upon Vaughan's sharp command to 'Come!'

Vaughan looked up briefly from his desk, irritably motioning Carne to a chair and writing for a time in silence. Then he laid his quill aside. 'Great House is to be sold!' he declared without preamble.

'Sold, sir?' Carne echoed stupidly, 'but it cannot be.'

'Cannot?' Vaughan permitted himself the briefest of smiles. 'I beg to correct you. The sale has already been legally agreed and the new owner awaits to take possession.' Remarking the boy's pale face, and experiencing not pity but irritation, Vaughan continued implacably, 'It has been sold to an ironmaster and his family. The money received will be set against your father's debts although, generous as it is, it will barely defray the grosser of your father's excesses.'

'I do not understand, sir.'

'Do you not? Then let me explain. Your father was a libertine; a scoundrel and fornicator, who squandered his inheritance and good name. He left you nothing, sir, save poverty and I remind you that you exist solely upon my charity and without it you would be destitute, a pauper.' For the first time, Vaughan's face was animated, alive with malicious satisfaction, since Rice Havard's superiority in birth and breeding had been a bitter yoke to bear. 'There is one other matter.'

Carne waited apprehensively.

'I have secured the services of a tutor for you, a gentleman of the highest erudition, one well versed in the classics, a distinguished scholar who will demand the highest standards of literacy and numeracy and expect intelligent discourse. In addition he will attempt to instruct you in the polite arts and instil strict moral and ethical values.'

Carne stood in awkward silence, unsure of how to

respond, until Vaughan rebuked sharply, 'Well! Have you no observation to make? No word of appreciation for what is done on your behalf? I do not expect fawning gratitude, nor even acknowledgement of my part in the affair. I am a Havard and as such regard it as a moral obligation to ensure that you, and Mostyn too, are educated in a manner befitting your . . . our . . . birth.' Vaughan's intended diatribe was interrupted by a manservant's announcement that the gentleman whom he was expecting had arrived and was awaiting without.

The visitor entered and Vaughan stated coldly, 'This, Carne, is your new tutor. You will address him appropriately and give sensible account of yourself.'

'There is no need, sir,' said Morrish, 'for we are already firm friends, since our encounter at the coach. He is a boy of courage and kindness, as I saw in his conduct towards his young brother.' He held out his thin hand towards Carne who was beaming with unashamed pleasure.

Morrish was, Vaughan thought, for all his breeding and erudition, a shambling, unprepossessing dolt of a fellow: shabby, rudely clothed and, with that untidy shock of fair hair, as childlike as the pupil before him.

'Perhaps we had best discuss his education,' said Morrish.

Vaughan mumbled, 'You will no doubt expect remuneration, sir. What figure had you in mind? Name your proposed fee, that we may discuss it and reach some compromise.'

'There will be no fee,' Morrish said dismissively.

Vaughan made token mild objection but was relieved when Morrish remained adamant. 'My duties are pressing as, no doubt, are your own, sir. If you have no other matters to bring to my notice . . . ?'

'There is the question of the pauper, Marged Howell, sir,' said Morrish. 'The woman who was sentenced to the pillory for some offence at Rice Havard's graveside. She has fled to the hills above Penavon . . .'

'What would you have me do?' Vaughan demanded

curtly, 'Take her into my household too? Add her to my list of dependents?'

'No, sir. I thought that, perhaps, you might persuade some of our parishioners to search for her, to take her what little food and warm clothing they can spare and that you might, perhaps, speak out on her behalf.'

'If she is discovered,' declared Vaughan inflexibly, 'she will assuredly be returned to the boundary as the law decrees, and set upon the road. Should any unlawfully assist her, they will be judged guilty of a crime and suitably punished. There is an end to the matter! I trust, Morrish, that you have no such misguided intentions? I remind you, the bishop would not be best pleased.'

'Nor would he, sir, should she die of hunger and neglect,' insisted Morrish stubbornly. They stared at each other in hostile silence, neither willing to cede, until Morrish declared, 'It seems, sir, that by the very nature of things we will not agree. What you see as interference, and guilt by association, I see as my pastoral obligation and as caring.'

Vaughan, disdainfully watching his curate mount his disgraceful parody of a horse, felt a small maggot of doubt stirring within his mind as to Morrish's suitability to instruct. His academic qualifications were excellent. His pedigree above reproach. Moreover, he had offered his services freely. It would be churlish to spurn such charity. Ultimately both Carne and Mostyn were in his own guardianship, his own care, and they were his to influence and mould. He could make as much, or as little, of them as he chose.

Chapter Fifteen

Carne was to begin his studies upon the morrow and had spent a restless night forcing himself to stay wakeful lest he oversleep, and the servants forget to summon him early for breakfast. His leather satchel, specially commissioned from the saddler, had been packed and unpacked, arranged and rearranged a thousand times. Everything within, from books and paper to ink and quill pens had been inspected so often that they were in danger of being worn clean away. His mind had been anxious, swinging absurdly between elation and despair. Perhaps Mr Morrish would think him a dolt, a dunderhead, as his cousin, Penry, assuredly did. He might send him back to Penavon vicarage in disgrace, declaring that he could teach him nothing! Carne felt cold with apprehension, then the certainty that he was the equal of any boy of his age at his lessons reasserted itself. His tutor had told him often that he was a good student, diligent and quick of mind . . . and yet? The candle in the chamberstick beside his bed guttered and died, its wax a frozen waterfall. Sleep tugged insistently at the corners of his mouth and his eyelids drooped and shut, despite all his efforts to prise them open. When he awoke, early dawn was filling his room with rose light and the sky beyond streaked with saffron, gold and red. When the servant rapped upon his door to awaken him, he was already washed, dressed and seated at his writing desk, the satchel clutched firmly in his hand.

As Carne set out in the carriage with Probert at the reins, Penry Vaughan appeared briefly in the stable yard, saying with singular lack of warmth, 'I need not delay you. I come merely to remind you, Probert, that Master Carne must, under no circumstances, be permitted to halt upon the way. He will speak to none but Mr Morrish and be fetched immediately his lessons are completed. You will collect him at mid-day and he will be returned at precisely one o'clock when he has dined here at the vicarage. Do I make myself clear?'

Probert intimated that he did. Vaughan nodded stiffly to Carne, scrutinising the boy carefully to see that he was suitably attired. Finding nothing amiss, and that, in fact, his young cousin looked elegant and every inch a gentleman, pride and annoyance battled within him. 'It is to be hoped, sir,' he said curtly, 'that you will conduct yourself circumspectly and apply yourself with diligence to your books. Your future will depend upon it.'

'Yes, Cousin,' murmured Carne, adding hesitantly, 'I will try to be a credit to Mr Morrish, and to you.'

Vaughan grunted non-committally, 'Well, you had best be off,' he instructed. 'I wish you good-day.'

'Good-day, Cousin Penry.'

As the coach entered the village of Penavon, Carne felt his stomach muscles contract, as if caught in some ferocious grip, and the sour taste of sickness rose in his throat. I am afraid, he thought. Afraid and alone, and I do not know what is expected of me or if I shall be able to achieve it. He was seized with such alarm that he found himself trembling uncontrollably, sweat moist upon his skin, and the satchel he had clutched with so much pride fell, unhindered, to the floor. He was only dimly aware of Probert crying out to alert the horses and of the carriage drawing to an urgent halt. Before he had time to gather his senses, the door was pulled determinedly open.

It was a surprise and excitement for him to see the attorney, Mr Randall Walters, standing upon the highway, plumply benign face wreathed in jocular smiles. Fidgeting, pulling at his brocade waistcoat as if he would make room

133

for the distended belly beneath, he said, 'So today you begin your lessons, Carne?'

'Yes, Sir.' Carne's face was as delighted as Walters' own.

'Then you had best take this.' Walters thrust a small suede pouch into the boy's hand. 'A man must make the best use of time. Fill the hour, Carne. Fill the hour. That is happiness.'

Carne murmured his agreement, slipping open the thongs of the pouch to reveal his father's silver watch and the engraved message upon its case: 'To Rice Havard, Squire of Penavon, from his grateful tenants.' His fingers traced the words, his eyes alight with rapturous delight and gratitude.

''Twas from the auction at Great House . . . A small remembrance.'

'Thank you, sir! Oh, thank you!' Carne had leapt from the carriage and was pumping Walters' hand with such ferocity that the attorney's fingers were numbed. 'Oh, it is the kindest gift I have ever had in all of my life, sir. I will treasure it until I die.'

His young face was so like Rice Havard's, and so grave in its intensity, that Randall Walters could not trust himself to speak again lest emotion unman him. He helped Carne back into his seat within the carriage and nodded to Probert to drive on, watching until the carriage disappeared in a blur of dust and noise. Then he blew his nose hard, blinked rapidly and, with his shoulders squared, turned back towards his chambers.

Carne's welcome at Myrtle Cottage was so warmly unfeigned that his misgivings evaporated upon the instant. Peter Morrish hurried out upon sound of the carriage and helped Carne dismount, shaking his pupil's hand vigorously, thin face alight with childlike pleasure as he exclaimed, 'Welcome, Carne! Welcome! Upon my soul, what a fine figure you cut! The very epitome of the well-prepared scholar.' His voice was generous in its admiration and there was much animated discussion about the pristine satchel and its contents, and cries of approval over the

134

newly acquired watch. 'That is a most splendid gift,' declared Morrish, 'and one to treasure all of your life, Carne. It will serve to remind you of times past and present, and holds promise of what is yet to be. There is nothing upon this earth, I am sure, which could bring you more pleasure.'

'Excepting Papa's being here, sir,' said Carne quietly.

Morrish's intelligent eyes met Probert's above Carne's bowed head. 'I believe, my boy, that he is with you in mind and spirit,' he returned gently, 'as he will be at all times of joy and sorrow in your life. It will please him that his son feels pride in his memory, for that is what every man would hope to leave to others.' With his arm placed affectionately about Carne's shoulder, he led him within.

Mrs Hodges, warm hearted and comfortably unchanged, came bustling from the small kitchen, a wooden spoon still clutched in her large, fire-reddened hand, to enfold him in her rough embrace. She smelled of warm flesh and baking. It was the smell of Great House and his infancy and Carne knew that here, in these modest, unprepossessing cottages, clumsily knocked into one dwelling, he had found both welcome and haven.

Peter Morrish's study was a glorious magpie-clutter of books, maps, globes and navigating instruments scattered in seemingly haphazard profusion over every surface, and spilling on to the floor. The walls were host to a prodigal display of diagrams, maps, drawings and paintings, together with sketches of ships under sail and numerous likenesses of wild animals and birds. Jostling below were crowded display cabinets of shells, rocks, birds' eggs and curios. All were scrupulously tabulated and arranged and, to Carne's youthful eye, the room was a treasure trove of things curious, fascinating and desirable. He stared in wondrous admiration at the sparkling minerals and crystals, the cases of stuffed animals, the fossils. Awe at such magnificent abundance robbed him of words, then, 'Oh, Mr Morrish, sir! This must be the most treasure-filled room in the world . . . well, anywhere,' he breathed reverently.

'There is so much to look at and to touch!'

'Then we had best begin our lessons,' declared Morrish, face wreathed in smiles of amusement at Carne's rapturous face. 'Since curiosity is the spur to true learning, we will put aside our textbooks for today, Carne, and talk informally about those things which interest us most.'

'Yes, sir,' agreed Carne, unable to hide his relief that he was not be tried and tested upon his knowledge and deficiencies. Yet, skilfully, and without Carne's suspecting it, Morrish drew him into discourse upon the subjects in which he had been instructed. Morrish, a pedant by nature, felt his interest quickening at the child's lively intelligence and acuteness of observation. Here was a pupil deserving of guidance, he thought, and whose future horizons need not be limited by the restriction now forced upon him. Education would be both comfort and escape.

'I have spoken to Mr Walters, the attorney,' Morrish began, 'and he assures me that . . .' he paused, wondering how best to phrase it, 'that the money set aside under your cousin's administration will be sufficient to pay for your education. Has it been discussed with you?'

'No, sir, but I would dearly love to attend the university of Oxford. My father was at Jesus College, sir,' Carne's face was gravely intent as he admitted, 'but I do not know if I am clever enough.'

'That is what we must endeavour to find out,' said Morrish, 'and we must work to that end, since it is your avowed ambition. I will teach you most sedulously all that I am able, and you, in turn, must promise to work wholeheartedly.'

'Oh, yes, sir! I will work, and work, until I drop.'

'But merely memorising your lessons will not be enough,' cautioned Morrish, 'for a fool may recite by rote, and it signifies nothing. You must learn to think and to reason, to argue, not hot-headedly, but with logic and assurance, you understand?'

'Yes, sir,' Carne's voice was low, 'but I do not think my cousin will accept a contrary opinion, for he says I am insolent and stupid.'

'Then you must act judiciously,' suggested Morrish unabashed, 'hiding your light under a bushel, if need arise, and revealing it only to those who might appreciate its illumination.' He hesitated, 'We have discussed many subjects, Carne, but there are sometimes those questions which trouble the mind, things trivial perhaps, and known only to us. Is there something you might care to ask of me, some difficulty you would have me explain?'

'That pauper babe, sir . . . the infant within Penavon church . . . the one which died. I cannot believe that it committed sin, nor was born into it.'

'I see. So what conclusion did you come to?'

'I thought, sir,' he began tentatively, face flushed in anticipation of mockery, 'that I do not always like nor understand God.'

'No more do I . . . nor even my fellow men!' admitted Morrish cheerfully, 'although I try wholeheartedly to love them. Still, even to think about it is a beginning. We had best consider it carefully, then compare our conclusions.'

Carne nodded, face gravely intent, as though plucking up courage to speak.

'There is something else which troubles you?'

'My watch, sir. I fear Mr Vaughan will be angry with Probert, for he was told, most specifically, that I must speak to no-one upon the way, and that if I disobeyed, he would be held responsible. I would not have him harmed on my account.'

Peter Morrish reflected upon the problem for a moment, then opened the door of his study and called loudly, 'A moment, Mrs Hodges, if you please.'

Mrs Hodges lumbered in, breathless and unbecomingly flushed with heat, and Morrish briefly explained Carne's dilemma. Then he took the watch from Carne's keeping and placed it into Mrs Hodges' hands saying, 'Now Mrs Hodges, I beg that you will give it to me, that I may return it to its rightful owner. There,' he declared with satisfaction. 'You must say that it was delivered first into my keeping and then into yours. I do not think you will be questioned further. As a man of the cloth, your cousin could not, in all conscience, countenance the lie direct; no more could I, yet we may all applaud initiative. If Mr Vaughan demands detail of what we have discussed today, say that I have tested you stringently in all subjects, from scripture to grammar and philosophy, and have found you to be unusually accomplished in every respect.'

'Oh, thank you, Mr Morrish, sir,' said Carne, face aglow with sincerity. 'I truly thank you. I have never enjoyed my lessons more.'

'Nor I,' declared Peter Morrish, smiling in return, and adding, to Carne's puzzlement, 'it is a rare privilege to be taught to recapture true innocence of mind. It is I who am beholden to you.'

Morrish saw Carne driven away in the carriage, and with a smile of satisfaction set out for the inn to saddle his horse. It had been a good beginning and much had been achieved, for he had gained Carne Havard's trust. He was an intelligent boy, honest and sensitive, with a lively curiosity of mind.

There was, however, one small errand which needed to be undertaken on Carne's behalf. Morrish raised himself delightedly into the saddle and rode off to Holly Grove Farm. Penry Vaughan had given rigid instructions that the coach should not be stopped, and neither Carne nor Probert must openly defy him. There was no reason on earth why Jane Prys should not visit her friend, Mrs Hodges, at Myrtle Cottage, or Prys either, should he take a notion. It was the most natural thing in the world!

Over the last few months he had become a welcome guest at Holly Grove Farm and found peace and relaxation there. Sara was a thoughtful, kindly woman who welcomed his presence, and Jethro showed plainly that he delighted in relaxing in his company after a hard day's toil, especially since, apart from his labourer, Tom Hallowes, and occasional visits from Prys, the farmer was seldom in the company of his fellow men.

He had also grown fond of Charles, who was a well-mannered intelligent boy, but it was to little Saranne he was inevitably drawn, bewitched by her artless shining pleasure in all things. She was like an infant taking its first adventurous steps into a world where all was new; curious, enchanted, eager to share the joy of her discovery with others. If he wondered briefly, as did others, from whom Saranne had inherited the startling beauty of those exquisitely unexpected violet eyes, then he thrust the thought from him. When he recalled the pitiful sight of her at the pillory, and her ferocious courage in protecting the pauper woman, he was grateful that life was now kinder. She was as much a part of Sara and Jethro's family as if born of their flesh, like Charles, and her brother's affection for her was an added blessing. Saranne followed him slavishly, hanging upon his every word, trying always to please him, as if she would repay him for his unselfish acceptance. Yet, now, Morrish was gratified to see, she no longer clung so fiercely to Sara's skirts, growing ever more independent and venturesome, and taking over small duties such as feeding the hens and gathering the eggs from their nests. Sara had stitched several pretty dresses and muslin aprons for her and the child wore them with such pride and appreciation that her delight could not be construed as mere vanity.

'She is a joy and blessing to us,' Sara admitted to Morrish as they watched Saranne perched high upon the old cart-horse's broad back whilst it plodded across the yard. Charles was dancing attendance at its head and Jethro was keeping a steady hold about her waist, for she was so small and frail-boned that her thin legs were splayed out straight at each side, and she could get no purchase upon its rough mane. Saranne was crying out aloud with helpless pleasure, her laughter filling the air, and Sara smiled and shook her head as the child impulsively bent over and dropped a kiss upon Jethro's wide, upturned face.

'Charles has started learning at the Dame school,' Sara said. 'Jethro is willing to spare him, since the harvesting is done. It is a halfpenny a day for every subject he attends.'

There was no mistaking her pride. 'Already he can write some of his letters, and with a neat hand. I hope he will be a scholar and learn to read and figure. It would be a rare help for Jethro, for we can neither read nor write, not having been taught.'

'And Saranne?'

Sara shook her head. 'Jethro's firm upon it, and he is a stubborn man, Peter. He does not think it fitting for a maid to be as clever as a man. He thinks she should be contented to cook and sew and do those things he judges womanly.'

'And what do you believe, Sara?' he asked quietly.

'I would not go against his wishes. He is a good husband and a loving father, and does what he believes to be best. I would not humble him by calling him wrong before others.'

'It grieves you then that her future is already decided?'

She looked directly at him, mouth prettily upturned, vivid blue eyes creased with laughter. 'I think, Peter, that someone has resolved that dilemma for herself, offending none. Every eve, upon Charles's return, she makes him recite all he has learnt and works beside him at his lettering. For all that she is so young, she has a quick mind and a clever hand. She will not attend school, 'tis true, but she is determined to read and write, and none will prevent it.'

'I am glad of that, Sara. It will broaden her horizons, make her future assured.'

Sara flushed and stiffened, believing his words a slight upon her for her lack of scholarship. Peter was immediately contrite at his stupid clumsiness.

'Saranne will find her own way,' he said gently, by way of apology, 'as we all must, and the path she takes will be right for her . . . as mine, as a clergyman, has been right for me, and yours, Sara, for you. You are the heart and soul of this family,' he said with sincerity, 'and none can measure the good you have done.'

She stared at him for a long moment, strangely moved, yet aware of him for the first time as a man rather than as a clergyman.

'I had in mind your kindness to Marged Howell,' he offered awkwardly, 'for I have tried so hard, and failed, to still the devils within her.'

Chapter Sixteen

Jethro, arriving at the market with Tom Hallowes upon the waggon beside him, was aware of a sullenness in the faces of the stallholders, an atmosphere of hostility which could not be hid. Farmers and those few labourers for hiring stood about in uneasy groups, their habitual jesting and gossip stilled.

'What is amiss?' he asked of a neighbour.

'The Ironmaster has come to Great House, Rhys Llewellyn. You have heard of him?'

Jethro shook his head.

'You will! It is rumoured that he will make offer for all the land hereabouts. You had best look to your farm, Jethro, for he has money enough, and bully boys enough, to wrest it from you!'

''Tis naught but lies and gossip!' Jethro maintained stoutly. 'Why should he have need of our few poor acres? They will barely feed those who labour upon them.'

'It is a richer harvest he seeks . . . that which lies below the soil; minerals and such. He has made one fortune as ironmaster from the wars with the French, and now seeks another. He will have few scruples about how he earns it!'

'Then he'll be damned to hell before he makes it on my back!' Jethro's voice rose belligerently, 'for I will protect my own land as Huw Thomas protected his!'

There was a murmur of angry assent from all about him, and fierce discussion as to how best to act. When Jethro, his meagre offerings sold, finally returned to Holly Grove upon the waggon, his quick temper had abated, but the

fear and resentment remained. Tom Hallowes had declared
that he would return on foot, with whatever news he could
glean from the market place and taverns, for everywhere
folk gathered there were small groups lingering still, their
voices raised in bitterness.

As Jethro neared the farm, his misgivings lightened, for
all was unchanged. He was a credulous fool, he scolded
himself, to listen to such idle gossip, and would not inflict
his misery upon others. It was the last day of the old celtic
year, he recalled guiltily, and Sara had invited Jane and
Hywel Prys to sup with them, and Megan too. Indeed, it
often seemed to him that now he had acquired not two
children, but three! With little to occupy her at Jane's
cottage, Megan had taken to helping upon the farm. She
was ever eager to scour the dairy pail with the mare's tail
brush, to aid with the milking, carry the wooden piggins,
turn the heavy cheeses, or labour fiercely at the washing
tub or kneading trough. She was proudly industrious and
willing to take turn at any menial task, only too grateful to
be paid in kind rather than pence, that her mother and kin
might be fed. How little Megan demanded of life, and how
freely she gave. He felt a sense of shame at his own ill-
humour as he halted the waggon and unharnessed the mare.

It was a jovial, contented company which sat upon
the wooden benches and settle surrounding Sara's well-
scrubbed table, rejoicing in the warmth of the fire, and the
victuals which Megan and Sara had prepared. Jane and
Prys were welcome guests, and the children and Megan,
who was but little older, aglow with bright, inconsequential
chatter.

'You had best take care, Megan,' warned Charles amidst
laughter from the rest, 'for tonight is the last day of the
old year, and the great black sow without a tail will run
behind you to gobble you up.'

'Oh, will she?' declared Megan, rolling up her sleeves
threateningly over her thin arms and making fists of her
hands. 'Let her try then, I say! She will soon learn my
measure, and her lesson! I have seen enough of pigs, black,

143

pink and mottled, to know how to shape their stumps!'

Charles crossed his eyes and made a hideous face, with tongue lolling. 'Ah, but if she snorts and snuffles behind you in the woods, Megan, with howling demons and devils . . .' He gave a realistically blood-curdling howl.

'Then I will kick its backside,' Megan said, unperturbed, 'and recite "The Lord's Prayer", and the devils will disappear like mist on the mountain.'

The company applauded her appreciatively for her boldness, although Jane was quick to see that Saranne was troubled, despite her hesitant laughter.

'Will that sow go running up the mountains?' she asked, her mind upon Marged Howell's cave. 'The black sow will not come to live here in our sty, Papa?' she persisted.

'She would not dare to show her snout hereabouts,' Jethro declared, 'else she would be brawn and trotters and herbed faggots, and eaten right down to the grunt! No, Saranne, it is a fine excuse to light bonfires for dancing and fun before the winter comes. The young girls must leap over the fire, then rush home before the flames die down. 'Tis my opinion that they have most to fear from the young bloods of the village who chase them through the dark, and not from that poor sow without a tail!' His eyes met Sara's in amused remembrance. Under cover of the ensuing laughter, he bent to recite the old rhyme, slyly, so that she alone could hear, 'I captured a greater prize that night . . . or perhaps she captured me, for although I ran and ran to escape her clutches, she would not let me be.'

Sara flushed, pretending crossness, but laughter bubbled up reluctantly within her and would not be checked. Soon Saranne was laughing, fears forgotten, and all the company besides.

It was then that Tom Hallowes came seeking Jethro, although he would not join their celebrations. When Jethro returned from the yard, it was Charles alone who noticed the weariness upon his father's face, and the uncertainty, and felt a chill of fear.

Long after Prys's mule cart had rumbled away across the

cobbled yard, and the truckle of its lantern beams were swallowed into the darkness, Jethro lay wakeful in the familiar comfort of the shared double bed. Sara lay flushed in sleep beside him, her copper hair a spilled brightness against her pillow, hand protectively cradling her cheek. The paleness of light through the latticed casement grew bright as the moon emerged nakedly from the wisps of cloud, thin as vapour, which had clothed it. With a murmured reassurance to Sara, he arose and dressed himself by window light, for the taper had long been extinguished in the chamberstick. Then, with a glance towards the bed to reassure himself that Sara slept undisturbed, he crept down the staircase, boots clutched tightly in his hands. In the huge, open-raftered living room where the fire smouldered 'neath its covering of turf, he paused, fearful that Charles might awaken in his cupboard bed. The moonlight, falling softly upon the boy's pale skin and the brightness of red-gold hair, showed that he slumbered unaware. In a moment Jethro was beside the door, feeling the coldness of the bare flagstones pierce his stockinged feet as, with jaw clenched and face fierce with concentration, he eased the key back in the lock as soundlessly as he was able. It seemed to Jethro that the sound of it wrenched and grated as abrasively within the bones of his skull as in the silent house. Yet the silence settled and grew deeper, and with a barely perceptible sigh, he drew the vast oaken door ajar and stepped out hesitantly into the moonlit night, closing the door gently behind him.

Pausing only to fasten his boots, he crossed the yard and sought the shelter of the great stone barn. There, from behind a bale of hay, he brought out the carefully hidden candle lantern, tinder box, and rags, and with the lantern aglow and the rags safely extinguished, he searched amidst a carelessly heaped pile of loose hay. Finding the objects he sought, he concealed them carefully 'neath his coat. Then, with the barest hesitation, mouth dry and heart thudding nervously in his breast, he took the track through the woods towards Penavon village.

Charles, who had been jolted raggedly from sleep by the rasping of the key in the lock, lay bewildered in his bed. His father's movements were stealthy, furtive, even, as if he went in fear of discovery, and Charles felt a cold premonition that this was not some ordinary late-night venture to settle an animal in sickness or birth, or to check the fowls against marauding foxes. He hesitated but a moment then, swiftly, and with resolution, he dressed and quietly followed his father without. The light from Jethro's lantern bobbed and wove before him, his father's broad figure rendered grotesque by moonlight. On and on Charles followed, trudging through mire and tussocks of rough grass, clothing and flesh torn at by briars and brambles, his breath raw, pain bursting in his chest, but now he dare not return, or lose sight of the hurrying figure, or he would be alone in the dark.

The thought of the black sow was fresh in his mind and it seemed that it lurked behind every boulder and isolated tree, greedy, rapacious, small eyes watchful, its tusks of teeth bared in savagery. Jethro and his lantern had disappeared into a wood and, as suddenly, the moon was obscured by a cloud, the darkness heavy and oppressive. Charles, near blind, and made clumsy with fear, stumbled awkwardly, and could only right himself by grasping at a briar for support. He felt it pierce his palm, then the swift pain and warm surge of blood, but he drove himself on, unwilling to halt. Fear clawed at his ribs as he entered the blackness of the wood with the trees, although bereft of leaves, so densely branched that they formed a canopy above. Then, before him, once more, he saw the glow of Jethro's lantern, swift and elusive as a firefly, tantalising, luring him inexorably onwards.

Suddenly the moon emerged again into the clear sky and the trunks of the trees shone silver and wet. The stitch in his side was so sharp that he was forced to halt, clutching his ribs, gulping air, as terrified to linger as to push ahead. The blurring of his eyes might have been sweat or tears, and he was painfully aware of his own sobs amidst the rustle of dried leaves and grass and the night sounds of small, unseen creatures. A screech owl called and, with a cry to equal it, Charles was running, terrified, wiping the dampness from his face as he ran, fancying that the great black sow was pounding at his heels, snout twitching, hooves scraping curled leaves and rock and the roots of trees.

When he emerged, gasping, into the moonlight, he glimpsed his father's lantern far ahead, and although he tried to call out, he could not. His throat was constricted and weakness made him unable to utter a word, only a hoarse rasping, as useless as a croak. Through bracken and heather, marsh and copse, he followed, not knowing what lay beneath his feet or ahead, seeing naught save that beckoning light that showed him where Jethro and safety lay.

Finally, when his strength was all but gone, he saw before him the familiar track that told him he was within sight of Penavon village. Steadying himself against a tree, Charles braced himself for that last surge that would force him into the open, and the familiar comfort of Jethro's arms. Yet what he saw made him slither down in revulsion beside the tree, wanting to bury himself in the dark earth.

In a moment he was vomiting and retching upon the coarse grass. He had seen not one black sow, but many, faces menacing and evil, lost in some grotesque ritual. Some carried lanterns, other burning brands, and some the severed heads of dead pigs upon staves, bloodstained, obscene, mouths agape, sightless eyes glazed. Yet, more terrible than all, was that the black-headed sows had the bodies of men and were clothed like them. What he had witnessed was a vast, surging herd, not of swine, but some strange beast, half-human, half-animal. It was the creation of the devil, Charles knew, and to stumble upon it was to court madness, or death.

He would have fled back into the woods beyond, yet he could not, for his father had fallen foul of the demons as unthinkingly as he. Whatever hell awaited him, he must brave it and endure, for he could not let Jethro face torture and damnation alone. He blundered into the open, then into that whirling leaping throng. He moved among them, terror prickling his spine, barely able to open his eyes for disgust. He was pushed roughly aside by one of the capering creatures and the head of a devil-pig fell from the bloodied point of a stick to lie upon his feet, bones and sinews raw at its severed neck. Despite himself, he screamed aloud, 'Papa . . . Papa!' The black-headed pigs surged furiously about him. One seized him firmly in his grip. 'Oh, dear God . . .' Charles kept repeating. 'Oh, dear God,' for so great was his terror that the words of the Lord's Prayer, which Megan had said would serve, would not come to his lips. He saw that the black sow which clutched his arm had a pistol in its hand, and he found himself sobbing.

All about them the creatures were chanting and surging, and Charles was carried with them, trapped with his captors in a heaving, sweating mass, borne inexorably towards the gates of Great House. The creatures were setting fire to the rags they carried, breaking windows with their staves and axes, hurling their lighted brands through the shattered panes. Everywhere Charles looked, they were hacking frenziedly at windows and doors, ruthlessly battering down all that threatened their crazed advance.

There was a furious uproar as the owner and servants of Great House surged out, the sound of their gunfire exploding fiercely into the crowd. There was a moment of horrified silence before the creatures, maddened and outraged, surged forward, unmindful of the danger, trampling him beneath their feet. Charles must have lost consciousness for a moment because he awoke to find himself clutched in the arms of his father. Jethro was pushing his way through the horror, tears streaming unchecked down his face. There was a cry to halt, but Jethro did not pause or slow his pace, running wildly towards the shelter of the woods, lantern still clutched in his hand. He hurled it away savagely, then set Charles upon his feet, half pushing, half dragging him onwards. There was a crack, as of a bough being snapped underfoot, and Charles saw his father stagger and almost fall. Then Jethro's fingers were at his waistcoat, and the pistol shone in his hand.

'No, Papa! No!' He flung himself upon Jethro, knocking the pistol from his grasp and Jethro let it lie, gripping Charles's wrist and forcing him through the fern and scrub, into the darkness of the wood itself. When they emerged, Charles saw, by the light of the moon, that his father's arm hung awkwardly, his coat sleeve stiff with dried blood. Jethro's face was pale and glistening with sweat and Charles could hardly make out his words, for his father's voice was thin and lost.

'Run! Run, Charles, I beg of you! I . . .' With a groan Jethro stumbled and fell, face down, upon the grass, unable to stir despite all Charles's efforts to aid him. 'Go!' the word was uttered with such urgency that Charles could not help but obey. So it was that as the longcase clock at Holly Grove struck the midnight hour, Sara Hartrey, seated upon the farm cart with Charles at the reins of the old shire horse, somehow took strength enough to lift Jethro's body on to a heap of soft straw, and to carry him home to the farm. Charles had learnt that there was less to be feared from the black sow without a tail than from men, as Jethro had foretold, but the knowledge brought him no comfort.

When daylight came, and full account of the night's ravages taken, it was seen that Great House had been little damaged. Its structure remained firm; as firm as Rhys Llewellyn's declaration that he would not be intimidated by 'a lawless band of cut-throats and arsonists', and would see them hanged or set upon gibbets, as they deserved. He would hunt them, he vowed, as ruthlessly as the vermin they assuredly were, and none should escape punishment. He set his complaints before the justices, and a hue and cry was called, for each of the magistrates feared that the next attack might be upon his own property and kin. Yet the Brotherhood of the Black Sows, like the myth which gave them birth, seemed to lack all substance and flesh.

If Rhys Llewellyn had hoped to find a scapegoat, he was disappointed. Apart from the wounds received, and secretly

149

treated, there was but one fatality. He was a pauper labourer upon the farms, a creature known to be simple-minded, 'touched by the moon'. Even had he survived the gunshot wound inflicted upon him, then he would have been able to tell them nothing, for he was a deaf mute. Nor could his incitement to riot be laid at the feet of any who employed him, for he had worked but casually upon the farms, sleeping in hedgerow or sty. He was buried in a pauper's grave, unmarked and, of necessity, publicly unmourned.

Marged Howell's skills at folk medicine, practised in secret, saved many such as Jethro from the corrupt and festering wounds, and the noose. The damage to Rhys Llewellyn, as to the peace of Penavon, was less easy to mend but, for the moment at least, the poisons within him remained as deep buried as that poor wretch of a pauper, James Hogg.

Chapter Seventeen

Within Great House, Rhys Llewellyn, the damage to his property restored, prepared to take upon himself the role of Squire of Penavon. He would bring to it, he believed, that strong single-mindedness which had made him the richest and most influential of the ironmasters.

He did not doubt for an instant that the mineral harvest which lay ripe beneath Penavon land was his for the gathering. Yet the assault upon his house, and the danger to his wife and child, had disturbed him more than he would own. He did not regret firing into that mob of cut-throats and vandals which had threatened him. It was no more than their lawlessness deserved. Any man who showed weakness in the face of savagery was a fool. One could not reason brutes into submission, merely enforce it, since strength was all that they recognised. Nevertheless, he had given orders that the bully-boys and enforcers should be discreetly returned to whence they came.

If his experience as an ironmaster had taught him the value of ruthlessness, it had also convinced him that there was sometimes a greater profit in waiting. Already the countryside was flooded with those escaping the disease-ridden hovels of the towns, their labours ended with the wars. Such flotsam could only add to the burdens of those farmers and tenants whom he sought to buy out. Poor harvests and crippling taxes had already reduced them to penury. He could afford to wait.

Clarissa, Rhys Llewellyn's wife, was a timorous, gentle-natured creature, so meek and self-effacing that few could recollect her venturing an opinion. Indeed, few could recollect Clarissa at all. Yet, despite her inadequacies, Llewellyn was forced to admit that she possessed impeccable taste, absorbed naturally perhaps from having always been surrounded by exquisitely beautiful things.

He knew that the invitations sent out from Great House to the few sprigs of minor aristocracy and the landed gentry would be avidly accepted. They would come either from curiosity, or in the hope that he might help them increase their fortunes. Llewellyn did not fear that they might scoff at the changes he had wrought in Great House, nor attempt to patronise him. If they feigned indifference to his wealth and success, or affected to despise it, they would be swift to recognise in Clarissa a gentlewoman of superior quality and breeding. He only wished she were not so excessively dull.

As he had expected, the conversation had been congenial, the refreshments and victuals provided perfectly chosen and prepared, and the brief entrance of his young daughter, Laurel, in the hand of her governness an enchantment to all. Laurel's golden curls had gleamed as extravagantly as her smile, and the minx had enjoyed the adulation and praise, for she was a vain little creature, as she had every reason to be. As convention demanded, Llewellyn was modestly deprecating about his winsome child, but delighted that his guests were as bewitched by Laurel as he. No doubt, there would be careful plans laid by his guests to secure her future inheritance, young though she be. He let fall with studied casualness that Clarissa and he regretted that there were so few suitable companions of his daughter's age to make her hours less tedious, and names and invitations were not slow in coming. Lord Litchard's motherless daughter, Lady Henrietta Danfield, had proved a congenial companion, and it had not escaped Llewellyn's notice that Litchard's son was of an age with Laurel. However, a child whose name returned time and time again was the vicar's ward, Mostyn Havard.

It amused Llewellyn to invite the child to his former

home since the boy's pedigree was impeccable, even if his circumstances were cruelly reduced. Besides, it would earn him a reputation for tolerance and charity among his neighbours in Penavon which might work to his advantage.

So it was that Mostyn, attired in the most elegant shirt of silk and Honiton lace, with knee breeches and coat of blue velvet, white stockings, and exquisitely silver-buckled shoes, arrived by carriage to pay his respects to Miss Laurel Llewellyn.

His manners were charming, his deportment exemplary, and he was certainly the most handsome boy that either Rhys Llewellyn or his daughter had ever seen. If Clarissa, observing signs in him of Laurel's carefully cultivated charm, was less than enamoured, then no-one gave any more credence to her views on this matter than on any other.

Rhys Llewellyn was amused and delighted by Mostyn's ingenuous enthusiasm for everything he encountered, from the changes in the fabric furnishings within Great House to the litter of pups in the stables, and the refreshment offered. He showed such lively curiosity and quick intelligence that Llewellyn was captivated, asking him jocularly, 'And what shall you aspire to when you are a man, young Havard?'

'A gentleman like you, sir.'

Llewellyn laughed immoderately, assuring the boy that he was already well advanced upon that road, adding, 'Well, young sir, and would it please you to return to Great House? It would benefit Laurel to have a gentleman to partner her at her dancing lessons and in civilised conversation. What do you say? Will you join her at her lessons, and instruct her in the polite arts?'

Mostyn was not sure if Llewellyn spoke in jest, but considered before replying gravely, 'I should like that, sir. To return would give me the keenest pleasure.'

He bowed extravagantly, his reply so plainly well rehearsed that Llewellyn laughed aloud, declaring, 'Upon my soul, young Mostyn, you have all the makings of a fine

153

young dandy! I shall speak to your cousin as soon as I am able and see if he is amenable to your attending lessons here. If he has no objections, it shall be arranged.'

Penry Vaughan was relieved and delighted, for his own sporadic efforts to educate his young kinsman had bored Mostyn and irritated Vaughan beyond endurance. He praised Mostyn lavishly and immediately ordered him two new outfits from the local tailor, salving his conscience by weighing the extravagance against future benefits. The Havard jewels and *objets d'art* removed from Great House had raised a not inconsiderable sum at the London auction rooms and his cousin's debts had been honourably discharged. With the added sale of Great House to Rhys Llewellyn, there remained a generous portion to pay for the boys' education, their board and 'incurred expenses'. That their education would cost him nothing disturbed Vaughan not a whit. By God's good grace, and Mostyn's, Vaughan had once more gained a foothold within Great House, and in Penavon society. He would guard it jealously.

Mostyn ingratiated himself as effortlessly with the household staff at the vicarage as with those at Great House, all, that is, save with Clarissa and, more importantly, Laurel. Laurel bitterly resented his demands upon her father's attention and, however hard Mostyn tried to disarm her, she showed him only cool indifference. He used his entire armoury of social weapons without effect; coaxing, wheedling, flattering, only served to deepen his isolation. From extravagant admiration of the playthings she possessed, he lapsed into an indifference as coldly calculated as her own. Laurel, puzzled and resentful, unused to being ignored, thawed, and grew conciliatory. Mostyn brushed her aside, eager to return to some plaything which called his attention. Her impassioned pleas and tantrums ignored, she tried to bribe him with the promise of sweetmeats, gifts, anything she owned, which would buy his friendship. Mostyn, satisfied that he had unwittingly discovered how best to intrigue her, did not shrink from putting Laurel to the test. It was to

Rhys Llewellyn that she always made appeal, coaxing and fawning, importuning shamelessly, 'Oh, say that we may! Please, please, Papa! If you do then I will love you for ever.' She would hug him fiercely, willing him to agreement.

'I hope, my dear, that your love is not entirely dependent on my indulgence,' he would reply with mock severity, awaiting her denial and the inevitable flurry of kisses. Amused, although undeceived, he would concede. 'Clarissa, you will arrange it.' It was a command, not a request. Clarissa could not help but observe the sly smile of triumph upon her daughter's face, and the swift irritation upon her husband's before he returned his gaze to Laurel, whom he loved.

To Penry Vaughan's satisfaction, for he was an incurable self-seeker and social opportunist, Mostyn's friendship with the Llewellyn family ensured him continued acceptance by the landed gentry and minor nobility beyond Penavon. Lord Litchard tactfully suggested that Mostyn might care to share his son's tutelage at fencing, riding and other masculine arts, an offer accepted by his guardian with indecent alacrity. In the normal order of things, Vaughan would have been expected to return the hospitality which Mostyn received, but his bachelor status and parochial duties gave him excuse to forego that expense, and pleasure. He would not, he made known, compete with the extravagances of others, for he was a man of the cloth, with his mind upon higher, more spiritual matters. Nevertheless, he would accept the many invitations proffered on Mostyn's behalf, with that same warm generosity of soul which had prompted them.

Carne, meanwhile, if he had not achieved his brother's social distinction, was happy at his studies, and in Peter Morrish's company. He was allowed now to take luncheon at Morrish's cottage so that he might give more time to his lessons and books, and Ann Hodges delighted in tempting his appetite with his favourite dishes. His friendship with Jane and Prys had been secretly renewed, and he was happier than he had been since Rice Havard's death and his own banishment from Great House.

Peter Morrish was convinced that his pupil's academic achievements would gain him a place at Oxford, as he desired. Thus the rigid curriculum agreed with Vaughan was widened gradually beyond narrowly academic subjects. Astronomy, navigation and knowledge of the natural world were all explored, and what Morrish did not already know, he either studied carefully or bade others instruct Carne upon. So irresistible was his enthusiasm that few felt able to refuse. Morrish was pleased when Jethro agreed to let Charles share Carne's lessons. It was a concession owed to Sara, for Jethro had declared, 'He is a farmer's boy, not a gentleman! What need has he of mere book learning? It will serve only to make him dissatisfied, and to give him ideas above his station!' It was the pence saved from the Dame school, as much as Sara's insistence, which had finally persuaded him to relent, and he did so with misgivings, declaring obstinately, 'He may go now, while there is little to do upon the farm, but come Spring, he will remain at his duties, without argument!' So it was agreed, with a proviso from Jethro that he should 'only be taught those things a farmer might need, like figuring and such, for all else would be wastage!'

Charles and Carne became immediate friends and were soon inseparable. It was not a friendship which Vaughan would knowingly have encouraged. Morrish, with his usual ingenuity, set his own plans. When he discussed with his pupils the inequalities of slavery, oppression and other social injustices, he bade them accompany him on his visits to the old and indigent sick, that they might learn the reality of suffering. When need arose, he borrowed a cart from the innkeeper and took Carne and Charles into the countryside to Holly Grove Farm to learn the practical needs of agriculture. Jethro was pleased to display his knowledge before them and soon Carne was as much at home in the barns and byres as in Mrs Hodges's kitchen. Peter Morrish insisted that it was all part of a rounded education, for life and learning were inseparable, and his pupils were not inclined to disagree.

Morrish found in Charles a keen pupil, one naturally quick in perception, and with an aptitude for mathematics beyond the ordinary. Yet of Carne, Morrish thought, given opportunity, this child will excel. He will advance beyond my instruction or knowledge. He has a scholar's mind and curiosity which he will strive always to satisfy. It pleased him that he had a part in Carne's growing awareness, but most of all he was pleased that Carne's sympathy for others lay deep, and that neither the loss of his parents nor Vaughan's harsh rejection could kill the core of it with bitterness.

From his window, Morrish watched them now in the stable yard of Myrtle Cottage, shaking his head indulgently at their antics as Charles strove to mount his Welsh cob. They were as roughly boisterous as puppies at play, yet with as little real malice or viciousness. He hoped that whatever befell them in future, however divergent their ways, that this was a friendship which would endure.

It was with warm recollection of the day's lessons, and satisfaction for Morrish's praise at what had been achieved, that Carne alighted from the coach at Penavon vicarage. Probert seemed about to caution him about something, his face unusually troubled, but even as he hesitated, Mrs Groves hurried into the stable yard, lips grimly compressed, and Probert faltered and walked away.

'Mr Vaughan will see you in the library,' said Mrs Groves.

'Yes ma'am. I will put my books away.'

'No! Now, at once! He will brook no delay!'

Carne followed her, bewildered, but without apprehension. Mrs Groves rapped upon the door importantly and, at the muttered command, 'Come!' pulled the door ajar and forced Carne within. His cousin was seated at the desk, face set, eyes unreadable. Before him lay Carne's miniatures of his parents. He walked forward, unthinking, to retrieve them, his overwhelming emotion one of anger that Vaughan had dared to search among his private possessions and then to defile his treasures by touching them.

'My miniatures, sir.' His voice was strained, hoarse with the need to restrain his fury.

'No, sir, they do not belong to you!' Vaughan's voice was swift and cutting as a whip lash. 'They were listed among the contents at Great House. I have proof of it. You will tell me how you came by them!'

'My mother and father, sir.' Carne's words faltered and died away.

'Do not add lying to your thieving! Yes, thieving, I said!' His face was ugly with rage. 'These likenesses were stolen, deliberately and maliciously! I repeat, how did you come by them?'

Carne felt a prickle of fear at his spine, but held his gaze steadily. 'They belong to me, Cousin,' he repeated staunchly, 'by virtue of inheritance. My father would have wished it so. I beg you will return them.'

The boy's certainty and apparent lack of fear so infuriated Vaughan that he could scarcely summon the power to speak. When he did, his words were garbled and barely coherent. 'Have you no shame? No sense of guilt?'

'No, sir, they are mine.'

'Yours, you say? You are a liar and a thief! These miniatures, if not stolen by you, were gained from another's theft, were they not? Admit it!'

'No, sir.'

Vaughan rose, face inflamed with fury, and delivered him a blow to the cheek which sent Carne reeling, but he steadied himself resolutely upon the corner of the desk. Vaughan, beside himself with anger, said between clenched teeth, 'I see, sir, that you need to be taught a lesson in honesty and truthfulness. Go to your room!' As Carne moved to gather up the ivories, Vaughan swept them into his own hand, declaring, 'No! You shall not have them. Go to your room, I say, and await me there. You will be punished, I swear, and will not stand defiant against me again!'

Without a word, Carne left the library and, heavy footed, climbed the staircase to his room. He felt no terror of what was to come, only an overwhelming shame that his cousin's treachery should have soiled the memory of the two people he had loved best. From his father's looking glass, his face stared back at him, mutinous and cold; the face of a stranger, the weal of Vaughan's blow savagely disfiguring his cheek, lip swollen and beginning to bruise.

'Well?' Vaughan's voice from the doorway alerted him. 'Have you come to your senses? Will you apologise?'

Carne shook his head.

'You will admit that it was Jane Prys who stole. Admit it freely, and write it down, and then we shall see.'

'She did not steal them, sir.' Carne's voice was clear, the birch switch in his cousin's hand notwithstanding. 'Nor did she give them to me. They were my own, by right, and only a liar or a fool could deny it!'

Vaughan's face grew so suffused with fury that a vein rose hard and throbbed at his temple, and even his eyes grew reddened, seeming to swell. 'Take off your coat and your shirt, sir,' he instructed, 'for I can see that my words and sympathy are wasted, and only punishment will serve to bring you to your senses!'

Carne did as he was bidden, trying not to flinch or cry aloud as the switch descended. Again and again it fell, until the fierce, lacerating pain consumed him like a flame, licking, devouring, burning him into ash, so that he could believe that he was weightless, fleshless, a mind bereft of all feeling and thought. He was not even aware that Vaughan spoke, or when he walked away, anger spent.

That night he could not suffer to lie beneath the sheets, the weight of them too painful to bear. His flesh seemed to be on fire and his mouth dry, but he could not ease himself to reach for the carafe of water upon his bedside table. Sleeping or awake, he was consumed with hurt, every movement a new punishment as hard as the beating he had borne. When the first cold light of dawn crept into the room, he forced himself to drag himself upright in his bed slowly and, crying aloud with the intensity of it, walked haltingly to the window that he might rest his head against its coolness. He wept then, but not in remorse, or from the violence of his beating, but because the miniatures of Rice Havard and Rhianon were no longer his solace.

He did not sleep but, when the sun rose higher, and the room was filled with morning brightness, he dressed slowly and with difficulty, biting his lip until he tasted the salt of blood, lest he cry aloud. He rested often, unable to bear the anguish of movement, and felt filled with a tiredness that deadened his limbs and seeped into his spirit. He could not summon the will to pour the water from his washstand jug into the bowl but simply dipped his hand into its coldness, wiping it carefully across his eyes, as though wiping away hurt. The burning heat had left him now and there was a coldness in its stead that had nothing to do with the day. He looked at his scarred flesh and felt neither surprise nor horror, nothing but the brief curiosity of one glancing shamefacedly at the affliction of a stranger. All that had passed seemed unreal to him, yet he could not dismiss the memory of it. It lingered, insistent as a broken dream, its menace surfacing when all else had been forgot. Carne put on his coat and bent to pick up his boots, then walked out on to the cobbled yard where Probert awaited him with the coach.

Probert, seeing the boy's pallid face and the bruised hollows about his eyes, felt his anger against Penry Vaughan rise, although he did not know the full cruelty of what had been done. He gripped Carne's hand in reassurance as he helped him within the coach, and Carne attempted to smile yet the unspoken sympathy was harder to bear than Vaughan's violence and tears pricked treacherously at his eyes. He entered the coach, head bowed, and the pain as he straightened his shoulders against the cold leather of the seats was so sharp in agony that the tears dried, unshed. He had taken his history book, and tried to read, but the printed words blurred and danced before his eyes, meaningless characters upon a foreign page, as alien and useless as he.

Peter Morrish, aware of some unease in his pupil,

stretched out an arm to encircle Carne and draw him companionably within the house. Immediately, Carne's involuntary cry and flinching away from his touch confirmed what he had long feared, that Vaughan's mental violence had given way to physical harm. He helped the boy to a chair, then gently removed Carne's coat and the linen shirt, its whiteness already stained with new blood. Some of the fabric lay fused to the re-opened wounds. Morrish eased it away, mind bleak with foreboding. When the full savagery of Carne's wounds was revealed to him, he felt such sickness and pity that he stood helpless, unable even to speak a word of comfort to the child. Then he was filled with such a murderous rage and hatred against the man who had inflicted such hurt that he felt himself shuddering, as if the blows descended now upon him. Morrish knew, with certainty, that if Vaughan had stood before him, he would have killed him without pity or remorse. I have so faithfully preached forgiveness, he thought, made it my creed, but there is none in me. He stared at the child's bruised flesh, the raw weals which disfigured chest and back dried and crusted, others oozing clear, or viscous with fresh blood.

'A man of God!' Morrish heard himself crying aloud. 'He is a devil, vicious and depraved! He insults the very name of God by his existence! The man is a brute, a madman!' He broke off his tirade to call furiously, 'Mrs Hodges! Here! This instant! Leave everything and come at once, I say!'

Mrs Hodges, alarmed by his unexpected anger, hurried at his command, sniffing, wiping her hands anxiously upon her apron.

'Quickly, woman. Go at once and summon the doctor! Bid him come without delay!'

Mrs Hodges, taking in the violence of the wounds upon Carne's body, hesitated, hands flying to her mouth in disbelief, and would have run to comfort him, but he shrank away, fearful of any touch, and she began to weep helplessly, unable to do as Morrish bade, or to halt the flow of tears.

'No, sir!' Carne cried, 'I beg you will not summon the doctor! Please, sir, it would vex me sorely, and my cousin might . . .' He left his fears unspoken, adding with quiet dignity, 'I would not give him the satisfaction, sir, of knowing that I am hurt, and complaining to another.'

'But your wounds must be treated,' Morrish insisted. 'What would you have me do?'

'I should like to see Jane and Prys, sir, if you will allow?'

'If you will stay beside Carne, Mrs Hodges,' Morrish said, 'and see to his needs, then I will saddle my mare, and go at once to Hillbrook Cottage, and will return as soon as I am able. If I see Charles upon the way, I shall bid him ride with me.'

She nodded and purposefully wiped her eyes, settling herself awkwardly in a chair beside Carne before rising to heap more kindling upon the fire, lest he take a chill, then demanding of him if he had need of a blanket to cover him, or food or drink. He had but to say the word and she would fetch them at once. Her plump, good-natured face was ugly with concern for the boy, and Morrish had no fears upon leaving him in her care.

'You will keep the door locked and barred, Mrs Hodges.' There was implied warning in his words. 'Allow none to enter until I return.'

Mrs Hodges brought Carne spice cakes and buttermilk, and set his chair nearer the fire's warmth, covering him with a clean linen sheet, lest a blanket stick to his wounds. Then she helplessly touched his dark hair, as if in blessing and grief, and stayed watchfully beside him until the heat of the flames and exhaustion had eased him into sleep.

The unmistakable sounds of Prys's mule cart clattering and scraping to a halt without had her rushing to unbolt the door, and when Carne, startled awake by the uproar, leapt agitatedly from his chair, it was to the loving tenderness of Jane's reassurance and Prys's calm presence.

There had been another beside them whom he did not, at first, recognise, for when he had seen her at his father's graveside, she had been distraught with rage and grief, a

162

poor demented creature whom he had believed deprived of her wits and reason. Yet he had thanked her courteously that she had shown the courage to declare her love for Rice Havard before all, knowing the revenge it must bring. He found it strange that such a wild, disordered creature stood once more beside him, somehow grown young, and with a calm serenity that brought a sense of peace to the turmoil he endured. There was no strangeness between them, only a mutual recognition of a grief shared and a punishment survived.

'I have come to help you, Carne, if you will allow me,' Marged Howell said.

He nodded, and Jane came forward to take his hand, bidding him squeeze her fingers as hard as ever he could, should he feel the need. There was no need for Marged Howell to say, 'I will not hurt you, my dear,' for he knew it, even before the sweet smelling unguents spread by her deft fingers cooled raw flesh and took away pain.

Marged smiled at him, although her eyes were soft with tears, and Jane knew that in risking her freedom by coming so willingly and publicly to Carne's aid, the wise-woman had poured balm not only into Carne's wounds, but her own.

It was a long time before Peter Morrish returned and, when he did, Charles Hartrey was not beside him. Upon Morrish's explanation and bidding, Charles had returned, although unwillingly, to the farm. His ready sympathy, Morrish believed, would at last have caused Carne to weep and that would have proved a greater humiliation than any he had been forced to endure.

He was never to learn how his friend, the advocate, had ridden with Morrish to the vicarage, nor what words were addressed to Penry Vaughan. Carne only knew that, for some unexplained reason, his cousin raised no more objection to Jane and Prys meeting him openly. Vaughan had informed him brusquely that to use the coach every day was a wasteful extravagance, and that thereafter he might take a horse from the stables and ride alone, or with Charles

Hartrey as companion, should the weather be fine. His attempts to thank his cousin were irritatedly cut short before he was dismissed with the surliest of acknowledgement to his room. There was no cessation of hostilities between them, simply an armed truce, a regathering of weaponry until need arise. Of one thing Carne was sure. His cousin liked him no better.

Chapter Eighteen

Penry Vaughan never again raised a hand in wrath against Carne, nor did he make mention of the thrashing he had administered. The day after Peter Morrish and Randall Walters had paid the vicar an unsolicited call, the overweight attorney had once more halted the Havard coach upon the highway, and delivered the miniatures into Carne's hands. Walters' plump, cherubic face had been wreathed in smiles, his waistcoat buttons straining beneath a surfeit of flesh and goodwill as he declared, 'These are yours, my boy, by inheritance and law. None can now dispute it. The . . . er . . . legal documents are in my safe-keeping.' He paused, eyes twinkling with mischief, before adding innocently, 'Perhaps it is wiser so, since there are more thieves and villains abroad than honest men of God.'

When Carne made to thank him, Walters brushed his gratitude aside to wave Probert grandly upon his way. There was a spring in the obese attorney's step, and within him that virtuous glow of one who has done good by stealth, only to have it thrust admiringly into public view. He smiled delightedly as he crossed the cobbled street, walking with delicate lightness upon small feet.

He looks, thought Higgs, his clerk, peering benignly at him through his office window, like a genial cockroach learning to walk upright. Higgs's withered brown face wrinkled into a smile as he turned to busy himself at his desk. He was recalling Carne Havard's impulsive visit to the attorney's chambers, begging to be 'allowed a word', and the conversation he had shamelessly eavesdropped upon.

'I beg, sir . . .' Carne had blurted to Walters, face scarlet with mortification, 'that you will tell me if my father's estate allows small purchases. Things of an improving nature?'

'I believe, Carne,' Walters had replied with the gravity suited to addressing a client, 'that Mr Penry Vaughan has that facility, but may I enquire as to why you ask?'

'Because, sir . . .' Carne had flushed awkwardly, 'because there are books which Mr Morrish has said I should buy. I cannot tell him that I have no means of doing so. I know that he would willingly buy them for me, but it would humiliate me to accept. He already offers me his services as tutor without fee.'

'Does he indeed?' muttered Walters. 'Then have you approached your cousin, Carne? Told him of the need?'

'Yes, sir, many times.' Carne's voice was low, his cheeks and neck mottled with shame. 'I thought, Mr Walters . . . I wondered if you would reason with my cousin, sir? I would not ask this favour, sir, except that I know that you are a gentleman whose opinion is valued by others.'

Walters had felt pity at the child's discomfiture, saying brusquely, 'Give it no more thought, my boy! If you will take a list of what is required to the bookseller, then I will see that it is presented to your cousin, and honoured. You have my permission, no, my *instructions* to obtain whatever is necessary to further your studies, both immediate and in the future. You understand?'

Carne had thanked him courteously and with evident sincerity, his young face transfigured with relief that he need no longer beg Penry Vaughan's indulgence, nor acquaint Morrish with his poverty.

Higgs, deep in reflection upon the matter, started guiltily, stirred into needless activity as he heard the attorney's footsteps upon the stairs. Carne Havard, like many another, would never know that payment had been made from Randall Walters' purse.

Carne's newly won freedom to ride to his lessons at Myrtle Cottage gave him a growing independence and maturity. It also served to diminish his unhappiness at

Penavon vicarage by setting his feud with his cousin into perspective. He could not forget the past, but his life beyond the vicarage walls now made the indifference shown to him within them bearable. As to the future, the prospect of studying at Oxford University was always clear in his mind, and he worked assiduously to achieve it. There was a freedom in education, Peter Morrish had said; it was the key to other men's minds, and one's own. Carne did not doubt it, nor that it would prove the key to free himself from Penry Vaughan's guardianship and cold contempt. It was a spur and a goad, as keen as his honest desire to please Peter Morrish.

The young curate, in turn, was aware that his secret knowledge of Penry Vaughan's cruelty to his ward armed him best. Should news of the boy's ill-treatment reach Morrish's godfather, Bishop Copleston, it would effectively kill Vaughan's hopes of preferment. Morrish would have been as little moved to see Vaughan himself killed, but there was no denying that the vicar's removal by more orthodox means would be of benefit to all . . . all save Carne, that is. Should Vaughan uproot himself and his wards from Penavon, as he was legally entitled to do, then their future would be bleak indeed, with none to watch over them or to curb Vaughan's cruellest excesses. In the meantime, like every other, Vaughan's actions must seal his own destiny and his own salvation.

It was Charles Hartrey's friendship and Carne's acceptance at the farm which had done most to heal the past. Given Sara Hartrey's maternal warmth and Jethro's simple kindness, he had relaxed and grown more confident of his own worth, for he knew he was accepted unconditionally. Vaughan's dislike had served only to make Carne awkward and tongue-tied in his cousin's presence, exacerbating his clumsiness and Vaughan's contempt. Now, with Jethro as his mentor, he worked on the farm, growing in physical strength and sense of purpose, with Charles and his casually thrown invitations to lead them into adventure and challenge against others of their kind.

The only Hartrey who would not accept him unconditionally was Saranne, whose past had made her suspicious
of strangers. Her wariness was slow to fade. Whenever
Carne appeared, despite his gentleness to her, she hung
back, shy and unspeaking.

'Do you not think, Saranne, my dear,' observed Jane
with seeming casualness, glancing up from her mending,
'that you might, perhaps, try to be kinder to Carne?'

Saranne fidgeted and looked towards Sara for guidance,
but found none, for her mother was intent upon her stitching. 'I do not like him!' blurted Saranne, clenching and
unclenching her fists in nervous agitation. 'He was cruel to
Marged. He had her locked into the pillory! I do not like
him!' she repeated fiercely.

'No, my love,' said Jane conversationally. 'I think you
are misled. It was the workmaster who ordered her punishment. Carne begged me, most earnestly, to see that neither
you nor Marged came to harm.'

Saranne regarded her in silence, strange, violet-coloured
eyes perplexed, but unyielding.

'Was it not kind of him, Sara,' Jane asked, 'to think so
generously of others in his grief at his papa's death?'

'Indeed,' agreed Sara, purposely not looking up, 'I have
always found him to be a most considerate and gentle-
mannered boy.'

'Does Charles like him better than me?' demanded
Saranne.

'My dear, how could he?' asked her mother, laying down
her sewing and immediately drawing Saranne close before
hugging her and smoothing the child's dark hair. 'Carne is
a new friend for Charles, just as Jane is a dear friend of
mine. You are my own little daughter, and Charles's sister.
I do not love you the less because of my friendship with
Jane. Come, let us set out the victuals upon the table, for
Papa, Mr Prys and the boys will soon be returning, and as
hungry as hunters, I do not doubt!'

Carne and Charles entered the farmhouse together, hair
ruffled, faces flushed, their disordered clothes giving evi-

dence of some friendly scuffle.

'Carne,' ordered Jane, 'you had best remove your shirt, since the cuff is torn. It would not do to return to the vicarage so dishevelled. It would earn you the sharp edge of Mrs Groves' tongue, and, very likely, your cousin's! Unbutton it, and I will stitch it neatly for you.'

Obediently, Carne did as Jane bade, to a sharp intake of breath from Sara as she saw the savagery of the lesions still unhealed. 'Oh, Carne! My dear child!' Sara ran to him in horror, voice treacherous with tears. She stretched out a comforting hand, but withdrew it, fearful of hurting him.

'It makes no matter, ma'am,' said Carne, embarrassed by his naked flesh and the tense silence in the room. 'It does not hurt, I swear . . . I beg your pardon most humbly, if I have offended. I had forgotten the ugliness of the scars.' He was crimson with shame, and had taken the shirt from Jane's hand to cover himself, declaring awkwardly, 'I believe the worst of them will soon be faded and forgotten. Yet I will not forget that Mistress Howell risked imprisonment to give me ease from hurt . . . or how willingly Jane and Prys came.'

He put out a hand to touch Jane's fingers affectionately.

Saranne had crept, unseen, to stand beside him, eyes watchful, sensitive to rebuff, as she said, 'You are a brave boy, Carne, and I will be your friend, if you will let me.'

The eyes of all within the room were upon Carne, willing him to speak kindly to the child, for her darkly flushed face and nervous agitation were evidence of the effort the words had cost her.

'I shall be honoured, ma'am, to count you so,' declared Carne, lips twitching, but bowing gallantly nonetheless.

'Then 'twould be fitter, young man, if you were suitably dressed,' declared Jane to break the tension, as she reached purposefully towards his shirt, needle poised.

'Handsome is as handsome does,' said Jethro quietly, 'and that was handsomely done, my lad.'

Saranne pulled tentatively at her father's finger to gain

169

his attention, 'And as handsomely said, my maid,' he admitted amid laughter.

Thereafter, Saranne attached herself as slavishly to Carne as formerly she had to Marged Howell, anticipating his every need, defensive or protective against others, utterly devoted to serving him. Carne was alternately flattered and aggravated by her worship, unsure of how best to react. He did not wish to hurt the child by a display of indifference, for, as Peter Morrish gently chided him, Saranne had faced cruelty and rejection enough. Even so, Carne was reluctant to encourage her newfound passion, or to alienate Jethro and Sara by appearing uncharitably brusque. Consequently, he walked a precarious tightrope, balancing uneasily between restraint and affection, and never wholly at ease. Charles was only grateful for a respite from Saranne's adulation, and would give Carne no lead, lest his sister's undivided attention return to bedevil him. As the two boys grew progressively more adventurous, climbing, wrestling, exploring further afield, the problem of Saranne's slavish attachment was resolved. The restrictions placed upon her by Jethro and Sara, for her own safety, were obeyed, secretly with some relief. Saranne was mindful of her pretty clothes and shoes, for she had too long been denied such luxuries, and it was pride in them, not fear alone, which made her cling closer to Holly Grove.

With the two boys occupied, and the farm demanding less of his labour, Jethro was able to devote more time to 'the womenfolk', ready always to take them by cart into Penavon village, or to visit their friends in the countryside. There were Saranne's small duties in the dairy to attend, with Megan ever eager to amuse and instruct her, then the kittens to be played with and fed, or help given in the kitchen with the baking, and Jane was teaching her to sew. The days were always too short for the excitement they held. When Charles and Carne returned from their sport or some task Jethro had set them, Saranne's pleasure and devotion were welcomed rather than spurned. Carne had learned to treat her casually but affectionately, as a real sister, taking his pattern from Charles. Yet even as they grew older, and they and their expectations changed, Saranne's did not. She loved Carne dearly, and with a love quite distinct from that which she felt for her parents and Charles. The only difference was that she had learnt how best to hide it.

When Mostyn was twelve years old, Rhys Llewellyn came to a decision which not all Laurel's wiles and impassioned begging could change. It was no longer circumspect, Llewellyn announced, for his daughter and Mostyn to share their lessons. They were no longer infants, but of an age when their academic needs and their interests were bound to diverge. In future, Laurel would take lessons alone.

His reasons for separating the pair, who had grown as comfortably familiar as brother and sister, deceived no-one, least of all Clarissa. They were not related by blood, and the older they grew, the more liable their relationship was to be remarked upon and misconstrued by others. Rhys Llewellyn's sights were firmly set upon a good alliance for his only child. Laurel was wayward and tempestuous it was true, but already she showed signs of real beauty. As a considerable heiress in her own right, there would be no shortage of suitors for her hand, and dowry. Already there were tentative overtures from those who would willingly ally an ancient name with new money, since it was their only means of dignified survival. Rhys Llewellyn loved his daughter as he loved no other, yet he did not delude himself. She was his greatest negotiable asset. It was in Laurel's interest, as his own, that her disposal yielded the richest possible return.

Mostyn had somehow contrived to hide the raw terror and resentment which raked him when Llewellyn had told him of his decision. The thought of permanently returning to the boredom and frugality of life at Penavon vicarage was unthinkable, and it was all Mostyn could do to prevent himself from begging Llewellyn to allow him to remain, but instinct told him that it would serve only to harden the

171

Ironmaster's resolve and rouse his contempt.

'I shall, of course, continue to treat you generously, as in the past,' Llewellyn declared sententiously, 'for we all consider you to be part of our household . . . our family.'

Mostyn, cold with humiliation, waited in silence.

'I will employ your own tutors for you. You shall continue your lessons here at Great House . . . Nothing will change.'

Mostyn thanked him with easy courtesy, his manner contriving to be suitably respectful, yet assured. Damn him! he thought impotently, damn him for his smug patronage and hypocrisy! It is Laurel he fears for. He has no real care nor liking for me! Mostyn swallowed his rage, as he had swallowed his pride and the gifts and bounty which Laurel and his benefactor had doled out to him from their charity. He accepted because there was no other way.

Llewellyn, watching him leave, thought what an arrestingly handsome boy he was, already showing firm promise of the polished and successful gentleman he had vowed to become. It pleased and flattered Llewellyn that Mostyn had taken him for his mentor, and it was true that, despite himself, he had grown fond of the boy. If only Mostyn had been his own son. He dismissed the thought guiltily. The boy would not suffer. He would groom him for a place within his business empire, until a son-in-law, or grandchild, showed greater claim to take Mostyn's place.

Mostyn was quick of intelligence, amusing, well liked, and would be an asset to him, Llewellyn felt sure. Yet there was a sharp edge to him, a determination to succeed; more than that, a need to excel, to prove himself the best. Llewellyn had studied him at riding lessons and at fencing with Litchard's son, and Mostyn's skill and unselfconscious grace had been a joy to watch. Yet he showed such fierce determination to win at all costs that he was not averse to catching his opponent off guard, and inflicting a sly wound. It was a trait which Llewellyn could not condemn, for he was aware of it in himself, the planned distraction, then the swift stroke which drew first blood from others. Yes,

Mostyn would excel at business for he had a core of ruth-lessness well hidden, but as indestructible as Llewellyn's own.

At seventeen years of age, Carne was a handsome, spirited boy, as dark haired and complexioned as Mostyn was fair, and so like Rice Havard in build and arrogance of move-ment and features that Jane, who was sometimes confused about the swift passing of the years, would call him by his father's name. He had surpassed Peter Morrish's expec-tations as a student, and both knew that his future was already decided. He would gain a scholarship to Oxford University, as he had hoped. Beyond that lay uncharted adventure. Escape.

It sometimes disturbed Carne that he now felt closer to Charles in friendship and interests than to Mostyn. The lives of the two brothers had inevitably diverged and they had grown increasingly distant. There was still the tie of blood between them, but in all else they were as strangers. Mostyn no longer relied upon Carne for protection, for Rice Havard was dead, and each exorcised the ghost of him in his own fashion.

In their earliest days at the vicarage, Carne's pleas that Mostyn should visit Jane and Prys had found no favour, perhaps because they reminded him too vividly of a past he sought to forget. 'It would anger Cousin Penry,' he had declared, and later, 'I would have nothing to say to them. I was but an infant, and have all but forgotten their exist-ence. I could not treat them as friends, you understand? I would patronise them, unwittingly, and make them awk-ward and ill-at-ease, and make you ashamed.' He had spoken with honesty, and regret, and Carne did not seek to persuade him. After a while, Jane's and Prys's gentle enquiries and urgings had ceased.

Penry Vaughan had taken to visiting London with increasing frequency upon 'matters of pressing business', the nature of which were never disclosed. Mostyn regretted his cousin's absence, for evenings spent alone, or in Carne's company, offered little diversion. Carne was so intent upon studying that he barely tolerated Mostyn's restless presence in his room, finding him disruptive, and easily bored.

'Damnation, Mostyn!' he exclaimed when his brother proved more than usually irritating. 'Stop your incessant whining and fidgeting! Have you no studying to do?'

'No. I am not for ever stuck in my books like you!'

'Then it might be better if you were!'

'Why? What will it avail you?' Mostyn drawled insolently. 'Do you have plans to become a tutor or a curate, like Peter Morrish?'

Carne was stung into retorting, 'No. I do not! And if I did, it would be more fitting than turning into an empty-headed little coxcomb like you, with no thought save for clothes and amusement. You are a dandy, Mostyn, and as mindless as the society you ape!'

'And you, Carne, are as cloddish and ignorant as the farmers and servants you are pleased to call friends! You are a damnable boor, and I will have no more truck with you.'

'Please yourself!' Carne snapped, adding abrasively, 'I do not doubt you would be happier in your own company, for you have such a high opinion of yourself.'

They glowered at each other furiously, unwilling to concede, until finally one or the other had seen the absurdity of the situation, then they dissolved into shamefaced laughter.

'I wish Cousin Penry had taken me as travelling companion to London,' Mostyn murmured petulantly. 'Penavon is as dull as ditchwater. I shall be glad when he returns, for you are neither company nor amusement!'

Carne grimaced, and reluctantly laid his textbook aside, wishing as fervently that whatever urgent business drew his cousin to the capital, it might keep him occupied for ever.

It was upon one of Vaughan's absences in London that Charles tried to prevail upon Carne to ride out to a meeting of the Religious Dissenters at Golden Grove.

'It will be a rare spectacle!' Charles exclaimed with enthusiasm, 'and there is bound to be argument and fisticuffs, since the cottagers will be determined to drive them away. Your cousin preached so wildly about the devil they bring! We might even see him,' he urged, 'the devil . . . not Penry Vaughan!'

Carne hesitated, objecting half-heartedly, 'I do not think that Peter Morrish would countenance it.'

'He is not invited!' Charles punched companionably at Carne's shoulder, chivvying, 'What hinders you, you milksop? Your cousin is not to know. It will be fun! An adventure,' he persisted. 'We are not seven but seventeen, Carne; men, not infants to be wet nursed! What harm is in it?'

Carne, unconvinced, said uneasily, 'Perhaps more harm than we know . . .' Then, glimpsing his friend's scornful face, he said defensively, 'It is not the devil I fear, you idiot! I have lived with one long enough. It is people! I'll wager there will be dolts enough, intent upon disrupting those whose aim is to worship peacefully in their own way. They will taunt and ridicule them, and when they do not respond, will turn their threats to violence. To them it will be but blood-sport, and one I have no stomach for.'

'Then I will go alone!' declared Charles, undeterred.

They stared at each other in angry silence, neither willing to yield.

'Will you join forces with the zealots and bigots?' Carne demanded at length. 'Ally yourself to such scum?'

'No,' answered Charles quietly, 'I will stand beside those who have the courage to speak out for what they believe to be right.'

'But you have no such convictions!'

'It makes no matter,' Charles insisted stubbornly. 'They have a right to worship freely, else what value is there in a religion which allows of no doubts nor alteration? You have heard Peter Morrish declare often enough that religion is a personal communion. He urges us to question, evaluate, then come to our own conclusion. That is all I shall do.'

Carne shook his head ruefully, declaring, 'You are a fool, Charles! An idealist . . . but ideals are as easily broken as flesh and bone! I will come, but only because I would not see you martyred! I have learnt to tolerate you as a fool; as a martyr you would be quite insupportable!'

They clasped hands upon it amid laughter, and Charles, good humour fully restored, offered, 'Ride over to the farm by six o' the clock and eat with us. Then I shall harness the ploughhorse to the cart and claim we drive to Myrtle Cottage . . . that there is some text or other which causes us concern, and we would ask Peter Morrish's opinion. You will come?'

'Yes, I have already promised, although I do not relish the thought of deceiving your parents.'

'We do it but to spare their grief,' dismissed Charles blandly. 'The end justifies the means.'

'It is how it will end which worries me most,' murmured Carne resignedly, 'although, I have as little stomach for its beginning.'

When the meal was ended at Holly Grove Farm, and Charles had brought the horse and waggon into the yard, Sara, seeing Carne's anxious awkwardness and her son's flushed face, felt a momentary unease. She was certain that some mischief was afoot, and that the boys had no notion of seeking Peter Morrish's aid with their studies. She smiled ruefully, berating herself for lack of understanding. It was plain to her now that the boys had plotted together, in Penry Vaughan's absence, to ride out to do a little harmless flirting with the more nubile of the village girls, or to display their new-found independence at some ale-house beyond Penavon. They were of an age, and it was in the very nature of things to put on their courting feathers and display themselves to advantage. She felt a warm surge of affection for the two handsome young creatures, poised so uncertainly on the edge of manhood. She felt amusement, and pity too, although whether her pity was for them or for herself she did not know. They were young enough to face the sorrows and disappointments which must come as surely as the joys. The whole of life lay before them, a challenge and adventure. She envied them that. Sara's hand strayed involuntarily towards Jethro's, and he clasped it in his strong fingers, firm and reassuring, glancing at her, and nodding his understanding. He turned to Charles, 'You will remember to take things easily, and to behave as you ought,' he cautioned, 'for there is always tomorrow.' He spoke quietly, holding the shire's harness to still it as Carne clambered aboard the waggon.

'Yes, Papa.'

'Yes, Mr Hartrey, sir.'

Their responses were low, subdued by guilt, and Jethro's lips flickered in a smile as he surrendered the reins to Charles's keeping. ''Tis not a funeral you ride to, but your tutor's house,' he reminded, adding innocently, 'You have faces dark as thunderclouds and fitted to scare the plumpest pigeons from the corn. Saving your fine clothes, I could set you in my fields for scarecrows!' Jethro grinned widely at his slyness, until Sara gave him a gentle nudge, and he delved into his pocket, saying, 'Carne, you had best take sixpence apiece, for it is owed you both from your labours upon the farm.' He pressed it into Carne's hand as Carne blurted his thanks, face wretched with guilt at deceiving him. 'You will not need it now, since you drive to Myrtle Cottage,' Jethro said equably. 'Best save it for a sunny day, rather than a rainy one.'

The pair drove off, with Jethro and Sara waving and admirably straight-faced, until Carne climbed down to open the farm gate, then remounted the waggon, and it disappeared from view. Then they erupted into good-natured laughter, indulgent, and the better for being shared.

'Saranne will be vexed that she missed their leaving,' said Sara, wiping her eyes and glancing about anxiously for sight of her daughter.

'Let her be,' advised Jethro. 'I believe she has gone on purpose to feed the stable cats. She is growing up, Sara, and has not learned to dissemble, to hide what is better hidden from others.'

'Carne, you mean?' asked Sara, startled that Jethro had perceived what she already knew; their daughter's growing fondness for the boy. 'She is barely fifteen, Jethro,' she objected.

'Then the feelings are deeper, and more raw.'

'Perhaps,' Sara admitted, 'but they will change a dozen times and more before she grows to womanhood. She is a comely, intelligent girl, and there will be many a young farmer anxious to walk out with her.'

'Then I will protect her for as long as I am able,' declared Jethro stiffly. 'She shall not go to some lewd clod of a farmer with brutish carnal needs. I am firm upon it!'

'Perhaps, like me, she will welcome his coarse advances,' suggested Sara, tongue in cheek.

'You are a forward hussy!' declared Jethro, laughing despite his efforts to remain sober faced. 'It is as well that you were chosen and wed by a decent, honourable man who knew how best to curb your wantonness.'

'Now there,' said Sara, taking his arm and leading him within, 'I must beg to disagree.' She continued in answer to his enquiring look, 'It was I, my love, who made the choice the very first time I set eyes upon you. I loved you then as I love you now, and you will never curb my wantonness, not until my blood is stilled, and I am laid within my grave. I confess it openly, without shame!'

'Since confession is good for the soul,' said Jethro, smiling down at her, then gathering her into his arms, 'I confess 'twas the only reason I wed you.' He stilled her exclamation with a kiss.

Chapter Nineteen

The farm waggon bumped and rattled upon the narrow, stone-ridden byways, the shire horse's great hooves clopping sturdily beneath their fringing of coarse white hair.

'We should not have lied to them,' ventured Carne, to break the silence, the pieces of silver burning their betrayal into his palm.

'We have but to call upon Peter Morrish upon our return,' said Charles, guilt making him defensive, 'and we shall have absolved ourselves.'

He seemed as unconvinced as Carne, and they relapsed into uneasy silence for a while.

'You are set upon going, Charles?'

'Have I not said so?' demanded Charles, stung into justifying himself, although he would have welcomed a chance to withdraw. 'If you are too pious or lily-livered to come, I will drop you by the wayside, and you may return to claim your cousin's horse!'

'*My* horse,' corrected Carne with unusual asperity, 'and I have no wish to renege upon my promise. I have given my word, and I shall not budge from it. You may depend on it.'

'I would sooner depend on *you*,' said Charles stiffly, turning his attention to the reins, 'for your heart obviously is not in this adventure.'

'Damnation!' cried Carne vexedly when one of the barrels on the cart rolled and bounced as the wheels struck a cart rut. 'Can you not steady the confounded things? You are neither use nor ornament.'

'My hands are occupied with the horse, as any but an idiot would see!'

The sacks heaped upon the cart floor rose under Carne's kick as he gave vent to his spleen, and an aggrieved voice cried out as Saranne emerged. 'If that kick was meant for Charles, then it was misaimed!'

Charles had almost lost control of the reins, and Carne studied her in open-mouthed amazement as she calmly brushed the husks of corn and dust from her gown and endeavoured to repair her dishevelment. Saranne laughed aloud at their comical expressions of disbelief, saying composedly, 'Papa was wrong when he said that your faces were like thunderclouds! You look more like gaping lunatics.'

'You are the lunatic, Miss!' countered Charles, halting the shire with an abruptness that all but overturned the cart. 'If you think that I will not return you to the farm this instant, then you are sadly mistaken!'

'Then you will miss your great adventure,' said Saranne coolly, 'for you cannot set me down to walk the lanes alone.'

'I will walk beside you!' promised Carne grimly, 'and give full account of your foolishness.'

Saranne had brightened at such a delightfully unexpected outcome to her wilfulness, but Charles quickly forestalled it, declaring, 'Yes, you would return and tell all, Miss! And with the greatest of relish. No, you shall stay, and to hell with the consequences! You have none to blame but yourself if you are manhandled and made a laughing stock! Settle yourself! Hell and high water will not divert me from driving to the meeting as I planned!'

He flicked the horse angrily into movement, the cart rattling and swaying along the lanes so perilously that both Saranne and Carne had to cling to its sides for dear life, lest they be tipped into a hedge. Thus it was that, with teeth gritted and knuckles clenched white to keep her hold, Saranne arrived, breathless, at the small copse where the dissidents were to gather. Ignoring Carne's outstretched hand, she clambered unaided to the ground, dark hair wildly disordered, violet eyes behind their thick fringe of lashes glinting with ill-suppressed fury. Strangely, Carne thought that he had never seen her look so becoming, with her cheeks whipped to colour by the fierce pace of the ride and her own resentment. She could scarcely find the words to speak, her softly rounded bodice rising and falling with each outraged breath as she demanded irately, 'What are you gaping at? You great ninny! Have you lost your few wits as well as your manners?'

As Charles exploded in mirth, she turned upon him, boxing his ears savagely, declaring, 'And you, Charles! Shame upon you for taking out your vexation on that poor horse! It ill becomes you to smirk! You are a brute and an imbecile! You drove that wretched creature like a bat out of hell!'

It was Carne's turn to erupt into laughter, which slowly died as he saw the gleam of tears upon Saranne's lashes. He felt a totally strange feeling of protectiveness within him, and a sensation which seemed to touch every nerve of his flesh and the blood which surged beneath, with such a confusion of pain and joy that it bewildered and shamed him. 'You had best stand beside me!' he commanded roughly. He stretched out a hand and took her wrist, but Saranne wrenched herself free.

'I would sooner stand with a serpent!' she said hotly.

'Your knowledge of the scriptures does you credit, Saranne,' interrupted Charles, straight-faced. 'For the moment you had best join the rest of the womenfolk,' he instructed drily, 'for it seems we are to be segregated, lest temptation recur.'

Followed by his laughter, Saranne turned and abruptly strode away, not even pausing to bid goodbye to the old shire, who was surrounded now by a coterie of raw-nosed urchins, measuring their puny height and reach admiringly against his.

Saranne settled herself upon the grass beside a quartet of women with young children, huddled in the lee of a copse of hazel trees. They greeted her courteously, making room, and one bade her share the washed sacking placed

181

upon the ground. They cautioned their older children to 'mind your manners' and 'keep watch upon the babes'.

Saranne, who had been happily absorbed in watching the children's inventive play, turned to view the wider scene. There was a crowd of perhaps thirty or forty adults all told, dividing almost equally into men and women, with as many children spread haphazardly about, seemingly unsegregated, although their elders were strictly set apart. They were ordinary, unremarkable country folk such as she, neatly dressed, and come to listen and make quiet judgement rather than to cause an affray, as Charles had feared. There was a carefree holy-day atmosphere in the crowd and the scene itself, for all were relaxed, and perhaps grateful to stretch their limbs in the clean air, the day's labours ended. The younger men, she hazarded, were labourers upon farms or roads or in the small quarries and brickyards, for their faces were weathered and their shoulders hard-muscled. Beside them, Saranne thought, a bubble of laughter rising irrepressibly within her, Charles and Carne looked like pampered gentlemen; as out of place as flaunting peacocks in a sober gathering of crows. Did she, Saranne wondered, stand as vividly apart in her dainty blue dress of sprigged cotton with its collar of lace? If so, then none had made her look or feel conspicuous, welcoming her into their midst, as Charles and Carne were being generously drawn into the flurry of chatter and bustle about them.

When the preacher rode in upon his chestnut mare, her first reaction was one of amusement, and she deliberately refrained from glancing towards Charles and Carne. The preacher was a small, frail-boned creature with deep set, lustrous dark eyes which seemed altogether too large for his small childlike face. Indeed, he was little taller than a healthy girl of thirteen or fourteen years, and seemed to embody an almost feminine grace and delicacy, which was accentuated by the blatant solidity of the broad-shouldered labourers who made way for him. He was black-haired, its cut longer than any man's present, its ends curling naturally about his thin shoulders and falling free. Yet, strangely, it seemed less an affectation than the indifference of a man as unconcerned by his appearance as the rag-bag of clothes he wore. Such a pathetically unprepossessing little man, Saranne thought.

'I have heard that he is a fine scholar, able to read and write like a great gentleman,' she said to the woman beside her.

The old woman's straw bonnet brim quivered with disapproval. ''Twill need more than a brain to convince us, I fear; it will need a soul and spirit. We are people not used to fine words and ways. Simple folk all . . .'

Saranne tried desperately to recall what Peter Morrish had said about the Calvinistic Methodists, for it was to that persuasion that Carne had declared the preacher belonged. All that she could clearly bring to mind was that such converts poured scorn upon what they called 'idols and artifice', and abhorred common frivolities and indulgences like dancing, the harp and folk singing, and those rough masculine games which profaned a Sunday. All of which Saranne secretly enjoyed.

The preacher walked towards the group of menfolk who had risen to their feet, their ranks parting to allow him a pathway. He walked confidently, hands outstretched to grip the hands of those he passed, smiling, exchanging greetings, and bidding them welcome. Diminutive as he was, there was a stature about him which seemed to raise him above all others; a joyous serenity which emanated from within, as if his flesh itself glowed with the flame of his conviction. There was no mistaking that, despite his poverty and the ascetism he practised and demanded of others, he was a truly happy man.

His voice, powerful and well modulated, reached effortlessly into every part of Golden Grove. It was a voice such as Saranne had never before heard; deep, and with a strange resonance which commanded attention. When he began to speak of his religious conversion, it was with a simplicity and sincerity which could be understood by all. He emanated such joyfulness, such love, that it seemed an actual physical force which reached out to embrace each one of them with the same intensity; a warmth of spirit. The whispering and unease which had greeted him had died away into silence and, despite his urging that they remained where they sat, the listeners had crept forward involuntarily.

The violence, when it came, was so savagely unexpected that, for a moment, the preacher and his silently attentive listeners seemed neither to comprehend nor even be aware of it. His deep, impassioned voice flowed on, cadences rising and falling; a fierce poetic tide of words and emotion.

The calm absorption of the crowd in the words of the preacher was suddenly jarred by the sound, first of hoof-beats, then the raucous blasphemous cries of the horsemen as they rode among the crowds, cudgels raised, striking indiscriminately at any within their reach. The children, terrified and screaming, ran wildly, often into the very path of the riders and the flailing hooves and clubs, their terror heightened by the eerie, black-masked faces of their attackers. The younger women ran fiercely to scoop up the infants, clutching them to their bodies, others stumbling pitifully at their skirts, their cries bewildered and lost.

Saranne, filled with horror at the senseless cruelty and bloodiness of the scene, could not at first move, limbs and senses paralysed. Then she ran heedlessly to snatch a small child into her arms as a horseman bore down with cudgel high. The child had been rooted to the earth, too rigid with panic to even cry aloud, and Saranne, grateful only that they had escaped the trampling hooves, halted and cradled the child to her, shielding its face. In a split second, sanity returned, and she began to flee but, too late, she heard the thud of returning hooves upon the turf, then felt the air cold with its swift passing, pain agonising through flesh as the cudgel met the bone of her shoulder. Saranne fell to her knees, trying to protect the child with her body, pressing it into the turf suffocatingly. She covered her head with her arms to ward off the expected blows, too fearful even to open her eyes. When she did, it was to see her attacker being dragged from his horse, which reared up, eyes rolling, hooves frenziedly raking the air, before running free. Carne wrenched away the man's weapon and was belabouring him with it with as little mercy as the wretch had shown to others.

'Quick, Saranne! Run! Follow me!' He lifted her bodily from the child, heedless of the piteous wails which came with its return of breath. Then he pulled Saranne's arm, the all-consuming pain of it so piercingly intense that she all but lost consciousness. Terrified, she stumbled after him.

'The child, Carne . . . What of the child?' She managed to sob out the words.

'We must take it . . . there's no other way.'

She followed blindly, raw with pain and fear.

'Dear God! Dear God!' she kept repeating helplessly. 'Why? What reason?'

They were nearing the safety of the cart now, and there was naught but noise and confusion all about. The menfolk, incensed with rage at the unprovoked cruelty of the attack, were trading blow for blow with the few horsemen remaining and deprived of their mounts. It seemed as if the victims had become the aggressors, whipped to blood-lust by their hatred for those too cowardly to declare themselves, yet striking at women and children from behind the protection of their masks. They found no protection now from the flurry of blows and curses, or the contempt of the crowd. What, Saranne wondered helplessly, had become of the little preacher?

As she came within sight of the waggon, Saranne suddenly remembered her brother. 'Charles? Where is Charles?' she exclaimed, horrified and ashamed that in the violence of the furore, she had forgotten him. 'Oh, Carne! Where is Charles?'

The child's mother came rushing to Carne's side, a gash upon her scalp still oozing blood which was smeared upon her face and hands. Crazed with anxiety and relief, she tore the infant from Carne's arms and ran determinedly towards

the trees, her child clutched to her in an embrace so fierce
that its cries rose louder yet.

'I must find Charles!' Saranne insisted desperately. 'It is
no use, I cannot go home without him, Carne! I must stay,
lest he is hurt.'

He started to bundle her roughly aboard the waggon in
order to take the reins but she resisted him fiercely, clawing
at his face, tearing away from his grasp, almost beside
herself with grief. Carne glanced up at a sudden shout to
see Charles running towards them, dishevelled, copper hair
matted with congealed blood, cheek so bruised that an eye
was already half closed.

The journey to Holly Grove Farm was completed in near
silence, for all three were too shocked by the savagery of
what had occurred to speak of it openly. When Jethro and
Sara ran to the waggon, Charles tried to blurt explanation,
but his parents were too vexed to hear him out.

Carne's thin inadequate apologies to Sara and Jethro had
been awkwardly stammered, and answered by the farmer
with a firm handshake and bluff reassurance. Sara, however, had merely nodded with bare civility, making no
mention of his returning to the farm. Saranne had started
to run to his side as he placed his foot in the mare's stirrup,
but her mother had clasped her firmly by the shoulder,
Saranne's involuntary scream of pain and her anguished
face betraying the severity of the blow she had tried to
hide. Carne had taken his foot from the stirrup, and stood
irresolutely for a moment, but Sara had said coldly and
with finality, 'Carne, your cousin awaits you . . . And you,
Charles, stir yourself, and be off to fetch Marged Howell.
I would as soon you were out of my sight! There has been
violence enough today. I would not add to it!'

She had tossed her head dismissively, cheeks burning,
lips compressed, and turned angrily away, her copper curls
a tangled brightness about her shoulders. Charles had
nodded to Carne, and they had ridden away in a silence
broken only by the impatient snorting of their mounts and

the clatter of hoofbeats upon the cobbled yard.

They had parted listlessly, Charles to seek out Marged Howell, and Carne to return to the vicarage. It was the longest, most cheerless, journey that Carne could recall. Upon the way his thoughts were mainly upon Saranne and the strange mixture of love and protectiveness he felt towards her, the stirring of some deep, unexplored feeling which he was powerless to subdue. It was not the affection of a friend or brother, despite his pretence. What he had felt for Saranne when he had seen her almost trampled beneath her attacker's horse, and snatched her to safety, was the love of a man for a maid. Even now, he could feel a warmth which stirred in his breast, and in his loins, at the thought of Saranne's dark beauty and her wide, affectionate violet eyes.

It was nigh on a week later that the preacher's body was found on the high mountain. He had been beaten almost beyond recognition, wrists and ankles savagely bound. He was buried, unblessed, in a pauper's grave, as the law and the church demanded, in a plot unmarked, for none had dared to come forward to claim him friend or kin. Penry Vaughan preached, grim-faced, from the pulpit that any known to be sympathisers of such heretics would be denied the rites of baptism, the Eucharist, marriage and death. Carne was appalled when he heard the news and rode despairingly to Peter Morrish's cottage.

'Freedom to worship should be a man's right!' Carne insisted to Peter Morrish. 'It is not right that a man's wages should buy not only his labour but his mind and soul! No man can own another!'

'Then you must work towards setting it right,' Morrish said quietly. 'It will avail you nothing to rant and rave, for idle words are poor exchange for actions. You know the source and remedy for such inequality? The root cause?'

'It is . . . because they . . . are cruelly dependent upon others for all they own. Without food and shelter, families will starve.'

Morrish nodded as Carne continued. 'It is corrupt, degrading, that a man's beliefs and allegiance can be sold for pence.'

'Indeed,' agreed Morrish. 'Our real hope is that a man may buy another's labour, even his flesh and obedience, but not his mind and soul. They are inviolate, and one day others of like mind will rise up and demand this right.'

'But the preacher is dead, murdered!' Carne reminded bitterly. 'What comfort can it bring to him?'

'It is the price he chose to pay, and he would not regret it,' Morrish said, 'unless others lay the purpose and memory of it to waste.'

After talk of the preacher's death, Peter Morrish refused to allow Carne to return immediately to Penavon vicarage. Instead, he kept him sternly at his lessons, believing it the kindest way. Charles came late to his lessons, awkwardly shamefaced, his face as bruised and misshapen as a windfall plum, and Morrish was hard pressed to hide his amusement.

'My mother holds us responsible for Saranne's injury,' he confessed ruefully, 'and will not be swayed from it! I have told her that you were loath to come, Carne, and Saranne has insisted that you saved both her and the child . . . but it is of no use.' He hesitated. 'I am to tell you that, for the moment, you are not welcome at Holly Grove.'

Morrish, knowing how the events at Golden Grove bedevilled Carne, glanced up from his desk, but made no comment.

'What of Saranne?' Carne demanded.

'Marged has mixed an ointment to heal her shoulder, and believes that when the swelling and inflammation are gone, it will mend.'

Carne nodded, mouth wry, as Charles blurted out, 'She feels guilt at your being unwelcome at the farm, insisting that she alone is to blame. And she begs news of the preacher.'

There was a tense silence, with Carne looking imploringly

towards Morrish, but Morrish nodded his head, reasoning that Carne's fears might be eased for the telling of it. Charles listened in disbelieving silence.

'I pray to God that whoever wrought such violence will be brought to justice!' he murmured at length. 'For they have made Penavon a place of shame.'

Morrish allowed their rage and distress to flow unhindered, then called them firmly to order, setting them written lessons to complete. Soon after he saddled his horse and rode away without explanation to Holly Grove Farm to plead for Carne.

After much discussion, he believed that he had convinced them to be lenient towards him, especially when Jethro had explained earnestly, 'It was some whim of Sara's, naught else, you understand? 'Twas fear for Saranne, no more. Let the boy return, and welcome, for he has done no wrong. We are beholden to him, Peter, and will make apology, for that much is owed.' He had stared fixedly at Sara, and she had flushed, but made shamed agreement.

When Peter Morrish had left, Jethro turned to Sara to ask quietly, 'But why are you so set against their courtship, my love? He is an honest boy, and you cannot doubt his courage.'

'She is beholden to him for her life,' Sara answered. 'She has worshipped him these many years. It will not do, Jethro!'

'You fear that it is gratitude and not love she feels for him?' asked Jethro, confused.

'No! I am fearful that her gratitude and devotion will ensnare him against his will. They are too young, Jethro. If he were a boy like Charles, his life bounded by the farm, it would be different.'

'You think Saranne is not good enough for him?' persisted Jethro. 'It is her pauperdom that troubles you?'

'No!' cried Sara vexedly. 'It is of as little consequence to him as his birth and breeding are to her!'

'Then I do not understand,' Jethro confessed, broad face creased with the effort of understanding. 'Saranne can

figure and write well – nigh as neatly as Charles, and Peter
Morrish is so taken with her that he swears that she is as
well learnt as he. Her nose is forever deep in some book
he has brought and you cannot fault her for her work upon
the farm. Like you, my love, and Megan, she is never idle.
I do not see the harm in it.'

'Do you not?' exclaimed Sara, 'then I vow that I do!
Carne is meant for greater things than Penavon. He will
attend that great university, be away for many years. He
will change, Jethro! If he woos and marries Saranne, and
forfeits that, he will regret it all his life and grow to hate
her. If he does not sacrifice himself, but returns to wed
her, will she then still love the man he has become? There
will be other women, other places. Saranne will be
unchanged. I love her, Jethro. I would not have her
heart broken for, after Carne, she would choose no
other.'

'I cannot see, my dear, why you fret so,' protested Jethro.
'They are man and maid, like any other.' Smiling, he
declared triumphantly, 'Think of Peter Morrish.'

'Peter Morrish?' repeated Sara sharply. 'What has he to
do with it?'

'Why, my love, he has attended so great a place of learning too, yet he is at one with all, scorning no-one. Be they
paupers or gentlemen, 'tis all the same. Can you not believe
that Carne will do likewise?'

'No, Jethro! 'Tis different!' Sara was emphatic. 'Peter
Morrish chose his life. He chose to dwell among the poor
and to be unwed. He wants nothing more; regrets nothing.
I would not see Carne's choice made for him by another,
even Saranne. You must promise me that you will help me
in this and do all in your power to keep them apart. As
lovers, at least, until they are older and Carne's future is
set.'

'If that is what you truly feel, Sara,' he said reluctantly,
'and are fixed upon it . . . although you were but sixteen
years old when we were wed . . .' Jethro knew full well

190

that however much Sara schemed to keep Saranne and Carne apart, she would not succeed. They were man and maid, and that was an end to it.

Chapter Twenty

At close on sixteen, Saranne Hartrey had already attained an unusual and haunting loveliness with the promise of true beauty to come. Jethro was so proud of her that he delighted in showing her off to others, like some rare and precious object. Marvelling at the fine bones and planes of her face beneath her pretty straw bonnet, he said, as he lifted her to sit upon the waggon beside him, 'That gown and bonnet become you well enough, Saranne. 'Tis the colour I have a fondness for. You will do. You will not disgrace us.'

As the waggon halted at the approach to the main highway, Jethro heard a distant rider, and when he had come clearly into view, Carne reined in his horse beside them.

'Saranne! Mr Hartrey, sir!'

He dismounted, smiling delightedly, his gaze upon Saranne. He was a handsome young man, there was no denying it, Jethro thought, and tall and well proportioned, his flesh and muscle honed by labour upon the farm. It was small wonder that Saranne favoured him. There was an easy arrogance about the boy, natural and unselfconscious, which drew the eye. Jethro fidgeted with the reins, then, making up his mind, said gruffly, 'We were away to the village, an errand to the corn merchant. Saranne would need to wait without, and I do not doubt that she would grow bored. Shall I leave her in your care, Carne, your safekeeping?'

He stressed the word 'safekeeping' and his gaze held enquiry and warning.

'Yes, Mr Hartrey. She will be safe with me until you return.'

Saranne scrambled eagerly from her perch upon the waggon and Jethro cautioned, 'I shall be half-an-hour, Saranne, no more. Hold yourself ready against my returning.'

'Yes, Papa.' She reached up to where he sat and hugged him impulsively, settling a kiss upon his cheek as he bent low. Jethro, warm with goodwill and embarrassment, found himself smiling foolishly before he stirred the shire into life.

Sara was wrong. She could not save them from hurt. It was part of living. The cruelty would be in denying them the right to shape their own lives. Whether it ended in happiness or pain was all one and the same, for sometimes they were inseparable.

Carne tethered the horse to a tree where it might safely crop the grass, and he and Saranne seated themselves upon a mossy log beside a small stream through a pasture. They were, at first, awkward and tongue-tied, each stiff in the company of the other.

After discussing the Methodist meeting at Golden Grove, she said, 'The preacher was not deserving of such hatred.' Her eyes filled with sudden tears and Carne watched them tremble upon her lashes, then overflow. He was filled with such tenderness that he drew her to him without thought, cradling her, stroking her hair, whispering words of love and comfort until her weeping ceased. Then he gently eased away the tears with his fingertips, kissing her eyelids, her cheeks, the soft curve of her throat. Saranne drew him to his feet wordlessly, her eyes appealing, then led him into the shadowed quietness of a copse nearby. She raised her face to his, lowering his dark head until his mouth met hers and they were kissing, gently at first, and with the sweetest tenderness. Her lips were softly yielding under his own, and he could smell the strange, elusive fragrance of her flesh and hair, and the scents of damp earth and decaying leaves. He felt the rising of her breasts against him and a hardening and desire within his own flesh, too fierce to

193

be stilled. He was kissing her eyes, her neck, her exposed skin, feverishly now, his mouth hard. Dear God! he thought. What madness! With a cry of despair that was wrenched from him and a real physical anguish, he forced her away. He was aware that his whole body trembled. Saranne's face was flushed, her eyes soft and unfocused, as they stood awkwardly apart, trying to still the longings which raged between them.

They spoke no word as they walked back to where Carne's horse quietly cropped the grass, raising its head enquiringly at their coming. Jethro, arriving soon afterwards upon the waggon, saw them gathering violets beside the brook, their dark heads bent close in companionable laughter, teasing each other.

Carne helped Saranne, clutching her nosegay of violets, on to the waggon beside Jethro, then rode away with a wave of the hand and a smile. Saranne pressed her face deep into the fragrance of the flowers, her eyes, when they met Jethro's, alive with a pleasure she thought secret.

Had he been right to leave them? Jethro wondered. They were not, as Sara believed, children.

There were many such meetings in the weeks and months that followed, their love growing deeper and more tender. Jane, who could deny Carne nothing, aided them in their assignations, and Charles was a splendid ally when, with Saranne's shoulder healed, they set out on horseback upon their companionable rides. Jethro, despite his initial misgivings, placed no obstacles in the way of their growing love, and Megan, romantic and tender-hearted, would never betray them. Sara, alone, remained bitterly opposed to any courtship, and made her feelings plain. In her presence at Holly Grove, Carne's and Saranne's behaviour was stilted and artificial, their awkwardness at their deceit plain. Yet Saranne's glowing happiness could no more be hid than their meaningful glances, or the tenderness of an accidental touching of their flesh, as intimate as a caress. Sara spoke no more of their affection, not even to Jethro, but she put her hope in the fickleness of youth to set them apart. Yet memory of what Saranne had endured for Marged's sake, and Carne's defiance of Penry Vaughan, even when thrashed so brutally, gave her little cause to feel sanguine.

It was Charles's last day at lessons with Peter Morrish. Jethro had declared that the boy had learning enough, and now his life and labour must be directed solely to the land. Such an outcome had been inevitable and made clear from the start and yet Morrish felt a dissatisfaction, regret for a task uncompleted. Charles had thanked him generously for his instruction and promised that he would not neglect his reading but keep to his studying whenever tasks at the farm allowed. Yet he had been more than usually subdued and Carne's good-humoured ribbing and confessed envy at his escape from lessons brought little response.

Morrish, studying him covertly, thought him a handsome, intelligent boy, with Jethro's mighty build, his frame not fully muscled and fleshed, yet already giving firm promise of the man he would become. If he shared Jethro's build, then his colouring and temperament were all Sara's. There was a vitality and quickness within him, a fierceness of purpose which burned as brightly as the glowing redness of his hair. He lacked Jethro's gentle passivity. Charles was, Morrish searched for the word, a catalyst, drawing life and people inevitably towards him in the same way as Sara. He was restless and filled with insatiable curiosity. Would life upon the farm be enough for him? Morrish could not be sure. If it were not, then Jethro would hold Morrish and education to blame. Yet would it have served the boy better to have remained illiterate? It would not have soothed his restlessness, but neither would it have given him a way of escape from the drudgery and frustration of a life thrust upon him, the burden of inheritance.

He watched Charles pick up his books for the last time and, with his head bent low, walk from the study and into the yard to saddle his horse. Carne made to follow but Morrish called out, 'A moment, Carne. I would have a word with you.' As Carne halted and turned enquiringly,

Morrish declared, 'I have submitted your name . . . put you forward as a candidate for the entrance examinations to Oxford.'

To still the surging of excitement, confidence and self-doubt within him, Carne asked, 'You think, Mr Morrish, sir, that I have a chance of success?'

'I believe that you will succeed, Carne. Yes, I am convinced of it.' He paused. 'I admire you for the resolution and single-mindedness you have brought to your studies, and the trials you have overcome. It has not been easy.'

He extended his hand to Carne, shaking his young pupil's hand warmly as Carne said quickly, 'It is all owed to you, sir. Without your belief in me, I would be as useless and contemptible as my cousin declares me to be.'

Morrish shook his head, saying firmly, 'You must keep a belief in yourself and your value, Carne, or all else is wasted.'

'But I will succeed, sir, at my examinations. That is the only way I can show my gratitude, to prove that your efforts to educate me have not been in vain.'

'Oh, my dear boy!' exclaimed Morrish, laughing delightedly, 'that will not be proof of your education, but a new beginning. Knowledge alone is but the barest bones of an education, a skeleton, without flesh or life.' He recalled himself abruptly, declaring, 'I must preach neither sermon nor lesson! There will be too many in future. Go now, and tell your cousin that we have taken the first step upon your future pathway. It is more honour than he deserves.'

He watched Carne go, gazing after him with affection and sadness as he saw him ride away. A beginning, he had told Carne, but an ending too, for Carne and Charles were no longer children. Rather, they were young men, their futures planned and divergent.

Carne, astride his chestnut mare, books safely fastened within his leather saddle-bags, paused at the modest entry to the highway which led to Penavon village and, after a moment's thought, reined her instead towards Holly Grove, thinking to intercept Charles upon his return from the chandler's. Once there, he dismounted and tethered the horse to a tree, then lay in wait for him at the edge of the copse. Charles would take the fine news that Peter Morrish had entered him for the examinations for Oxford to those at the farm. He would not go himself, lest they think him conceited, or trying to belittle Charles's achievements by trumpeting his own. Jethro and Sara would be pleased, and Megan too, but for Saranne, as for him, the joy would be alloyed by the knowledge that success would inevitably bring a parting. Carne had tried to quell the feelings of desire he felt for her, yet, still, they rose strongly within him. No, he decided, he would not tell Charles awhile, but let Saranne hear of it from his own lips. It would be kinder to them both than to lay her feelings raw before others. Besides, he knew, although it had never been spoken aloud, that Sara had set her face against his courtship of her daughter and he would not deliberately antagonise her.

Instead, he would ride out to Hillbrook, and bask in the warmth of Jane's and Prys's unstinting praise. They were as dear to him as grand-parents, and he owed *them* first knowledge of Peter Morrish's faith in his worth. It grieved him to see how frail Prys seemed to have grown, how unsteady upon his feet, although his mind remained clear and active, untouched by age and infirmity. Often, these days, his body was wracked by fierce coughing which left him exhausted. So Carne helped Prys often now to collect peat and coal from the surface of the land. Jane was unchanged, and Carne thanked God for it. Without her, he thought, life would still have been bleak and comfortless as the days following his father's death, when Penavon vicarage seemed scarcely more welcoming than Rice Havard's cold tomb. How long ago it seemed, and how young he had been.

Carne walked into the small copse to retrieve his horse and had actually put a boot into the stirrup to swing himself into the saddle when the horse, alerted by some unexpected sound, grew tense, ears pricked, head raised in alarm. Charles returning, perhaps, Carne wondered. Yet there was no sound of hoofbeats or harness, simply the quiet stirring of leaves, as of some animal disturbed or fleeing. He dismounted hurriedly and stood beside his mount, soothing her, bidding her stay silent.

It was Saranne who came, unsuspecting, through the trees, a shallow basket upon her arm, filled with moss and clutches of wild primroses, starry and pale against the greenness of their leaves.

'Carne?' She hesitated, unsure, then sped towards him, feet scattering the fallen leaves, dark hair flying. There was no mistaking her incredulous joy as she flung her arms impulsively around him, heedless of her scattered flowers. 'What are you doing here? Did you hope to see me? Come seeking?'

Carne felt the warm softness of her flesh pressed yieldingly against him, and breathed in the scent of hair and skin. He knew a great surge of tenderness and a deeper fierce emotion that held both pleasure and pain as he drew her to him, arms tightening about her, burying his face in her hair, then his lips against the pale curve of her throat, her cheeks, her eyelids and her moistly parted lips. It was like no sensation he could describe. Nerve, blood and flesh seemed first to pulse, then quicken with heightened awareness, fusing with Saranne's own, so that they were one body, one emotion. Carne felt his hands straying from her small waist to the firmly rounded breasts, raised against the smooth cotton of her bodice then, in fear of Charles returning, he pushed her guiltily from him. His fingers still held the sleeve of her dress and Carne let his hand fall uselessly to his side, for the desire to draw her back against the harshness of his breast bone and crush her to him was so intense that he dared not touch her. Saranne's face was flushed, her violet eyes dark and heavy-lidded, as though with sleep, lips reddened and full from the pressure of their kisses. Carne thought he had never seen anyone so desirable and beautiful and, in his shame and humiliation, he exclaimed with a sharpness born of anger against himself, 'You should not be walking in the woods and byways alone, Saranne! It is foolish and irresponsible! I wonder your parents allow it!'

'I came to meet Charles. I promised I would roam no further than the entrance to the copse.' She bent swiftly to retrieve her fallen primroses to hide her distress at his brusque refusal of her. Carne bent to help her, ashamed to see that his coldness had made her mouth quiver and brought tears to her eyes. Then made clumsy with remorse and affection, with infinite tenderness, he stroked the tears from her lashes with his fingertips. He made no attempt to kiss her again, but that protective gesture was more revealing than he knew and Saranne cherished it more deeply than any word or caress.

'Saranne . . .' His voice sounded strange to his own ears. 'I must . . .'

She raised her head, alerted by some uncertainty in his tone. Suddenly there was the jarring, alien sound of a horse and rider coming close, the cracking of twigs and branches, the thud of hooves upon soft earth. Charles emerged into the small clearing, riding too fast, head lowered against the threatening lacework of intertwined branches. Saranne and Carne had distanced themselves instinctively, springing guiltily apart as he reined in his horse, startled and uncomprehending. They viewed him warily from opposite sides of the copse where they had fled to safety, Saranne awkwardly smoothing at her skirts with her free hand, then staring into her basket, Carne fidgeting with his horse's reins.

'A fine welcome!' said Charles, dismounting. 'I thank you for your enthusiasm!' His fresh, amused face glowed with goodwill and whipped colour from the gallop, as he blundered innocently, 'I am sorry that I was delayed so long. Some difficulty at the chandler's, but it is now sorted.' When neither responded, he looked from one to the other perplexedly, taking in their embarrassment and misery. 'Ah, I see you have ridden before me to the farm, Carne, and told them of your good news? I met Peter Morrish in the village. He was afire with it.'

Saranne looked to Carne for explanation, but did not speak.

'Why so long a face, my friend?' Charles had clasped Carne's shoulder jovially. 'Is he not a dark horse, Saranne? A genius? I would not be skulking so modestly, but shouting it from the tree tops were I to enter Oxford University . . .' Charles broke off, puzzled and offended, as Carne shook off his friendly grasp.

Carne's gaze was upon Saranne's face as she said with a smile, 'Why that's wonderful news! How pleased you must be, Carne, that your plans . . .' She did not finish the words, and Carne felt her anguish as she stepped forward, hand outstretched in congratulation. Her smile, as her voice, had not wavered, but remained fixed and unalterable as a mask. 'You will outgrow us,' she said.

'No!' said Carne. 'I will not do that! Nothing will change.'

If the urgency of his denial reached her, then she gave no sign, but said, so low that only Carne could hear, 'You should have told me. It was owed to me, that I might not hear it from another.'

Carne explained helplessly, 'It will not be for several months or more! It will make no difference, Saranne, I swear it.'

Saranne's head was held high as she called out lightly to Charles, 'Will you let me ride your mare home, Charles? Or, better still, set me behind you, as of old. Mama will fear some ill has befallen me. I would not have her vexed.'

'Carne?' Charles invited. 'You will ride beside us to the farm? You would have good welcome, I promise.'

Carne shook his head. 'I beg you will make my apologies and regrets . . . to *all*.'

The words were for Saranne, but she resolutely kept her face averted. 'I must ride on to Hillbrook, to tell Jane and Prys.'

'Yes,' Saranne said. 'They are deserving of that, and will

200

be as eager as you for your escape to . . . better things than Penavon has to offer.'

Without another word Carne swung himself from stirrup to saddle and rode off through the clearing, face dark as a thundercloud. Charles helped Saranne on to his mount, saying, 'I will take the bridle and lead you home. You had best give me your basket to carry. You have picked them carelessly, Saranne, and held them too close! Their stems are broken and they are wilted already and near dead.'

He looked at her in astonishment, remorseful, face bewildered under the thatch of red hair as he asked, 'What have I said to make you weep, Saranne? Did I take you too hard to task? I swear I did not mean to.'

Prys hobbled to the door of the cottage as soon as he heard the drumming of the mare's hoofbeats, his lean, cadaverous face transfigured with pleasure as he helped Carne dismount, crying out, 'Jane! Jane! We have a visitor.'

He clasped Carne's hand, exclaiming warmly, 'And there is no-one more welcome in all the world.' The fleshlessness of the old man's fingers and their coldness were a shock to Carne, for the change in Prys had come so violently that he was ill-prepared. Prys said gently, 'Should Jane ask if you think I look unwell, I beg you will set her mind to ease by denying it. 'Tis kinder to lie than cause her hurt. It will come soon enough.'

As he spoke, Jane was emerging from the small garden at the rear of the cottage where she had been hanging the clothes upon the line.

'Carne, my dear,' she ran towards him, basket forgotten, and enfolded him in a swift embrace. 'Oh, my dear boy,' she cried delightedly, stepping back a pace to inspect him the better. 'I declare you grow taller and more handsome each time we meet. Does he not, Hywel?'

Prys gave Carne a glance of mingled exasperation and indulgence, saying, 'I had best take Carne's mare to the new outhouse.'

As Prys took the mare's bridle in his grasp, Jane glanced

anxiously at Carne to ask, 'There is nothing amiss at Penavon?'

'No, no, Jane, I promise. My cousin cherishes my company as little as I cherish his. We have learnt to exist together.' Carne put his arm about Jane's shoulder to guide her within. 'I have come to bring you good news, Jane. The best you can imagine!'

Despite all his efforts to stay calm and detached, the excitement of it blazed through him, and Jane, who knew him better than any other, was not deceived. 'We had best wait until Hywel returns,' she declared, 'although, I can scarce contain my curiosity! It is fitting that he shares such pleasure with us, as well as all else.'

They watched him leading Carne's mare to the stone outhouse, his steps awkwardly hesitant, then he stopped suddenly, body wracked with the fierce coughing which left him exhausted.

'Shall I go to him?' Carne offered, distressed, but Jane stayed him with her hand.

'No. It would grieve him if he thought you had seen. Let us go within.' Jane's expression was patiently resigned and she seemed to Carne to have suddenly grown older, less in control of herself, as she said, 'I need not ask if you see him changed: it is there in your face. You are as powerless to hide it from me as he to hide his sickness. It is a stupid game we have learnt to play, you understand? Each of us fearful to admit it, lest we hurt the other, as if admitting it will rob us of time.'

'You have called a physician, Jane?'

'No, he will have none of it, vowing it is but a springtime chill, no more. Although Marged Howell has begged him to seek the services of a doctor.'

'Do you know what it is, Jane, that ails him?'

'Marged fears that it is scrofula, the king's evil, and there is no cure on God's earth for that affliction. He will worsen ere summer is ended.'

They looked at each other helplessly, neither able to comfort the other, unable, even, to speak of death. It seemed so alien a thing in this comfortable room with its familiar furnishings and the bright fire of apple wood throwing its scented flame.

'What will you do?' His voice was low.

'I will survive, my dear, as we all must, whatever the good Lord sends. Oh, but it will not be easy, for I have known the love of a dear, good man. It should be blessing enough, no doubt, and I should not ask for more . . . but it will make my loss the greater, I fear.'

Carne reached out protectively to her, cradling her head against his chest, soothing her as she had so often soothed him in those cold, nightmare hours of his own childhood. They were still locked together when they heard the sound of the outer door opening, and drew apart as Prys came in, smiling and demanding to know all of Carne's news.

The story of his tutor's good opinion told, and reinforced a thousand times and more, Carne reluctantly took his leave, kissing Jane with more than his usual tenderness.

'Oh, how proud we are of you, my dear boy,' she said. 'It pleases us that you are so clever . . . but our greatest pride is in your loving concern. It is so rare a gift, and one to treasure. I dare to hope that Prys and I had some small share in the growth of it.'

Carne's thoughts on the ride back to Penavon vicarage were upon Prys's sickness and the pitiful changes it had wrought in him. How could he have been so blind? So immersed in his studying, and in his need for Saranne, that he had failed to notice the changes in the old man? Carne's young, firm-muscled hands, gripping the reins, tightened as he remembered Prys's fleshless touch, skin stretched tight over bone, brittle as a dead leaf. It was natural, inevitable, yet he could not imagine the living flesh and warm blood that surged within himself cold and stilled. At that moment, he recalled the image of Saranne as she ran towards him, hair streaming, mouth curved into a smile, to greet him eagerly within the wood. Yet he knew: 'Earth to earth'.

He rode through the gates of the vicarage, the mare's

hooves striking the cobbles of the yard, clear as a tocsin bell. How little joy his brave news about Oxford brought him now!

Penry Vaughan waved Carne wordlessly to a chair, barely looking up from his writing at the library desk. While Carne waited he thought of Mostyn lingering without and hoped that, in spite of his brother's invitation to dine at Great House, he would remain long enough to hear his news. First, though, protocol demanded that his cousin hear it before his ward.

'Well?' Vaughan demanded at length, austere face scowling, 'perhaps you will explain this unlikely yearning for my company. I take it that it is not the usual recurring plea for money which your brother makes? My purse, sir, is not bottomless.'

'Yes, sir. It is a question of money, but mine . . . my father's, rather than your own!'

'Indeed,' Vaughan's smile was amused as he pulled fastidiously at his cuff. 'I believed that he died penniless, a spendthrift and pauper, sir, with neither estate not assets. Perhaps you will correct me?'

'I have spoken to Mr Walters, the attorney-at-law, and he has told me that there is money enough to attend Oxford University, as my father intended me to,' said Carne firmly.

Vaughan's face had lost its colour, and with it its air of mocking assurance. He seemed, Carne thought, uncomfortably ill-at-ease. 'It can hardly have come as a surprise to you, Cousin,' declared Carne. 'It was always my avowed intention, and Mr Morrish considers me to be ready. He has already entered my name for the examination.'

Vaughan seemed to be having some difficulty in breathing, and had thrust a finger beneath his neckerchief for ease. There was a beading of sweat upon his upper lip, and his skin gleamed pallid and unhealthy.

'You are ill, sir?' asked Carne. 'Would you have me ring for some brandy? Summon Mrs Groves perhaps?'

Vaughan made no immediate reply, moistening dry lips,

fingers gripping the edge of the desk until the knuckle bones showed white. Then he said distinctly, as if with great effort, 'You will not be attending Oxford, Cousin. You may put the idea from your mind.'

'No!' The denial was forced out of Carne. 'You shall not vent your spite upon me longer! I will go . . . whatever the cost!'

'It is not possible.'

'You had best explain yourself, sir!' Carne's voice was coldly menacing as he held his fury in check. 'Explain, sir, else, by God, if you do not, I shall not be held responsible for my actions!'

Vaughan, seeing that there was no way of escaping it, hauled himself awkwardly to his feet, declaring, 'There is no money! It is gone . . . gone, I tell you!'

Carne, who had raised himself from his chair, looked at Vaughan stupidly, murmuring, 'Gone? How? What have you done with the money from the sale of Great House . . . the rents, the farms?'

Vaughan stared at him helplessly, too frightened to speak. Carne leaned over the desk and grasped Vaughan's collar, twisting it relentlessly, choking the words from his throat.

'It is spent.'

'Damn you!' Carne's hands had found his cousin's throat and tightened upon it, forcing the breath from him, regardless of his whimpering moans. Vaughan's face had grown mottled, swollen, his eyes starting fiercely from his head, but Carne would not release him. He was filled with such a white heat of rage that he was all but crazed, blind to Vaughan's terror. When he finally let him go, Vaughan cowered in fear, clutching at his throat, vainly seeking some way of escape, but there was none.

'What have you done with the money?' Carne spat out the words. 'Tell me, or, upon my oath, I will kill you!'

'Spent.' Vaughan's face had crumpled like a child's, and tears coursed helplessly down his cheeks, splashing off mouth and chin. Yet Carne felt no pity, nor even revulsion.

'You robbed me,' he said tonelessly. 'It was ever your intention. You robbed me coldly and with deliberation, knowing it was all that was left to bring me hurt.'

'No.' Vaughan had fallen to his knees beside the desk, trying vainly to crawl to safety beneath it to evade Carne's wrath. 'Investments. I swear it was not my fault . . . bad investments . . . It was no more than your father did.'

'Do not dare to speak of him! Damn you!' Carne hauled him, trembling, to his feet, Vaughan's head striking the corner of the desk. A slow trickle of blood escaped from his forehead, but Carne ignored it, saying contemptuously, 'You are a liar and a thief, sir! Those are the words you once spat at me, using your strength and warped nature to curb me. Yet, thrashing me was not triumph enough. It did not wholly satisfy. You tried to steal from me the likenesses of my parents to deny me the comfort of my past. You will not steal my future, sir, else I will kill you for it!'

Vaughan was staring at him, wild eyed with terror, as Carne lifted a fist and smashed it down into his face, releasing his coat so that he reeled away awkwardly, staggering against a torchère upon a stand, his efforts to find support bringing it crashing about him. He lay ominously still, and Carne, bending over him, felt his rage ebb and die away.

When he straightened, Mostyn was beside him, his face as bloodless as Penry Vaughan's, his eyes wide with horror. 'You bloody fool! What madness possessed you? He is dead! You will hang for it!' He made to reach to the bell-pull to summon the servants, but Carne frustrated him, barring the way.

'You owe me some allegiance . . . some aid, Mostyn! We are kin!'

'I owe you nothing! You are a stupid, blundering fool, undeserving of help! What good has your violence done you? You will end on the gallows, as you deserve.'

'I will ride away,' Carne declared wildly. 'I will go where none can follow.' He glanced to where Vaughan's body lay, face translucent in its paleness, its only colour the darkness of the wound upon his forehead and the trickle of congealing blood. He felt no regret for what he had done, no guilt; such a conclusion had been, from the start, inevitable.

Dear God, he prayed silently, let him not be dead! It would be too cruel if he were to triumph again at the last.

Mostyn, following Carne's gaze, declared contemptuously, 'You can never escape! Whether he is alive or dead, it makes no difference. The penalty for murder is death. It will be the gibbet or gallows, you may depend upon it. You are a blundering fool, Carne! Your own worst enemy! The justices will be told, and they will set up a hue and cry throughout the whole country.'

'Then you must keep the matter secret until I am clear of Penavon!'

'I?' Mostyn was frankly incredulous. 'Do not involve me in your infamy! I will have none of it! It is enough that my brother is a knave and a criminal! It will bar me from society . . . destroy all I have planned and worked for!'

'Then you had best help me flee, and salvage what little respect and social standing you may.'

Mostyn deliberated for a moment, glancing towards Vaughan who lay crumpled awkwardly, the torchère and stand fallen beside him, tapers scattered haphazardly about. 'I will not lie for you,' he conceded, 'but will ride to Great House as planned, saying nothing of the affair. None will dare enter the library until dinner is served, for the servants are forbidden to disturb him.'

Carne nodded, urging, 'And when you return, if all is well, you must plead ignorance of the affair, and seek shelter with Jane and Prys at Hillbrook. They will take you willingly, and treat you as kin.'

'Kin?' Mostyn cried, outraged. 'Are you mad? I cannot believe I heard aright! They are servants, common country peasants, no more! I would sooner be dead! No . . . I shall return to live with my cousin, as before.'

'You are an idle self-seeking parasite!' declared Carne with contempt, 'and I wish you well of your fine friends at

Great House. They are welcome to you . . . Jane and Prys deserve better!'

Mostyn grimaced, saying with boredom, 'It ill becomes a criminal to lecture me, brother! You had best be upon your way. My unpunctuality will earn me a mild rebuke, yours might well earn you a place upon the gibbet!'

'If Vaughan recovers . . .' Carne began hesitantly.

'Then I will plead ignorance, and offer my condolences,' finished Mostyn. 'Should he die, then I must make other arrangements. If they believe it to be the work of some thief and blackguard, then it may even earn me a place within Great House.'

There was no mistaking his satisfaction. Carne thrust out his hand, saying quietly, 'Since we must part, at least let it be as brothers and friends, for there is no other of our blood-line.'

'Indeed there is!' Mostyn ignored Carne's out-thrust hand. 'Our cousin, should he live. If he dies, I have no doubt that he has named me his heir.'

Carne let his hand fall impotently to his side and turned upon his heel.

'Wait! Have you money? A plan of escape?' demanded Mostyn.

'I have a few coins saved, and will take my mare from the stables. It is better that you do not learn of where I plan to ride. It will ease your involvement.'

Mostyn nodded, making no protest, as incurious about Carne's destination as to what his brother's future held. 'I would stake you with guineas, if I were able . . . but I have barely enough for the gaming that must surely follow our dining at Great House. Those miniatures, Carne, of our parents . . . You will have no need of them now, and they would fetch a fair price at auction.'

'Be damned to you for the heartless, grasping little swine you are!' exclaimed Carne, beside himself with vexation. 'You shall not get your greedy hands upon them . . . all else that I leave, you may sell, and welcome! It will be the last I shall ever concede to you, so mark it well!'

'And you, sir . . . Have a care how you ride,' cautioned Mostyn mockingly. 'Your own carcase may be worthless, but your horse may bring a few sovereigns, if returned to Penavon vicarage.'

'I thank you for your concern,' muttered Carne, unable to hide his bitterness. He hesitated, then declared, 'I bid you farewell, brother, until we meet again, as we assuredly will.'

'In heaven or hell,' agreed Mostyn, still smiling, 'if the devil wills it!'

Chapter Twenty-one

Carne had feverishly packed his parents' likenesses and the few possessions he cherished within his leather saddlebag, and had ridden unhindered from the vicarage. Despite the need to appear calm, he was aware of his heart beating suffocatingly and the tremors in his limbs which he was powerless to control.

His rage and hatred for Penry Vaughan had faded to a cold realisation of what he had done, and of the punishment he must expect should he be halted. Inevitably there was remorse too, for he could no longer recall Vaughan as that brute who had thrashed him and stolen his birthright. He saw only the wretched, cowering creature of the library, then that bloodstained flesh, pitiful in its stillness.

Carne's every instinct was to flee Penavon, to put as many miles as he could between himself and the crime he had committed, but some stubbornness held him back. 'No! Dammit!' he cried aloud, 'I will not be driven away like a craven!' Those he loved were deserving of better. He turned the mare towards Hillbrook and rode there as by a fiend possessed.

The urgent clatter of hooves upon the cobbles sent Jane hurrying to the cottage door. This was no ordinary visit, she felt sure; something appalling had occurred. She had only to look at Carne's anguished face for confirmation as, without a word, she watched him dismount, then put an arm comfortingly about him and drew him gently within.

'There is nothing in all the world which cannot be eased for the telling of it,' she said. Yet the burden of his story when he confided it was almost more than she could bear. Hywel fetched, unasked, the four half-sovereigns prudently set aside for a rainy day, murmuring in answer to Carne's awkward protestations, 'Take it, I beg. It is better spent upon the living than the dead.' To Jane he had warned in agitation, 'Do not hinder him more, my love. He had best leave at once, for the justices might already be informed, and a hunt begun.'

'No!' Jane's denial was firm. 'Time enough when darkness falls. Then he may leave unseen. I will ride out in the mule and cart to fetch Jethro. He will know of other, safer tracks. Besides, they will believe him to be already far from here.'

Not all Carne's pleas nor Prys's mutterings of pig-headed stubbornness would move her, and as the decrepit waggon and the ancient mule moved off, Carne darted towards Jane as she flicked at the reins, stirring the mule into life.

'Jane!' He cried anxiously, running over the cobbles, alongside her perch upon the cart.

'Yes, my dear?'

'Please. I beg you will bring back Saranne. There is something which must be said.'

The conflict upon his eager young face tore at her heart. Sara and Jethro would assuredly set their faces more strongly against any involvement with Saranne, and who could blame them? Yet, like Rice Havard before him, she could deny him nothing. She turned her head briefly from the track ahead to look back at him and nod. The sudden radiance of Carne's smile spoke of a burden unexpectedly lifted from his shoulders.

The wait at Hillbrook was long and tense, with Carne and Prys fearful of every unexplained sound, and ill-disposed towards idle chatter. It was a relief to both when the waggon rattled and creaked to a halt upon the cobbles without. To their surprise, it was not Jane returning but Charles at the reins, with Morrish's lanky frame stretched out along the cart floor, and a windswept Randall Walters cramped uncomfortably on the perch beside him. They had been summoned at Jethro's command.

Morrish descended, and gripped Carne's hand, declaring, 'I am a peaceful, God-fearing man, Carne, as well you know, but that creature's treachery brings me near to violence! Penry Vaughan is a cheat and a scoundrel, a disgrace to the cloth!'

Randall Walters, plump chins quivering agreement, tugged down his straining waistcoat over his corpulent belly, blinking rapidly, and affirming, 'The man's villainy does not surprise me! There have been rumours of his forays to London. Crude talk that he has been entering gaming houses, gin dens and stews, dissipating himself and his money. I had thought it idle gossip; malice from those as degraded as he. Yet, now, I am forced to the truth of it. It grieves me most that it was another's money he squandered! But there is one small comfort to be gained in this.'

Carne looked at him uncomprehendingly.

'I believe, Carne, that if Vaughan survives, you will have little to fear, since he will be reluctant to summon the justices, for he must needs acquaint them with his part in the affair. It does him scant credit!' He drew Carne quietly aside and pressed into his hands a small pouch containing fifteen gold coins, ignoring his protestations that he could not accept such a gift. 'It is not a gift, but a loan,' Walters declared testily, 'and one I shall expect to be repaid, with interest; I make no bones about it!'

'But I have no means of repaying you, sir, and who knows when, or if, we shall meet again?' Carne protested despairingly. 'I shall be hunted and, if caught, my life will be forfeit.'

'Then we will consider the debt paid in full,' said Walters unconcernedly and with grim humour.

Carne smiled involuntarily and made to thank him, but Walters continued, 'I would rather it were Vaughan's death than yours, I swear. You have my promise that somehow, wherever you may be, I shall send word to you as to whether your cousin is alive or dead, and when it is prudent for you to return. Meanwhile, I have brought you another mount,

212

a grey, for your own will be too easily recognised, if its description, and yours, is widely circulated. Tomorrow your own mare will be found wandering upon the highway by my clerk, Higgs, if he has strength and wit enough to halt it. He is such a mild, inoffensive old creature that none could suspect his involvement.'

Carne thanked him sincerely, as he then thanked Peter Morrish, adding ruefully, 'I regret, sir, that in striking my cousin, I descended to his level. Physical abuse, as you so often reminded me, was ever the refuge of the bully and blackguard.'

'I am not wholly inflexible upon that point,' admitted Morrish, smiling. He gripped Carne's hand, eyes twinkling, as he averred, 'No, Carne, I hope I am never too rigid not to allow of the exception which proves the rule.' His face grew serious. 'You have my blessing and my friendship, Carne, whatever may befall. I beg that you will write word to me, when you are able, of your fortune, that I may tell Jane and others who love you. I fear she will grieve for you most when her need will be greatest.' He glanced towards Prys.

Carne answered quietly, 'I know you will offer her your comfort, sir.'

'And God's greater consolation. You have my word upon it.'

'I had best be away,' began Carne awkwardly, 'for I fear I have tarried long enough, and cannot wait longer, although I would have been glad to learn from Mr Hartrey the safest pathway to take.'

There was the sound of the violent halting of a waggon upon the cobblestones as Jethro and Sara leapt hurriedly down and, after them, from the well of the mule-cart, Megan, Jane and Saranne. Jane embraced him warmly, and Jethro gave him a map with directions, drawn to his instructions and lettered by Charles.

'Make for the docks at Bristol, my boy,' Randall Walters interjected, 'and take with you this letter to an acquaintance of mine, Sir Robert Crandon. I have explained all to him within.' He smiled self-consciously. 'Well . . . with a few well-judged exceptions. He owns a prosperous shipping line, and I have begged his indulgence over "a small matter of family disagreement", asking that he find place for you upon a vessel of his line, until all is forgot.'

Carne's gratitude was lost in the flurry of excited approval which greeted Randall Walters' plan, as Megan came forward to make her farewells and to add a modest half-crown to his store. Carne received the coin with the courtesy and goodwill with which it was offered, knowing what pains had gone into its saving.

Charles murmured, 'Mr Morrish has offered me the use of his mount, that I may ride part way with you, Carne. You will not refuse me?'

'No. I will not refuse you.'

Saranne hung back hesitantly, not knowing if her indifference upon their last meeting within the wood had angered him and caused him to turn away from her, but Carne, gently taking her hands within his own, and speaking so low that only Saranne could hear, said, 'I can offer you nothing now, Saranne, save my love, and the promise that I will return.'

'It will be enough.' The deep violet eyes were unwavering and filled with certainty.

'I cannot ask you to wait. It would be too cruel.'

'The only cruelty would be if you did not. I shall wait, Carne.' Her fine compassionate eyes were filled with tears as, regardless of all those watching, he kissed her upon her mouth with the greatest tenderness, then Saranne took his hand and pressed it to her lips.

Sara, disturbed, stepped forward, for there was no mistaking the loving declaration the two had so publicly made, although they were so fiercely intent that it was plain that, for them, no other existed. No! Sara was crying inwardly. It must not be! I will not allow it. Cannot! But Jethro gripped her arm and pulled her firmly to his side, saying with unusual harshness, 'Leave them, Sara! Leave them be, I say! They must work out their own salvation. Saranne will have need of your comfort. Do not make her hate you and turn away!'

Sara restrained herself, but she, alone, knew the effort it had cost her. When Carne turned to bid his final farewells, Jethro, as Morrish and Walters and Megan before him, clasped the boy affectionately, and with real regret for his leaving.

'You will return ere long, I have no doubt of it,' Jethro declared. 'You are a good, honest lad, Carne, and I count you as one of my own. What you have done, you were driven to by goading past endurance. I think no less of you for that.' He held Carne in swift embrace. 'A blessed journey and a safe return.' Embarrassed by the length of his speech he quickly pushed Sara forward. She looked at Carne in silence for a moment, struggling to compose herself, but when she spoke, the coldness of her voice betrayed her reservations, and her hand was stiff within his own.

'I wish you well,' she said, and it had grieved him that her usual warmth had died. She made no attempt to embrace him.

'Jane . . .' he turned aside and held Jane close.

'Do not forget us, my dearest boy.' Her voice was not quite steady.

'There is no danger, ma'am, that I shall ever do that,' he responded quietly. 'You and Prys are all of family that I possess, save Mostyn.' He smiled wryly, 'And I fancy that your love for me is deeper. Yet, you will watch over him for me, Jane?'

'Yes, my dear, I will do what I can.'

Carne shook Prys's hand, then impulsively drew the old man to him. 'Good-bye, Mr Prys, sir.'

'Good-bye, my dear boy, and may God go with you.'

'And with you, sir.'

Without a word, he walked outside to where Charles had already mounted his horse and held the grey, saddled and waiting for Carne, beside him. Carne nodded to Charles, but could not turn to those clustered anxiously before the cottage, lest he betray his sorrow.

'I will ride the first few miles with you, Carne.'

'I shall be glad of your company.'

Saranne watched them ride away with such extreme sadness that she feared her heart would break within her. Jane took her hand and held it tight for comfort, although her bleak emptiness was every whit as cold as the girl's own.

'He will come back,' she promised Saranne. 'He must. It is where he belongs.'

There was a strange confusion in Jane's mind that grew, perhaps, from tiredness and grief. She saw in her mind's eye, not Carne, but Rice Havard, face dark and brooding, his love for Rhianon as fierce in death as in life.

'He will love but one . . .' Jane murmured. 'There will be no other,' and Saranne, hearing the words, took solace in them.

Upon the high mountain, Marged Howell felt the cold wind upon her face and a fear that pierced her like a dart driven through flesh into bone. Strange, she thought, that I can bring healing and ease to others, but not to my own wounds. Like Jane, it was Rice Havard she thought of. People believed that she stayed upon the hills to escape recapture, fearful of punishment. She stayed because Rice Havard's spirit still roamed here, held captive in death as restlessly as in life. It was all that she was permitted to share. They called her the 'Wise Woman' and 'Conjuror', Marged thought ruefully, yet how foolish and useless were her powers. How much easier to heal another's flesh than one's own troubled spirit. She was a true Christian woman and believed the raising of spirits and devils to be corrupt and dangerous. She would not countenance such wickedness. Could not! Yet Rice Havard, that heedless, unloving devil, came to her unbidden to haunt her with what was past and done. Whether in memory, or flesh, he possessed her. It was not enslavement that Marged feared, but that, one day, his restless spirit might find the peace it sought at the sacrifice of her own.

★ ★ ★

The chillness of fallen dusk was deepening about them as Charles bade farewell to Carne. They had spoken little upon the way, save to discuss the rough map which Jethro had devised, always keeping to those paths and byways where they were least likely to be remarked. They halted their horses at a tiny crossing, but did not dismount, Charles riding forward into the centre of the intersecting paths to turn his mare. He paused briefly beside Carne to say, 'Well . . . I shall leave you now, my friend. I would it were possible for me to travel with you all the way.'

'And I that I might return with you to Holly Grove.'

'It seems,' said Charles wryly, 'that the wrong one is adventuring. It was ever the way that another's pasture looks greener.'

'But you would not quit the farm, Charles? Not willingly?'

'Willingly, and with relief!' exclaimed Charles fervently. 'But my future is already decided. I cannot change it.'

'But . . . can you not object? Declare that you have other plans?'

'It would avail me nothing, save to antagonise my father and unsettle me. Without me the farm could not be worked. It is my inheritance, and a millstone about my neck.'

'Better, perhaps, than the noose promised mine,' said Carne with a poor attempt at humour.

'Well . . . I had best go,' Charles touched Carne's shoulder awkwardly, 'else they will think I have ridden to Bristol beside you. If you can send some word of how you fare?'

'I will do what I can.'

Their gazes met briefly, revealing the words deliberately unspoken.

'Take care, my friend,' said Charles.

Carne nodded. 'And you.'

He shortened the reins within his hands, the horse fidgeting and pawing the ground, eager to be away. 'Charles?'

Charles turned his head enquiringly.

'Take good care of Saranne. She will have need of

comfort. Tell her that I will return. Whatever befalls, I will return. She has my promise.'

'She does not doubt it, no more do I . . . Until we meet again!'

Charles raised a hand in salute, and set his mare along the path towards Penavon.

Carne sat, unmoving, in the saddle, until the last hoof-beats of Charles's mare had faded into silence. Then, with a coldness of loneliness and regret, he set the grey towards the highway that led to the town of Cardiff and its quays.

Mostyn, driving the curricle to Great House, was in no happier mood than Carne. If his pity was more for himself than his brother or his poor wretch of a cousin, then it did not lessen his sense of desolation and hurt. He had little enough liking for Penry Vaughan and could not grieve that his cheating and rapacity had brought revenge. Mostyn could not wish him dead, although it was Havard money that he had filched so brazenly. Yet, should Vaughan die, it would be of no more consequence than the death of a servant or modest acquaintance, regrettable but easily enough overcome. What Mostyn could not overcome was his grief at Carne's leaving, his abandonment. Mostyn had cultivated an air of sophistication, that languidity of manner which fashion and society decreed. He affected boredom, a studied indifference, taking others like his friend Danfield and Llewellyn, as pattern. He had learnt to imitate, absorb, and finally to convince. Yet it was no more than a pretty carapace, a protective shell. The old vulnerability remained. The need for approval and affection which his father had denied. He had treated Carne with cynicism, that shallow flippancy which had become second nature, too afraid to express his honest fears and need. Always, Mostyn knew, he was held back by the fear of rejection, the crippling power of hurt.

'Hell and damnation!' he cried aloud, and the horses, startled, trembled and ran on, the carriage swaying peril-ously. It is none of my affair, he told himself. Carne must

make his own way. Should Vaughan die, then I stand only
to gain from it. Yet, constantly, memory of Carne's past
defence of him returned unbidden to flay him with raw
regret.

Once within Great House, he would be diverted with
wining and dining and the scandalous barbs of dinner-table
gossip. He would set himself to entertaining the company.
Laurel would hang upon his every word, although her
mother Clarissa would be harder to impress, but impress
her he must, for one day he would need her as an ally. It
might have served him better, he mused, had Laurel looked
more like her mother; pale, unappealing, and hence,
pathetically grateful for any man's interest and proposal of
marriage, believing herself unworthy of love. There were
many who would offer for Laurel's hand, even without the
lure of her inheritance. Yet none with so all-devouring a
passion to possess Great House as he. If possession of
Laurel Llewellyn was the means, then that was no real
obstacle. There would be none dining at Great House as
handsome, stylish or amusing as he.

When the evening was over, he drove the curricle back
to Penavon, the whale-oil lamps flickering fitfully in the
cool spring darkness. Mostyn knew that he had acquitted
himself well and felt a small surge of triumph. He wondered
idly if Penry Vaughan had been found, and whether he
lived. Then he thought briefly, but with more emotion, of
Carne. We all make our own way in the world, he comforted
himself. If we do not, then the deficiency lies in us and not
Providence. We reap what we sow.

When he had left the horses in the care of a bleary-eyed
stable boy to be uncoupled and returned to their stalls,
Mostyn returned unhurriedly to the house. Here, he was
greeted with tears of distress by Mrs Groves, and a garbled,
almost incoherent, account of the vicious attack upon her
master.

'Oh, sir . . . Oh, sir . . .' she kept repeating helplessly.
'It is past believing that any could be so vicious and
depraved. To attack a man of God! It is unthinkable!'

'And my cousin, Mrs Groves?' Mostyn's hand had tightened upon her arm, a measure, she believed, of his distress. 'Is he alive?'

'Yes, thanks be to God! It was the hand of Providence which saved him, sir, and that alone.' Mostyn's fingers loosened their hold "Tis no wonder you are distressed, sir,' she said, 'and who can blame you? You are known to be fond of the poor gentleman, as are we all.' She started to snivel again and Mostyn looked at her with distaste. 'I swear, sir, that the sight of the blood, and that wound upon his poor head, made me all but swoon. Thank the Lord that you have returned, for Mr Vaughan has been asking most particularly for you.'

'A physician has been summoned?' asked Mostyn to hide his unease.

'Indeed, sir. And he is with him now.'

'Then I will go at once to seek his advice.' Still clutching his silk hat in his hand, Mostyn mounted the stairs with a haste which made Mrs Groves later declare that 'the poor young gentleman was all but out of his wits with despair! Pale as a ghost, he was, and looking as lost and wraithlike, poor soul. His only thought to be at his cousin's bedside.'

Mostyn had indeed one thought; to discover how much Penry Vaughan remembered. It occurred to him as he mounted the staircase that not only Carne's part in the affair might be recalled, but his own. He entered Vaughan's bedchamber hurriedly, scarcely acknowledging the presence of the physician, Dr Tobin, who was bending solicitously over his patient, face gravely intent. Penry Vaughan was propped against pillows, his cadaverous face as blanched as the bandages fastened about his head. His skin was sallow, bloodless almost and, by the jar of engorged leeches at the bedside, Mostyn saw that he had already been cupped and bled. He could not hide the flicker of nausea which assailed him at the sight of the bloated slug-like creatures. 'I see, Mr Havard, how the sight of your cousin's injuries distresses you,' said the doctor. 'Your concern does you credit, sir, but you had best be seated upon this chair and compose yourself, else I will have not one, but two, patients to attend.'

He eased Mostyn, protesting feebly, into a chair, then mixed and delivered him a potion from his cabinet of medicines. As Mostyn swallowed it obediently, Vaughan's blue-veined eyelids opened.

'Mostyn? It is you, Mostyn?'

'Yes, Cousin Penry.'

Vaughan's eyes closed involuntarily, as if he could not suffer the weight of his eyelids.

'Who did this vileness to you, sir? Who is responsible? I beg you will tell me!'

Mostyn's voice was so impassioned that Dr Tobin started towards him anxiously as, startled, Vaughan reopened his eyes to stare at him, saying so feebly that Mostyn was forced to bend low to hear, 'A thief . . . a villain who broke into my own library.'

'You recognised him? Knew the man, Cousin?'

Vaughan closed his eyes again and hesitated, the silence stretching so oppressively that Mostyn all but leapt upon the bed to shake him into speech. Vaughan's lips formed the words with effort, 'No . . . a stranger.'

'They have caught this scoundrel? Brought him to book for his crime, sir?'

'No.' Vaughan's voice had died away and Dr Tobin, alarmed at his patient's agitation, rose and signalled to Mostyn that he must leave at once.

'Carne? He has returned? I would speak to him alone,' insisted Vaughan.

Mostyn hesitated only briefly. 'Perhaps the blow to your head, Cousin . . . Do you not recall? Carne is absent upon a visit. It is not known when he will return.'

Vaughan's eyes opened wide and there was no mistaking the plea in them as they met Mostyn's unwavering gaze.

'Yes. I had forgotten,' Vaughan murmured. 'It is all ended then.'

Dr Tobin's plump, dark-jowled face was puzzled, uncomprehending. 'Perhaps the young man should be sent for. His presence might ease Mr Vaughan's mind?' he suggested uncertainly.

'No . . . it is better not.' The voice from the bed was tired but authoritative. 'It would serve no purpose to warn my young kinsman of my . . . accident, and survival.'

The blow to the clergyman's head had undoubtedly weakened and confused him, Dr Tobin decided in concern, but if Vaughan was determined not to summon the boy, then to insist would simply aggravate him further. 'You must do as you think fitting, sir.' He began gathering his instruments and medicines and replacing them with scrupulous precision within his fitted travelling box. 'I think it is wiser that your cousin is left to restore himself in peace,' Tobin decreed, hustling Mostyn before him to the door of the bedchamber. 'Sleep is a great restorer of flesh and spirit.'

Meekly, Mostyn allowed himself to be chivvied on to the landing where Dr Tobin declared, 'You may see him again in an hour or two . . . but for a few moments only. It is to be hoped that your cousin will soon be recovered enough to swear out a warrant for the justices and to give a description of the scoundrel who so brutally attacked him. I wish you good-night, sir. You may be assured that I will return later to check upon the condition of the invalid.'

Mostyn made him a courteous reply and, bowing stiffly, walked dispiritedly to his room.

When, later, Mostyn returned to Vaughan's bedchamber, there was a nurse in attendance. His cousin was still pallid and waxen beneath his bandages but had his eyes open and was seemingly in full command of his senses. Dear Lord, wondered Mostyn, how much does he recall of the affair, and my part in it? Perhaps it is better to brazen it out, to pretend ignorance of the whole affair?

'Cousin Penry . . .' he began, seating himself anxiously in a chair beside the bed. 'I fear from what I heard you tell the physician that you know the culprit, and are seeking to conceal his name for reasons of your own.'

'Yes, Mostyn. You are right.'

'I pray, sir, that you will set my troubled mind to peace.' His wide blue eyes under the cluster of pale curls were softly blurred with tears. 'Could it be . . .' Mostyn faltered miserably. 'Could it be that it is my brother, Carne, whom you wish to protect? I beg you will tell me, for I am sick with apprehension lest he be in some way involved in this.'

'Oh, my dear boy,' Vaughan's thin hand met Mostyn's upon the coverlet in reassurance, 'it grieves me to admit that your fears are justified. It was indeed Carne who struck me so cruel a blow, and it wounds my spirit more deeply than my flesh. I beg you, Mostyn, not to take upon yourself that burden of guilt and remorse which should rightfully be your brother's. You must not castigate yourself so cruelly for another's sins. I beg that you will not distress yourself more.'

'How can I not be distressed?' Mostyn's tear-stained face was raised in appeal. 'It breaks my heart that there is such viciousness in a brother of mine! To strike down a kinsman, one who has so generously opened to him both heart and home, with no other thought than to provide solace . . . It is unspeakable! Depraved! I cannot bear to speak of it!'

'Then we will mention it no more,' promised Vaughan, but Mostyn would not be consoled and buried his face in his hands. 'I swear, Cousin Penry, that you will be revenged.' Mostyn's voice was muffled, thickened with grief. When he finally roused himself to look at Vaughan, his cheeks were flushed, his eyes unnaturally bright.

'No, Mostyn!' Vaughan rebuked with gentle forbearance. 'One must learn to forgive . . . that will be your true strength. A test of character.'

'I will never forgive him!' Mostyn's voice rose fiercely. 'I no longer count him brother! He is a coward and a villain! I only ask that you will not associate me with his villainy in your mind, and think me the less for it. As far as my life is concerned, Cousin Penry, Carne is already dead!'

'My dear Mostyn,' Vaughan was touched despite himself, 'you may set your mind to rest upon that score. You have always been a most gentle and obedient boy, never causing

223

me a moment's worry or grief.' His arm crept comfortingly about Mostyn's bowed shoulders and he patted him reassuringly, as if he were a small child.

'Oh, Cousin Penry,' Mostyn said, 'how I admire your good nature, your capacity for forgiveness. It shames and humbles me.'

There was no mistaking Penry Vaughan's extreme satisfaction as he modestly brushed aside Mostyn's praise. 'When you are as old and experienced as I, my dear cousin, you will learn the true value of being temperate and slow to exact vengeance. There is a virtue in forgiveness which brings its own reward.'

'It is more reward than Carne deserves, sir, that you will tell others that he is away upon a journey at your request, and in no wise implicated in this affair.'

Vaughan looked at him in surprise, but did not deny it.

'That is a master stroke, sir. An inspiration,' approved Mostyn, 'and a true measure of your generosity to others.'

'We will say no more about it,' declared Vaughan magnanimously. 'We each understand the other better for what has occurred. But if you could find it in your heart to forgive your brother, Mostyn . . .'

'Never!' Mostyn stood up resolutely to take his leave, and, surprisingly, leaned over to kiss Vaughan's cold cheek. 'Had the blow fallen upon me, Cousin Penry, I believe I might have understood, and forgiven, but I cannot, and will not, forgive Carne's ingratitude to you.'

'You were ever a comfort to me, Mostyn,' Vaughan's tired head fell back upon his pillows, 'as Carne was ever his father's child! It is true that the way the green bough is bent, so will the tree grow.'

Chapter Twenty-two

Carne was intent upon travelling to Bristol as quickly as he was able, fearing that the justices might have already sworn out a warrant for his arrest upon a charge of attempted murder, or murder itself. He would keep to the highways by night, when most honest, God-fearing folk were abed, and a lone rider passing in the darkness would be no more than a shadowy figure, hard to recall to mind. In the daytime he would rest at some ill-frequented inn, asking that refreshment be served in the innkeeper's private parlour. He thanked Providence and his friends that he had gold enough to pay for shelter, for, otherwise, he would have been the sleeping target for every rogue and footpad. There were those so desperate that they would maim and strip a man for his clothes and the few coins he carried, or kill merely to secure a horse. Carne was also grateful to Randall Walters for his foresight in providing him with the letter of introduction and the grey. It was a good, strong animal, intelligent and swift to respond, and none would be searching for him upon such a mount.

He passed but one coach by night, and that a gentleman's small travelling coach, its whale-oil lamps dim and the ancient coachman all but asleep upon the box. There were distant lights of isolated cottages and farms and occasionally a rider, solitary as he, would pass by and make self-conscious greeting, face averted, quickening his horse's hoofbeats, his lantern a dying glow. The night was alive with sounds strange to him: the creaking of dry branches; the soughing of wind through hedgerow and grass; the stirring of small, unseen creatures and their squeaks and rustlings amidst the fallen leaves; the wild, near-human cry of some animal caught in the teeth of a trap or in the talons of that single white barn owl, gliding and swooping wraithlike across the startled grey's path.

As dawn broke, the sky lightened, then blazed into a brilliance of red, gold and saffron, fiery and devouring as flame. It brought Carne no joy; his mind was on Penavon and its people. He knew that, with every fresh stride, the grey carried him nearer to freedom, yet separated him from the past, and he did not know when, if ever, he might return. Yet he must return. There were people like Saranne and Jane, as much a part of himself as his own flesh. And these hills near Penavon were his very life blood, and the source of every thought and action. He was bonded to them in the future as well as in the past. They were inescapable. There was no other place on earth, Carne knew with certainty, which would ever hold the power to move him so deeply, or to draw him so strongly.

He rode until the sun was high, with only occasional pause to rest and water the grey. At a stream he quenched his own thirst, lying full length upon an outcrop of flat stone and dipping face and head into the cold crystalline depths, its edges clotted with wild cress. Once a buzzard circled above, its wings darkening the sky, to hover seemingly motionless, its shadow misting the grass. Then, with hair dripping and a cool freshness upon his face, Carne remounted the grey and urged it onwards. Upwards they climbed, mile after mile, hour after hour, through bracken and thorns, over hill and hollow, marshland and rock-strewn turf, close cropped by sheep. Their forlorn cries followed Carne hauntingly as he rode, their lost bleating an echo of the sadness he felt within.

It was with a sense of incredulity that he eventually and unexpectedly breasted a hill to see the coastal plain and sea spread out below. The first was verdantly green and the second glowed like pewter in the late afternoon light. Carne knew a surge of exhilaration, a new optimism, as he stroked the grey's damp neck and set her on the last lap of her journeying, and his own. Taking his leave of the hills, he rode towards the tree-sheltered plain, with the grey River Taff slithering, snake-like, across it, its movements curled and sinuous.

So it was that Carne rode into the small town of Cardiff. The breeze was cool and the late afternoon sun cast long shadows but the air was full of familiar scents and sounds; the singing of birds and the insistent murmur of insects upon the wing. Too soon the man-made squalor of the town and docks made stark contrast. The streams and cataracts upon the hills were now a sluggish grey-black river, its bed a graveyard for the slop and detritus of urban living. The stench of rotting things repelled him and, as he rode by, a water rat emerged from the foetid slime to struggle on to the bank. The houses alongside were ill-built and packed so closely together that the alleys between were dark and sunless, with scarcely space for a horse and rider to pass unscathed. The upper storeys leaned so perilously inwards that those who dwelt within might have flung open their casements and touched fingers with those upon the opposite side. Worse, what little sky might have been glimpsed from the narrow alleys was hidden by the tawdry lines of washing strung across the straw ropes. It hung in tattered folds, grey and damp, ill-served by sun or breeze.

Carne, dispirited now, and as ravaged by uncertainty and guilt as by exhaustion, wished only to find a ship to Bristol. Yet he knew that first he must sell the grey for whatever it might bring.

As he rode along the cobbled way to the dockside stables, Carne saw, with pity and disgust, those forsaken creatures more desperate than he, their haunts the gin and opium dens. Men and women, filthy and unkempt, crouched within whatever shelter they could find. A beggar woman with pock-marked skin stretched out a hand to Carne's bridle, trying to drag him from the saddle but, with an oath and a cry, he thrust her fiercely away. Her face twisted with hate, she spat at him contemptuously, her malignant curses following him upon the way. Despite himself, Carne shivered, for there had been such evil in her maledictions, such foulness of mouth, that he felt unclean and exhausted by the event.

The proprietor of the stables had witnessed the attempt to unseat Carne and ran forward to hurl abuse at the woman. He was a thin, whey-faced creature and, noting Carne's fine dress and mount, said respectfully, "'Tis best to keep your wits about you, sir, for this is a port where all creeds and colours meet. Men of all persuasions, aye, and women too. There is no evil too vicious, nor perversion too debauched, that it cannot be bought. You would be wise to encourage none, and trust none. It is a sadness to me and shaming that I must give such warning. I hope, sir, that you will not take it amiss.'

'No. I am grateful.'

'But you will want stabling for your grey, sir, and a clean, honest place to rest your head?'

'I would sell my horse.'

The man looked at Carne shrewdly, taking in his youth, fine speech and air of breeding and he inspected the grey with no less thoroughness. Posing Carne no questions as to ownership, his bargaining was incisive but fair. It grieved Carne to part with the animal, for it had been companion upon the long way and was his sole living link with Penavon and all he knew.

Did his cousin still live? Had he been branded murderer? Had a hue and cry been called? Carne was too travel-weary and drained by emotion to care. With the guineas for the grey and his other few treasures clutched within his saddlebag, he made his way to the inn which the ostler had pointed out to him, the Travellers Rest. The irony of it made him smile wryly. There would be little rest or sleep for him that night, and his travelling had scarcely begun. He could not hazard where it might take him.

The inn near the quayside was hardly more than the roughest tavern. It was a crowded bustling place, frequented by the sailors, fishermen, traders and craftsmen of the port, those industrious sailmakers and repairers, rope workers, carpenters, net menders, farriers and chandlers, whose work was done in the timbered huts aside the wharves and in the lofts above. Yet although the fare was simple and the furnishings sparse and functional, it was tolerably clean and the atmosphere convivial. The landlord came over to greet Carne and was a jocular, rubicund fellow in apron and shirtsleeves, face shiny with sweat or overindulgence.

'Is it victuals and refreshment you seek, sir?'

'I had thoughts of renting a bed, if you have one to spare.'

The landlord's smile grew wider, more expansive, and he rubbed a hand across his stubbled chin while considering. In truth, Carne thought, he had as many chins as he would have laps, were he seated, his flesh falling in generous folds like a paper concertina.

'If you will come this way, sir,' he invited, 'you may inspect my bedchambers. There are three, sir, and only one is presently taken. You may have the choice of the larger room with four straw palliasses upon the floor, if you are not averse to sharing with strangers. However, should you prefer it, being a gentleman, there is one small room with a trestle bed and, in addition, a small cupboard for your clothing, as well as a washstand with bowl and jug, and the usual chamber pot. It will cost one shilling and sixpence more than a room shared.'

'Yes, landlord, I will take it.'

'You are wise, sir,' declared his host delightedly, 'for I cannot always vouch for the company you might inadvertently be forced to keep.'

Carne smiled and offered the landlord the shillings required from a small pouch hanging securely beneath his befrilled shirt.

As the landlord took Carne up the staircase to the bedchamber, he asked, 'Would you have me send a serving maid to the livery, that your mount may be delivered here when you leave?'

'No . . . I shall be leaving by boat, as soon as I am able. I travel to Bristol.' He had flushed under the landlord's keen scrutiny, mumbling, 'Although I have not yet found a vessel.'

'Then it would be as well to jettison your saddlebags and, if you will excuse the impertinence, for it is kindly meant, purchase a cheap straw basket, such as is used for mackerel and sprats, or a canvas sack threaded with rope, for that is what sailors carry. 'Tis not so easily remarked, or stolen, if you take my meaning. You would be wise to pack away your fine clothes within it, until you have need of them again and to buy some canvas trousers and a short jacket and hat, that you might be taken for a fisherman or tar. If you prefer, I can send my potman to the chandler's to secure what you need. He has seen you, and will choose a fair fitting, you may depend upon it.'

Carne thanked him and gave him the money he required, with a little extra to be offered to the potman for his trouble.

'There is no disguising the quality of your speech, or that you are a gentleman bred,' the landlord mused, 'so when in doubtful company, it would be wise to keep your mouth firmly shut, sir, begging your pardon, and pretend to be one who keeps his own counsel.' He smiled. 'And I fear, sir, your hands might also betray you, for they are neither dirt-grimed nor broken-nailed.' He shook his head regretfully.

'I think,' said Carne quietly, glancing at his palms, 'that if I board a ship at Bristol, they might soon pass inspection, for favours will neither be asked nor given.'

'Then I will not say that it will make a man of you, sir, for you are already that,' his host said, preceding him carefully up the narrow stairway, 'but it is safer to mingle and blend, rather than be set apart. It is a fact of life and nature both. If one searches for a single black sheep, it is harder to distinguish it in a flock of the same colour. You get my drift, sir?'

'I do,' said Carne delightedly, adding with a touch of wry humour, 'and this black sheep thanks you, sir.'

'And your name, Mr . . . ?'

'Grey,' he said decisively. The horse had proved an honest companion.

'Grey,' the innkeeper repeated, smiling. ''Tis plain and fitting, sir. A good name . . . safe and anonymous.' His eyes twinkled knowingly. 'Midway 'twixt black and white.'

In Penavon, opinion was divided as to the reason for the assault upon Penry Vaughan and the most likely aggressor. If Carne Havard had struck his cousin in anger, as some at first suspected, it was inconceivable that the vicar would not have unleashed upon him the full fury of the justices and the law. He would be the last person to shield the boy! No, it was plain that some escaped prisoner or lunatic, intent upon robbery, had set upon Vaughan in a fury, enraged perhaps at being disturbed.

Few enquired as to the victim's condition or the extent of his injuries, for they nursed wounds enough of their own. Besides, Vaughan had preached so many times that suffering was ennobling that it seemed a God-given opportunity for the vicar himself to test the truth of it. If the blow to his head had mellowed him, or blessed him with forgetfulness, it was the will of the Almighty. They could only pray that it was a permanent state of grace.

However, Mostyn's apparent distress at his cousin's injuries had convinced Rhys Llewellyn that his young protégé felt gratitude, and even affection, for Penry Vaughan. The Ironmaster, who considered the clergyman to be an austere and unlikeable fellow, was strangely moved by Mostyn's loyalty. It was a trait which he found admirable and which he was keen to foster. The boy had, after all, suffered the loss of his parents and his inheritance and it was to his credit that Mostyn had grown neither bitter nor dissolute but a young man of easy charm. Llewellyn must take some credit for that upon himself, for he had encouraged the boy and financed his education and his instruction in the polite arts. Now, none could claim his patronage wasted for Mostyn was all that Llewellyn himself had striven so desperately to become. Yet he still felt a lack of breeding that even his wealth could not remedy. By an accident of birth, Mostyn had that advantage. Perhaps, Rhys Llewellyn mused speculatively, the boy might yet become a useful tool to him in business. Certainly he was intelligent enough and had a modest flair for figures and a quick grasp of essentials. But competent accountants were two a penny, and easily replaced. What was needed was a social director; a business host who, in Llewellyn's absence, could meet directors confidently and charm men of influence into investing in new schemes. He would groom Mostyn for that position. The boy was a good conversationalist and, despite his youth, at ease with both women and men, of whatever age and circumstance. Besides, Laurel was amused by him, and treated him more as a kinsman, a brother. Mostyn was well mannered and a steadying influence upon her, calming her wildest exuberance and not above correcting her should need arise. It was a restraint which Laurel would take from no other, save himself, and further proof of young Havard's influence and powers of persuasion upon others.

Llewellyn sighed. He could wish his daughter to be truly at ease in the presence of gentlemen, unlike those silly twittering creatures with their affected airs and empty chatter, who served only to ornament a drawing room . . . or to drive men to escape into the gaming parlour and bawdy houses. Worse, she might become as frigid and self-effacing as Clarissa. He had bought his wife, he reflected, with as much deliberation and lack of emotion as if she had been a high-bred mare, or a piece of fine porcelain, to add to his collection. An acquisition to display to others as proof of his discrimination and wealth. She had proved a poor bargain and he had lived to regret it. Unlike any other ill-chosen *objet d'art*, he thought ruefully, he could neither relegate her to a closet, nor exchange her. She was a permanent and bitter reminder of his lack of judgement. Still, she had given him Laurel. He could make his daughter all that Clarissa was not, and none should take her from him excepting the husband of his choice, and her own, he amended generously, always providing of course that their tastes agreed.

Laurel left the house unseen and hurried across the yard to the stables, pretty skirts and petticoats lifted over delicate shoes. She was so intent on delaying Mostyn that she was completely unmindful of the filth and dampness underfoot. When she entered the stable block, it was to see Mostyn leading out the mount from Penavon which the groom had already saddled and bridled. Mostyn was, Laurel thought, the most handsome and elegant young man she had ever clapped eyes upon, and despite his classical, almost effeminate, good looks, he was disturbingly masculine. There was a suppressed energy about his lithe muscular body; an animal grace of movement and limb echoed in the pure bred mount he led.

'Mostyn?' she cried, running forward impulsively and taking his arm. 'You were not thinking of leaving without a word of farewell?'

The scowl already on Mostyn's face deepened and he shook off her hand with irritation, saying petulantly, 'Farewell, ma'am! There. I have said it! Now, if you will excuse me.' He had pulled the horse out into the cobbled yard and had set his highly polished boot into the stirrup, when Laurel took his arm once again.

'Hell and damnation, Laurel!' he cried vexedly. 'Why must you plague me so? I have enough on my mind without your constant badgering!'

Her cheeks flushed at his reprimand, but she clung firmly to his arm, demanding coaxingly, 'Tell me what ails you, Mostyn? What has set you in such a flux? Perhaps I can help you?' Her eyes were pleading.

'You?' He pulled away scornfully, saying with vexation, 'It is a matter for men! You can know nothing of such affairs.'

'Affairs, Mostyn?' A coldness touched her, sharpening her voice. 'It is some woman . . . some entanglement from which you seek to free yourself?'

'Hell's teeth, Laurel!' he exclaimed furiously. 'What do you take me for? A fool? A dissolute rake? Would you have me confess to whoring?' His anger was so fierce that he spoke to her cruelly and without restraint, forgetting the normal courtesies. Surprisingly though, Laurel did not seem to have taken offence. Indeed, she was brushing aside his sullen apology.

'Let us go back within the stables, Mostyn, to discuss what might be done to ease the affair,' she said reassuringly.

He hesitated only briefly, then, after glancing about him surreptitiously to see that they were not observed, he hurried her within and followed, tugging the horse's bridle since it was reluctant to re-enter. When he had satisfied himself that no grooms or stable lads were within earshot, he said brusquely, 'I do not care to linger here! It is foolish, Laurel, and ill-advised. If your father discovers us, I shall be held responsible. I have troubles enough, without adding to them!'

'They are matters of honour, Mostyn? Gaming debts?' she probed hesitantly.

'And if they are, ma'am? 'Tis none of your affair! I am wretchedly poor and disadvantaged and have not the income of a gentleman, merely the tastes,' he declared sourly. 'My cousin is a cloddish provincial without knowledge of such things. He keeps me deucedly short of money. A pauper! I have to beg for the meanest shilling and am a laughing stock, the butt of my friends. I tell you, Laurel, I can stand it no longer!' The handle of his whip clutched tight in his hand, he slashed so fiercely against his boot that the horse, startled, fidgeted and tossed its head, so that he had to struggle to control it.

'Then it is only money you seek?' Laurel's voice was light with relief.

'Only! Only, you say! The lack of it will see me shamed and disgraced! I will be unable to lift up my head before my friends; a known cheat, unwilling to pay my wagers.'

'But all gentlemen run up debts, Mostyn,' said Laurel,

puzzled 'It is a way of life in dealings with tailors, wine merchants, coachmakers. It is set upon one's account. I have heard Father say so . . .' she broke off, frightened of the blazing anger she had aroused in him.

'Gentlemen have accounts, ma'am,' he corrected bitterly. 'The poor have debts. I am poor . . . God help me.' He made to drag his mount without, pushing her aside irritably in his haste.

'Wait! I will get you the money. Tell me how much you owe.'

He halted.

'How much, Mostyn? I must know.'

'Seventy pounds.'

'You are sure you have told me all?' she asked anxiously, 'that there is no more to be reckoned?'

'Is it not enough? I have told you I am a beggar!' he exclaimed abrasively.

'I will get it for you, Mostyn.'

'You? How?' He was frankly sceptical. 'You have no use for money. All your needs are supplied. All your extravagances met without murmur. I do not believe you, Laurel. No!' He thrust her away from him with such force that she had to steady herself against a beam lest she lose her balance. 'You are a liar, and seek only to deceive me, to ingratiate yourself with me. I will not be used!'

Laurel flung her arms about his neck, resisting all his efforts to free himself of them, and planted a kiss upon his mouth, clinging, yielding, so that he could feel the soft curves of her breasts and the fragile slenderness of her bones. He had been forced to loosen his hold upon the horse's bridle and, as he pushed Laurel away, he was aware of the warm scent of her flesh, the fragrance of her hair, and the stirring of response within him. Even as his yearning grew to return her kisses and cover her body with his own, sanity returned, and he thrust her viciously from him, crying out in frustration and rage.

'Would you have me banned from your house? Destroy me?'

'No, Mostyn. No! I love you dearly! It would break my heart, I swear!'

Laurel was trembling and ashamed, hurt by his rejection. Tears had gathered in her eyes and were coursing miserably down her cheeks. 'Forgive me, Mostyn, I cannot bear it when you are cross with me. I shall get you the money, I swear, and none shall know I have given it to you.'

Mostyn retrieved his horse's bridle, scarcely glancing at her ravaged face, before leading his mount into the yard. 'Stay where you are until I have ridden out,' he commanded, 'lest we be seen together, you understand?'

'Yes, Mostyn.' Her voice was subdued and soft with tears. 'I will get the money for you, you may depend upon it.' He did not reply. 'But you do like me a little, Mostyn? More than any other?' she asked helplessly. 'There is no-one else who would do so much for you. No-one.'

But Mostyn had already swung himself into the saddle, and was away, the horse's hoofbeats upon the cobbles drumming out her words.

Laurel had rehearsed her speech carefully in her mind before she entered the library where Rhys Llewellyn was engaged in familiarising himself with some business documents. Clarissa and the household servants knew better than to disturb him when he was thus occupied, but Laurel was a law unto herself, and had been a cherished visitor from the time she first escaped her nurse's surveillance to open the door and clamber, unaided, upon his knee. She entered now with a pretty rustling of gown and petticoats to where he sat, head bent over the papers upon his desk in silent scrutiny. Then she dropped a swift kiss upon his dark hair and, as he looked up in confusion, Laurel sank into a most graceful curtsey. The flickering taper flames threw a halo of light about her face and hair and upon the sapphire-blue folds of her gown. Pride at the innocent loveliness of her caught at Llewellyn's throat as he exclaimed brusquely, to conceal his absurd pleasure, 'Well,

Miss? And to what do I owe this unwelcome invasion of my privacy?'

'There is something I would ask of you, Papa, a favour. I should like my own money, Papa.'

'Money?' he asked sharply. 'For what reason, Laurel? I deny you nothing.'

'Because, Papa . . .' she blurted out, 'there are things I would buy.'

'Things? Things?' he repeated testily. 'I do not understand you. You must be specific. It is not fitting that a mere . . . young gentlewoman,' he amended quickly, 'should be in possession of money. It is unnecessary and demeaning. A young man is different. He has need of coins to wager and pay his bills, to give him independence.'

'There are things I would purchase, Papa. Small trinkets for Mama's birthday, and yours, to feel that they were truly my own choice, or those small necessities of which a young lady . . .' she broke off with a small sob, tears welling to shimmer in her eyes then spill through her lashes, '. . . things which cannot rightly be discussed before gentlemen, Papa.' She finished brokenly, preparing to rise and take her leave.

'Confound it, my dear!' he declared, unnerved by the misery he had unwittingly wrought. ''Tis not worth a candle! You may have your own money, and welcome. I had no notion of making you weep. Now, dry your tears, my dear, and forget that we have spoken of it.' He delved into his pocket and dried her eyes tenderly upon his silk handkerchief. 'There, my love . . . do not take on so! It was remiss of me not to have thought of it for myself. I will arrange it at once and, should you have further need, you may simply remind me of it when your capital is exhausted. Will that do?'

'Oh, Papa, you are the best and kindest of men, and I love you dearly,' cried Laurel, almost overturning the foot-stool in her urgency to rise and fling her arms about his neck. 'And you promise that you will not ask how, and where, I have spent it?'

237

'I promise,' he replied with mock solemnity, pretending to cross his heart, to Laurel's great amusement. 'You shall keep your little secret, my love, for my lips will be sealed upon it until death delivers me.'

'Oh, Papa! You are funny and absurd,' she exclaimed affectionately.

'Now . . . What shall we say?' he demanded. 'One hundred guineas, to see you through the year? Was that the sum you had in mind?'

'Oh, Papa, but it is too generous,' exclaimed Laurel. 'It is a fortune. I cannot accept such a sum. It is too much. I had no thought . . .' Her face was such a picture of incredulous delight that Llewellyn laughed aloud.

'Nonsense, my dear. It is a trifling sum. Less than I spend on horseflesh at a single sale. Come, I insist upon it! I will brook no refusal.'

'Then I accept,' said Laurel, kissing him upon his forehead, then laying her cheek against his. 'Since you claim it will bring you pleasure, it would be churlish of me to deny it to you, Papa!' she teased, smiling. 'Besides, I will provide better conversation at your table than a mere filly . . . and I am so much prettier.'

'I cannot dispute it,' he said gallantly, offering her his arm to escort her to dinner. 'Although, it is fair to say that they do not hanker after gowns and pretty trinkets and are satisfied with a diet of hay.'

'Would you have me ask the housekeeper to order that cook prepare a dish of it for us both, Papa?' she asked wickedly.

'No, my love. I would have you remain exactly as you are,' he said amidst shared laughter. 'I would change neither hair nor hide!'

Clarissa was engaged in penning a letter at the delicately carved *bonheur-du-jour* in her small private drawing room. The pretty desk, as most of the room's other furnishings, was from her childhood home, Dornford Abbey, and sometimes, with the mullioned windows heavily draped and the tapers flickeringly aglow upon the chandelier, she could fancy that she had returned there, in flesh as in spirit. She laid aside her quill, writing abandoned, and moved restlessly about the room, touching the smooth, polished surfaces of the furniture lovingly and caressing the familiar silver and gold snuff boxes and *objets-de-vertu*. Things of virtue, quality. She smiled despite herself. Was that what she had been to Rhys Llewellyn? An acquisition to be displayed? Certainly her provenance had been faultless and none could doubt her virtue or quality. Clarissa's lips curved in a wry smile. These small trinkets, souvenirs, were dear to her. When she touched them, it was with love, as if she sought to absorb the very shape and essence of them through her fingertips that she might store them within, feel them a part of her. Yet, Rhys had never touched her with love, never allowed her to belong, never valued her for what she was. To him she was of no more worth than some inanimate object; useful, decently unobtrusive, yet not desirable enough to be coveted by him or any other.

Clarissa wandered slowly to the casement. The thin spring sunlight that seeped through its leaded panes held no warmth, but reflected a soft glow upon the linenfold wainscot and the mellow, polished surfaces. A movement in the yard without caught Clarissa's attention, and she drew closer to the panes, unseen. 'Laurel!' she spoke the name aloud and would have rapped upon the glass to call her daughter's attention, for the air was chill and the child was wearing her pretty new dress of muslin which was altogether too flimsy and delicate for venturing abroad. The silly girl wore neither bonnet nor pelisse, and would, as like as not, fall victim to some ague. Even as Clarissa raised her hand to alert her daughter, another movement from within the stable stayed her, and she instinctively moved aside from the casement, lest she be observed. Someone had eased out from the shadowed doorway, movements furtive and hesitant, to stand beside Laurel, and had taken her arm possessively. But who? Clarissa felt a rising fury at the impudent familiarity of the gesture, and her outrage

grew as she recognised Mostyn Havard. The impertinence
of it! The brazen effrontery! Laurel would be hopelessly
compromised. She would descend at once and put a stop
to such antics!

Yet she did not go, but remained motionless, watching.
It was a meeting of those who shared some secret which
they wished to conceal, an understanding, a tryst. But
trysts were meetings of lovers, amorous moments greedily
snatched. Dear heaven! Surely that could not be? They
were almost like brother and sister. No! It was not possible!
Laurel's movements were too stringently watched, her
hours planned and spent always in the company of her
governness or tutors. That Mostyn Havard's taking of her
daughter's arm had been proprietary, Clarissa could not
deny. There was some bond between them. For what purpose had they met? It was clearly more than a casual
encounter.

She saw Laurel take a leather pouch from the reticule
she carried, and press it into Mostyn's hand. Although she
could not be sure, for he had moved to shield Laurel from
her prying gaze, she thought she had seen the boy bend to
kiss her. Surely he would not be so absurdly foolish? It
would mean the end of his acceptance at Great House and
of Rhys Llewellyn's indulgent patronage. Indeed, it would
be the end of his acceptance in society anywhere, for Rhys
would see that every door was closed and barred to him.

Dear Lord! Clarissa thought despairingly. What am I to
do? She pressed her forehead to the window pane, but its
coldness brought no comfort or relief. I will go, at once,
and accuse them openly . . . but of what? Laurel will deny
anything improper has occurred, and declare it to be simple
spite and imagining, knowing how I dislike the boy. Her
ridicule will make me appear foolish and vindictive. Nevertheless, she resolved, I will speak to her and demand to
know what passed between them. I shall do it circumspectly, before Rhys, so that she will be too startled to
prepare herself and lie. It is my right as her mother, my
duty, although she will not thank me for it. She has never

pretended to love me, nor even to liking.

Clarissa turned dispiritedly from the window and returned to her desk, the unfinished letter spread before her. Although she dipped the pen into the ink and set the quill to the page, the words she sought eluded her. With a sigh she placed her writing materials in a drawer and closed it.

Clarissa had steeled herself to say what needed to be said when Rhys, Laurel, Mostyn and she found themselves gathered that evening at the dinner table, with no other invited company. Although her heart was then beating so suffocatingly that she felt its nervous pulsing at her throat, she said with feigned innocence, 'How pretty you looked this afternoon in the stable yard, Laurel, but I fear, my dear, that you should have worn a pelisse for warmth. Mostyn was more sensibly attired with a warm riding cape to keep away the chill.'

Mostyn's face reddened with embarrassment, and he fidgeted awkwardly with his dinner napkin before blurting out uncomfortably, 'I offered Laurel the protection of my cape, ma'am, when we met by accident, but she would have none of it.'

'Really, Mama!' Laurel's voice was sharp with anxiety. 'I was out of doors but a moment, seeking a brooch I had lost.' Her flushed face and indignation gave the lie to her artless claim and Rhys Llewellyn stiffened and watched her intently.

'Did you find it, my love?' asked Clarissa with seeming negligence. 'I thought it was a pouch . . . of coins, perhaps, which I saw you pass to Mostyn's possession? Perhaps I was mistaken, for it was the merest glance from the window of my small drawing room.' She paused, then went on eating, apparently unaware of the turmoil she had created.

'Mostyn?' Rhys Llewellyn's voice was harsh.

Dear God, Mostyn thought, I am finished! She has set a trap to snare me. How will I answer? He felt the dampness of sweat above his lip and trickling at his neck and hairline.

241

He glanced helplessly towards Laurel but, by the trembling of her mouth and the soft glint of tears which quivered upon her lashes, he knew her anguish was as deep as his own.

'Oh, Mama! Mama! How could you?' The tears had spilled now and were coursing down her cheeks. Laurel made no effort to stop them, or even to wipe them away, her face beautiful and tragic, her despair real.

Mostyn thought resignedly, I am done for, I had best confess all . . . salvage a little of my pride before I am sent packing in disgrace. He tried to speak out, but the words burned sourly in his throat and died away. Dear God, he thought helplessly, I am a fool! An imbecile! What madness could have possessed me!

Clarissa alone seemed unmoved by the drama unfolding all about her. Rhys Llewellyn had noisily thrust his chair away, and had risen to go to Laurel's side. Appalled as Mostyn was, he could not help but observe how, in Laurel's grief, her youth and vulnerability were intensified, her fragility enhanced. He even felt a brief stirring of protectiveness towards her before the full import of his own peril overwhelmed him. Laurel had buried her face hard against her father's waistcoat, sobbing heart-renderingly as his arms encircled her. 'Oh, Papa! Papa! Now all is ruined . . . the secret spoilt. Oh, I had planned such a lovely surprise for you . . . a birthday gift, and Mostyn was so kind . . .' Her sobs broke off, only to redouble in anguish. She fought to control herself, her pained cries diminishing to gulps, then a whimper. 'Mostyn took the coins to make the purchase for me, vowing he would tell no-one, lest the secret be ruined.'

'There! There, my love!,' Rhys Llewellyn was stroking the pretty fair hair, his gaze turned furiously upon Clarissa who, flushed and helpless, was stammering her awkward apologies. 'It is all a stupid mistake, my dear, a misunderstanding. Mama would not willingly put you to such distress.' His voice held little conviction. 'Mostyn?'

'Sir?'

'I beg you will continue with your meal, sir, and forget, if you can, this aberration of my wife. That is if this needless fiasco has not deprived you of all appetite.'

'No, sir,' Mostyn, reprieved, gratefully did as he was invited.

'Now, Laurel,' declared Llewellyn, wiping her eyes with his silk pocket handkerchief, 'let us have no more tears. It was wrong of Mama to have . . .' he hesitated, seeking the right phrase, 'to have watched you so secretively and to have so absurdly misinterpreted what she saw. It was worse to have shamed and embarrassed a guest at our table.' He turned to Mostyn, his brief glance towards Clarissa stiff with disapproval. 'I hope, Mostyn, that you will be generous enough to accept my wife's apologies, and my own.' At Mostyn's quick nod of agreement, he continued, 'I thank you for being honourable enough to keep Laurel's small confidence, even at risk to yourself. It says much for your loyalty and discretion, sir.' Glancing up, Clarissa thought she surprised a fleeting smile of satisfaction upon Laurel's face, then a glance of triumph towards Mostyn, but she could not be sure, for Rhys was calling her attention, saying testily, 'Clarissa.'

'Yes, my dear?' She was aware that she had paled at the harshness of his tone.

'I have already settled one hundred guineas upon Laurel, given it into her keeping, and told her she may spend it as she chooses, with neither advice from nor accountability to others. You understand?'

'But you did not consult me or inform me,' she reminded him helplessly.

'It was none of your affair, a matter discussed and decided between Laurel and me. You understand?' he insisted.

'Oh, yes, I understand, sir!' The bitterness with which she spoke seemed only to irritate him.

'Damnation, Clarissa!' he exploded. 'Must I consult you upon every trivial affair? Are you my keeper? My gaoler? Have you not done damage enough by your prying and suspicions? I swear, ma'am, you are so obsessed with social correctness and pious platitudes that you forget what it is to be human, a creature of flesh and blood!'

'No, Rhys. I do not forget.'

There was a poignancy underlying the words which made Mostyn look up, startled. He squirmed uncomfortably under Clarissa's unwavering gaze before lowering his own in confusion, blurting out clumsily, 'You were correct, ma'am, to watch so carefully over Laurel. Your concern for her does you credit.'

Clarissa bit back the instinctive retort that she neither sought his opinion, nor valued it, to say with deceptive mildness, 'It is the natural duty of a mother, as any other, Mostyn, who seeks to protect against harm.'

There was an implied warning in the seemingly innocuous response, which told him that she had not been deceived, although Rhys Llewellyn and Laurel seemed unaware of it.

'I have decided, Clarissa, that Laurel is now at an age when she requires the services of a personal maid, a lady's maid. That is, of course, if you have no objection?'

It was less a question than a taunt, a ploy to make her look ridiculous, but Clarissa answered equably, 'No, my dear. It is a splendid idea. I approve it wholeheartedly.'

Llewellyn looked only briefly disconcerted before recovering himself and urging with false heartiness, 'Let us finish this excellent meal, then, while we are in accord and our appetites remain.' *She is a damnably cold creature,* he thought sullenly, picking negligently at the food upon his plate, *emotionless and bloodless; too high bred by half! She is like so many of her kind, with the blood-line thinned by interbreeding. Weakened in looks and spirit!*

Clarissa, the impeccable hostess, gave him a gentle smile, the custom of long training re-establishing her ease at her own table. She drew them all expertly into conversation, watching their boorishness and resentment dissolve under her unobtrusive guidance. Rhys Llewellyn could not but admire her expertise, her cool composure, however grudgingly. None could fault her grasp of the social niceties. Did she never feel rage, rebellion, hurt? Did she feel anything?

I should hate Rhys, she thought. I should loathe him for the years of bondage, the subservience I have been forced to accept. Coldness is my only weapon and, if it were lost, he would humiliate me further. Yet, in spite of all, I have a need for his love.

Chapter Twenty-three

Saranne's anguish at Carne's leaving had drained all the joyous warmth and spirit from her and she felt as empty and bereft as she had upon that terrible day when Marged Howell had fled into the hills, leaving her abandoned. Throughout her early childhood, try as she might, Saranne could not truly understand the despair of loss which had sent the wise woman to forsake her. She knew now the full depths of Marged Howell's grief; that pain of separation.

She was young, Jethro said, and would soon enough forget. Sara felt an ache within her for her daughter's sadness but was fearful of showing her compassion too openly, lest it serve to feed Saranne's loss. She had become silent and withdrawn into herself, even the newest kittens and the animals upon the farm failing to rouse her from apathy. Sara had persuaded Jethro to drive them to Penavon village, that they might choose and purchase cotton muslin to make a dress and cloak for Saranne, thinking the stitching of it might keep her daughter occupied by candlelight when her tasks upon the farm were done. Jethro had even suggested that she might order a pair of the very best quality shoes at the cordwainer's and buy a pair of cotton stockings – an extravagance which would usually have elicited cries of delight. Saranne had murmured unhappily, unaware of Jethro's hurt pride, 'No, I thank you, Papa, but the money would be better saved, or spent upon Mama. I have no occasion to wear them.'

It was Charles, alone, who treated Saranne as of old, teasing, harassing, pretending naught was amiss, and it was to him that she spoke of her regrets and before him that she wept unashamedly. He, too, felt the loss of his friend keenly and, remembering his promise to Carne, did his best to give her solace.

When Sara broached the subject of Saranne's misery to Peter Morrish without Jethro's knowledge, he said gently, 'Do not deny her time to grieve, Sara. It is the way of healing from within, as necessary as our mourning for the dead. Whether by death or circumstances, the pain of separation can never be fully felt by another, or the void filled.'

'Why do you preach at me when I am so worried for her, and so confused?' she demanded, anguished. 'Words! Words! It is comfort I have need of: the strength of another; human warmth!' Sara buried her face in her hands despairingly and could not see the hurt she had caused him, nor the tentative movements of his hand towards her copper hair, as swiftly stilled.

Morrish's voice was strangely thickened and warm with compassion. 'You may help her, by the loving protection of your arms and the generosity of spirit and acceptance you offered her when first she came to Holly Grove as an outcast child. She is still that child and all you can do is offer her the same comfort.'

'And who will comfort me?' The words were wrung out of her and, when she raised her eyes to his in pleading, she saw the same torment within his own. It was but a step towards her and he could take her in his compassionate embrace, as he had taken so many others who were lost, fearful or grieving. Yet he made no move to touch her. His face was ugly with the burden of the decision to be made, and Morrish thought that never before had he felt such all-devouring torment of flesh and spirit. He knew that if he stretched out a hand to touch her, all would be betrayed. There could be no turning back. He must lose God, Sara, the work he had given his life to – and be in peril of losing his immortal soul. Yet, how much would be lost in his rejection of her? Even could he endure the separation from

247

all he held dear, he could not demand a greater sacrifice from her. Sara would lose Jethro, the children she loved, her home and name. She would be ostracised by all, as much a fugitive as Carne. No, it was too cruel a sacrifice for it would mean, at the end, the sacrifice of love itself.

Sara, knowing love and pity for Peter Morrish deeper even than her feelings for Jethro, Charles, and Saranne, said quietly, 'I asked you not to preach at me, Peter, but that is your vocation, your life. What good you have done, my dear friend, with your patient listening and eager help! All who come to you are better for your kindness.' There was such conviction in her voice that Peter Morrish could not speak. 'You told me that Saranne must find comfort in my loving. In turn, I shall find my own comfort in Jethro's. He is a warm and gentle man, and none can doubt his strength and constancy. He values you as his most honest and dearest friend.'

Morrish knew that Sara was giving him the answer *he* sought, and it brought him both joy and a sense of indescribable loss.

'When Jethro told me of your walk beside the paupers so long ago, I knew you for a good, brave man.' Her voice was low. 'A man who was not afraid to humble himself to help the wretched and dispossessed. How rich your life has been, Peter, and how full of kindness and self-sacrifice. You have helped so many, and given hope and peace to those who had none.'

To all save one, Peter Morrish thought, but he suffered her to put a hand upon his arm and lead him within, into the warm company of friends who loved and trusted him.

Carne had spent a restless night, his thoughts upon the events which had driven him from Penavon and upon its people. The roistering and carousing of those in the tavern beneath and the strange, unrecognised noises of dockside and quays alerted his senses so that, despite his bodily exhaustion, his mind was in a state of heightened awareness. When he finally found sleep it brought no ease, for his mind was filled with restless images that spilled over into his dreams. Grief and guilt bedevilled him. The love and yearning he felt for Saranne burned hot within his flesh and he could not still it, nor hope for its consummation. No more could he still the conflict of emotions within him. Rage. Regret. Self-recrimination . . . they would not give him rest.

With the first glow of dawn, Carne gratefully rose and washed himself in the cold water set out for him and dressed himself in the seaman's clothing. The canvas trousers were stiffly uncomfortable and the clogs seemed to drag at his feet, making his movements clumsy and halting. Even should he be able to keep his balance at sea, he did not doubt that his leg muscles would ache with the weight of them. Resolutely, he placed the soft, broad-brimmed hat upon his thick dark hair, then hauled the canvas sack atop his shoulder.

As his hand fastened upon the knob of the door, there was an urgent knocking and coughing without and, for a moment he stood irresolute, unable to summon the courage to open it, lest a justice's warrant awaited him. Finally, his nerves taut, he inched the door open to reveal the spare, spry figure of a man of middle years, face brown and deep-grooved as a walnut. No justices' man, Carne decided with relief, but a sailor of sorts, weather-beaten, and honed lean by seafaring. Indeed, his visitor's clothing so ludicrously resembled Carne's own that, but for the fact that Carne was a good head and shoulders taller, and perhaps two stones heavier, they might have been images reflected in a glass. They stared at each other for a moment, unspeaking, Carne's mouth curving into an involuntary smile as he saw how tattered and well-worn was the man's clothing, the canvas trousers as wrinkled as their owner's face, and seemingly as aged. The sailor studied Carne with equal interest, his own face dissolving into humour as he took in the pristine newness of the boy's attire.

'Well, sir,' he said, grinning, and thrusting out a lean hand to grasp Carne's in its calloused palm. 'I fancy you will be more passenger than aid upon deck . . .'tis plain you are as much a sailor as I am the Duke of Wellington!'

'You will take me to Bristol, sir?' asked Carne, delighted.

'Upon your landlord's, Jed Priday's insistence that you are as honest and trustworthy as he.' The visitor's face wrinkled into good-natured laughter as he added, 'I'll own that, but for Jed's recommendation, I might have mistaken you for some snuff-box fancier, or Beau Brummel himself!' There was no rancour in his tone or expression, just honest amusement. 'I warn that 'tis not a clipper or a barque you will be boarding, but a ketch, with less space for ease than a lodging house bed!'

'And I am indebted to whom, sir, for my passage to Bristol?'

'To the owner and skipper of the *Bronwen*, sir . . . Harry Fox . . . at your service, Mr Grey.' He inclined his head fractionally and Carne, suppressing his immediate impulse to bow formally, inclined his head in return.

'I am in your debt, Captain Fox, sir.'

'Then we had best settle upon your fare, that you may rest easier in your mind,' suggested Fox, smiling expansively. The ridiculously low sum agreed, parted with, and pocketed with due ceremony, Carne's new master acknowledged gruffly, 'The fee and service are a courtesy, sir, a favour for a debt I owe to Jed.' He did not elaborate, but added, 'Since you are now both passenger and crew, Mr Grey, I will speak frankly, as is my right. I do not question your purpose in voyaging, sir; that is your own affair and, the less I know, the better it will please us both. May I suggest, however, that the clogs you wear, although suitable for labouring upon the dockside, will serve you ill on deck.' His lips twitched. 'I fear, Mr Grey, that should you accidentally stumble, we might find it hard to haul you aboard again, for the weight! Most deckhands go barefoot, their soles grown thicker than the planks they tread, but I fear, sir, as a gentleman, your own feet will betray you as remorselessly as your fine new clothing.' Seeing Carne's discomfiture, he added, more kindly, 'You would have fared better had you acquired clothing already well worn, although a little honest grime and sweat aboard will soon enough remedy that! As for your feet . . .' he said doubtfully, 'we will surely find something more suitable on board the *Bronwen*, else you will need to be bodily carried ashore at Bristol and set upon a horse, for you will be incapable of walking.'

Carne mumbled his gratitude, but Fox airily dismissed it, declaring with a smile, 'Believe me, Mr Grey, I speak from harsh experience. 'Tis trouble enough to find your land legs, without the vexation of blistered feet! I recall my first voyage as a cabin boy: I could have sworn my oath that when I came ashore, I walked upon burning cobbles doused in pitch!' He broke into good-natured laughter in which Carne soon joined. Then, hauling his canvas sack upon his shoulder again and setting it firm, Carne tipped the brim of his soft flat hat at an angle, like Captain Fox's, and followed him down the rickety staircase of the Travellers Rest, and out to the quayside.

Although early dawn was breaking and the morning air was chill, Carne did not feel the bite of it upon his skin as he followed his companion from the Travellers Rest. He was aware only of the fierce surge of exultation within him, the confusion of sights, noises and smells which quickened his senses. He thought that for all of his life he would remember this urgent activity about him, the mingled odours of the sea, the wharves heaped with cargoes, aromatic or as malodorous as the gleaming fish, bloodily gutted by the bonneted fishwives. Harry Fox, turning to glance at Carne, saw with amusement the fierce concentration upon the boy's rapt face, his gaze restlessly devouring the changing scenes.

'Cardiff is a small enough port, Mr Grey,' he said disparagingly, 'not a patch upon Bristol, for trade nor vessels: small smacks and ketches mostly, and Severn trows for coastal trade. They load and unload where they may, in creeks and small bays or natural harbours. You will not see the great square-rigged sailing ships here, the four-masted barques, the schooners brigs. There is nothing upon God's earth more pleasing to the eye than a full-rigged sailing ship. My ketch, the *Bronwen*, on the other hand, lays no claim to beauty,' he said by way of apology.

'It is not beauty which I seek, Captain Fox,' said Carne, unthinking, 'but a means of escape.' His embarrassment at the ease with which he had betrayed himself caused colour to flood his skin and he stumbled awkwardly, wooden soles clattering against the cobbled stones, before a clog wrenched itself adrift.

As he bent to retrieve it, Fox said quietly, 'Yes, you are right, Mr Grey. The sea offers escape to us all, whether we flee from ourselves or others. It is all things to all men . . . But one can never be free of it!' Fox shook his head, as if impatient with himself, to say indulgently, 'But you are young, Mr Grey, and would not understand.'

But I do understand, thought Carne. Am I not a prisoner, too? Of my past, and the life which formed me? Those shadows which, even as one believes them fled, return to haunt with memory and regret. Saranne, my father and Mostyn. Jane and Prys. Aloud, he said, smiling, 'I am not too young, Captain Fox, to feel the lure of the sea and the thrill and excitement and adventure. It is a new beginning. All is so strange and different here, new people, new sights. I have never before seen the sea, or even breathed in its smell. It is like nothing I have ever known!' He stood for a moment, transfixed with pleasure, breathing in the strange, tantalising odour of iodine, salt and wet sand and the pungent aroma of fruits, spices and fresh-caught fish mingled with tar, pine-resin and a host of other scents, subtle and indefinable.

Harry Fox, warmed by his companion's fervour, declared, 'The sea is a demanding mistress, Mr Grey, and I have felt the need for none other. She is fickle, capricious, a creature of moods . . . sometimes tender, sometimes cruel . . . but never dull or predictable. She is the love one always returns to at the end.' Even as he spoke, he was smiling and exchanging nods of greeting with the ropework-

252

ers, net menders and fishwives upon the quay, weathered face alight with pleasure. A contented man. 'And here,' he said, motioning towards a small, unprepossessing craft moored alongside, 'is the other woman in my life: the *Bronwen*.' He helped Carne clamber awkwardly aboard, feet heavy in his wooden-soled clogs, before making swift introduction to the crewmen who were intent on their tasks upon the battered ketch.

'Mr Grey has a fancy to help us sail,' declared Fox enigmatically. 'He would have you show him the ropes.'

One of the crew, an ancient with a grizzled beard and gnarled leathery skin, looked up swiftly, taking in Carne's pristine clothing and immaculate hands and hair before glancing down meaningfully at his own calloused, tar-stained palms. He spat over the side. 'Well,' he said with a good-natured grin, ''tis a poor sailor who would judge a craft by the beauty of her sails!' He tossed a rope towards Carne, who caught it deftly. 'We will see how you shape, young sir,' he chuckled mischievously. 'If all else fails, we can but hope to trade you as a figurehead.'

Carne was swift to lead the crew's appreciative laughter.

Mostyn regarded himself with approval in the looking glass, tweaking the frills of his shirt front into symmetry, studying himself critically from every angle, and not finding himself wanting in elegance or style. There was no denying that he was handsome. It was a fact which none could dispute. With his pure classical profile beneath the mass of artlessly disarranged curls, his fine figure and excellent complexion unpitted by smallpox scars or pox, he had a presence which commanded the eye.

What pleased him as much as his reflection was that he was once more free of debt. Laurel had cautioned that he must curb his passion for gaming and life's small luxuries. She would not, in future, lie for him. He smiled. Luxuries became with usage the barest of necessities. He had no doubt that his wildness and profligacy secretly excited her and she relished her small power in freeing him from debt, not realising that it was he who held true power. Laurel's obsession with him was a well which would not run dry, any more than her purse, for she would scheme and deceive endlessly to bind him to her. Yet he must take care not to overreach himself, for she was shrewd. There was, however, a wager with his companions which he must fulfil, despite the risks. It would give him the greatest satisfaction to carry it through and win. He turned from the looking glass with reluctance and went to seat himself at Carne's writing desk at the window, for he had demanded use of Carne's room from Penry Vaughan, keeping his own as a dressing room. Fastidiously flicking back his ruffed sleeve-cuffs, lest they be soiled by ink or the beeswaxed surface of the desk, he took some writing paper from a drawer, dipped his quill into the ink, and began to write. A light, secretive smile curved his lips. Yes, this was one wager it would please him to win.

Saranne had taken the byway to the beech copse, despite Sara's firm insistence that she stay at all times within sight and call of the farmhouse. Sara and Megan were engaged upon turning the vast cheeses in the dairy, a messy and delicate endeavour which demanded all their concentration. Jethro had driven the waggon into Penavon village upon some errand to the carpenter's yard and, not ten minutes since, Charles had set out upon his mare for Peter Morrish's cottage, bidding her ride with him if she would, for she would be assured of a welcome.

'No, Charles,' Saranne had put a hand to his arm in gentle acknowledgement, 'I am my own worst enemy, I know, and should not inflict myself upon you or others. I would not be fit company – I beg you will forgive me, and understand.'

Charles set a foot into the stirrup, swinging himself easily into the saddle, before leaning over to drop a brotherly kiss upon Saranne's dark hair. She held firm to the bridle, raising her head to nod at him, violet eyes warm with understanding.

254

'There is nothing in the world to understand or forgive, so there is an end to it!' he said gruffly as he gathered up the reins. Hesitating for a moment he added, 'You will be all right? You would not have me stay, keep you company? We could ride out to see Jane and Prys at Hillbrook, or walk the hills to Marged's cave?'

'No . . . it is better not. Tomorrow, perhaps.'

'You have heard that Mostyn Havard has been sent for by Jane, unbeknown to Prys?' he asked awkwardly. 'I heard Mama discuss it with Megan.'

'You think he will go?'

'No. It was Megan who delivered the message to him at Jane's behest, saying that she would be pleased to take back his answer. He spoke most curtly, bidding her be gone, for he wanted no truck with scullery maids or servants, past or present. He swore at her, it seems, claiming that Jane already had use of a cottage which was rightfully his, and must expect no more charity. Like Carne, she had made her own bed and must be prepared to lie on it without whining and importuning others.' At mention of Carne, Saranne's face had grown taut and Charles cursed himself for being so insensitive.

'I expect Jane was grieved,' she said quietly, 'and humiliated for the asking . . . and his refusal.'

'No doubt, although Megan softened it in the retelling. It seems he relented and threw some silver upon the stableyard but Megan turned upon her heel, and let it lie.' His hands fidgeted upon the reins as he blurted angrily, 'Mostyn Havard is a stupid, ignorant little coxcomb! I wish to God he had gone in Carne's stead!' Then, urging his horse away so violently that Saranne was forced to leap aside, he was away across the cobbles of the yard and out through the open gate of the farmyard without a backward glance. Later, his anger spent, he halted the mare beside the entrance to the highway, dismounting to still her trembling, a prey to shame and regret as he gripped the snaffle to soothe her lathered neck.

'There, my beauty,' he said, ''tis all over, and none of

your doing. Bide quiet now. I should not have vented my anger upon you, for you are undeserving of it.' His broad good-natured face was repentant, eyes concerned 'neath the thatch of copper-gold hair. ''Tis all over,' he repeated as the mare tossed her head restlessly above the high-arched neck and pawed the earth and fallen leaves, before quivering into calmness.

But for Saranne, he thought bleakly, it is not over. No more for Carne and me. Our lives are changed, and for the worse, and none can ease the truth of it. I should have told Saranne to take care, sent her back to the house. He remounted his mare and rode her slowly and with gentleness towards Myrtle Cottage. Saranne had always been a law unto herself, and did not take kindly to advice. Whatever he told her, she would go her own way, work out her own salvation at the last. She had been in a strange mood, Charles reflected uneasily, but perhaps no stranger or more violent than his own. One day, when Carne returned, as he surely would, Saranne's grief would be over, her problems solved – while his would continue. The farm had served many generations and would stand for many more, but he hated the shackles it forged upon him as deeply as he loved Jethro, Sara and Saranne.

Saranne, wandering through the familiar copse of beech and hazel trees with its overgrown paths and drifts of dry coppery leaves, was aware only of a sense of loss, a desolation. She had come here secretly, needing the salve of loneliness, and believing that she might feel nearer to Carne in some place whose isolation they had shared. Yet all was changed! Spring had given way to winter and she could no more regather the joyousness of their meeting than could those clusters of primroses flower again which had earlier bloomed upon the banks and woodland floor. She settled herself upon the fallen branch of a dead tree, its surface crusted with moss and lichens, her fingers absently tracing the curve of a tiny fern, its curled leaves struggling from a fissure in its coarse bark.

A rustling in the leaves and a snapping of dry twigs underfoot startled her and she sprang up fearfully to gaze in the direction from which the noises came. Her nerves were tense as she awaited sight of the intruder. She hesitated indecisively, uncertain whether to flee. Stronger than her apprehension was a cold rage that a stranger should come blundering into her special secret place. It was untenable; an intrusion she could not allow. Fiercely she stood her ground and waited. The sigh she let fall was sign of her relief as she recognised Tom Hallowes, booted feet shuffling amidst the dried leaves, bones gnarled and twisted as the blackthorn all about.

'Tom!' she called. 'There is something amiss at the farm? You have come seeking me?'

He paused beside her, shuffling, ill-at-ease, his creased face unhappy. 'No, Saranne.' He hesitated. 'I have not been sent. I have come of my own free will, thinking I might find you here. 'Twas always here you ran to when life was hard.'

'You always knew where I would be hiding,' she admitted, linking her arm with his under his frayed coat sleeve, 'and were sure to guide me back in a mood more kindly. Charles always teased that you kept a special magic in your coat; a charm to make me smile against my will. I am glad you came searching me out, as of old, Tom. I could bear no other company.'

'Miss Saranne.' He halted, awkward and distressed, and Saranne felt a sense of unease to match his own, a feeling of foreboding.

'What is it, Tom? Something has alarmed you? I beg you will tell me, else I shall have no peace.'

'I have a message for you,' he confessed, 'and I do not know if I shall do harm in delivering it to you. I would not deceive Jethro and Sara or do them ill,' he finished.

'A message? A letter, do you mean? A note?'

Hallowes nodded, unspeaking.

For a moment she was filled with a wild hope that it came from Carne. 'This note, Tom. Who delivered it to you? How did you come by it?'

'It was set into my hands by three young gentlemen, strangers, their faces unknown to me. They stopped me upon the byway to the farm, where they had been lying in wait. They asked that I deliver it to you, and no other, nor speak of it to any.'

'These gentlemen,' she asked sharply, 'they did not threaten you or seek to do you harm?'

'No, although I do not mind confessing that I thought their presence boded no good. Well dressed, they were, and spoke with that insolence affected by some gentlemen towards those they consider to be their inferiors.'

'Yes, Tom, I have seen such arrogance in so-called gentlemen,' she confessed wryly, 'but you are sure that they spoke of me by name?'

'Yes, Miss Saranne. I could not mistake it, although my heart was thudding at my ribs, and my every instinct was to run to the farm and alert your father and young Charles, lest they meant you harm. I have not told Jethro,' he said wretchedly, 'although I am sick at heart for deceiving him.'

'You recollect the exact words they used, Tom?'

'They gave me a shilling, Miss, for my pains, declaring that it held news of one you were seeking. But if I told another, then you would never learn his whereabouts or fate,' he said simply. 'I could not deny you that, for I knew well enough of whom they spoke. Master Carne . . .'

'The note, Tom,' she ordered quietly. 'Give me the note.'

'Oh, Miss Saranne!' he exclaimed despairingly, 'I do not know if what I do is right, or if evil may come from it! It will near break my heart if they mean you harm.'

'As it will break mine, Tom, if you deny me sight of it.'

He stared at her helplessly, then produced it from the ragged lining of his coat saying, as he thrust it into her hand, 'There! I have done what was asked of me, and out of affection for you. I pray God I have not done wrong.'

Saranne opened the note, afraid almost to read the words penned upon it. The message was curt and unsigned: 'Miss Hartrey, I have news of him. Meet me within the beechwood tomorrow eve at six o'clock.'

Tom Hallowes, alarmed by Saranne's stillness and the pallor of her face, asked solicitously, 'It is a message about Master Carne? You would have me fetch your mother to you, or Megan?'

'No, Tom. It is naught but a stupid prank; a foolishness by those who should know better. Not worth the expense of the paper which it is scrawled upon!' She tore it into useless shreds and scattered them, declaring, 'There! Let that be an end to such nonsense! It is all it deserves!'

He was not convinced.

'A childish rhyme,' she continued lightly, 'verses from some lovesick young jackanapes who had seen me passing by in the waggon with Papa. I would as soon he learnt naught about it, Tom, for he would seek them out in a rage, and give the affair more weight than such foolishness deserves.' When he made no reply she said gaily, 'Come, let us return to the farm and I will pour us both a measure of shot.'

He hesitated, then walked beside her, his footsteps slow.

'These young gentlemen, Tom? How did they leave? On foot?'

'No, Miss Saranne, their mounts were cropping nearby, tethered to the trees. Fine horses all, and with extravagantly tooled saddles. Gentlemen of means, certainly, yet I could not bring myself to trust them. I was glad, I confess, when they rode away.'

'They said nothing more in parting?'

'One, more arrogant than the rest, called out, "Deliver the message, ancient, else, when I return, you will feel the full sting of my whip, and you may thank God that you are an ignorant peasant and unable to read. Otherwise you would be poorer by a shilling." ' Hallowes flushed. ''Tis you who are ignorant, sir, for all you are a gentleman! I called out after him but I think the wind must have carried my words away, for he did not falter or reply.'

He turned his head away that Saranne might not see his wretchedness and shame.

'It was well said, Tom,' she said gently, 'and with the dignity of a real gentleman, not counterfeits like them. I'll wager my all that he heard, but was too craven to return!'

'Perhaps, Miss Saranne. Perhaps,' he conceded, voice low.

Chapter Twenty-four

Carne's first glimpse of the great, bustling seaport of Bristol was burned into his memory as indelibly as a brand mark seared upon flesh. He was never to forget it. There was such a confusion of things to hear, see and savour that he abandoned all efforts to separate them, content simply to breathe in the tantalising essence of the whole.

'You will be eager to step ashore, Mr Grey,' Captain Fox's voice intoned on his reverie.

Carne turned abruptly. 'No, sir. I shall be eager to set sail again as soon as I am able.'

His gaze returned to the great sailing ships in the waters beyond, the graceful three-masted schooners, the barques and the barquentines, sails proud. 'Do you not miss it, Captain Fox, sir?' he exclaimed impulsively, his young face alight with enthusiasm. 'The excitement of adventure, of sail? I can scarce wait to feel the sea-winds upon my face and hear the sounds of the canvas.'

Fox's weathered face was amused as he added drily, 'And the lashing of hail and storm, with the skin flayed raw by wet hemp and labour? No, Mr Grey. I would as soon end my days upon the *Bronwen*. 'Tis the same with ships and boats as with women. When a man is old, he will settle for a familiar comfort rather than beauty. It brings less grief.'

Fox's swift smile creased his leathery skin, settling deep grooves from nose to mouth and a myriad of tiny lines upon his cheeks. Yet his eyes remained expressionless and he was aware that he had deceived neither Carne nor himself. There was a momentary awkwardness. 'Heave to, Mr

Grey,' he ordered curtly. 'We are about to make fast and you must learn to look sharp if we are to make a seaman of you!'

Fox turned away abruptly with shouted commands to the crew and Carne's energies and thoughts were lost in the disciplined clamour of tying up and unloading the *Bronwen*'s cargo upon the wharf amidst the moored sailing ships drying their sails.

The cargo unloaded and formalities completed, Carne made to take his leave of Captain Fox, finding him among the clutter of horses and waggons and the waiting carriages alongside St Augustine's Wharf.

'I will bid you farewell, sir, and offer you my gratitude for your kindness in setting me upon the first leg of my journey.' Carne surrendered his canvas sack to the cobblestones and offered his hand cordially to Fox, with a bow of acknowledgement.

'No kindness, Mr Grey. A matter of business conducted to our mutual satisfaction, sir.' Fox smiled disarmingly. 'If you will permit it, I shall deliver you to whomsoever you seek.' His keen eyes were warm with understanding sympathy. 'Your business is your own, sir, as the *Bronwen* is mine. I seek neither to interfere nor probe.'

'Then I accept with gratitude, Captain Fox.'

'We will eat first, Mr Grey. It is wiser so for, whatever befalls, 'tis more easily met upon a full stomach. It is a truth I early learnt, and I have never found cause to alter my opinion.' He set off at a swift pace, with Carne, burdened with his canvas sack, shuffling manfully to keep within distance of him as Fox wove and bobbed his way expertly along the heaped wharves and dock basin. The port seemed to run deep into the heart of the city, the quaysides bordered with iron posts and chains, linked at intervals by small bridges, gently arched, or set upon squat pillars of stone. On either side lay tall elegant buildings; dwelling houses and the offices of merchants, bankers and ship owners interspersed with an occasional church, square-turreted, or with a tapering, needle-point spire. To Carne's surprise, the daily life of the people of the city and commerce seemed to exist side by side as amicably as the water and highways, each lending the other a charm and unexpectedness enhanced by the towering masts of the sailing ships, their rigging a delicate tracery against the heaped cargoes and solid masonry beyond.

Fox halted briefly beside a dock basin to watch the progress of a schooner being towed to her moorings, her cargo of salted cod pungent in the cool air and blending with scents of tobacco, spices and heaped fruit, as well as the iodine tang of the sea and the animal odour of horse sweat and droppings from the stables beyond.

'*Newfoundland Trader*,' observed Fox, jerking his head towards the slow-moving ship as Carne came to stand beside him, grateful for the respite and for the brief opportunity to divest himself of the canvas sack.

'A handsome vessel,' ventured Carne, knowing a verdict was expected of him. 'Though I know little of ships or sailing, Captain Fox,' he admitted sheepishly, 'save theory learnt from my tutor, and a master mariner.' Then, aware from Fox's expression that he had revealed too much, he added quickly, 'But I am most eager and willing to learn, sir.'

'If you will take some advice well meant, Mr Grey; say nothing of those lessons you have learnt to others of the crew. It will serve but to aggravate, and tell against you. You will be the butt of cruelty and ill-humour, you understand?'

'No, sir. I cannot say that I do,' confessed Carne, 'but I will take your advice, for I know it to be sound, and born of experience.'

'You will be the lowest of the low aboard, Mr Grey. 'Tis the order of things, and you will do well to accept it first as last. Keep a cool head and your own counsel.' He hesitated, as if weighing his words carefully. 'I know you are a gentleman by birth, sir, and that clothing you wear cannot make you a common sailor any more than a crown could make a hog a king!'

263

Carne's instinctive laughter died as he saw the earnestness of Fox's expression, for he had no wish to offend him.

'Believe me, Mr Grey, you will do well to keep your learning well hid,' Fox repeated. 'Pretend ignorance and there are those who will help you, for there is no man on earth reluctant to belittle another by a show of his own superiority. 'Tis the way of things, with animals as well as men. They will run with the herd. It can render them brutish, and they will fight and kill if the need arise to prove their leadership.'

'I will take your advice, sir, and be circumspect,' said Carne quietly.

'It will be to your advantage.' Fox bent and lifted Carne's sack from the stones and delivered it to him, saying gruffly, 'If I have made the life sound hard, and the men callous, it is because I have learnt by my own errors that it is prudent to be cautious.' He watched Carne steady the canvas upon his shoulder before walking on. 'It can be a hard, demanding life, Mr Grey, and one to make you curse and rage with the pain in your limbs, and the loneliness, for all that there are men about you. But, at the end, it will make a better man of you than at the start, if you will let it. There is not a moment of it, good or bad, I would not relive if I had the chance, for all I revile and deny it.'

Carne said awkwardly, 'I am grateful for your confidence, sir, it is not always easy to confide the truth to a stranger.'

'But easier, perhaps, than to one who knows you, and must deny the knowledge after,' added Fox.

They strolled together through the crowded port; a rich kaleidoscope of swift-changing colour and pattern, with Fox offering and returning greetings with cordial good humour to those thronging the quaysides and identifying for Carne the vessels of interest, their routes and their cargoes, the names of the places to which they were bound which were as strangely poetic as the great sailing ships themselves: Valparaiso, Cape Horn, The Americas, The Indies. There was a rhythm and a splendour in their names and cargoes. Iron ore from Bilbao, pit props from

Scandinavia, coffee beans from Brazil, tea from the Orient, bales of cotton and tobacco from North America, coal and minerals, comestibles, bolts of silk and coloured cottons everywhere piled high and jewel-bright. While all around went on the making and mending, the clearing and cleaning, the ceaseless burden of everyday toil. Carne's eyes and ears were sated with the newness and variety of it all, so that the shops of the carpenters and the blacksmiths, the chandlers and the foundry, the stables and the wheelwrights, the sail lofts and the rope walks blurred and grew indistinguishable one from the other.

'We are here, Mr Grey. It is a small tavern with little to recommend it, save good ale and simple fare aplenty. Best eat well, sir, for you will not taste its like when you are under sail, God help you! It will be hard tack then and brackish water to sustain you, with weevils and maggots, and brown rats in the bilges for company.'

'Then I must make the most of yours, sir, while good fortune prospers,' said Carne, 'for who knows when I may again dine in such refined and salubrious company!'

Fox's bellow of laughter accompanied them within, eliciting swift smiles and greetings from those seated, and a hearty welcome from the landlord, a tall, gangling fellow, whose leanness was in inverse proportion to the richness and variety of his fare.

It was with reluctance that Carne finally emptied his jug of ale and set it aside, and Fox doused his clay pipe of tobacco. They arose to be about their tasks and Carne retrieved his canvas sack from beneath the table.

'Mr Fox,' he said haltingly, 'I should be glad of your considered opinion, sir . . .'

'Then you may have it,' declared Fox jovially. 'What is it you would have me decide?'

'This gentleman whom I am to meet, to proffer my letter of introduction . . . Should I change into formal clothes, sir, do you suppose, or greet him as I am?'

'This gentleman,' asked Fox, 'he is a stranger to you, Mr Grey?'

265

'Yes, sir. I present a letter of credence from a friend, an attorney-at-law, in the confidence that he will find me a place aboard a ship of his line.'

'Indeed?' Fox took Carne's elbow and carefully guided him through the crowded table and chairs of the tavern into the fresh air, before asking quietly, 'And the name of this unknown benefactor, sir?'

Carne's hesitation was so fractional that he hoped Captain Fox was unaware of it. His voice was firm as he replied, 'Sir Robert Crandon.'

'Crandon?' It was both question and exclamation. 'Then you move in august company, Mr Grey!'

'You know him, sir?' Carne demanded eagerly.

'Of him,' corrected Fox, adding with humour. 'He is a gentleman with sights set higher than the captain of the *Bronwen*, I declare. It is not a mere shipping line he owns, Mr Grey, more a fleet!'

'Then I should dress accordingly to greet him, sir?'

'I think it unlikely that he will be personally involved, Mr Grey.' Captain Fox's eyes were kind, yet there was something in his tone which did not accord. 'No doubt it will be one of his minions you will see, some shore-based clerk, anonymous and unknown to his employer. One, perhaps, who would begrudge you ease of access to those in authority, and the fact that you are a gentleman. No, Mr Grey, present the letter by all means, but do not wear your fine clothes. It will but serve to accentuate the differences between you, and lend malice to resentment.'

'I thank you, Mr Fox,' said Carne with sincerity. 'I confess that all is new and strange to me, and I have need of your counsel. You will accompany me to the shipping offices, sir? I should be glad of the support and company of a friend, if it will not discommode you too greatly.'

'No, Mr Grey. It will be my pleasure.'

Carne fell into step beside him and they walked in silence for a while.

Eventually, Fox lingered for a moment, gazing about him indecisively, before striding across the quayside and towards a high, narrow building with mullioned windows flanking a squat, splendidly becolumned edifice of stone, not unlike a Greek temple. Carne, hurrying to keep up with him, heard Fox murmur, so low that the words were barely audible, 'I have done as you asked, Mr Grey, and brought you here.'

'You will not accompany me within, Captain Fox?'

'No, sir, for I must return to load the *Bronwen* and sail the tide.' He hesitated before saying unexpectedly, 'You are welcome to return with me, Mr Grey, and face whatever it is that bedevils you and drives you away. You will be forced to it at the last.'

Carne did not pretend to misunderstand, but replied simply, 'I cannot.'

Captain Fox scrutinised Carne's face carefully, then nodded slowly, 'I bid you be cautious then for sometimes, in our haste, we flee from a known danger to a greater one unbeknown.' He held out a raw-boned hand, its skin as minutely wrinkled and weathered as his face, and Carne, releasing his sack, took Fox's hand in his own firm grasp. 'I know that you are a young gentleman, and to be trusted,' Captain Fox said quietly. 'If you choose, I will willingly return with you from whence you fled, and speak out on your behalf.'

Carne's grip tightened upon Fox's hand. 'I thank you, Captain Fox, sir, but there can be no return,' he said with finality. 'I do not doubt that we will meet again, as friends, in kinder times. I shall make it my pleasure to seek you out. Where shall I find you?'

'You have but to ask for the *Bronwen*. Wherever she is moored, there I will be while the good Lord sees fit to give me breath.' He smiled. 'She is all I own, Mr Grey, or, perhaps, 'tis truer she owns me.'

Carne watched Fox go with an ache of regret and, as he turned aside, Fox turned, calling out, 'I said I did not envy you, Mr Grey. I was wrong. I envy you your youth, the future, and the sea. It will be an adventure such as you have never known. Make good use of it.'

'I will, sir.' Carne's voice was confident, brave with the arrogance of the young.

It was Captain Fox, then, who paused and gazed after him. May God go with you. He did not speak the words aloud but continued soberly upon his way, reflecting. You might have sore need of Him, my friend, before your journey's end.

'I think, Mama, that I shall go for a small stroll,' Saranne was busily tying a bonnet over her dark hair and taking her cloak, 'as far as the farm gate, perhaps, since the table is laid and the soup will not spoil.'

Sara fought down her impatience, demanding tersely, 'What can you hope to see? Already it grows dusk.' Then, conscious of Saranne's hurt expression and of her own unfairness, she added, seeking to make amends, 'A quarter of an hour, then, no more, else supper will be spoilt.'

Sara glanced towards Jethro and Charles but neither made demur, seemingly too absorbed in the farm accounts to show interest or raise objection.

'You had best take a lantern,' insisted Sara.

'To the gate, Mama?' Saranne would have argued but seeing the implacable obstinacy upon her mother's face, merely nodded, lest she be forbidden from leaving altogether.

'The cobblestones in the yard are uneven,' murmured Sara, 'besides, who knows what strangers might be abroad. You would do well to heed me.'

'I shall take a lantern, Mama,' said Saranne, stifling her irritation, 'and see that I step in neither cow-pat nor puddle, if it pleases you. And if anyone seeks to abduct me and hold me to ransom, I shall go willingly, and save Papa the expense, for I think that I shall not be too grievously missed.' Sara was not able to hide a smile as Saranne glanced meaningfully towards Jethro and Charles, absorbed in their discussion. 'I have been neither use nor ornament of late,' Saranne confessed, her voice low. There was an underlying poignancy in her appeal to Sara to deny it, as of old.

'I would not change you.' Sara's reassurance was swift and without reserve.

With her hand upon the latch of the door, Saranne turned abruptly. 'Mama?'

'Yes, my dear?' Sara had started towards her, alerted by some strangeness in her tone, but Saranne, face shadowed by the brim of her bonnet and the dimness of the flickering candlelight, had already moved out into the yard. It was with a sense of unease that Sara watched through the leaded casement the girl's progress towards the farm gate, the lantern bobbing and weaving, settling a dancing arc of light about Saranne's slight figure. She turned impulsively towards Jethro to tell him of her fears, but the words died unspoken, for she could not have explained, even to herself, why she was filled with such dread. She moved to the fireside and busied herself with stirring the soup in the iron pot suspended from a crane-jack above the fire. Against the firelight, her hair glowed like burnished gold and copper, and her skin grew warmly flushed with heat. Yet within her there was only coldness, too deep to reach.

In that eerie strangeness of half-light which precedes dusk, Saranne's lantern was of little use to illumine her way. She would have snuffed out the candle within, but dared not, for she was aware of Sara's unseen presence at the casement, anxiously watching, waiting.

Fearful that she might be called back, or that Charles might take it into his head to accompany her, she forced herself to walk to the farmyard gate at a leisurely pace, although her every instinct was to hurry to the beech grove and learn news of Carne. She placed the lantern atop the wooden jamb of the gatepost and eased the gate open as quietly as she was able. Its jarring creak upon its hinges seemed to rip through the silence, setting her teeth and nerves upon edge, and she half expected a cry from the house to halt her, but none came. With a sigh of relief and

269

apprehension, she slipped through the narrow gap and into the byway. Then, closing the gate carefully behind her, she retrieved the lantern. The farmhouse was soon hidden from view.

The high pleached hedges enclosed her on either side and the branches of the ancient trees, with their last remaining leaves, formed a tracery overhead, so that she could have believed that she moved through some desolate, long-ruined church, its rafters laid bare to the sky, its windows broken stone. Yet there was neither peace nor silence here, nor the ghosts of things past. The sounds were of things real and living: the movement of small creatures scrabbling and hurrying to hide, the sigh of branches, the crack of twigs underfoot, the far-off screech of an owl filling her with sudden terror. She hurried on, grateful now for the lantern glow, although it seemed but to distort and darken the shadowy shapes of trees, so that their black trunks seemed to menace her above their gnarled roots, like shapeless bodies, their branches grotesquely twisted limbs, fingers outstretched to grasp her. The protruding stems of bramble and blackthorn ripped at her cloak and skirts, so that she tore herself free, too terrified to halt, yet fearful to go on, her small bewildered cries an echo of the sounds all about her. The raised boles of the sycamores were eye sockets, the eyes within watching her every movement, the excrescences upon their cracked barks, hideous disfigurement upon the desiccated flesh. What she did not see, she imagined, and her imaginings were grosser and more terrifying than any known threat.

With a scream, Saranne fled towards the beechwoods, believing, even as she ran, that she heard the crashing of footsteps behind her, as if something, or someone, stalked her relentlessly, observing her terror, but content to await the claiming of its prey.

In the clearing in the beechwoods, Saranne raised her lantern nervously, seeing only the smooth trunks, silvered in light. It was, she felt certain, past six o' the clock, and she wondered uneasily whether summoning her here had been no more than a cruel jest, or if her unknown informant had grown weary of waiting and hurried away.

She would willingly have done likewise, but the need to know that Carne was safe overrode her apprehension, and kept her rooted to where she stood in the mossy clearing with its ferny floor. She must wait, she counselled herself sternly, or all would be for naught. Yet she knew that she could not tarry overlong, lest Sara grow impatient, and send Charles or her father in pursuit.

A sudden stirring of the fallen leaves, deep in the copse, alerted her with a crackling underfoot and the impatient snapping of twigs that perhaps barred the way. Saranne's mouth ran dry, and the thudding of her heart was so violent in her breast that she heard the sound of it filling her ears, and felt the pulse of its throbbing at her throat. She almost cried out in fear, but did not move, biting her lip for sheer terror until she could taste the salt of blood upon her tongue. The figure that emerged into the clearing was that of a man, she felt sure, yet, even with the lantern held high, she could not discern his face, only that he was darkly cloaked and wore a high silk hat in the manner of a gentleman. She could give no word of acknowledgement or greeting, for her tongue cleft drily to the roof of her mouth, and she was as incapable of speech as of movement, her limbs useless, even to flee. She saw in the lantern beams only the fluttering of moths and small insects, driven by some inborn urge for self-destruction. The lantern shook in her grasp as the stranger's gloved hand reached out and, with deliberation, took it from her, raising it high to illumine his face. It was then that she knew she had just cause to fear him.

271

Chapter Twenty-five

'I see, ma'am, that you recognise me.' The intruder's bow was slight, his tone insolently mocking. 'Pray do not remove yourself so far from me. Stand closer. It is my wish that we become better acquainted.'

'Then it is not mine, sir! I warn you, keep your distance!'

Saranne raised the lantern high, and would have brought it crashing down upon him had he not retreated.

He surveyed her with a smile of derision, removing his gloves with affected languor, and then his silk hat, placing the gloves within. 'It is not fitting that my head be covered in the presence of . . .' he paused, '. . . a lady.' His mouth twitched with wry amusement.

'A gentleman, sir, would not need to explain his actions to another! Courtesy would be natural to him. He would be incapable of boorishness.'

In the lantern beams, Mostyn's carefully disordered curls shone pale. His full girlish lips had grown petulant, but his voice was coolly controlled as he asked, 'And how, ma'am, would a pauper and common labourer upon the soil learn of the polite arts and social mores?'

'From others, sir,' Saranne's reply was swift and incisive. 'From gentlemen of true quality, who need no uniform to prove their status to others.'

'Damn it, ma'am!' Mostyn flushed. 'Do you try to teach me my manners?'

'No, sir,' Saranne's voice was dismissive. 'If years of patient schooling have failed, 'tis my opinion it would be time and effort wasted. A true gentleman is born, not made!' She gathered up her skirts in her free hand and, lowering the lantern, turned to take her leave.

'Stay!' Mostyn's hand reached out to grasp her wrist and the lantern swayed and shuddered, the candle guttering as she fought to escape his fingers' hard grip. She was in terror that the candle flame might die and she be left with him in darkness. Mostyn had hurled his silk hat and gloves to the earth to free his hand, the better to secure her, but fury and panic made Saranne wrench herself free, her nails raking his cheek with drops of blood.

'Vixen! Bitch!' Surprise made Mostyn draw back, his fingers straying to his pained flesh, eyes wide with disbelief as he gazed at the smeared blood. Saranne should have run then, but her shock was so intense that her brain seemed as numbed and useless as her limbs.

'You promised me news of Carne,' she said dully. 'It was why I came. It was naught but a lie, a cruel jest to deceive me.'

'No! You are wrong!' he said viciously. 'You shall have the news you seek! He is a near-murderer! A common criminal with a price upon his head! He will be hunted down, and when he can run no more, he will be strung from a gibbet until his flesh rots, his bones picked clean by carrion crow and rat!'

'That would be no worse a betrayal than your own,' declared Saranne scathingly, 'for who but filthy carrion could find pleasure in the death of one of its own?' She was aware that Mostyn was glancing restlessly all about him, his face venomous, but her contempt for him killed all discretion. 'You have battened upon him, and others, all of your life!' she accused. 'He is well rid of you, for you would have bled him dry!'

'Hell and damnation! I will have no more of this!' Mostyn strode forward, hand raised, and struck her a blow across her cheek which sent her stumbling to her knees, the lantern flying from her hand. 'You dare to lecture *me* about kinship and breeding! The whelp of God knows what filthy coupling . . . Carne's whore!'

Terrified, Saranne had turned to flee, stumbling awkwardly through bracken and thorn, for she dared not pause to gather the lantern from where it lay. In an instant, he was upon her, wrestling, struggling, throwing her to the ground, the thin beams of the lantern showing his pale face contorted with a hatred close to madness.

Saranne was weeping now, struggling furiously to throw off his weight and the fierce bones of his fingers which drove into her flesh. Kicking, raging, praying aloud, she fought, but to no avail, for he was possessed with a madness of rage and lust for revenge.

'I *will* take you!' His eyes were wild, his face a pale blur above Saranne's. 'I have made a wager upon it, and must win!'

There was a noise of laughter and a crashing in the undergrowth beyond, as, weak with terror and despair, Saranne glimpsed three others of his kind emerging from the shelter of the trees, concealed lanterns brought from the protection of their dark cloaks and held aloft, their leering faces grotesque masks in the glow. Then she could see no more as Mostyn's engorged lips pressed triumphantly over her own, fingers pressing hard into her breast and the full weight of his flesh upon hers a torment.

'Dear God in heaven,' she wept aloud. 'Help me! Help me!'

She was no longer aware of the coarse mocking laughter of Mostyn's friends, their crude encouragement, nor of the grins of lasciviousness upon their faces – Saranne knew only that she must fight with every nerve of her body and her dying strength to be free of the obscenity of being raped by him. She would kill him if need be.

There was a sudden violent explosion of sound and fury as Mostyn was torn from her, and a flurry of furious blows and curses, screams and thuds. Dazed and petrified by the fury of the attack, Saranne cowered where she lay, neither knowing nor caring to whom, or to what, she owed her deliverance. She did not know how long the fight continued all about her, as she wept and shook in a terror greater than any she had known.

Then Charles was lifting her from the earth, holding her close, soothing and protecting her as of old, and wiping the tears from her cheeks with gentle fingers. Saranne put her hand to her hair, knowing that her bonnet was lost, as was her cloak, and that the bodice of her dress had been ripped away to expose pale flesh. Charles covered her with his jacket and, when she finally dared to raise her head from the comfort of her brother's shoulder, it was to see in the beams of the lantern in Tom Hallowes' gnarled hand, Mostyn's bruised and bloodied face, sullen with hatred, as Jethro held his coat collar in his vice-like grip. Two of his companions, their faces ravaged, and with clothes disordered as Mostyn's own, were struggling with difficulty to their feet, their groans and sighs a measure of the punishment they had taken. The fourth of their company, barely conscious, was trying to inch himself painfully, on his belly, across the clearing and into the haven of the copse beyond.

Jethro spat the words at Mostyn, face contorted with such blind rage that Saranne was chilled. 'You are scum and filth! Too low and brutal to be called animals, for none would show such savagery! You are a gutless, cowardly pack, unwilling to pit yourselves against men! Fit only to terrorise and prey upon defenceless women!'

'I will set the law upon you,' Mostyn blustered, trying to wrench himself free of Jethro's grasp. 'Let me go, I say, or you will rue it, I swear! I have friends in high places.'

'Friends in high places?' Jethro's voice was the more menacing for now being calm. 'Then I caution you that you think well before you lay complaint. And if you persist, then, as God is my judge, I will hunt you down as remorselessly as I would track any blood-crazed fox, each and every one of you, and kill you with as little regret!'

Mostyn, unable to retrieve his pride and dominance before his peers, protested childishly, 'Let go my collar! I am not frightened of your stupid threats. It was naught but a stupid jape, a jest in high spirits. The girl was willing, and ready. She spurred us on!'

Jethro released Mostyn, only to strike him so fiercely across his mouth that Mostyn reeled and would have fallen, had not a companion steadied him, counselling awkwardly, 'It is best we leave, Mostyn.'

Mostyn stood indecisively, blood reddening his lips and running from the corner of his mouth, only to cry furiously as he wiped a hand to stem the flow, 'We will go, but not at your command! We go because we are finished here. That is all.'

'No! That is not all!' Jethro's voice was harsh. 'You will make your apologies to the one you have wronged, my daughter. You will beg her forgiveness most humbly for the vileness forced upon her. And if you do not, then, upon my oath, I vow that you will never more utter a single word!'

Mostyn stood defiantly apart, although two of his chastened companions had raised the third of their number unsteadily to his feet and were awkwardly supporting him. Cowed and shamefaced, they made apology, eyes downcast, unwilling to raise their heads to meet Saranne's eyes.

'Let them go,' ordered Jethro curtly to Tom Hallowes who would have barred their way.

Tom fell back obediently, calling out as they limped sheepishly away, 'If you seek your mounts, they are no longer tethered. I have set them free, for they have the good sense to return from whence they came. They will not venture here again. You would do well to heed their example!'

Lest they demur, Jethro's warning was absolute. 'Should you ever attempt to molest my daughter, or harm or threaten any upon my land or in my employ, then my gun will make answer!'

Mostyn had sidled away, and would have slunk after his companions unobserved, but Jethro said implacably, 'Your apology, Havard! Before I give you leave to go.'

Fuming at being so addressed by a mere farmer, yet reluctant to take further punishment, Mostyn moved towards Saranne, but, seeing her terror, Charles halted him, declaring, 'Stay where you are, Havard! Come no nearer . . . and say what must be said. It would please me to knock you to your knees and watch you beg! You are a whimpering bully and a brute. A posturing, pathetic little peacock, all show, and no spirit or sense. For all Carne's loyalty to you, you are not fitted to breathe the same air as he. I fear for your life, should he return!' He drew Saranne protectively into the shelter of his arms.

Mostyn's face was tight with suppressed anger, his eyes aglitter with resentment as he spat out the words as if they choked him, 'My apologies, ma'am. I trust you will accept them.'

Saranne crept from the shelter of her brother's arm to face Mostyn fearlessly, her voice as hard as the expression in her eyes. 'I will neither forgive nor forget. There will be a reckoning and the price will be high, and paid in full! I swear it on all I hold most dear!'

Mostyn shrugged and attempted a derisive smile which did not quite reach his eyes. He was more shaken than he cared to admit by Saranne's threat, for he knew that it was not idly made. To hide his unease and the strange sense of foreboding which so disturbed him, he bent with seeming nonchalance to take up a discarded lantern from the ground, and thence to retrieve his silk hat and gloves from nearby, replacing them with insulting fastidiousness before bowing and taking his leave.

'We should not have let him go,' said Tom Hallowes with quiet conviction, 'we should have killed him. He is an animal, and an animal allowed to savage and go free will always return.'

'No!' declared Jethro bleakly. 'It would not do to go to the gallows for him. He is not worth the sacrifice of one single life. He has learnt his lesson.' He turned to Saranne. 'And you, Miss? Have you learned yours? The price of your deceit and folly?'

'Oh, Papa! Papa!' She ran to him despairingly, and buried her face in his waistcoat. Jethro patted her dark hair helplessly, the tears in his eyes as fiercely burning as Saranne's. He knew that if he had lost her in death, or had she been defiled by such brutes, then he would have killed them without remorse, every last one.

'What will Mama say?' Saranne's voice was scarcely more than a whisper. 'She will say I am wicked and heedless,' she answered herself, 'and so I am . . . So I am.'

'We had best be off home . . . and you with us, Tom,' said Jethro gruffly, 'for you are deserving of Sara's thanks, as well as my own. I thank God that you had the wisdom to tell me of what you knew.'

Tom Hallowes nodded, and fell into step beside Charles and Jethro, his arm still about Saranne's shoulders as he led her gently home.

Sara, forewarned of the purpose of the quest, and seeing with sick horror the extent of Saranne's hurt and the injuries inflicted upon her three protectors, hugged her daughter close, drying her tears. 'A good night's work you have made of it, Miss!' she said briskly to hide her distress. 'It is as well that you took the lantern, and that Tom, at least, had the good sense to confide his fears. Seat yourself at the table, Tom, and share our meal, for that is owed to you, and more, as Saranne will own when she recovers her manners. You, Miss,' she instructed Saranne, 'make yourself clean at the washbowl and jug, and change your gown.'

Saranne went silently and did as her mother bade. Sara's eyes met Jethro's in terrified alarm, the question that bedevilled her unspoken.

Jethro shook his head. 'She is unharmed, save for the bruises to her flesh and pride,' he said quietly, knowing how nearly Saranne's body had been violated, and her innocence lost.

Sara's voice was taut with fear, 'And those who attacked her? Were they known to you, Jethro?'

'No.' His denial was firm, and none contradicted him.

'She is a wickedly heedless girl!' cried Sara, banging the pot of hot soup upon the scrubbed table with a fierceness that sent a shudder through flesh, bowls and spoons alike.

'Saranne cares for nothing and no-one! She will see me to an early grave! It comes of you spoiling and indulging her, Jethro! You have made a rod for your own back, and for mine!'

'Hush, my dear, 'tis all right now; she is safely home. Do not take on so!'

But Sara would not be pacified, crying, 'And where is her new bonnet? We are not made of money! Bonnets do not grow on trees!'

'Nor daughters, my love,' reminded Jethro as, with understanding, he rose to stand beside his wife, an arm about her rigid shoulders.

Mostyn was deeply humiliated. He had been made to look ridiculous before his cronies, and smarted from the shame of it. Not only did his companions show scant sympathy for his injured pride and face, they insisted he honour his wager in full, and at once, as if he were some common street-jack who might abscond, and not a gentleman of honour. It left him feeling cheapened and demeaned, but he had paid upon the nail, although it had near beggared him, and further increased his resentment towards Saranne and those cloddish oafs of yeomen whom Carne had chosen to befriend. Mostyn's only consolation was that he had branded the Hartrey chit 'whore' and 'bitch' before his peers, although, to his chagrin, Danfield, whom he most admired and strove to emulate had declared scathingly, 'You are a fool, Havard. No fox hunts close to his lair, but has the sense to strike farther afield. It is a rule of the game! You had best heed it.'

'What harm has it done, save to fetch us a few taunts and bruises? You are lacking in humour, sir!' Mostyn had declared, aggrieved.

'I see no humour in such a sordid little escapade!' Danfield had been dismissive. 'If you value your neck, you will save your excesses for the gin dens and bawdy houses, or for willing whores! The girl was plainly unwilling, and her father of honest stock. Despite your blustering of "friends in high places" such people have the ear of the justices, and the sympathy of all. Be warned, Havard! Or, like the brother who prompted your childish jealousy, you will end upon the gibbet!'

Mostyn, incensed by Danfield's self-righteousness, and his own crassness in letting slip rumour of Carne's escape, turned his rage upon his accuser, declaring maliciously, 'What I said of Carne was nonsense – designed to provoke! Nothing more! It is well known that he fled the place to escape entanglement with that pauper creature, who would have leeched upon him and bled him dry. She is naught but a common doxy, for all her high flown airs and graces, and those men her willing procurers.'

Danfield was unconvinced. 'I vow they came out of the affair with more dignity and honour than we,' he said regretfully. 'Take care that neither Rhys Llewellyn nor your uncle learn of this fiasco, for if they do, they will not take it lightly, should some complaint be laid against you.'

'Against us!' corrected Mostyn peevishly. 'The three of you are as much a part of the affair as I! I will not be made a scapegoat.'

'I have no doubt that you will survive,' said Danfield drily, 'scheming and talking your way through, and setting others in danger. It is one accomplishment at which you excel, Havard.'

His two companions who had hitherto remained silent, too spent and dispirited to join the debate, added their recriminations to Danfield's. Mostyn, outfaced, tried to make light of the affair, coaxing shamelessly, 'Let us not fall out about so trivial a matter. I own that the idea was mine, and I am wholly to blame. It was an ill-conceived adventure, clumsily executed. I have received my come-uppance, my friends, and will bear it like a man.' His well-practised smile, marred as it was by his swollen lips, did not disarm them.

'Keep your wiles for women, Havard!' advised Danfield carelessly, 'although, judging by tonight's showing, your efforts will bring you little success.'

There was an appreciative ripple of laughter from his supporters.

Although inwardly seething, Mostyn feigned amusement, saying expansively, 'Let us set ourselves to order, then make for some gaming house or tavern. I have free use of my cousin's coach and can convey you all. Where would you have me take you?'

'I would have you remove yourself!' said Danfield abruptly. 'You may go anywhere you choose, as long as it is clear of my sight, Havard! I have surfeit of your ill-conceived schemes, and of your company. You begin to bore me, as well as offend!'

'Then I shall go,' promised Mostyn stiffly, 'for it is plain that you are in need of rest to restore your humour and sense of proportion. I am surprised that such a triviality has so deranged you all. It has barely affected me.'

'Then it is you who are deranged, sir,' countered Danfield abrasively, 'for having planned such an ill-considered outing. You must take the consequences.'

'If we discuss our defence to any wild accusation made, and hold to our story well enough,' began Mostyn, 'then . . .'

'Be damned to you for a fool, Havard!' interrupted Danfield, abandoning his habitual languidness to grasp the cravat at Mostyn's throat, and twist it so tightly that his victim could scarce breathe. 'Hear this, for I will not repeat it. Should harm come of tonight's work, then I for one will neither hide nor condone your part in it. Understood?'

'You have no cause to harass and threaten me,' mumbled Mostyn sulkily, removing Danfield's hand and setting his cravat straight. 'It will be over and forgotten by morn, you may depend upon it.'

'We had best make our ways singly,' instructed Danfield, as if Mostyn had not spoken. 'We must go on foot, since our horses have fled. Should any harm come to my mount, Havard, I shall hold you responsible. I bid you all good-night!' he said curtly, and set out upon his way.

His companions murmured inaudibly, and self-

consciously took separate leave. Mostyn was alone. He
hesitated for a moment only, Penry Vaughan would hardly
be in the best of humours if he returned to the vicarage
without his cousin's mare, and so disgustingly dishevelled.

The thunderous knocking upon the door of Great House
brought a footman hurrying to investigate. Such disturbance spoke of some disaster, he felt sure, for dusk had
fallen and unexpected visitors were rare. Besides, there had
been an urgency about that thudding of the heavy iron
knocker that troubled him. He called out to the under-
footman to lend him aid, then, taking a stout stick from
the hallway, he eased open the door.

'Dear heavens above!' He stared in disbelief and helplessness at the crumpled figure lying inert upon the carriageway
'neath the pillared *porte-cochère*. Then, seemingly restored
to action, the footman thrust the stave at his companion
and bent over the awkwardly splayed body, the light from
the lanterns above illuminating the unknown visitor's
pallid, blood-encrusted face. 'It is young Mr Havard,
Bowles,' he said, shocked. 'Be quick! Lend me a hand.'
Then, irritably, 'Drop the stick to the ground, man! He
has been soundly beaten!'

The under-footman, who was little more than a boy, ran
to help him, struggling to support the limp body under its
dead weight. 'Is he dead, Mr Grace, sir? Is he dead?'

A faint, barely audible groan from Mostyn answered his
question as Grace commanded, 'Help me lay him upon the
hall floor, then run at once to inform the housekeeper and
Mrs Llewellyn. Gently! Gently, boy! Then ride out for
Doctor Tobin or Doctor Jordan. Bid them come without
delay. 'Tis a matter of urgency.'

There was no doubting that young Mr Havard had been
beaten most viciously and without mercy, for he seemed
barely alive. His face was bloodied and swollen, dark
bruises already disfiguring his palely translucent skin. His
bright hair was matted with filth and remnants of twigs and
grass, as if he had lain senseless in some ditch or copse. As

for his clothing, it was all but torn from his flesh, so furiously rent that it barely covered him decently. He was so unlike the elegantly arrayed Master Mostyn that the housekeeper, Mrs Radford, did not at first recognise him.

Clarissa, rushing out from the drawing room to discover the cause of the commotion, was horrified. She knelt beside Mostyn anxiously, her face a mask of concern, chafing his cold hands, stroking his poor, bloodied head. 'If Rhys were here,' she began tremulously, 'he would know what to do. He would alert the magistrates, seek out the villain responsible.' Then, with a supreme effort of will and long-engrained training, she forced herself to take charge. 'The doctor has been summoned?'

'Yes ma'am. Young Bowles has ridden out for him.'

'Fetch blankets, Mrs Radford, and a stone hot water bottle to set at his feet,' she ordered crisply. 'Perhaps it is better not to move him until the physician comes, lest it cause damage to broken bones or flesh. Yet the marble of the floor is so cold and comfortless. I do not know how best to help him,' she said despairingly, kneeling once more beside him, heedless of her pale silk gown, as she held his hand for comfort, although he seemed neither to see nor hear.

Clarissa was, at heart, a sensitive, kindly woman, and could not bring herself to desert him. To her horror, she recalled that she had not warned Mrs Radford to keep news of the accident from Laurel. Before she could rectify the omission, Laurel was at her side, distraught, weeping, almost hysterical with grief, accusing her mother of shamefully keeping her in ignorance of Mostyn's plight.

Mostyn, who had set the stage most convincingly by tearing at his clothes and rolling in the most execrable filth, was content to have salvaged fortune from disaster. He opened his eyes fractionally and, with pained effort, whispered confusedly, 'Mrs Llewellyn? Is it you, ma'am? There were some men . . . they set upon me . . . robbed me.'

His eyelids flickered and closed and Laurel wept anew, declaring pathetically, 'Oh, Mama! He will die, I know it.

I can't bear it! It breaks my heart to see him so.'

'Hush! Hush, my dear!' Clarissa remonstrated. 'It will do him no good to hear you so distressed and put about. He shall be given a bed in the Green Room, as soon as the doctor says he may be moved.'

When Dr Tobin had arrived and examined him thoroughly, he declared to Clarissa that although young Havard had indubitably been set upon by ruffians, and violently beaten, there was no immediate danger to his life.

'I fear, ma'am, that my enquiries of the boy have elicited little of use to the authorities in the matter. It seems his remembrance of events is poor and I do not feel it politic to pursue such questioning, for he is shocked and weakened. I believe he must have suffered a severe blow to the skull, although he has no recollection of it. His only concerns were for the welfare of his mount, and fear lest he incommode you. I have promised, most particularly, to determine if the animal has returned to the stables, for such worries serve him ill!'

'Then I must set his mind at rest about his stay here,' offered Clarissa at once, shamed by her former suspicion and dislike of the boy, and eager to make amends. 'I shall be pleased to minister to him.'

'Oh, no, Mama!' blurted Laurel impulsively. 'You shall not be troubled a whit. I shall nurse him most devotedly, I promise, and read to him and amuse him by the hour.'

Dr Tobin smiled upon Laurel indulgently. 'A kind offer, made to spare you, ma'am. Such thoughtfulness is rare in the young, and must warm you greatly. It is plain that your daughter is devoted to you.'

'Indeed,' Clarissa's voice was expressionless.

'I must trust you to see that the patient is not over-tired or taxed too much for he is still weakened and in need of rest. Yet it would be a pity to dampen Miss Llewellyn's selfless enthusiasm,' he said pleasantly.

'I shall make it my business to care for him, nonetheless,' said Clarissa with surprising tartness.

284

Chapter Twenty-six

Mostyn was beginning to tire of the elaborate charade he had so carefully contrived. The pleasure of duping Dr Tobin was starting to pall, and he found his incarceration in his bedchamber boring, despite the luxuries showered upon him, and the diversions offered by books and chess. Rhys Llewellyn had not returned from London, whence he had travelled on a matter of business, and Mostyn did not relish the intense questioning which he was sure he would be expected to undergo on Llewellyn's return. Most of all, he missed his carousing with his acquaintances, for he had few friends save Danfield and one or two others who shared his fondness for gaming and philandering. So it was with real pleasure that he welcomed Peter Danfield to his bedside.

'Well . . .' Danfield exclaimed languidly when they were alone. 'I have to admit, Havard, that you show a certain panache, for all that you are a devious, self-seeking little swine.' His face was as carefully expressionless as his tone, yet he could not conceal a certain reluctant admiration. Mostyn was so plainly delighted to see him that Danfield, despite his private misgivings, warmed towards him.

'You have heard nothing more of the . . . that affair at the beech copse? There have been no enquiries by the magistrates?' Mostyn asked tensely.

'None. I fancy the girl's father would have it bruited about as reluctantly as you. It would do her reputation no good, nor, I fancy, would it ingratiate you with Mrs Llewellyn.'

'Her husband might take a broader view,' dismissed Mostyn impatiently. 'I cannot believe that he is blameless in such affairs.'

'He would not thank you for taking refuge upon his doorstep, and in one of his bedchambers,' countered Danfield mildly.

'Doubtless he has taken himself into the bedchambers and beds of many upon occasion,' declared Mostyn with sly relish.

'There is cant and hypocrisy in all such matters, Havard, as you well know!' Danfield's handsome face had lost its expression of cultivated boredom, and he did not attempt to conceal his exasperation. 'A man's philanderings, well hidden, are adjudged a harmless conceit – crudely exposed they become sins.'

'Perhaps the real sin lies in being found out!'

'Perhaps.' Danfield's easy smile did not quite reach his eyes. 'One cannot but applaud your ingenuity, Havard, but take care not to be too clever! You might lose more than you gain!'

'If you have come to lecture me in morals and manners,' said Mostyn petulantly, 'you had best be precise. My head aches damnably, and I'll be hanged if I take your meaning.'

'Then I shall set it out plainly. Rhys Llewellyn is your patron and friend. You depend upon him for survival, physical and social. Do I make myself clear?'

'Perfectly,' Mostyn said stiffly.

'Without Llewellyn's patronage and the pittance your cousin offers, you would be destitute. You are dependent upon their goodwill for what you eat, drink, wager and wear . . . for your education and acceptance. Without them you could scarcely exist.'

'Then I am grateful to you for reminding me of it,' declared Mostyn sarcastically. 'It is a knowledge that I have been at some pains to try and forget, without conspicuous success. I am reminded of it at every twist and turn by those to whom I am indebted, and worse, by others with large incomes and small minds! It is easy enough to preach continence to a beggar when you have wined and dined to excess!'

Danfield could not control his amusement, although he tried manfully to keep a straight face, and soon Mostyn had joined in his merriment, and they were laughing companionably together, their altercation all but forgotten.

'There is an aspect of the affair which you seem to have given no heed to,' Danfield reminded soberly. 'You are known to those at Holly Grove by name and reputation . . . that much was made clear. It is you they will come seeking, Havard, you may depend upon it. But whether openly or in secret, and when least expected, who can say? I cannot believe it will be easily forgotten by the girl's kin.'

'You swore they would hesitate to make it known, lest it humiliate her,' Mostyn accused. 'She would be ostracised by all, her hopes of marriage ended, her reputation gone. If they value her, they dare not take that risk! They *have* not spoken out . . . else Mrs Llewellyn and Laurel would be distraught, unable to keep news of it from me.' He made no attempt to hide his self-satisfaction.

'I declare, Havard, you are the most odiously smug, conceited wretch!' Danfield said, vexed and irritated. 'I doubt you have feelings for any save yourself. You seem as incapable of shame as of remorse. You are concerned for nothing but your own worthless hide!'

'And you, Danfield, are fast becoming a prig and a bore.' Mostyn smiled disarmingly. 'And were you not so confounded elegant, handsome, intelligent and rich, I'll wager that I would not think so highly of you, nor be pleased to call you "friend".'

Danfield tried his best to remain aloof, but his irrepressible good humour defeated him, and reduced him to reluctant laughter.

'You have not told me how you explained away your own cuts and bruises,' Mostyn reminded. 'You were in a state almost as sorry as my own, and Jefferies could scarce stand upon his own two feet without Caborne's assistance, I recall.'

287

'I claimed my horse had bolted,' Danfield confessed. Then, seeing Mostyn's eyebrows raised in derision, 'I admit it was ludicrously uninspired, but then I lack your vivid imagination and skill at lying. It is an art form at which you excel, Havard!'

Mostyn bowed his head in graceful acknowledgement.

'My horse, good creature, arrived at the stables before me, to give credence to my claim . . . as yours, I hear, returned to Penavon vicarage.'

'As must I . . . as soon as I am able.' Mostyn's voice held little enthusiasm. 'Tobin's questions begin to irk me,' he declared in answer to Danfield's enquiring look, 'although I have him convinced that I suffer concussion and chronic memory lapses. Idiot that he is, he begs Mrs Llewellyn not to catechise me too harshly, lest it weaken and confuse my brain.'

'I am amazed that he finds evidence that you possess one!' observed Danfield drily. 'It speaks more highly of your acting ability than his professional skill.' He hesitated. 'You know that Rhys Llewellyn returns tomorrow eve?'

'No. How did you come by the information?'

'He has travelled to London with my father and others of his ilk. They plan to form a consortium, I am told, to invest in mining for iron ore and coal here at Penavon. Llewellyn has a certain expertise in such affairs, and the money and land to explore for minerals. You did not know of this?'

'No.' Mostyn had paled and his voice grown tight with resentment. 'I am not privy to such confidences.'

Danfield, seeing how the news had distressed him, said quickly, 'Then I offer you some news which will please you better, for I know how fiercely you are plagued by Laurel's pursuit of you.'

'Well?' Mostyn was regarding him with unusual intensity, the linen bed sheet clutched so fiercely that the knuckles of his fist were white as bone. 'Well?' Mostyn repeated irritably.

'I cannot pretend it is a prospect I greatly cherish, but

it seems part of the bargain is that Laurel and I must wed.'

'But that is ludicrous! Obscene!' The words were torn from him.

'I am deeply touched, my dear fellow, that you protest so vehemently on my behalf.' Danfield's smile was gently mocking. 'But I do assure you, Havard, that I will offer no serious objection. Arranged marriages are meant, after all, to be marriages of convenience. I intend to make mine precisely that. It will be convenient for me to marry an heiress, and there can be no denying that Laurel has beauty and spirit. It seems to me an admirably civilised arrangement. I affirm that I intend to change neither my habits nor my way of life save, perhaps, to wager higher stakes, and to live altogether more prodigally. Our friendship will in no wise suffer, Havard. You have my word upon it as an honest broker.'

Mostyn merely nodded, masking the chagrin he felt at Danfield's carelessly delivered news. Laurel's betrayal rankled within him as sourly as the knowledge that Rhys Llewellyn had dismissed him as unworthy of his confidence. Damnation! he thought furiously, do they think I am nothing? A nobody? They live in a house that is mine by right, yet dole me out charity. Llewellyn offers me scraps from a rich man's table, his unwanted leavings. He may yet learn that the best-trained cur, if provoked too far, will turn and savage the hand that feeds it.

Danfield, glimpsing the smile of wry satisfaction upon Mostyn's lips, asked resentfully, 'How will you take the change in *your* fortunes, Havard?'

'I shall be grateful to be spared Laurel's nursery devotions. I own, Danfield, such constant worship, although deserved, is apt to grow tedious. I wish you a surfeit of it.'

'I meant how will you treat me, as your new patron and employer?' drawled Danfield provocatively.

'With the same intolerance and contempt as the question deserves.' Mostyn's tone was equally light. 'I am no man's ready harlot . . . I live by my own rules.'

Despite his feigned indifference, Danfield recognised the warning underlying Mostyn's words and heeded it. He deftly turned their conversation to talk of fashion, scandal, and the harmless trivia that enlivened drawing room and dinner table, then took his leave. Mostyn had ostensibly regained his good humour, commenting on all with his habitual acuity and wit. Danfield found him vastly entertaining. It was a skill which Mostyn had early learnt. If others do not please you, outwit them by pleasing *them*.

It was an inflexible rule that on no account was Laurel to visit Mostyn's sickroom without her mother being present, and, in addition, it was required that a nurse or companion act as chaperone to the pair. Throughout dinner, Laurel had persisted in childishly coaxing her mother to return with her to Mostyn's room, declaring that he would be bored without company, and grateful for diversion.

'Peter Danfield visited him only this afternoon,' reminded Clarissa reasonably, 'and Dr Tobin was adamant that his patient should not be overtaxed.'

However, so insistent were Laurel's pleas that Clarissa reluctantly allowed herself to be persuaded, taking her needlepoint with her to while away the time. Mostyn, contrary to Laurel's hopes, seemed almost indifferent to her efforts to amuse him, rejecting proffered books, board games, puzzles, and an offer that she read to the invalid with less than his usual grace.

On several occasions, Clarissa glanced up, concerned, once to ask if there were some salve or potion that she could order to be brought, or if he would care for a negus or cordial.

'Mrs Llewellyn . . .' he began hesitantly, after more civilly declining those comforts she named, 'I think, ma'am, it is time I returned to Penavon vicarage.'

Clarissa was immediately all concern, advising against leaving hurriedly and without Dr Tobin's consent. 'Besides,' she reminded quietly, 'your cousin is absent in London, and you will have little companionship and diversion. Will you not at least stay until my husband returns?'

'No, ma'am.' Despite Clarissa's generous entreaties and Laurel's impassioned pleas that he remain, he was adamant. He would leave upon the morrow, and would discommode them no further. They had already been kinder than he deserved. Clarissa, glancing at Laurel's white face and her tensely clenched hands, felt a spasm of pity for the child. How foolish, she thought, to wear her heart so vulnerably upon her sleeve. Like Rhys, Mostyn Havard was not the sort of man to treat her with the tenderness she deserved. He would fight only for those things which were inaccessible, and defied all his efforts to seduce. He would value nothing that was willingly, generously given. With a sigh she set her needlework aside and, ignoring Laurel's appeals to stay 'but a few minutes more', ushered her firmly without. Mostyn, she thought, was looking wan and strangely pathetic. The blow to his skull and the shock of the experience must have taxed his strength more than he knew. That he would be well cared for at Penavon vicarage she did not doubt, for there were few, Clarissa felt sure, who could resist his unctuous charm, or count it less than a privilege to nurse him.

As soon as it grew dark, Laurel threw back her covers and, taking up the wax taper in its chamberstick, crept to the door barefooted. She could not bear the cold indifference that Mostyn had earlier shown towards her, nor the thought of his leaving. She would beg him to stay, for, despite Papa's promised return, the house would be cold and empty, denied Mostyn's presence.

She had eased open the bedroom door, grimacing for fear the sound of it would alert the household. Then, making certain that the passage outside her room was clear, she secured the door carefully behind her and soundlessly made her way to Mostyn's bedchamber, the candle guttering and flickering monstrous, swift-changing shadows upon the high ceiling and walls.

'Mostyn?' She eased herself gently through his door,

her heart thudding uncomfortably in her breast with nervousness and fear of discovery.

'What do you want? What are you doing here?' His voice was thickened with sleep, his senses dulled. Then, 'Dear God, Laurel! Are you mad? Would you have me thrown into the street?'

By the light of her taper, he saw her face illumined and ghostly, fair hair flung loose, eyes wide and glittering with a mixture of fear and excitement. Worse! There was no denying that she wore only her cambric nightgown, its softness clinging to the soft contours of her pointed breasts and the delicate line of her flesh.

'Get out!' The words were hoarse. 'Get out, I say, before you are discovered! Whatever possessed you to come here? Are you mad?'

Disappointed and hurt at Mostyn's brusqueness, she hesitated, then began to weep, the candle in her hand trembling so violently that it guttered out. The burnt wick sent up a stench of smoke and melted wax that caught at her throat. Laurel's tears fell faster and more fiercely as she stumbled to the bed, seeing, in the light of his candle, Mostyn's face angry and filled with dislike.

'Look, Mostyn . . . I brought something.' She offered him the knotted handkerchief from within the pocket of her nightgown. 'You see . . . ten pounds, Mostyn. I have saved it for you. No-one need ever know. I brought it because you were robbed! Take it, Mostyn. Take it,' she urged.

'Hell and damnation!' he gave vent to his fury and rage, sending coins and handkerchief hurtling to the floor. 'Are you an imbecile? Deaf? Would you destroy me?'

His anger bewildered her, for she had meant only to ease his hurt. 'If I could but slip between the covers with you, Mostyn,' she pleaded despairingly, 'you could hold me close, keep me warm. I am so cold, I swear, and trembling.'

He pushed her away fiercely as she tried to insinuate herself beside him, begging, 'If you do not want the money,

Mostyn, no matter. But do not send me away, Mostyn. I cannot bear it.'

Laurel's tear-stained face was ugly in its torment. He felt no pity, no need to comfort her, only an overwhelming surge of disgust. He recoiled from her fastidiously, unable to hide his revulsion. The candle flame at his bedside made plain to her the contempt upon his face. Shocked by his rejection, Laurel stood uncertainly beside his bed, sore with shamed humiliation. Yet she could not bring herself to leave, would not, until she learned what had occurred to make him suddenly despise her so.

'You are to marry Danfield,' he accused. 'It is already arranged.'

'No, Mostyn, I swear. It is a lie! I know nothing of it!'

'No lie,' he said viciously. 'It is your aim, and his, to sneer at me, and betray me, making me a laughing stock before others! I cannot bear it!'

'Oh, Mostyn.' She believed his anger sprang from love, his fear of losing her. 'I will never marry him! I will have no other save you!'

Laurel's voice was as soft and yielding as the flesh that she offered, her body pressed upon his own, her hair falling upon his face as her lips touched his, gently, then with increasing hardness and yearning. Mostyn felt a warm response within his flesh; a rushing of desire for her in his loins, a quickening of blood. There was, too, a sense of surging power, a knowledge that he alone held the means to subdue or rouse her. As quickly as it had come, desire left him, and he cried harshly as he thrust her callously from him, 'Go to your bed, Laurel! You are a fool to . . . stir me so! I will not be tormented! Go, I say!'

Mostyn had forcefully pushed her away upon hearing muffled sounds of movement without, his senses alert despite his desire to humble her and punish her for her father's rejection.

The door was swiftly opened and Clarissa stood there, a candelabrum in her hand, the candles casting a glow about her pallid face, her eyes wide and incredulous. 'Return to your bed, Laurel! Go at once! Do not hesitate, nor argue . . . go!'

There was such anger in her voice that Laurel obeyed without question.

Before she had reached the door, Clarissa commanded coldly, 'Do not go noisily, or awaken the servants with your wailing, or I swear that I shall thrash you soundly, and tell your father all!' When Laurel had obeyed, she said stiffly, colour rising to her face and neck, 'I heard your refusal of Laurel, Mostyn. I thank you for it.' She clutched her cloak tightly at its edges, drawing them together. 'She is a stupid child. Wilful and impetuous . . . not knowing what dangers might be aroused,' she hesitated, 'what tragedy might follow.'

'I swear to you, ma'am, that no harm has come to her.'

Mostyn's handsome face beneath the cluster of disordered curls was earnestly pleading. 'I do not know what devil possessed her. I beg that you will believe that her coming here was neither planned nor known to me.'

'Yes,' agreed Clarissa quietly, 'I believe you . . . but I do not know what best to do . . . how best to handle this affair.'

Mostyn heard the appeal in her voice and said reassuringly, 'I shall leave tomorrow, as I earlier vowed. None will find it strange, I do assure you. The servants at my cousin's house have already been alerted by Danfield at my request.'

'Yes, perhaps it is best.' Clarissa's resolve and firmness had deserted her, and she suddenly looked older, confused. 'Your own servants have no knowledge of Laurel's coming here? You did not alert them?'

'Alert them?'

'As to Laurel's absence from her bed.'

'No . . . I had been unable to sleep . . . I would have descended below, to the library . . . to take a book for solace.' Tiredness, or shock, had made her speech halting. 'I looked into her room, as I sometimes do, to make certain that she slept . . . It is an old habit . . . Hard to break.'

'It is not my affair, ma'am, to advise you, or interfere.'

She stared at him, puzzled, awaiting his explanation.

'But I believe it would be kinder to all if no word of this were spoken to Mr Llewellyn. It would anger and grieve him to no purpose.'

Clarissa moved to the bed and touched Mostyn's shoulder lightly in gratitude, and he felt the sudden heat of the candle flame as she bent towards him, her eyes unnaturally bright, skin fragrant with the scent of some flower he could not put a name to.

'Thank you, Mostyn.' For the first time there was a warmth for him in her voice, real affection. 'I shall not forget.'

He watched her make her way to the door, the silver candelabrum gripped firm, the light from its candles casting shadows over all. Mostyn settled his head upon his pillow and slept. There is virtue in making an enemy into a friend. He had not taken the revenge so easily offered, and was glad of it. There would be time enough for that. When he awoke, he carefully gathered up the coins he had hurled so intemperately to the floor.

Chapter Twenty-seven

To Jethro's relief, Saranne appeared to have recovered from her ordeal in the beechwoods. Indeed, the violence of the assault seemed to have shocked her out of her former apathy, and she once again surrendered herself obediently, if not wholeheartedly, to her tasks upon the farm. At all events, Megan welcomed an extra pair of hands to help her with the chores in dairy and farmhouse, since her time now was further occupied in helping Jane at Hillbrook. Sara, too, spent every moment she could at the isolated cottage, taking whatever victuals could be spared to tempt Prys's appetite and relieving Jane of the stitching, baking, and small duties which would have kept her from her husband's side.

Jane sat for long hours beside him as he slumbered fitfully in his box bed beside the fire, his frail hands transparent upon the coverlet. His face had grown so wasted of flesh that, in the sunken hollows of his eyes and the gauntness of stretched skin, she saw already the skeleton beneath. There was about him the dry brittleness of aged parchment. He spoke seldom now, for the wasting disease had taken its toll. His strength was sapped by the coughing that wracked him and the uselessness of his lungs was clear from the brightness of the blood on his pillow. Jane took little rest, dozing beside him in a chair by night, and by day ever watchful. Often Peter Morrish came to settle beside her, his gentle presence a balm, his companionship enfolding her in warmth. He neither preached nor prayed aloud. Yet Jane could not doubt that the words of comfort he spoke in his own mind gave Prys the peace of spirit he so desired.

Megan often begged Jane to allow her to remain at Hillbrook, that she might minister to their needs and take turn with her at the bedside, but Jane thanked her gravely and declined. Peter Morrish, and Sara too, had also protested their willingness to remain, but Jane would not countenance his staying.

'I thank you,' she said warmly, 'for your kindness and the loving help you offer. But I beg that you will not take it amiss if I say that I choose to watch over him alone. I have no fear of loneliness, or the dark.'

One morning, when Megan returned at dawn after the long walk by lantern light from the Griffin's cottage, she opened the door to see Jane seated beside the box bed, her head cradled in her arms upon the counterpane. At first Megan supposed she was asleep but Jane raised herself awkwardly to say, 'He has gone, Megan. I have done what needs to be done, set him tidy at the last.'

Megan, glancing at Hywel Prys's waxen face, saw the coins weighting his eyelids, the knotted kerchief that bound his jaw and the strange tranquillity of flesh no longer heir to the pain of grief. 'Oh, Mrs Prys! Mrs Prys!' she wept. 'I would have stayed with you . . . kept you company, but you sent me home!'

It was Jane who cradled Megan's head to her, feeling the wetness of her tears, holding her close in comfort. I was wrong, Jane thought. I said I had no fear of loneliness and the dark. Without Hywel, the loneliness will be unending. I will be for ever in the dark.

Higgs, Randall Walters' clerk, glancing from his desk at the window of the attorney's office in the main highway, saw Jane in the crudely made cart draw up outside. He hurried downstairs to greet her and to escort her within.

'Mistress Prys. I beg you will allow me to accompany you within, ma'am. Mr Walters will attend to you personally, I do not doubt, for he has the highest regard for you, ma'am, as have we all. You have had a sad loss, ma'am . . . and I will not speak further of it, save to say I . . . we . . . feel for you in your grief. Yes, we do indeed.' Higgs's creased brown face, transparent as a child's, showed the depth of his feelings and Jane put a gloved hand gently upon his frail arm and nodded her gratitude.

Randall Walters, corpulent and dishevelled, blundered noisily from his inner sanctum to greet Jane and escort her within. His wig was knocked askew, giving him a curiously lop-sided air, and his gold-rimmed spectacles were perched so perilously near the end of his nose that a sudden sneeze might have dislodged them. Jane suspected that he had been indulging in a post-prandial doze but so genuine was his pleasure at seeing her that she could not be critical. He was as clumsily appealing as a large, bounding puppy or a dancing bear; all shambling awkwardness and desire to please, she thought, amused.

'Well, Mrs Prys,' he began when he had tipped some ledgers from a chair on to the floor and she was settled to his satisfaction, 'I confess I am delighted to see you. Delighted. It is a social visit, I may hope, and not a problem which affords me this pleasure?'

'No problem, Mr Walters, for it is settled in my mind. But business certainly.'

'Indeed,' he said vaguely, raising his eyeglasses which were cutting into the fleshy sides of his nose. 'Then perhaps we had best discuss it over refreshment, ma'am, for the mind works better upon a full stomach.'

Jane thanked him gracefully, but declined, and he looked quite absurdly disappointed.

'Well then, ma'am,' he prompted, 'the nature of this business?'

For answer, Jane unbuttoned her coat and, after fumbling awkwardly with the neckline of her gown, unfastened the opal and gold necklace and laid it upon the desk. 'I would have you take this into your safekeeping and draw me up a will, Mr Walters,' she said briskly.

298

'A will.' Randall Walters' eyes, magnified behind his lenses, grew larger yet, but, to his credit, he did not question how she came by it, simply nodding acquiescence. 'It shall be done, ma'am. Shall we settle the disposition of your property here and now, or would you prefer that I visit you at your cottage? There might be bequests you wish to ponder more deeply?'

'There are two only, Mr Walters. My few personal possessions, my straw chairs and poor sticks of furniture, I leave to Megan Griffin with whatever money remains to me.'

'I will see that it is set out as you require.'

'The house and the necklace I leave to Carne Havard, upon his return. They are owed to him, gifted to me by his grandmother.'

The silence stretched long before Randall Walters said gently, 'And if Carne does not return, Mrs Prys?'

'I cannot doubt that he will, sir, but if, at my death, some awkwardness should prevent him . . . I beg you will wait two more years.'

'And then?'

'Then the necklace to go to Saranne Hartrey and the cottage to Megan, with all else. I have set aside enough money to see me buried with Hywel Prys. If you will see that it is Peter Morrish, sir, and not Mr Vaughan, who speaks the words.'

'Yes. I promise that it will be done exactly as you wish.' Randall Walters rose from his chair and walked to Jane, the necklace in his hand. He held it outstretched towards her, urging, 'Will you not continue to wear it, ma'am? You will feel its loss.'

'No, Mr Walters,' Jane's voice was firm. 'I have worn it for nigh on fifty years by night and day. It has been my consolation and my joy, you understand? Yet, now . . .' There was no need for her to explain further.

'I will keep it safely under lock and key, ma'am. You may rely on its safety and my discretion. None shall hear of it, save those involved. You have my solemn word upon it.'

'Yes. I was sure of that, sir.' She paused. 'I knew I could count upon you, since you are a man of integrity and reputation.'

At the quayside offices of Sir Robert Crandon's shipping line, Carne's letter of credence from Randall Walters had produced no appreciable response. He had been kept waiting in a bleak corridor for an hour or more, growing increasingly tense and nervous. That it was a ploy to detain him and force his arrest, Carne felt sure, and it was all he could do to stay calmly seated when his every instinct urged him to flee the place.

The bored clerk, into whose room he was eventually admitted, was a sallow pock-marked fellow who wasted no time upon civilities. The preliminaries grudgingly completed, he finally said dismissively, 'You will join the crew of the schooner, the *Bristol Maid*, lying alongside the Parade. She sails upon the morning's tide. You had best make ready.'

'Where, sir, is she bound?' Carne said, unable to hide his delight.

'The Indies.' The reply was terse, disinterested.

'Her cargo, sir?'

'That is a matter for the owners and captain, not for you! You will be a swab, Mr Grey, a deckhand. I suggest that you forget any grandiose ideas as to your position or worth.' He motioned towards the letter before him. 'Your past, and influence, cease here, in this office. Once aboard, you must rise and fall by your own endeavours. You will be the lowest of the low. Less than vermin.'

Carne quitted Bristol upon the early tide, against a sky ablaze with a brilliance of rose, saffron and crimson light. There was a savagery about it that was alien, he thought; for the dawns he had witnessed at Penavon arose gently above the mountain heights from a softness of mist. Here, the horizon, sea and sky were aflame; the vessel so vividly aglow with reflected light that the decks and sails appeared to burn with it. Air and sky fused, billowing canvas became rose-edged cloud, sanguine light spilled over to stain the scrubbed boards as if with blood.

A fierce blow to his shoulder sent Carne crashing painfully to the deck. Dazed, and with palms numbed and skinned, he awkwardly scrabbled to his feet. A brawny, ill-tempered face glowered into his as a fist grasped at his shirt and swung him aloft, half choking him.

'Look hard at me, Mister Grey! Mark well the cut of my jib, for you will grow to fear it, and my fists. My name is Isaac Savage! Savage by name, as by nature!'

As Carne attempted to gather his wits, a resounding slap across his face all but dislocated his neck.

'Now, shift your idle carcase! We want no bloody passengers!'

The seaman spat out such an obscenity of oaths that Carne stood frozen when released. He would have suffered a crueller and more disabling blow had not an older seaman dragged him clear, urging, 'Come, lad, follow me, if you value yourself. 'Tis plain Savage has your measure. He would sooner it were for a canvas shroud than a seaman's rig. Here!' He thrust a bucket of greasy water and a broom into Carne's stinging hands. 'Scrub that deck as if your very life depends upon it, as well it might!'

'I am beholden to you, sir,' said Carne, chastened. 'Whom have I the pleasure of addressing?'

His rescuer smiled, showing ruined stumps of teeth, shaking his head incredulously, weathered face amused. 'You will address no-one, my lad,' he warned, 'if you do not, straight away, use some elbow grease. Take off your clogs and swab barefoot, 'twill give you a firmer grip upon the boards. Look lively, should Savage return, and give him no lip, nor cause him to find fault. There is always one in the crew he makes the butt of his vicious ill-humour. I fear you have earned yourself that burden.'

'What shall I do, sir? What say?'

'Do everything; say nothing. Bide your time, your chance will come. If you work for the devil, you must learn his tricks to survive.'

By that day's end, Carne could not be sure that he wanted to survive. The decks were scrubbed clean enough to eat off, but the thought of food sickened and disgusted him. His hands and feet were painfully blistered, the broken flesh beneath reddened as raw meat. He could scarce raise his arms for the ache in them, and his every movement of neck and spine was a torture. All he yearned for was sleep. Yet, when he finally lay upon the boards of the foetid, airless hole that stank of unwashed bodies, urine and sweat, he remained feverishly awake. His stretched muscles would not relax, but twitched rebelliously, his legs so agonised by cramp that he all but screamed aloud. The scored flesh of his hands burned incessantly, and his head throbbed, his mind confused. He had not attempted to pluck the splinters from the swollen soles of his feet, where they smarted a reminder, because he had neither the strength nor will to remove them, nor, indeed, the sight, since his eyes were blurred with tiredness, their lids raw-edged from wind and spray. He was too exhausted even to weep.

'Well, my lad, you acquitted yourself well. None can fault you for courage, although Savage will take no joy from it.'

The seaman who had delivered him from the third mate's spite was bending over him, creased face sternly approving. He touched Carne's shoulder reassuringly and felt him wince with pain, although he affected not to notice, continuing, 'You earlier asked my name . . . well, I shall tell you, since you have earned the right to address me as a fellow seaman. I am Septimus Fortune, and you?'

'Grey,' murmured Carne through awkward lips, 'Mansel Grey.' Then, 'You are well named, sir,' he added with an attempt at a smile. 'It was my rare good fortune to meet you.'

'Well, Mr Grey,' said Fortune, smiling in return, 'I'll hazard that this has been the longest day in all of your life.

Grey by name, and grey by nature.' His pale-washed eyes were warm with understanding. ''Tis a name that is plain and anonymous, a good name to take refuge behind.'

Carne made no reply. The questioning he awaited did not come.

'Try to be as inoffensive as your name, my lad,' advised Fortune dourly, 'but do not confuse it in your mind with who and what you really are. That must never be forgot.'

'And your own name, Mr Fortune?'

'Ill-chosen, lad,' he admitted. 'Yet it serves to amuse others and set them at ease in my company. Who could rightly fear a man called Fortune?'

'You chose it for that reason, sir?'

'I chose it because I had need of a new name, a new life, like many another aboard. I was young, then, and rash enough to think I could shape life and fortune both.' He smiled wryly. 'In the end, as is the way of things, it was life that shaped me.'

'Then it has been good to others, if not to you, sir,' blurted Carne, 'for your kindness has greatly eased my path today.' Despite his efforts to remain alert, he yawned involuntarily, barely able to force his tired eyelids apart. Sleep weighed heavily upon him.

Fortune smiled and nodded, saying quietly, 'Best rest now, while you can.' His hand hovered compassionately above Carne's shoulder but fell uselessly as he recalled the boy's hurt. His young shipmate was a gentleman, Fortune thought ruefully, and Savage would make him pay harsh dues for it. He would protect the lad as best he could, but discreetly and unobserved else it would do him no favour. Fortune felt a sharp pleasure as he recalled the boy's words of gratitude, for they were honestly spoken.

'It will be better tomorrow, Mr Fortune, will it not?' Carne's words came poignant, and slurred with fatigue.

'I cannot doubt it,' assured Fortune, knowing full well that he lied.

The labour that Carne and others as lowly as he were forced

to was both back-breaking and demoralising, and purposely so. Carne determined that, whatever befell, he could not allow it to break his spirit. No more would he allow Savage's brutality and spleen to humble him and lay him low. Septimus Fortune continued, unobtrusively, to help the boy; instructing him as how best to tackle each new and degrading task that the Third Mate thrust upon him; tending the sores and blisters upon his broken flesh; trying always to damp down the smouldering grievance Carne felt against his persecutor. There were many, now, amongst the crew who felt sympathy and liking for Mansel Grey. He worked uncomplainingly, often taking upon himself, unbidden, those labours which others were too weak or sickly to fulfil, in order to spare them punishment. Yet he never spoke of it to any and sought neither praise nor gratitude. His hands and feet healed and, steeped in sea water, as Septimus Fortune decreed, his skin grew hard and impervious to hurt. After a time, he seemed to grow impervious even to Savage's public jibes and taunts, remembering, perhaps, how viciously he himself had called Penry Vaughan to account. Carne believed that his cousin's death, or maiming, at his hands, had wrecked not only the victim's life, and his own, but those of innocents such as Saranne and Jane. It had been a harsh lesson, and one he was not anxious ever to repeat.

Septimus Fortune, however, knew that Carne's voyage of self-discovery on the *Bristol Maid* had scarcely begun. For the moment, fresh food and water were still plentiful, the sea calm, and the cramped quarters and the habits of others had not begun to irritate and rub raw. The lad was intelligent, and slow to anger, it was true, but he was neither a saint nor a willing martyr. There were those who, in the past, had been broken by Savage's brutishness, and others who had tried to break him and ended up by being flogged before the ship's crew. Savage was a bully and a coward, protected by his rank. At sea, his word was absolute. None dared to question his commands but, on land, he was simply a man, human and vulnerable.

Septimus Fortune, wherever they finally docked, would strive to keep Mansel Grey securely in his sights, and Savage, too. Savage's death would undoubtedly be violent, and by another's hand. It was in the very law and nature of things. He who sows the wind must as surely reap the whirlwind.

After weeks at sea, and with Septimus's tutelage, Carne believed that he had learnt how best to avoid the Third Mate's cuffs and blows. Rather than be caught idle and feed Savage's wrath, he would press his help upon others, or even invent duties, in order to keep himself constantly occupied. Perversely, his industry only served to provoke his tormentor the more and the scathing lash of Savage's tongue grew harsher and more frequent, aided by a core of sycophants whose brutishness matched his own. Septimus tried always to stand watch with Carne, sometimes offering some small concession or bribe to fellow crewmen, should their hours on watch conflict. It was a time of unease now, for the weather had worsened and the enforced closeness of the crew and lack of privacy and escape grew irksome. The fresh provisions, taken on at Bristol, had run low, and the water had grown as brackish and unpalatable as the salt herring and hard tack, which was now their staple fare. Savage seemed to take a sadistic delight in pushing Carne to his physical and mental limits. He forced him to climb the rigging in squalls and gales when the furious whipping of the hempen ropes and the crash of the sails near deafened him or threatened to send him crashing to the deck below. His first ascent had seen him trapped like a fly against the spider's web of rigging, eyes clenched tight, terrified to mount or descend, unable to open his eyes lest vertigo, and the sheer horror of losing his grip, send him plunging to sea or boards. Yet, knowing that Savage waited eagerly below to jeer at any cowardice, Carne made himself do what was demanded of him, although his heart pounded so violently against his ribs that he felt it as a physical pain. There was the taste of vomit souring his mouth as he inched relentlessly upwards but, when the task was completed and he climbed down to the deck, Carne looked into his adversary's eyes, unable to hide the violence of triumph which possessed him.

'Well done,' Septimus's voice had been quietly approving. 'It will never be as hard again, I swear.' Seeing the boy's sudden loss of colour and the wretchedness upon his face, he had gone quietly to support him, saying, 'Lean hard upon me. It is over now. 'Tis but shock and relief.'

'No,' Carne denied, his voice so low pitched that only Septimus could hear, 'I have disgraced myself . . . I have fouled my breeches.'

'They are more easily washed than blood from the deck,' said Septimus, unimpressed. 'Be grateful. A corpse would have small need for breeches!'

Septimus was not the only friend and ally that Carne, in his new identity as Mansel Grey, was to make among the shipmates. The brutes and braggarts gravitated unerringly towards others of their kind. These were the dregs of humanity, scraped and stirred from the stinking refuse of prison, opium den, gin-palace and slum. 'Cockroaches,' Septimus called them, 'maggots grown fat upon the rottenness of others, and on their own corruption.' They had not escaped their former lives, nor even fled them, for their diversions, save for whoring and the cruelty of bear pits and bull baiting, had changed little. Like the cockroaches and rats in the bilges and holds, they carried their vices with them. Gambling, drunkenness and knife fights were rife, as were other less venial perversions. Shipboard life, of necessity, bred an enclosed and intimate society and, since they were denied the indulgences of bawdy houses and the cheap release of field whores, sexual jealousies and revenges were commonplace.

If Carne had expected that the ship's officers would exert discipline, and be of a different calibre from some of his companions of the lower deck, he was soon disillusioned. With few exceptions, they were either indifferent to the grosser excesses of the crew, or were too cowardly to inter-

306

fere. The captain, a surly, rough-necked individual, barely left his cabin and, when he did, his colour was suspiciously high and his speech slurred. He was never known to address an ordinary seaman, nor even to nod an acknowledgement. Those below decks were, to him, a remote and alien breed. He had no wish to cultivate them. He was, Septimus observed disparagingly, 'a ruin, and a caricature of a man, ill-fitted to sail a rum keg!' The First Officer, whose uniform and speech were as impeccable as the captain's were slovenly, devoted himself entirely to the studying of instruments and charts, their checking and correcting.

One of Carne's closest companions was a gentle, inoffensive fellow, an ex-pauper who had been farmed out since early childhood to earn a living as and when he might. From the small fragments of his past history that Carne and Septimus had managed to draw out of him, William Oates was no stranger to hardship and abuse. His labour had been cheaply bought, and valued less, and beatings and hunger were the most constant memory of his scarred childhood. Now, at sixteen or seventeen summers, he was a thin, gangling youth.

Carne and Septimus were constantly surprised by his small acts of undeserved kindness. He was a sensitive, good-natured boy and, although slow in movement and thought, quick with generosity to those in need. There were those, like Savage, who mistook William Oates's quietness and hesitancy for doltishness, and believed him ignorant and idle. Like Carne, he was the butt of the Third Mate's crude humour and unprovoked violence, and he responded with a passivity which served to inflame the bully the more. It was true that Oates was slower than many at his duties, but his tasks were attended scrupulously and, when finished, none could fault them. Yet his sometimes plodding perseverance was held up to ridicule before all by Savage.

It was for Oates's sake that Carne inwardly fretted and strove to keep his fury under control. Septimus sometimes had to stand bodily between the two men, lest Carne's contempt for Savage's brutishness towards his friend cause him to lash out at the offender. Such violence, Septimus knew, was what the Third Mate courted. Rebellion would inevitably end with Oates being made a more pitiful scapegoat, and with his defender in irons. Savage would have triumphed, and his sly arrogance might well prove harder to bear than leg-irons and chains.

During one raging south-easterly gale, when Carne and Septimus took eight-hour watch together, they could scarcely keep to their feet for the violence of wind and storm. They were drenched to the bone from the iciness of spray, the ship rolling and heaving against the suck of the waves and their crashing violence which seemed set to splinter masts and deck. Almost blinded by the lash of hail and sea, their voices dying unheard above the screams of the blast, they somehow endured the physical agony of it, feeling, when all was over, as if their bodies had been pounded by blows as relentless as those which battered the wounded ship. They were grateful to return to their cramped cells, and for the blessing of warmed ale and sleep. Lying upon the boards where they fell, exhaustion claimed them almost before their salt-reddened eyelids closed.

It was only upon the morrow that they learned how Savage had first made Oates struggle aloft to secure the foresail, wrenched free from its gaskets by the ferocity of the storm. Then, upon his return to deck, all but frozen by cold and weather, he had sent him aloft again with three others, claiming to be dissatisfied with the speed with which he completed his task. He would have sent him aloft a third time but Oates, barely having survived the appalling savagery of it, was unable to stand and had been carried below by some of the crew, their resentment against the mate so bitter that even he had faltered and let Oates rest.

Upon the following day, Savage descended to where Oates still lay, feverish and drenched in sweat upon a straw palliasse. He had been barely able to open his eyes, or to recognise Savage, and although he struggled to stand, he fell to his knees, shuddering violently from a spasm of ague and the exhaustion which gripped him. Savage jerked Oates angrily to his feet, although he was forced to take the seaman's full weight, his massive fist wrenching at Oates's sweat-stained shirt front.

'Get up, you lazy sod! Show lively! I have had a bellyful of your moaning and idleness!' Repelled by the stench of his victim's corrupt sweat and his sickliness, Savage let him fall and the crack of Oates's head against the boards did not stay the mate's hand. He dealt Oates a fierce blow across the mouth, believing himself unseen.

Septimus, entering the open doorway, cried out in fury, 'Leave him be! Leave him be, I say, or, by God, I swear I will kill you . . . even if I swing from the yardarm for it!'

Savage hesitated only for a brief moment, the contorted anger of Fortune's face persuading him to do as he was bidden. 'Oates is a fool,' Savage blustered. 'A weak-minded fool. There is naught troubling him! He is idle to the bone . . . a malingerer!'

Septimus stared at him with such contemptuous loathing that Savage shifted his feet uncomfortably and dropped his gaze. Then, with aggravating slowness, he sauntered towards the open doorway, and turned, 'See that he makes ready for his watch,' he ordered abrasively. 'Let no-one stand in for him, you understand? I will not countenance it!'

'He will stand no watch this day,' declared Septimus with cold finality. 'You have my word upon it!'

'He had best be there, else either you or he will bear the charge of insubordination, and the flogging it demands, and you, Fortune, have my word upon *that*.'

Oates tried to rise, his agitation so fierce that Septimus knelt beside him and placed an arm securely under his neck to raise him, frightened by the rasping of the boy's breath deep in his throat. Blood trickled from the corner of Oates's mouth where Savage had struck him, but although his lips moved feverishly, he could utter no word, only harsh, unintelligible sounds. His hand gripped Fortune's arm with unexpected force, his eyes clouded and unfocusing.

''Twill be all right,' promised Septimus, with more assurance than he felt, but the boy's nervous grip with his thin fingers dug deeper into his flesh. 'Calm yourself, lad, he cannot do you harm. You must needs set your mind to ease on that, and rest awhile. 'Tis but a feverish ague, no more.'

Septimus felt the boy's neck grow limp and his head lying relaxed against the supporting curve of his arm. He cried aloud for someone to come and relieve him, his cries growing louder and more urgent.

It was Carne who came running, young face ravaged with pained disbelief.

'Care for him . . . Do not leave him!'

'He is not dead, Septimus?' Carne's voice was shrill and plaintive as a child's.

'No . . . Look to comfort him, lad, lest he awakens and be afeared. I will seek aid.'

Septimus felt as cold within as if his blood had congealed. 'If Oates should die,' he told himself, 'then I will murder Savage, as he has murdered him.'

Chapter Twenty-eight

Septimus was a seaman who had early learnt the value of living by the rules. He was neither inquisitive nor a trouble-maker, and by his very dependability he had earned acceptance by authority and his shipmates alike. It suited him well, for there were areas in his past which he jealously guarded. Indeed, until his unlikely friendship with Carne and Oates, he had deliberately held himself aloof, wanting no ties of loyalty to man or vessel.

With Savage's brutality towards Oates, he broke the rules of a lifetime and went to seek help. Moreover, he went directly to the cabin of the First Mate. The First Officer, a desiccated, remote young man by the name of Flanders, had been so astonished by Septimus's unorthodoxy in approaching him, and at his urgency, that he had invited him within and listened in silence to his outburst. Flanders had acted swiftly. With barely a glance about him at the austere desk with its racks of brass navigational instruments and the meticulously ordered charts, he had taken his boat-cloak from a hook on the cabin wall and accompanied Septimus without.

Flanders had always seemed a dry, pedantic individual, more at home with precision dividers and sextant than the untidiness of flesh and blood. Yet his concern for Oates had been real, and his action immediate. He had given orders that Oates be carried at once to a minute cabin, little more than a large storage cupboard, where a rope hammock had been set up, and one of the stewards detailed to attend him. When Septimus had made to thank him, he had brushed it irritably aside, 'You say no man is responsible for this seaman's condition, his injuries?'

'No, sir.' Fortune's response had been low, his expression guarded.

'How did he come by the blows to his face, the cut to his head?'

'I believe, sir, that he fell . . . He had been ordered aloft twice during the storm to secure the foresail. Exhaustion and cold must have forced him to stumble.'

'The injuries are recent, Fortune. The blood barely congealed.'

Septimus kept silent.

'Why did you not approach Mr Savage, or the Second Officer, Mr Hill? You are aware of ship's regulations!'

Septimus hesitated only fractionally, 'I could not locate them, sir . . . so not wishing to lose time . . .' His voice faltered beneath the First Mate's scrutiny, and died away. Then he added, more firmly, 'I would request your permission to visit Oates, sir.'

'And you find it more expedient to ask me, rather than go through the normal channels? Why?'

'Because you are here, sir, and aware of the gravity of Oates's condition.'

Flanders studied him keenly before conceding, at length, 'You have my permission.'

Septimus thanked him gravely, then hurriedly sought escape.

'Fortune?'

He hesitated and turned, filled with unease. 'Sir?'

'There is nothing you want to confide to me? Nothing I should know?'

'No, sir. Nothing.' What mattered now was William Oates's recovery, naught else.

When the time came for William Oates to go on watch, Carne confided to Fortune, his voice troubled, 'I had best take his place, Sep. There has been no new instruction given. Savage will expect it.'

'No! Leave it,' Septimus ordered.

nnation, Flanders. They will see the flogging!' the
had blustered, his mind so befuddled that he could
speak coherently. 'That is your justice . . . rough
dy . . . Savage will see it rendered.'
age?' Flanders' tone had just the right air of amused
cension to rouse Huskings. 'But he is the officer
d, the prisoner's accuser.' He smiled deprecating-
, no, sir! It would not be correct procedure at

n you must make it your affair, Flanders, not mine,'
gs said irritably. 'Must I do everything on board?
t enough that I assume command? I arbitrate over
must I dispense the damned punishment too?'
sir. I will attend to it,' promised Flanders smoothly.
am senior in rank and service to Savage, and have
pressed authority, I may lawfully overrule him.'
cipline, Flanders,' mumbled Captain Huskings, 'you
and? We shall have need of officers of strength and
ment like Savage. Not squeamish . . . willing to
is confused ramblings broke off. 'Steward! My hat
at-cloak! Where is that confounded fool? Hurry,
becile, I have not got all day!' His cloak fastened,
gs turned abruptly, then staggered and all but fell,
ly by Flanders' supporting hand. 'Steward! Get
n made ship-shape!'
ervant's expressionless eyes met those of Flanders
e squalor and disorder of the captain's living quar-
rumpled bed with its curtain drawn haphazardly
e cluttered desk, the stench of spirits and stale
ke.

d already settled upon one of his toadies from
lower deck seamen to serve as 'flogger', a duty
ld have disgusted any in his right mind, for it
l and degrading ritual for all concerned. The
sen, Joe Fields, was a shambling bear of a crea-
sy and slow-witted, but of massive strength
une had once, jokingly, remarked barely made

'But he will turn his anger against you!'
'Then let him!'
Savage, as Carne had predicted, came blundering and
cursing below, infuriated that Fortune had made direct
appeal to Flanders, and fearful that complaint had been
laid against him, and entered in the ship's log. His coarse,
pock-marked face was malevolent as he ordered, 'Get yourself on watch, Fortune! Shape yourself, you idle sod, else
the weight of my hand will help you!'
Carne made to intervene and to go in his stead but
Septimus stayed him with a restraining hand, declaring
calmly, 'No. I am called for the night watch. I cannot take
both, nor can Seaman Grey neither. So, which is it to be?'
'Hell and damnation!' Savage's florid face was engorged
with anger, 'I have given you an order. Obey it!' He started
to turn on his heel.
Septimus declared clearly, 'I cannot stand watch for sixteen hours. It is more than flesh and blood can tolerate! So
there is an end to it.'
'You insolent bastard! Would you defy me? I have given
you an order! Obey it!' Savage grabbed Fortune by his shirt
front and shook him like a terrier shakes a rat, then released
him abruptly and hurled him hard against a wooden beam.
'Damn your insolence!' Savage's voice was thick with rage.
'Go, or it will be a charge of mutiny you will be facing!'
'Then that is what it must be.'
Septimus, despite the mate's rough treatment, was oddly
composed, setting his clothing to rights phlegmatically. In
a moment, goaded beyond all sense and endurance, Savage
was upon him, striking at him with his fists, kicking, raining blows. Instinctively, Carne ran to tear Savage away
from his friend, for the seaman appeared paralysed, helpless
to shield himself against the insane onslaught of violence.
'No, lad!' Septimus screamed, the anguish in his voice
halting Carne. 'You must swear witness! I have not struck
Savage a blow . . . not even to defend myself.'
Savage, the cry somehow penetrating the fog of his madness, faltered and his fists dropped to his side. Fortune's

face was a bloodied mess, barely recognisable, and Carne, feeling nausea and rage within him, would have leapt upon Savage to force revenge yet Septimus painfully shook his head, eyes imploring him to stay aloof, and, sick with pity, Carne obeyed.

Savage stood quite still for a long moment. 'You, Seaman Grey,' he ordered, voice coldly controlled, 'will bear witness that Seaman Fortune wilfully disobeyed a command of his superior officer.'

'Bear witness, sir?' Carne glanced in bewilderment towards Septimus who was supporting himself with difficulty against the scarred upright of an oak beam, but Fortune's eyes were fastened upon Savage. He did not speak but his mouth twisted wryly in the rawness of his face as, with painful effort, he straightened himself and spat contemptuously at Savage's feet.

Captain Huskings had been irritated at being disturbed, and showed it. By his rudely flushed face and choler and the reek of spirits in his cabin Savage knew that Huskings had been drinking steadily. His gait was unsteady and his speech undeniably slurred. When Savage had made complaint about Septimus Fortune, declaring him to be an agitator and born rebel, the captain tried to concentrate upon what was being said and form an opinion. His senses were befuddled and his wits slow, but he managed to absorb the gist of the Third Mate's diatribe against indiscipline and the dangers it posed.

Savage congratulated himself upon the way he had dealt with the situation. Having persuaded the captain to his own way of thinking, he left the man to his drink and returned below in rare good humour.

'You, Seaman Grey,' he ordered, voice coldly controlled, 'will alert the ship's company. See that all are assembled on deck. Captain's orders! I will except no-one. Every man – save the helmsman – will attend. That is an order, obey it!'

Carne looked helplessly towards Septimus, who had drag-

314

ged himself upright and was supporting culty against the scarred oak of a downl

'What would you have me tell the asked.

'That they will witness a flogging.'

'All of the lower deck, Mr Savage?'

'All!'

'But what of the sick, sir?

'Those who cannot walk unaided others.'

Defying regulations, Carne had gone to direct appeal, knowing even as he did expect no countermanding of the captain offered to stand witness for Septimu Savage's brutality to Oates was at the and Septimus had struck no blow. Ca been unshakeable and bore the seal of h had been equally obdurate. The decisi and was irreversible. Carne had pleade Oates be at least spared the hideousne had been denied. Flanders had been Rules and regulations must be adhere all future petitioning be made thro Third Mate.

Flanders had appeared to Ca unmoved by the flagrant injusti ordered. Yet, to his credit, he had tain Huskings, asking that the flo the alleged offence be commuted

'Alleged?' Huskings had dem alleged, sir, but proven! Have officer? Would you accept the above his? They are the filth thieves, vagrants, prisoners fle

'I ask only, sir, that you them opportunity to state the seen to be done.'

'Da
captai
scarce
and re
'Sav
conde
involv
ly. 'O
all!'
'Th
Huskii
Is it n
all . .
'No
'Since
your e
'Di
unders
comm
ang.' '
and b
you im
Huskin
saved
this cab
The s
above th
ters: the
aside, th
cigar sm

Savage h
among th
which wo
was a cru
seaman ch
ture, clum
which For

up for the weakness of his head.

However, on this occasion, Flanders used his authority to overrule the Third Mate's choice, declaring it to be brutal and malevolent. Savage was incensed, yet also well drilled enough to know that Flanders' position was inviolate, and his ruling law.

'What were your orders for this seaman? How many lashes did you demand?'

'Thirty,' mumbled Savage reluctantly.

'Thirty! Dear God in heaven! Are you mad? Would you murder him?'

"Twas a crime near to mutiny.'

Flanders stared at him with ill-concealed loathing to say contemptuously, 'I, sir, will be the arbiter of that. Fortune will be punished, as he deserves, with five lashes. It is justice, not revenge, we seek.'

The rebuke did nothing to diminish Savage's sullen ill-humour, and although he made no overt protest, it was plain that Flanders' usurping of his authority rankled. Flanders was aware of his enmity and festering resentment and he was aware, too, that although his uniform and rank provided immediate protection, it might not always be so. There were opportunities enough aboard ship for old scores to be bloodily and secretly settled, and Savage was not a man to forget a slight. He would brood, and plot retribution, and Fields might well be the instrument to deliver it, for the Third Mate was too cunning to stain his own hands with violence. Flanders sighed as he took his place beside Captain Huskings. It was a hellish business, filthy and degrading, and his stomach and mind rebelled at the obscenity of it. Yet he had work to do and must not weaken. He had chosen an honest seaman to deliver the whip, a man who, unlike Fields, would not revel in the undertaking of it. He had reduced the punishment. There was no more he could do.

At midday the sun was at its height, its glowing intensity so fierce that to look at it burned the eyes. There was no

317

relief from its heat or brightness. As Captain Huskings had commanded, all save the helmsman were gathered on deck to witness the flogging of Septimus Fortune. Even William Oates, feverish and barely conscious, had been carried aloft upon a canvas stretcher. Carne stood guard rigidly beside him, so gripped with anger and pain at the barbarity of what was to be publicly enacted that he was as little aware of his surroundings as Oates. Despite the fierce heat and the oppressive airlessness that seemed to weigh upon him, he felt colder than at any moment in his life.

He knelt beside Oates, trying to make sense of the sounds that the boy made, and wiping the fevered sweat from the seaman's flushed face.

'Stand upright, Seaman Grey!' Savage commanded harshly.

Carne rose despairingly to his feet. Sick with apprehension, he watched as the heavy iron grating was manhandled awkwardly into position, then firmly lashed to the ship's mast. His mouth was dry and his palms moist with sweat. This was like some nightmare of the past returned, unbidden, to haunt him. It was Penry Vaughan's face he saw, cruelly malevolent, and his own flesh that burned and broke at the lash of the whip. He knew that he would relive and feel, with Septimus, every gout of blood drawn, every rupture of skin.

Next, two seamen brought Septimus from below, hands tied, feet loosely bound, lest he be tempted, perhaps, to hurl himself bodily over the ship's side. Septimus's face was ugly and swollen with the beating he had taken, yet he held himself tall and his eyes, from their bruised pouches, were steady as they met Carne's. Beside him, William Oates stirred restlessly and groaned.

Septimus, the bonds at feet and wrists untied, was pressed, face down, upon the iron grille, his cords refastened more tightly. Savage stepped forward to inspect them and, with a swift pitiless gesture, ripped the shirt from Fortune's back, leaving its paleness exposed. There was an indecency in his eagerness and in the slight smile that curved his lips, and Carne felt his fingernails cutting into his clenched palms as he fought to control the hatred he felt towards him. Septimus's flesh bore a lacing of old scars; lesions which had healed and faded. That he was no stranger to deprivation or savagery was clear.

Harding, the seaman who had been ordered to flog him, stepped forward. His face, despite its weathered skin, was grey and pained. It was he who knelt beside Fortune, bidding him in a low voice to unclench his jaws that a leather 'bullet' might be inserted between his teeth, lest agony force him to bite through his tongue. He could not look directly into Fortune's eyes as the head of the cruelly spreadeagled man twisted awkwardly towards him, mouth agape, to take the leather.

Harding stepped back uncertainly, bare feet pressed hard against the boards to bolster him against the insistent pitch and roll of the ship. Savage prised the whip from the grasp of another seaman standing by and thrust it into Harding's hands.

'Brace yourself!' Savage's voice rang out clear warning, and it was not Fortune alone who flexed himself, muscles held rigid, but all of the ship's company. The whip rose with a hiss, lash snaking unerringly towards exposed flesh, laying it raw. The cut gaped into a mouth, open, surging blood. A silence seemed to have stilled the sea and the creaking of mast and board, until the expulsion of the watchers' breath escaped in a sigh, echoing the upward flight of the lash. Once more it fell, on Savage's command, lacerating, raking up blood. There was a cry from a man's throat, wild and despairing, raw as the scream of an animal in pain. Oates had somehow willed himself to his feet. His face gleamed palely with sweat, features swollen and distorted; a drowned man surfacing. Before Carne could reach out to lend support, there broke from Oates such a wail of anguish that it made every man's blood congeal. He lurched forward, hand raised to stay Harding's whip, then faltered, and fell to the boards to lie still.

'Leave him!' Savage cried. 'Leave him, I say! That is an

order! Seaman Harding,' he instructed stolidly, 'continue with the punishment.'

The whip rose and fell, biting, splitting flesh wide, but mercifully Septimus could no more feel its pain since his body was now hanging limply, flesh and mind unable to bear the obscenity of it.

It was Flanders who ordered, after the final stroke, 'Cut Seaman Fortune down. Take him below.'

A deckhand threw a bucket of sea-water over Septimus's sore flesh, its surface scored with raised and bloodied weals, and cut away his bonds.

Savage made as if to follow the two men who carried his inert body below, but Flanders halted him, declaring forcefully, 'Mr Savage, you will stay, sir, and supervise the cleaning of the deck. Too much blood has been spilt.'

Savage flushed but obeyed, tersely directing men to dismantle and return the grating, and ordering Joe Fields to scrub away Septimus's spilt blood from the boards.

'Seaman Grey!'

'Sir?' Carne stiffened at Flanders' call.

'You may accompany Seaman Oates below, with his bearers.' The eyes of the two men briefly met and, although no further word was spoken between them, each was as aware of the other's pity and understanding as if it had been declared aloud. Flanders assisted the captain to his cabin as Huskings stumbled inelegantly, skin florid and moist, cursing volubly at the heaving of the vessel and the obstacles in his path.

Until his midnight watch, Carne spent what time he could tending Septimus, trying to ease the worst of his torment. In his agony, Septimus cursed aloud, gripping Carne's hand so fiercely that he had to prise his fingers apart. When he was able, he went to William Oates's side, kneeling helplessly beside his gaunt form, able only to sponge his fevered brow.

When he returned from watch exhausted in flesh and spirit, Carne went once more to Oates. But Oates was dead. He had died alone.

Chapter Twenty-nine

Late autumn was gradually yielding to winter. There had been a dampness of November mists which soaked into the bones as insidiously as they crept across Penavon land, and then several sharp, piercing frosts so intense that even the branches and twigs were cased in ice. It had been hazardous to venture abroad and, for the first time, Jane knew true loneliness, denied Prys's company, and all sight and knowledge of Carne.

She spent many hours in the straw chair before the fire, thawing her bones and remembering the past. One afternoon, the sound of a horse clattering on to the cobbled yard jolted her from her musing, its iron shoes ringing with unusual clarity upon the frosted air. Charles or Jethro, she wondered, hurrying to see, or Peter Morrish perhaps. When Jane opened the door, the snow was already falling in flakes large and soft as curled feathers. Through its soft veil, she could not, at first, make out the features of the figure which had dismounted.

'Mostyn? Master Mostyn? Is it you?' The old, childish name had sprung to her lips.

'Yes, ma'am. It is Mostyn Havard.' The slight emphasis upon his last name was intentional.

'Oh . . . Mr Havard!' exclaimed Jane, flustered into awkwardness. 'I had not expected to see you . . . I have heard no word . . . Not this long time.'

'If you will invite me within,' he said pointedly. 'It has been a cold ride, and perilous, my mare grew hesitant upon the icy byways.'

'You will forgive my discourtesy,' Jane declared, with a hint of her old self-possession. 'Surprise and pleasure have robbed me of the few wits and manners I possess. I beg you will come inside and warm yourself at my fire.'

Mostyn merely nodded and fastened his mount's bridle to the iron ring set into the wall of the house. Following her within, his supercilious gaze carefully took in the cramped smallness of the place and its apparent poverty. He stood, fingering the brim of his elegant silk hat.

'If you will seat yourself, Master . . . *Mister* Havard,' she corrected herself, flushing, 'I will bring you refreshment.'

He waved the offer aside impatiently, declaring, 'I shall not be remaining. It is a fleeting visit only. Business presses hard upon me . . . There is, however, a purpose in my coming.'

'Carne? You have news of Carne?'

'None,' he said dismissively. 'I have no doubt that he will return when he deems the time right, and he is no longer in fear of the gibbet.'

Jane, hurt and disappointed, searched Mostyn's face in vain for some sign of the timid, terrified child she had known. He was handsome, certainly, but there was an arrogance about him, a discontent about the weakness of his mouth, which troubled her. She did not doubt that he had prospered, for his clothes were of the latest mode, and clearly expensively tailored.

'You were not at the funeral of my husband . . . Hywel Prys.'

The unexpectedness of the remark, so expressionlessly delivered, surprised him into discomfiture. He was silenced only briefly before declaring urbanely, 'To my regret, ma'am. My own grave illness prevented it. I was set upon by common rogues who attacked me, leaving me all but dead. But for the courtesy of my good friends, the Llewellyns at Great House, the outcome might have been disastrous.'

Jane merely said, 'It is fortunate that your employer treats those who serve him with consideration. It is not always so with master and servant.'

Mostyn's lips tightened fractionally, but he quickly recovered his usual composure to correct, languidly, 'I fear you are mistaken, ma'am. I am an equal, not a servant.'

'Indeed?' Jane's tone was deceptively mild. 'As you will know, I could not be expected to fully appreciate such a relationship, although it was my privilege in times past.'

Mostyn, looking bored, made no answer.

'Oh, and I fear that I could not thank you for that shilling you had sent out to me lately, when I drove to Great House seeking news of Master Carne. I hope that it was returned to you, as I instructed?'

'It was crass and foolish of me,' Mostyn admitted stiffly, 'but charitably meant. I have no doubt that the fool of a manservant gave garbled explanation.'

'No,' said Jane innocently. 'He gave precise explanation. He could not be faulted.'

'I was engaged upon business – a conference with Lord Litchard, Mr Llewellyn and others – but it is not of that I wish to speak.'

'Then I shall be seated, if you will not,' declared Jane firmly, waiting for him to show her the courtesy of offering her a chair. When he did not defer to her, she lifted one and set it beside the fire.

'I have come, ma'am, to offer you a cottage in the village. A dwelling nearer Penavon.' He glanced around him disdainfully. 'A place more convenient and better furnished than this . . . pitiful ruin, so far removed from the beaten track.'

Jane stared at him in astonishment, a cold fury mounting within her.

Taking her silence for gratitude, he continued brashly, 'You are old, ma'am, and alone. You could be set upon by vandals, or die here, untended.'

'Your concern does you credit.' In her anger at his impertinence, she could scarce spit out the words. ''Tis a pity it comes so late! Do not dare to patronise me, sir, nor salve your conscience at my expense!'

323

'I had no such intention,' he rebutted irritably.

'This is my house, my land.' She spoke distinctly and with venom. 'I will trouble you to leave it! You are trespassing here!'

'Damnation, Jane!' he exploded.

'You will call me Mrs Prys, for that is my lawful name, as this is my lawful property. You have no claim upon it! No rights! I do not know why you have come, nor at whose bidding, if it is not at your own. But I swear that neither threats nor bribes will move me. You understand?'

'You are a foolish, senile old woman. Obstinate, and not worth a candle. You are undeserving of pity and help!'

'I am too proud for pity, and have no need of help – save from my friends, who offer it freely. You may tell your master, equal, or whatever you choose to call Mr Rhys Llewellyn, that when I leave here, it will be in my coffin. When God calls, and not he.'

Mostyn gave her a look of such malevolent loathing that she feared he might strike her, and he actually moved towards her, then turned abruptly upon his heel, and left without a word. When she heard the muffled sounds of his horse's hooves fading, she went to the door and peered without. The yard and mountains beyond were shawled with drifted snow, and the air had grown warmer, yet there was a chill within her. Mr Randall Walters would know what to do. He would make sure that none could put her upon the road. The cottage was hers by rights. Surely none could trick or wrest it from her? Jane returned slowly to her chair and, with her arms clasped tightly about her shoulders, rocked herself to and fro for comfort, but none came. Her grief was not only because she was afraid, but for what Mostyn, Rice Havard's son, had become.

Mostyn set out sullenly upon the frozen byway from Hillbrook, imprudently whipping his mare into action to relieve his resentment. The terrified mare tried valiantly to respond, yet her metal shoes could find no grip upon the treacherous surface, slithering awkwardly, ears laid back, eyes showing their whites.

'Hell and damnation!' exclaimed Mostyn, venting his spleen and whipping her the harder, 'Are you stupid? Lame? Get on with it, I say!'

They had reached a small stream, fed by waters gushing from a fissure in the rock of the mountainside above, yet so fierce was the cold that the tiny cataract was now a fall of ice, white as spilled candle wax, and the stream as solid. The mare had halted abruptly, fearful to leap, but Mostyn, his mind still upon the slight which Jane, a mere servant, had inflicted upon him, was in no mood to be denied.

'Jump, damn, you! Jump.' He laid the whip so viciously across the mare's shoulder that it flayed her raw. In an agony of pain and terror, she reared up, hooves raking the frosted air, and threw him to the ground. 'Damn your miserable hide!' He set a hand to the bridle, and was about to leather her beyond endurance, blind and deaf to all but his own rage to inflict hurt.

'Havard! A moment of your time . . .'

Mostyn, fuming with annoyance, spun around, jaw clenched, to face the interloper. Charles Hartrey, who had been painstakingly leading his mount along the icy pathway, was regarding him contemptuously from the other side of the stream.

'It seems,' Charles accused coldly, 'that you treat animals as cruelly, and with as little regard as you treat ladies.'

'I treat ladies as ladies, and common women and trollops as they deserve,' Mostyn snarled, too incensed for caution. 'You have my answer, Hartrey. Now get clear of my way, your face offends me!'

'And your manners, sir, offend me! Or your lack of them!'

'And what will you do to improve them, farmer?'

In a trice Charles, his square solid face set pugnaciously, had leapt the stream and was at Mostyn's side, snatching the whip from his hand and belabouring him with the force and accuracy that had bedevilled the mare. Mostyn, in a white-hot rage, would have snatched the whip from him, but, despite his swiftness and his skills at fencing, was no match for sheer brawn and outraged righteousness. All Mostyn could do was shield his face from the raining blows as Charles beat him remorselessly to the ground, revenge and hatred killing all reason. When his anger was spent, Charles broke the whip across his knee, effort reddening his features, his breath a frosted cloud.

'Get up, Havard!' he ordered scathingly, kicking at Mostyn's boots as he lay cowering beneath his arms, as if to ward off further blows 'I have finished with you.' Charles put out a hand to steady him but Mostyn brushed the gesture aside, struggling unaided to his feet. One cheek was streaked with globs of dark blood and he shook them aside viciously, trying vainly to restore his dishevelled clothing to order.

'You are an oaf, Hartrey, and will answer for this, I swear!' There was a whiteness about Mostyn's mouth, his lips so stiff with mortification that he could scarce spit out the words, 'You will pay for your damned interference, farmer!'

'What? Will you beat me as bravely as you beat a defenceless woman, or that wretched dumb animal you own?' Charles, goaded, cringed in mock fear. 'Then try it now! We are both unarmed, and better matched.'

Mostyn muttered angrily, but made no move.

'No?' taunted Charles, 'but then, I am neither defenceless nor dumb.' He spat contemptuously at Mostyn's boots. 'You are not a man, Havard, but a pathetic apology for one! A foppish, affected, little charlatan, more concerned with the cut of your breeches than proving your worth! You sicken and disgust me!'

'And you . . .' sneered Mostyn, face disfigured with hatred, '. . . are a clod. A common labourer, with neither birth nor breeding! I do not bandy words with inferiors, the servant class! You are beneath my contempt! Scum!'

'Beware, then, Havard,' warned Charles, drily amused, 'for scum has a habit of rising.'

Outfaced and humiliated, Mostyn made to retrieve his mare, which tossed her head rebelliously, and tried to pull away, fearful of punishment.

'Shall I hold her steady for you, sir?' demanded Charles. 'Lift your boot into the stirrup, perhaps? 'Tis plain that your horse has as little liking for you as I.'

Mostyn mounted in hostile silence.

'Why were you riding from Jane Prys's cottage?' Charles demanded.

'It is none of your damned business!' exclaimed Mostyn petulantly. 'I ride where I please . . . see whom I please.'

'No,' corrected Charles quietly, 'there are places and people forbidden to you, Havard!'

'Damn you! You dare to utter threats against me!' blustered Mostyn, gripping the reins more tightly.

'I make no threat, Havard. I state a fact, and remind you of what you already know!'

Mostyn made to move off, but Charles cried imperiously, 'Wait!' He bent and retrieved Mostyn's silk hat from the wayside where it had rolled, dislodged in the fracas. Mostyn made to snatch it away, but Charles set it firmly to the frozen earth and stepped hard upon it, then he placed it in Mostyn's outstretched hand.

'You are a fool, Hartrey! A stupid, puerile idiot!' He hurled the hat savagely away, 'Empty-headed and ignorant!'

'Then perhaps I had best retrieve it for myself,' declared Charles, unruffled, 'for it will be as much at home on my head as yours!' He did so, battering it straight and then doffing it extravagantly as Mostyn urged his horse back, then forced it onwards to clear the stream. 'Take care!' called Charles solicitously. 'The path is icy, and I would grieve to see your mare break a leg!'

'The devil take you,' exploded Mostyn as, smarting from his double humiliation, he rode on without turning his head.

On riding through the pillars of Great House, Mostyn's outrage had given way to self-pity. He felt the old, treacherous burn of tears at the remembrance of the humiliation he had been forced to endure. Thank God it had not been witnessed by others! He could not have borne it if Danfield and the others had seen him so disgraced and made the butt of that great lout's clumsy humour. How was he to explain the bloodied weal across his cheek, congealed and crusted now? His clothes were ruined, as was his plan to distinguish himself in Rhys Llewellyn's eyes by acting boldly, and upon his own initiative. Oh, damnation! he thought vexedly, I can scarce credit the stupidity of Jane Prys and Hartrey! They are simple-minded lunatics! They speak the language of the farmyard and do not comprehend anything beyond muck and filth, too ignorant to be helped or instructed! He dismounted at the stables, each movement a pain he could scarce endure, biting his lip fiercely to avoid crying out. A groom led his horse away swiftly, his face a polite mask, but his eyes insolently amused. Had he his whip, Mostyn thought, he would have set it about the wretch's shoulders, taught him a bitter lesson!

Laurel ran across the cobbles of the yard to greet him, colour fading as she stared in dismay at his disordered clothes and the bloodied cut across his cheek. 'Oh, Mostyn! Mostyn! You have been hurt. Oh, your poor face! Has Danzig thrown you? Was it the icy roads?' Her voice and face were filled with concern as she stretched out a comforting hand to his shoulder to help him within. The pain was so savage that he cried aloud.

'Hell's teeth!' he exclaimed. 'Must you always creep about and fondle me? I am a man, not a lap dog to be for ever petted and fussed over. I tell you, Laurel, I am sick to death of your mooning and harassing me. I can scarce breathe for your confounded pestering.'

Laurel's face had flushed red, then grown drained of all colour as she said in a tight, high voice, 'I know you are in pain, Mostyn. But you have no cause to treat me so. It is cruel . . . and I am not deserving of it.' She turned back to face him, hands clenched. 'Well, and was it another fight, Mostyn? Someone seeking revenge for you cheating at cards? A gaming debt unpaid?'

Despite the fierce agony it caused him, he grasped her arm, saying clearly, and with venom, 'No . . . a woman. It was about a *real* woman, of flesh and blood, not a cool, bloodless imitation, Laurel, like you! Someone of flesh and fire, and passion to match my own.'

He was actually shaking with rage, the tears coursing down his cheeks. Laurel, wide-eyed and sick with jealous anger, stared at him, then ran wildly within and to her room. Mostyn's face, she thought bleakly, had been spiteful, evil almost, in its loathing, as he had flung those words at her. Yet Mostyn had not seen Laurel's face, nor Saranne's but another's, tortured by childish memory of something witnessed, but not fully understood. The face he saw was Marged Howell's: passionate, tortured and grieved to near madness as she hurled the coppers into Rice Havard's tomb.

At Hillbrook, Charles listened in silence to Jane's explanation of Mostyn's mission. The offer of a fine cottage nearer to Penavon did not ring true. What possible use could Havard find for Jane's poor isolated dwelling? It had neither value nor workable land. Perhaps, Charles reflected, Havard was determined to claw back from her what he considered to be rightfully his own. Yet, it was more likely that the cottage's very inaccessibility was the key. It would make an ideal venue for gaming, cock-fighting, or for conveniently housing common doxies and field whores for 'gentlemen's' sport. He could not even hint at such heresy to Jane, so contented himself with comforting her and assuring her that he would ride, that very afternoon, to ask advice of Randall Walters, despite the icy highway.

That brought him, most conveniently, to the true purpose of his visit. The attorney, upon Peter Morrish's recommendation, had agreed to take him into his chambers as a clerk, for the winter months. The farm had little need of him before early spring, and Jethro had finally been prevailed upon to allow it, since the money offered would be a godsend.

'I am glad, my dear,' said Jane truthfully, 'but you must go easy in the telling of affairs at home. Jethro is a good man, but afeared that your heart does not lie in farming. That you are clever, and a scholar, is a threat. Do not unman him by showing, too proudly, that you are the breadwinner, and he survives by charity.'

'No, Mrs Prys. I will tread carefully.'

'And ride so, too!' she adjured sternly, 'for you are as restless as a moth at a candle flame, and as open to courting danger.'

Charles promised to behave most soberly, smiling indulgently, and kissing her withered cheek. She weighed barely more than a child, he thought, and the loss of Prys and Carne had left her increasingly frail and vulnerable.

'You will take care,' he said impulsively, 'to keep the door well chained? And do not wander into the yard, for fear of slipping upon the ice. I have brought fuel enough for the fire, and fed the mule, and mucked out his stable. There is little enough water, but the snow I have gathered will soon melt in the buckets before the fire. Take heed that you boil it well, Mrs Prys, and be wary in handling the kettle, lest it spill and scald you.'

His earnest young face was creased with concern.

'Be off with you!' cried Jane laughing, yet touched by his thoughtfulness. 'I learnt such things before you were in your cradle, or your mother before you! Do not try to teach your grandmother to suck eggs!'

'Indeed, I would not,' disclaimed Charles, wry-faced. 'It is an art I have not acquired, and I do not intend to persevere.'

'But, with your farming?' Jane asked quietly.

'I do not know, Mrs Prys. I honestly do not know.'

Jethro walked with difficulty towards the hay bale in the great barn and sat down gratefully upon it. He hoped that no-one had seen him crossing the yard with his shot gun for he had walked unsteadily, unable to hide the weakness in his limbs and the trembling that possessed them. He could not remember when he had first become aware of it, for it seemed to have been with him so long; that great weariness that lay deep within the blood itself. He sometimes felt as if his arms and legs were shackled with iron chains, and he could scarce bear their weight, nor breathe, for the effort it took to move them. It was not the farm alone which troubled him, nor Charles, nor yet the violence that had so nearly destroyed Saranne's life, and with it his own. No, it lay deeper even than that. It was a blackness of the spirit that overshadowed all else, a cloud that cut out light and warmth, so that he grew numbed of feeling. A blind man grasping at darkness.

He had tried to keep the terror of it from Sara, ashamed of his weakness, forcing himself to the tasks that had once been pleasure. Yet his head ached constantly with a throbbing hurt, and he knew that his vision grew poor, for he saw all as through a film of tears, blurred and unrelated. Sometimes the light seemed to fade, so that it was hard to distinguish between night-time and day and, if he stretched out a hand to reach something, a tool or such, his fingers could not reach it. Sometimes, if they did, it fell from his awkward grasp, and he could not clearly see to retrieve it. He did not know what ailed him, but he was afeared that it was the same creeping sickness from which his father had died; some slow paralysis that had taken movement, sight and speech, leaving him a useless husk, tended like a helpless babe.

Dear God! The palsied shaking of his hands and limbs began again, then the fiercer jerking he was powerless to control. With an effort he lifted the gun, feeling it jump within his grasp, as if it, and not he, were possessed with life. Then, clumsily, and with the greatest difficulty, he removed the safety catch. He sat uselessly for a while, thinking of what the future might hold for those he loved, and for himself – the cruel erosion of dignity and respect, the dependency. Yet he could not bring himself to pull the trigger that would end it all. His head ached, and there was a burning, crushing violence in his breast. He wept aloud for the stubborn flame within him that still burned and would not be extinguished, that helpless clinging to dead life. The pain had grown intolerable now, and he could scarcely struggle to his feet. It was beyond bearing. He could believe that his ribs were being crushed between the great grinding stones of a mill. He stood for a moment, a cry of despair breaking from him as he was devoured by an all-consuming pain. I will go to Marged, he thought. She will know what ails me . . . Lend me her help. He tried to cry out for Sara or Saranne, but he could neither move nor make sound. He knew that he stumbled, and there was a noise so violent that it ripped apart the air with his flesh. There was a red mist clouding his eyes, and the salt taste of it within his mouth. Jethro could not know that it was his own blood.

Sara, returning carefully upon the waggon with Saranne along the frozen byway to the farm, heard the sound of a gun and steadied the cob which had taken fright at the sound, soothing and calming it.

''Tis Tom Hallowes,' she declared as Saranne, white faced, made to leap down. 'He is searching some hare or bird for the pot . . . or else 'tis Jethro fending off a fox, or keeping rats from the grain.'

Charles, riding behind them down the barren approaches to the farm, urged the mare on, despite the dangers. He scrambled down at the gate and ran to the barn from whence the sound had come. When he beheld Jethro's ravaged flesh, he could not, at first, move for horror and disbelief, nor bring himself to advance towards such bloodiness. The sickness of gall rose to his lips and he turned away as if to flee; then, to his shame, he retched and vomited upon the loose hay of the barn floor. He could not doubt that Jethro was dead and sorrow, rage and guilt so fiercely possessed him that he could have lifted the lifeless corpse, shaking it in a frenzy, willing it to breath and feeling. He rested his head against the coldness of a beam and wept until he could weep no more. Then he took off his jacket and laid it over Jethro's poor, torn flesh, to cover his face and those sad, unseeing eyes. He walked listlessly without and padlocked the doors of the barn, that none might enter.

With Saranne and Sara weeping and left to the care of Megan and Tom Hallowes, Charles rode to summon Peter Morrish, and thence to Randall Walters' office. His decision had been made. His life and future must be upon the farm. It was owed to his mother and Saranne, and it was all he could do now for Jethro.

Why? he asked himself. In the name of pity, why? The answer he returned to was always the same. Because of me. I failed him. I was not the son he wanted me to be. He killed himself from bitterness and hurt. Guilt will lie heavily upon me. I shall never be rid of it, nor the sight of that bloodied, defeated face.

Peter Morrish tried to give him ease of conscience, but Charles would take no comfort. He had been tried, and found wanting. He must redeem himself by being all that Jethro had hoped.

Saranne ran to Peter Morrish, embracing him, burying her head against his breast, weeping inconsolably, and he stroked her hair as if she were that poor, bewildered child again, keeping vigil at the pillory through the darkness of long night. Sara, too, was shocked and all but deranged by grief. She also would have fled to him, seeking the warm comfort of his understanding, yet, although he spoke to her gently with words of encouragement and affection, he did not gather her instinctively into his protective embrace. His heart bled for her and he felt her grief and bewilderment as rawly as if they were his own. Yet, in touching her, drawing her close in physical embrace, he would have denied all that he believed most devoutly. In doing so, he would have betrayed Jethro's friendship, and forfeited all right to future love. Sara felt only his coldness and the deliberation with which he set himself apart, neither touching her in gentleness nor stemming her tears. Although she had loved Jethro dearly, like all others when death comes, she was wracked with guilt and regret for things done and undone, spoken or left unsaid. Help me! she wanted to cry aloud to Morrish. Comfort me; hold me in the shelter of your arms; lift me from my grief, as you raised up Jane and Saranne. Why do you turn away from me? I am forsaken, bereft. If she wept into her pillow, and agonised, it was because she feared that Peter Morrish truly believed that Jethro's death was owed to her. It accounted for his rejection, the contempt for her that killed all warmth. She could never forgive him for turning away.

Peter Morrish had wept and agonised too; begging God to show him the way that would bring the least crippling hurt. One day, if God willed it, he would tell Sara that he had stayed aloof, denied her, so that one day he might come to her openly, and without guilt, to offer his love. Still, his chosen vocation set him apart. He had always known that it would be a lonely path, bitter, and beset by temptations and sacrifice and he could only pray that, in denying temptation, he had not sacrificed Sara's trust. It was a cross he did not know if he was strong enough to bear.

For those at Penavon, it had been a long cruel winter and even the promise of a warm and early spring could not mitigate the harshness of it. For the living, life went on, funny, tragic, unpredictable and as inevitable as the changing of the seasons, the unalterable cycle of existence itself. Jethro and Prys were dead and Carne alive to them only in memory. The lives of those who survived were changed, as they were changed. For Jane, whose memories of Prys were kind, it meant a using up of days and she thanked God that such days must now be few. Her hopes of seeing Carne again were growing weaker with the weakening of her own strength and limbs, but she would not admit her doubts, even to Megan. Megan, who loved Jane dearly, grieved at the changes in her, the forgetfulness, the encroaching feebleness. Yet she was sensitive that in its blurring of the senses, and time, age was not wholly cruel. It was a means of survival when reality had become too hard to bear.

Saranne missed Carne increasingly, and the days were long. She had loved Jethro unquestionably from that first moment when he had lifted her upon the farm waggon and carried her in his arms to a new life. He had been both father and deliverer to her, and his wilful abandonment, for that is how she thought of his death, revived all the old fears. Was it her heedlessness in going alone to the beechwoods which had so disturbed him that he had taken his own life? Had he felt she was worthless? Had her misery over Carne's leaving caused her to be blind to Jethro's hurt? If she had been kinder, more loving, would he have survived the darkness of his mind, and the greater darkness which lay beyond? She could never be sure.

Sara, too, bore a burden of guilt. What terror had forced Jethro to take his life so violently? She could not believe, as Charles had claimed, that it must have been some hideous accident, a moment's unguarded carelessness. No. Jethro had been too well disciplined and careful a man to unthinkingly allow such tragedy. She had observed some change in him, a restlessness, and remarked with laughter his added clumsiness. How could she have been so cruelly self-absorbed as not to have seen his need of her? She might have reassured him, as he had so often reassured her in the blackest hours. She had told Jane prophetically that she was not always worthy of Jethro, the man who had chosen her. That was a truth that she must learn to live with and bear alone. There would be no more clumsy reassurance of her worth, no indulgent laughter at Jethro's awkwardness. No laughter at all. It was too late to make amends. Perhaps, Sara thought regretfully, that was the real burden of the living, harder even than the acceptance of death.

Charles settled into planning how best he might improve the fortunes of Holly Grove. He pored long and sedulously over the farm accounts which Saranne had so meticulously kept. They brought him neither comfort nor solution. Disastrous harvests, taxes, and the shortage of seed had rendered the small holding all but bankrupt. The stock had dwindled, and those few beasts remaining were of poor quality and hard to feed, since the barns were nearly empty. Yet feed them he must, and either sell their produce or the animals themselves, for without the necessary money for purchasing what was needed to enrich the soil and stock, they would lose all. It was a vicious circle; a treadmill of plodding existence, without rest or reward.

Yet, unlike Jethro, Charles would not recognise the possibility of defeat. He would work, beg, importune others to come to his rescue with money if need be, promising them a generous return. He would approach Randall Walters, the seed and corn merchants, the provisioners, any who might ease the burden of debt. He would beg Peter Morrish to ask certain renowned breeders, friends of earlier days, for advice on rearing healthier cattle and sheep. He would hire an honest drover to drive his animals to Hereford, or London even, where the need was greatest and the prices high. If needs be, *he* would take them with Tom Hallowes and Megan, and leave the farm in Sara's care until their return.

Charles was young and energetic, and his optimism was unquenchable. He would succeed, he vowed. He was driven by a resolute urge to prove himself, and it would not be denied. Sara and Saranne were convinced that Charles was impelled by the need to make restitution for his father's death, and from fear for their future. Charles, alone, knew that what impelled him lay deeper. Success would be the means to release him from the farm. He would employ and direct others to tend his land, as did men like Rhys Llewellyn, Lord Litchard and others. Landowners and investors all. That it might prove difficult to bridge the chasm between poor farmer and gentleman of substance, Charles did not acknowledge. It was a challenge he had already accepted in his own mind. If a man believes in himself, he was convinced, then nothing on earth will stay him. Consequently he saddled his mare and thrust the neatly folded accounts into his saddlebag, and rode confidently towards Peter Morrish's cottage.

There was a warmth in the early spring air, and the hedgerows were breaking with new greenness, the purity of birdsong piercingly sweet. Inspired by a common stirring of blood, Charles began to whistle quietly, then to sing triumphantly aloud.

Chapter Thirty

They buried William Oates at sea the very next day, since
the weather grew hot and the presence of a corpse aboard
did nothing to ease the fears of the superstitious crew.
Flanders had spoken the age-old words reverently and with
real regret. 'We therefore commit his body to the deep . . .
Looking for the resurrection of the body . . . when the sea
shall give up her dead.' Carne had been one of the six
crewmen who had borne the frail, pathetically light burden
to the water. He had watched the chained and weighted
canvas strike hard upon the surface, then slide gently to
the ocean floor. The sea had closed about William Oates,
who had perished as if he had never been.

The heat then became suffocating, settling like a thick,
impenetrable blanket, slowing all movement and thought.
The ship was becalmed, its sails shrouded and useless, and
the seamen suffered the same lassitude, despite a lessening
of their duties. Water supplies ran dangerously low, with
no hope of rain, or of touching land, to provide replenish-
ment. Salt beef and smoked ham were an infrequent luxury
and fresh vegetables and fruit non-existent. The lower
deck's staple diet was hard unappetising biscuits, and even
these seemed tasteless and were alive with weevils and maggots. Tempers flared upon the slightest provocation, and
fights and petty revenges were commonplace.

Once, when Carne and Septimus were standing watch,
both men made listless and enervated by the unmoving air,
Carne asked, 'What cargo do we carry aboard, Sep?'

The older man hesitated before admitting with seeming

casualness, 'I'll be damned if I know!'

'But are you not curious, Sep? Did you not help load the cargo into the hold at Bristol?'

''Twas done by others before I set foot aboard, same as you.'

'Have you not enquired? Asked of someone?' Carne persisted.

'I have not!' declared Septimus, abruptly. ''Tis the business of a seaman to sail, and that I do as best as I am able. You had best do the same, lad. As like as not, the owners would resent my prying into their affairs as fiercely as I would resent their snuffling into mine! Let that be an end to it!'

But Carne's face remained troubled, his manner awkward, until finally, glancing anxiously about to make sure that they were alone and could not be overheard, he confessed, 'I think, Sep, from the crates I glimpsed in the hold, that we carry rifles.'

'Rifles? Perhaps you were mistaken.'

'No. I am sure of it. It was stencilled in black upon the raw wood.'

'What business took you into the hold?' asked Septimus sharply.

'I acted upon Mr Flanders' orders. He gave me the key to the officers' pantry . . . bade me bring up some wax-sealed bottles from the shelves, and boxes of victuals.'

'And?' Septimus's tone was harsh.

'The door was barred across with iron and padlocks. I set the lantern upon a box to lend me light to open it. It was then that I saw the crates.'

''Tis none of our affair!' exclaimed Septimus agitatedly, 'and you had best forget it!' He paused. 'You have spoken of it to no-one but me?'

'No-one,' admitted Carne, puzzled by his friend's vehemence.

'Then do not! Nor confide to any that it was Mr Flanders sent you.' Septimus gripped Carne's arm hard in his urgency, then, shamefacedly, let his hand relax and fall to his side, adding with awkwardness, 'It is plain that he suspects that you can read, else he would not have sent you.'

Carne was puzzling over why this should so distress Septimus when Septimus adjured quietly, 'Do not ask for explanation. I can give none. I hope that you have learned to trust me?'

Carne nodded, bewildered.

'Rifles . . . guns, are a common trading cargo,' Septimus continued. 'They may be lawfully exchanged with copra for varnish, ivory, tortoise shell, reptile skins . . . you understand?'

'Indeed, but . . .' Carne considered for a moment, '. . . why, then, may I not speak of it openly?'

'You are an innocent,' declared Septimus fiercely, 'and it will serve you better if you remain so . . . else others will see you buried, with William Oates. Be satisfied with that. Ask me no more. I will not answer. I beg you, do not speak of it again, or we must part, no longer friends.'

With this Carne had to be content, for Septimus was adamant upon it, and the subject closed.

In the weeks and months following Carne's flight from Penavon, Mostyn had gradually, imperceptibly, taken upon himself those tedious small duties which irritated Llewellyn most. In striving to gain his approval and trust, and to make himself indispensable, Mostyn had found, by accident, that direction which his life had formerly lacked. There was an excitement and stimulation in dealing and creating new money which held him in thrall. The pity lay in that the money was not his own. Llewellyn paid him handsomely, it was true, but in order to keep apace with Danfield and his friends, Mostyn ran himself increasingly into debt. Pride would not allow him to parade himself in their company any less modishly outfitted than they, so, as his tailor's, hatter's and bootmaker's bills grew more ruinous, Mostyn's wagering grew proportionately bolder and more desperate. His creditors, aware of his straitened circumstances, pressed him accordingly. Danfield and the others had expectations of inheritance or title and were never dunned, which only aggravated Mostyn the more. Laurel's patience had grown thin and Penry Vaughan, who was incurably parsimonious, refused to be held responsible for his young cousin's extravagances.

Mostyn was therefore persuasive in cultivating the good-will of Evan Lloyd, a minor employee of Rhys Llewellyn, who boasted a small office above the saddler's shop in Penavon village. Lloyd, who was of simple yeoman stock, held the ironmaster in awe and was flattered that a young gentleman of Mr Mostyn Havard's position and intellect should single him out for notice. It was Lloyd's responsibility to collect and make account of those dues delivered to him by tenants upon the Great House estate, including the rentals of the farms, saw mill, flour mill, brickyards, and all other small businesses and dwellings. He had learnt to read and figure at a Sunday School and was an earnest and assiduous scholar, grateful for the privilege of his lowly education. He was also honest and cautious at his work and, when Mostyn showed an interest in it, was proud to enlighten him. Lloyd had a natural respect for the integrity and feelings of others and, because of it, was respected in turn.

Mostyn, whenever buying new saddlery on Vaughan's account, or ordering riding boots at the cordwainer's, made it his business to call at the small, airless room where Lloyd worked, up the long flight of uncarpeted stone stairs. He would sometimes take a jug of ale with the delighted accounts clerk, or seek his advice upon some fictional project or endeavour, subtly gaining his confidence and trust.

'It is time, Lloyd, that you had assistance here,' he ventured upon one such visit. 'Would you have me speak to Mr Llewellyn upon the subject?'

'Oh, no, Mr Havard, sir,' Lloyd protested nervously. 'I would not have him think that I complain . . . or am incapable.'

Mostyn laughed, declaring, 'Nonsense! None could

341

accuse you of any such deficiency! You are an example to all.' He thought hard for a moment before suggesting, 'Will you not allow me to assist in some way? Your industry puts me to shame, sir! Let me, at least, take those bags of coins to a safe place. I have use of the carriage, and can deliver them to Great House without the slightest trouble. Mr Llewellyn is absent until tomorrow eve but I am expected to dine.'

Lloyd hesitated briefly, then declared, lest Mostyn be offended, 'Why, Mr Havard, I should appreciate that above all, sir. I will allow that I feel at risk carrying the money so openly, and in the saddlebags upon my mount. Everyone hereabouts knows my movements and the times I ride out, and others beyond might learn of them too.'

Without further hesitation, Lloyd fetched the bags and, with some effort, lifted them on to the desk.

Mostyn smiled and took them up, finding them heavier than he had expected. 'I will take the money directly to Great House, and place it in the safe. Mr Llewellyn has given me possession of the key,' he said.

'If you are sure, sir?'

'I am sure.'

At Great House, after cursory explanation to Clarissa, Mostyn shut himself securely in Rhys Llewellyn's study where the great iron safe was kept. Calmly and unhurriedly, he rifled through the bags of coins and promissory notes, extracting only notes enough to settle his outstanding gaming debts, and thrusting them into the pockets of his riding breeches. The rest he placed within the safe, and locked them away. He then emerged calm, and lacking the slightest twinge of conscience, to greet Laurel, who was awaiting him without.

'Oh, Mostyn!' Laurel's exquisite face was prettily animated as she took his arm. 'I am so glad that you will be dining here tonight. It is so dull here and tedious when Papa is away.'

Mostyn, his immediate money worries eased, smiled at her indulgently, and said with mock indignation, 'I am honoured indeed, ma'am, that it is only your father's absence which makes me a desirable escort in your eyes.'

'No, Mostyn,' she protested, face serious. 'You are the only escort I would choose, now, or in the future. I could wish you always to be at my side.'

Mostyn glanced about him anxiously, lest Clarissa be within hearing, before saying with cruel deliberation, 'But your affections are promised elsewhere, ma'am. I hear that your betrothal to Danfield is to be officially announced on your seventeenth birthday, and you are to be wed six months after that. If you will excuse me, I must go to my dressing room and make ready.' He removed her arm firmly from his own.

'Oh, Mostyn . . .' Laurel's lip was quivering, her eyes soft with unshed tears. 'Why are you so unkind to me? I swear that I will not marry Danfield. They can never make me . . . not ever!' She took his arm again, fingers pressing insistently through his sleeve. 'Look at me!' she commanded fiercely. 'Why do you not believe me? What can I do to convince you that I will take only you? I will do anything to prove it, I swear!'

Mostyn, singularly unmoved, once again firmly disengaged his arm from hers, saying with evident boredom, 'You might behave circumspectly, Laurel, for a start, and not hound me, or fawn over me before others, else we shall be forced apart altogether, you understand?'

'Yes, Mostyn,' she said, voice subdued, 'I understand.'

'You must, on no account, show any disquiet about the plan to marry you to Danfield, nor any aversion nor incivility to him.'

'But, Mostyn,' she protested, 'it is so hard to . . .' she saw the irritation shadow his face and subsided miserably, to nod agreement. 'But we shall still meet, Mostyn? Here at Great House, and out riding? I know you are fond of me. You will not let me go to him?' she pleaded. 'It would break my heart, I swear it! You will find a way, promise me?'

'I will find a way,' Mostyn said expressionlessly. 'Trust me.'

'I will, Mostyn, with my life, if need be,' she exclaimed, alive to the drama.

With a brisk nod, Mostyn turned and started to mount the staircase to the room set aside for him. There was a smile of amusement on his lips at the ease of his duplicity, and a warm self-satisfaction within. It would have been so easy to steal all the money put into his hands, and to swear that Evan Lloyd was the thief, or some footpad to blame. Yet, by stealth, he could continue to appropriate enough to pay his debts without arousing suspicion. The money was, in any event, owed to him for the work he did on Rhys Llewellyn's behalf. He was doing no worse than claiming his own; a debt repaid. The irony of it pleased him, and Clarissa, glancing at him as they encountered each other upon the stairs, thought, with some disquiet, that young Havard was a most handsome and prepossessing young man, and that today there was an unusual warmth and gaiety about him. He would, assuredly, break some woman's heart, as Rhys had broken her own, with his inner coldness and self-absorption. She only thanked God, and Danfield, that it would not be Laurel's.

Yet she could not know that Mostyn's thoughts were already upon what more he must do to secure his future, beyond the power of others to destroy.

Rhys Llewellyn was to be absent for some weeks upon urgent business which would take him, with Lord Litchard and several of his London associates, to France. Mostyn had hoped that he would be invited to travel as Llewellyn's aide and amanuensis but, to his acute disappointment, he was ordered to remain at Penavon to deal with financial matters in his employer's absence, as a test, it was disclosed, of his efficiency. Mostyn would be empowered to take full responsibility in all local business affairs and Llewellyn had declared it to be an opportunity to show his mettle; to prove his acuity and self-reliance. Mostyn would have preferred to show it on the continent of Europe, and before the *haut ton*, rather than the Penavon peasantry, yet he accepted Llewellyn's decision with every show of grave appreciation.

A few days after Rhys Llewellyn's departure, the lady's maid whom he had provided for Laurel was unaccountably called away to resolve some family crisis. The young maid-servant had been apologetic, begging Clarissa for a few days' grace to settle matters. She could ill afford to hazard the position she held at Great House, she admitted in agitation, so, if Clarissa ordered it, she would make it her duty to stay. Clarissa, who was kind at heart, and could not bear to see the poor woman's future imperilled, gave promise that she might leave, and her position as lady's maid would be held secure until her return.

If she missed her maid's ministrations, Laurel made no complaint, although, when her riding lesson was due, she deftly turned the girl's absence to her own advantage.

'I absolutely forbid you to go riding, unchaperoned, with your riding master, Laurel!' Clarissa declared stonily. 'You may pout and throw as many tantrums as you choose! Your father would not allow it. No more will I!'

'But, Mama . . .'

'There will be no argument, Laurel. It is unseemly and quite inexcusable. That you should even entertain such an idea is beyond understanding!'

'Will you not ride with me yourself, Mama?'

'You know I will not! I would not, at my age, make such an exhibition of myself.'

'Then, please, Mama, may I not take a groom and let Mostyn ride with me? He has done so, often, in the past.'

'You were a child then, as he,' rebuked Clarissa stiffly. Then, seeing Laurel's downcast face, she reluctantly conceded.

Laurel threw her arms around Clarissa and kissed her with real warmth. 'Oh, Mama,' she declared impulsively, 'you are a sweet, good woman, and I love you most dearly.'

If Clarissa felt scant joy at this outpouring of affection, it was because there was little difference between the wiles of Laurel the woman and Laurel the child. It was affection bought, and not freely given. In buying it, Clarissa knew that she was feeding her daughter's selfishness, and proving her own weakness. She consoled herself with the knowledge that at least *this* indulgence could do no harm.

Mostyn arrived early and, at Clarissa's command, took himself off to summon a groom to accompany them, and to deliver their horses to the yard. From the window of the small drawing room, Clarissa watched them ride out. How young they were, and how sure in their arrogance and youth, squabbling, chattering like young starlings, and as filled with affectionate rivalry.

'We shall make for Penavon woods,' Mostyn decided, 'then we may gallop the horses across the low moorland and the edge of the mountains.'

'Agreed,' said Laurel equably, then, with a sudden slash of her crop, her horse was off, mane flying, tail streaming, as it streaked away. Mostyn was swift to follow, and the groom, startled, galloped in their wake.

There was a sudden wild cry and Mostyn turned his head enquiringly. The groom, distracted perhaps, had ridden beneath a low, overhanging bough, the sudden force unseating him as it struck. He had been thrown heavily to the stony earth beneath the tree, its dry surface scarred with tree roots.

'Laurel!' Mostyn's harsh cry reached her, and she reined in her horse, turning apprehensively, and riding back. The groom, shaken, and grimacing with pain, was trying to rise to his feet, using the tree trunk as support. Yet he was barely able to set his right foot to the ground, wincing, and crying out with the effort.

'His horse!' exclaimed Laurel, looking about her anxiously.

'Unharmed, Miss Llewellyn,' the groom reassured her, 'he took fright and bolted into the small copse yonder. He will soon tire and come cantering back.'

'Then we must return with you to Great House,' she

declared briskly, although, try as she might, she could not hide her disappointment.

'No, Miss Llewellyn.' His denial was swift, conciliatory. 'If you will allow it, I shall ride back alone, leaving you safe in Mr Havard's care. Then if Mrs Llewellyn wishes it, I shall send another groom in my stead.'

'Oh, but I do not think . . .' Laurel glanced anxiously towards Mostyn, expecting him to make objection, but he was gazing restlessly about him, indifferent to her unease. I can hardly object that Mostyn is unfitted to protect me, Laurel thought confusedly, for that would certainly anger him, and shame him in the servant's eyes.

Seeing her uncertainty, the groom ventured innocently, 'I'm afraid, Miss Llewellyn, my progress will be halting and unsure, and I would hesitate to slow you and become a burden. I shall manage more easily alone.'

'If you are sure . . .'

Mostyn, fretful and irritable at the delay, ordered sharply, 'Do not fuss so, Laurel! Perkins is quite capable of retrieving his horse and riding back. He has already told you. If you would have us return with him, then say so! Otherwise, let us ride on, or it will be nightfall before we set out!'

Smiling ruefully, Laurel turned her mare to stand beside Mostyn's. As he petulantly flicked his mount into action, she followed and soon they were jostling neck and neck, racing fiercely along the track towards the great wooded slopes of Penavon.

The groom flexed his injured ankle, grimacing involuntarily with pain. He set it tentatively to the ground, testing it with his weight. Then he raised his fingers to his lips and let out a shrill, piercing whistle. His horse came immediately from the copse where it had been lingering, cropping the cool turf beneath the trees.

'Well done!' he exclaimed, smiling, then setting his uninjured foot into the stirrup and swinging himself aloft. 'We had best take our time returning along the byways.' He chuckled aloud as his fist fastened hard upon the three gold

347

coins in the pocket of his breeches. Mr Havard had paid him handsomely. A sprained ankle was a modest enough return.

Mostyn and Laurel, revelling in their freedom, raced each other determinedly across meadow and along lower mountain paths, cutting wide swathes through the knee-high bracken, then, finally, reaching the cool, shadowed darkness of the woods. Still laughing and arguing, they breathlessly dismounted, their horses steaming and lathered by the chase. Mostyn led his mare to a tiny rivulet that meandered through the peaty soil, its waters made shallow and laggardly by a thickness of fallen leaves. Laurel followed silently and allowed her mare to drink, then Mostyn led the animals to a small clearing where they might safely graze.

Laurel, frowning, and with a keen excitement, watched him return, tapping her riding crop aimlessly across her skirt to hide her nervousness. When Mostyn was abreast of her, she said hurriedly, 'I think I shall drink from the stream, Mostyn . . . bathe my face perhaps.'

Mostyn shook his head, eyes unnaturally bright, and reached out to take the riding crop from her, tossing it amidst the drift of fallen leaves.

'We had best turn back, Mostyn.' Her voice rose high, 'Mama will send a groom for us . . . if . . .'

Mostyn merely moved closer, and her weak protests died in her throat. In the split second that she saw and recognised the purpose in his eyes, she felt panic, then a wild, fierce elation rise within her. She longed to flee, to run and hide herself away, and yet she found herself unable to move, willing him to come closer. There was such a conflict of emotions rising within her that she felt scarcely able to think, or act. Yet, naturally, instinctively, she moved towards him and, in the hardness of his body and the strange, fierce arousal of her own flesh, she knew with certainty that this was what she had long awaited and been denied. The reality was so much crueller and more violent than the chasteness of her childish dreams. Yet, as his kisses and caresses grew more intimate and passionate, her own fervour matched and exceeded Mostyn's own, and it was she who pulled him to the soft bed of earth and leaves, his lips hard and demanding upon hers.

There was such a wildness of rage and feeling, pain and surrender, that she cried aloud, unable to bear the ecstasy and the hurt, seeking only the intensity of fused flesh and the need to feel his body within her own.

Then it was over, and a long calmness assailed her: the gentle fulfilment of coming home.

'Mostyn . . .' She wanted to touch his face and kiss him, to stroke the fair springing hair at his brow. She wanted to tell him it was as if every nerve and cell within her cried out with fierce pleasure. She wanted to share tenderness.

But Mostyn had already pulled away, and was brushing the dead leaves from his breeches and jacket, lips pursed fastidiously as he tidied his dishevelled cravat and pulled at his cuffs. He did not attempt to take her hand and raise her to her feet, but watched coldly as she struggled awkwardly to rise.

'Hurry!' he admonished. 'Make yourself tidy! Would you have yourself taken for a field whore?'

'Mostyn!'

He had the grace to look ashamed, sullenly murmuring, 'I . . . would not have this known.'

'Not known? But we belong now, Mostyn . . . as if we are wed.'

'We are not wed! And should your father suspect, then we will be kept apart!' He grasped her arm so harshly that she cried out with hurt. His eyes were hard now, all gentleness gone. 'Is that what you want?'

'No, Mostyn. No. I shall do as you say, but . . .' The appeal she might have made was lost. Mostyn was already with the horses, untying them, leading them to where she stood. There was still the dankness of moist earth, the salt smell of Mostyn's sweat and the sickly sweet odour of pomade in her nostrils; scents she thought would stay with her for ever. Yet, as Laurel settled herself upon her mare, there was no joy in her. This seemed not a beginning, but an end.

Chapter Thirty-one

Sara had genuinely grieved Jethro's sudden and violent death and relived, many times, the desolation that must have engulfed him in that last conscious moment of utter despair. She was convinced that he had taken his own life, and adding to her sorrow was the belief that, in doing so, he had cut himself off for all eternity from those who had loved him. Peter Morrish had refused to accept that it was other than a tragic accident and gradually, with his support and gentle persuasion, Sara had begun to regain confidence and hope and to exorcise her feelings of guilt.

It came as no surprise, therefore, when, some twelve months after Jethro Hartrey's death, Morrish asked Sara to become his wife, and she accepted him willingly. Their union was a joyous revelation to both, and if Jethro was in their thoughts, then it was with no sense of betrayal. Rather, they were grateful for times past and to those people who had fashioned and moulded their clay into what they now were, strengthening them in the white-hot kiln of their loving.

Saranne and Charles gave the union their unreserved approval but, despite Morrish's pleas, Saranne would not make her home with them, declaring that newly-weds must enjoy the blessing of privacy. Mrs Hodges also would not stay on as housekeeper and packed her few possessions lest Sara felt her position as mistress of the house threatened. Morrish was troubled, wondering how best to reconcile the needs of the two women without giving hurt, but it was Sara finally who persuaded Ann Hodges to remain.

When Sara's new life brought her to Myrtle Cottage and Peter Morrish's side, she took on the responsibilities, not only of a husband and a household, but a parish. Soon she was as immersed as her husband in the affairs of the parishioners. Her natural compassion and commonsense endeared her to all and they felt at ease in her company, for she had shared their lives and their poverty. Sara was happy and fulfilled in every way, and the beauty that had diminished at Jethro's death, as if her vitality and joy in living had been buried with him, blossomed again. Looking at her sometimes, Morrish could scarcely believe his good fortune, or that he had ever thought his life without her complete. He would put out a hand to smooth back her glowing copper curls, so bright and voluptuously abundant, or to touch the smooth curve of her cheek. Sara would cover his hand affectionately with her own, smiling warmly into his eyes, or press her lips into his palm, relishing their closeness in mind as in flesh. She was, he thought delightedly, a miracle come to pass. He thanked God for her, most humbly and devotedly, as she thanked God for him.

Meanwhile, Charles found solace from Jethro's death in his obsessional fight to build up the farm and make it profitable. That capital, which he had succeeded in borrowing from Lord Litchard and Randall Walters, he put to excellent use, first enriching the parched, neglected soil and pastureland. Then, with a small team of labourers, he back-breakingly improved the land and visited cattle markets, fairs, stock breeders and estates, seeking, wherever he travelled, advice upon the healthy feeding of fine animals and the selection of more suitable breeds.

Gradually, and by trial and occasional error, he brought in more profitable flocks and herds, turning hitherto neglected outlying areas of the farm to arable use and setting most to pasture. The small Welsh runts gave way to fine Glamorgan cattle; large, round-headed beasts with short hair, red or speckled in colour. He bought Jacob sheep, renowned for their superior wool and hardiness, and fine

Tamworth pigs, with ginger bristles and pricked-up ears; also curly coated Lincolnshire hogs as well as excellent geese, ducks and silkie hens. Great plodding shires arrived to plough the arable land and the dairy was re-equipped.

Despite his commitment to making the farm pay, Charles was troubled by the amount of capital swallowed up in the venture. Yet, although the new stock, feeds, materials and wages were expensive he knew that profit must come, for he had planned and executed his schemes meticulously. So, armed with that confidence, and his prognosis of what yield he might expect, he once again visited Lord Litchard, and invited him to see for himself the progress that had been made. Intrigued, Litchard agreed, bringing with him his estate manager. They carefully scrutinised the stock and accounts and were quietly enthusiastic about what had been achieved, but made no direct promise of financial aid. Therefore, when, a week later, Charles was summoned to Litchard House, his spirits were low and he was resigned to a polite refusal of financial aid. Lord Litchard, face carefully expressionless, congratulated Charles upon his industry and his articulate defence of the project.

'I have decided,' he said, 'to put one thousand pounds into your venture, Hartrey, with the usual legal safeguards, and if you concur.'

Charles's face was a study, first in suspense, then joyous incredulity. He was so transparently delighted that Litchard laughed aloud, before cautioning, 'If you are to join me in investment, Mr Hartrey, it would be as well were you to cultivate a gambler's inscrutability – for your face is quite absurdly readable!' Yet, even as he cautioned him, Litchard thought ruefully, How much would I sacrifice to feel that same enthusiasm and energy, or to see it, for once, reflected in the face of my son.

Later to his consternation, Charles received an invitation to dine at Litchard House and was in a ferment as to whether or not to accept. Saranne insisted that it would be foolish to refuse since it was clearly a measure of Lord Litchard's faith in him. Besides, there would certainly be those present who might be of use to him in his business ventures. Charles could not deny the truth of it, yet he knew that he could not feel wholly at ease in such fashionable company.

When he came seeking anxious approval from Saranne, before leaving for Litchard House, she examined him from his well-polished boots to the top of his silk hat, declaring honestly, 'There will not be a man as handsome, nor as well fitted, in all of Penavon, my dear. Have no qualms about it.' Then she reached up and kissed his cheek affectionately. Reassured, Charles made her an exquisite bow, and she returned a faultless curtsey.

'You have hired a gig, Charles,' she demanded, 'or asked for one to deliver you?'

'No,' Charles said quietly, 'I dress as is expected of me, and as a courtesy to my host but I am a farmer and all know it. If they do not respect me for it, then a fine carriage will not make alteration. No, I shall take the waggon.'

Saranne smiled, 'They will respect you, Charles,' she said with conviction. 'If they do not, the deficiency is in them, not in you.'

In all, it was a pleasant and congenial evening, and none treated him with other than courtesy. There had been an initial slight stiffness on the part of Lord Litchard's son, Sir Peter Danfield, but it was so soon past that Charles was inclined to think he must have imagined it. Could they perhaps have met before? No, it was unthinkable that they had ever been acquainted. Charles put the idea resolutely from him. It was some trick of speech, a resemblance to another which had misled him, he was convinced.

Peter Danfield, recalling the shameful encounter in the beechwoods when Havard had all but taken Hartrey's sister by force, had briefly lost his composure upon recognising Charles. Yet habit and training had steadied him and, although he was aware of his father's questioning gaze upon him, he did not again falter.

When Saranne, on his return, asked every last detail of the ladies' gowns, the entertainment and the conversation,

354

Charles was unable to satisfy her natural curiosity, for his attention had been all for Lord Litchard's daughter, Henrietta. He thought her the most exquisitely beautiful creature he had ever, in all his life, seen. Slender, dark-haired, and with that pale delicate skin which is so fine as to seem almost translucent, she captivated him from the first. Surprisingly, he was neither tongue-tied nor gauche in her company, for she made him feel as if he were the most witty, desirable company on earth. Her gaiety and warm sympathy were irresistible. Lady Henrietta's eyes were the brightest, deepest blue, and, had Saranne asked him, Charles could have described her mouth, her throat, her small expressive hands, and her sweet voice – haunting, and without mockery. Charles Hartrey had finally found a woman he could truly love. The irony was that he could never claim her for he was, as he had boasted to Saranne, a farmer with no pretensions to aristocracy, or even to the landed gentry. It was one thing to accept a yeoman at one's table, another to accept him as an equal.

Rhys Llewellyn returned from his business negotiations on the continent in an unusually benign frame of mind. His foreign interests were prospering beyond all expectations and new and profitable agreements had been signed. Lord Litchard, and others of rank and title, were his eager associates and soon, with Clarissa's and Laurel's connivance, his descendants might well inherit estates and peerages and the wherewithal for their upkeep. Yes, he thought with quiet satisfaction, he had acquitted himself well and was worthy of congratulation.

His extreme good humour spilled over into a generosity towards Laurel and Clarissa which was extravagant even by Llewellyn's standards. Laurel received a collar of fine matched seed pearls, lustrous, and with a subtle milky sheen; a most suitable present for a young gentlewoman, Clarissa had declared, pleased. Her own gift was, surprisingly, a suite of necklace, bracelet, earrings and cross pendant of emeralds set in gold, the whole exquisitely designed, and delicate. She kissed him with genuine delight, touched that he had selected his offerings with taste and care. Too often in the past, Rhys had sought to demonstrate his successes by buying jewellery of the utmost vulgarity; ornate, tawdry and crudely executed. Already, Clarissa thought with a smile, *he begins to imitate the restraint of those he aspires to join.* She did not doubt for an instant that he would succeed in his ambitions, both business and social. Rhys Llewellyn was a man who did not recognise the existence of defeat.

There was a modest family celebration on his return and to Mostyn's satisfaction he was invited to attend. To his surprise also, Llewellyn gave him a gold half-hunter as a reward for his services and spoke with appreciation of his reliability and initiative. The reports he received of Mostyn's work from his business colleagues had been excellent, and therefore he had decided to appoint him formally to the position of 'Administrator' of Penavon Estates.

Mostyn's mind turned calculatingly to what this new designation might offer. Would there be increased financial rewards, or was it merely an impressive name? A ploy, perhaps, to give him extra responsibility, but no real power or position? However, Clarissa's and Laurel's delighted congratulations were so spontaneous and sincere that he forced himself to thank Llewellyn with that same generosity, voice affectingly proud and hesitant.

Altogether a most satisfactory evening, Mostyn thought as he rode home through the starlit darkness in the open cabriolet. He had acquitted himself quite admirably. His hand strayed from the rein to touch the gold half-hunter in the pocket of his brocade waistcoat, as if it were a talisman. Carne had inherited their father's silver watch. It was a poor thing, of little value, but he had coveted it at the time. Yet a gold watch was the first acquisition permitted a young gentleman; a measure of his status and expectations. He would acquire all others, Mostyn pledged confidently, by hook or by crook.

★ ★ ★

'It was kind of you, Rhys, to buy Mostyn the watch, and to speak so highly of him,' Clarissa said warmly to her husband at the evening's end.

'He has earned it,' Rhys Llewellyn declared abruptly. 'I spoke no more than the truth.'

'Still, it was generous,' she persisted.

'I have learnt that a horse will work more willingly for a treat than a goad,' he said dismissively. Then, 'I thought Laurel did not seem entirely herself, Clarissa. She was lacking her usual gaiety and nonsense. She is not unwell?' His voice was sharply anxious.

'No, my dear . . . perhaps it is some natural indisposition,' she said discreetly. 'It will soon be set to rights.'

Llewellyn merely grunted non-committally.

''Tis more than likely she is over-excited at your returning, and with the present you brought her. That was thoughtful and generous of you, Rhys.'

'Nonsense, my dear!' he rebuked. 'It is only fitting that you both represent me properly. You are as much on display as my house and its other contents.'

'Yes,' agreed Clarissa quietly, all pleasure in her gift and the evening gone. 'It would be foolishness to neglect one's goods and chattels, lest they make poor return. I bid you good-night, Rhys.' She slipped within her room, shutting the door carefully behind her, and he was left wondering at the sourness with which she had spoken.

For several weeks afterwards, life at Great House settled into its former pattern of leisurely elegance, save for Mostyn who found that his new appointment was no mere sinecure. His work doubled, as did Rhys Llewellyn's expectations of him, and he found himself increasingly preoccupied with new schemes. To his credit, Mostyn acquitted himself well and without complaint and was rewarded by being invited occasionally to attend major business meetings as an aide to Llewellyn, and at lesser ones to act on his own initiative. In addition, he earned a handsome increase in salary and a small, but elegant, carriage of his own, that he might attend his duties more easily. He had therefore no more need to 'appropriate' a just salary from the dues collected from the tenants of Penavon estates and, as if he missed the scheming and danger it had involved, he resurrected them by wilder, more excessive, gaming.

Mostyn found his first visit to London at Llewellyn's bidding to be stimulating, although he was obliged to behave with the utmost circumspection because of his employer's presence. The hubbub, the crowds, the fashions, the many diversions offered, fascinated him but the return journey was made distinctly hazardous and uncomfortable by the filthy state of the inns and the execrable highways. The coach ride itself was hard and tiring, bedevilled by tollgates, and there was constant fear that a broken wheel or spring might delay them and make them easy prey for highwaymen. The party reached Great House exhausted and irritable, and in sore need of refreshment and washing.

Clarissa was surprised to see that Rhys had brought an unexpected guest, an elderly gentleman, whom she immediately made warmly welcome. Hot baths and a leisurely meal soon restored the travellers to good humour. It was all too soon dissipated, however, when Rhys Llewellyn, disturbed by Laurel's continuing lassitude and pallor, invited his guest Sir Frederick Haycraft, the noted London physician, to determine the cause of her indisposition. The doctor was of the firm opinion that Miss Laurel Llewellyn was with child.

There could never have been such an uproar at Great House as that produced by those few incisive words. Under any other circumstances Rhys Llewellyn's stupefaction would have been cause for mirth as disbelief, horror, resentment and rage clouded his face in swift succession.

'It is monstrous! A lie!' he spat accusingly at the physician. 'You are plainly incompetent! Such a thing is not possible!'

Sir Frederick Haycraft, who knew only too well that not only was it possible, but undeniable, strove to calm

Llewellyn, declaring, 'I suggest you be seated, Mr Llewellyn and compose yourself, while we discuss this matter rationally.'

The hand he put to Llewellyn's elbow was shaken away with ill-concealed fury. 'Compose myself! Discuss the matter?' he bellowed, almost incoherent with shock and outrage. 'I will have you know, sir, that my daughter is chaperoned at all times, as one would expect! I am aghast at your effrontery . . . your sheer stupidity at making such a claim!' He looked about him wildly, awkwardly attempting to loosen his necktie by thrusting his fingers beneath it, for it had grown unaccountably tight and was all but choking him.

Haycraft, seeing with concern his empurpled face and his choler, was fearful that he might suffer apoplexy. He said sharply, 'It is a plain fact, sir. Control yourself. It will do you no good to be abusive, for it will alter nothing. We are alone here and cannot be overheard. You have called for my advice and I have given it.' He saw by the pained comprehension in Llewellyn's eyes that, despite himself, he was beginning to accept the truth of it. Haycraft poured a stiff measure of brandy from the decanter upon Llewellyn's desk, urging, 'Drink this, sir. It will help recompose you. It would not do were your wife and servants to see you in such pitiable disorder.'

'Damn the servants! Damn Clarissa too! This is her doing!'

'I do not think . . .' declared the physician reasonably '. . . that you can make such assumption.'

'I can make any damned assumption I please. This is my house! My wife! My daughter!'

'Indeed,' agreed Haycraft evenly, 'and were it not so, I would not have taken your abuse and rudeness so tamely.'

Llewellyn's heavy, dark-jowled face was now drained of colour as he murmured apology, his fierce anger seemingly spent. He looked old, careworn. 'You have told my wife of this?' he asked listlessly.

'No. I thought it my duty to apprise you. Would you

359

have me inform Mrs Llewellyn? I shall do it as gently and tactfully as I am able.'

'Please.'

Llewellyn's plea was scarcely audible. He was pitifully chastened, Haycraft thought, and it would take him long to recover. Yet had he not made mention, when he had first sought medical advice, of some expected engagement to a young nobleman? If they had anticipated the match, it was a situation easily remedied and none save the immediate families need be made aware of the fact. The young man's parents might even prove grateful for this assurance of the bride's fecundity. It was often the case.

'You would do well, Mr Llewellyn, to approach your daughter with reserve, sir,' Haycraft cautioned quietly in leaving. 'Hers is a delicate condition, ill-served by blustering reproaches. It is the young man concerned who is in need of your censure, and deserving of your wrath.'

Llewellyn nodded.

'Your daughter has been betrayed more cruelly than you.'

Has she indeed, thought Llewellyn, feeling his anger rise again. Has she? Well, Danfield would make amends, and soon, or Litchard and he would know the reason why! It was infamous that the boy had behaved so disgracefully, and with such slyness. God knows, there were plenty of whores and low-born trollops, eager and ready to slake his lust. There was an order and way of doing such things discreetly. Still, it would bring him Danfield as a son-in-law, even if the glory of it were, of necessity, muted. He sat at his desk, head held fast in his hands, and awaited Clarissa's coming.

Clarissa, when she came, had evidently been weeping. She had been too shocked and overwrought by Dr Haycraft's prognosis even to approach Laurel but her fear was that it was Mostyn Havard, not Danfield, who was at fault. Her memory of their groom returning to Great House injured, and Laurel's seemingly innocent ride into the hills with Mostyn, filled her with sick guilt and misgivings. She prayed most earnestly that Peter Danfield was the father of Laurel's expected child.

By rigidly controlling her expression, she kept calm before Rhys, saying simply, 'I think, Rhys, it is Laurel you had best question, for she alone knows the real truth.'

'Then send her to me!' he ordered ungraciously. 'You may take your leave, ma'am!'

'No.' Clarissa's reply was unequivocal. 'The bell-pull is at hand. Summon a servant to fetch Laurel, if you wish it. I will stay. She is my daughter, as well as yours! Whatever is said or decided will affect us all.' She had not raised her voice nor spoken with passion, yet, to Llewellyn's surprise, he found himself doing as she bade.

When Laurel entered, tearfully, looking towards her father for the first time in terror, he felt a quickening rage. She was his child, perfect in her unfolding beauty, yet her innocence had been violated savagely, to bring each one of them almost unbearable hurt. Despite his anger and sense of betrayal, he felt for Laurel only pity and grief. He held out his arms to her and she ran to him weeping repentance, seeking the comfort he had never denied. He soothed her hair, holding her helplessly as, shaken by sobs, she begged his forgiveness.

'Hush, my dear. Hush,' he said. 'Papa will set it all to rights.'

His eyes met Clarissa's above their daughter's despairingly bowed head and they exchanged a look of shared sorrow and understanding. 'I shall ask Lord Litchard to come at once. The marriage shall be brought forward, and none shall learn of your disgrace.'

'Lord Litchard, Papa?' Laurel raised her head, face puzzled. 'What has he to do with it? How can he help?'

Clarissa was suddenly appalled and thought she might faint.

'It was Mostyn, Papa. Mostyn.'

'Dear God!' The exclamation was wrung from him.

Clarissa made to move and comfort him, but he thrust her away, unseeing. It was more than Laurel's seduction that tortured him, she knew; it was the betrayal of all he had worked for and planned. Without a word she crept from the room to seek Dr Haycraft's aid. How strange, she thought stupidly, that Mostyn should repay them so shabbily, when she had at last grown to trust him. Her instincts had been right from the first. Clarissa would have given Great House itself, and all she owned, to have been proved wrong.

Even Mostyn's self-possession deserted him in the face of Rhys Llewellyn's white-hot anger. His employer's tongue was like a whiplash and Mostyn had barely been able to defend himself against the viciousness of the verbal assault. Indeed, he feared, at one stage, that Llewellyn might assault him physically, so frenzied and vindictive was his attack.

'You are a coward and an ingrate, Havard!' he accused bitterly. 'I brought you into my house, treated you as I would a child of my own! You have abused my kindness.'

Mostyn mumbled inaudibly.

'For God's sake, speak up for yourself, if you can!' Llewellyn exclaimed contemptuously. 'You have acted like an animal! Behave now like a man, not a snivelling underdog!'

'I am sorry . . .'

'Sorry?' echoed Llewellyn incredulously. 'Sorry, you say! And is that enough? You have dishonoured my friendship, and brought disgrace to my house and family! You are a thief, and an opportunist!'

For a moment Mostyn, fearful of discovery, felt sickness rise into his throat.

'Yes, a thief!' reiterated Llewellyn scathingly, 'for you robbed my daughter of her good name, her hopes for the future.'

Mostyn's taut nerves relaxed.

'You have neither the grace to make proper apology, nor the manliness to claim you love the girl, or make defence! You disgust and offend me, Havard! I am tempted to throw you bodily out of my house.'

But you will not, thought Mostyn with certain pre-science, because then all will be lost.

'But I *do* love Laurel, sir,' he protested fiercely. 'I have always loved her, and always will. If I did not defend myself, or claim so, it was because I am miserably aware of the grief I have caused. I merit all the anger you heap upon me, and more. If I could undo the wrong, the misery I have caused, then I would let you kill me, and willingly. It is only what I deserve. I beg that you will forgive me in time and let me make amends.'

Llewellyn said coldly, 'I will never again trust you, Havard . . . Never like you . . . nor forgive. That is God's honest truth!'

'Then, sir,' Mostyn's voice was grief-stricken, wavering pitifully, despite his effort to control it, 'I had best remove myself from your sight. I would not distress you further.'

'Damnation!' Llewellyn exploded, enraged. 'You will stay and listen to what I have to say! I dislike you, Havard, and have made it plain, but I love my daughter, in spite of all – I will not see her disgraced publicly, and her life ruined. Despite my misgivings, you will marry her as soon as ever it can be decently arranged, you understand? Have I made myself clear?'

'Yes, sir.' Mostyn's voice was low.

'My God, Havard! If you, in any way, mistreat her, or bring her a moment's grief, then you will pay for it, and pay dearly. You have my oath on it!'

'I will treat her always with tenderness,' Mostyn affirmed, 'knowing how little I deserve her trust, and your own, sir.' He held out a hand, but Llewellyn ignored it, scowling and thrusting Mostyn aside as he strode towards the door. Mostyn stood there helplessly, head bowed and shoulders hunched, a picture of the cruellest dejection. Only he was aware of the fierce surge of elation within him; the certainty that he had won.

In the flat, suffocating airlessness of the doldrums, the

Bristol Maid had been so long becalmed that it seemed to Carne that they must perish, like some forsaken tribe, as powerless as the ship to make the movement which might save them. He felt sucked of life and feeling, lassitude and hunger so weakening him that the lightest task became a burden. The brackish drinking water was exhausted and the depleted barrels of ale so jealously rationed that drinking became more penance than pleasure. The men grew increasingly emaciated and irritable, their bodies disfigured by carbuncles and scabs, tongues painfully swollen, lips cracked and plagued with sores.

Carne and Septimus, standing uneasy watch, cursed the endless, oppressive stillness. The heat was so intense that it seemed to scorch the eyes, making the horizon shimmer and dance, as though seen through the sea itself, blurred, and robbed of all colour.

'Dear heavens, Sep! Will it never end?' Even to form the words seemed an effort. 'Will we never sail?'

'In God's good time.'

'Then I fear we are here for all eternity!'

Even as he spoke, the first whisper of breeze came, so lightly that it was scarcely more than a breath. Carne, fearful that he had imagined it, said nothing, but then a stronger breeze ruffled the sea. Carne raised his face and felt its touch, hot, fleeting, but unmistakable.

'A breeze, Sep! A breeze! It has broken!' He cried aloud, so fierce in his joy that he grasped Septimus and whirled him exultantly across the deck, as if impelled by uncontrollable madness. Septimus, infected by the same fever, responded as wildly, and they were laughing and dancing, leaping and cavorting, as if they had taken leave of their senses.

Savage's scowling commands, for once, had no power to still them nor any other of the crew. Within moments they were on deck, shouting and capering like fiends possessed, their inertia and ill-humour forgotten.

There was barely need to give them shouted commands before the topsails were unfurled and, as the wind gradually increased in vigour, the mainsails were set to trap each capricious gust and breath. With sails full bellied, the *Bristol Maid* was under way.

Carne, caught up in this bustling frenzy of activity, felt a resurgence of strength and energy as if, like the barque, he too had been becalmed, life suspended, until recalled to motion. Oh, but she was a beautiful ship: elegant and proud as a swan upon water. Running easily now with fore and main masts square rigged, and mizzen with a gaff and boom sail, there was nothing on God's good earth and oceans to match her.

Like Captain Fox and Septimus, Carne was learning the hardship and romance of the sea, a devotion, running deep in the blood. He sighed with satisfaction. There would be a time when all this was a memory, with no more reality than the clouded edges of a dream. Yet, for now, he could breathe in the noise and sights and that strangely evocative mingling of odours: pungent and cloying. Over all, the smell of the sea rose sharp with iodine and salt, as if it seeped through air and boards alike, invisible, ineradicable. It accentuated the natural odours of wood and hemp and of the melted tar and pine-pitch. It heightened the raw pungency of the varnishes and vegetable oils until the piquancy burned in the nostrils and eyes, and could even be tasted in the mouth.

'You are fast getting your sea legs,' approved Septimus, studying Carne as he descended, sure-footedly, from the rigging, 'but do not get too cocky, my lad, else the sea will humble you.'

Carne smiled, confessing, 'I swear, Sep, that when I saw those barques and schooners lying off at Bristol, I thought them silent and graceful as birds in flight. Yet all is noise and creaking, shuddering and groans. It is as if the wood is alive and cursing and ranting more fiercely than the crew.'

'And so it is,' said Septimus soberly, 'and the ship herself. Each vessel is different in character and feel. They are like women: beautiful, ugly; good-natured and bad. There are some which entice you, and some which repel. You are aware of some defect in them, some evil the moment you step aboard. There are ships so prone to disaster that no man would knowingly sail in them.'

'You believe that, Septimus?'

'I know it to be a fact.'

'And what about the *Bristol Maid*, Sep?' he asked jokingly, but Septimus's face showed no amusement.

'There are those things which bleed into the ship itself . . . I will not sail in her again.'

'William Oates?' asked Carne quietly. 'You speak of him?'

'No. It was Savage alone who was to blame for that. One man's violence cannot curse nor corrupt a vessel. In killing another, it is himself he crucifies.' Sep turned away abruptly to busy himself needlessly with a cable bit. He was shirtless and Carne saw with pity the raised cicatrices upon the flesh of his back from the flogging.

'Then what is it that corrupts a ship, Sep?' he persisted uneasily. 'What makes men afeared to sail in her?'

But although he probed and questioned remorselessly, Septimus would not answer.

Soon the winds freshened and grew stronger. There came squalls and occasional gales, the rain falling as slanting sheets of water. Yet, after the heat and fearful calm, none resented it. Those on deck turned their faces eagerly towards it, mouths agape to hoard and savour every precious drop, then set the barrels and buckets upon the boards the better to conserve it.

The weather had once more turned around, the sky clear and cloudless, yet the suspicion that had been troubling Carne over the weeks could no longer be subdued or hidden. He blurted out his fears to Septimus when they were alone and could not be overheard. 'There is something sadly amiss, Sep. Yet none speaks of it.'

'Indeed?' Septimus's eyes were guarded, watchful.

'I am not fool enough to believe that we sail to the Indies . . .'

'Then you would be more fool to question it openly.'

366

'For God's sake, Septimus! I am not a child, an infant to be hushed and lulled into quietness. If you do not think me fitted to know, then I shall take myself to Flanders, and demand to know.'

Septimus seemed to be weighing his response very carefully, before finally nodding and saying with a sigh of regret, 'I would have told you ere long but must have your oath of secrecy else I cannot confide it. There is too much at stake!'

'Then you have it,' declared Carne, exasperated by such a childish bid for secrecy, 'though I cannot for the life of me see the need for it.'

'There *is* need.' Septimus's voice was low. 'What I tell you might well set your life, and my own, in danger, and that of Mr Flanders too.'

'Flanders?'

'We move together in this. It has been planned by us, from the start.'

'But what, for God's sake? You speak in riddles. I swear I cannot understand you! Is this some joke? Some jest?'

'No jest.' Sep's mouth twisted wrily. 'We sail to Africa for a cargo of slaves.'

'A slaving ship!' Carne all but shouted it aloud. 'God Almighty, Sep! I would not have believed it of you. You knew – and came willingly?'

'Quiet, you fool!' Septimus took his arm in a vice-like hold, detaining him. 'We work to trap them, to give evidence against them to the Society for the Abolition of Slavery. You understand?'

Carne nodded, chastened to silence.

His arm was released and Fortune watched him intently, face inscrutable.

'I am sorry, Septimus. I am truly sorry,' he blurted. 'Tell me how I may help. Set me work to do. Whatever you order, I shall do it uncomplainingly, I swear.'

'Then I order silence upon what has been spoken,' Septimus said curtly. 'Do nothing, say nothing. Should any man aboard suspect . . .' There was no need for him

367

to continue: it was clear by Carne's expression that he understood.

Carne felt fear and revulsion twisting his stomach, knotting the muscles beneath his ribs. 'I do not know if I will be able to suffer it, Septimus,' he confessed despairingly. 'The thought of it sickens me. It is evil . . . depraved.'

'You will bear it because you must. There is no escape,' declared Septimus flatly. 'My choice was made freely and knowing the risks.'

'Then it would have been better to keep me in ignorance, for now I shall know no peace,' protested Carne.

'I have learned that you cannot buy peace with the suffering of others.' It was a quiet statement of fact. 'A life is all we have. No man has the right to kill, or to own another, body and soul. It is an obscenity, a sacrilege against God Himself.'

Carne, humbled by the older man's quiet conviction and his simplicity of faith, said truthfully, 'You are a good man, Septimus. It grieves me that I cannot help.'

'But that is why I trusted you!' he said with wry smile, 'for whatever happens to Flanders and me, I know that you will revenge it.'

Carne nodded assent.

'Not by violence,' cautioned Septimus, 'but by denying us, and all knowledge of what we do. If need should arise, you will side with Savage and his brutes, eager to see us killed and raising no hand to help us, or to halt theirs. Then you will return to Bristol, bearing the evidence we sought.' Septimus patiently awaited Carne's questions or objections, but none came.

The boy looked at him steadily, eyes grief-stricken and grown old with knowledge. 'It will not be easy,' he ventured.

'No,' said Septimus. 'It will not be easy.'

Save for the inevitable bullying and skirmishing among the lower deck seamen, and useless bickering about the monotony of the diet and the lack of drinking water, the rest of the voyage proved harsh but uneventful.

Carne dredged from his memory all that he knew about the anti-slavery society and Wilberforce, its inspiration and advocate. The morality of his stance, and that of the society, was not in doubt. Slavery was a filthy, degrading trade and none could convincingly argue for its survival. 'Yet argue they do, and actively support it,' he remembered Peter Morrish had observed with contempt, since financial profit was the strongest antidote to morality and ethics.

That individuals and countries were prepared to trade in human flesh and misery for gain was indisputable. The very ship on which he sailed was involved in it. Did Sir Robert Crandon, her owner, actually condone it, Carne wondered, sickened. Or did he leave the practicalities of such a venture to others; concerned only with profits and losses. It seemed unlikely he would soil his hands or his conscience, with such base commerce since his milieu was the drawing room and the board room, where hypocrisy was obligingly lost amongst the tinkle of tea-cups and coinage.

'I cannot understand why slavery is allowed to continue,' Carne protested to Septimus on another day, when they were set to work varnishing the capstans and were in little danger of being overheard.

'Can you not?' he replied cynically, pausing at his labour. 'Then you have not allowed for human greed.'

'But countries, Sep, parliaments and rulers . . . Spain, Portugal, Brazil . . . Why will they not condemn or control it? They flaunt it openly.'

'Countries are governed by men,' Septimus reminded, 'and a man's nature and needs do not change, whether he be rich or poor, famous or unknown.'

'Then the treaty signed is of no import?'

'Treaties are but paper, and as easily broken,' said Septimus discouragingly.

'But our own law forbids it!' countered Carne. 'Are there not naval patrol boats, determined to stamp out the trade in slaves? Were we caught with such a cargo, the ship would be forfeit as prize.'

'Ay, and we poor fools sailing her held to account, while

those who reap the greater profits claim innocence and immunity,' agreed Septimus, adding forcefully, 'It is those who finance such vileness we need to bring to account.' He swung around suspiciously at the sound of a footfall, then his eyes gave Carne clear warning as he returned to his labour, effort redoubled. When they were again able to speak freely, Septimus warned, 'It would be as well for your own safety if we were seen to disagree. Were we sworn enemies, then they would never suspect your involvement.'

'No!' Carne's objection had been instinctive, but he would not alter his decision for all Septimus's chiding and persuasion. 'No!' he reiterated obstinately. 'Your friendship aboard is all I have. I will stand beside you in all else, and do as you ask, but not in this! Nothing you say will influence me to do otherwise.'

For all his blustering and protestations of anger at his friend's intractablility, Septimus was secretly relieved. Like Carne, he would sacrifice all that was needed in the struggle against slavery, but friendship was a blessing too prized to needlessly forgo.

It was with fresh eyes, and alerted by Septimus, that Carne now beheld the ship, searching for those signs which spoke of her as a 'slaver'. He could not again descend into the hold without a firm command, so could not know whether shackles and leg-irons were stowed below. Even had he the opportunity to read the captain's manifest of cargo, or the names upon the wooden crates and boxes themselves, he would be no wiser. Such things were too easily counterfeited. He would need to inspect every crate within that hold before he could be sure. It was a course too risky to embark upon since, with Septimus and Flanders, his first consideration must be to survive.

Yet there had been tell-tale signs, of which Fortune, who was better informed and more experienced, had taken note. That the hatches were covered with open gratings so the slaves might take air below decks was certain, although they had been skilfully covered to avoid detection, should a naval vessel approach.

Despite the claim that all the drinking water was exhausted, there were casks and barrels stored below in quantities ludicrously excessive for the small number of crew – and with them copious barrels of rice and cereals, and the wherewithal to boil and serve them. Yet none had ever been offered to the hungry crew aboard. This information came to Septimus by way of Flanders, as did the knowledge that there was matting stored below for bedding. It was a commodity unsuitable to trade, or to sell, and there were rifles, certainly, since Carne had seen them marked. In itself, that proved nothing, but taken in total, it left little room for doubt.

When land was at last sighted, Carne felt, not the fierce exuberance of a man too long at sea, but a sense of real apprehension. 'What will happen?' he demanded anxiously of Septimus as they gathered with others of the crew to see the land rise shimmering through a grey mist of heat. 'Will we make port? Take on fresh supplies?'

'No. They will not risk entering a busy dock, nor even anchoring off, for fear of Royal Naval vessels which cannot be prevented from boarding and making search. Slaving is an act of piracy north of the equator and, should we attempt to outrun them, they have guns enough to blast us out of the water.'

'Where will we head, then?'

'Along some river estuary, to find a creek or sheltered inlet unseen. It has all been meticulously planned, do not doubt it. We will anchor undisturbed, and the boats be launched to travel up river.'

'You – Fortune!' Savage had come noiselessly to stand beside them, scowling. 'Shape your idle carcase! I will have no passengers aboard! Get below and unload the cargo, and you, Grey, with him!'

They went as ordered to the vast cavern that was the ship's hold, the oil lanterns swaying and spluttering with the restless surging of the sea. It was piled high with crates and boxes, their topmost lids pressed almost to the main-deck above and covered with a protective canvas, large, and all-embracing as a tent. They were but two of a working army and, at Savage's command, toiled relentlessly, man-handling the crates, lifting them through the hatches to those stationed above, labouring until the sweat dropped from their reddened faces. It was perilous, awkward unloading, with constant threat of loosened cargo shifting, or a careless fall. Carne had little time or inclination to read the stencilled letters upon the bare wood, his energy spent. Yet, like Septimus, he had glimpsed within those few broken, mishandled crates, the pathetic lures of trade beads and chequered Lancashire cloth, the 'Kaniki' that would be a trader's currency, along with cases of rum, muskets, ammunition and powder.

When all was set ashore, save for the heavy rope-handled, iron-studded crates in the far corners of the hold, and those casks bolted to the bulkhead, Septimus and Carne were ordered brusquely on deck. The hold, dank and echoingly vast with massive wooden pillars piercing the decks where the masts dropped to meet the keel, was left all but deserted. Like some forsaken pagan temple, Carne thought, emptied and cleansed for the ritual of blood sacrifice.

He stood, exhausted, beside Septimus, who was breathing greedily, hungry for air after the suffocating heat of the hold. As the iron-bound boxes were delivered on deck and the hatches replaced over the grilles, Carne could not help but glance towards Septimus who stood stolid and unmoving, his gaze upon the sea. Carne had no need to see his friend's face. The weight of the unwieldy boxes, and the metallic shifting of chains within, were proof of the horror to come and what they contained: the bracelets of Death.

Chapter Thirty-two

The cargo had been loaded upon the bumboats and Savage and Hill had chosen seamen from the crew to accompany them up river, whilst Captain Huskings and Flanders remained on board. Predictably, Savage's chosen henchmen were the brawniest and least squeamish of those aboard, epitomised by Joe Fields, whose coarse strength barely surpassed his dull-wittedness. Hill had chosen Septimus for his boat and Carne, fascinated but repelled by the mission, had been in a fever lest he be picked as one of Savage's crew. Yet Flanders had intervened, his cool, incisive voice overruling all others as he had ordered, 'You, Seaman Grey, will remain aboard and help with preparations.'

Savage, face hostile and scowling, had started to make objection but at a muttered word from Hill he subsided silently while the First Officer coolly designated those others who would remain. Septimus had not looked at Carne but settled himself with the seamen in Hill's boat, to the habitual imprecations and oaths from the Second Mate as to their idleness and ancestry. From the deck of the *Bristol Maid*, Carne watched impassively as they rowed off, their boats, and those they towed, awkwardly humped with cargo. They receded from view, like a small string of water beetles, clumsy and ungainly, stirring the surface of the cocoa-brown water, then disappearing around a bend in the river. There was an unnatural stillness about the river and the air; a heaviness, stifling and oppressive. The upper banks were clothed in vegetation, made lushly abundant by the richness of river silt. The trees behind were tall and attenuated, their foliage a dark, matted coarseness, like seaweed adrift upon a motionless tide. It would be black and impenetrable within, Carne thought, and filled with a fury of sound that came to him now only faintly; the faraway cries of birds, the screeches and trumpeting of animals of tree-top and earth, and those that slithered through mud and water, or made their homes in holes in the river bank. As it was, there was a constant buzz and humming from the insects that he brushed furiously from his face and exposed skin, but they would not be discouraged, returning to bite and suck, obstinate and greedy as leeches. A log slid down the bank and towards the muddy waters. Only a quickly raised head that showed the slug-white skin beneath the clenched jaws, and small reptilian feet, revealed it as a crocodile. Carne watched it glide and sway into the river, hideous and graceful, repugnant, yet barely rippling the water, as much a part of it as the drifting weed, the fallen leaves, and floating branches. Only the coarse-skinned head, its nostrils and the watchful amber eyes, hooded and malign above the surface, betrayed its existence.

'There are many such cruel and predatory creatures hereabouts, Mr Grey.' Flanders had come to stand beside him, his expression as controlled as his voice 'It is always as well to be on guard, to know one's enemies, and act accordingly. One false move, or a stupid show of bravery could end in death. Nature, red in tooth and claw!'

'Yes, sir.' Carne's reply was almost inaudible.

'Get below! Every man jack of you!' Flanders commanded, manner changing to briskness. 'There will be slave decks to place in readiness and make fast upon the supports jutting from the masts and the ship's sides. You will find the planks laid across the upper deck already measured and prepared. There will be four decks in all.'

Dear God, thought Carne, toiling with the rest of the crewmen to manhandle the decks into place. How can they hope to survive in such arid, airless cells, denied light, or even space enough to sit upright? It is inhuman! Such greed and viciousness profane the very name of humanity. The sweat was coursing down his face in runnels. He paused and ran a dry tongue over his lips.

'Grey!' Flanders' voice rose harsh. 'Stir yourself! You will rest when you have earned it, and not before!'

Without glancing at him, Carne returned to his labour, muttering savagely beneath his breath, working to dull his senses and the misery of his task. As each deck was secured in place, those erecting it crawled out, oppressed by a fierce need for space and ventilation, their limbs cramped beyond endurance.

'Come on! Heave-ho!' Flanders chivvied them irritably, urging them to begin anew. 'There is work to be done! You, Grey!' he accused. 'Have you been asleep in there? Shape yourself, man!'

Carne, who had been unable to crawl through the low cavern without difficulty because of the closeness of the deck above, said quietly, 'There is not enough room there for an animal, much less a man.'

'Then it will suit them well enough!' grunted a seaman beside him. 'They are less than animals; they are savages all! They should be housed with the rats in the bilges.'

There was a bellow of laughter from his companions, and Carne, despite his efforts to control himself, felt his fury mounting. His hands were clenched so fiercely that the knuckles showed white as raw bone, and the urge to crash his fist into the man's face was so overpowering that he could scarce contain himself.

'Grey!' He looked up abstractedly into Flanders' eyes, 'Your work, man!' His voice was coldly lacerating. 'Have you forgotten why you are here?'

As swiftly as it had sprung, Carne's rage left him. 'No, Mr Flanders.'

His reply was firm and Flanders saw the boy's hands relax and his body lose its tenseness as he resumed his labour with increased diligence. Carne's thoughts turned towards Septimus and his journey to some small, imagined native village where, for rifles and cutlasses and a parcel of china beads and cloth, a human cargo would be sold. When he tried to recall Savage's face, he could not, only the gnarled, coarse-grained head of the crocodile, eyes watchful and without pity. Fatigue and confusion blurred them in his mind and, although he tried to separate them, he could not. They were one and the same.

When the shore boats came back down the river, it was early afternoon on the morrow. The sun was at its highest, an orange-red glow of fire, its heat rawly suffocating. Every small movement brought a fresh surge of sweat to the flesh. Even to breathe was an effort, for it drew heat within, as stifling as that which burned without, filled with the stench of the river and the stagnant corruption of decaying vegetation.

The sound which alerted Carne to the boats' return was a wailing and moaning of such despair that, hearing its eeriness drifting across the water, he all but fled below. It could scarcely have been human, he thought, so fierce and instinctive was its abandonment to grief. He felt the soft hairs at the nape of his neck rise.

'That sound . . .' His throat was so dry that the words were a croak, and he found himself trembling.

'The cries of the slaves. They are bringing them by river and along the shore,' Flanders said abruptly. 'It is a sound you will hear by day and night, Mr Grey, without pause or ceasing. You will never forget it.'

Even as he spoke, the first craft turned the bend of the river, with a seaman bearing a rifle in the bows, and the six oarsmen the only paleness among a heaving, writhing mass of black bodies. The screams and cries of the prisoners rose pitifully and Carne, seeing the chains, leg-irons and cuffs that shackled them, and the cuts and weals upon their flesh, felt such a blind rage of disgust against himself and all others who were party to such degradation, that he turned and drove his fist into a wooden stanchion, the pain of it forcing tears to his eyes.

Flanders, seeing the stupid, punitive gesture, put a hand upon Carne's shoulder saying, 'You will need your strength,

Mr Grey. Make ready to haul the cargo aboard, and make safe the boats.'

There was a shouting and wild screaming from one of the boats below as if terror and madness had caused affray. Flanders and Carne were at the ship's side in an instant while a native, crazed by shock and fear of what was to befall, struggled to his feet despite the restricting shackles. His furious, lashing energy, as he struck out wildly with his chains, threatened to overturn the boat and send him and the others plunging to their deaths. Yet the cries of Hill and the oarsmen went unheeded. The slave was past reason or caring, his only thought to flee. The boat was rocking perilously now as he raged and cried aloud, its boards a seething mass of chains and fallen bodies. Then a rifle crack hung upon the air, and another, as, with a slow inevitability, the man staggered blindly and fell over the boat's side and into the brown waters, manacles bearing him inexorably downwards. At once, there was a flicker of life at the bank and a swift writhing of tail and scrabbling of claws. The crocodile was in the river, blood staining the rusted water as it re-emerged with a darkness of flesh in its jaws.

'Kill it!' Carne screamed aloud. 'Use your rifle, you stupid swine!'

But no shot came, and even those within the boat fell silent, awed by the swift transition of life into death.

'I fear, Mr Grey,' murmured Flanders compassionately, 'that there are many who would welcome such an end before this voyage is done. That is their tragedy, and ours.'

It was with sickness of spirit that Carne helped secure the boatloads of slaves in their bleak prison between decks. Some were defiantly screaming and lashing out indiscriminately in their chains, their blows and curses for gaolers and prisoners alike. Others wept and shuffled, bewildered as old men without memory or hope. These scarcely seemed to heed their leg-bracelets and cuffs, nor the restricting shackles that bound them, one to the other. Despite their youth and vigour, they were hollow-eyed and listless as the dead. Perhaps they already felt themselves to be so, the past beyond recall, the future unknown, the present too terrible to bear. Others, younger than Carne, whimpered and whined beneath their breath, seeking reassurance of others, and finding none. Whether defiant, listless or subdued, there was hardly room enough for each to lie awkwardly upon one side, or to sit doubled beneath the low roof formed by the deck above. Hampered by chains and irons, always pressed against the sweating flesh of another, and fouled by human urine and excrement, they huddled like exhausted animals in a cage, beaten, cowed, all resistance broken.

Carne, leaving them below, returned dispiritedly on deck, his spirits as crushed as their own. If he had hoped for respite from the tragedy of it, there was none. Along the bank of the river and into a clearing aside the trees, piteous screams and cries for deliverance once more ripped the air. Shackled and braceleted at ankle and wrist, they were yoked together at the neck by a continuous iron-forged chain. If one stumbled and fell, he dragged with him those on either side, their only defence against the cruel excoriation of iron upon flesh the strength to haul him to his feet, and support him when terror and fatigue made them barely capable of supporting themselves. There was no rest, and no escape. They were a sad, bewildered body, moving ponderously like some strange, unlovely insect, crushed and harried, moving fitfully at another's goading. There was silence from river, sky and land; no sound save for their thin cries and the metallic rise and fall of the chains, stark and monotonous as the recurring call of some harsh-toned bird. Their bodies and limbs gleamed with sweat, their hair close curled, and showing the shape of skull and bone, eyes wide and blue-white in the blackness of flesh, lips widely bared over gleaming teeth. Some wore small cloths which barely covered their loins, others were naked, their muscular bodies showing scars from the rhino-hide whips of the traders who had beaten them into submission; their women-folk strong-boned, firm breasted, their skin burnished to ebony, and cradling unweaned infants to them, with others scarcely older stumbling upon their chains that shackled them all. Men and women bore the newer, livid weals and the open wounds of cutlass and knife, crusted and congealed, or still agape, the flesh raw beneath or oozing blood under a crawling scab of flies. Their plight, if possible, was worse than those already below, terror and exhaustion adding to the burden of their chains, the cruel iron biting into flesh, flaying them raw. Their feet too were torn by thorn tree and stone, and as they were hauled roughly aboard, the unexpectedness of the pallidness of their soles and palms revealed suppurating sores, deep and neglected. The pain of their hurt must have been scarcely endurable, but they were assailed by an even deeper one; the loss of those they had loved and given birth to, the loss of home and the freedom to exist as men, women and children in their own right.

Carne had been anxiously searching those coming aboard for sight of Septimus. Except for Savage, he was the last to come aboard, face haggard with exhaustion and grief, his rifle carefully unloaded to avoid needless harm.

'Septimus! You are all right?' Carne demanded urgently.

Septimus lifted a hand tiredly to his face, reddened by heat. He rubbed his eyes and said tonelessly, 'I am all right.'

Carne pushed his way to stand beside him. 'It was a long journey?' he began awkwardly.

'I have been to hell and back this day,' Septimus's voice was factual and without self-pity. 'Let me be,' he said quietly. 'I am not yet ready to speak of it. Leave me to dwell on it alone. I am not fit company.'

Carne nodded and with compassion turned to help the captives to that hell which lay below. Long ago, in another life in Penavon, Peter Morrish had told him that, disguise it as they might, the captain and crew of a slaving vessel could never keep their purpose hid – the stench of its cargo under the crippling man-made decks could be detected a mile and a half away across the water. He knew now that it was no mere exaggeration by the anti-slavery lobby, intent upon stamping out the vile trade. It was the simple truth. The heavy, foetid odour of human faeces and urine pervaded all, its rotten, decomposing matter left uncleared. The vileness of it seemed to taint the very air above the decks, thick and malodorous as marsh gas. The slaves lay in their own stinking filth and that of others, the native matting beneath them soaked and adding to their discomfort since it rubbed their flesh raw. Unable to move, their skin broke down into festering sores, so painful that they could scarcely turn in their shackles without involuntarily screaming aloud. From the hastily constructed decks above, the excreta of others seeped between the boards, a leaking cesspit, foul and contaminating.

Those seamen who were ordered below to dole out the meagre rice and cereals and the water, had been known to retch and vomit upon reaching the upper deck, and, save for Savage, Hill, Joe Fields and others of their kind, none remained unaffected by their suffering. It was not the slaves alone who remained trapped in misery and an anguish of despair, but all those with the least vestige of human pity. Guilt at the part they had played in the capture, and memory of the atrocities inflicted by the Arab traders, all served to haunt them and cause regret. It was a ship that stank of corruption and Carne realised, now, what had prompted Septimus to declare that he would never sail on her again. Even when the matting upon which the captives lay was burned and every last board of the slave decks renewed, the stench of spilt blood and savagery would remain. All the waters of the oceans and rivers they crossed would never cleanse it.

When they reached the doldrums, and the *Bristol Maid* lay becalmed in a furnace of searing heat and airlessness, sickness grew rife. Vomiting and purging bedevilled the slaves anew as, in the greater violence of winds and tide, they succumbed to seasickness. The women and children grew weaker, their misery compounded by the shortage of food and water. Those who died were granted as little dignity in death as in living. Their bodies, denied even a canvas shroud, and with no word of committal spoken, were slid over the side.

'I have a mind to jump ship, Sep . . . as soon as we reach land. I can no longer stomach this. I feel degraded, unclean,' Carne told his friend. 'I will not wait to collect my wages, nor see them sold to the highest bidder like so many cattle.'

Septimus looked at him in silence for a long time before saying heavily, 'Yes, it is best you go. You will have need of money. I have a little set aside.' As Carne made to protest, Septimus declared firmly, 'No . . . hear me out! I shall have little use for it, for my place is here, on board. My voyage, and my work, will end at Bristol.'

'I have not your strength of will, Sep,' Carne confessed awkwardly, 'and I am sickened beyond endurance by what I have seen. I can bear no more. I beg you will think no worse of me for it.'

Septimus shook his head and put a comforting hand to Carne's shoulder. 'We will find a way of escape for you, never fear . . . and you shall take the money I offer, and with good grace, for it is but a simple gesture of friendship. It is money from other voyages, honestly earned. I swear that it has neither blood nor taint upon it.'

'I thank you, Septimus, for the offer,' Carne said in a low voice, 'and for understanding why I could not claim payment for the cargo we carry.' Septimus's words had so vividly recalled Marged Howell hurling the few pauper-coins into Rice Havard's tomb that he suddenly felt unendurable sadness. 'I think, Septimus,' he said, 'that I must tell you who I really am, and what I have done . . . that you may properly know me. It is owed to you.'

'No!' Septimus's harsh denial gave place to gentleness as he declared, 'I know who and what you really are . . . and whatever you have done is God's province, and your own, and for no man to judge or condemn. You are an honest friend, and I have known too few of them to do other than accept the blessing of that with gratitude and humility. Friendship denies the need.'

Carne, deeply affected, had remained silent for a time, then said quietly, and with conviction, 'I would not have forsworn this voyage, Sep, for all the horror I have witnessed. It has burned itself into my mind and spirit and can never be forgotten.' He paused, searching for the right words. 'I have learnt of the cruelty of man, and of his vileness to others, but I have also known loyalty and friendship too, from you and from William Oates.'

'Ay . . . he was a gentle lad . . . and brave,' said Septimus with regret, 'and he will not be forgotten, nor Savage's part in his dying. There is a venom in Savage, a core of corruption: he is flawed beyond salvation.' Septimus's words lingered in Carne's mind, tragic and prophetic, as if sentence had been passed.

It was but three days later that Septimus came up from the slave decks below in a white rage of fury and despair. He had all but come to blows with the Third Mate for his cruelty to a woman captive, and the infant at her breast. The child was obviously dying, sickness and lack of nourishment making it too weak to suckle. She had begged for water for it but Savage had brought only a cupful and had dashed it in the infant's face, wasting every precious drop. When the child made no response, he had declared it to be dead and had taken it from the mother, callously indifferent to her screams of distress. He had thrown the child's body overboard with no more thought than for the filth and rubbish he threw to the screeching sea-birds. 'I do not believe the child was dead.' Septimus's voice had been toneless, as if all life and energy had been drained from him. 'That woman's cries will haunt me for every moment of my life, waking or sleeping.' His eyes, as he looked at Carne, were tortured with despair. 'I could not defend her . . . nor wrench the child away . . . There is too much at stake, do you see? I could not take the risk.'

Septimus had gone blindly to his quarters and Carne had

not sought to go with him, nor to reason, for there was nothing to be said.

As day inexorably followed day, the stench of sickness and decay hung over the vessel like a miasma. So noxious and depressing was this to the spirits of the crew that, when the weather finally turned, their nerves were as raw and unpredictable as the wind. Despite Carne's protestations that he would take night-watch beside Septimus, Hill over-ruled him, claiming that Savage had ordered that Grey was to go below to feed the captives. Savage, Carne was told curtly, would take watch beside Fortune, and no other. If he valued his hide, Hill declared maliciously, he had best do as he was bidden, and quickly, else Savage's full weight would speed his way!

When Carne returned upon deck, he could barely see for the force of the rising gale, with the relentless lashing of rain and fierce wind taking away all breath and sound. He had seen the feverish activity and the fury of concentration upon the faces of the crew, but despite catching at the arm of a passing seaman to demand explanation, the man's hastily shouted words were carried away upon the fierce wind before he tore himself from Carne's grasp.

'What is amiss? Is there a naval ship close by?' he demanded desperately of Flanders. 'What of the captives?'

Flanders dragged him into the lee of a mast for shelter, his voice thin above the storm. 'Mr Savage has been swept overboard!'

Carne held the lantern high to see the First Officer's face, palely illuminated. 'And Septimus?'

'He raised the alarm. It was already too late. The storm and sea will have done for him. The ship cannot be turned.' Did he imagine it, or did Flanders' lips twist into the barest parody of a smile as he declared, 'Mr Savage is most certainly dead. You will excuse me now. It is my sad duty to carry the news to the captain.'

Septimus had been relieved of duty and another detailed to take his place on watch. Carne waited apprehensively below as the storm without raged on, tossing the ship capriciously so that decks and bulkheads tilted sickeningly and eyes and ears grew confused, every movement treacherous. Septimus's face and hair were streaming with water, his clothes plastered wetly to his flesh. Carne ran to support his friend, seeing the pitiful weariness that assailed him. It seemed, with the sea and rain, to have been driven into the very marrow of Septimus's bones. Carne supported him gently to the matting that was his bed.

'Savage is dead!' Septimus was kneeling, as if at awkward prayer, hands covering his face, jolted and thrust by the ship's heaving.

'I think, Sep . . . that you have nothing to fear. Mr Flanders swears it was the cruellest accident,' he blurted clumsily. 'God's will,' he said.

'And man's . . .'

With the noise of the gale, and Septimus's words muffled by fatigue and his hands, Carne could not be certain that he had heard aright. He settled him upon his bed and Septimus slept as he lay, wet clothes untouched. Carne knew that he must never speak of it again, whatever befell. It was not through fear of causing his friend pain in reliving memory of it, but through fear of hearing him lie.

Later, despite Septimus's most forceful entreaties, Carne stubbornly refused to take the money which the seaman offered to help make good his escape. Septimus sniffed expressively, but made no other reply.

'I have a little money remaining from . . .' Carne hesitated '. . . from earlier times. Enough to serve me. What you have earned has been hard won, and by your own sweat and toil. It were better used to free others.'

There was no mistaking his real meaning and, after regarding him intently, Septimus merely nodded, murmuring, 'If you are sure . . .'

'Yes. I am sure.' His voice was firm, but his companion sensed a diffidence in him, a certain unease.

'There is something you would have me do?' he prompted. 'Come, then! Steel yourself to ask me this

384

favour, lad! I can but refuse,' he warned, smiling.

Carne's expression was so unexpectedly sober and troubled that Septimus himself grew serious. 'What would you have me do?'

'I would have you care for the few treasures which I possess.' He surrendered into Septimus's keeping the ivory miniatures of Rice and Rhianon Havard and his father's watch.

Septimus studied the paintings gravely before saying, 'Well, Mr Grey, they are treasures indeed. I need not ask if they are yours by right, for the likeness is plain to see. 'Tis certain they are gentlefolk born, as you. There is love there, and goodness of heart. I envy your return to them.'

'They are dead, Sep. Both. These many years.'

Hearing the tremor in his voice, Septimus said briskly, 'It is true that such things are better protected on ship, or land, than in salt water. You will need to leave hurriedly, without warning, by leaping ashore, perhaps, should chance arise.' He touched the ivory reverently, tracing Rhianon Havard's exquisite young face with gnarled fingers, eyes gentle, as he promised, 'They will be safe with me. I will protect them at risk of my own life, if need be.'

'Then I would not leave them in your care,' said Carne quietly, 'for I value your life above all inanimate things, Septimus. That is the simple truth.'

Looking at his intense young face, Septimus could not doubt it. 'I thank you for that,' he said with dignity, 'for I have done things of late which lie heavily upon me.' His voice faltered and died away. 'I am not always deserving of such trust and friendship.'

'William Oates would not claim it to be so,' Carne reminded, voice low, adding, 'I would have you possess the watch, Septimus, as a keepsake, a bond between us. It is the best thing I own.'

Septimus did not make false protestations, but said, 'Then it will be the greatest pride of my life, and I will not be parted from it, save to return it to you.'

'If all goes well,' promised Carne, 'then I will come to

Bristol, searching for you, to those of whom we have spoken, Sep.'

'Ay . . . they will know my whereabouts, should God spare me.' He carefully placed Carne's treasures in their leather pouch within his shirt front.

They clasped hands firmly upon the promise, grateful, yet sad at heart.

Chapter Thirty-three

When the *Bristol Maid* finally neared the coastline of America, her long voyage all but ended, the captives in the slaves' decks were too weakened by hunger and adversity to make resistance. Many had died of sickness and grief, and those surviving were too broken in spirit to rebel. They were bound for work in the cotton fields of Louisiana, and would soon have to suffer the further indignity of public auction.

The ship anchored offshore and the weather was hot and humid, exacerbating the foul conditions below. Captain Huskings made a rare appearance on deck, dark-jowled, sluggish of mind, his clothing filthily stained. Neither officers nor crew had respect for him, since he had none for himself.

'He is of as little use as that figurehead upon the prow,' Septimus muttered tartly, 'and with as little beauty!'

'Perhaps it is guilt which bedevils him so,' suggested Carne, 'and drink is but a quick way to forgetting.'

Septimus was not impressed. 'He is as much a stranger to guilt as to command!' he declared contemptuously. 'His only concern is for money. It is the means to drink himself insensible. In that, at least, he has a head start!' He applied himself more diligently to his task, murmuring disparagingly beneath his breath.

'But is that not an advantage?' persisted Carne.

'Perhaps, since it places Mr Flanders in direct command. Yet it is dangerous too, for were we to be taken for piracy, a drunken oaf of a captain would put all others at risk, Mr Flanders most of all.'

'But could not his innocence be vouched for? By others?'

'No. It is the risk we take. We act alone, and of our own volition, once aboard. We will be judged . . .'

'Fortune!' The harsh call silenced Septimus.

'Sir?' He abandoned his task and went at once to where Flanders stood waiting, face intent.

'We go ashore. You will take to the oars with Seaman Grey.' He named four others of the crew to row beside them, and the seamen hurriedly began to lower the shore boat.

'You are sure, Flanders, that you know what to do? How to recognise these people?' Huskings' tone was high and petulant, voice slurred.

'Yes, Captain. I am quite sure. I have studied the sealed orders most carefully.'

'Then see that you carry them out to the letter,' he blustered. 'You go on my behalf, at my command! You are answerable to me. Do not forget it!' He turned clumsily then staggered and all but fell, righting himself against a capstan before walking unsteadily below.

In silence, Flanders watched him go, expression unreadable, then he climbed down the rope ladder at the ship's side and entered the boat that would take him ashore.

Even when the shore boat was made fast, the stench of the slave ship drifted from the sea, its putrefaction a stinking blight over all.

'If Mr Flanders cannot find those he seeks,' mumbled Septimus, 'then it is certain that they will find him! They have but to follow their noses to know where the *Bristol Maid* lies.'

'Fortune. You will accompany me,' Flanders ordered. 'You, Caudle, will guard the boat. My business will take me half-an-hour, no more. The rest of you will stay within the port and return in good time, sober and capable, you understand?' It was upon Carne that his gaze was fixed. 'I have no fear that any man would be foolish enough to jump ship. There is money owed to you and, should you not return, it will be forfeit.'

Carne glanced towards Septimus and saw his friend's eyes signal recognition that the time for escape had come. There would be no leavetaking, no acknowledgement of what had passed between them. Nothing. Carne moved away with the three other seamen who had taken turn at the oars, careful not to look back or betray his nervous agitation. When they became separated by the crowds upon the quayside, he made his way, with slow deliberation, to a small coastal vessel, and fell into conversation with the captain of the four man crew. It was sailing north and was short handed.

'She is a trim little craft,' Carne offered with enthusiasm, 'much like one I once had the pleasure to crew to Bristol port. Will you consider hiring another hand, sir?' Carne demanded. 'It would please me to sail in her.'

His escape was as easy and unremarkable as that. Hardened as Carne now was from his labours aboard the *Bristol Maid*, his experience held him in good stead and he was readily accepted by the crew. His greatest relief was to be free of the cesspit that was the *Bristol Maid*, the sights and cries and the smell of her. He was aware that the rank odour of her clung to him still, foetid and offensive, and he was at pains to cleanse his flesh of her taint. He bought clothing from members of the ketch's crew and it was with acute relief that he made a bundle of his old clothing and hurled it over the ship's side. Yet, even as it struck the water, there came to mind the burial of William Oates and the loss of the dead slaves, and his exhilaration died.

When they set him ashore at Baltimore, it was with real regret that he said his farewells to the captain and the crew. He would dearly have loved to spend more time exploring the city at leisure but had very little money remaining from the small hoard which he had brought from Penavon, and could not long survive without work. His sole negotiable asset was his seamanship, so he had no choice but to barter it for whatever return it might bring. It could hardly produce a lower or more depressing yield than that of his disastrous voyage upon the *Bristol Maid*. Yet even that had given

389

him the friendship of Septimus and William Oates. It had given him, too, a knowledge of man's inhumanity to man that pedantry and rhetoric could never have conveyed. It had changed him from a child into a man, and life could never again be as it was.

Thus, it was with a new sense of assurance and purpose that he visited the shipping offices of the port to secure a working passage upon any trading vessel that would take him. Here, where he was unknown, there was no need to hide his advanced knowledge of seamanship, navigation and charts. None would delve too deeply into his past experience, nor check upon it, but take him at his word. Should he be tested, or questioned, then he was confident that he could give good account of himself.

There was indeed a catechism before Carne was accepted as a member of the crew of the iron, four-masted barque *Fort Jackson*. Those who interviewed him tested his knowledge and capabilities until he was drained by exhaustion. Yet, somehow, he dredged the answers from schoolroom memory, sounding, despite his nervousness, capable and assured. There were reservations about his youth and inexperience, but he believed that he had been able to dispel them. He told the truth about his background, as far as he was able, concealing knowledge only of his reason for leaving, and his true name. His practical grasp of sailing, under Septimus's clear instruction, stood him in firm stead. When he left the shipping offices and his board of investigators, it was with their congratulations that he was now Third Mate upon the *Fort Jackson*.

There was pride in his step, and a straightness to his shoulders, as he walked through the bustling, prosperous dockside with its heaped, aromatic cargoes. The ships moored nearby, or anchored off, showed rigging fine and delicate as spiders' thread, canvas drying, or full bellied in sail upon the far horizon.

'Mr Havard?'

Carne felt the gorge rise in his throat and, for a long moment stood transfixed, unable even to turn to his questioner. When he finally found courage, the man was already beside him. 'Havard?' he repeated, his voice sounding hoarse and unnatural, even to his own ears. 'I fear you are mistaken, sir. My name is Grey, Mansel Grey.'

The stranger, a seaman of some five and thirty years or more, paused, weathered face briefly confused, then said quietly, 'It has been a long time, Mr Havard. Yet I cannot think that I am mistaken. Penavon? The church? Jane and Hywel Prys? You do not recall? I admit that I am much changed.'

Carne studied him intently, but could not recollect the strong-featured face and spare-muscled frame of his interrogator. He shook his head, saying stiffly, 'I fear that you have me at a disadvantage, sir.'

'John Bessant. You recall the pauper given refuge in the church?'

'And expelled from there by my cousin, Penry Vaughan . . .'

John Bessant nodded.

Carne asked gently, 'And your wife, sir?'

'Dead of a fever . . . these six years and more.' Bessant's voice was flat and filled with hurt. 'That is why I took to the sea, you understand. I have worked and studied to fill my days, and my mind. There was an emptiness . . .' Then, fearing he had revealed too much of himself, he added briskly, and with a wry smile, 'You will forgive me if I do not enquire too keenly as to the health of your cousin, the vicar of Penavon. I recall his treatment of you was as uncharitable as that meted out to me and mine.'

Memory of the blow Vaughan had struck him, and of his callousness towards Ruth and the dead child, kept both silent, until John Bessant ventured hesitantly, 'If it is through him that you have cause to deny your name, then I will never again refer to it, before you, or any other. You have my word upon it.'

'I thank you for that.'

'It is I who have cause for gratitude to Hywel and Jane Prys, and those friends who offered me a new life, denying themselves for our sakes. You have news of them?' he asked eagerly.

'I fear, Mr Bessant, that Prys might already be dead. For when I left Penavon, he was gravely sick of some cruel wasting disease of the lungs.' Carne hesitated, face stricken, as he admitted, 'As for Jane, I do not know . . . Nor if I will ever return.'

Pitying his distress, John Bessant said quietly, 'I have promised to return there, for my sake, and Ruth's, and the child's. I will tell Mrs Prys that I have seen you and that you fare well.' He paused before asking awkwardly, 'You have found yourself a ship, Mr Grey? If not, I shall be pleased to add my efforts to your own.'

'Yes, I thank you. I sail on tomorrow's tide upon the barque *Fort Jackson*, as Third Officer.' He could not conceal his pride.

Bessant's expression was a comical mixture of delight and incredulity as he thrust out a hand, exclaiming, 'Then as Second Mate upon that very ship, I welcome you aboard, Mansel Grey. It seems our paths are destined to cross, whether upon land or ocean. We can but hope this voyage will be kinder. The past cannot be forgotten, for it has brought us to what we are.' He added with painful honesty, 'I am no longer that poor, down-trodden wretch of the church, Mr Grey, whining, abrasive, wallowing in self pity. I have travelled a hard road, and it has taught me the truth of what matters. If there is anything you wish to know about the *Fort Jackson*, you have but to ask.'

Carne hesitated, unsure of how to phrase it, then asked baldly, 'Her destination, sir? She is not a slaver?'

'Dear heavens!' Bessant regarded him with real astonishment. 'A slaver . . . ?' Then, seeing that Carne's fear was real, and divining the reason for it, he answered gently, 'She is bound for the Indies, and her cargo of machinery and tools is lying on the quayside, for all to view. No, Mr Grey, you need have no fear that she is a slaver. I have known the servitude and meanness of a pauper's life – I would not willingly deliver another human soul into a bondage crueller than my own. I could not live with it, or myself. Now, if you are ready to follow me, I will take you on board, for I know every timber and bolt in her.'

'I am ready,' said Carne.

The morn of the wedding between Miss Laurel Llewellyn and Mr Mostyn Havard was cold and crisp, with that blueness of sky and clarity of light which sometimes makes December memorable. Rhys Llewellyn, from perversity and a desire to assert his pleasure in the union before the doubters, had surpassed himself in providing luxuries for his guests at Great House. Indeed, were it not for Clarissa's restraining influence, his lavishness might well have slipped over into vulgarity. Nevertheless, with the tables elegantly damasked and swagged with greenery and exotic flowers, and the frosty sparkle of finely cut crystal, the effect was enchanting. Glittering epergnes spilled waterfalls of ivy, ferns and sugared fruits, while candelabra gleamed beneath their pastel-coloured tapers of beeswax and spermaceti. Over all, the subtle elusive fragrance of pot-pourri and fresh petalled blossoms scented the air.

The village church at Penavon, and the villagers themselves, had rarely seen such a gathering of the affluent and fashionable. Great House itself, and all those elegant and servanted households in the surrounding areas were abustle with discreet activity. Coaches and carriages arrived in such prodigal numbers that they overflowed on to the carriageways and there was scarcely space to stable all the horses. Distinguished guests were bed-chambered in considerable luxury and comfort, while their scores of retainers were installed in considerably less salubrious style.

The nuptial service was conducted impeccably and the streets lined with obediently cheering well-wishers, men, women, infants at skirts and babes in arms. Their glimpse of wealth's vanity and excesses aroused no envy in them, no resentment. It was a world apart, glittering and iridescent as a bubble, and with as little substance. The reality was free ale and victuals, dancing in the frosted air, scrambling for hot pennies at the churchyard gate, a few hours respite from labour. If they did not consciously wish Laurel Llewellyn well, then they did not wish her ill. She was as remote from them as a shooting star, her pathway as glittering.

Laurel, too, felt herself set apart. It should have been a day to remember with delighted gratitude, feeling all eyes and attention upon her, as indeed they were. She was a most graceful and elegant bride, slim and fair as a lily, and with the same waxen delicacy and purity. Yet she was not pure! She saw it in the eyes of all, assessing her coolly. Even the servants, she was aware, thought of her as a disgraced wanton. She knew Papa held his breath when he saw her in the slender dress of creamy Macclesfield silk with the veil of Honiton lace, and grandmama's headdress of diamonds and seed pearls. Yet, even as he admired her, she saw by the emptiness of his eyes and the cold set of his lips that he had not forgiven her, and she wept within, despite her answering smile.

'You are feeling all right, my dear? You would not have me stay awhile?' Clarissa's voice was concerned, her eyes gentle.

'Yes, Mama . . . I am perfectly all right.'

Clarissa had been asking Laurel for some sign of affection, some declaration that she had need of her comfort, but Laurel was too proud and stubborn to give such assurance, so her voice was coldly dismissive. Clarissa, elegant in clover-pink, and with colour flaring high, nodded and kissed Laurel's cold cheek.

Oh, Mama! Mama . . . stay! Laurel wanted to cry out. I am not all right. I am frightened and alone and do not know if Mostyn truly loves me, for he shows me neither affection nor kindness of late. Instead, she said with a poise and self-possession which Clarissa herself could not have surpassed, 'I thank you, Mama, for all you have done for my sake, now, and in the past. You have been an example to me in your elegance and dignity. Today's celebrations cannot fail to go well, for you succeed in all you do.'

Oh, my dear, Clarissa wanted to reply, studying with compassion the set, strained face of her daughter. Oh, my dear child, if only you knew how little I have succeeded in the things that matter to me. But she parried gracefully, 'I thank you for that, my dear. You are the most beautiful of brides, and I am so proud of you.'

She is *not* proud of me, Laurel thought helplessly. She regrets this marriage and feels naught but shame. She lifted her head high to hide the bleakness that engulfed her, her expression cold.

If only she had told me she loved me, Clarissa grieved silently.

If only she had taken me in her arms as of old, and shown me forgiveness and affection, Laurel thought with regret as Clarissa smiled and left, exquisitely gowned and coiffured, and seemingly at ease.

Mostyn awoke on his wedding morn with an aching head and a mouth as wry-tasting as sour milk. He tentatively eased open his eyelids, but even the pale winter sunlight scalded his eyes, and he groaned aloud, inwardly cursing his intemperate celebrations of the previous eve. He could recall little of what had occurred, save that the amount drunk, and the amount spent, had been excessive to the point of lunacy. There were sharply fragmented memories of taverns and bawdy houses, with ribald jokes and horse-play from his three equally inebriated companions, and other indulgences mercifully less clear. Despite his feeling of nausea and fragility, Mostyn could not suppress a grin of purest satisfaction. It was not every day that a man married an heiress and returned in triumph to take possession of her and his family home.

He glanced towards the wooden butler stand beside the window which held his wedding finery. The sky-blue coat with its rolled and quilted velvet collar and elegant silver buttons; the slim-legged unmentionables of grey doeskin; the new hessian boots, his snow-white shirt, frilled and pin-tucked most stylishly, with the pale blue cravat and 'elegant pearl pin, a gift from Laurel.

Laurel. His mood of euphoria dissolved as swiftly as it had arisen. He could not pretend that he loved her, at least, he *could* pretend, and would, for as long as it suited him. She was pretty, certainly, and biddable and indulgent when he coaxed her into being so. Well, he was a master at the art of pretty words and easy deception. He did not doubt that he would soon enough find her boring, and her clinging ways tedious, but business, and men's pursuits, would offer respectable escape. He frowned fleetingly. It was by a damnable ill chance that Rhys Llewellyn had discovered, only a week or so since, that there were discrepancies in the estate accounts. Evan Lloyd had been taken before the justice, Lord Litchard, and accused of embezzlement and fraudulent conversion of funds from the Penavon Estates. The clerk had been barely able to speak a coherent word in his own defence. He had glanced fearfully towards Mostyn, making awkward appeal for his superior's support. Mostyn had stared back at him with contempt, despising the man for his spinelessness and lack of spirit, then turned abruptly away.

'Any man fool and scoundrel enough to cheat an honest employer is undeserving of pity. He should face his punishment like a man!' he said coldly.

Rhys Llewellyn had remained silent, but Lord Litchard had stared at Mostyn so keenly that he had almost forced him to drop his gaze. 'I would remind you, Mr Havard,' Lord Litchard had cautioned stiffly, 'that this man, Evan Lloyd, has not been brought before the courts. His guilt or innocence is a matter for the judiciary, not for idle speculation! His punishment, if needed, will be determined by them, and no other.'

'Indeed, sir,' Mostyn had agreed meekly. 'I apologise unreservedly if I have caused offence but theft from a gentleman like Mr Llewellyn, who treats those he employs with concern and generosity, well . . . it offends me, too!'

When the luckless prisoner had been returned to his cell to await trial, Lord Litchard and Rhys Llewellyn sat in uneasy contemplation over their glasses of Canary wine.

'Well, Llewellyn?' Lord Litchard demanded quietly, 'I confess that I have always found Lloyd, and all the man's family, to be honest and dependable in their dealings. It is strangely out of character and I will own that it troubles me.'

Llewellyn, who had similar reservations, did not voice them, merely observing, 'Whelps do not always run true to breed. There are always mutants, oddities. Some are born flawed, Litchard.'

Lord Litchard was unconvinced. 'Damn it, Llewellyn!' he protested, 'I am no mean judge of character. I would have wagered my life on Lloyd's veracity. He took a pride in his work. It was his whole existence! A man does not lightly sacrifice all that is of value to him upon a mere whim.'

'If the stakes are high enough, he will wager all,' murmured Llewellyn.

The two men had parted civilly enough, although Llewellyn fancied there was a slight reserve on Lord Litchard's part.

Llewellyn sighed as he stepped into his carriage, absently fingering the brim of his silk hat as he settled himself against the cold leather. Should Mostyn be called upon to give evidence against Lloyd, then he would undoubtedly acquit himself well. His future son-in-law was articulate and convincing; a practised charmer, as Laurel had learnt to her cost! Was he also a liar and a thief? The picture of Evan Lloyd's wretchedness stayed with Llewellyn, defying all attempts to banish it.

Yet the Ironmaster knew with certainty that to protect his good name, and his family, he would act as ruthlessly as Mostyn, even to the sacrificing of another.

Mostyn, with his white favour pinned to his coat, made ready to set out for Penavon church where Penry Vaughan and the bishop were already ensconced and waiting. Peter Danfield, his groomsman and supporter, had already arrived to accompany him, his complexion as unhealthy through over-indulgence as Mostyn's own.

'Are you ready, Havard?'

'As ready as I shall ever be! It is a damnable bore, and I would as soon it were over.'

'That is not the remark of an eager bridegroom,' chided Danfield mockingly. 'Perhaps you have been over-eager, and the conquest offers no new challenge?'

'Would you have me trembling and swooning like a nervous bride?' demanded Mostyn languidly, staring at himself critically in the looking glass atop his shaving stand and meticulously adjusting his cravat and pin.

'No . . .' Danfield's voice was hostile '. . . but a little enthusiasm would not go amiss, and a little concern for Laurel. She loves you, Havard, that much is plain, but I'm hanged if I can fathom the reason for it! She is deserving of better.'

Mostyn turned from studying his reflection to regard Danfield with surprise, remarking his high colour. 'Who had you in mind, sir?' he drawled provocatively. 'Yourself? Or was it a general observation upon my unworthiness?'

'That is a damnable impertinence, Havard.' Danfield's voice and expression were cold. 'But I will ignore it . . . making allowances for the exigencies of the day, and your state of mind. You are clearly unbalanced.'

'Yet not incapable . . .' Mostyn's lips twitched with wry amusement, 'as I have indisputably shown. I took what was offered, as I will take all else. Laurel will respond more readily to indifference than affection. Believe me, I know. I have her measure.'

Danfield regarded him steadily before saying quietly, 'Then I hope, most devoutly, that she has yours, Havard, or, by God, I do not envy her.'

They stood silently for a moment, Danfield's dark saturnine elegance a perfect foil to Mostyn's handsome fairness, each painfully aware of the antagonism which lay between them. Finally Mostyn smiled, saying disdainfully, 'I

398

apologise unreservedly, Danfield. It was but foolishness to bolster my morale, absurd nonsense. I would not endanger our friendship.'

Danfield nodded and smiled a pardon as they walked together to the carriage.

'Friendships are rare,' confessed Mostyn contritely, 'and should be nurtured and cherished.'

'As marriage,' countered Danfield urbanely, 'for they are alleged to be created in heaven.'

Mostyn allowed him the privilege of the last word, but could not resist congratulating himself that his own, most assuredly, had been created upon earth. The damp earth of Penavon woods.

Laurel remembered little of the nuptial service, save that she somehow walked the length of the church aisle, glad of her father's arm to support her own. She was filled with such queasiness and weakness of limb that she had to steel herself against dissolving into a faint. She was briefly aware of the blurred colours of the gowns and bonnets of the women and the old dowagers wearing their original wedding veils, their faces pinched and grotesque, skin and veils discoloured to the brittleness of parchment. She felt a sudden terror of what might be her own fate but the terror passed and Laurel seemed to have recovered herself. But the whispering among the guests ran soft as a breeze through grass: 'A nervous bride,' they murmured approvingly, one to the other, 'modest, shy . . . sensitive to the solemnity of the occasion, and what must inevitably follow.' There was no denying that Laurel Llewellyn was beautiful. Her fairness and the translucency of her skin lent her an ethereal, almost spiritual, quality. There was a delicacy about her which was infinitely touching in its purity. Laurel, seeing Mostyn turn, and the charming radiance of the smile which greeted her, smiled back wanly.

She survived to smile benignly at the Poor Law children, lining the aisles and the vestry porch. She beamed dutifully upon villagers and infants crowding the church green as they stared and cheered. Then, when she and Mostyn finally entered the newly refurnished west wing of Great House, Laurel felt once again an unusual shyness and apprehension. Mostyn was a stranger to her, as was this vast, echoing bed-chamber, with none of the familiar intimacy of her childhood refuge. She was listless and drained of energy, yet strangely reluctant to discard her wedding dress for a nightgown and mount the bedsteps to the cavernous four-poster bed. It seemed to dominate the room. Alien. Hideous. Symbolic, not of future happiness, but the shame and humiliation within her, already conceived. She disrobed in her small boudoir, her 'sulking place' as Mama called it, while Mostyn retired to his dressing room. For tonight, she would have no lady's maid, and he, no manservant, but she was grateful for that. Laurel's fingers were painfully slow and clumsy at their task, but, at last, she was dressed in her nightgown of creamy silk and lace. She looked, she thought, like a wraith, a poor shade, lacking all substance and colour. Gathering up her courage, she returned to the bedchamber where Mostyn awaited in a nightshirt nearly as splendidly belaced as her own.

'The wedding went well, Mostyn.'

'Of course.'

His voice was slurred, not with exhaustion, but over-indulgence at wining and dining, his face unbecomingly flushed and heavy. There was a grossness about him, a self-satisfaction which she had never before noticed.

'It is an occasion to remember. A Havard returning to Great House.'

He had clambered into bed and was sitting upright, hands behind his head, curls gleaming, eyes blue-white in the taper light. She mounted the steps and eased herself self-consciously under the sheets beside him. Now, she thought, he will tell me that I looked beautiful, and how proud he was of me, and how it gladdens him that we are wed. He will hold me gently, lovingly, to him, and all will be right again. The harshness of his neglect, and the crude coupling within the woods, will be exorcised, forgotten.

But he did none of those things. His drunken lechery

400

was crude and fumbling; a sweating turmoil of greed and pain. He took her without love or real desire, and spoke no words of affection. As swiftly as he had entered her, he rolled heavily away, and was asleep. Laurel lay sleepless in the flickering candlelight, the heaviness of his breathing and his drunken snoring the only sounds. She felt shamed and degraded, as cheap as the lowest field whore. She had taken a tiny white sprig of myrtle from her bridal wreath and pinned it to her bodice, and had pressed a spray of it within her prayer book. Myrtle, symbol of love.

The blossoms fastened at her breast were bruised and dying, their delicate petals crushed. They fell as uselessly now as Laurel's tears, and brought as little comfort.

Chapter Thirty-four

Mostyn regretted his drunken ineptitude upon his wedding night and, like Laurel, could have wished it otherwise. Yet he was too proud to admit it openly, fearing that an apology would demean him and make him less of a man. He could recall little of what had occurred, save that his clumsiness had disgusted her. There had been no concern for her, no intimate caresses, simply the quick gratifying of a sexual urge; cold, brutish. Laurel had turned away from him and wept as, sated and befuddled, he had fallen into sleep. The coldness, now, was on her side; a frigid distaste which shamed and humiliated him and made him increasingly vindictive in private. He took refuge in accusation. Laurel's condition, he declared petulantly, made her ugly and ungainly. It ruined her looks. He was bored with her clumsiness and lethargy. She revolted him. How could he find her lovemaking pleasing when she grew daily more hideous and bulky, face puffy, hair lank – a great lumbering parody of a woman? Yet, even as he spoke the words Mostyn felt a stirring of resentment that Laurel's coldness had forced him to such viciousness. That she loved him he was sure, but some devil within him drove him to punish her, and himself. Always he was testing her; scorning, belittling, seeking to degrade her in order to demonstrate what her love would endure. Laurel could not know that the wound of Rice Havard's rejection festered within him still and that Mostyn was as bewildered and powerless as she. She never spoke of Mostyn's disaffection, nor her own hurt, and in public played her part as convincingly as he.

But Clarissa, loving her, saw in their estrangement a harsh reflection of what she had borne in her marriage to Rhys, and grieved inwardly.

Rhys Llewellyn seemed unaware of the undercurrents of stress within his own household. He could find no fault with Mostyn's work and now that his coal mining ventures were gaining in importance and becoming increasingly profitable, he was grateful to delegate responsibility to his son-in-law. If he occasionally thought that Laurel looked defeated and unhealthy, then he dismissed it as being an inevitable adjunct to childbirth. No doubt Mostyn found her indisposition wearisome and her pleas for affection and reassurance an irritation. All would be well when the child was born. If it were a boy, then the future of his enterprises, and his succession, would be assured.

Mostyn had asked to speak to Rhys Llewellyn privately and on a matter of some urgency, and the two were consequently immured in the library of Great House. Llewellyn, who had expected to learn of some business difficulty, was plainly disconcerted when Mostyn confided that he intended to speak out boldly in Evan Lloyd's defence at his trial. Moreover, he asserted, he fully intended to offer to make restitution for the money which the clerk had embezzled.

'Why?' Llewellyn demanded curtly.

'I feel that it is owed to him.' Mostyn hesitated before adding with conviction, 'He is part of the Rhys Llewellyn Company. I cannot deny him that loyalty owed to an inferior, however worthless.'

Llewellyn considered before cautioning firmly, 'I do not think, Mostyn, that you should appear in court.'

'You feel, sir, that it might reflect discredit on our family to become publicly involved?'

'I do indeed.' He paused. 'Your generosity does you credit, Mostyn. Yet, I have grave reservations about your championing such a man publicly. If you are called upon to give evidence, then it is best that you do so impartially, and remain aloof from the affair. Besides, it need no longer concern you. As from today, you are not an employee, but a director of the "Rhys Llewellyn Company".'

Mostyn did not need to simulate pleasure; it was genuine as he replied with a gravitas befitting his new responsibilities. 'I am grateful to you, sir, for the confidence you place in me . . . and will take your advice, for I would do nothing to harm the company, or the family to which I now belong.'

Llewellyn nodded and gripped Mostyn's hand, as if to congratulate him and seal a bargain. If he thought that the damage to his family and to Evan Lloyd had already been done, then he gave no sign of it. His face remained impassive. As far as future business was concerned, he was convinced that Mostyn would prove every whit as shrewd and reliable as he.

Mostyn's mood was briefly disturbed when, later that day, an unknown ruffian forced his way into the new office within Great House, demanding to speak to him. The creature, claiming to be Evan Lloyd's brother, became vilely abusive, and had to be forcibly restrained by Grace, the footman, and Bowles, the underfootman.

'You are a liar and a thief!' he accused, beside himself with rage and grief. 'You have crucified an innocent man . . . I swear, Havard, that should Evan be convicted, then I shall break you as you have broken him!' He lunged at Mostyn with the blackthorn stick gripped in his palm, bringing it down ferociously across his shoulders, before the footmen were able to intervene and imprison his arms. Helpless, and impotent to break free, he railed at Mostyn in a frenzy, calling him every vile name he could lay tongue to.

Alerted by the fracas, Rhys Llewellyn hurried into the room, white-faced, to hear the man's screamed curses and blasphemy. Despite his urging that the attacker should be detained and taken before the justice for aggravated assault, Mostyn would not hear of it.

'It would be pointless,' he reasoned, 'for the fellow is

clearly deranged by pity for his brother's plight. He will bear a harsh burden of remorse when sense and reason return and he is able to think clearly. I could not, in all conscience, add to the sorrowing family's grief.'

'I do not think it wise,' declared Rhys Llewellyn gruffly, 'but if you are determined upon it . . .'

Mostyn nodded before answering quietly, 'I, too, have lost a brother and keenly feel his loss, although he had as little care for the anguish he would cause. I beg you will let this man go without hindrance.'

It was inevitable that before Evan Lloyd was taken before the justices, Mostyn's selflessness and generosity were discreetly made known. Lloyd was sentenced to five years detention at a house of correction, the first weeks to be spent on public display in the stocks, with a later spell upon the treadmill.

'But for the public-spirited action of an unnamed benefactor,' the justice declared, 'there might have been another of the prisoner's family standing accused beside him.'

Mostyn would neither take credit for the affair, nor discuss it. 'A man must benefit from example,' he observed quietly to Rhys Llewellyn, 'as I, sir, have benefitted from yours.'

Saranne's grief at Carne's absence had given way to a restlessness of spirit and she sometimes despaired of his ever returning to Penavon. His loss and Jethro's death were inseparable in her mind, resurrecting all the old childhood doubts and her terror of rejection. Was Carne's life as miserably bereft as her own? she wondered. Had he settled in some far-off town, or country even? Was there a new love more compelling than the old which would make him forget his promises? They had been so innocent in their affection, and so sure, and yet, had she not also been as sure of Jethro's love, and of its protection?

There was too little now to occupy her since Charles had, of necessity, added to the staff of both household and farm.

His business accounts were the province of a financial adviser and, although she still kept scrupulous household accounts, those mundane duties which had previously absorbed her were in the care of a competent housekeeper and kitchen and sewing maids of her choosing. Even Megan, her longtime confidante and friend, was more often at Jane Prys's cottage, for the old woman grew increasingly frail and dependent.

Troubled by Saranne's despondency, Sara persuaded her daughter to help the deprived and indigent sick of the parish. With the beginning of coal mining in the area, there was a worrisome influx of people from the large industrial towns seeking work. They fled from the filthy, overcrowded slums, their factories closed by the ending of the wars and the slump in trade. They sought to escape dereliction and exchange poverty for wealth. They could not know that they had exchanged one prison for another.

Saranne's charitable work among the newcomers soon absorbed her as remorselessly as Sara had hoped, leaving her little time or energy for self-pity. She worked tirelessly beside Peter and her mother to ease the poverty and squalor which was the common lot of those deprived, whether native to Penavon, or forced there through circumstance. She shared their humiliation, and memory of pauperdom gave her the spur and the compassion to do what needed to be done. As Peter Morrish had long known, in seeking a solution to the needs and suffering of others, Saranne found a partial solace for her own.

Perhaps because she was no longer wholly absorbed in her own loss, Saranne was aware of some change in Charles. He seemed quiet and withdrawn, lacking his old bantering cheerfulness. He had endured her questioning patiently, declaring that, no, he was not still inwardly grieving Jethro's death. He had long come to terms with it. His business affairs were prospering. He felt neither ill nor overworked. There was nothing in the whole world to vex him, or that he might wish to change. Saranne was not deceived, for she knew him better than any other upon earth. There had always been a closeness between them, from the day when, as a child, he had accepted her with that generosity of spirit he was never to lose.

'It is Henrietta Danfield you are pining for!' Saranne accused.

Charles flushed under Saranne's scrutiny, his cheeks as fiery as his mane of springing red curls, as he strove to deny it. 'No, Saranne. Henrietta's world and mine are set too far apart, even for friendship – and that would not be enough. She is superior to me in every way. In birth, breeding, in all that matters.'

'I have never known you be so easily defeated,' she accused sharply, 'nor to be influenced by position and wealth. You have never taunted me with being a pauper, nor despised me for it. You have always claimed you judged people on what they are and what they make of circumstances, not what circumstances make them!'

Charles looked at her in astonishment. 'You are right,' he said contritely. 'She is a kind and warm-hearted person in her own right, as you are, Saranne. Yet I cannot think that Lord Litchard has not already planned her future.'

'If she has any worth, or spirit, she will decide for herself!' declared Saranne, 'as I have chosen Carne, and Mama has chosen Peter Morrish, despite the differences in birth and all else. Henrietta would be a fool not to see you for what you are, Charles, a good man, who will make a success of all he does, but will never lose his compassion and humility. A man to depend on, and whose love will never alter with circumstances. It is all any woman could hope for, and more than she dare ask.'

Charles said gently, and with affection, 'You are always my fiercest advocate, Saranne. Were Henrietta to see me with your eyes, then I do not doubt she would look upon me kindly.'

'And if she does not,' declared Saranne impetuously, 'then she is both blind and insensitive, and undeserving of you.'

'Agreed,' said Charles, and their laughter echoed from

the farmhouse walls, and rose to the smoke-blackened rafters, touching them with their honest delight.

Henrietta Danfield was a pretty young lady of quite remarkable spirit, and sure in her own mind. She was Peter Danfield's fraternal twin, and their mother, who had long been an invalid, had died of a wasting sickness three days before their seventh birthday. She had been no more than a shadowy sweetness in their lives; gentle and elusive, and as haunting as a half-remembered fragrance.

But Lord Litchard had loved her deeply and was for a time made desolate by his loss. He had never remarried, but had turned his left-over misery to business and the care of his daughter and his son. If he loved Henrietta more than her brother, he was careful not to show it, treating them with scrupulous fairness and sternness, when need arose. Yet Henrietta was so like Charlotte, her mother, that he was inevitably drawn towards her, feeling, perhaps, that she was the flesh and blood embodiment of that gentle spirit.

Henrietta, he had learnt, was no pale counterfeit of another, but a person in her own right. Being delivered into the care of a succession of nurses and governesses made her neither wilful nor over-demanding. Yet neither was she weakly submissive. She was a happy, intelligent girl, articulate and sensitive to the moods of others, her kindness spiced by a wicked sense of humour. To her credit, it was usually directed at herself, or her willing twin, for she was devoid of cruelty and never deliberately sought to give offence. In time, Henrietta became Lord Litchard's accomplished hostess, delighting in making elaborate preparation for dinners and luncheons; mixing her guests with skill, drawing out the timid, calming the over-exuberant, making each one feel witty and assured. She genuinely liked people, and they, in turn, blossomed 'neath her approval. If Mr Charles Hartrey's name appeared on the list of guests with ever increasing frequency, then Lord Litchard did not remark upon it. That his position at table was invariably near her own was the merest coincidence, she assured herself. It was designed to set her father's guests and business associates entirely at their ease. Charles was a model guest: courteous, well informed, amenable. He treated her with exemplary respect and civility. It was this that she determined to undo.

One morning, Henrietta was persuading her brother to rise early, despite the ravages of a night spent gaming and carousing with Mostyn and his cronies.

'You are growing indolent and stout, Peter,' she accused, adding pertly, 'you will very soon have need to corset yourself, like the Prince Regent, merely to stand upright!'

Since this was palpably untrue, as Peter cut a figure of the utmost elegance, he was amused rather than offended, and intrigued as to the real purpose of her attack.

'Beau Brummel might well have had you in mind when he put that outrageously indiscreet question to Lord Alvanly,' she persisted, returning to the assault with renewed vigour. 'You recall what Brummel asked, in order to humiliate the Prince?'

'Who is your fat friend, sir?' her brother supplied obligingly and with good-natured tolerance, as they dissolved into shared laughter. 'I'll be damned, Henrietta, if I can fathom why you need me to ride with you,' he objected mildly, 'but I will come nevertheless . . . if you think I can be hauled into the saddle without use of a pot-crane!'

'At seven o' the clock, then,' said Henrietta briskly. 'We shall ride as fast and furiously as of old, over the mountain and through Penavon woods, then wherever whim takes us.'

'Then that will surely defeat your purpose,' he observed.

'Why? What do you mean?' Her reply was sharp, abrasive.

'Simply that I shall eat an enormous breakfast upon my return, and wax stouter by the mouthful.'

Henrietta seemed to relax perceptibly and, although his curiosity was aroused, Danfield knew better than to question her directly. Tomorrow would bring him answer, he knew.

'I hesitate to inflict my . . . gross weight upon some unsuspecting mare,' he declared languidly, 'but if you think it will survive . . . ?'

'The groom shall bring a cart-horse,' she replied equably, 'and you will be well matched for girth and hindquarters.' Before he could make reply, she smilingly quitted his room.

Danfield presented himself in the stable yard at seven o' the clock precisely, handsome and sartorially splendid. Their mounts were groomed and already awaiting them, and the pair rode off in high good humour, the crispness of the winter air sharply invigorating.

There had always been an element of good-natured competition between them in childhood, and now it spilled over into recklessness as Danfield challenged, 'The first to reach Penavon woods, Henrietta . . . loser to forfeit a gold sovereign! Are you game?'

'Certainly . . .' Henrietta's eyes were alight with mischief, '. . . but you must give me a head start, else it will not be a fair contest. Agreed?'

'Agreed.'

She stirred up her horse and soon was cantering away fiercely, face intent, so furious in her concentration, that she scarcely heard the pounding thud of Danfield's mare as it thundered past relentlessly. For a time they were absorbed in the contest, Danfield always galloping slightly ahead, but occasionally turning back to goad her to swiftness. Their laughter and cries rang out clearly in the chill air and it was with regret that Henrietta finally hung back at the entrance to a small copse, then stilled the horse and climbed down from the saddle. With a swift slap to its hindquarters, she sent it to graze, then knelt upon the soft leaf mould, regardless of her dress, scrabbling with her bare hands, then feverishly streaking her face and clothing with the wet earth.

Danfield, seeing no sign of her approach, slowed his mare and waited within a clearing under the beech trees, remembering with guilt Mostyn's ill-fated adventure here with Jefferies and Caborne. Well, it had served Havard well enough in the end, since it was the Llewellyns' patient nursing of him at Great House that had led to his marriage to Laurel.

'Damnation!' he cried aloud in vexation. It was just like Henrietta to be diverted by the sight of some small animal or bird, and to linger, forgetting their wager. He waited with increasing irritation for her to reappear, then, annoyance giving way to concern, he rode back to find her. To his distress, she was lying, crumpled and insensible, upon the damp earth, face pallid, and with one leg lying awkwardly beneath her. Fear tightened his throat as he scrambled from the saddle, helplessly chafing her cold hands, calling her name without response. Unsure of what best to do, he lifted her into his arms, staring around him uncertainly, fearful that in her cold stillness she might already be dead, neck broken in her fall.

'Henrietta . . .' He kept murmuring her name despairingly, but her eyelids remained closed, and he could detect no signs of movement or life. He had thought, at first, that it was a jest, some foolish trick that she played upon him, and that she would leap from his arms, laughing her triumph, and ride away to victory, wager won. 'Henrietta . . .'

She stirred and her eyelids quivered and opened, eyes gazing at him uncertainly, as if she were trying to recall his face to memory. 'Peter? What has happened?'

'A fall from your horse. You recall?'

She nodded, wincing with pain as she moved her head, her hand rising to ease the hurt of it.

'Are you badly hurt, Etta?' The old childish name came to his lips unbidden. 'If I set you in the saddle, and lead you home . . . ?'

'My ankle, Peter . . . I fear I have injured it in falling . . . I will try to stand upon it, if you will set me down.'

He set her gently to earth, supporting her carefully, but

411

she bit her lip to suppress the agony of putting her weight upon the injured limb, unable to prevent herself from crying aloud. Tears welled into her eyes.

'It is no use, Peter . . . Is there not a cottage nearby, a farm perhaps? If I rest awhile, perhaps the pain will ease.'

'But I cannot leave you alone here, Henrietta!' he objected miserably.

'Please . . . I will come to no harm. Perhaps there will be a waggon, or cart even.'

Slowly, reluctantly, he remounted his horse and rode to Holly Grove Farm. It was a strange quirk of fate, he thought, as he unfastened the gate to the farmyard, that brought him to Charles Hartrey's door seeking aid. It would serve him ill if Saranne Hartrey recognised him for one of her assailants in Mostyn's attack, and turned him away in disgust. His father would hear of it and his wrath would be hard to bear. Danfield understood now a little of the terror and fury that had ripped Charles Hartrey at his sister's suffering. It was with sick foreboding he dismounted at the farmhouse door and put out a hand to touch the iron knocker.

Charles, upon hearing of Lady Henrietta's accident, showed the greatest possible concern and kindness to Danfield, instructing Tom Hallowes to go at once and find Sir Peter's horse, and that of Lady Henrietta, and to return with them to the stables at Holly Grove. Hallowes, who had been present on the night of Saranne's ordeal, started visibly upon seeing Danfield and, by the look of scorn upon his face, the old man seemed to be about to make protest. It was Saranne whose gentle self-possession retrieved the situation. She came forward of her own volition to give instructions to Mrs Clarke, the housekeeper, and to greet Danfield with more dignity and civility than he deserved, treating him as an unknown gentleman, forced to seek aid for a member of his family in distress. Danfield was abrupt with awkwardness, guilt robbing him of his normal poise and ease of manner. He was painfully aware that Saranne was more in command of the situation, and herself, than he.

'You had best go, Tom,' she reminded Hallowes quietly, 'else the horses might wander or bolt, and do themselves some injury.' Although the words were quietly spoken, the look she gave the old servant was one of entreaty, which he could not ignore. He nodded his understanding and went obediently on his way.

Later, Danfield determined, he would make full apology to Charles, whatever humiliation and self-searching was involved, and would most humbly beg Miss Hartrey's pardon. Mostyn was, at best, an ill-natured fool and, at worst, a near-rapist, and he, Jefferies and Caborne as much to be blamed for their weakness in being influenced by him. For the moment, however, Henrietta was all of his concern, and he was grateful that Hartrey offered his help, and his house.

Henrietta, with an arm around her brother's neck, and a hand upon Charles Hartrey's shoulder for support, managed to struggle rather inelegantly to Holly Grove. Under Saranne's direction, she was soon comfortably ensconced on a sofa before the fire, her ankle bound in strips of damp linen, under which a liberal application of Marged Howell's arnica lotion had been spread. It was already cooled and less painful, she confided with gratitude, and the swelling was beginning to subside.

Saranne said quietly, but with sympathetic warmth, 'We must be grateful, Lady Henrietta, that you were so conveniently near at hand.'

'Indeed, Miss Hartrey. It was most providential.'

Their eyes met in shared amusement as Henrietta added devoutly, 'One might call it a miracle almost!'

Charles and Danfield appeared to be engaged in a deep and most intense conversation at the far end of the long, high-raftered room but, try as she might, Henrietta could not make out the substance of their talk. She had hoped that the curious antipathy between them might somehow be resolved, for they were the two people whom she most

413

admired, with the exception of Papa. Yet her brother's face was so earnest, and Mr Hartrey's shoulders so stiff and unyielding, that it seemed more argument than discussion. Then, suddenly, they seemed to glance in her direction, or was it at Miss Hartrey they looked, and whatever it was that divided them and caused their animosity, faded. Charles Hartrey smiled and thrust out a hand in friendship to her brother, and Peter responded with a strange humility and eagerness. Together they returned to confront her.

'Mr Hartrey . . . Charles . . . has kindly offered to send a servant for Dr Jordan, Henrietta, but I have told him that we will return to Litchard House and summon his services there . . . if you are agreeable?' Peter explained.

'Yes.' Henrietta's reply was low as she looked at Charles. 'Perhaps it would be better . . . I have imposed upon your generosity, Mr Hartrey, and your sister's, too long. I regret the trouble I have caused you.'

'Not trouble, Lady Henrietta, but the warmest pleasure in your company. My regret is for your indisposition alone. I am . . .' he paused uncertainly, continuing more firmly '. . . I am pleased that you do me the honour of considering our friendship strong enough to call upon my aid.'

Lady Henrietta made modestly appropriate reply, but there was no doubting that she was indeed grateful to her host, for she gave him a smile of the utmost radiance. Peter had turned away briefly to speak to Miss Hartrey, and the housekeeper was engaged upon some errand elsewhere, when Henrietta murmured, speaking so low that only Charles could hear, 'I hope, sir, that our friendship will deepen and grow, for that would give me the greatest satisfaction.' Then, aware that she had revealed too much of herself, she said, by way of apology, 'I fear that I am inclined to be forward and impulsive, sir, or so Papa scolds me. My behaviour is not always lady-like.'

'Indeed, ma'am?' Charles replied with admirable gravity. 'Then I hope I may counter it by behaving always like a gentleman.'

'That would be a great pity, Mr Hartrey,' she said

demurely, a smile curving her lips as he laughed aloud in delighted response.

Danfield turned to regard them with curiosity. The housekeeper had returned and, after a brief conversation with her, Saranne crossed the room to be at Henrietta's side.

'The curricle is at the door, Lady Henrietta, and your brother is anxious to drive you home, if you feel able to endure the journey.'

Henrietta declared her readiness to depart, although she appeared to take her leave with some reluctance, thanking both Charles and Saranne for their hospitality, and declaring, 'I hope, Miss Hartrey, that you will visit me often, to ease my indisposition and my loneliness. It would be a kindness I would truly appreciate. I have need of friends and diversion.'

Saranne readily agreed, but Charles was puzzled by the quick smiles of complicity which had passed between them at mention of Henrietta's indisposition. It was not, he thought, vexed, a subject to cause Saranne amusement, even if Lady Henrietta had bravely made light of it. He was surprised at Saranne's insensitivity.

'You have a charming and most enviable house, Mr Hartrey.' Henrietta's vivid blue eyes were glancing about her with admiration for the blazing log fire upon the inglenook hearth, and the lived-in room, with its comfortably worn furnishings and the pearly hams and faggots of dried herbs hanging from their hooks upon the rafters.

'It is a working farm and home, ma'am,' he said, pleased. 'I have known no other.'

'It would grieve you then to leave it?' she questioned gravely. 'For all your memories are here.'

'All the people I have known and loved have lived here,' he responded with equal gravity, 'and some are now gone. It is people who make a home, not stones and mortar . . . living things.'

'Yes,' she said, as if his answer pleased her. 'Yes . . . One day I shall be forced to leave Litchard House, since it

will be Peter's by right. It will sadden me but . . .' she left
the words unspoken.

'But you will keep the memory of past happiness, and
begin anew, ma'am?'

'Yes.'

'Then it is my fervent hope that you will find greater,
lasting happiness, Lady Henrietta.'

'As you, sir,' she responded gently. 'As you.'

Chapter Thirty-five

Sara was delighted by the new-found friendship between Henrietta Danfield and Saranne. For the first time since Carne's leaving, her daughter seemed to have regained some of her vitality and carefree good spirits. The two young women had quickly become the closest of companions, for they shared not only humour and intelligence, but a deep affection for Charles. They discussed him endlessly, and plotted quite shamelessly to lure and entrap him, a ploy which was absurdly unnecessary, since he had been besotted by Henrietta from the first time he had set eyes upon her.

Danfield, too, had cultivated friendship with Charles and Saranne, treating them with that natural courtesy and charm which was so often obscured by his public show of languid affectation. They became frequent and welcome guests at Lord Litchard's house, a circumstance which pleased him, for he had scant regard for some of his son's earlier friends and their gaudier excesses. If he observed the growing fondness between Henrietta and Charles, and he would have been blind not to, then he did not overtly discourage it. He liked and respected Charles Hartrey and, moreover, he trusted him. Litchard was a private man, schooled from childhood to hide his emotions, yet he knew that his love for Henrietta was so deep that he would have killed, without remorse, anyone who deliberately caused her hurt.

As Peter Morrish and Sara were drawn closer into Lord

Litchard's friendship, so the tentative warmth between Sara and Henrietta grew into open affection. Indeed, Sara had been heard to declare indulgently that she appeared to have adopted not one daughter, but two! It did not escape her that the remorse which had caused Danfield to offer Saranne friendship had grown into genuine liking, then unconcealed admiration for her darkly disturbing beauty. Saranne, in turn, seemed wholly at ease in Danfield's company, and content to be a part of a society which she had hitherto affected to despise.

To Henrietta's bewilderment, Danfield had insisted that Mostyn and the Hartreys should never be invited to dine together at Litchard House. Although she pressed him for explanation, he would give none. Yet, so adamant was his objection that she agreed in order to please him. It was as well, Henrietta thought, that Laurel was *enceinte*, and therefore unable to present herself in society. She liked Mostyn's wife as little as she liked him. Mostyn she mistrusted because he was devious and self-seeking; Laurel because she was so incurably empty-headed, and both were intolerably vain. Henrietta could not take seriously Danfield's warning that to invite them as fellow guests would be 'to invite disaster'. However, it was no great hardship to be spared their company.

Mostyn's absences from Great House had become notice-ably more frequent and Laurel was painfully aware of the reasons for it. She would have welcomed his reassurance, for she was embarrassed by, and resentful of, the changes in herself. She took no joy in her new gowns, which, for all their skilful cutting and expensive embroidery, were frumpish. Mostyn had told her rudely that since she had neither waist, nor shape of any kind, she could scarcely expect a mere seamstress to work miracles. Laurel's reproachful tears had sent him in a fury to seek more agreeable company. The stews he frequented grew ever more squalid and the trollops within them more amenable

418

to his demands. Nor did he confine himself to the known harlots and bawdy houses, but amused himself with the willing sluts among the cottagers and the bawds flooding into the place in search of easy money.

Finally, after a night of carousing, Mostyn returned to Great House to find Rhys Llewellyn awaiting him, his face so grim and choleric that Mostyn was alarmed.

'Laurel?'

'I am surprised, sir, that you have the interest to inquire.' Llewellyn's tone was cutting. 'Your wife . . . if that is a word you recognise, has been in labour this six hours and more.'

Mostyn tried to focus his eyes, but found it impossible since he was in such a drunken stupor that Llewellyn's words scarcely penetrated his befuddled brain. He tried to gather his wits, but succeeded only in looking more sottish and confused.

'Has she . . . has the child been born?' he asked stupidly.

'It has not!' declared Rhys Llewellyn icily, 'but your presence would have been seemly, and some show of concern, however hypocritical.'

'I am concerned . . . deeply . . .' Mostyn defended himself, voice slurred.

'Are you, sir? Are you?' demanded Llewellyn, 'about whom? Yourself? You disgust me, Havard! You have enquired about the child, because this is to your advantage. Not one word have you asked about your wife, and how she fares! By God, Havard, it would give me the keenest satisfaction to flay your selfish hide, and throw you into the gutter where you belong!'

'No, sir . . .' Drunkenness made Mostyn incautious. 'It is you who have risen from the gutter; I merely return to the house from whence I sprang!'

'Be damned to your insolence!' Llewellyn struck him a blow to the face which sent Mostyn reeling, and he fell, clutching at a chair to steady himself, but awkwardly overbalancing and striking his head against the corner of the chimney piece. Blood sprang from the cut above his eye and dripped upon his shirt front and coat, a crimson stain, sobering them both. However, shocked as he was, Llewellyn was unrepentant.

'You have been dealt only a portion of the violence you deserve,' he declared contemptuously, 'and, by God, Havard, it would have pleased me to have killed you, as you deserve! You are a cheat and a parasite, an apology for a man!'

Frightened by his rage, and the blow he had been dealt, Mostyn turned to scurry from the room.

'Wait!' The harshness of Llewellyn's voice halted him. 'Clean yourself up, as best you can and return to await the summons from Dr Tobin. You are filth, Havard, and I would as soon be rid of you – but Laurel has need of you, God help her! As long as you are under my roof, you will behave with decency, to avert a scandal . . . you understand?'

Mostyn nodded, a silk handkerchief held to the gash upon his brow, its whiteness crimsoned with blood.

'Your place is here, beside Laurel!' Llewellyn's savagery had ebbed, and he looked defeated and old. 'Should she die, Havard . . .' his voice faltered and broke entirely.

Mostyn felt a coldness which had nothing to do with pain and loss of blood. He knew that Laurel's death, even if the child survived, would be the loss of all.

Dr Tobin's demeanour, as he came slowly into the room where, despite the hour, Clarissa, Rhys and Mostyn waited, was tense. After the first protesting wail that showed how fiercely Laurel's child had ripped its way into the world, the three had waited in silence, unbroken even now with joyous congratulation.

Dr Tobin's face was flushed and solemn, his hair and clothing dishevelled and stained with sweat and blood. Yet he looked no more exhausted and distraught than the three who awaited him. Rhys Llewellyn's face was taciturn, Clarissa's anguished, and Mostyn's as pale as the bandage which padded his brow.

'Laurel?' There was fear and pleading in Clarissa's tone.

'It has been a difficult birth . . . long and complicated.' He spread his hands expressively.

'And the child?' Llewellyn's voice was hoarse.

'A boy! Strong and healthy.'

'Thank God!' The cry was torn from him as he turned spontaneously to embrace Clarissa.

They clung together in wordless relief, until Dr Tobin said quietly, 'Do you not wish to comfort your wife, Mr Havard?'

Mostyn hesitated, and Tobin, puzzled and concerned, glanced from one to the other, unable to fathom the hostility between them.

'Go, Mostyn!' Rhys Llewellyn's voice was as lacerating as a knife, and Mostyn, fastidiously adjusting his clean shirt and necktie and his pristine cuffs, braced himself and went within.

At Saranne's eager prompting, Charles had made Megan a surprise present of a pretty little donkey cart, light but sturdy, and fashioned by the master cartwright over at Golden Grove. To draw it there was a pretty wide-eyed donkey; a jenny with a coat soft as crushed velvet, her delicate hooves burnished as chestnut falls. Megan had been so overwhelmed by the sheer magnificence of the gift that, for once, she had been rendered speechless. She was able only to shake her head in wonderment, incredulously touching every shining surface of the contraption, unable to believe it real. Then, flinging her arms about the startled donkey's neck, she burst into tears of joy.

'Dear heavens, Megan!' Charles cried, alarmed. 'Had I known it would distress you so, I would never have ordered the damned thing!'

Megan and her elegant little equipage were soon a common sight in Penavon and beyond, travelling the lanes and byways between her mother's house, Holly Grove Farm, and Jane's Hillbrook Cottage. For the first time in her life, Megan had time for relaxation, the long, tedious journeys on foot a thing of the past. She was grateful that she could now more easily keep a watchful eye upon Jane, for the old woman was growing feeble and forgetful, and Megan was afraid that she might do herself injury. Yet Jane would not hear of Megan removing herself from her mother's cottage to care for her permanently at Hillbrook.

'I cherish my independence, my girl,' she would declare if ever the subject were tentatively broached, 'and I am too old to know fear or loneliness . . . No, you are too young to bury yourself here, Megan. Time enough for a tomb when you are dead!'

Megan had tried to reason with her, but Jane was adamant.

'You are as dear as a daughter to me, Megan. But, my dear, Spring and Winter will not mix. Winter is too crabbed and Spring too tender. That is the nature of things, Megan. To survive, they must be kept apart. To everything a season.'

Jane had slept ill, even in the warmth of the box-bed beside the fire. There was a chill in her old bones, an ache that spoke of snow to come. Her bones, she thought with a smile, were a better barometer than the fir cones upon the sill, or even the ears of wheat fastened to the card that Saranne had painstakingly made for her as a child. Jane felt strangely light-headed, almost as if she were someone else, set apart, somehow removed from her own body, and watching Jane Prys from a place far distant. There was a heaviness in her limbs and a confusion clouding her mind, and she wondered, in sudden fear, what she was doing here in this unfamiliar room in a house in which she was a stranger. She tried to make sense of it and the objects around her, and could not. She sat down heavily upon her bed, holding her aching head in her hands for a long while. Then memory returned, and frightened and bewildered, she rose to her feet.

'Prys?' she called his name, looking about her anxiously, but saw no sign of him. 'He will be feeding the mule. I had best take the water.' She walked barefooted to the kitchen and tried to lift the heavy wooden water bucket, but could not. With an effort that brought the breath rasping to her throat, she pulled it fiercely behind her, the water slapping at its rim, then awkwardly overturning, soaking through her nightgown, and upon bare flesh. Slowly, painfully, she dragged the bucket behind her, not knowing where she went, or why, unaware even that it was long emptied, and the water swirling uselessly at her feet. She set down the bucket and unlatched the door, then walked out into the yard, the wind dragging at her hair, whipping her nightgown against her thin bones.

'Prys?' The wind carried her voice away, forlorn and lost. She felt neither cold nor fear, only a great relief, as if a burden that had borne her down had been suddenly lifted from her. Then, because she was tired, she lay upon the cobblestones of the yard and waited for sleep to come.

Carne and John Bessant had become firm friends during the eighteen months of their voyaging together and, despite the grief of his enforced banishment from Penavon and Saranne, whom he loved, Carne had known times of real contentment. It had been a period of adventure and growing, and Bessant had watched over him discreetly, protecting him from known dangers yet never curbing his independence of spirit. He had seen him grow from hesitancy into self-reliance; a man able to command others and to convince them of his worth. As Third Mate, Carne had taken on a responsibility far beyond his years but his judgement was sound and his seamanship exemplary. He was industrious and fair minded and respected by officers and lower deck seamen alike, for he never set men a task he could not strive to accomplish himself. He was stern when occasion demanded but equally swift to praise a labour well done or to admit fault and take blame upon himself. His life was hard and his pleasures, as those of the other seamen, taken wholeheartedly. There had been ports and ships he would always recall, some with pleasure, some with less, and there had been women and diversions he might in future years care to forget. Yet there had never been a place that filled him with such a yearning to return as Penavon, with its fox-red hills, and no woman who had filled him with such tenderness and desire as Saranne.

John Bessant, homeless and rootless himself, was aware of Carne's longing to return and his sense of loss. In a way, he thought, it was even greater than his own despair at losing Ruth and the babe since, now, there was nothing and no-one to draw him back. How bitter it would have been had they lived and he was unable to take sight or touch of them. If there was a place left on earth which John Bessant thought of with special affection, it was Penavon, for there he and Ruth had known the most selfless kindness they had ever encountered, and from strangers and not kin. It was a link in the chain of responsibility and caring he felt towards Carne, and it bound them together securely. John Bessant did not forget the promise he had made before Jane and Hywel Prys . . . he would pass on to another in need the kindness and warmth of spirit that they had so generously offered to him. Yet, when the time came for Carne to return from whence he had come, John Bessant knew how fiercely he would grieve the loss of his young companion. Carne had confided to him, and no other, the reason for his leaving Penavon and why he could not return. Bessant, in whom memory of Penry Vaughan's callousness towards Ruth and their dead child bit deep, could not honestly regret Carne's violence towards his cousin, only that it was the catalyst for his exile. However much he pondered upon the subject, Bessant could think of no solution that might not end with Carne imprisoned, or sent to the gallows. He did not confide that for the rare consolation of knowing Penry Vaughan to be dead, he would willingly have stood trial in his attacker's place and taken his punishment.

One warm springtime day, when the *Fort Jackson* had berthed at Baltimore, Carne remained on board the vessel, supervising the unloading of cargo, while Bessant went ashore to arrange for the taking on of supplies for a return voyage to the Indies. He would, he declared, spend his time usefully on the quayside, finding what pleasure and diversions might greet them in the seven days they would spend ashore. There were mariners, too, he would have need to interview for lower-deck crew, since two of the seamen were changing ship, and a third sick, and to be put ashore for treatment.

'Mr Grey, sir.' The clear, authoritative voice hailing him from the dockside made Carne stiffen, then swing around in disbelief.

'Mr Flanders! Is it you, sir?' Even as Carne spoke, he bit back the question, for there was no denying that it was indeed the lean upright figure of the First Officer upon the *Bristol Maid*, looking every whit as commanding in his gentleman's clothing as in his impeccable uniform.

'Will you consent to come aboard, sir?' Carne called down invitation. 'My duties are all but done.'

Flanders signalled acceptance with a gracious raising of his silk hat before he turned to the driver of his open carriage, bidding him wait. Then, with the practised ease of a mariner, he made his way on board.

In his small cabin, Carne offered Flanders refreshment, although barely able to stem his curiosity about so unexpected a visit and visitor.

'A chance visit, Mr Flanders?' he had ventured conversationally.

'No, Mr Grey. I came not by chance, but by design. I have charted your progress at sea, as determinedly as on shore, and knew I should find you here.'

'The reason, sir?' Carne asked.

'Because of a promise made, a debt owed.' Flanders drew a pigskin pouch from the pocket of his coat and handed it to Carne, saying, 'I return these to you, placing them in your hands, and yours alone, for that was the duty entrusted to me. I beg that you will open the pouch in my presence, for that, too, was demanded of me.'

Carne knew before he loosened the thongs that within

were the ivory miniatures of Rice and Rhianon Havard and his father's silver watch. Yet, patiently and carefully, he did as he was asked, then placed the precious mementoes upon the desk before him, touching them with sensitive fingers, as if in committing them to touch, he might convince himself that they were truly in his possession.

'Septimus?' His question was abrupt, harshly spoken.

'He died of yellow fever when voyaging off Africa, and was buried at sea.' Flanders's voice was carefully expressionless, although his eyes were bleak. 'He asked that I make it my solemn duty to track you down and return your belongings.'

Carne, strangely wearied and grieved by Septimus's loss, sat heavily upon a chair beside the desk. Flanders was awkwardly beside him, putting a strengthening grip to his shoulder, then handing him the draught of brandy which he had poured.

'Fortune was a good friend, Mr Grey, and an honest man, and brave. I shall mourn his death as deeply as you.' The words were stiffly spoken, for that was Flanders' way, but there was no mistaking his sincerity and compassion. Carne drank the brandy at a single gulp, feeling its warmth take away the physical coldness within him.

He looked up, to ask intently, 'And the trial, sir; the evidence you gathered about the *Bristol Maid*? Was Septimus beside you to speak out that it was a slaving ship?'

'No.' Flanders' voice was low, scarcely audible. 'But you may be certain he would have stood beside me on that, Mr Grey, as on all else, for none could sway him from the truth, nor doubt his honesty. That is why I have come to you. I believe you to be an honest man.'

Carne looked at him without comprehension, blurting, 'What is it that you ask of me, Mr Flanders?'

'To return to London with me, and stand beside me at the trial.'

'The trial?'

'The *Bristol Maid* was lately taken when entering the Bristol Channel, seized by a Royal Naval vessel. Her captain

426

and crew are to be charged with smuggling.'

'Huskings?'

'The same . . . that drunken lout of a fellow, corrupt, and unfitted for any command, save upon a slaver, as well you know . . . for no other would have plied such a sordid trade. I all too often damned him for his idleness and the brutality he allowed to flourish above deck and in the holds. Yet I had need to keep my purpose hid and was slow to intervene. That was why I could not halt Septimus's flogging, although it grieved me bitterly.'

'He would have believed it the price he had to pay,' ventured Carne, seeking to ease Flanders' anguish of mind. 'His commitment was as fierce as your own, sir. You bear no guilt.'

'I thank you for that, Mr Grey. Fortune, himself, bade me pay it no more heed, declaring that one man's pain counted for little against the sufferings and deaths of so many. Yet it grieves me still.'

They looked at each other in silence for a moment, before Flanders admitted awkwardly, 'I know, Mr Grey, that you have never returned to the place from whence you came . . . and I do not ask the reason. I ask only that you tell me, tomorrow at this hour, if you will agree to stand beside me at Huskings' trial. I would have him and his masters charged, not merely with smuggling but piracy – which is the charge for slaving.' As he saw the conflict of emotions upon Carne's face, the terror and indecision, he said quietly, 'Confess nothing to me now, Mr Grey. This must be of your own volition, your own choosing. It is a decision none can make for you, and none shall blame, nor think the less of you, if you feel unable. I bid you think well upon it. Should you return, I can promise you nothing save that you will be in the public gaze, your every word recorded and used. You, and your past, wherever it lay, will be open to scrutiny, and nothing can be spared or hid.'

Carne nodded his understanding as, heavy at heart, he escorted Flanders without, and watched him disembark, to be driven away. When he returned to his cabin, he took the miniatures of his parents into his hands, gazing at them as if he might find the answer he sought in their gentle, youthful faces. He felt love for them, and fear, a fierce confusion of mind. He did not know, when Flanders returned, what he should answer. Like Septimus and William Oates, he wondered, was death the price he would have to pay?

Chapter Thirty-six

Carne had spent a restless night in his cabin, his mind tortured with the decision he was forced to make. He was no longer that callow youth who had fled Penavon, but a man of responsibility, trained to immediate action and command, and yet he felt the same coldness of panic as when he had struck down Penry Vaughan, his life and future forfeit.

He would have sought John Bessant's advice, but the Second Officer was still ashore, and there was no other to whom he could confide the truth. Dear God! How could he return, and how *not*? Sleep would not easily come and, when at last it did, Carne was plagued with restlessly disordered dreams, only to awaken before dawn. He was drenched in sweat and trembling like a child delivered from a nightmare, but still unsure. The difference was that his nightmare was reality.

His cabin was cramped and oppressive but he would not venture on deck until his mind was clear, his decision firm. It was his choice and his alone, Flanders had said, and none would blame him, nor think the less of him. None, save himself, and those whose suffering and deaths had forced him from the *Bristol Maid*. None save Sep and William Oates. What were the words which Septimus had used? 'There are those things which bleed into the ship itself.' Yes, Carne thought despairingly, and into the minds and very souls of men. But I am not as brave a man as you, Sep, he cried inwardly. I cannot face the terror of death as stoically, nor the promise of pain.

The words spoken between them came back anew to mock and haunt him, 'I do not know if I will be able to suffer it, Septimus.' . . . 'You will bear it because you must.' . . . 'I have learnt that you cannot buy peace by the suffering of others.' . . . 'A life is all we have. No man has the right to kill, or to own another, body and soul. It is an obscenity, a sacrilege against God Himself.' . . . 'If need should arise, you will side with Savage and his brutes, eager to see us killed, and raising no hand to help us, or to halt theirs. Then you will return to Bristol bearing the evidence we sought.'

But I am alive and Septimus is dead, Carne anguished silently, and would not hold me to my word! He could not know he would be sending me to a death as violent as those he strove to end. If I return, God alone knows what will become of me, and if I do not, then I alone will know what I will have become.

When Flanders returned upon the morrow, Carne was on the quayside, waiting. Flanders helped him load his belongings in the carriage and nodded, speaking no word of consolation or praise. The captain of the *Fort Jackson* watched from her bridge and raised a hand in last acknowledgement, then turned away. In his uniform pocket lay the letter which Mansel Grey had entrusted him to deliver to John Bessant when he came aboard.

The journey by passenger vessel was tedious and seemed interminably long. Time hung heavily, although Flanders, who had learned of Carne's flight to sea, and the reason for it, was a sensitive companion; unobtrusive, generous to listen, and sparing with advice.

'Without your evidence, Mr Havard,' he acknowledged in a rare burst of confidence, 'we could not substantiate the charge of piracy. We are grateful that you come, at risk to yourself.'

'I have wondered, sir,' Carne began hesitantly, 'if, should I be taken before the justices, you would send news of it to those who have my wellbeing at heart?'

'Yes, I promise that it will be done, exactly to your

430

wishes.' He paused. 'You are wondering, perhaps, why Septimus Fortune's written testimony would not suffice as evidence?'

Carne nodded.

'He could neither read nor write, Mr Havard. His mark, in the swearing of one who sought only to bring Huskings and the owners to justice, would have counted for naught. Your own written evidence would have been as suspect, I fear. As Mansel Grey, none could vouch for you, nor prove your identity. You did not exist.'

'And now? If I am proved murderer?'

'You have returned of your own free will, knowing what you face and the outcome. No man prepared to risk his own life to end the virulence spawned by slavery could tell other than the truth. You will be believed, Mr Havard.' He glanced determinedly out to sea to hide his discomfiture. 'You are as brave a man as Septimus Fortune . . . as he and I knew from the start. It was why you were chosen and why we gave you our friendship and trust.' Flanders turned abruptly upon his heel and hurried below.

When the ship docked at the Port of London, it was upon a warm mid-summer's day, and the sky a vivid, clear-washed blue, its thin vaporous clouds already dissolving. The port was like every other Carne had known, familiar yet strange, the heaped cargoes upon its wharves spicy and aromatic. He was home, voyage ended. Yet Carne's heart was beating painfully, throat tight, and he felt only an overwhelming impulse to flee back to the sea and the life which had claimed him. He did not belong on land. He even moved as one long used to drifting with the rhythm of the tides, like the seaweed at the water's edge.

He glanced anxiously towards Flanders, whose gaze was raking the small crowd upon the quayside. Then, with a hand to Carne's elbow, he was steering him towards a cluster of grave-faced gentlemen, introducing them as officials of the Society for the Abolition of Slavery. Their greetings to Carne were warm, their praise honest and unstinting. There was no turning back.

431

The four clear days before Carne and Flanders were called upon to give evidence in court remained no more than a fevered blur in their memories. There seemed scarcely time enough to eat and sleep between the remorseless questioning and probing of the Society's attorneys-at-law and their underlings. The two men could not believe that the trial itself could take more toll of their strength and energies, as they strove to affirm and rebut, to accuse and deny, to marshal their wits and their proof. They relived the stinking squalor of the *Bristol Maid*; the stench of her; the brutality; the cries and desperation of the slaves. They stumbled and halted in their speech, raged in their tiredness. When all seemed purged and ended, the ferocity of the court trial brought it as cruelly to life again, and the torture of it began anew.

Carne stood purposefully upright in the chastening formality of the court, affirming his oath, and all that had gone before. When he spoke, his voice was clear of the nervousness which he had feared would betray him. He declared his name to be Carne Havard of Penavon in Wales, a ship's officer, and formerly domiciled at Great House, Penavon, and Penavon vicarage. He spoke, as Flanders had predicted, with a conviction and honesty which none could doubt.

Without the court, the trial ended, Carne railed angrily at Flanders, 'It is infamous! Corrupt! I cannot believe that the owners were acquitted of all guilt and blame.'

'My dear Havard,' Flanders' mouth was twisted wryly, 'power and wealth create their own immunity.'

'But is there no way such filth can be called to account?'

'No. There is no way. You had best dismiss all thoughts of retribution from your mind, else it will fester within you, to no purpose other than your own destruction. Too many have already been destroyed.'

When Carne made no reply, Flanders said quietly, 'Their hands are clean of blood and none can prove it otherwise. The murdered are a world and lifetime apart, Mr Havard,

432

their rotting corpses unseen, and their fate never acknowledged.'

'But it is shameful! The worst of hypocrisy! What can
you hope to achieve?'

'The support of those of like mind,' answered Flanders
simply, 'then, slowly perhaps, to awaken the consciences
of those ignorant of its evils, and uncommitted to abolition.
If we cannot convert those who stand to gain, then we must
arouse the disgust and condemnation of all those ordinary
people who have voice.'

'That will not be enough!' Carne protested despairingly.

'It is a beginning. The trial has served to open people's
eyes to the horrors of slavery, as it will serve to open their
minds. We have not lost in all, Mr Havard,' he rebuked
gently. 'The *Bristol Maid* and her cargo have been confis-
cated, and will not sail again. Huskings and his crew have
been convicted of smuggling and piracy, and sentenced
with the severity they deserve.'

'But not Sir Robert Crandon!'

'If he has not been sentenced by law, then he has been
sentenced by association. His name will be for ever linked
with slavery and the *Bristol Maid*. He has been sentenced
in people's minds, and will be powerless to act again, do
not doubt it.'

'Yes,' Carne agreed. 'Septimus is owed that.' He looked
keenly at Flanders and said with honesty, 'I thank you for
returning those things he kept safe for me, and ask you to
believe, sir, that I would sacrifice each one of them willingly
to give Septimus but an extra hour of life, even were I to
see him no more.'

'Yes, Mr Havard, I believe you.'

There was silence between them until Flanders
demanded abruptly, 'And where do you go now, sir? What
are your plans?'

'I have none. I do not honestly know what the future
holds, Mr Flanders, and until I do . . .' He hesitated,
before repeating more firmly, 'Until I do, I will not involve
those who await my return, nor add to the grief I have

433

already caused them. It were better I were thought dead, forgotten!' He held out his hand in parting, saying earnestly, 'I shall not forget the work you do, Mr Flanders, you may be assured of it, as I shall not forget Septimus, and all he is owed. I hope, sir, that we shall meet again when life is kinder.' He made to leave.

'A moment, Mr Havard!' There was an urgency in Flanders' command. 'There is a gentleman come, seeking you.'

Carne nodded, for he had been expecting to be detained since he had first declared his name in open court. Surprisingly, the cold sickness of apprehension had left him and he felt only relief. He would no more need to hide, nor act a part. He stood rigidly controlled as the coach drew to a halt beside him, and waited.

'Carne! Carne Havard!'

He turned incredulously to Flanders and then back to Peter Morrish, too shocked and bewildered to seek explanation. Then Morrish was embracing him, and exclaiming between laughter and tears, 'Oh, my dear fellow! My dear fellow! Can it really be you? Oh, how proud we all are. I have come here to bring you home.'

'I do not understand,' Carne murmured stupidly, when he could at last find voice. 'I do not understand. How can this be? What of my cousin?'

'Penry Vaughan is well, Carne, and pressed no charges.'

'But why? Why should he not do so? It does not ring true.'

'Because the fault was his,' said Morrish simply. Then seeing that Carne was all but exhausted by the emotional turmoil of the trial, and stress and confusion, said gently, 'Mr Flanders sent word through the Anti-Slavery Society at Bristol. They provided the coach and coachman which brought us here, that we might take you home to Penavon.'

'Us? Mostyn has come with you?'

Morrish shook his head.

'Prys, then, or Jethro?'

Flanders stepped aside and opened the door of the carriage, that Saranne might descend. Carne and she paused for a long moment, staring at each other, separated by the years and the changes in them. They were no longer children, on the edge of love and maturity, but a man and a woman. Strangers. Too much, Carne thought, had happened. Then Saranne was in his arms, kissing him, weeping with happiness and love, and he was touching her hair, murmuring tenderly, his senses alive with the sweetness of her skin, the softness of her flesh, the familiar dearness of her. The years between were as nothing. She was his own dear love. Yielding, more beautiful, but unchanged in her constancy. The scent and feel of her flesh was tangible, real, and not imagined. In Saranne was relief from all that he had suffered; his pity for the slaves, his grief for Septimus and Oates; his yearning for home. She was his own warm flesh. His sanity. His hope for the future, atonement for what was past and could never be forgot. Even as he embraced her, Carne's gaze met Morrish's, warm with pity and understanding of what he had endured.

'It is time to come home,' Peter Morrish said.

'Yes,' said Carne. 'It is time.'

Flanders nodded and stood stiffly erect, but spoke no word as they drove away.

During the tedious three-day journey from London to Penavon, Carne was grateful for the boon of a private travelling coach and that they had not been forced to suffer one of the cramped, inferior company stages. Despite his urgency to be home, he had a need to purge himself of those memories and emotions resurrected by the trial, and to accept that he was no longer hunted, and an outcast, but free. The journey had been most meticulously charted by the Society for the Abolition of Slavery, with excellent tavern fare upon the road and overnight inns which offered clean bedchambers and bedding as well as courteous service. There were frequent halts for refreshment and resting and gradually Carne's fears and tension relaxed and he

435

grew comfortably at ease in Saranne's and Peter Morrish's company.

At first, exhaustion bedevilled him and, despite the questions which crowded his mind, he was barely able to remain alert, or even awake. The steady rhythmic clopping of the horses and the swaying of the coach were strangely soporific. Often, drowsiness so dulled his senses that he fell asleep, his head upon Saranne's shoulder, only to be abruptly awakened in some tavern yard, to find Saranne still cradling him protectively and scarcely able to move for the cramped numbness of her limbs.

Her nearness was a comfort to him and Carne thought she had never looked more beautiful and appealing; her childhood slenderness matured into a rounded softness of flesh, feminine and infinitely desirable. Saranne, in turn, was, at first, shyly overawed by the saturnine good looks of the self-possessed stranger. To Peter Morrish's secret amusement, she took eager opportunity to study Carne as he slept, head resting upon her shoulder, in the coach. And there was no disguising her pleasure in the spectacle. To Saranne's eyes, the Carne of youthful memory was most agreeably enhanced. Although his darkness remained unchanged, he had grown commandingly tall; his body broad shouldered, his muscles hardened by toil. Carne's skin, burnt bronze by the salt-laden winds, had drawn firm over the strong bones of his face, deepening the network of fine lines about his eyes and mouth. He was altogether more handsome and impressive. A gentleman of elegance, but a man of authority and distinction, too. Her love for him was an ache and a joy within her, a tenderness and a passion too fierce to be borne. She wanted always to be reaching out and touching him, to feel the warmth of his sleeping flesh, the caress of her skin upon his, as if the flow of his blood might somehow seep through his very pores and nerve-ends, and mingle at one with her own. Saranne loved him, as she had loved him unchangingly through the long years. There was a part of Carne's life now too dark and troubled to speak of without hurt and she could offer

436

him a loving refuge. She could offer him the only thing in his life which would never change; the constancy of her loving, and must pray that it would be enough.

Before they reached Penavon, all that had occurred there in his absence had been told. He had grieved at the confirmation of Prys's death, and wept openly at learning of Jane's death too, and also that of Jethro. Yet there was happiness too. His delighted surprise at Peter's marriage to Sara was sincere, as it was towards Mostyn's marriage to Laurel, and at the birth of their son. One of Carne's most pleasurable reunions, he felt certain, would be with Charles, and he was as jubilant at the news of how well his friend's projects at Holly Grove were succeeding as with the news of his courtship of Henrietta.

'It seems then,' ventured Carne, as they dined in the landlord's parlour at the last stopping inn upon their way, 'that much has changed in my absence.'

Peter Morrish and Saranne paused in their eating and the glance exchanged between them was hesitant and concerned.

'Penavon itself is changed,' warned Peter. 'You are returning to a new landscape, a new life. It is not the Penavon of old.'

'I am changed too,' reminded Carne. 'Life does not stand still.'

No, nor should it move so cruelly and with such violence, thought Peter Morrish.

When they set off, eager and refreshed, upon the final stage of their homecoming journey, Carne felt a new excitement stirring within him. The villages became increasingly familiar, the fields and copses giving way to undulating hills, and then the familiar bracken-clad mountains, wild, and broodingly unchanged.

Morrish and Saranne, who had tried to warn him of the quest for coal, and Mostyn's and Llewellyn's part in it, sat beside him in silence, afraid for him. There was a fierce elation in Carne, an expectancy so all-consuming that he spared no thought for those beside him, his mind and gaze feasting hungrily upon the changing landscape without the coach.

The outskirts of the village, when they came to it, were an unrecognisable sprawl of makeshift dwellings. Tents, huts and an unsightly huddle of canvas-covered carts, with all the slops and detritus of living, erupted all about, like some vilely sprouting fungus; an excrescence on the face of his valley. Everywhere there was filth and disorder; in the piles of bricks and quarried stone, the unfinished houses in ugly, straggling rows, in the unkempt animals and milling people. It was, Carne thought, appalled, little different from those mean dockland streets which had filled him with such pity and despair. As the carriage approached, the men, women and children fell silent and moved aside, lest they block its way. Dear God! Carne thought, what squalor and misery they share! Then he glimpsed beyond the settlement's edge the mines driven deep into the hillsides, with their cluster of sheds and rusting trams, the heaps of coal, the narrow-gauge railway lines, and, more distant yet, the vast unwieldy shape of the drill which bored into the rocky earth like some feverish insect with ceaselessly devouring jaws.

'It is an abomination! An eyesore!' he exclaimed furiously. 'How can such desecration be allowed to exist?'

'Because men exist,' said Peter Morrish simply. 'They must work or starve.'

Saranne's hand moved to cover Carne's, then to grasp it comfortingly, but he paid no need, too incensed even to notice.

'I had expected to see the cottagers' old bell-mines,' he exclaimed helplessly, 'small pits, like Prys's, dug into the earth . . . but this! It is monstrous! They are turning Penavon into a desert, destroying its beauty remorselessly, and for gain! And these people are alien, strangers all!'

'They are Penavon people, Carne, deserving of help and kindness,' Morrish rebuked with a coldness which made Carne flush, for he had never before given him occasion to use such a tone. 'They are but one step removed from those for whom you gave testimony. Slaves to men's greed, and forced to labour for others or starve.' His voice softened as he said with compassion, 'You will forgive that I speak harshly, for I am as grieved as you for all that is lost. It is a cold homecoming for you.'

'But I am free, as you reminded me.' It was an admission and apology as Carne's hand closed protectively over Saranne's small fist, firm in its reassurance. Yet he felt no reassurance within. Jane, Prys, and Jethro were dead and others like Charles, Mostyn and Peter Morrish had made new lives and progressed beyond him. He did not even know if he could endure to stay. He had nothing to offer Saranne save affection and the money he had earned and saved. He owned no home, had no future prospects, his only skill was seamanship. There would be small enough demand in Penavon for that.

Chapter Thirty-seven

Carne was given an immediate and unreserved welcome by Sara at Myrtle Cottage, where a comfortable room had already been prepared for him. The old anger and mistrust she had shown towards him had gone and she had raised no objection to Peter's and Saranne's journey to London to bring Carne home. Like Jethro, all she had wanted from the first was her daughter's happiness. Sara accepted that, for good or for ill, there could never be happiness for Saranne without Carne.

Mrs Hodges had prepared a veritable feast of his favourite dishes to tempt and nourish him and the meal was joyously shared by Charles, Megan, Randall Walters; those friends who had patiently awaited his return. Then, immediately after luncheon was ended, Saranne drove out upon the donkey cart with Megan to tend a sick child at the encampment. Peter Morrish and Sara were intent upon their charitable work, begging Carne to excuse them and to rest himself well in their absence. He pretended agreement to put their minds to ease but could find no ease for his own. Bedevilled by restlessness, he had a notion to call upon Mostyn at Great House, to pay his respects to Laurel and his nephew, but after some hesitation crossed the highway to the livery stables of the inn instead. There he hired a mount and rode out to see Marged Howell on Penavon mountain.

She greeted him warmly but without surprise, her serenity settling a calmness upon his spirits. In the unde- manding quietness of her company and the mountains,

Carne found himself unburdening his mind of those terrors which still possessed him in his sleeping as in his waking hours. She listened compassionately as he rid himself of the evils and savagery he would never confide to another. Her acceptance was a catharsis; her gentle presence a healing balm. When all was ended and his wretchedness spent, she said quietly, 'There is no ready salve, my dear, for the wounds of the spirit, or for grief. I know, for I have too long sought it.' The confession was full of pity and understanding. 'One must let wounds bleed before cleansing and healing begin.'

Carne exclaimed contritely, 'I should not have come! I had no right to burden you with my useless fears and ramblings.'

'You have every right,' she said with honesty. 'You are part of one I loved: Rice Havard; his flesh and bone. You came to me from need, and I am grateful for it.' She paused before adding quietly, 'Sometimes our hurt is eased by the telling of it; acknowledging it openly.' She smiled wryly, 'For despite all that we are and all we may achieve, we are children still – vulnerable, uncertain, ravaged by childish fears.'

They looked at each other in compassionate understanding, bound by past griefs and knowledge shared. It seemed to Carne a moment set apart in time; when minds and spirits meet in recognition and perfect harmony.

Carne's unexplained absence from Myrtle Cottage and the lateness of his return caused consternation.

Peter cautioned the womenfolk not to show agitation upon Carne's return, nor to question him too urgently, although their concern, he knew, sprang from affection alone. 'He has need for solitude,' he advised. 'He must have peace and quietness – the chance to come to terms with the past, and himself, and to rechart his future. So much has changed. It will not be easy.'

Carne entered full of remorse at his lateness and made awkward apology, although he gave no reason as to why he had felt the need to ride out to see Marged. Nor did he

441

speak of what had passed between them.

'You are free to come and go whenever you choose, Carne,' Sara replied warmly and with sincerity. 'Our life here is without pattern or formality,' she explained, 'since a clergyman's house must be freely open and welcoming to all.'

Upon thanking her, Carne was rewarded with a glance of tender approval from Saranne, then a smile as radiant with pride as that which Peter Morrish had bestowed upon his wife.

It was thus a relaxed and congenial company which awaited Charles on his return from dining with Henrietta at Litchard House. He had brought the new carriage to return Saranne to Holly Grove, and while Sara and Peter and Mrs Hodges were ostentatiously engaged in inspecting and praising it, Saranne and Carne were discreetly allowed to make their farewells. Restricted as they were by the nearness of others, their kisses were more tender and passionate, their embraces the warmer for being urgently snatched. In the conflict of emotions which churned within him, and the uncertainty of what his future held, Carne was certain of one thing. He loved Saranne, and could face life with no other beside him. He would ask her to wed him, and soon, and make whatever changes in his life their marriage demanded. For the moment, though, he was content to breathe the scent of her skin and hair, to feel the soft yielding of her flesh, and her lips to his own. She brought him forgetfulness, and there was much he would choose to forget.

After the carriage had left, Carne and Peter talked of Mostyn and his marriage to Laurel, and of how he was faring at Great House.

'I believe that he is . . . comfortable there,' Morrish prevaricated. 'It has always been a second home to him and I have found the Llewellyns to be kind.' He paused, as if debating whether to speak further and more frankly, then subsided into silence.

'It was always his intention to return to Great House,' Carne's voice was low, troubled. 'He swore that he would possess it. It was his one ambition, from childhood.'

'Then it is to be hoped that he has not achieved it at the sacrifice of others,' Morrish said wryly. 'It would be too high a price to pay for bricks and mortar, and one he will repent. One cannot trade in human flesh and blood without disaster, Carne, as you have learnt!'

'You think, then, he married without love? That he has no feelings for his wife and child?' Carne asked awkwardly.

'You had best ask him,' counselled Morrish quietly, 'for he does not confide in me, and I hold no store by rumour. But what I have seen of him shows me that he is restless and unhappy. His is not the behaviour of a man who has achieved his aim. I think it might be wise to seek him out. He has need of uncritical acceptance.'

'The understanding of a brother?' Carne's voice was drily unconvinced. Then he admitted quietly, 'It is true that I know Mostyn better than any other. But I swear, Peter, that I do not understand him, and never shall.'

'You do not need to understand in order to accept and forgive,' Morrish's voice held no hint of rebuke, but his eyes were shrewdly questioning.

'I will go to Great House and speak to him . . . see if I can help in any way,' promised Carne, 'and then make my peace with my cousin, Penry Vaughan, since it pleases you.'

Peter Morrish hid a smile, saying, 'It is you who have to be satisfied, Carne, that you have done all in your power to heal the rift.' He hesitated. 'Whatever cruelties or misunderstandings separated you, they are over . . . past. It is time to begin anew. You owe it to Mostyn as a brother, and to yourself.'

'Brothers . . .' Carne murmured to himself. 'It seems that there is always some conflict between them, a resentment and misunderstanding. Cain and Abel, Jacob and Esau . . .'

'They are examples meant only to shame and inspire others to greater efforts,' declared Morrish drily. 'I dare to hope that they will prove salutary.'

* * *

Penry Vaughan made a rare uninvited visit to Great House in his cousin's absence, to inform Rhys Llewellyn that Mostyn was in grave trouble for allegedly seducing a young girl in the village. The girl, a parishioner whom Vaughan scathingly dismissed as 'low-bred, dissolute, and a practised liar and whore', had given birth to an illegitimate son, one month after Laurel had been delivered. The girl's father, a farm labourer, threatened to make the matter known to the judiciary, alleging that Mostyn had shamelessly ensnared his daughter, and taken carnal knowledge of her, violently, and against her will.

'You have approached Mostyn on the subject?' Llewellyn demanded testily. 'Accused him?'

'Certainly,' Penry Vaughan replied stiffly, 'since it was my duty to do so, both as priest and kinsman.'

'He denied it?'

'Indeed not! He was most arrogant and offensive in his manner, admitting it freely, and with evident satisfaction. He showed neither shame nor remorse.' Vaughan's face was flushed with righteous indignation. 'Should such indelicate matters come to the ears of your wife and daughter . . .' He broke off expressively, before continuing, 'So I considered it to be my Christian duty to inform you of this unsavoury affair. The girl's father even had the brazen temerity to threaten me, and demand recompense.'

'A payment for his silence, you mean?'

'Indeed.'

'Which, I am sure, being the gentleman and honest clergyman that you are, you strenuously resisted?'

Vaughan, who thought he detected a note of irony in his questioner's voice, said defensively, 'I thought it better to put the matter into more worldly hands, since your business dealing makes you better equipped to bargain with such rabble.'

'Yes,' Llewellyn agreed, no flicker of expression betraying his rising irritation. 'It is true that I have had practice in dealing with such people of late – and Mostyn is, assuredly, my son-in-law.'

'Then I may safely leave this affair in your hands, sir, to deal with as you think fit?'

Llewellyn merely nodded, coldly watching the clergyman take his leave.

'Mostyn is not really a wicked boy. He is more sinned against than sinning,' observed Vaughan, flurried into defensiveness. 'Such women are Jezebels! Whores and temptresses . . . Wantons, undeserving of sympathy . . .' Vaughan broke off, unnerved by Llewellyn's contemptuous stare, then added unctuously, 'I am hopeful, sir, that you will treat him as he deserves.'

'You may be certain of it!'

Vaughan paused, startled by Llewellyn's vehemence as his host continued, 'And may I echo that hope, sir, for the people in *your* care . . . that you treat them as they deserve.'

'With respect, sir, I believe you may take that for granted.' Vaughan bowed stiffly and with infinite conde-scension as he climbed, seething, into the carriage and bade Probert drive him away.

Laurel was unable to shake off the feeling of pessimism, or the inertia which possessed her. She could scarce summon the effort to allow herself to be dressed, or permit her hair to be attended to by her maidservant. She knew that she was ungrateful and causing her parents grief, for they spared nothing in their efforts to divert and humour her. Yet she was unable to make response, although she tried to rouse herself from her lassitude. It was, she thought, des-pairingly, like being engulfed in some dense, all-pervading fog, a blackness which deadened all sight and sound, and stifled feeling. She could take no interest in her son, a strange, alien creature, timid and fretful who seemed tied to her by neither flesh nor emotion. She felt nothing for him, not even resentment for the pain and humiliation of his birth. Yet, cruelly, perversely, despite his indifference to her and his frequent cruelty, she knew that she loved Mostyn. She could not understand why and berated herself for her weakness, but to no avail. The more she abased

445

herself, the more vicious and degrading grew his rejection of her and the deeper her desolation. She saw little of him now and when she did he was dismissive, declaring her to be gross and unlovable. Her mind, he said dispassionately, had become unhinged by childbirth and he doubted that she would ever recover her wits. She could end her days in an asylum for the insane, for that was the fate of those obsessed, as she, by fears and darkness.

'It is not my mind, but my spirit which grieves,' she protested with a first sign of spirit, 'for you show me neither love nor respect.'

'How can one respect a slut?' he countered, 'a woman devoid of all charm or appeal to the flesh? You bore and disgust me, Laurel!' He continued dressing imperturbably. 'It is small wonder that I spend my time elsewhere, in the company of others more congenial.'

'But, Mostyn . . .' She knew even as she spoke that it was useless to plead with him. Submissiveness would only anger him and earn his contempt, yet she could not help herself. 'But Mostyn . . . I am your wife; you owe me something.'

'I owe you nothing!' His tone was harsh. 'Neither respect, love nor fidelity. You cannot buy affection, Laurel. It has to be earned!'

'Then I will earn it!'

'How? Your looks? Your intelligence? Your wiles?' He picked up a handglass from her dressing table, thrusting it before her face. 'Look, Laurel! Take a long, hard look at yourself, and tell me what you see. A drab, unkempt caricature of a creature, without warmth or excitement. As useless in mind as flesh.' He watched, untouched, as her tears fell.

'I am not for sale, Laurel!' His words held arrogance, but bitterness too. 'The Llewellyns have bought Great House, but they will not buy me. I have sold you my name, and spawned your child, but you will not own me! You have my oath upon it!'

He strode imperiously from the room, slamming the door with finality.

Rhys Llewellyn, who had been awaiting him in the hall below, steered him remorselessly towards the library, taking no account of his protestations that he had a meeting planned elsewhere. 'Your meeting, sir, will be with me!' he declared unequivocally. 'You had best accept it, and listen to what I have to say, for I still hold the purse strings.'

Mostyn nodded sullenly, and obeyed. Laurel paused at the head of the staircase but, despite her distress, curiosity forced her to follow them. In his fury to remonstrate with Mostyn, Rhys Llewellyn had unwittingly left the library door ajar, and Laurel crept unashamedly towards it to eavesdrop.

'This . . . woman, this harlot you visit so blatantly in the village . . .' Llewellyn began scathingly, 'I hear that you have fathered a bastard upon her!'

Mostyn regarded him steadily, a slight smile upon his lips. 'So?' he demanded superciliously. 'You wish an introduction to her? You would avail yourself of her services?'

'Damn you for your insolence!' Beside himself with rage, Llewellyn grasped him by his collar and raised a hand to aim a blow at Mostyn's cheek, but, instead, released him, his hand dropping uselessly to his side. 'I would not soil my hands in striking you,' he said contemptuously. 'You are filthy, corrupt. You are no more than carrion, Havard! I should have forbidden Laurel to marry you.'

'And raised a bastard for a grandchild?' Mostyn's smile was mocking. 'I am surprised, sir, that you consider it, since you call the mother of my other son . . . what was it? Harlot? It seems to me there is little to choose between them.'

Shock drained Llewellyn's face of colour, save for the spots of burning colour high over his cheeks, and his fists were clenched so tightly that the knuckles gleamed white! When he spoke, his voice was so filled with controlled fury that even Mostyn was afraid, and retreated nervously.

'It is you, sir, who is the whore!' Llewellyn spoke distinctly and with venom. 'You have sold yourself for money, for bricks and mortar, and to pay your creditors! You are a seducer and lecher, a fornicator with the morals of a goat!'

Mostyn smiled, and bowed insolently, before saying languidly, 'I thank you for that testimonial, sir. It will stand me in good stead.'

'With whom?' Llewellyn's voice was lacerating. 'The trollops you entertain? I have a mind to forbid you the house. You are an affront to decent society!'

'I think, sir, you will not do that,' Mostyn warned, unable to hide his self-satisfaction, 'else you will forfeit my son, and your daughter's inheritance. They are mine, my property, and I will allow no-one and nothing to rob me of them.'

'You are a cheat, Havard!' Llewellyn accused disgustedly, 'a liar and a cheat. You care for neither Laurel nor the boy, and have denied her the affection and support that are her due. You are a parasite! She would be well rid of you.'

'I think not,' said Mostyn coolly. 'Strangely enough, she holds me in deep affection. She would not thank you for your interference. Her hatred would be for you, not me. She is a natural underdog, sir, the more she is whipped, the more she cringes, and the better she obeys. I do not think, somehow, that you will mention my little . . . consolation.'

The door was flung open upon its hinges with a crash that had both men turning in alarm. Laurel stood there, lips compressed, face white with anger, but standing erect and self-possessed. 'Get out!' Her voice was coldly incisive. 'Get out, Mostyn, before I kill you, as I am minded to.' Rhys Llewellyn had moved towards her to take her arm but she motioned him away. 'You may take your "consolation" as and where you choose, and be damned with you! But mark this and mark it well, you will never again share my bed nor lay a finger upon me. I will bear no more brats of yours, nor will you influence my son against me, nor take control of him.'

Mostyn made to sidle up to her, smiling placatingly, and trying to disarm her with a claim that it had been no more than a foolish jest. He placed a hand at her waist, and she wrenched it away, warning fiercely, 'Do not touch me, Mostyn, now, or in the future . . . and do not add lying to your deceit and betrayal. I cannot stomach it!'

'I will come back,' he blustered defiantly, 'and when I do . . . then . . .'

'And when you do, it will be as a guest in my father's house . . . with neither power nor privilege,' she said wearily.

'You will not be rid of me so easily,' he raged impotently. 'You have need of me.'

'No. I have no need of you.'

'My son? My name?'

'*My* son,' she corrected flatly. 'As for your name, it is nothing. You have made it a joke and obscenity. It grieves me that my son bears it, and the stigma of it.'

'Then you will not care that my love-child bears the name Rice Mostyn Havard!' he flung at her, enraged.

'Love-child?' she demanded scornfully. 'Love is a word you cannot know the meaning of, Mostyn. As for his name, and the woman who bore him, I feel no anger towards them, no resentment. They have taken nothing of value from me, but I pity them with all my heart. God knows, I pity them!'

'Damn you, Laurel!' He took a threatening step towards her.

'Go, Mostyn!' Rhys Llewellyn's voice was so harshly commanding that Mostyn halted.

'Yes. Go to your paid woman, and your by-blow,' said Laurel quietly. 'I no longer have need of you.'

'We will speak of it upon my return, when we are alone and you are more amenable to reason,' mumbled Mostyn, edging towards the door.

'If you return, then it will be on my terms.'

'Be damned to hell with you, Laurel!' he exploded help-lessly.

'I have been since the day we met,' she said with honesty.

Chapter Thirty-eight

Mostyn, fuming with resentment at Rhys Llewellyn's high-handed treatment and at Laurel's daring to lay down conditions for his acceptance at Great House, walked blindly across the cobbles of the stable yard. 'Hell and damnation!' he muttered aloud. 'Am I here on sufferance? A nobody?' He strode into the stables, his face so contorted with anger that the stable lad who had often felt the sting of Mostyn's whip for his slowness, retreated into a far corner of the stall, trying in vain to make himself invisible. 'You, there! Saddle my mare, and be quick about it!'

The boy led the mare into the yard, then interlaced his fingers to support Mostyn's riding boot, as, with a surly grunt, Mostyn swung himself into the saddle. Barely pausing at the pillared gateway, and about to whip the horse savagely on, he was diverted by a cry.

'Mostyn! . . . Wait!'

He reined in his horse and it gave him no pleasure to see that it was Carne who hailed him from a well-fashioned gig, with excellent horses and dressed like a gentleman. 'I heard that you had returned,' he declared sullenly. 'Say what you have to say, for I have little time to waste.'

Carne's grip on the reins tightened as he strove to suppress his annoyance.

'If it is money you beg, or an introduction to people of substance, then I cannot help you. You had best return when the time is convenient. I have an appointment to keep.'

'I came to renew acquaintanceship with a brother.'

450

Carne's voice was low. 'I have friends and money enough to support me, Mostyn. I do not seek your charity.'

'Then I am glad to hear it, for there are demands enough on my purse and my patience.' He made as if to stir his horse into action, then hesitated. 'You will know that I am now in possession of Great House.' There was no mistaking the triumph in his voice. 'And that I have a son, who will inherit.'

'I congratulate you,' said Carne drily, 'upon both. From all accounts, you have worked strenuously and single-mindedly to that end.'

Stung by Carne's cynicism, and still smarting from his tongue lashing by Laurel and her father, Mostyn taunted spitefully, 'Well? And what have you achieved that gives you the right to gloat and belittle me? How do you measure your success? By a suit of out-moded clothes and a third rate gig?'

Carne smiled, recognising in Mostyn that childish out-burst of temper in his fury to be always the first, and the best. Despite himself, he felt a stirring of pity and protectiveness. 'Come, Mostyn,' he coaxed, descending from the carriage to stand beside him. 'Let us meet again, after so long a time, as brothers and equals.'

'Equals.' Mostyn's tone was cold. 'I hardly think we meet as equals. Were it not for me, you would be languishing in some house of correction, or strung from a gibbet!'

'Damnation, Mostyn!' Carne cried in vexation. 'What is it that ails you? I cannot believe that it is my return which so embitters you. It is something deeper and more corrosive that eats away, poisoning from within.' He put a tentative hand upon Mostyn's arm. 'If you have need of friendship . . . help . . . ?' he offered.

Mostyn pulled away, declaring, 'What arrogance to suppose that you can help me in any way! Damn your insolence, Carne! You are nothing, and no-one. It is jealousy that bedevils you, anger that I have achieved your old aim to inherit Great House!'

Carne shook his head wearily.

'Do not deny it! Why else then did you come, save to insinuate yourself into my life, and try to wrest it all from me?'

There was a wildness in Mostyn's manner, a strangeness which fuelled Carne's suspicion that his brother was near to breaking point, and he said sharply to hide his compassion, 'I came to invite you to my wedding, and to ask that you stand as my supporter . . . my groomsman.'

The expression of rage upon Mostyn's face gave way to a look of furtiveness and unmistakable fear.

'Who is it that you wed?' he asked harshly.

'Saranne Hartrey . . . of Holly Grove Farm.'

Without a word, Mostyn whipped at his horse with such violence that it all but dragged Carne beneath its flailing hooves.

'I do not consort with peasants,' he shouted back, 'rabble and scum . . . but I wish you all the happiness in marriage that I enjoy!'

Carne watched him go, cursing him for his vicious arrogance, yet strangely troubled, in spite of all. Mostyn's back was rigid, his face grim, as he whipped ferociously at his terrified horse, urging her on. Yet his eyes were blurred by tears of hurt and self-pity.

Rhys Llewellyn had watched Mostyn ride from the stable yard and had hurried without to remonstrate with him for his fierce handling of the mare, distressed to see her so treated. Instead, he had been inadvertent eavesdropper upon Mostyn's and Carne's acrimonious exchange.

Awkwardly, but with dignity, he introduced himself and invited Carne within, apologising for Mostyn's ill-humour and lack of manners. Carne accepted courteously and followed him as Rhys Llewellyn ventured sympathetically, 'I have followed with interest the *Morning Post*'s reports of the trial of those upon the *Bristol Maid*. Slavery is a vicious and degrading trade, Mr Havard. I admire you for the courageous public stand you took upon the issue. It could not have been easy.'

'No, sir. It was not easy,' Carne admitted.

Llewellyn studied him keenly before asking shrewdly, 'But easier, perhaps, than to stand aside and allow it to continue?'

Carne nodded agreement.

'Do not let it grieve you, Mr Havard, that those who were plainly implicated denied all responsibility, and were allowed to go free!' he adjured unexpectedly. 'They will pay a harsh price. Their lives and livelihoods will be forfeit. Society is quick to condemn, but slow to forgive. In the final reckoning, imprisonment might have proved the kinder punishment.'

Before Carne could make reply, Llewellyn shepherded him within, saying with an abrupt change of mood, 'I hope, Mr Havard, that it will cause you no distress to revisit your old house and see it changed.'

'No, sir. It will give me pleasure,' said Carne honestly. 'My grief was in leaving it. I was but eleven years old, and all of childhood and kindness lay here.'

Rhys Llewellyn was studying him carefully as Carne confessed, 'I am glad that it is not empty, but a home to you as once it was to me. No, my regret is not for bricks and mortar lost to me, Mr Llewellyn, but for people. It is one thing I have learnt.'

Llewellyn nodded. 'It is more than some learn in a lifetime,' he said quietly, and both knew of whom he spoke.

Great House was, as Carne kept reminding himself, cold stone and mortar, yet he could not subdue his treacherous memories. Upon descending the great staircase at Llewellyn's heels, so violent and unexpected was remembrance that he was forced to halt. Llewellyn turned and saw Carne's pallor and evident distress and inwardly cursed himself for his insensitivity, saying quickly, 'I fear that in my enthusiasm, Mr Havard, I have overtaxed us both. The day is humid, do you not find? If you are agreeable, I suggest we return to the library and I will summon refreshment.'

Carne had, by then, recovered his colour and composure and he followed him below. Still, he could not shake off the vividness of the scene recreated in his mind. The bearing of Rice Havard's lifeless body across the flagstoned hall and a terrified boy crouched, unseen, against the balustrade to await his father's coming, then running to greet the emptiness of death. Yet Carne knew with a shame which in no way lessened his conviction, that he would fight, work and scheme, as ruthlessly as Mostyn, to repossess Great House. Whether it took him five years or fifty, no matter. He would have no peace until he could reclaim it and lay to rest the ghost of Rice Havard, and those other shades which so restlessly haunted his mind.

Carne was duly presented to Clarissa, whose social poise allowed her to mask her surprise and curiosity at his unheralded arrival. Carne liked her immediately, for she was entirely without affectation. Clarissa, who might have resented him because of his kinship to Mostyn, was wise enough to reserve her judgement, for which she was later grateful. She found in Carne a reflection of her own innate courtesy, and his real appreciation of the beautiful objects she cherished and gathered about her made her warm towards him.

Laurel, however, greeted him with an almost febrile anxiety to please; a quicksilver gaiety and chatter which could not hide her inner sadness. He saw the concern for her in the glances exchanged between her parents, and her fragility raked him with pity. She was little more than a child, with a child's vulnerability and need of assurance; an assurance he was convinced that Mostyn denied her.

Dear heaven, he thought, how could my brother have so carelessly destroyed her? He glanced up and saw Llewellyn's watchful gaze upon him and knew he had betrayed his feelings.

'Perhaps, Mr Havard, you would care to see our grandson, your nephew?' he asked pleasantly. 'Clarissa, my dear, perhaps you will ring for a servant to ask his nurse to bring him?'

454

Clarissa did as he bade and they waited in awkwardness until the child was brought. Laurel ran to relieve the nurse of him, face flushed and animated, and held him jealously to her, caressing his face with a soft-fingered touch, kissing his cheek 'neath the lavishly trimmed bonnet.

'You see, Mr Havard . . . Carne,' she cried delightedly, 'how handsome he is, and intelligent. His eyes follow me . . . he knows that I am his mother, I am sure of it. Is he not the sweetest and most handsome of babes?'

'Indeed, Laurel . . . he is the handsomest infant I have seen, in all of my life. He does you credit, ma'am. I do not wonder you are so proud of him, and love him so dearly.'

He saw by her radiant smile that his words had pleased her and wondered why the look which passed between Rhys Llewellyn and Clarissa was one of joy, and yet Clarissa's eyes were filled with tears.

Carne's sombre mood lightened as he left Great House and approached the attorney's office in Penavon village. He held Randall Walters in real affection and was looking forward to seeing him again.

Once inside the office, Walters, rubicund and smiling expansively, looked just the same as he remembered. 'Carne, my dear fellow . . .' he said, grasping first his hand, then enveloping him totally in a massive, bear-like embrace. He held him at arm's length the better to study him, nodded approval and declared extravagantly, 'You are too grand, I fear, to be told how you have grown, and given a sixpence as of old! But oh, my dear fellow, how pleased I am by your return! You cut as fine a figure, I declare, as your father did in his youth . . . and are the very spit and image of him!' Before Carne could make reply, he continued ebulliently, 'I must hear all from the very beginning, for we could not speak freely at your homecoming.'

'First, there is a debt owed to you, and which I would repay, sir,' Carne insisted. 'I do so with my warmest gratitude, for I despaired that I would ever find the opportunity.' He took a leather pouch from his pocket and poured out

455

its contents, fifteen gold coins in all.

'But there are too many,' protested Walters. 'You are mistaken, Carne.'

'No, sir. I simply repay, with interest, the money advanced to me. I beg you will not refuse it, for that was always my declared aim. Without your generosity, I would never have found the means of escape. Do not treat me now with less understanding and kindness than you showed to me as a child.'

There was a pride and entreaty in his tone, and Walters studied him intently before gathering up the coins within the pouch and placing it wordlessly in the drawer of his desk.

'And now, Carne, I, too, have something to return to your safekeeping, a gift from someone who loved you as deeply as you cared for her.'

'Jane?' he asked quietly.

'Yes. Jane Prys.' Walters placed a document and a linen-wrapped bundle upon his desk, sweeping away the clutter to make space. 'The will is straightforward and easy to understand. Save for some furniture which was bequeathed to Megan Griffin, she left her property, and this one item, to you. Would you have me open it?'

Carne murmured the single word, 'Please', his voice hoarse and barely audible.

Walters carefully unwrapped the simple bundle to display the gold and opal necklace, then placed it gently into Carne's hands.

'The necklace was a gift from your grandmother, Sophia Havard, to Jane, a recognition of the debt of affection and loyalty owed.'

'And Jane asked that it be returned to me?'

'To be held in trust for your wife, and thence to your female issue. She wished to return it to those to whom it rightfully belonged.'

'But she could have sold it, bought herself out of poverty and servitude!' Carne exclaimed passionately. 'My grand-mother must have meant it to be used so!'

'That was Jane's happiness, Carne, the returning of it to whom it belonged,' said Walters. 'She knew you would treasure it most. The cruelty would be in resenting or rejecting her generosity. It would devalue the gift, and the giver.'

Walters reseated himself at the desk and fidgeted with the papers before him, continuing, 'Now, to the residue of your inheritance. Jane Prys has bequeathed you the property known as Hillbrook Cottage.' He wrinkled his face in apology and sucked in his underlip. 'It is a poor place, part ruined, I fear. The roof is sagging and open to the weather, and the land surrounding it poor and unfit to cultivate.'

'I remember it, sir,' Carne confessed.

'And what use will you make of it? It is too remote for use by any but passing drovers and vagrants. It was, I am led to believe, a tied cottage upon the Havard estate.' He frowned. 'That is no doubt the reason for Mostyn's attempting to buy it after Hywel Prys's death.'

'Mostyn?' echoed Carne in bewilderment. 'I cannot see the purpose in it, unless he is attempting to restore the land sold upon my father's death, and the farms and cottages.' He hesitated, then said with regret rather than anger, 'I would like to believe that it was to ease Jane's poverty he made offer and yet, I cannot. It does not ring true.'

'Your friend, Charles Hartrey, was alarmed. It seems Mostyn threatened and brow-beat her and she grew confused and terrified. Hartrey begged me send a letter of warning, which I did most willingly. I can tell you no more.' He hesitated, seemingly searching for how best to phrase the words. 'Since Jane Prys's death, the house has lain empty. Yet its deterioration has been swifter and the dereliction greater than can be rationally explained.'

'Vandalism?'

'Deliberate, and with purpose,' said Walters with conviction.

'Vagrants? Or the strangers and itinerants pouring into Penavon?' asked Carne sharply.

'No. I cannot believe it. It would be of no use to them.

It is too far removed from the new drift coal-mines that Llewellyn and Lord Litchard finance. The newcomers are mostly good people, intent upon work, but with the usual cut-throats and charlatans amongst them. They live in tents or waggons, forsaken houses and empty barns, wherever they may find shelter until the colliery company's cramped hovels are built. No man would willingly move far from the encampment, lest another be hired before him. They might fight to wrest work from another, rather than see their children starve. But . . .' He broke off expressively. Then his heavy, good-natured face relaxed, dewlaps gathered into a dry smile, as he demanded, '. . . since we speak of violence, it is appropriate to enquire after your esteemed cousin, Mr Penry Vaughan. You have renewed acquaintanceship?'

'No,' Carne admitted sheepishly. 'That is a pleasure as yet deferred. I intend to make a formal call upon him this very afternoon.'

'Indeed?' The attorney's eyebrows rose questioningly. 'Then I hope your reception is less frigid and acrimonious than before. The reason for this change of heart?'

'I hope to make my peace, since Saranne and I are soon to be wed.'

Walters leapt up with surprising agility for so well-fleshed a man and pumped Carne's hand in delighted approval, declaring, 'Then it is as I hoped! Oh, my dear boy, I congratulate you most sincerely, yes, most sincerely! Saranne is altogether a most exceptional and charming young woman, spirited and intelligent.' His kindly, avuncular face grew unusually serious as he added, 'I truly believe that such loyalty and devotion as you have shown for each other will hold you in good stead, for trust is the basis for all good relationships, whether they are inspired by love or by duty alone.'

'Yes, sir. I have found it to be so in all your dealings with me, and others.'

Walters grew crimson with pleasure. 'I believe that we shall soon be celebrating another betrothal, Carne,' he said.

'Indeed, sir?'

'My goddaughter, Henrietta, appears to be quite inordinately fond of your friend, Charles Hartrey,' Walters confided with sly mischievousness. 'If she is to be believed, he is such a paragon of all the virtues that he should be quite odiously conceited and unlikeable.' He smiled widely. 'In fact, he is a most excellent young man, and despite a little natural jealousy and scepticism on my part, for I have known and doted upon Henrietta from her infancy, I am forced to concur.' He regarded Carne shrewdly. 'He has convinced Lord Litchard of his worth in personal and in business matters. Have you plans to remain here and join Charles in his ventures?'

'I honestly do not know.' Carne's hand reached out involuntarily to finger Jane's opal necklace upon the desk, as if it were a talisman. 'The sea is strong in my blood.'

Walters nodded his understanding.

'Charles has tentatively broached the subject, invited me to join him, but I am no farmer.'

'Neither is Charles!' exclaimed Walters unexpectedly. 'I believe his success at Holly Grove Farm springs mainly from a debt to Jethro; a need to repay his father's years of struggle against poverty and his tragic death.'

'Perhaps, sir.'

'I believe that he is a shrewd and intuitive businessman and that you would be well matched in wits and temperament should you take up his offer. Do not dismiss it out of hand, Carne. Think on it carefully,' he advised, 'but do not rush blindly into a partnership. Consider well, for it is as vital to do so in business as in marriage.' Suddenly he turned the conversation and asked, 'What would you have me do with Jane Prys's necklace?'

'If I may leave it in your safekeeping until Saranne and I are wed. It would be better so.' Carne hesitated. 'I will do as Jane asked, but not now. It is too raw. I would give it to Saranne in joy rather than hurt, as Jane deserves.'

Walters gathered it up and folded it within the linen cloth, then placed it in the safe, venturing no word. When he returned, he rummaged amidst the clutter within his desk and, after much impatient muttering and fumbling, brought out a document neatly rolled and beribboned, and thrust it hastily into Carne's hands.

'A small gift, a token set aside against your return and marriage,' he mumbled. 'I never doubted, do you see, never doubted . . .' Embarrassment had roughened his voice and made him sound brusque.

Carne looked at him in bewilderment and tried to murmur his thanks. Walters waved them aside dismissively, 'It is nothing. A small worthless old house in the village I was eager to dispose of. Those are the deeds, if you will accept them as a favour to me. I shall not take offence if you or Saranne consider it to be too lowly a place. It is damnably cramped and inconvenient.'

There was silence between them before Carne thrust out his hand, gripping his friend's firmly and with gratitude.

'It is to be hoped I have not caused you offence, Carne,' said Walters, eyes downcast. 'That was never my intention. I am a man alone and unwed, with no prospect of child. Yet, I hope I may claim some small part in your growing, and in your remembrance.'

'No, sir!'

Walters looked at him in consternation, his eyes clouded by disappointment.

'You are not a small part of my growing, sir. You made the cruelties which I endured from others bearable. I thank you for that, as for the gift you offer me now.' He gripped the attorney's hand more firmly. 'I admire and respect you more than any living person.'

'My dear Carne,' Walters said, his eyes clear and amused. 'Am I to understand that I stand higher in your estimation than Penry Vaughan and Mostyn both? You do me too much honour. It is more credit than I deserve!'

460

Chapter Thirty-nine

Carne's visit to Penavon vicarage was not a conspicuous success. That it was anything but a pleasure to Penry Vaughan also was immediately apparent. His face showed shock, disbelief, then disapproval and, finally, outrage at this unwarranted intrusion.

'I wonder, sir, that you have the unmitigated gall to show your face here!' he offered by way of greeting.

Carne said quietly, advancing and holding out a hand in friendship, 'I come, Cousin Penry, with the best of intentions.'

'Then you will know that the road to hell is oft paved with them!' Vaughan ignored his proffered hand and would have tugged at the bell-pull to summon assistance, had not Carne stood before it determinedly. 'Have you returned to harass a defenceless man?' Vaughan accused sourly, 'to complete that cowardly assault you began? I warn you, there are servants within call. I have but to raise my voice.'

'I have come to make amends,' said Carne patiently, 'and ask only that you listen. Then, if you choose, you may raise your voice as violently as you raised a whip to me as a child.'

'It is I, sir, who bear the scars of your brutality,' Vaughan reminded frostily, his hand rising involuntarily to his forehead.

'As I, sir, bear deeper scars. I do not speak only of flesh . . .' Carne broke off abruptly, only to plead disarmingly, 'Let us not speak of violence and what provoked it, Cousin Penry. It is past and done with.'

'Is it? Is it, indeed?' Vaughan's gaunt face was suffused with rage. 'You might still be indicted, upon my word alone, for inflicting grievous bodily harm upon me, and attempted murder!'

Carne regarded him in silence.

'Ah! I see the truth of it renders you speechless. You can neither deny it, nor defend yourself!'

'If you wish, sir,' said Carne equably, 'you may summon a servant and make accusation. You may summon the justices, if you so desire. I shall be pleased to inform them of the circumstances of our disagreement.'

Vaughan raised a hand towards the bell-pull, then let it fall to his side. He cleared his throat loudly.

'Would you have *me* summon assistance for you?' offered Carne ingenuously.

'No!' Vaughan exclaimed harshly. 'As a man of the cloth,' he began sententiously, 'it is my obligation to . . . well, to . . .'

'Abjure violence and preach charity and forgiveness? Quite so, Cousin Penry.'

Only a nerve flickering beside the clergyman's eye gave indication of his suppressed anger. 'Well, sir,' Vaughan invited with effort, 'perhaps you will now give me the true reason for your return to my jurisdiction, since you have allegedly found it so irksome in the past. What has changed?'

'I have, sir.'

'Indeed? I am glad to hear it. One may hope it is a permanent conversion, and not a passing whim,' Vaughan muttered sourly.

'I believe, sir, that it would serve us both were we to become reconciled. We must live within this community, and it would serve no purpose, save to shame and demean us, should our enmity continue and its true cause be known.'

Vaughan regarded him steadily, but made no answer.

'I may hope that you, sir, and Mr Morrish, will officiate at my nuptials.'

462

'Nuptials? To whom?'

'Miss Saranne Hartrey, of Holly Grove Farm; the Reverend Peter Morrish's stepdaughter.'

'But she is a pauper-child, without birth or breeding! It is unthinkable!' he objected.

'No, sir. It has been thought about and discussed copiously. I am pleased to say that, after careful consideration, Miss Hartrey has graciously consented to accept me.'

'But . . . were you not aware of her . . . background?' persisted Vaughan. 'Her unsuitability?'

'No.' Carne feigned surprise. 'I confess that I thought her guardian, Mr Morrish, to be a man of the utmost sensibility and refinement, and his scholarship was never in doubt. However, if you feel unfitted to officiate . . .'

Vaughan did not reply.

'. . . then Mr Morrish's godfather, Bishop Copleston, has declared his eagerness to take part.'

'I shall be honoured to assist him,' Vaughan said stiffly. 'You are aware, I trust, that your brother, Mostyn, is in possession of Great House, and has a son and heir? His business affairs are prospering and his future expectations limitless. He is a gentleman of substance in Penavon, and much respected.' He frowned. 'It is to be hoped, sir, that you will emulate him, and add lustre to the family name.'

'I will do my best,' promised Carne, straight-faced, 'to equal, or better, his achievements.'

'Pride goeth before a fall, sir!' reminded Vaughan tartly.

'But surely a man's aims must exceed his grasp, Cousin?' countered Carne innocently, 'and we must each constantly strive towards perfection?'

Penry Vaughan, tight lipped, ventured no reply.

Rhys Llewellyn, despite Mostyn's whoring and drunken insolence, could not bring himself to force his son-in-law to quit Great House. He was all too aware of the harm it would bring to Laurel and his grandson, and the danger to his own ambitions and his standing in society.

It was true, he reflected irritably, that he still held the

purse strings but ironically it was Mostyn who now held the real power. In all but name, his son-in-law was master of Great House. Through marriage to Laurel, he had made himself inviolate. In law, a husband possessed his wife's body and her child, as he possessed her inheritance. She was as much a chattel as his house, his stable and the contents therein.

It was therefore to the home of Mostyn's harlot that he decided to ride. He would go alone and with his pockets full of gold. He would buy her silence as easily as Mostyn had bought her flesh. He would lay down as condition for her bounty that she leave Penavon and not return, her bastard with her. There were by-blows of the gentry and aristocracy in every village and hamlet, God knew, but fathered discreetly. Mostyn's crime was not his venery but his boasting of it before his wife.

So, with distaste, and because he could delegate the matter to no other, Rhys Llewellyn bargained for Laurel's peace of mind and his grandson's possession. He paid liberally and ungrudgingly for both, if less readily for Mostyn's self-indulgence. There was a dignity in the manner of the girl's parents, despite the hovel that housed them, although their daughter was clearly a drab, a common trull. He did not glance towards the child, asleep in the crude wooden cradle beside the solitary window. It held no interest for him. The girl, for victim she clearly was not, was delighted with her recompense and quick to agree to his final offer, declaring that she would be better off in a place with life and adventure, for Penavon village was little more than a graveyard tomb. Llewellyn, who found the hovel filthy and malodorous, was convinced that it was verminous too. He was a fastidious man and would demand clean linen on his return to Great House, as well as a quantity of warm water and fragrant herbs to purify his hip-bath, and himself. With that comforting thought, he dwelt no more upon the plight of the Durston family or Rice Mostyn Havard, but dismissed them from memory.

* * *

464

Those last days of summer before Carne and Saranne were wed were, to Sara's mind, the happiest and most carefree she could remember. There was a pure heat to the sun, unchecked by autumn's nearness, and it seemed to her that its golden warmth touched and transfigured all.

The invitations to the wedding were to be delivered by a 'bidder', for few in Penavon could read. Sara had invited old Tom Hallowes to take on the task, promising him a new suit of clothes and a straw hat and stave as custom demanded. Charles, knowing the old man's memory to be failing, had sedulously coached him in the words to say and Megan had driven him out upon her donkey cart so that she might be on hand to prompt him. Hallowes had confounded her by not only reciting every word perfectly, but slyly inventing rhymes of his own.

The written invitations on the other hand, were delivered by messenger. When Mostyn received his, he tossed the card away contemptuously, making some scornful remark to Laurel. To his chagrin, Rhys Llewellyn insisted that he accept and that his wife attend with him. He would brook no argument upon the subject. Mostyn chafed and objected but finally consented with bad grace. His resentment still smouldered but he knew better than to defy Llewellyn outright.

Betsy Durston had disappeared, and Mostyn was convinced that Llewellyn was somehow to blame for the girl's defection. She was a hussy, it was true; a sluttish baggage with little appeal save her willingness, but there were always others like her to be had for the paying. Mostyn had the sense to know that what mattered was his legitimate son, Adam. He was the source of his prosperity and power, his future salvation. He would never relinquish his guardianship of the boy.

Henrietta, who dearly loved both Sara and Charles, was touchingly eager to make Saranne's wedding memorable. She was so innocent in her generosity that Saranne was loath to snub or hurt her. She had already made tactful refusal of Litchard House for the wedding feast, the glass-sided coach, the engraving of nuptial cards, and an extravagance of hot-house flowers.

'It will be a simple wedding for family and friends,' Saranne explained with gentle honesty. 'Your wedding will be different, Henrietta; all pomp and circumstance, and a social occasion to treasure.'

'No,' said Henrietta quietly, 'it will be the same. The exchange of vows between two people. All else will be but trappings. I will endure them because it is expected of me, because to refuse them would be to cause hurt. I shall not even be aware of them, Saranne. I shall see only Charles.'

The morn of the wedding was bright and clear, with that crispness of air that hints at the first breath of autumn. When Carne arose from his bed, the ground still glistened with rime, the sun's warmth already dissolving it into a silvered mist. His clothing was set out upon the wooden butler aside the window, his fashionable pigeon-grey unmentionables of fine doeskin, his coat of deeper grey with its rolled and quilted collar, the handsomely frilled and bestarched shirt, and his hessian boots. His high silk hat and the silk favour which Sara had stitched for him lay upon the mahogany gentlemen's chest beside it, with a pristine silk handkerchief and his cravat of shadowed silk. He glanced towards the shaving stand with its looking glass and the newly purchased toilet articles ranged upon it. How strange it still seemed to be at Penavon once again, and how long a road he had travelled since the day his father died, all those years before. No. He must not think of what was over and done, lest sadness mar his mood and the day ahead.

At Holly Grove, Saranne stood unseeing before the looking glass in the familiar bedchamber. She was, Henrietta thought, a most beautiful bride, despite the modest simplicity of her wedding gown. The white sprigged muslin was fresh and delicate and matched to perfection by the wreath of fresh, petalled orange blossom which circled Saranne's free-flowing dark hair. The tiny pelisse which draped Saranne's shoulders to keep off the chill was of a fine creamy wool, with frill and binding of delicate lavender blue, a colour which heightened the intensity of her deep, violet-coloured eyes. In her gloved hands she clasped a simple posy of flowers, freshly culled from the gardens and conservatories of Litchard House.

'You were right to choose so delicately pretty a gown,' admitted Henrietta gravely, studying Saranne's image in the glass. 'It becomes you well.'

From Saranne's stillness, Henrietta knew her thoughts were on Jethro and that his death was a heaviness within her.

'I do not doubt that you are feeling sad and perhaps a little fearful,' Henrietta said compassionately, 'but without the sadness of the past, you would not have known Carne, nor have become who and what you are today. To change the past would be to sacrifice the present and to deny the future.' She looked suddenly anxious as she asked, troubled, 'It is not the thought of marriage to Carne which makes you afraid? You have no fear on that score? No reservations?'

'None.' Saranne's denial was clear and confident. 'It is what I have waited and yearned for this long time . . . and you are right, Henrietta. I can regret no moment of the past, no misery or deprivation, which has led me towards Carne's safekeeping. I love him!' she confessed simply. 'There is nothing I would ask, save for his nearness all of my life . . . whatever comes.'

Sara, in an attractive new gown of pale silvery green, and with a matching bonnet which showed off the richness of her abundant copper hair, was seated in a pew in Penavon church. Her eyes were upon the two straight-backed and elegant young gentlemen standing before her: Carne Havard and Charles, her son, her son and Jethro's. For a moment grief rose in her throat and tears blurred her vision as she delved blindly into her reticule for her handkerchief. Shamefaced, she blew her nose as inconspicuously as possible, then dabbed at her eyes, hoping that no-one had remarked her grief. How young Carne and Charles looked, she thought dispassionately, scarcely more than children. Then she checked herself with the severe reminder that in all eyes, save hers, they were men. Charles had demonstrated it in his will to overcome his father's death and in his revitalisation of a farm dying of poverty and past neglect. Carne had suffered banishment and God alone knew what deprivation and horror before returning to Penavon and Saranne. Whatever the future brought, there was no doubting his constancy, nor his love for the daughter who was as dear to her as Charles, even though she had not been born of her own flesh and blood.

The sound of Handel's Processional March upon the small church organ roused Sara from her introspection and alerted her to Saranne's coming. She turned to see her daughter's face composed and so radiant with sureness that tears burned in Sara's throat. Peter Morrish smiled at his wife and Saranne, following his gaze, raised her violet eyes to Sara's and dropped her a small curtsey. Then Saranne's eyes were upon Carne, who had turned and was gazing at her with such naked pride and love that, despite her resolution, Sara's tears fell in warmth and joy, for Jethro's poor sake, and for the unknown future of her chosen child.

Henrietta, glimpsing Sara's confusion of joy and grief, gave her a gentle, reassuring smile, hesitant, but caring. How dear a child she was, Sara thought, and how much a part of their lives she had become. She was good-natured and compassionate, devoid of all affectation. Henrietta accepted others as gratefully as they accepted her. How proud Jethro would have been of this slender, golden girl whom their son loved. In her muslin dress and pelisse she looked fragile and palely delicate beside Saranne's glorious darkness. The contrast between sunshine and moonglow, candlelight and flame.

She glanced to where Bishop Copleston stood resplendent in his lavishly embroidered cope, golden crozier held regally in his hand. He dominated the small church and his vestments, against the drab grey stone, were colourful and strange. Beside him, Penry Vaughan stood eclipsed by such magnificence, overshadowed and diminished in every way.

Saranne, gazing up at the bishop, saw, not his dazzling splendour, but the kindness of his eyes and the sweet warmth of his smile. His deep, mellifluous voice began to intone the age-old words and give them new and special meaning, as if they belonged to Carne and to her, and no other.

'Dearly Beloved . . . Wilt thou love her, comfort her, honour, and keep her in sickness and in health; and, forsaking all other, keep thee only unto her, so long as ye both shall live?'

'I will.' Carne's voice was strong and sure.

'. . . Wilt thou obey him, and serve him, love, honour, and keep him in sickness and in health; and, forsaking all other, keep thee only unto him, so long as ye both shall live?'

'I will.' Saranne's reply was quietly subdued, but as wholly committed as Carne's.

'With this ring I thee wed, with my body I thee worship, and with all my worldly goods, I thee endow: in the name of the Father, and of the Son, and of the Holy Ghost. Amen.'

It was a commitment of flesh and spirit before all; an echo of what they had known and cherished in their hearts through the years of long absence.

'Those whom God hath joined together let no man put asunder.'

After the service, Carne and Saranne stood at the doorway to Myrtle Cottage, with Sara and Peter Morrish beyond, to welcome their guests. Penry Vaughan had been forced to take Saranne's hand and murmur a few conventional words of goodwill, although, to her relief and Henrietta's open amusement, he had not attempted to kiss the bride.

'Congratulations, Carne. Felicitations, Mrs Havard.' The words were curt and seemed to stick in his throat.

Carne responded as stiffly, 'Thank you, Cousin. It will please you, I know, to call Saranne kin.'

Vaughan coloured angrily and, but for the watchful eyes of the bishop, might have been tempted into reply. As it was, he looked discomfitted and walked wordlessly away.

Saranne, for Carne's sake, was pleasant and amenable to Mostyn, although his kiss burned upon her cheek like a brand. She had to plead mutely with Charles not to rush forward in disgust and vent his resentment publicly, for Mostyn's attempted rape upon her in the beech copse was fierce in their minds. Yet Mostyn, sure that Carne was unaware of it, and that Saranne would never dare to disclose it, was brazen in his spurious display of affection, and she could only endure it silently.

Sara and Peter Morrish were at pains to set Laurel at her ease and Henrietta was equally solicitous for her comfort, setting her in a chair before the fire and fetching and carrying for her attentively. They were all moved to pity by her new gauntness and dry, lack-lustre skin and hair. It seemed that her child's birth had robbed her of her former prettiness and strength and she was painfully slow to recover. Laurel showed interest and animation only when speaking of Adam, her son, and Saranne, who had joined Henrietta and her mother, was as eager as they to listen and encourage her.

Mostyn, who had been trapped in desultory conversation with Penry Vaughan, turned aside to chide contemptuously, 'Laurel, my dear, you are undoubtedly boring everyone with your adulation of our son. He is a perfectly ordinary child, with no claims to superior looks or intelligence. You will be judged dull and provincial to be so besotted with the infant.'

Laurel flushed cruelly at the reproof, but Saranne was fierce in her defence.

'Indeed not, Mr Havard!' she smiled coldly. 'I judge only that she is a mother with a natural affection for her child. Were it otherwise, it would be a cause for sadness and regret.'

Mostyn, who was plainly bored, merely raised his eyebrows eloquently and moved to Peter Danfield's side where his presence appeared to be as little welcomed. After a while, he returned peevishly to Laurel's side, commanding loudly, 'Come, my dear, we had best return to Great House . . . a dinner party is planned for this evening. It promises entertainment of the highest quality. I would be loath to miss it.'

Bishop Copleston, who could not help but overhear the insult which had been spoken deliberately to humiliate Sara and Peter Morrish, moved forward before any other could intervene, declaring smoothly to Laurel, 'What a pity we must lose you, Mrs Havard, for your company has been most congenial. Dinner parties are often most tedious affairs and a penance too often self-inflicted. Here you would have been assured of intelligent company, courtesy, and the finest refreshment and entertainment. You have my sympathy, ma'am, on every count.'

Mostyn bit back an angry retort and bowed coldly in return, although inwardly seething. Laurel was earnest in her thanks, before following him awkwardly without.

'You showed unconscionable rudeness, Mostyn, and I felt nothing but shame for you!' she rebuked when they were within their coach.

'And I, my dear, felt nothing but an agony of boredom.'

'They were kind and hospitable people, undeserving of rudeness, and the marriage ceremony was admirable in every way.'

'It was a dull and dowdy affair,' he said dismissively, 'with no pretensions to distinction. A poor dispirited display, unlike our own.'

'Your brother treated his bride with tenderness and love. I swear, Mostyn, that I would gladly have changed places with Saranne,' she said bitterly. 'I recall that on our wedding night, you showed me neither tenderness nor understanding.'

'When one has anticipated one's marriage, Laurel, and behaved like a common whore, one cannot expect to be

471

treated with the delicacy due to a virgin,' he declared vin-
dictively.

Laurel, biting her lip until she tasted the warm saltiness
of blood, stared fixedly through the window of the carriage.
She saw and heard nothing, conscious only of the humiliation that ripped through her, and the need to hold back
her tears.

Within Myrtle Cottage the festivities and celebrations continued far into the night with all the traditional music,
dancing, spontaneous singing and bawdy good humour that
a village wedding inevitably evoked.

When the time came for the bride and groom to leave,
there was a wild undignified scramble into the yard, with
the bishop nobly sprinting at its head. The horses were
ready and waiting and the bride was swung into the saddle
in all her wedding finery by the groom, who leapt upon his
mount behind her. Then, cradling her to him, they were
away, granted a sporting chance to flee by their impatient
pursuers. Saranne, weak from laughter and the excitement
of the day, was barely able to cling to the horse's broad
neck as, bumping and jolting on to the rough highway,
they fled the chase. Had it not been for the security of
Carne's encircling arms and the firm support of his breast,
she would certainly have been thrown to the cobbles. As it
was, with shared hilarity and Carne's good horsemanship,
they kept ahead of the pack. The mare's fleetness took them
effortlessly through brook and mire, over meadow and hill,
yet always the wild cries of Saranne's would-be abductors
spurred them onwards, their sole purpose to reach the
haven of their own roof and bed. Carne frenziedly skirted
the itinerants' huddled waggons, his horse's hooves striking
clear as a tocsin upon the stony track.

At Thatched Cottage, he leapt down swiftly to bear his
bride within and to secure the doors. Without the house,
the bawdy revelry went on until cockcrow, but within the
unfamiliar bedchamber at the rear, Saranne took off her
bridal finery, the wreath of flowers from her dark hair wilted

now and the petals bruised. In this simple room, with only the muted cries of the revellers without, there was a new beginning, the promise of new life. Carne carefully extinguished every candle flame and the room grew softened by moonlight. It shone through the latticed casements, strangely luminous, its paleness deepening the shadows. Carne watched Saranne as she stood motionless in the diffused light, the filminess of her muslin gown translucent above the flesh of her arms. Carne saw her escape her gown's diaphanous folds, then watched the fall of her petticoats and bodice and heard the rustling of starched lace as the garments dropped, swirling and foaming at her feet. The moonlight touched the naked contours of her skin; her breasts, her shoulders, the generous curves of her hips, her flesh pearly and haloed in soft light.

She was so beautiful, and so long desired, that Carne could scarcely breathe for tenderness and longing. He stood, silent and unmoving, content to take in the revealed perfection of her lovelines. Then, with a cry torn from deep within his answering flesh, he was beside her, savouring the silky touch of her flesh and the warm, sweet smell of womanhood.

He took her gently and with near-reverence, afraid to hurt with clumsiness – but her passion and giving was as total and all-consuming as his own. Then, in the great calm that came after the penetrating and fusing of flesh, he kissed her neck, her shoulder, and the rounded breasts that belonged now to him, and no other. Finally, when he fell asleep he felt the peace of a wanderer who had come, at the last, to his home.

Chapter Forty

Laurel's new-found maternal instincts and her fascination with Adam had proved her daughter's salvation, Clarissa thought with gratitude. She had overcome the effects of his birth, and, upon the surface at least, Mostyn's neglect and betrayal of her. There were few traces of the hoydenish, self-centred creature of the past in Laurel now. She had shed her vapidity as she had shed her youth; forced from childhood to womanhood in those few harsh months. Her slenderness had returned, and her beauty was heightened and intensified with a refining of flesh and bone. Perversely, Mostyn began to feel a pride of acquisition in her; a new stirring of interest, since she so clearly fascinated others. Laurel, who had been forced to endure the cloying pity or contempt of his cronies, was sure of one thing. She would no longer allow him to patronise or belittle her.

There was to be a dinner party for Papa's business associates, Lord Litchard and Danfield, and some gentlemen from London who were to remain at Great House as guests for a week. Laurel was determined that she would do her father justice and be as elegant and assured as he would wish. Her dress was of deepest rose pink, styled in the high-breasted, softly flowing fashion of the Regency which suited her slenderness so well. The shade enhanced the blue of her eyes as well as the colour in her cheeks and flatteringly emphasised the pale gold of her hair, gathered now into a pretty top-knot, such as Lady Henrietta wore. Was it, perhaps, a little daring? She thought not. Her shoulders were prettily white and her breasts more prettily rounded since Adam's birth.

Mostyn knocked upon her door, as she now insisted, and awaited her call before entering the room. He was undeniably handsome and stylish, she thought, and, despite her vow that she would remain aloof and dispassionate, she could not entirely quell the pride she felt in him. In looks and stature, he was the superior of any man she had seen, and there was no denying that he could be charmingly attentive – but it was no more than a practised art, like fencing, riding, or a hunting skill.

'You look exquisite, my dear.' There was no mockery in his tone. Laurel jerked her head aside irritably as he made as if to touch her, and his hand fell uselessly to his side. She studied herself critically in the looking glass before her, turning her head to view herself from all angles, but would not pronounce herself satisfied. His gaze meeting hers in reflection was wry, quizzical, her own dissatisfied.

'My neck is too bare . . . the neckline low.' She reached for her jewel case beside her to make selection. 'Papa's collarette of pearls and filligree, I think.' She hesitated, disturbed, then began to search frantically amongst her treasures, more and more despairing. 'Mostyn!' she exclaimed in disbelief. 'My pearls! My pearls have gone!' Her eyes were wide with shock and apprehension.

'Hush, my dear. You have mislaid them,' he said to quieten her. 'Do not distress yourself so. They will be found, you may depend upon it.'

'My maid! Quickly, Mostyn! The bell . . . Summon her now, at once! I must know . . . oh papa will be so vexed with me. How can I face him? He will think me stupid, careless . . . oh Mostyn!' she wailed helplessly. 'What shall I do?'

'Wear your rose quartz . . . or moonstones, Laurel; they will do very well. Hurry! Do not work yourself into a state. It will serve no purpose and your papa need not know until they are found, as they surely will be.'

'But, Mostyn . . .'

'Do as I say Laurel! Your father will not relish a scene before Lord Litchard and his London guests. Control yourself and think no more about it, for it will all be easily explained. It is the result of some confusion, or your maid's carelessness, I do not doubt.' He fastened the rose quartz necklace upon her slender neck. 'There . . . Now you look perfect, my dear, and none will know of the omission, the mishap.'

'I will know, Mostyn,' she said, her pleasure in the evening already dulled, 'but I thank you for your trouble. You have been sensible and kind.'

The dinner party was a success, despite Laurel's misgivings and her distress at mislaying her cherished necklace. Her parents' outspoken pleasure at her prettiness and elegance, and the evident admiration of the gentlemen guests, did much to restore her equanimity. Mostyn behaved admirably, showing unusual solicitude towards her; unobtrusively drawing her into conversation, and, in turn, keeping their guests amused and stimulated by his frequently outrageous wit. The atmosphere was relaxed and the company so congenial, that, for a while at least, Laurel was able to thrust all thoughts of her loss from her. Despite the evidence of the past, she was forced to admit to herself that Mostyn had acted with sensitivity and real concern. He was the Mostyn of old; carefree, equable and utterly charming. The mellowing effect of the wine and her gratitude almost undermined her determination to be free of him. When she and Clarissa retired, leaving the gentlemen to their port and discussion, Laurel smiled at him with undisguised warmth and Mostyn had smiled back, and bowed with teasing gallantry.

Laurel did not lock the door of her bedchamber that night, and, had Mostyn wished it, he might as easily have re-entered her life as her room. She waited in a turmoil of expectancy and self-recrimination, hoping that he would come, and fearful that he would not. She awoke as she had fallen asleep, alone.

The morning brought reason and resolve. As soon as

476

she had made certain that Rhys Llewellyn's guests were occupied and her father alone, she went to his study to confess her loss.

'Have you spoken to anyone of this, Laurel?' he demanded sharply.

'Only Mostyn, Papa.'

'Then you may leave me to deal with the household staff, although, I find it hard to believe that any one of them would be so foolish as to steal. Suspicion would, inevitably, fall upon them and such a valuable necklace would be too easily identified. How could they hope to dispose of it?'

'No, Papa,' she admitted with heavy heart. 'It does not seem likely.'

'You have searched your jewel case, and your dressing table, Laurel? You have not mislaid it?' he asked severely. 'I would be loath to make accusation against the servants, were it missing through your own carelessness.'

'No, Papa, I have not mislaid it. I have searched most carefully, I do assure you. It is always kept within my jewel box. I swear I cannot understand it.'

Distress made her agitated and Llewellyn, seeing that she was trembling and close to tears, said more gently, 'Do not upset yourself, my dear. It will be found. You have my promise upon it. Besides,' he said, thinking to calm her, 'it is of no great value. It can be replaced.'

'I loved it, Papa!' she exclaimed despairingly, 'and it can never be replaced. It was special. A gift from you. Do you not understand?'

'Yes. I understand, my love,' he reassured, placing an arm about her and kissing her cheek affectionately. 'And it pleases me that you cherish the giver as dearly as the gift.' He hesitated. 'Have you tried to recall when last you wore it, my dear? When you last saw it even?'

She shook her head helplessly. 'I truly cannot say exactly, Papa, for I keep it separated from all else, in that small drawer of my vanity case.'

'You cannot remember when you wore the necklace last?' he insisted. 'Think, Laurel. Think hard.'

477

'Not since before Adam's birth, Papa.'

'You are sure?'

'Yes. I was not seen in company for some weeks before and so had no occasion to wear it. Since then I have been unwell, and reluctant to return to society, save for Carne Havard's wedding, and I did not wear it then. Oh, Papa . . . I am so sorry, so sorry. I loved my necklace, and cannot bear to have lost it.'

'You have not lost it. It will be returned to you,' said Llewellyn with absolute certainty. 'So not another word, not another tear.'

Laurel could not doubt his determination to find it, and was relieved in her mind. Llewellyn, if he regretted his extravagant claim, showed no sign of it after he was left alone to dwell upon it. As he had remarked, it was a distinctive, easily identifiable piece, difficult to barter or sell, even for a fraction of its true worth. He would have its description circulated to the nearest towns where it might be offered and alert goldsmiths and jewellers with whom he did business to its loss. Should all else fail, when he next returned to France, he would have the craftsman make a replica, authentic in every last detail. Laurel need never know that it was not the original. It touched him to know that his daughter valued his small gift so deeply.

With little enthusiasm for the task, he tugged at the bell-pull to summon the household staff for questioning. Despite his reassurances to Laurel, it seemed likely that it had been taken upon an impulse by someone unaware of its value. A knowledgeable jewel thief, or even a casual house-breaker, would undoubtedly have taken all Laurel's jewellery. If Llewellyn's thoughts turned instinctively to Mostyn, the conclusions he came to pointed unerringly to his son-in-law's innocence. Mostyn, had he wished, could have bought such a necklace a thousand times over from his own pocket. The salary he was paid, and his own business investments, had made him prosperous. He would not risk all for a pretty trinket; a trifle of such little comparative worth. No, whatever faults Mostyn possessed, and there were many, he was not a fool, nor a common thief. They must look elsewhere for the culprit.

As tradition demanded, there was a huge, informal 'wassail party' at Thatched Cottage, in order that the newlyweds might proudly welcome their friends and acquaintances under their own roof. There was a vast thirteen-handled wassail bowl, filled with apple brandy, to refresh their guests; delectable spiced apple cakes made by the ubiquitous Mrs Hodges, and an exchange of laughter and good-natured chaff, which set the tone for an evening of spirited music and dancing.

Saranne, deep in conversation with her stepfather, was overheard by Charles to confide that she felt it was high time she returned to her duties alongside Sara in the parish.

'I cannot stay uselessly at home, Peter!' she said, 'and since Megan will not allow me to lift a finger, I am becoming a drone and parasite!' She glanced towards Carne, adding earnestly, voice low, 'I am so happy, and have been so fortunate in my own life, Peter, I feel that I owe it to others . . .'

Charles repeated the gist of the conversation to Carne later, saying, 'I think, Carne, there will soon come a time when you will be forced to decide where your future and Saranne's lie. Will you return to sea?'

'No. That part of my life is ended. It was thrust upon me by circumstance.'

'The farm, then?' Charles persisted. 'Will you not consider joining me at Holly Grove until you purchase a holding of your own? There is money to be made breeding and raising fine stock.'

'No.' Carne's denial was unequivocal. 'I must earn my living, certainly, and soon. But I have no aptitude for farming, and no knowledge.'

'But have you the interest, Carne?'

'No,' Carne admitted honestly.

'Business, then? Speculation in land, or mining iron-ore or coal? Henrietta's father and Rhys Llewellyn are already embarked upon it, and confident that it will bring swift and lucrative returns. I have a fancy that that is where my own future might lie, with what is under the land for the taking rather than what may be grown in it, or grazed upon it.' He hesitated. 'Will you not give it serious thought?'

Carne, seeing the enthusiasm upon Charles's face, and his excitement, gave his promise to consider it, saying with rueful smile, 'I fear, Charles, that I am best suited to being a lotus eater!'

'Then you will soon enough starve,' declared Charles uncompromisingly, 'for lotuses in Penavon are scarcer than hens' teeth!'

Charles finally, at Henrietta's insistence, formally asked Lord Litchard for his only daughter's hand in marriage. The interview, as Charles had expected, was thorough, yet he emerged bloodied and triumphantly unbowed, to the good-humoured congratulations of Danfield and to Henrietta's irreverent delight.

Before Charles left Litchard House, she managed to whisper to him, under cover of bidding him farewell, 'Well, Mr Hartrey, and will you agree to take the rest of me, as well as my hand, should it be offered?'

'With the greatest of pleasure, ma'am.'

'And will you try to change me, sir? My papa insists that I am self-willed and unpredictable.'

'I would not change hair nor hide of you, Lady Henrietta,' said Charles, 'although I thrive upon challenge.' He bowed extravagantly.

'You would not seek to improve me?'

'Indeed, no. One cannot improve upon perfection.'

Henrietta smiled mischievously and dropped him a most elaborate curtsey, accusing, 'Why, I do believe that you are trying to flirt with me, sir, and before Papa! What impertinence! You had best leave, sir, before he is made aware of it, and forbids you the house!'

Henrietta thought that life had never been happier or as

filled with promise. She basked in the goodwill of all who knew her, secure in Charles's love, and as sure of her own for him. It was a joy to her that, now, she had gained, through Charles, a sister in Saranne and a surrogate mother in Sara Morrish. The days seemed too short for all that had to be accomplished before the betrothal party at Litchard House. There were so many things to be arranged; so much to purchase or organise, and all must be absolutely perfect. Her betrothal to Charles was, after all, the most important event in her life, and nothing must mar the celebration of it.

Danfield, who saw that Henrietta's enthusiasm was taxing her strength and patience, grew concerned for her. As twins, there was still a bonding between them; an unusual awareness of the other's emotions. Finding her hunched disconsolately at her desk, checking yet another of her ubiquitous lists, he said coaxingly, 'Leave it all, Etta . . . and come riding with me.'

'No, I cannot, Peter. There is so much still to do. I cannot see an end to it,' she declared, exasperated.

'Nonsense!' He took her shoulders firmly and helped her to her feet. 'You will be no better for stewing over it uselessly. The fresh air will do us both good – I am in need of exercise and company.'

She needed little persuasion to accompany him and smiled to see their horses already saddled and waiting in the yard. 'You are a bully and a tyrant, Danfield!' she exclaimed ruefully, 'and all too sure of yourself!'

'No, Etta . . .' he said with unusual hesitancy, '. . . I am not that.'

He looked for a moment as if he would confide in her, as of old, but in a moment his humility was gone, his devil-may-care brashness reasserted, as he whipped up his horse and rode for the highway, with Henrietta in startled pursuit.

They rode furiously and impetuously, Danfield allowing her no quarter, over meadows and mountain paths, through copses and streams, until, pleasantly exhausted by the race, they made their way into a beechwood and dismounted to water their animals at a small leaf-clogged stream. The water flowed pellucid and clear and Henrietta bent to splash some upon her face, and then cupped her hands to drink of it. The sound which disturbed her and sent her scrabbling to her feet was a thin mewling cry, pitifully weak, like a despairing whimper of a lost kitten.

'Danfield?' She ran in alarm to grip at his sleeve.

'Some animal,' he said, 'caught in a trap perhaps, and unable to free itself. Come, Etta!' he tried to lead her towards the horses. 'It is time we were away. We can do nothing.'

'No!' She wrenched herself from his grasp and ran towards the sound, grown subdued now, and barely audible. 'I cannot leave it.'

'Etta! Stop!' His voice was harsh, but it failed to halt her. 'Etta! For God's sake! There is danger.' He ran furiously after her, but she was already hidden from sight, lost amidst the crowding, silver trunks of the beech trees. Her cry rang out, startled and grief-stricken, and, for a moment, he halted, unable to move for the terror that gripped him. Then, with an effort of will, he forced himself to follow.

'Etta? What is it! Are you hurt?' His voice was hoarse, but she made no reply. Her face was turned from him and he could see from her hunched back only that she was rocking herself helplessly, as though for comfort. When she turned, her eyes were bleak and filled with pain, her arms cradling something grotesquely obscene.

'Etta? Is it an animal? Wounded?' He made to take it from her, but she clutched the ragged bundle more fiercely to her, and shook her head.

'It is a babe, Peter . . . a newborn babe.'

He moved closer, peering at it warily, then recoiling with horrified disgust at the sight of its monstrously swollen face and blackened flesh. A suffocating stench came from it, rancid and offensive, the sourness of vomit and faecal decay.

'Leave it, Etta!' he ordered. 'There is nothing to be done.'

'I cannot.'

He stood there irresolute, then said firmly, 'Whoever has abandoned it cannot be long gone, else it would not have survived.'

'But who would leave it, knowing it would die of hunger and cold?'

'Someone too poor to succour it.' His abruptness shocked her into weeping, and he said, ashamed, and to comfort her, 'I will see if I can find the woman who has deserted it, and offer money and aid, Etta.' He put a comforting arm about her shoulders. 'It will be all right, Etta, I promise. It will be all right.'

She nodded, and Danfield strode along the small, winding path along the stream's edge, and thence into the overgrown thickets of bramble and briar, striking at them viciously with his whip, feeling the thorns tearing at his riding boots and piercing the cloth of his sleeve. It was a fool's errand, he knew, but he owed Henrietta the comfort of a search. Yet, at best, he would find a woman as sick and weakened as the infant she had been forced to abandon. At worst, he would find her corpse. He found nothing, living or dead, and when he returned, exhausted, to where Henrietta stood, he found her silent and motionless, as if carved in stone. The bundle lay at her feet, its rags hidden beneath that of her coat.

'Etta?'

'It died,' she said. 'It died, here, in my arms.' She neither wept nor moved towards him, her voice as dry and emotionless as her eyes.

'We will go home, Henrietta, and send someone to . . . to see to it,' he promised. 'It shall be buried decently, Etta, you have my word.'

She went with him, unresisting, to where the horses stood, and he helped her mount. She did not speak, nor did she glance towards the dead child. He took the reins of her horse and led it, with his own, out of the beechwood and into the lightness of the day.

'Etta?'

She looked at him enquiringly.

'It is as well if we do not tell father,' he said. 'It will do no good to alarm him . . .' He broke off uneasily. '. . . he will say I neglected you, and we will no longer be allowed to ride so freely.'

She did not reply.

'Do you understand, Etta?' he persisted.

She nodded.

'I will send someone to the woods, I promise.' The bleakness of her eyes and her pallor troubled him.

'They had left it so near to the water,' she said, 'that its hand was touching it. It was too young . . .'

'It is kinder so, Etta,' he blurted clumsily, but even to his own ears Danfield's voice held no conviction.

Henrietta, as she had promised Danfield, kept the tragedy of the infant's death from her father. She could not even bring herself to speak of it to Charles, so raw and bewildered were her emotions. She had several times been on the verge of blurting out the full horror of it to Sara or Saranne, but she could not bring herself to speak of it. By putting it into words, she felt that she would be forced to accept the reality of it, and relive her anguish before others. It was cowardly, she knew, to keep the memory locked within her; to delude herself into rejecting what had occurred. There was no other way to exorcise the hurt of it, yet . . . the tears she wept in secret brought no relief.

Charles and her father, seeing the change in her, set it down to her feverish preparation for her betrothal party, and begged her to delegate the tasks to others, lest she be too exhausted to enjoy the celebrations to the full. But she would not. She must crowd every moment, she knew, to block out memory – for that alone could be her salvation. Danfield had done as he promised and sent the undertaker with his cart to collect the child and give it decent burial because, as a pauper and outcast, it was denied all Christian rites. To do him justice, Danfield had pitied the child, although he could not recollect the memory of it without a feeling of revulsion and disgust. He had considered asking Peter Morrish to give the corpse Christian burial, but, in the end, decided that to do so would only make his part in it, and, consequently, Henrietta's, known. He had seen more of life than Henrietta and knew that the spheres of the rich and the poor were cruelly set apart. God had created the world, and one must accept it with all its imperfections and tears. It altered nothing to shed one's own.

It needed but seven days to the betrothal party, and Henrietta felt such lethargy and heaviness of limb that even the fitting of her finished gown left her listless. She had admired the dressmaker's skills, and the gown itself, most lavishly, for it was delightful in every particular. Yet, as she surveyed it critically, and herself, in the cheval glass of her small dressing room, she was aware of how tired she looked, and how deeply bruised were the shadows about her eyes. The animation seemed to have gone from her, and her skin, eyes and hair looked distressingly lacklustre. Was it a trick of the light, she wondered, that made her appear so gaunt? Although she had always been slender and delicately fleshed, her bones now seemed to protrude starkly, deepening the hollows beneath.

Her mind returned, unbidden, to the memory of the dead child in the beechwoods, and she felt again its pathetic frailness, and heard its plaintive mewling as clearly as if she held it still within her arms. She pushed the thought of it angrily from her, berating herself for such morbidity. The party would be a success and Charles would be proud of her, upon that Henrietta was determined. She would not blight the reality of the present, nor the promise of the future, by useless regret for what was over and could not be changed. She must take off her party dress, lest she crush or disorder it, but she could not summon the will to walk towards the bell-pull, or the strength to undress herself. How strange she felt, and light-headed, almost as if she were remote from her own body and standing apart,

surveying herself with as much detachment as she had
surveyed her reflection in the glass.

Although it was but early afternoon, and the sun high,
she made her way awkwardly to her bed and lay upon the
covers. When she tried to open her eyes, she could not, for
they were weighed down. Her limbs, too, seemed as useless
and unresponsive. Her head ached abominably and her
throat was so raw that she could scarcely swallow. She felt
confused and afraid. She tried to calm herself and think
but her thoughts were pictures, bizarre, disjointed, without
meaning or sense. I am Henrietta, she thought, but am I
child or woman, alive or dead? There was heat burning
into flesh and bone. She could not escape it, for she was
impotent to move, unable to weep or cry aloud.

Danfield might more easily have sent a servant to Penavon
village to pay the undertaker's bill, but it was an errand he
could not trust to any other. He rode there upon his horse,
reasoning that in a carriage his arrival would be more easily
observed and remarked upon, since carriages were few and
easily identified. When he left the premises, he was unnaturally pale and distressed and scarcely seemed aware of his
setting foot in the stirrup, nor of raising himself into the
saddle and riding away.

It was not the entering of such a coldly depressing place
which affected him so, nor even the memory of what had
occasioned the visit, but the undertaker's apprentice who
had been hysterical and fearful, ill-fitted to practise the
trade he chose, Danfield thought. The reason for the boy's
terror was soon made plain. The undertaker was sick of
cholera, the dreaded miasma. The physician held little hope
for the man's recovery. It had come from the itinerants'
camp, Dr Tobin had said; a woman, newly birthed, it was
thought. She had been wrapped by the undertaker's hand
in a winding sheet, and buried, uncoffined, in Penavon soil.

Chapter Forty-one

To the villagers of Penavon, the rumour that the death plague, cholera, was in their midst brought uncontrolled terror. It had already claimed one of their own, and it was said that Lord Litchard's daughter was sick, and that there was little hope of her recovery. If wealth and influence were of no avail against the virulence of the disease, what hope was there for the peasantry in their mean, overcrowded little dwellings? Their fury and hatred turned upon the itinerants. A woman had died of cholera, and it was said that her newborn infant had died of it too. The grieving husband, unable to find the money to succour it, or to treat its sickness, had abandoned it to a slow death. Their rage at his inhumanity, and their terror at the spread of the disease might well have caused them to band together to attack the newcomers, and drive them from Penavon, but fear and superstition held them back. The sickness was caused, the ancients of the village claimed, by 'the evil eye', that curse which could be visited upon man, woman or child by a stranger possessed of the devil. No word need be spoken; no touch exchanged. It was a force as malevolent as the devil himself.

It was in treating the dying undertaker that Dr Tobin's diagnosis of cholera had been made firm. The woman and babe whom he had buried manifested the same affliction. It was a fever which wasted the flesh with vomiting and purging, so that they stank of corruption and decay and became mere skeletons, with bloated, blackened faces, as if choked or drowned. It was a vileness such as the doctor had never before seen; even the child had been grotesque and barely human, a wizened, pathetic little carcase, scarce larger than a skinned rabbit. Yet its eyes and head had been bloated, the skin charred as though burnt.

When the eminent physicians summoned by Lord Litchard had emerged from Henrietta's bedchamber, he knew by the gravity of their faces and their air of defeat that it was indeed cholera, as Tobin had feared. The words they spoke were conciliatory, soft-toned, as if they were already solacing one bereaved. He heard only the single word 'cholera', their conventional phrases washing over him as sea over sand, coldly obliterating all else. He did not remember making reply, but thought, irrelevantly, how strange it was that they had entered dignified, a little pompous in their eminence, arrogantly sure. Yet, now, they left chastened, murmuring apology. They were men as helplessly defeated as he.

Danfield, standing beside him, put an arm about his shoulders and led him into the library, seating him beside the fire, chafing his father's cold hands, murmuring meaningless comfort. I am to blame, Danfield thought bitterly. It is all owed to me. I should never have persuaded her! He tried to speak the words aloud, to confess that he, alone, was culpable, but the only sound was a harsh croak, ugly and unintelligible. Lord Litchard heard it, then also a sobbing that came from the throat, hard and guttural; a man's awkward tears. He should have reached out a hand to comfort his son, but could not, nor raise his head. There was no help he, nor any other, could give.

With cholera confirmed, Litchard House became a house of depression and fear. Some of the newer household servants gave notice and left, and as many others abandoned their duties with no word. Yet the solid core of retainers, who had known and loved her from infancy, willingly stayed to render what services they might to ease the family's grief.

Charles, unwilling to believe the truth of it, had gone at

once to Lord Litchard, declaring that other physicians must be brought in. He would ride to wherever such men might be found, to London if need be, and ensure that they return to Penavon with him. He would take no refusal. Lord Litchard, seeing in Charles's impotent rage an echo of his own, spoke to him compassionately, but with firmness, setting out boldly the reality which he, himself, had been so loath to accept. Charles had begged, then, to be allowed to see Henrietta, to stay beside her, sure that his presence would strengthen her will to fight and survive.

'I swear that I will neither show my distress, nor demand response . . . It will be enough to be near her.'

'I do not know . . .' Litchard was irresolute, swayed against his judgement by Charles's promise, yet afraid. 'I do not know . . .' he repeated helplessly, '. . . for it broke my spirit to see her. She is so much changed.'

'Shall we not go together, sir?' Charles persisted quietly. 'It will do Henrietta no hurt, I am convinced of it.' Then, 'May not our very presence reach through to her, to be a comfort and reassurance, that she is loved and not forsaken?'

'Yes.' Litchard's voice was low. 'Yes, that may well be.' He arose slowly and steadied himself against the chimney piece, as if his limbs were stiffened with pain. Then, together, they mounted the staircase in silence and entered Henrietta's sickroom. The nurse, a coarse-featured creature, rose officiously from a chair at the bedside and made vociferous protest but Lord Litchard waved her peremptorily aside. Charles stood beside him, looking down with overwhelming love and pity at Henrietta, and spoke her name. She showed neither recognition nor response, set apart in some dark, impenetrable world of sickness beyond his reach. He turned, and walked blindly from the room, unable to bear the knowledge of a torment he was unable to share. He would willingly have borne her suffering, or have given his life for her return from that alien place. Lord Litchard, who had followed him to the head of the staircase, looked at him in understanding, but did not speak. Charles stood back and watched him stumbling awkwardly down the stairway. Litchard's hand upon the balustrade rail was transparently frail, his body hunched with grief, as if age had come upon him suddenly.

Charles could not doubt that Henrietta was dying, and the acceptance of it filled him with pain, and a new clarity. It is not Henrietta alone who is changed, he thought. We are as broken in spirit as she is in flesh. When her suffering is ended, ours will be beyond enduring. He could no longer pray that Henrietta be spared, or believe it. If God were a truly merciful God, then He would gather her, swiftly, in death, to spare her intolerable hurt. Charles had earlier thought that he would willingly have taken upon himself the burden of her death. Yet the burden he and Lord Litchard now bore was crueller, and without hope of release.

Later, Dr Tobin, in visiting Henrietta, was angered to find the woman who was paid to tend her by day in a drunken stupor, her patient neglected. She was a foul-mouthed, slatternly creature and he dismissed her upon the instant. Yet he did not know where he would find another willing to replace her, for the remaining nurse declared herself overburdened and had little stomach for the harsh discipline that the care of a cholera victim demanded.

Sara, upon hearing of it, went at once to Lord Litchard, asking to be allowed to tend Henrietta, and Megan went with her, brushing aside all protests.

'I would do it for my own kin,' she remarked tartly, 'I think of Charles and Henrietta as family, for none at Holly Grove ever treated me as a servant, but as one of their own.'

Peter Morrish, far from attempting to dissuade them, went to Litchard House with them to offer his own services by day or night.

It was Danfield who gripped Morrish's hand and spoke their gratitude, for Lord Litchard was able to do no more than nod grave acknowledgement of such kindness, emotions too treacherous for speech.

* * *

Morrish left Litchard House for the itinerant camp with a cold heaviness of spirit; his care as much for Sara and Megan as for Henrietta and her kin. He had found it hard to dissuade Saranne from following her mother, but had at last convinced her that her help was sorely needed both in the parish beside him and to comfort Charles. Yet Charles, he knew, was beyond comfort in his rage of fury and grief. Beneath his railing against God, and his bitterness, his stepson was as broken and bewildered as Lord Litchard, who spoke no word of accusation, his grief too deep-buried.

Peter carefully loaded Megan's donkey with the produce he had persuaded the smallholders and farmers to sell to him cheaply, for the itinerants were no longer welcomed in Penavon village, even to purchase the meagre food they could afford. He took with him, too, kindling for their fires and buttermilk for the infants, and all the worn clothing which could be spared. They would pay him in pence, and he would not refuse it, lest their dignity grew as threadbare as their hopes.

It was while he was halting the donkey cart before the eager crowd that the curate learnt something which disturbed him deeply. It was let slip by Ed Brimble, a former ironworker whom Morrish knew to be a trouble-maker. He was a large, aggressive fellow, his manner surly and his mouth pulled into permanent lines of discontent.

'Where are your wife and daughter?' Brimble demanded abrasively. 'Afeared of the plague, I do not doubt!' He spat derisively at Morrish's feet.

'My wife is tending a cholera victim.' His voice was cold. 'She goes by choice and from compassion for others but I do not doubt that she is afraid. Only a fool would willingly court death and disaster.'

'Then you are a fool upon your own admission!' responded Brimble contemptuously.

'I do God's work,' said Morrish equably, 'and do it as best I may. I cannot think that He is entirely lacking in wisdom.'

There was a ripple of good-natured laughter from those

491

helping Morrish with the unloading and from the others standing about. By the glint of anger in Brimble's eyes and the thrust of his jaw, Morrish knew he had made an enemy.

'Will you not help with the unloading?' he invited innocently. 'It is said that God helps those who help themselves.'

Brimble flushed but, hearing the mutinous murmurs of the crowd, did as he was bade, muttering savagely, 'There was a woman here . . . a while ago . . . some so-called "wise-woman". For all the good she did, she might have stayed where she belonged, like many another come to poke and pry, pretending pity and concern.'

'And why did she come?' Morrish asked sharply, ignoring the intended jibe.

'To that woman . . . the one who died of the plague.'

'Then it was brave of her, for she risked her life and freedom to do so,' said Morrish quietly.

'She was a fraud and a charlatan . . . a witch, I do not doubt!' Brimble's tone was scornful, his face contorted with hate. 'It was she who killed the woman with her tricks and potions! She put the evil eye upon her!'

'Nonsense!' Morrish's anger made him reckless. 'Marged Howell is a woman of integrity, and would harm no-one! There is no such thing as the evil eye! No man with an ounce of intelligence would accuse her of such a monstrous crime! None save a villain or a lunatic!' Morrish was surprised to find his hands shaking and he knew that rage and distress had tightened his throat and voice. He tried to calm himself, conscious that it was his fear for Henrietta and Sara which so deeply disturbed him. Yet his fear was for Marged Howell too.

'Has the witch . . .' Brimble hesitated, '. . . that wise-woman been called to the house of the sick girl? The gentry?' Brimble waited arrogantly for Morrish's reply.

'No,' he admitted honestly, painfully aware that Sara's offer to bring her to Henrietta had been curtly refused. Lord Litchard had declared it to be 'unchristian', an obscenity he would not allow. Morrish repeated stubbornly,

'Marged Howell is a good woman, and would do no harm.'

'She is spurned by the rich, but good enough for the poor?' sneered Brimble. 'We are considered to be filth, the dregs of humanity, no better than animals.' He looked around him fiercely, seeking support. 'The villagers hate and distrust us! We are scum, unfitted to mix or eat with "decent folk".'

There was a murmur from the crowd.

'Even our dead are buried without the church walls. One God for the rich, but none in paupery!'

The murmur had swollen to an angry roar of agreement and Morrish, sick at heart, could not deny that what Brimble had accused, of burial, was true, but he could not let it go unchallenged.

'Where a man is buried is decided by man!' He raised his voice above the noise of the crowd. 'It is cruel and wrong, and I do not defend it. I cannot. It is indefensible. But rich and poor are equal in God's sight and, after death, will receive justice and reward.'

Brimble spat again derisively. 'Yet now we are to suffer? Persecution or dying . . . without complaint? We are to be content?' He turned upon his heel and strode contemptuously away.

Morrish looked helplessly at the faces about him, hostile, questioning, anguished; some with eyes cast down in shame, but all demanding a reassurance he could not honestly give.

'I promise,' he vowed, 'that not one of you gathered here shall lie in unconsecrated ground in death. I will conduct Christian service and burial. None shall lie in a pauper's grave.'

They looked at him, quiet and unforgiving, their expressions guarded, then, one by one, they lifted their burdens from the ground and from the cart and silently walked away. He had failed them. Worse, he had failed God, and himself. He had promised them eternal life, but that was remote and far away. They wanted instant salvation. It was survival upon earth, they demanded,

493

deliverance from hunger and hurt. It was a promise he could not give.

Henrietta groaned and stirred restlessly, and Sara went to her instantly, smoothing back her pale, damp hair, wiping the sweat from her face, setting a wet cloth upon her burning brow, then at her temples. How thin the child had grown, a poor skeleton, frail as a bird. The vomiting and purging were unceasing, the air of the sickroom, despite the herbs and burning pastilles, malodorous with putrefaction and some sweetly sickness which spoke of decay.

'Poor gentle little Henrietta, loved and indulged by all.' The tears gathered in Sara's eyes and fell upon Henrietta's hand, its skin parchment thin and bloodless. Sara wrang out the cloth, then dipped it in the china jug beside the bed and tenderly bathed Henrietta's palms. The girl neither drew away nor made any sound, her restless agitation had given way to stillness. Sara saw that her face was no longer flushed, but darkened, as though bruised; a steadily encroaching blackness.

'Megan!' Sara's cry was high with anguish, and Megan, sleeping nearby, awoke and stumbled towards her, breastbone raw with fear. 'You had best fetch Lord Litchard . . . and send a servant to Myrtle Cottage. Tell Peter he is needed. Go! Megan . . . for God's sake . . . Go!'

The sound of the horses' hooves clattering upon the cobblestones, and the confused noises of a coach creaking and grumbling to a halt amidst the jangle of harness and human cries, took Morrish running to the door of Myrtle Cottage. He had placed all that was needed for the sacrament upon the table in the small hallway, and returned only to gather it to him. Then, with a few murmured words to Mrs Hodges, he entered the coach and was gone.

The man who battered feverishly upon Carne Havard's door was no-one known to him, but poor, thin, ill-dressed and trembling. Agitation had at first robbed him of speech but, when he finally blurted his mission, Carne did not delay.

'They are hunting down Marged!' he called out to Saranne. She hurried to him, watching, wide-eyed and terrified, as he took the pistol he had carried at sea from the locked drawer of his desk, and with it a pouch of shot.

'I must ride with you, Carne!'

'No!' His voice was harsh with distress. 'You would prove more hindrance, Saranne! My fears would be for you only!'

Carne feared that she would bar his way, or fling herself upon him in an attempt to dissuade him from arming himself. Yet, after a moment's indecision, she stood aside resignedly to let him pass.

'Carne?'

He turned.

'Take care . . .' The banal words, quietly spoken, were a cry of love and despair.

He nodded and went out into the yard where his visitor, Jack Hollis, stood with the horse and gig, prepared and waiting. Carne murmured his thanks and mounted the gig to take the reins.

'I will come with you, sir, if you will have me.' Hollis's pinched face was strained, tense with the fear of rejection.

'You are sure?'

'Yes, I am sure.'

He clambered awkwardly beside Carne and, with a swift tug at the reins, they were away, the light carriage swinging and swaying across the cobbles. As they negotiated the gateway from the cottage, Carne glanced at the man hunched beside him, his fists clenched so hard that his knuckles rose hard as stones. He was a poor enough ally to stand against the bullies, louts intent upon violence, Carne thought. As if he had spoken aloud, Hollis gave a wry smile before admitting, 'I fear I shall not carry much weight in battle, sir.'

'You will double the strength of my army,' said Carne with an answering smile.

'Since they travel on foot, we might prevent them, sir?'

Carne shook his head. 'There is only a narrow pathway, and the way overgrown and treacherous. We must leave the carriage.'

They were travelling recklessly and in such acute discomfort from the jolting and shuddering of the lightweight gig that Hollis murmured with unexpected dryness, 'That will surely inconvenience us, sir!'

Carne's easy laughter momentarily broke the weight that had hung over them as Hollis added, 'At least the way is known to you, sir, and must give us advantage.'

'Yes. The horse is sure-footed, and will ease the way, but I rely upon my pistol to surprise and halt them.'

Hollis was silent for a moment. 'I fancy, sir, that their greatest surprise will be in seeing me!' he confessed with wry humour. 'If I serve no other purpose, I may hope to deflect them. Ed Brimble and his louts will be so enraged at my impudence that they will forget their victim and set upon me.'

'It is a dangerous notion,' cautioned Carne as he awkwardly negotiated a bend in the pathway. 'You are unarmed, and they will not spare you punishment. Are you not afraid of the outcome?'

'I am, sir,' Hollis admitted honestly, 'for as Mr Morrish told Brimble but an hour or so since, 'tis only a fool who would willingly court death and disaster.' He smiled tentatively. 'Yet perhaps it is better to be a fool in God's cause than the devil's?'

'I think Mr Morrish's first care would be that you stay alive,' declared Carne, bringing horse and gig to a perilous halt at the mountain's foot.

'As my own, sir,' agreed Hollis with gentle irony, scrambling eagerly to the close-cropped turf.

Marged Howell had been washing her spare clothing in the stream beside the cave, absorbed in her task of rubbing the garments with a lye of wood-ash, before plunging them into the clear water, then pounding them against a flat stone.

She would dry them upon a sloe thicket, for although the late autumn sun was pale and weak, the mountain breeze would dry and air them swiftly. Marged had grown used to her own company and had no yearning to return to a life that had often proved hostile and cruel. She had also grown used to the birds and small animals whose habitat was so like her own, and they, in turn, had grown to trust her, and grew venturesome and tame. Now the birds, as the mountain creatures, called a fierce warning, their movements and cries sharp with an urgent agitation she could not ignore. This was not the visit of friends, Marged felt sure, for the fury of the birds' anguish spoke of hostility, some deliberate menace. She would not return to the cave, for there the marauders might more easily trap and imprison her, denying her all chance to flee. She had no time to gather up her garments since, already, she heard in the distance the raucous shouting and blundering of her seekers. With the swiftness of terror, she ran towards an outcrop of rock, and beyond that, to the darkness of a nearby copse where she might find refuge and a chance to gather her senses and wits.

Megan left Henrietta's sickroom to beg Lord Litchard to go to her at once. He did not hesitate, but hurried to be at Henrietta's side, with Charles and Danfield trailing, grim-faced, at his heels. Megan, in a wretchedness of anxiety and doubt, sent a groom to summon Dr Tobin. She was shaking uncontrollably and plainly shocked when Peter Morrish gained entry to the hall.

'Henrietta is worse?' he demanded.

'Yes. Lord Litchard, her brother and Charles have been called to her bedside.' Her teeth were chattering so fiercely that her words were scarcely coherent, although she clenched her jaw hard to control the spasms that raked her through. Sickness and hard nursing had taken their emotional toll of her, Morrish thought compassionately, and she was close to breaking.

'I will go to them at once,' he said, adding gently, 'and

you, Megan, my girl, will take yourself to Saranne's cottage to tell her how we fare.'

'No. I must stay! Sara will have need of me.'

'Go! I will stay with Sara for as long as ever I am needed, and will do what has to be done. I am no stranger to sickness, or to . . .' He bit off the words sharply. 'Go, Megan, and take the carriage which delivered me here.'

She hesitated.

'You have been a rock and an inspiration to all, my dear,' he said with sincerity, 'and you have nothing in all the earth to reproach yourself with. No-one could have done more, or acted so selflessly.'

Megan tried to smile, her eyes filling with helpless tears as she nodded and walked out into the cold autumn air.

So it was that, burdened with her own grief, Megan arrived in the carriage at Thatched Cottage, only to find Saranne in bonnet and pelisse, as distraught as she. Megan's self-recrimination vanished in her overpowering concern for Marged Howell as, breathless, but now firmly in command of herself, she called out to the coachman to linger.

'There is another way to Marged's cave,' she confessed to Saranne, 'a track we used as children, to get to the mountain-cave. I do not doubt it will be well-nigh impassable, for it is many a long year since I set foot upon it. I am not even sure that I can recall it to mind.' She looked at Saranne keenly, 'It would be better if I were to go alone. There are quarries and gullies, heavily overgrown. I would not take you into danger.'

'It is a greater danger Marged faces,' Saranne said simply. 'I will come, Megan, or regret it always.'

Megan nodded her understanding.

The coachman, with little relish for doing so, left them near a small fissure in the mountain face which Megan claimed to recognise. He would ride at once to alert the justice, he said, and return with whatever help could be mustered in the village. Shaking his head at their foolhardiness, he watched Megan and Saranne pushing their way obstinately through the waist-high bracken and gorse that flanked the lower slopes, Megan slashing at the brambles and blackthorn with a fallen hazel branch. He drove off, filled with unease, turning his head to see them thrusting higher and higher through the reddened ferns. They clung for a while to the hillside, motionless, like two patient dark beetles, fearful of being dislodged, then, slowly, painstakingly, they stirred into movement, until a bend in the track hid them from the coachman's sight.

Chapter Forty-two

Marged, crouched helplessly behind a thicket of saplings in the copse where she had taken shelter, had one horrifying glimpse of her pursuers and knew that, try as she might, she could not escape them. There was a blustering savagery in their cries and behaviour which she recognised and feared. They came openly, as hunters, their sole purpose to track down their quarry and kill. It was there in their faces; an elation as wild as their shouts. She had seen it often in those who trapped and hunted for pleasure; a lust for the spilling of blood which only a death could satisfy – and the death they sought now was her own.

She heard their noisy approach; the cracking of twigs and the rustle of leaves beneath their feet, the whiplash of their staves as they beat aside thorned briar, as if they would see her revealed, as defenceless as any small forest creature, and rain upon her the same vicious blows. She would feel them shatter her flesh and bone as carelessly as they stripped bark from a living tree. Dear God, Marged thought, where can I hide? Where flee? If I run until I fall from exhaustion, what will it profit me? For a brief moment she thought she would stumble from her hiding place and let them kill her, if they must, for now she only prolonged her silent agony.

Their shouts grew closer, and suddenly, unable to bear the fierceness of her panic, she scrambled to her feet and ran blindly into the heart of the copse. Their shrill, triumphant cries redoubled in intensity. They had seen her. She must not escape. The ease with which she ran goaded them into a fresh fury of pursuit as, crashing wildly behind her, they gained ground. Marged was fleet of foot and knew every thorn and briar, every rock and crevice, every stream and bog. Yet they were stronger, and more determined. They pursued her cunningly, unremittingly, sometimes separated, sometimes together, knowing that terror and lack of stamina would bring her to grief. With her heart pounding within her breast, and a redness of blood filming her eyes, Marged ran until, beaten, and unable to escape from them or the weariness which engulfed her, she found the shelter of her familiar cave, and, stumbling and falling, she dragged herself to the far corner of her cave, away from the fire.

With the sound of her pursuers shouting at the entrance to her shelter, she began to whimper quietly; an animal cornered and unable to do anything save tense itself against the cruelty of that final blow. When the hand finally wrenched at her arm, fingers digging hard into her flesh, Marged, cowering in the darkness, was too terrified to open her eyes. She crouched there, an arm awkwardly shielding her head from the expected stroke, but it was Megan's voice she heard, high and fierce with urgency. Marged's mind, disordered by fear and exhaustion, could make no sense of it. Perhaps I am dead, she thought dully, or in the grip of some nightmare. The pain from the violence of Megan's grasp, and the anguish with which she was being shaken into arousal, were undeniably real.

'Quick! Make haste, Marged!' It was Saranne's voice now, ragged with alarm. 'Do not argue or question it . . . just come, else it will be too late!'

Marged, with Megan's arm encircling her for support, stumbled, bewildered, towards the cave's entrance. She could scarcely make her limbs obey for the pain and tiredness which possessed her, but she willed herself on, Saranne's and Megan's cries forcing obedience.

'Dear God in heaven!' Megan's grip had relaxed, and Marged would have fallen but for Saranne's steadying arm. In their fury to escape, and with the noise of their scrambling movements echoing and reverberating from the enclosing rock, they had heard no sound from without. Beyond the flickering glow of the fire at the cave's mouth, Ed Brimble and his two henchmen stood impassively, legs astride, mouth sneering their triumph.

Ed Brimble's hate-filled voice rang out. 'Burn the witch's poisons! She is a murderess! The devil's tool!' His face was vindictive, ugly with rage.

'Aye,' one of his roughnecks urged. 'And burn her too! Burn the witch at her own fire!'

He had taken a step forward and Marged, panic-stricken, would have run back within, but Saranne thrust her violently away, screaming despairingly, 'Run, Marged! For God's sake, run!' and Marged responded instinctively, leaping forward and dodging between the startled ruffians and out on to the mountainside. There was a moment of silence, as strangely ominous as that lull which presages the ravages of a storm. Then Brimble's stick descended, viciously, knocking Megan to her knees, splitting the flesh of her skull. Saranne's cry was strangled in her throat as she ran to her aid, fearful that the blow had killed her, but Megan, dazed, and with blood oozing sickeningly from the wound to her scalp, was vainly trying to haul herself upright, her nails scrabbling despairingly against the bare rock of the cave. One of the ruffians raised his stick threateningly and would have clubbed her to the ground had not Brimble's harsh command halted him.

'No! Leave her! She is of no account . . . not worth the effort it would need to kill her! It is the witch we have come to take.'

The man hesitated, mumbling sullenly, 'What would you have me do, then?'

'Hunt her down as ruthlessly as she deserves! She is weary and cannot long escape us.'

As Saranne made a wild rush to the entrance of the cave, thinking to flee and summon aid, Brimble dropped his stave and caught at her wrist, twisting it so viciously that she screamed aloud in pain. Then he hurled her contemptuously towards the third of the men, ordering curtly, 'You, Pegler! Do what needs to be done to ensure that they do not escape and raise the alarm! Silence them . . . you understand? Secure them, if needs be. Kill them if you must!'

Pegler nodded, demanding sourly, 'And when you catch the witch?'

'Then we will teach her the lesson due to a poisoner and a murderess . . . a killer of innocent women and babes. She will be ducked as a witch, thrown into some hillside pond or mire and, if she dies, it will but serve to prove her guilt. If she survives . . .' Brimble left the words unspoken, but none could doubt that, in being spared, Marged Howell's cry would be for the ease of death.

Saranne had seen Megan's hand slide determinedly towards an iron poker, abandoned beside the fire, but, by an almost imperceptible shake of the head and indrawn breath, she gave Megan silent warning that to attempt to escape now would be folly. The blood was making dark, viscous runnels down Megan's brow as it dropped from cheeks and chin, reddening her blouse. She felt it clouding her eyes and touching the corners of her mouth and wiped it away impatiently with her palm, surprised that she felt no pain. She was simply grateful that, for the moment, Marged ran free. She watched Brimble and his henchman leave, their hateful faces eager with expectancy; so sure that they could corner Marged and punish her as they planned.

Within the cave, Megan and Saranne sat huddled together in terror for Marged and themselves. The man, Pegler, who held them captive, was a coarse, awkward-limbed fellow, whose treatment of them had given them little hope that their freedom could be coaxed or bought. He had paid no heed to Megan's wound and Saranne's pleas that she be allowed to tend it had been answered with foul-mouthed scorn and abuse. Nervously, she had waited until he was occupied in breaking the few poor sticks of furniture that Marged possessed, and heaping them upon the fire with her meagre chattels and possessions. There was a fierce satisfaction in the way he destroyed everything he touched. He was someone who found joy in destruction; the devouring power of the flames. Megan, as Saranne, was fearful that when Pegler's unnatural preoccupation with the fire was ended, his urge for violation and destruction would be turned upon them. They did not speak of it, each afraid perhaps that putting it into words might give it reality. Saranne had begged him for a light within the cave. The early autumn dark was already falling, and she could not bear the thought of being imprisoned with him in darkness, unaware. He had mocked her and postured stupidly, mimicking her voice and fears, but in the end he had grudgingly lighted a candle and, securing it within a lantern, had thrust it at her, his hands closing fiercely over hers. She had willed herself not to recoil and show disgust, but had borne his touch silently, grateful that he had returned almost at once to his obsessive feeding of the flames.

Saranne was in terror that Megan's wound would cause weakness and unconsciousness from loss of blood, for it had not congealed but flowed unceasingly. In the lantern light, Megan's hair was stiffly matted, her face smeared with blood, her clothing dark-stained. When Pegler was intent upon breaking up a stool, splintering it fiercely against the rock at the cave's mouth, Saranne, under cover of its crashing, tore a strip of cotton from her petticoat to bind up the bound and staunch its flow. Pegler, alerted, turned, and in an instant had lumbered towards her, dragging her roughly to her feet, his ugly hands groping at her breasts, his mouth pressed suffocatingly upon her own. Saranne, sickened and appalled, tried to kick and wrench herself free, but his grip was so relentless that she was barely able to breathe. She felt the weight of his arms crushing her rib cage, the bones of his jaw bruising her own, the vileness of his open mouth and tongue. Then, suddenly, incredibly, she was free as his limp body bore her, gasping and sobbing, to the floor of the cave. She lay there helplessly for a while, pinned by the awful weight of his flesh, the air forced from her lungs, taking in deep, gulping sobs of breath. Then, horror lending her strength, she had somehow freed herself and crawled away. Megan was still standing motionless, the great iron pot with which she had cracked his skull clutched in her hands.

Saranne's words were scarcely more than a whisper. 'Megan . . . I think you have killed him.'

'It is no more than he deserved! He is a brute . . . a fornicator!' she stumbled over the word.

The iron pot went clattering noisily into the farthest corner of the cave and Saranne, despite her terror that Pegler would stir, began to laugh weakly and helplessly, until Megan shook her into shamed silence.

'We had best run while we may,' she ordered sharply, 'for if he recovers, it will be the end of us both.' Megan felt absurdly light-headed, and so giddy that she almost fell as she bent to take up the lantern. Her voice sounded slurred and strange and she would dearly have liked to lay her aching head upon something comforting, and sleep. Yet she forced herself into wakefulness and ran towards the mouth of the cave, lantern held high. In its beams, her face looked ghostly and blood-smeared, her eyes wide and unnaturally bright.

'Will they not see the lantern, Megan? Track us down?' Saranne asked hesitantly.

'Yes,' said Megan. 'That is why we must take it . . . not to light our way, but to lead them to us. It is Marged's only hope.'

Marged Howell ran blindly, despairingly, through the wild mountain fastness she had made her own. From the moment she had fled, she had been grateful for its solace. Its strange beauty and isolation had wrapped itself about her, comforting and familiar; a protective cloak. Yet, suddenly, the mountain seemed a strange and alien place, hostile, and filled with menace. There was a confusion in her

505

mind. She was no longer able to recognise who she was, or where she ran. She could not even recall from whom she fled. Her head ached and the exhaustion that slowed her limbs had seeped now into her bones, so that weariness seemed part of her very blood itself. She felt her feet dragging, yet could not summon the strength to hasten them. Yet some unnamed terror drove her on remorselessly. Thorn and bramble tore at her clothing and flesh and the trees and wind-stunted bushes threw out gnarled and twisted hands, grotesque, clutching. She knew she could run no more. Perhaps, if she skirted the old quarry, moving slowly to ease the pain in her side, she would be sure-footed enough to evade them and find shelter in that deep crevice in the mountainside where someone had once quarried stone for a hut. They would not be as confident of the landscape as she, and the coming dusk might slow and imperil them.

Even as she broke cover and urged herself upwards to the quarry rim, she heard Brimble's voice commanding harshly, 'Stop! Stop, I say!' but she did not stop, urging herself onwards, higher and higher, then, above her, upon a crag, she saw his companion, stave held shoulder high, and felt the wrenching force of the blow as it thudded against her shoulder. Even as she screamed and swayed, clutching helplessly at the thorn bush at the quarry's edge, the shot rang out. There was a piercing pain as her palms grasped at the thorns and she felt the warm flow of blood from their wounds. Then the roots of the blackthorn were torn away from the soil, and with them her own. She was falling, flying, drifting effortlessly to earth, without pain or hurt. There was a calmness within her and a silence all about, save for the plaintive cry of a windhover, distant and bleak. Someone is dying, she thought; there will be a death. When the darkness closed over her, she thought, briefly, of Rice Havard, without bitterness or regret. The hunter and the hunted were all one in death. It was simply a coming home.

The scream that rent the air was not Marged's, but

Saranne's. She had watched the brute raise the stave and bring it down upon Marged's shoulder, and heard the sickening thud of wood on flesh, which shattered bone. Marged had swayed perilously near the quarry's edge and Saranne's harsh sob had died in her throat as she saw her clutch despairingly at the blackthorn tree. For a brief moment it had seemed that she must steady herself, and survive, but slowly, inevitably, the torn roots had been prised from the arid soil, and Marged had fallen, the thorns still piercing her hands. There had been a sharp crack, as of the breaking of a dried twig. The cry of the windhover had ripped the air as Saranne's terrified screams had ripped her. Megan, pale, and barely able to stand, had dropped her lantern to the path and had run to her, cradling her to her bloodstained bodice, stroking her hair, murmuring words of helpless comfort. They clung together, making no move to escape, their danger forgotten in the tragedy of Marged's murder, as it had assuredly been.

When the violence of Saranne's sobbing had quietened into trembling, Megan said gently. 'We had best be away from here, Saranne.'

'No . . . If Marged is alive, I must go to her. I will not leave her alone, and in pain.'

'No!' Megan's cry was in vain, for Saranne was already at the quarry's edge, peering into the abyss below, to where Marged's body lay lifeless, a grotesquely twisted doll, smashed upon the quarry floor. 'No!' Megan was beside her, trying feverishly to hold her back, but Saranne was already descending, scrambling, slithering upon the sharp rock face, nails and feet scrabbling for hold. 'Saranne! One of them is armed! He will shoot you down!'

For a second Saranne halted, terror closing her throat as realisation of her peril gripped her. Her limbs were suddenly trembling and useless. She could neither descend nor scramble upon a ledge too narrow to take her feet with safety, her restless fingers finding no support. Dear God! she thought despairingly, I shall fall. I shall lose my hold and go hurtling down, be smashed upon the jagged rock and die beside Marged. Giddiness made her close her eyes and, when she opened them and gazed down, the acid gorge rose in her throat.

'Saranne . . . hold fast! I am coming.' It was Carne's voice, firm and reassuring and, too terrified to make reply or to glance above, she heard him descending in a shower of earth and small stones, until, covering her body with his own protectively, he had eased and coaxed her into a firmer foothold beneath, despite her tears and protestations. Then, inch by slow inch, he forced her to the quarry top where, exhausted, and retching harshly, she lay upon the soft turf. With Saranne comforted, and her tears dried, he set himself the task of descending to the quarry floor, and, with Marged's poor mutilated body covered with his coat, he began the long, tense climb from below. The horror of Marged's broken and disfigured flesh chilled him and he was filled with hate for those who had done so callous a thing. To him, as to Saranne, Marged had been a woman of special worth, a last tenuous link with childhood. She was one who had never shown cruelty or indifference to any living thing, whose sole desire had been to bring relief from hurt. Now the hurt was his, and his only comfort lay in that Marged would be persecuted and reviled no more.

When he had recovered himself from the harrowing sadness of the climb, he bade Saranne keep close beside him upon the track, and lifted Megan in his arms, despite her weary protestations, and carried her down to where the horse stood tethered to a tree, then lifted her on to its bare back. Jack Hollis walked before them with Megan's lantern held aloft to light the way. In his other hand was the pistol, primed and trained steadily upon Pegler, who had recovered his senses, and whose vicious blow had sent Marged to her death. Carne's single shot had been discharged to halt his violence and it had found its mark in the soft flesh of Pegler's upraised arm. It had been enough to sober and still him but, for Marged, it had come too late. Carne could not regret that he had wounded the creature, for he would have been content to see him dead. Now

508

Pegler walked before the frail, but upright, figure of Jack Hollis, his blustering arrogance gone, as cowed and biddable as a whipped cur. Ed Brimble, upon seeing his accomplice fall, had promptly deserted him, running wildly across the mountain, cowardice lending him fleetness. With the third man, he would not long escape, for the villagers would hunt them down and take them before the justices.

Megan began to weep, weakness and loss of blood unnerving her, so that Carne had to support her to keep her steady. She slipped awkwardly forward, burying her face in the mare's rough mane, sobbing despairingly as realisation came. 'It was too late,' she said. 'In spite of all, it was too late.' Her tears had made runnels in the smeared blood that had dried upon her face and Saranne's torn petticoat hem was still tied, incongruously, about her head, its whiteness blood-soaked and darkened.

Carne said compassionately, 'You are both still shocked and grieving, exhausted from the terror you have endured. When we reach the gig, I will take you at once to Dr Tobin's house. Megan's wound must be attended to without delay.'

'No!' Megan's refusal was passionate, despite her tears. 'Oh, may heaven forgive me,' she exclaimed penitently, 'I have forgotten Henrietta. In all this wickedness, I had thought only for Marged. I must go there at once, Carne. To Litchard House. They will surely think me wicked and wretched to have acted so.'

'They will think you brave,' said Carne steadily, 'for that is what you are, Megan. A woman of character, loyal and resolute.' His arm reached out and encircled Saranne, who was walking listlessly beside him. 'You are two good women, and Marged would have been as proud and privileged as I to walk beside you.'

Jack Hollis, walking ahead of them, lifted the lantern high and nodded his head.

Chapter Forty-three

The events at the quarry left Saranne increasingly withdrawn, plagued by a sickness which she could not throw off. Dr Tobin had declared it to be a natural result of grief which would gradually recede, but Carne could not be convinced, fear of Henrietta's death from cholera still too raw.

Henrietta's death, too, had left scars unhealed. Lord Litchard had grown painfully slow, halting in movement and speech, as if age had come upon him like a darkness of the spirit. Danfield, plagued by guilt, had thrown himself remorselessly into the affairs of his father's companies and the estate. Charles, who grieved inwardly, could find no consolation in work and all but abandoned it, since, without Henrietta, success would avail him nothing. Carne, deeply troubled, had taken over the running of the farm at Sara's pleading but, without Charles's knowledge and guidance, he could do little of value. Charles seemed unaware that his friend was trying to redeem his neglect, indeed, he seemed unaware that life went on, and that his mother, Saranne and Peter Morrish, as all those in his employ, grieved for him, and despaired of his reason. For Charles, as for Henrietta's father, life had ended with her death. Survival was a penance to be endured.

Autumn gave place to a harsh unremitting winter and there were three more deaths from cholera at the camp but no more in Penavon village. Dr Tobin and Dr Jordan gave it as their firm opinion that the pestilence was over. Perhaps the cold winter had frozen the contagion, there was no means of knowing.

If any good had come of the tragedy of Marged's brutal death, it was that it briefly served to draw the cottagers and the itinerants more closely together. They had been united in their shock and revulsion. The Wise Woman had treated their wounds and ills from compassion and simple kindness, and been repaid by a callousness which shamed and degraded them all. That her three assailants had been sentenced to death upon the gallows aroused no bitterness within the camp. A murder had been committed. Justice had been done. If their thoughts sometimes turned to the ease with which any one of them might have been incited by Ed Brimble to follow him and commit murder, then they did not speak of it. They had learnt something salutary of themselves, and others. Should they forget it, the shadows of Brimble and the scaffold were there to remind them.

After Marged's burial, Peter urged Carne and Saranne to return with him to Myrtle Cottage, since there was something of a personal nature he would confide to them both. They were surprised and uneasy to find Randall Walters and Higgs, his clerk, awaiting them there and Carne grew increasingly fearful for Saranne at what might be disclosed of the past.

Peter spoke briefly and with affection of Marged, before adding compassionately, 'It is to Saranne that I now speak, since what Mr Walters will now relate to you will be the legal niceties, emotionless, dry-as-dust facts, without heart. Marged spoke from the heart when she said that in all of her life she had only deeply loved two people – Rice Havard and Saranne. It was Saranne who fought for her and defended her with her own young life, and whom she had been forced to leave. It grieved her that there was no other way, but she would have me tell you, Saranne, before all, that you were as dear to her as a child of her own flesh and that she had never forgotten the debt she owed to you.'

Saranne had begun to weep quietly and Sara would have gone to comfort her but for Peter's warning glance. It was Carne she clung to for solace and who soothed her and stroked her hair until her grief was spent. Then Morrish nodded towards the attorney, who, with gaunt little Higgs at his elbow, and carrying a sheaf of papers, seated himself beside the curate at his desk.

'It is necessary,' the attorney began, 'that I read you the full details of Marged Howell's bequest, for that is what the law demands.'

For a moment Carne was a child again in the library of Great House, waiting despairingly for news of Rice Havard's estate. He knew by Randall Walters' pitying glance that he too remembered, and understood, how he had been delivered into poverty and Penry Vaughan's unloving hands. Carne was scarcely aware of the details which the attorney now recited and heard only the essence of his speech.

'In plain language, Marged Howell has left to Saranne Havard all that she possessed: the secrets of her healing potions and medicines, written in her own hand within a book, and to be passed to the eldest child of any issue of her marriage. In addition, she leaves to her that ruined house where she on occasion dwelt, and which Rice Havard ordered built for her, with thirty acres of woodland and hillside surrounding it, and which includes the source of Penavon river and its mountain spring.' He hesitated, saying gruffly, 'It is a poor and isolated place, but beautiful . . . unspoilt. She hoped that it would bring you the pleasure it once brought her.'

There was silence in the room before Saranne said despairingly, 'She gave me all she loved and valued in life. She owed me nothing.'

Peter Morrish said gently, 'No . . . Saranne. She begged me tell you that it was not a debt repaid, but a symbol of her love, as yours, freely given. She prayed that you would accept it as that.'

'I gave her so little,' Saranne said remorsefully.

'You gave her all you possessed,' said Peter Morrish simply.

When Morrish was alone, he took the letter which Marged Howell had given into his safekeeping from the concealed drawer in his writing desk. He knew the contents by heart, and yet, what she had written never failed to sadden him and move him to pity. She had told, with simple honesty, the story of her love for Rice Havard, and had made the confession she would never speak in life.

Morrish sat with his head clasped in his hands for a long while. Her story was stark and bore the mark of truth, yet the conflict remained for him, as it had once done for her. Was Saranne her child? Not of her love for Rice Havard, but her earlier rape and violation by another; those, masked and unknown to her, who had burned her home and savagely hounded Joel Howell to his death? Sickness had given her escape from remembrance of the birth and the ravages of nursing-fever had further weakened her. The child, her father had insisted, had been stillborn, and the midwife, a slatternly foul-mouthed creature brought from Golden Grove, had disposed of it. And yet?

When the child, Anne, had been admitted to the poorhouse, her mother dead of a fever, her father fled, an old woman had claimed to recognise her. She was a confused and senile creature, and none could rely upon her memory, but she swore that Anne had been sold by the midwife to a childless couple at Golden Grove. A strangely 'knowing' infant, with eyes of the most startling violet-blue, and who was claimed to be the newborn bastard child of a wise woman.

Marged had begged Peter to search among the records of the poorhouse and he had hastened there and found them already burning to useless ashes upon a pyre. Marged had believed Saranne to be her own. Her revulsion for the act of rape and the brute who had forced his flesh within her had been slow to overcome, but she had grown to love Saranne deeply, so deeply, Morrish thought compassionately, that she had never openly claimed the child, believing that Jethro and Sara would give Saranne that loving acceptance which would otherwise have been denied to her. Peter Morrish sighed. Then, with calm deliberation he took the letter, and that fragment of charred paper which bore Anne Hewlish's name, and threw it into the fire, seeing them blacken, then glow into sparks and die. Spent ashes.

'Dear God,' he prayed upon his knees, 'forgive me that I have sinned. Help me to take the burden of it upon myself, and keep it hid. It would bring naught but grief, for Saranne would believe herself again rejected, and could never forgive. It is kinder that she loves Marged, in death, as she loved her in life . . . and is freed to mourn her loss.'

He walked pensively from his small study to the fireside where Sara arose anxiously to greet him and lead him to a chair.

'Oh, my dear,' she said compassionately, 'it has been a long harsh day, and you are wearied. You will be glad that it is ended.'

'Yes,' he said. 'I am glad that it is ended.' And Sara, who loved him, knew that it was of something deeper, and more threatening than Marged's death, that he spoke.

Saranne's sickness gave her no ease, and at Carne's insistence Dr Tobin was called in again. He emerged from the consultation and examination preoccupied and expressionless, absorbed by thoughts of his own.

'You have discovered what ails Saranne, sir?' Carne's voice was sharp with concern. 'There is some remedy you would suggest?'

'None.' Dr Tobin's smile was expansive as he added, 'Nor should there be. Your wife is with child, sir . . . that is the simple fact. I offer you my congratulations.'

Carne, with Sara and Peter, was overjoyed at the news and Megan quite absurdly solicitous. Lord Litchard had granted her a small cottage in the village for her devoted care of Henrietta and, with Jane's furniture installed, she had found true comfort and independence. Its nearness to

Thatched Cottage delighted her.

Sara's and Peter's concern, however, unvoiced before Saranne, was that the news of the coming child might send Charles deeper into grief. It was all of two months since Henrietta's death, yet he showed no hint of recovery from hurt, and no desire to return to his work upon the farm or his business affairs. Morrish had offered to break the news of Saranne's pregnancy sensitively, to spare Charles deeper regret for what he and Henrietta might have shared, but Carne was adamant that he would tell him when he adjudged the time to be right.

Yet, when Carne did tell him, Charles showed his first hint of pleasure and interest in the world beyond his grief.

'Why, Carne!' he had declared, gripping his friend's hand delightedly, 'that is the best of good news! I cannot tell you how pleased I am.' His broad, honest face had been alight with vicarious excitement. 'This son of yours . . . this nephew of mine.' He paused. 'We must build him an empire fit to inherit.'

Carne had studied him anxiously and Charles had continued with all the conviction and enthusiasm of old. 'He shall take his choice . . . Holly Grove shall stay in my keeping, lest he has a yearning for the soil . . . but there will be better opportunities too. What do you say? Do you see yourself as an ironmaster? A coal-owner? A businessman, perhaps? The world is open to us, Carne, we merely take our choice . . .' He faltered, then demanded firmly, 'Shall we not give that brother of yours a run for his money? Beat him at his own game? I swear it would add extra spice to the competition!'

'I will do whatever you advise, and join you willingly in all your ventures.' Carne thrust out a hand to seal the bargain and Charles took it smilingly in his own. Yet the smile could not entirely hide the pain which darkened his eyes. It was a beginning, Carne thought with gratitude. A new life created, not only for his child, but Charles too.

'And if the child . . . the baby . . . should be a girl?' It was a question which Carne forced himself to ask, knowing the hurt it would cause.

Charles's grip remained hard and unyielding. 'Then you must name her for Henrietta,' Charles said, his voice warm with loving pride. There was sadness within him, but the beginning of acceptance too. There was a long, hard road before him, and he must walk it alone. He had taken the first step.

At Great House, Laurel was pleased to learn that Saranne and Carne were to have a child; an enthusiasm not wholly shared by Mostyn. His own son, Adam, was heir to the Havard line, he reasoned petulantly. Carne's child might well be a girl, in which case, Adam might fairly claim precedence. At least, Adam would be in possession of Great House, and of much of the former Havard estate, through Rhys Llewellyn's prudent investment in land. The first miners' dwellings would be ready for occupation in early Spring, and those drift mines being tunnelled deep into the hillsides would soon prove productive and profitable. His own fortune was prospering, and it had given him a feeling of intense satisfaction to have his cousin, Penry Vaughan, importuning him desperately to allow him to invest his meagre savings. How his cousin had managed to scrape together the money he offered was a matter of no consequence to him. Mostyn was as indifferent to whether Vaughan had begged, borrowed or stolen it, as he was to all else about him. No, that was not strictly true. He satisfied Mostyn's craving to be admired and flattered; a willing sycophant. It could do no harm to indulge him. Danfield had lately heard rumour that Carne and Hartrey were intending to open up new coal mines, in direct competition with the Litchard-Llewellyn mines. What arrant conceit! It was only to be expected that Carne would resent his brother's success. It was a damnable impertinence; opposition born of spite. Well, his jealous scheming would avail Carne nothing. He would learn a harsh lesson, and, as like as not, have the audacity to come crawling and begging

516

help, as if kinship gave him the right. Let him fend for himself! Mostyn thought disgustedly, as I have from the moment I was born. He was always my father's favourite, and life was made easy for him. Let him stand or fall by his own efforts, as I have done, and be damned to him!

Rhys Llewellyn was only grateful that Danfield had taken over the running of Lord Litchard's concerns and that Mostyn, for all his shortcomings, was reliable and adept at business affairs. Were it not so, Litchard's preoccupation with Henrietta's death might well have put their profitable partnership in jeopardy.

As it was, Llewellyn reasoned, with Litchard so broken and disinterested in the life of Penavon, then he, as squire, would need to take upon himself the mantle of benefactor. He was already a great landowner and a major shareholder in the Litchard-Llewellyn mines. Philanthropy inevitably brought a man to public notice and enhanced his business reputation, as well as the possibility of social advancement. Llewellyn, who was not a man dedicated to doing good by stealth, considered the matter well. He would set up some sort of public charitable institution in Penavon, he decided. Something to do with children perhaps, since Laurel had been so conveniently delivered of a son. He had a notion to resurrect the home for pauper children, which Rice Havard's death had closed. Yes, that might suit very well. He could hardly suggest that it be called after its benefactor, since that would smack of too much self-aggrandisement and vanity. What, then? The 'Laurel Llewellyn Home for Outcasts'? No. They would expect her to become involved in its affairs, and that Rhys Llewellyn would not allow. It would do Laurel no good to be mixing with infants who might be scrofulous, verminous, sources of disease, even cholera, as poor Henrietta Danfield had proved. The 'Adam Havard Home'? Yes. That had a ring of authority. Havard was a distinguished name in Penavon and there was a certain irony in that young Adam would be continuing the

517

philanthropic charity which his paternal grandfather had first begun.

Thus it was that the 'Adam Havard Home' came into being and, to the righteous indignation of those Penavon born and bred, there was no shortage of infants, orphaned or abandoned, from among the restlessly changing influx of those seeking employment in the newly developing mines.

To Clarissa's relief, some of the open hostility between those at Great House seemed to ease as Adam grew. It was true that they existed in a state of uneasy truce rather than in harmony, yet it was a beginning and she could but hope that, in time, the old conflicts and animosities might be forgiven, if not forgotten. Certainly, Mostyn was distinguishing himself in business and earning Rhys's regard as well as trying to redeem himself in Laurel's eyes. There was no doubting either that the pride which he felt in his son was real. That in itself persuaded Laurel, and Clarissa herself, to believe that Mostyn might have matured. Perhaps his past indiscretions were, after all, no more than a young man's kicking over the traces – the rebellion of one forced into marriage too soon.

Rhys Llewellyn too was relieved that Mostyn's dissolute ways had been mended, or were at least discreetly cloaked in decency. He thanked God, and his own foresight, that Mostyn's bastard was safely removed from Penavon. The payment had been absurdly generous, but he could not regret it since it had freed Laurel from humiliation and bought her peace of mind. He was therefore completely unprepared for the fury which descended upon Great House when that creature, Mostyn's hussy, forced her way boldly past the under-footman, and Grace himself, and into the guest hall. A gypsy, her lover, swarthy, fleshy-faced, unwashed and unkempt, was beside her, and in her arms she carried what could only be Mostyn's child. The likeness was inescapable.

'You will remove yourself from my house!' Llewellyn's anger was ill suppressed, his manner menacing, 'and if you

518

do not, then I shall summon the justices and demand your arrest.'

'Indeed?' The man's tone was deliberately offensive. 'I think you had best reconsider.'

'Damn you for your insolence!' Llewellyn's patience broke. 'If you have come here to threaten or blackmail me into paying more, then I will have none of it! Extortion is a crime.'

'No, sir,' the ruffian's voice was insultingly assured. 'We came to deliver what you have bought . . . your purchase!' He took the filthy, bedraggled child from the woman's arms and thrust him into Llewellyn's. The child screamed outrage, his cries so pitiful in his bewilderment that Laurel and Clarissa came running from the drawing room, fearing it was Adam.

'Papa?' Laurel rushed towards him, then stopped, silenced by the two grinning and filthily clad creatures aside the child.

'Rhys?' Clarissa's voice was shrill, horrified. 'What is it? What has occurred? I beg you tell me.'

It was Laurel who answered, voice raw with hurt. 'It is Mostyn's . . . Mostyn's woman, Mama, his mistress, and his by-blow!'

'Get out!' Llewellyn's face was engorged with fury, a vein throbbing fiercely at his temple as he thrust the child back into the trollop's arms. 'Get out, or, by God, I swear I will kill you! It is what you deserve. You are trash! Guttersnipes!'

The child, screaming furiously still, clutched at the woman's shawl, twisting it in his small fist. Laurel pushed her way forward to say, incredulously, 'That is my gold and pearl necklace, Papa! The one stolen.'

The woman clutched the child closer, making him scream the more, and there was no doubting her terror and confusion.

'You are thieves, then, as well as extortionists!'

The man was looking puzzled, his arrogance melting into uncertainty as he persisted stubbornly, 'It was given to

519

her . . . a thing of no value, she was told.'

'Payment for services?' Llewellyn demanded laceratingly. 'Then you have been grossly overpaid, madam. And the gentleman who rated your services so highly?'

Laurel ran to her father's side, declaring urgently, before the woman could make reply, 'Let her keep it, Papa! I could not wear it now. It is soiled, filthy! I could not bear to see or touch it.'

Clarissa, mindful that Laurel's outcry had been as much to deny mention of Mostyn's name as from disgust at the woman's sluttishness, said coldly and with contempt, 'Give the creature the necklace, Rhys. It is of as little account as she.'

Rhys Llewellyn made as if to protest, but Clarissa's savagely set face and warning glance silenced him. 'You had best return to the drawing room, my dear,' he said gruffly at length, Laurel's distress and pallor shaming him into contrition. 'This ludicrous charade has gone on long enough! It in no wise concerns you. I will see that it is ended.'

Clarissa took Laurel's arm and led her, unresisting, away. The child in the woman's arms had stopped its screaming, and, glancing back at it, Laurel was ripped with a conflict of rage and pain, yet pity too, so that her step faltered, and she would have fallen had not Clarissa steadied her. The child stared at her, unblinking. Beneath the filthily matted curls, which might have been gold or brown, the eyes which surveyed her were wide, blue, and unnervingly curious. They were more like Mostyn's than her own son's.

'Papa . . . do not let her keep the child! Do not, I beg you.'

Rhys Llewellyn, hearing Laurel's passionate cry, and seeing in her face a return of the old confusion which had dulled her reason after Adam's birth, said, 'No, my dear. She shall not take the boy. You have my oath upon it!'

The transaction was swift and eagerly accepted. The necklace was returned to Rhys Llewellyn and the child taken into the care of a servant, then transported to the

Adam Havard Home. Upon Llewellyn's insistence, he was entered upon the rolls as *Rice Mostyn Havard*; names which aroused no undue curiosity, for many of the offspring of the poor were given the names of those who were, or had been, of note in the small community, in the hope that they would inherit that same good fortune.

Llewellyn elicited that the child's grandmother was dead, and the old man incapable of caring for the boy. His mother and her 'keeper' had come to return him to Mostyn, hoping to threaten and bluster him into buying their silence. They would, with persuasion, grudgingly have taken the child with them, to later abandon him perhaps, or to initiate him into a life as violent and decadent as their own. They received no payment. Indeed, they had surrendered the two things of value which they possessed; the boy and the necklace. The pair had been relieved to evade the punishment of the law, and had made their sullen escape, scourged and chastened by the whiplash of Llewellyn's tongue. He set as little value upon them as the necklace he had insisted upon retrieving. It was proof, if proof were needed, of Mostyn's part in the whole tawdry affair. Neither Clarissa nor Laurel should ever know that it was in his possession. When its work was done, and he had confronted Mostyn with the evidence, it would be sold and the proceeds given to some charitable cause. His mouth twisted wryly. To the Adam Havard Home perhaps, to ensure the future of Mostyn's bastard brat and others like him. He thought, briefly, of his own grandson, sleeping comfortably in the nursery overhead, and felt only a warm surge of pleasure that the boy's future was secure. His conscience was clear. He had provided a home for Mostyn's by-blow through his own altruism. It would be fed, clothed, kept clean, and taught to labour usefully. It was more than Mostyn deserved, or that whore who had spawned him.

Chapter Forty-four

Mostyn, openly accused by Llewellyn of the theft of Laurel's necklace, reacted predictably. His blustering outrage and denial having failed to convince, he took refuge in blaming the slut he procured in the hope of deflecting attention from his own guilt. She tricked and seduced him, Mostyn claimed. She was no better than a common whore – trash, useless rubbish, and unworthy of attention.

'And do you place my daughter, your wife, beside her in worth?' Llewellyn demanded icily. 'Is she also to blame?'

'That is different,' Mostyn protested defensively. 'I loved her . . . still do. It is not unreasonable for a man to behave in such a fashion.'

'Like a beast of the field, do you mean?'

'No, sir . . . like a red-blooded man.'

'A man would not treat a gentlewoman like a field whore, sir!'

Mostyn, squirming under Llewellyn's contempt, demanded rebelliously, 'And am I to pay for it for the rest of my life?'

'If needs be.' Llewellyn's voice was chilling in its quietness. 'You live here, under my roof, sir, and eat my bread, and work at my behest. All you have is owed to me. I have made you, and can as easily break you. It would not cause me a moment's grief, you may depend upon it!'

'But you would not,' Mostyn mumbled sullenly, 'for Laurel's sake, and the boy's. You would bring disgrace upon them!'

'Damn you to hell, Mostyn! Are you blind as well as

dissolute? Are you too arrogant to see the truth of it? I shall put it plainly, sir, so that you need delude yourself no longer! You are a common thief, an adulterer. Worse, you have the audacity to force your trollop into my house, and her man, and your bastard with her!'

'I did not know what she meant to do,' he said resentfully. 'It was not my fault.'

'In the name of God, man, whose fault was it?' Llewellyn raged impotently. 'Did you not know that I had paid the woman to leave Penavon? To spare Laurel grief.'

'No . . .' Mostyn's voice was so low as to be almost inaudible. 'You were a fool to trust her!'

'And yet you trusted her with your child,' Llewellyn accused. 'Have you no thought for the boy at all? No interest in his future?'

'None.' Mostyn was, for once, positive. 'My concern is only for Adam. Would you have it otherwise?' he demanded scathingly. 'Should I acknowledge my bastard? Flaunt him openly? Tell Adam of his half-brother? It was for that you castigated me!'

'Confound your insolence!' Llewellyn had to steel himself against striking him. 'What sort of a cold-blooded reptile are you?'

'I am a realist,' admitted Mostyn, unconcerned. 'I know that you have need of me to keep your business and your family intact before others. If my reputation for honesty were smirched, then so must yours be, and Laurel and Adam would suffer social rejection and hurt. You will keep the necklace, believing it gives you power over me, that you hold it as surety for my good behaviour.' He smiled with a return of his old arrogance, knowing that Llewellyn could not deny it. 'You will never openly charge me with theft,' he continued, 'because you will destroy not only me, but all that you have worked for, and the people you love. It is too high a price.'

'Do not depend upon it.' Llewellyn's voice was as certain as Mostyn's. 'No price would be too high to be rid of someone who has made a mockery of loyalty with an act of betrayal in marriage, as in friendship. No, do not depend upon it!'

Mostyn hesitated, aware of a threat in Llewellyn's words and uncertain of how best to answer it. 'You have the necklace as surety,' he said finally, 'and I have my son. I am at liberty to remove him from your house, and none would question my right. I shall not do so while it suits me to live at Great House and enjoy its amenities and the society it offers. Should events force me to revise my opinion . . .' he shrugged expressively. '. . . I believe we understand each other well enough, sir.'

'Perfectly!' Llewellyn was tight-lipped with anger. 'Do not forget, Mostyn, no man is too devious, or too arrogant, to be spared a fall.'

'Precisely,' said Mostyn languidly. 'I suggest you take note of it.'

Mostyn's immediate encounter with Laurel did nothing to restore his self-esteem. Still smarting from Llewellyn's scorn, he turned his rage and accusation upon Laurel.

'Were I welcomed into your bed,' he declared peevishly, 'I would not need to seek solace elsewhere. It is you who are to blame!'

'Indeed!' Laurel responded coolly, 'then you have my permission to consort with any strumpet or street-walker undemanding enough to have you.'

'I do not need your permission!' Mostyn declared, outraged. 'I may go to any I choose, whenever I choose! It is no affair of yours!'

'Oh, but it is! Have you forgotten, Mostyn, that I have encountered one of your . . . sluts?'

'And cannot hide your jealousy!'

She smiled tolerantly. 'I am only relieved that you have finally found someone so exactly your equal . . . in cunning and worth.'

'Damn you, Laurel, for a cold bitch!' he exploded furiously. 'It is you who have driven me to it. You must bear responsibility. Ours was a marriage of convenience. I agreed to wed you, to spare you humiliation. You would have been ostracised, shamed, else . . .'

'As you, Mostyn, would have been denied a return to Great House. I do not delude myself that you married me for love. I am no longer so childishly naive. I ask only that you do not delude yourself either.'

'I have given you my name, and protection,' he blustered. 'I have kept to my side of the bargain. I promised nothing else.'

'You promised to love and to cherish.'

'As you promised to obey!'

'Then we have both broken our vows, and stand equal,' she said crisply, 'but I thank you nonetheless, Mostyn.'

'On what account?' he demanded sharply.

'On account of Adam.'

'And is that all, Laurel?' His tone was intimate, appeasing.

'No . . .' she hesitated, and saw his fleeting smile of triumph before she confessed, '. . . I thank you for teaching me to survive, Mostyn. It was a hard lesson, cruelly learnt, but it will stand me in good stead.'

'In good stead for what?' he asked with sarcasm. 'You are nothing without me. A woman alone is a prey for every rogue and philanderer upon God's earth! It is only in marriage that she finds identity. It gives her status before others. There is nothing as pathetic and shameful as an ageing woman unwed.'

'Is there not, Mostyn?' There was a wealth of meaning in Laurel's quiet response.

'Do not forget, Laurel,' he adjured spitefully, 'that all you have of property and inheritance is in my keeping, by law. I possess all. It is mine by right.'

'No, Mostyn. You do not possess all.'

Her cool composure angered him more, and he declared hotly, 'You are a fool, Laurel! You will learn the truth of it! Goods, chattels, money . . . Adam, even, are mine to order at will. Possessions all.'

'You do not possess me, Mostyn!' Her voice was calm with certainty.

'I have possessed you, for what it was worth!' His contempt was lacerating. 'You have served my purpose, Laurel . . . like . . . like a brood mare,' he concluded triumphantly. 'I have no more use for you.'

'Then we are at one,' said Laurel without rancour, 'and it is for that I thanked you!'

Mostyn, baffled and enraged, looked at her for a few tense moments, but, unable to make reply, turned upon his heel and left her.

Mostyn drove the curricle recklessly towards Caborne's house at Golden Grove, sweat rising from the horses' flanks in a vapour thick as their frosted breath. By the time he arrived, the horses were lathered with foam, their hides bloodied from the lashes of his whip, but his own temper had abated and he greeted Caborne with his customary nonchalance. The groom who uncoupled the horses shook his head ruefully, then dropped his gaze, leading them away silently, his back rigid with disapproval.

'You have heard then?' Caborne said, hurrying him towards the house, 'else you would not have come flying here like a bat out of hell!'

'Heard? Heard what?' demanded Mostyn impatiently.

'Jefferies! He has fled . . . God, alone, knows where!'

'Fled?'

'Absconded . . . with his investors' savings. Thank God we were not involved in his harebrained schemes! Money and friendship are soon enough parted.' He paused, bewildered by Mostyn's silence and pallor. 'Mostyn . . . You were not foolish enough to . . . ?'

'A trifling loan,' Mostyn disclaimed irritably, 'scarce worth the mention. It is of no account, I do assure you, Caborne . . . more in the nature of a . . . gift, to tide him over, you understand?'

Caborne was unconvinced. 'You will swear, Havard, that

there is no capital of your own involved? It will not ruin you?'

Mostyn laughed unaffectedly, declaring, 'I swear, Caborne, that not one penny is involved which cannot be spared! As for ruining me, the idea is ludicrous! I have as little regard for Jefferies' business acumen as for his taste in whores,' he replied as Caborne lifted his eyebrows questioningly. 'A case of enthusiasm and urgency over discrimination, would you not say?'

Caborne laughingly agreed. 'You have not given me the true reason for your visit?' he reminded. 'Had you some excursion in mind?'

'An impulse only!' said Mostyn dismissively. 'It will wait. I shall return later to discuss it. Will you have my carriage brought?'

'Now?' asked Caborne, startled.

'Yes, without delay. I have an errand which will not wait.'

Caborne gave orders that the carriage be returned, asking archly, when Mostyn was at the reins, 'Some . . . urgent mission, which will enhance your pleasure? Another impulse, perhaps?'

'One which will give me no satisfaction,' declared Mostyn, whipping the horses into life.

From any, save Mostyn, Penry Vaughan's bewilderment would have drawn sympathy and regret. It merely served to irritate Mostyn the more.

'I fear that I do not understand. Is this some jest, Mostyn? Some childish prank, as of old?' His voice sharpened anxiously.

'No jest, Cousin Penry. I repeat, your investment has yielded nothing.'

'But my capital? My capital is safe?' he persisted. 'There has been some necessary outlay, perhaps, some purchase to secure future profits?'

'No purchase. No capital. Jefferies, with whom you invested, has absconded with all.'

527

Vaughan steadied himself by gripping the edge of the desk at which he stood, demanding incredulously, 'With whom *I* invested, you say? Are you mad, sir? It was at your insistence I did so . . . You are to blame, and you alone!'

'Nonsense, sir!' Mostyn's voice was cool. 'Since your memory disobliges you, I will remind you of the true facts. You begged me to invest it for you, which I did reluctantly, although it was scarce worth the bother of handling such a niggardly sum. No, Cousin, I will not be made a scapegoat for your own cupidity, and the defection of another! Human greed is the culprit, in both cases. It is a lesson you have been at pains to impress upon others!'

Vaughan, ashen-faced, and shaking with rage and humiliation, asked, 'Does it not concern you, sir, that I stand to be ruined . . . my career and my future ended? All that I have struggled and schemed for lost? I shall be the object of people's pity and derision, a figure of scorn before all.'

'Damn it, sir!' cried Mostyn in exasperation, 'such whining self-pity ill becomes you! It is maudlin, and disgusts me! It was a beggarly enough sum, and should not cause you alarm!'

'You will reimburse me, then?' Vaughan cried eagerly. 'You will see that my losses are made good?'

'It it pleases you,' Mostyn agreed negligently, cutting short Vaughan's embarrassing fervour of gratitude. 'I have already told you there were but a few hundred pounds of yours involved.'

'But the rest? What have you done with it, Mostyn? Is it safe?' Vaughan demanded feverishly.

'If you would care to have it returned,' offered Mostyn languidly, 'I shall pay you from my own purse . . . and then consider your investments my own. It would give me the greatest satisfaction, since the company is already over-subscribed. It will be a rare opportunity.'

Vaughan hesitated, asking suspiciously, 'This company . . . Do I know it? Is it reputable?' His gaunt face was flushed with unease.

'You insult me, Cousin,' Mostyn's manner was curt. 'My own money and that of the Litchard-Llewellyn Company is already invested.' Mostyn had grown plainly bored, saying superciliously, 'I shall bring you the money owed to you by Jefferies at once, if that is your wish . . . and buy your share in the venture at full market value. Is that to your satisfaction?' He made as if to leave, smiling urbanely.

'No, Mostyn . . . perhaps I have been hasty, indiscreet,' confessed Vaughan, eager to placate him. 'I beg you will leave my shares untouched.' With sudden inspiration, he declared, 'If you could see your way clear to also investing that money you repay on Jefferies' behalf . . . ?'

'If that is your wish,' replied Mostyn indifferently. 'However, I must warn you that you do so at your own risk, Cousin. I shall not be inclined to cover your losses in future, should they occur. Is it clearly understood?'

'Oh, yes, Mostyn. If I have seemed remiss in my gratitude,' Vaughan admitted stiffly, 'I beg you will set it against shock and confusion, and not judge me too harshly. I am beholden to you. I do not deny it. The money was not entirely my own, do you see?'

'We will say no more about it,' said Mostyn magnanimously. 'We are kinsmen, and should be open and honest, one with the other. You are all I have of kin, through blood, Cousin Penry . . . save for my son, Adam, of course. I cannot accept Carne as such – his treatment of you still rankles and sours me.'

Vaughan gratefully nodded his understanding as he first gripped Mostyn's hand, then embraced him.

Mostyn returned to the carriage thoughtfully. Penry Vaughan had declared himself to be beholden to him. Well, he did not object to keeping his cousin securely in his debt, for his support might, one day, be needed. Mostyn adjusted his silk hat and climbed into the curricle, settling himself with unselfconscious arrogance at the reins. The money he had squandered upon Jefferies had been his own, and the loss negligible. It had gained him Vaughan's trust and gratitude, and he considered it well spent.

★　★　★

529

Carne was relieved that the apathy which had claimed Charles after Henrietta's death had given way to a fervour of activity for the newly formed Hartrey-Havard Mining Company. It was, Carne knew, simply a way to exorcise his grief; a means to forgetfulness. Yet, gradually, the excitement and stimulation of the venture had absorbed them both, then obsessed them with a determination to succeed.

Charles was already a successful stock-breeder and a business man in his own right, and there was no lack of local investors like Randall Walters, and other associates, eager to finance the enterprise. While Charles immersed himself in the financial details and the acquiring of leases to the land, Carne set himself to deal with the more mundane essentials, such as the hiring of transport, equipment and labour.

Geologists' reports were first commissioned and studied, then drilling equipment hired at exorbitant cost and experts well paid to oversee the operations. Their findings were unanimous. The old surface veins of coal drove deep into Penavon hills. The coal was of the finest quality and suitable for the smelting of iron. Supplies were rich, easily accessible, and virtually inexhaustible.

Some of Llewellyn's colliers had already been housed in straggling new terraces of houses, tiered like vineyards across the rocky hillsides. Their places in the makeshift camps were immediately filled by others, and it was these newcomers whom the Hartrey-Havard Company must attract into the mines in order to compete.

With Saranne so near the time for her child's birth, she no longer helped within the camps. Yet Sara was firm. It was the womenfolk, she declared, who were the final arbiters. They had suffered enough privation and hardship. The new company must win their trust. There must be a firm promise of good, affordable housing in the near future, the immediate supplying of nourishing food and working clothing for the men as evidence of good faith. With Megan's and Mrs Hodges' practical help, a soup-kitchen was set up in a disused coachhouse and stables in Penavon village, and tough clothing and wooden-soled boots provided for those men seeking employment. Help was also given for their dependents and the sum set against their future wages, with their surety that they would pledge to work for the new Hartrey-Havard Company. The first man to offer his services was Jack Hollis, and the respect and liking he inspired in others proved invaluable. There was no shortage of volunteers to work beside him. He was a brave and honest fellow, and his belief in the integrity of the new mine-owners was recommendation enough.

One morning, Carne, deep in earnest conversation with one of the company's mining engineers, was alerted by an anxious Peter Morrish to the fact that Saranne's labour had begun. Dr Tobin, he declared, had earlier been summoned.

The physician and Carne arrived upon the doorstep of Thatched Cottage at the same instant. Tobin, slow moving and placid, stood aside to let Carne enter, but Carne, overwrought with anxiety, bustled and manhandled the physician within, demanding tartly, 'Why are you not with her, sir? You should be at her side, not shilly-shallying upon the step like some hesitant dancer.' He was aware of his rudeness and would have made apology had not Dr Tobin raised an eyebrow in amusement before dissolving into spontaneous laughter. 'I see no cause for mirth, sir!' declared Carne, his good intentions forgotten.

'I beg you will forgive me.' Tobin stifled his laughter with an effort to explain, 'This is the second occasion I have visited your wife, sir.'

'The second . . . ?'

'Upon the first, your wife was delivered of a healthy son . . . handsome, and complete in fingers and toes, and with a bellow which would not have disgraced one of Mr Hartrey's prize bulls, sir!'

There was no disguising Dr Tobin's extreme satisfaction. Carne, torn between delight, disbelief and shame for his rudeness, would have spoken then, but Dr Tobin pushed him towards the staircase where Megan stood holding a pathetically small bundle, wrapped in knitted wool, cradling it with the greatest gentleness.

'Well? Do you not wish to make your son's acquaintance?' she asked.

Carne mounted the stairs as one in a trance. Megan turned back the shawl and Carne stared, amazed, at the small crumpled face, the shock of dark hair, so like his own, the tiny perfect fingers and nails . . . and stretched out a hesitant finger to touch the child's cheek. The eyes which reluctantly opened were of the deepest violet, thick-lashed as Saranne's. Carne felt such a fierce surge of tenderness that it was a pain within him.

'Saranne?'

Megan glanced below and Dr Tobin nodded briefly, mounting the stairs, cautioning as he did so, 'A moment only, pray do not overtire her! I shall follow you to make my examination directly.'

Saranne, flushed and exhausted, smiled to see him. Her eyes were feverishly bright and her pretty hair, still damp with sweat, clung in limp tendrils to her face and neck, despite all Sara's efforts to tame it. Carne bent over and kissed Saranne gently and with tenderness, as if she were as fragile and new to him as the child they had made. Her arms reached out to draw him to her, strong and firm, as she said, 'I had thought to call him Eynon Prys Havard. It seemed fitting, for Jane and Prys were parents, both, to you.'

Carne smiled and nodded. The look of love which passed between them spoke words enough.

Chapter Forty-five

Eynon Prys Havard, as he was duly christened, was as unlike his cousin Adam as it was possible to be. He was as dark as his cousin was fair; as strong-boned as Adam was delicate; as placid in temperament as Laurel's son was nervously high-strung. None could deny that he was a lusty infant, healthy, handsome, swift to smiles and slow to tears. He slept well and fed easily. Sara believed her grandson to be perfect in every particular and Peter Morrish was quite absurdly besotted with him. As for Megan, she was heard to declare to any who would listen, 'that child has the disposition of a saint, and the face of an angel'. Saranne only hoped that such flattery and ardent devotion would not turn her son's head. She need not have concerned herself. The love he received, and gave in return, was generous and undemanding. When Saranne had first expressed such doubts to Peter Morrish, he had replied quietly, 'It is a lack of love which sours and cripples, Saranne. No-one can be loved too much. It is what makes us grow in spirit and affection. Being loved is what assures us of our own value and worth.'

Saranne glanced towards Sara, then admitted truthfully, from her own past, 'Yes, I am certain that is so. The love which one gives to one's own child is natural, inborn, but to give as freely to a child unknown is true devotion. That is what Mama so readily gave to me.' She crossed the room to where Sara stood and kissed her soft cheek with affection. 'I do not know, Mama, how I would have survived, or what I would have become, had you not accepted me . . .

533

generously, and without question. I do not even know if I would have had the strength or the will to survive.'

'Oh . . . but you would have survived, Saranne . . . you had courage and spirit in your defence of Marged, and would not desert her, in darkness, hunger or cold. I count it my greatest blessing, my dear, that it was to me you came, and no other.'

Carne had come, unnoticed, into the room where the two women, with arms entwined, were watching over his son's cradle. He had heard the conviction in her words and glanced at Morrish questioningly, afraid that something untoward had occurred to provoke her distress. Morrish smiled and was about to speak when there was a sudden knocking upon the front door, sharp and peremptory, as if delivered by a raised stick. Saranne would have hurried to answer it but Megan was already there, and, within moments, had entered to consult them, face unbecomingly flushed, manner distraught.

'It is Mr Mostyn Havard, Mr Carne, demanding to speak to you. I did not know where best to put him, where to ask him to wait,' she said.

'It is of no consequence,' Mostyn was standing in the doorway, sartorially immaculate, his glance openly disdainful of his modest surroundings. 'A charming room, ma'am.' The languidly spoken words were addressed to Saranne. 'And as pretty a domestic scene as I have been privileged to observe . . . I beg that you will introduce me to my young nephew, since that is the reason for my visit. I have come to pay my respects.'

The silence in the room had grown oppressive, yet none seemed capable of movement or speech, until Carne strode forward to grip Mostyn's hand with every evidence of pleasure, declaring as he set an arm about his brother's shoulders and drew him proudly towards the cradle, 'How good of you to come, Mostyn. You are most welcome to see your nephew.'

There was no mistaking the genuine warmth in his manner and voice at this unexpected attempt at conciliation

534

on Mostyn's part. Saranne had stepped back involuntarily as Mostyn approached, and Sara, whose arm still held her daughter protectively, felt the tremor of revulsion which ran through her. Peter Morrish, aware of Saranne's distress, but not the reason for it, moved swiftly to stand beside her.

Carne, clumsily but with pride, lifted his son that Mostyn might see him the better, asking impulsively, 'Is he not handsome, Mostyn? See how eager he is to grasp my finger . . . and how strong his hold! He has such strength and determination! Is he not like father, with that mass of black hair, although his eyes are Saranne's? Do you not see it?'

'Yes. I see it.' Mostyn's voice was cold. 'There is a look of father about him, certainly. Yes, he is a fine boy. One must hope that it is in features alone that he resembles him, Carne.'

There was a tense, uneasy silence in the room before Carne said evenly, 'I cannot think that your memories of him are all your own, Mostyn – but are owed, in part, to Cousin Penry's hatred. You were an infant, barely able to recall him clearly, or to understand the grief he bore.'

Before Mostyn could make denial, Peter Morrish intervened firmly, 'We are what we make ourselves, Mr Havard. Circumstances, and the indifference or hostility of others, need not embitter us.' He reached out with deliberation and took Saranne's hand firmly within his own, saying with conscious pride, 'You may look to our daughter, Saranne, for the proof of it.'

Mostyn contrived to look both sceptical and insolently amused as Morrish continued undeterred, 'The cruelties of others can destroy us or make us strong, as they strengthened Saranne. We carry the seeds of self-destruction within ourselves, but they owe little to inheritance.' Morrish's eyes were upon Sara now and she returned his look with that same tenderness and approval. 'No, Mr Havard, I do not think you need fear for your nephew. It is not the strengths and weaknesses of others, but our own, which shape our lives.'

'I thank you for the sermon, sir . . . I must attend your church more often.' Mostyn's smile and ease of manner took all offence from the words as Carne bent to settle his son back into the cradle, plainly relieved. 'And what have you decided to call my nephew?' Mostyn asked Saranne. 'A Hartrey name, perhaps? Jethro, or Charles, would it be?'

'Neither, sir.' Saranne could not bring herself to address him by name, and was aware she sounded cold and uncivil. 'We have named him Eynon Prys.'

His astonishment and dismay cheered her.

'Eynon? But that was my grandmother's family name.'

'Indeed,' she agreed equably, 'and the name she bequeathed to her serving maid, Jane Prys. It is Jane and her husband we perpetuate, for their kindness and loyalty as friends. No, more than friends, as family.'

'A . . . pretty gesture, ma'am,' said Mostyn, 'and entirely apposite.' His voice was carefully expressionless, so that none could accuse him of the insult so clearly intended.

'I do not doubt that you and Mr Havard have much to discuss of a private nature, Carne,' interjected Morrish smoothly. 'Come, Sara, and you, Saranne, my dear.' He guided them towards the cradle. 'We shall take Eynon Prys with us.'

'No.' Carne's voice was firm. 'Stay, Peter, I beg of you. Mostyn and I will go to the study.'

Mostyn nodded, glancing towards Saranne, to say negligently, 'My postillion upon the coach has a small gift to deliver to you on Laurel's behalf. Some pretty trifle she has chosen for the boy's christening,' he added with affected languour. 'I dare hazard that it will prove decorative, but useless, as were all the gifts Adam received. Those born to affluence have little conception of the lives or needs of others less fortunate.'

'I am sure, sir, Laurel would give as much thought to choosing such a pleasurable gift as I,' Saranne rebuked gently, 'and as little to its monetary worth as the recipient's . . . I shall write and thank her for her generous impulse, and for the gift, or, better still, call upon her to assure her of my gratitude. It would not be fitting to convey it impersonally through a postillion . . . As a gentlewoman of discernment, she would consider it ill-mannered and churlish.'

Mostyn scarcely bowed, face set, and followed Carne without.

When the two brothers were seated in the small study, fortified with Canary wine, Carne found himself apologising awkwardly for Saranne's abrasiveness.

'Saranne is not yet fully recovered from the birth . . .' Even as he spoke the words, he felt a sense of shame and betrayal, but his sense of responsibility for Mostyn was long ingrained.

'It makes no matter,' Mostyn said earnestly. 'I understand. She mistrusts me and is suspicious of my motives in coming here. I must hope to persuade her of my goodwill and that I come only to heal the rift between us. I would have you believe that, Carne.' He was watching Carne with an expression of anxious pleading and humility.

'We have been too long apart,' admitted Carne honestly.

Mostyn said, 'I know what is owed to your care of me in the past, Carne. I am older now, and wiser, and see the depth of it, and the gratitude that is your due. It is hard for me to speak of such things coldly and without reserve.' His voice trembled painfully and the glass in his hand shook and spilled as he set it down.

'Then there is no more to be said.' Carne gripped Mostyn's arm reassuringly. 'We will not speak of it again.'

Mostyn looked up, eyes held wide as in childhood, and Carne felt the old sense of affection and protectiveness stir.

'Laurel and your son, Adam, are well, I trust?' he asked by way of diversion.

Mostyn, given time to compose himself, replied enthusiastically and, for a time their conversation was innocuous and pleasantly free from dissension.

Finally, Carne volunteered, 'I am glad that you have taken upon yourself to call, for there is a matter of business

I wish to discuss with you, on behalf of the Hartrey-Havard Mining Company.'

'Indeed?' The expression of displeasure was so fleeting that Carne might have imagined it. Mostyn's voice was carefully noncommittal as he asked, 'In what way does your business venture concern me?'

'I wish to buy a parcel of land which Randall Walters assures me is the property of the Litchard-Llewellyn enterprise, though not in use.'

'Where exactly?'

Carne produced a rolled map from the drawer within the desk and laid it upon the tooled leather surface, securing the edges with a paperweight and containers of sand and ink to keep it outspread. Then, taking a quill, he outlined the land in question.

'Why do you require it?' Mostyn demanded sharply.

'I am not at liberty to say.'

'There is no coal upon it. It is barren, less than useless. You cannot mean to build there? Or farm?'

Carne did not reply.

'It has been surveyed at some expense and drilled by experts at considerably more,' persisted Mostyn, 'and declared to be no better than arid rock. I cannot see what purpose it would serve.' He surveyed the map again, more carefully. 'Damnation, Carne!' he exclaimed triumphantly. 'You must have judged me blind, simple-minded at best, not to have guessed your intention. That is the spit of land between the two drift mines you have already begun to work!'

Carne did not deny it, claiming defensively, 'I promised Charles Hartrey that I would approach Lord Litchard or Rhys Llewellyn to secure its lease.'

'Litchard has left for London. He takes no interest in the company since Henrietta's death, and Danfield and my father-in-law have given me full power of attorney to act upon their behalf.'

'You have said the land is barren, worthless,' reminded Carne.

'To us . . . but not to you.'

'You will sell it, then?'

'At a price, and the price is one thousand pounds . . . take it or leave it. If you leave it, there will be others as greedy for land as you, or bent upon thwarting your ownership and expansion.'

'I must take the matter to Charles . . . seek his advice.'

'No!' declared Mostyn implacably. 'You will decide, here and now, unless you are no more than a hired lackey without voice or position. In that case, your hesitancy will cost you five hundred pounds, since the offer I make is to you, and no other. Should Charles Hartrey wish to negotiate, the price will be two thousand pounds.'

'Dear God, Mostyn! Are you mad? I swear I do not understand.'

'I am a businessman, as you claim to be,' said Mostyn with finality. 'I have offered you the land for one thousand pounds because you are my brother, and for no other reason. Such mawkishness is against my principles, but discharges any debt between us. I will never, again, be guilty of such weakness. We are rivals in business, and, in future, must bargain as such. Well? What is your answer?'

'I will buy.' Carne felt a sickness of doubt unnerve him, but took Mostyn's swiftly thrust hand to seal the bargain, bitterly aware from his brother's smirk of triumph that he had been cleverly outwitted. Whatever the cost, Carne knew that Charles would stand by his commitment, but the certainty gave him more unease than comfort.

'Lesson One in the art of negotiation,' instructed Mostyn crisply. 'Always keep to the rules of gaming. Never disclose your hand. Guard your expression as fiercely as your cards, and when you wager, Carne, do it confidently.'

'Even if it seems set to ruin you?'

'Especially if it seems set to ruin you! You must needs convince yourself in order to convince others. Like all else in life, it is a performance, an act, to deceive.'

'And you are a born actor, Mostyn.'

Mostyn smiled and bowed mockingly in acknowledgement

as Carne added drily, 'Although I cannot accept your philosophy on life.'

Mostyn broke into spontaneous laughter, amused and unrepentant, 'You have been too much influenced by Peter Morrish,' he accused.

'As you have by Penry Vaughan!'

'Perhaps,' Mostyn agreed tolerantly. 'In business, as in love, one must take whatever advantages are offered . . . forget one is a gentleman.'

'So I had observed,' agreed Carne drily.

'Then you have learnt a valuable lesson.'

'I have learnt another,' said Carne, straight-faced, 'which will keep me in mind always of our reconciliation.' To Mostyn's quizzical glance, he replied ruefully, 'In business, there are no kin, no friends. All are strangers.'

'A beginning,' said Mostyn approvingly, 'but incomplete.' He smiled ingenuously and with all of his well-practised charm as he replaced his empty glass upon the desk and rose to take his farewell. He clapped Carne companionably upon the shoulder, then embraced him, and stood back, eyes challenging and amused. 'In business,' he corrected, 'there are no kin, no friends, and all are not only strangers, but rivals and enemies. When you believe that, Carne, and act upon it, I, too, shall have learnt something.'

'And that?'

'To be afraid.'

Contrary to all Carne's expectations, Charles was plainly delighted that they had secured the parcel of land, even at so exorbitant a price. It was essential, he assured Carne, to link the two newly excavated drift mines. It would pay for itself a hundred times over, and more, in convenience and time and manpower saved. A shared, narrow-gauge tramway could greatly cut their haulage costs and the land would provide a common ground for the storage heaps of coal and waste mined, and for the stabling of pit ponies and the storing of equipment. They could divert the course of the streamlet running by, a small tributary of Penavon river, and use it to create a washery.

Charles was so forceful in his enthusiasm and appreciation of Carne's shrewd bargaining that Carne was finally convinced. However, on hearing a full account of the conversation with Mostyn, Charles declared firmly. 'I do not doubt, Carne, that he meant what he threatened, and would have doubled the price had you demurred.'

'But why?' Carne demanded, troubled. 'I have gone over and over it in my own mind, and can make no sense of it.'

Charles, who sensed how bitterly Carne had berated himself for accepting the price, said quietly, to ease his friend's anxiety, 'You must believe that he told the truth – that he appreciates your past care for him, and came with good grace to repay the debt. He is a man, now, and sees more clearly. You cannot for ever condemn him or mistrust him for what he was as a child.'

'Yes. You are right, Charles,' Carne agreed gratefully. 'It is I who am at fault, if I will not accept him for what he now is.'

Yet Charles had known, and reared, too many animals upon the farm to be fully convinced. He had observed and nurtured them from birth to death, and knew that what is born in the blood can be subdued, but rarely changed. In every herd there is a beast that has evil and violence inborn, and is not to be trusted. Yet, it would do no good to remind Carne of it. An older child will always protect and excuse a younger, even when both are fully grown. No outsider can change it. He knew this from his love for Saranne.

Chapter Forty-six

The New Year brought squalls with swiftly gusting winds that drove the snow relentlessly into every small fissure and crack, piling it against hedges and walls in sculptured drifts and baring frozen earth. Then came a sudden mildness and thaw. Rain fell in slanting rods, sharp as glass, piercing the snow which still lingered, eating into craters edged with ice. Those ewes and lambs which did not survive fed the predatory birds and foxes, their corpses revealed by the melting snow, carcases picked clean. There were human victims too; ancients, infants and the chronic sick, buried in Penavon's churchyard earth, and others in graves unmarked. An old year and a new one; an ending and a beginning.

The new Hartrey-Havard coalmines prospered, their workforce housed in terraces which clung precariously to the lower slopes. At the approaches to the drift mines, huts proliferated together with all the sordid debris of human exploitation. Shelters for the men, women and children employed, stabling for the pit ponies and donkeys, farriers' and blacksmiths' shops, sheds for harness and miners' tackle, workplaces for all those trades and crafts essential to the extracting of mineral wealth.

Charles Hartrey's special pride was the small surface waggonway which had been constructed to transport the mined coal by the force of gravity to the river below. The waggons rode upon the newest fish-bellied rails of iron, more durable, he believed, and more efficient than the wooden rails of the Litchard-Llewellyn mines. Without the mines, the horses were used to haul the empty waggons uphill for loading, and were allowed to ride down in open waggons; a trip which they jealously awaited, and plainly enjoyed. The horses were highly valued and kindly treated by the hauliers who cared for them. Within the mines, women and young girls crawled through the narrow passageways upon all fours, with leather belts strapped around their waists, and chains passing between their legs, that they might the better drag the trucks or sledges of hewn coal from the work face to the surface. They laboured by candlelight, and for twelve hours a day, with many a young child beside them. Such was the nature of things. They must labour or starve.

Rhys Llewellyn and Mostyn could afford to be tolerantly amused by the efforts of the small rival company, for it proved no threat to their plans or prosperity. Should he choose, Llewellyn knew that he could crush it as ruthlessly as his colliers crushed the brittleness of coal. The Hartrey-Havard venture, he made publicly known, was an absurd folly, and doomed to failure.

As an experienced ironmaster, he was well aware that Penavon coal was the finest grade of anthracite, vital to iron-smelting. It could fuel the rapidly expanding ironworks at Merthyr, by now the largest in the world, and also the copper smelting works newly built at Llanelli and Swansea. Such coal would be needed too for the making and running of factory machines, for the smelting of copper for the cladding of ships, and for bolts used in the dockyards of Spain, Holland and France. The fleets of war must give way to the trading vessels, and the hunger for coal would then be insatiable. It was the dawning of a new industrial age and of new prosperity for those bold enough to welcome it. The Litchard-Llewellyn mines would take him, and his grandson, into a wealth and distinction unimaginable to others. It was there for the gathering.

Ironically, the new business rivalry between Carne and Mostyn seemed to bridge, rather than widen, the rift between them. They met socially now, with increasing frequency, their exchanges amicable, if still tempered with reserve. Between Saranne and Laurel there was no such reserve, save on the subject of their respective husbands. Each remained discreetly loyal on that score. Adam and Eynon, although infants, formed a firm liking, one for the other; a natural attraction, perhaps of opposites. Megan, who adored Eynon, was fair-minded enough to admit that Adam was a 'handsome, affectionate boy, without malice or meanness'. Yet in Carne's presence, and even that of Peter Morrish, whose voice was gentleness itself, he seemed anxious and ill-at-ease, looking for Megan or Laurel always for reassurance, stretching out his arms to be held close.

'He is shy,' Saranne had exclaimed, 'for you men are great, clodhopping creatures with abrupt manners . . . your voices too loud and harsh!'

Laurel had said, and it was the only defensive criticism she was ever heard to make, 'I fancy his papa expects too much of him, and grows impatient. He will like him better when he is grown. Mostyn is ill-at-ease with infants.' She had flushed awkwardly, fearing that she had been indiscreet. 'He loves him devotedly, but cannot abide his crying. He would not have a milksop for a son.'

Carne had been about to protest but, seeing Saranne's warning frown, bit back the angry retort that Adam was no more than a babe. 'He is a good and handsome boy, in every way; a child to be proud of, and I speak not only as a besotted uncle.' He smiled.

Laurel and her son had relaxed and smiled too, and the moment of uncertainty had passed. Yet, later, Carne, in playing with his own chuckling, responsive son, and seeing Eynon's absolute pleasure and trust in him, felt oddly disturbed. How bitterly Mostyn had hated their own father, he reflected uneasily. Yet now he inflicted the same terror and stresses upon Adam, his son. It was none of his affair, and Mostyn would not thank him for interfering, nor would it serve to help Laurel and the child. He could only hope that Laurel was right, and that it was a brief aberration on Mostyn's part that would resolve itself as his affection for Adam increased. Laurel had said that Mostyn did not want a milksop for a son, but no more did Adam want a brute for a father. Mostyn should learn from his own experience – the pity was that Mostyn never had.

Charles had summoned an urgent meeting of the main shareholders in the Hartrey-Havard Company in order to discuss submitting a tender to supply coal to the giant Merthyr Ironworks. It was, he declared, the only logical step forward if they were to compete successfully against the Litchard-Llewellyn mines. The true difficulties lay in that the ironmasters were all-powerful and had created their own dynasties. Rhys Llewellyn had been one of their number and they looked after their own. To compete they must pare their estimate to the bone, and even be prepared initially to lose money in order to survive.

There was heated and occasionally acrimonious discussion before the final figure was agreed. It was low enough, Charles believed, to persuade the ironmasters. It meant that there would be no dividend returns for the investors that year but, should their bid be accepted, it would secure for them entree into a new and expanding market.

Charles and Carne drove to Merthyr together in Randall Walters' travelling coach to present their tender formally to the ironmasters. They were confident that they could supply all the coal that was required of them, and at a lower price than any other. They waited in a small ante-room with representatives of half a dozen or so mining companies, expecting to be called into the main meeting room and questioned. When they were finally called to give account, it was to see Mostyn leaving the meeting room, elegantly attired, urbane, and smiling broadly. He greeted them civilly enough, pausing briefly to murmur to his brother, 'You had best save your breath, Carne. The contract is ours. They needed little persuasion that the smaller, less

545

profitable, companies might overreach themselves, and default. They can rely upon us.'

Carne refused to be drawn by Mostyn's flagrant attempt to irritate and outface him. 'We shall see,' he said equably, adding with a smile as broad as Mostyn's own, 'It is upon facts and figures they will rely and make decision.'

'Indeed.' Mostyn fingered the brim of his silk hat, then meticulously adjusted his cravat, before glibly quoting the exact figure submitted by the Hartrey-Havard Company. 'Try by all means,' he said expansively, 'but we have undercut you by five hundred pounds.'

And so it proved.

There was bitter disappointment among the shareholders that the Hartrey-Havard bid had failed, but resignation too, for it would have been impossible to further reduce their offer. The contract was for a full year, and they could only hope that when the time came for its renewal, they would be better prepared.

Charles publicly congratulated their newly appointed Transport Manager for what he had already achieved for the company. Captain Harry Fox, hired upon Carne's firm recommendation, had early proved his worth. Through his personal contacts, he had secured shipping freightage to carry coal to small ports in Devon and Somerset and along the Welsh coast at impressively low rates. Yet, all were agreed that the need was to break into the wider, more demanding markets and to supply coal to the iron foundries and copper smelting works upon a long-term basis.

Surprisingly, it was Peter Morrish who came up with a possible solution. His own parents were long dead, he confided, but his mother's brother, one Charles Nevill, a Worcestershire industrialist, had lately opened a smelting works at Swansea. Another kinsman had obligingly turned his fortune, and talents, towards copper and had established a works at Llanelli. Would Charles care to accompany him to those towns, that he might effect introduction? Charles accepted the offer with alacrity.

'Perhaps,' Peter offered tentatively, 'Carne might wish to drive there with us? It is only a suggestion, you understand? I have no wish to interfere. Since you are now both kinsmen of mine, through marriage, it might serve to strengthen your case?'

They set off on their journey by coach within three days of their meeting. Yet, perhaps, they had been too open and trusting in their discussion, since, when they arrived at Swansea, it was to learn that Mostyn had earlier been dispatched by Rhys Llewellyn upon the same errand.

The meeting between the two brothers was outwardly cordial, but Mostyn took the deepest satisfaction in stressing Rhys Llewellyn's long friendship with Nevill, and in declaring that he, too, was a friend and intimate of the family. Carne, who knew how much depended upon securing the contract, would have answered curtly, revealing their own advantage, had Peter Morrish not touched him steadyingly upon the arm and shaken his head in warning.

'Mr Morrish, sir.' Mostyn's tone was familiar and faintly deprecating. 'I am surprised to see you. What has lured you so far from Penavon? You do not usually move in such exalted company.'

Morrish smiled, unoffended. 'I do not think, Mr Havard, that there are many who would convincingly declare themselves to be more exalted than God,' he rebuked mildly.

Mostyn, briefly robbed of his advantage, flushed, and bade them a swift 'good-day'. However, he turned in leaving to murmur, 'I shall be staying at the inn for a while. Shall I have the honour of your company? It is a deucedly uncomfortable place, crowded, and ill-equipped for serving gentlemen. I cannot honestly recommend it.'

Before Carne could make reply, Peter Morrish intervened hurriedly, 'No. We will not add to your discomfort, Mr Havard. We shall be staying with a family, relatives of mine.'

Mostyn lifted an eyebrow and shrugged, before saying mockingly, 'Then I wish you well in your common lodgings . . .' With a quick bow and a flourish of his hat he left, smiling.

Carne, who was still smarting from Mostyn's victory in securing the contract at Merthyr, would have been less than human not to seek revenge. The shock and outrage upon Mostyn's face when he arrived at the Nevills' for dinner, only to discover that they were Carne's hosts, were recompense enough. He quickly recovered his composure and set out to charm and flatter the company, but it was to Morrish that the interest inevitably returned and their pleasure in his society was evident. Their conversation and questioning were all directed to family matters and affectionate reminiscences of the past.

Mostyn, outclassed and outwitted, at first struggled to regain the initiative, then drank more than was good for him, growing steadily more pompous and assertive. When it was time to take his leave, he muttered accusingly to Carne, when his hosts were out of earshot, 'Damn you for your deviousness, Carne! And that confounded preacher with you. It was petty and childish to keep his kinship with the Nevills hid. Yet he will find that in business, it is money, not blood, which speaks louder.'

'Perhaps . . .' He bade Mostyn a pleasant 'good-night', adding his fervent hope that his brother would sleep soundly and in comfort. Mostyn departed frigidly to his carriage.

Upon the morrow, the contract with the Nevills signed, Carne, Charles and Peter Morrish returned in triumph to Penavon. Yet one grave worry remained. There would be need of an infusion of new capital to purchase waggons and barges for haulage and extra men to be employed. Yet all the shareholders were already fully committed and could be expected to invest no more.

Randall Walters awaited their return anxiously, plump face unusually grave and displaying no apparent excitement, even at the news of their success. 'You have money to finance these new ventures?' he asked brusquely.

'No,' Charles confessed, 'and I admit I have little hope of immediately doing so. All who have invested with us are fully committed and the Litchard-Llewellyn company have their own bankers and financiers firmly in their grasp.'

'Not all,' declared Walters, straight-faced. 'I took the liberty, in your absence, of sending a messenger to London to put a certain proposition to an independent banker of impeccable family and credentials – a gentleman who has the rare honour to be my elder brother.' He very deliberately took out a snuff box and, setting a pinch upon the back of his hand, sneezed eloquently.

'And?' prompted Charles, impatient at his slowness.

'He is pleased to oblige . . . upon my surety as guarantor!' Walters' delight at having sealed the bargain was as great, if not as vociferous, as that of the other three.

'You are a dark horse, sir! A saint! A veritable genius!' Carne cried, waltzing the portly gentleman around exuberantly.

'I try my modest best, sir,' declared Walters amidst merriment, as he puffed and gasped at his unaccustomed exertions, 'although I freely confess to having no great talent for waltzing.'

It had been a lasting pleasure to Peter Morrish to renew his family ties with the Nevills and he had seized as eagerly upon the opportunity also to visit his cousins at Llanelli. He had been as well received by them, for he was a generous-hearted man, intelligent, and without affectation. Carne and Charles knew, in securing this newest contract to supply the copperworks with anthracite, how much was owed to Peter and the affection in which he was held. To have offered him financial reward would have offended and belittled him, so, instead, Charles and Carne made Sara an outright birthday gift of some of their own shares in the company. She received them with the good grace and generosity with which they had been offered and Peter was delighted that they gave her security and financial independence.

In December of that year, to add to their unprecedented good fortune, Saranne gave birth to a daughter, whom Peter christened in the parish church at Penavon with the names Henrietta Rhianon Sara. During the service, her godfather, Charles Hartrey, holding her with awkward tenderness at the font, and feeling the living warmth of her through the cobweb-fine shawl which Megan had knitted, faltered in his responses. Saranne, seeing the shine of tears softening her brother's eyes, shared his ache of grief and regret, and his tentative joy at this new life's beginning. Had she done right, she wondered, in christening the child Henrietta? It had been at Charles's wish, but was it fair to burden the child with the name and memory of one dead and deeply mourned? Would this new Henrietta be a constant reminder to Charles of what was lost to him? The answer was in the gentleness with which he held the babe, cradling her to him with a special tenderness. Charles loved Eynon deeply, and treated the boy as affectionately as if he were his own son. Yet, between Henrietta and Charles there was always a special closeness; a rare, instinctive understanding which others envied and respected.

Carne, too, felt a strangely protective love for this, his daughter, named as solace for another, and to honour his own, long-dead mother, and also Sara, mother to Saranne in all but flesh. Was it from Havard blood her colouring and features sprang, or from some unknown forebear of Saranne's? Henrietta's pale-skinned delicacy and fairness were favourably remarked upon by all. She was exquisite; an enchanting child. How strange and ironic, Carne thought, that his daughter should so closely favour Mostyn. It was as if his brother's beguiling charm, irresistible, golden, had been born anew.

It was upon the afternoon of Henrietta's christening that the first real dangers which the drift mines might bring stirred Penavon. Carne had taken the gig and driven himself to the waggonway to inspect some new horses which Joe Benjamin, his farrier, had bought. As he drove, he passed by the men, women and children, black faced and weary, shuffling their way along Penavon Highway and those byways which led to their newly built dwellings and the newcomers' camp. The men touched their forelocks and murmured greeting, the women dropped swift curtseys, and even the infants, half asleep with tiredness and balanced perilously upon their fathers' shoulders, were coaxed or roughly jolted into acknowledgement of the mine-owner. It was a strange, subdued little procession, yet he felt a coldness within him that owed nothing to the wintry day. Their bowed heads and weariness reminded him of those other men, women and children chained and enslaved. It was but a foolish notion, he knew, and he must dismiss it from memory. These were a free people, fed, clothed and housed from the bounty of the Hartrey-Havard company. Their faces, behind the masks of coal grime, surely reflected the words of gratitude they spoke, not defeat and sullen suspicion? Yet the unease remained. Some of those infants looked barely older than Eynon, his son.

In greeting his farrier and the dealer and inspecting the fine horseflesh, Carne's mood of depression vanished. All about them waited a patient, gently curious crowd, little different from those he had seen returning upon the way, save for cleaned faces above their tattered clothes. The men carried the spades which they provided and the candles they supplied for themselves and their air-door lads, and the women who pulled the sledges and trams of coal held ready their harnesses and chains. They, too, had greeted him gravely and with respect, but the childrens' eyes were for the horses and his own pretty carriage and mare. Why did they not enter the mine? Carne wondered. What held them back?

The children were pointing and chatting excitedly. He turned and saw the strange grotesque figure approaching, and heard the cry of 'The Penitent is here! Ready and waiting!' Indeed, by the fellow's filthy rags and pathetic state, he might well have been clad in sackcloth and ashes and seeking to expiate some long-carried burden of sin. His garments dripped water and in his hand he held a lighted candle strapped to a wooden pole, to thrust into the far corners and roof of the mine, to make sure that there were no traces of the dreaded methane gas. A naked light could swiftly ignite it and envelop those who worked there, unsuspecting, in a sheet of searing, destructive flame. The man was, Carne reflected, less 'penitent' than human scapegoat, his life held forfeit for those riches below earth, and those who laboured to release them. Once inside, he would wriggle upon his belly through the darkened mine, thrusting his makeshift light into tunnels too narrow to enter, or towards the roof of coal where the methane rose and hovered.

Engrossed, all too soon, in conversation with the horse-dealer, Carne was, at first, startled by a fierce cry, then a screaming, so piteous that it chilled his blood. He turned to see, to his horror, the Penitent, a moving sheet of flame, his screams of anguish freezing those surrounding him to helplessness. For a long moment, Carne too was unable to move, made impotent by shock and disbelief. Then, instinctively, without thought, he tore off his cloak and, running forward, wrapped it despairingly around the blazing man, hurling him to the earth, rolling him, trying to beat out the flames with his bare hands. Others joined him in his efforts but he was as unaware of them as of the seared flesh of his hands. He saw only the man's own flesh, as black as the remains of the cloak which had covered him, and hanging in charred folds of skin to reveal the raw flesh beneath. The man's face was a hideously distorted mask, skin shrunken and seared, his eyes a whiteness in the swollen flesh and naked skull. The farrier ran forward, covering the disfigured body with his coat, urging those crowding and jostling about him to stand clear.

The man no longer moaned but women and children in the crowd wept helplessly for him, and for themselves. The sickness of gall burned in Carne's throat and he had scarce been able to form the words needed to order Joe Benjamin to lift the poor creature into the gig as gently as they were able.

'I will drive him, at once, to Dr Tobin's house.'

The crowd parted, awkward and confused, clearing a pathway. Benjamin lifted the shrouded figure as effortlessly as a babe and carried him gently to the gig.

'I will take the reins,' Carne said as he made to clamber up and take his place upon the gig, but Benjamin's hand fell, vice like, upon his arm, halting him.

'You had best return to your home, sir.' The farrier's voice was flat, expressionless. 'I will do what needs to be done.'

'He is dead then?' Carne demanded stupidly.

'Aye, and thank God for it.'

Carne watched in silence as Benjamin drove off, then turned to see Jack Hollis beside him, thin face raw with hurt. 'The victim, Jack, who is he? There are those who must be told.'

'A pauper, like me, come to make his living . . .' There was no conscious irony in the words, no condemnation in his voice, as he added, 'He had neither kith nor kin.'

'You had best send the colliers home . . . and the women and children with them.'

'No.' Hollis's voice was steady. 'He has done what was required. The mine is cleared of danger. It is better not, else they will feel fear to enter, do you see? It is kinder, in the end, that they conquer their fear at once.'

Carne looked at him long and hard, then nodded, saying, 'You must do what you think to be best.'

'There will be many such as he.' It was a simple statement of fact. 'It is what he was paid to do, Mr Havard, sir. He knew the risks to be taken.'

Already an overseer was at the mouth of the drift mine and entering first.

The men, women and children followed dutifully, and without complaint. None hesitated, none turned back. Sighing, Carne touched Jack Hollis's arm, only to cry out involuntarily at the pain of his blistered palms, biting upon his lips, then making shamed apology.

'I will take you home in the waggon,' Hollis said, 'for

you will not be able to take the reins of a horse. You will need treatment for the burnt flesh upon your hands.' Hollis's voice was brisk. 'You had best guide me to where the physician lives.'

'No,' said Carne dully. 'We will go home to my daughter's celebrations, as planned. Saranne has made an ointment from an old receipt given her by a friend who died some years ago by violence – a wise woman, whom she befriended and loved.'

Chapter Forty-seven

Henrietta's christening party, which Saranne, Sara and
Megan had planned with such eager excitement, had been
harshly overshadowed by the savagery of the Penitent's
death. Saranne, shocked by Carne's pallor and the severity
of the burns which blistered his palms, had been, at first,
too distraught to help him. So confused and useless did she
become that it was Sara who took command, fearful that
there would be not one but two invalids in need of treatment.

Charles had been as grieved as Carne by the accident at
the mine. The horrific burning alive of one of their own
men was as vivid an image in his own mind as if he had
been there. He saw him, a human torch, heard his screams,
saw his charred and blackened flesh, and was sickened
and filled with guilt. Meeting Carne's anguished eyes, as
Saranne gently spread the unguent upon his raw-
skinned palms, Charles knew that the pain Carne felt was
deeper than that of his physical wounds. In truth, Carne
welcomed the pain, for it gave him brief respite from that
which haunted him.

Peter Morrish, seeing Carne's lowered head and his eyes
so fiercely closed, stood beside him briefly and put a firmly
comforting hand to his shoulder. 'I will go and see what
can be done . . . what help or kindness I can render, for
there will be many in need of sympathy.'

'And I will ride with you, if you will have me,' Charles
said quietly. 'It is fitting that I am there to take responsibility.'

Carne looked up to say dully, 'No blame attaches to you, Charles. Your work is with the financing of the mine. The men are in my care. It is my failure. No other is at fault.' His eyes were bleak.

Peter Morrish, aware that shock and self-recrimination had forced him to desperation, halted, and would have murmured solace. But it was Randall Walters who spoke, his dry legal tones clipped and abrasive, 'No, Carne! To blame yourself so is puerile; a foolish self-indulgence! It helps no-one!' There was a moment of shocked silence before Walters continued with a confidence which allowed no argument, 'It was an accident . . . terrifying and tragic, but an accident nonetheless. The fault lay neither in you nor the victim. It was an Act of God.'

'Of the devil, more like!' Carne could not hide his bitterness.

'If you prefer . . . it is all the same in the end.' Walters dismissed Peter Morrish's startled protest with a querulous wave of the hand before demanding brusquely, 'Well, Carne? Have you the necessary arrogance to usurp God's authority, or the urge to play devil's advocate?'

'No!' He had been shocked into involuntary denial.

'Good.' Walters permitted himself a wintry smile. 'I confess it is a role all too often thrust unwittingly upon me.'

He was rewarded with a reluctant smile from Carne and a lessening of tension in those who listened, half fearful that his acerbity might give added hurt. 'There is none who would lay blame upon you, Carne. The colliers respect you as an honest man who has brought work where there was idleness. They know the risks and take them willingly. It is a lesser evil than seeing their children starve. If you are culpable, then so am I . . . as are Charles, Peter Morrish . . .' Walters' gaze turned towards Jack Hollis who stood awkwardly ill-at-ease in the doorway, as he added firmly, 'Yes, and all others involved. It is a burden and guilt we all must share, whether you allow it or not.'

There was a tense silence before Hollis, mindful of the fatigue and pain etched into Carne's face, claimed regretfully that he must needs return at once to the drift mine.

'Then I shall be pleased to take you in my carriage,' Walters offered, 'for I shall be grateful for your company, if you will allow it?'

Hollis nodded, undeceived, as Carne unexpectedly hurried forward to say to the attorney with quiet honesty, 'I thank you for treating me with compassion today . . . for taking my responsibility upon yourself, sharing my hurt, as so often before.'

The portly attorney beamed affably as he set an arm to Jack Hollis's elbow to guide him without. At the doorway, he paused to exclaim penitently, a hand pressed hard to his forehead, 'Oh, Carne. What an absent-minded old fool I am. I had almost forgot, for it was driven from my mind by all else.'

Carne waited, bewildered, for enlightenment.

Walters' hand had strayed to his pocket from which he produced a small package, sealed in a manilla envelope. 'A gift for Henrietta, for this is a good time to redeem all debts and pledges, as you declared,' he said, thrusting it towards Carne, whose stiffly bandaged hands precluded him from taking it.

'Damnation! I am a fool and a cretin!' exclaimed the attorney remorsefully, turning to give it into Saranne's keeping.

'A gift for Henrietta?' she chided. 'But you have already made her a generous one.'

'A gift from another, whose love reaches out from the past.' The attorney turned abruptly upon his heel and left, with no more said, shepherding a puzzled Jack Hollis before him.

Saranne broke the wax seal upon the envelope and opened the tooled leather box contained within. The sight of the exquisite gold and opal necklace rendered her silent, save for an indrawn breath of admiration at the sheer unexpectedness of its beauty.

'Jane's necklace! She bade me give it first to you,

Saranne, and thence to our daughter, should one be born,' said Carne.

Sara, hearing the emotion which affected his voice, and knowing the strain he had suffered, quietly escaped the room, leaving Carne and Saranne unmindful of her going.

'I cannot fasten it at your throat, Saranne,' Carne said, 'and that is what I would dearly wish to do. But I beg that you will wear it with the love and pride Jane knew in its possession.'

No. It is too valuable a thing . . . too ornate and precious for the life I lead, Saranne wanted to cry out, but knew that if she did, it would grieve Carne too deeply.

'Yes, I will wear it, my dear, and as proudly as Jane,' she promised, stepping before the fire to gaze into the pier glass above the chimney piece, that she might see it securely fastened.

In the firelight, with its leaping flames, memory of the Penitent returned harshly to wound him. Yet, as surely as if Jane stood beside him, he felt her strength and loving nearness, and, like the child of old, he took comfort.

The horrifying death of the Penitent had taught Carne a harsh and salutary lesson. With increased power came increased responsibility. Those in his employ, he now knew, were deserving of the same protection, the same concern, as Saranne, Eynon and Henrietta, for they were as dependent upon him for their future and their daily bread.

To its credit, the Hartrey-Havard Mining Company lost no time in appointing an experienced mining engineer, Edward Levis, to advise them upon all aspects of safety in the mines. Draining and ventilation had proved a lesser problem in the old open bell-mines and shallow drifts, but now the company was driving new roadways deep into the heart of the mountains where airlessness and seeped water were proving a hazard to those who toiled in the damp, stifling atmosphere.

At Levis's suggestion, pit-props were brought in as roof

558

supports, and, wherever practicable, wooden 'flooring' boards were laid, with a small drainage sough beneath, to run off water, to draw in fresh air and return the stale air through the upper part of the drift.

There was little to be done about the presence of methane gas, Levis declared, save to test frequently. Like marsh gas, it was naturally formed, a product of vegetable decay which sought escape from the soil. A careless spark from a pick-thrust or a naked candle flame could spread the flash-fire in an instant, like 'wildfire' as the scourge became known.

Those working in mines must learn to endure flash burns as an unavoidable hazard. Such injuries must be judged an acceptable risk, as the danger of asphyxiation from roof collapse or loss of limb, even death, through stumbling beneath the wheels of a tram. It was the price demanded for the extraction of coal.

Carne felt the attitude to be callous and defeatist, although he knew that Levis spoke honestly and from bitter experience. Carne pleaded with the shareholders of the company to be allowed to provide tramlines and waggons below ground, with pit ponies to drag them, or access in the narrower passageways where only the younger, smaller children could now work the cramped seams.

Peter Morrish supported Carne staunchly but Charles, Randall Walters and all the other shareholders asserted that the money was simply not available to implement it. The contract between the Litchard-Llewellyn Mining Company and the Merthyr ironmasters was to be offered for renewal. In order to compete, existing costs must be cut and no new expenditure embarked upon. Without this contract, Charles declared unequivocally, many in their workforce would face redundancy and some of their mines would be forced to close.

Levis, aware of the harsh need for economy, suggested that the timbermen who provided and rammed home the wooden pit-stays, should work by night, and, with them, the rippers who hewed away the roofs of the passageways to make space for the waggons to be dragged through by the women and young hauliers. Thus, no time would be lost before the colliers and those who loaded and dragged the coal to the surface could begin their daytime labours.

This proposal was voted upon and passed, with Carne's and Morrish's the only dissentient votes. It was also proposed by Charles that Edward Levis be given permanent appointment as Chief Mining Engineer and also Safety Engineer, to the Hartrey-Havard Mining Company. With this, Carne and Morrish were in full accord.

The meeting had been held at Holly Grove Farm and, as Carne made ready to drive Morrish back to Penavon in the gig, Levis came hesitantly from within to stand beside them and say earnestly, 'I would have you believe, Mr Havard, that my concern for those who labour in the mines is as honest and deep-felt as Mr Morrish's and your own.'

Carne murmured acknowledgement.

'In theory, sir,' Levis blurted awkwardly, 'the use of a penitent is an obscenity. It degrades and cheapens human life. Yet, the death or suffering of one may save the lives of many who are forced to labour below.'

Carne nodded curtly. He would have stirred up the horses had Levis not taken stubborn hold on the reins, continuing with conviction, 'In theory, sir, no man, woman or child should labour in darkness beneath the earth, chained and used like a beast of burden. They do. That is the reality of it.' His honest young face still flushed with earnestness, he let fall the reins, murmuring more quietly, 'I believe that yours is a good company, with the interests of your workers at heart. That is why I accepted your offer.' He walked away, stiff in his dignity.

Carne, shamed by his own gracelessness, called out impulsively, 'Mr Levis!'

'Sir?'

'I am grateful that you accepted. We work to the same end, to make things better.'

Levis nodded. Peter Morrish thought pityingly, Carne's burden is as crippling as those who toil underground. He

560

must weigh compassion against survival; guilt against success. He will anguish and bleed. He will believe himself slave-master and deliverer; devil and saint. He will never resolve the conflict within himself.

'Levis will be an asset to the company.' Carne's eyes were firmly upon the road ahead.

'Yes,' agreed Morrish. 'He will do what has to be done.'

Several months later, the shareholders of the Hartrey-Havard Mining Company were formally notified that they had secured the contract to supply coal to the Merthyr Ironworks for a period of two years. There was excitement and celebration among the workforce and, understandably, elation among the employers. That week, every collier received an extra five shillings in his wages, every ancillary worker and craftsman, four shillings; every woman and girl, a florin, and every child, even the girls who carried the colliers' tools and the air-door boys, a sixpence. If some, like Peter Morrish, counted the contract a mixed blessing, then they did not voice their reservations. It would have been churlish to cloud the celebrations and optimism of so many.

A week later, the grateful Hartrey-Havard Company provided a fête with dancing and refreshments for all upon the village green and a half-day's holiday with payment. Saranne and Sara, Megan, Mrs Hodges and the children were there, admiring and admired, as were the officials and overmen and everyone employed in the mines, from the greatest to the least.

Dr Tobin, deep in conversation with an elegantly attired Edward Levis, glanced up to see Charles Hartrey paying court to his infant niece, Henrietta. The pretty child, held in her mother's arms, was flirting with him with quite flagrant disregard for reticence. Hartrey appeared relaxed and happy, a sturdy, impressive figure with his fresh complexion and handsome head of copper-coloured hair. Charles, as if aware of Tobin's scrutiny, glanced up, and made both men a courteous bow. His manner to all was

561

charming and ostensibly relaxed, yet Tobin's trained eye was aware of a restlessness in the young mine owner, an energy damped down and firmly held in check. It was the loss of Henrietta Danfield which drove him so remorselessly, Tobin thought with pity. He would not let her go.

On the other side of the green, Sara Morrish had taken her husband's arm, saying pensively, 'It has been a good day, Peter, has it not? The colliers and their families have enjoyed it?'

She regarded him, he saw, with more intensity than the simple question deserved. 'Yes, my dear. It is a pleasure they will long remember.' His gaze, almost against his will, had settled upon a child of some four or five years of age, a sweetmeat clutched firm in his hand. The child's palms were raw-skinned with burns, as from a rope, and his eyelashes drooped heavily above the dark eyes, despite all his efforts to stay awake. His father bent low towards him and nodded at some murmured request, then raised the child high upon his shoulders. The man's face, although young and handsome, bore the mark of a blue scar, coal seared indelibly beneath the skin, and the child's face, although scrubbed to shining redness, still bore traces of the ingrained coal dust that veiled the pores of his flesh. The child's grip upon his father's forehead relaxed almost imperceptibly as fatigue slumped him forward into sleep, his sweetmeat falling unnoticed to the ground. Peter Morrish hurried forward to retrieve it and set it into the father's hands. The man thanked him civilly before pocketing it, awkwardly swinging the child from his shoulders and holding him, still sleeping, within his arms.

'It has been too fierce an enjoyment for him sir,' the young collier made awkward apology, 'the music, and holiday, and all . . .'

Peter Morrish nodded his understanding.

"'Tis three miles and more to the mine, sir, for we are settled near Golden Grove. We must leave at five o' the clock each morning, for it is a long walk, and we do not reach home until dark. But it has been a bright and shining day, and one he will long remember.'

'Yes . . . a bright and shining day,' said the curate, glancing down at the sleeping child's lips, gently parted, eyelids blue-veined as the bruised shadows surrounding them.

Sara had started forward to join them, but a fierce hail of cries and shouts and the marching of heavily booted feet upon the highway halted her. She stared in horrified dismay at the gaggle of colliers who had paused now at the edges of the green, their faces blackened by coal dust, only their eyes and the soft pinkness of lips and underlips showing bright. Their shovels and picks were gripped hard in their fists and there was no doubting that they came in anger and to provoke violence.

Dear God, she thought despairingly, it is the men from the Litchard-Llewellyn mines, come to revenge themselves. There will be bloodshed for certain. Her eyes went instinctively to Saranne who was standing, pale faced, clutching Henrietta more fiercely to her, and with Eynon holding, terrified, to her skirts. Even as she watched, Megan ran forward and gathered him to her, clutching him protectively; Peter, she thought despairingly, where is Peter? In her anxiety for the children, she had lost sight of him and he was nowhere to be seen. When, at last, she glimpsed him, her relief gave way to terror, for he was facing the band of noisy interlopers alone. There was a terrible coldness within her and she would have run to him, or called out his name, but in her anguish she could neither move nor make a sound.

Morrish's voice rang out clear, 'You are welcome to join with us, John Barnet, as are all who come here in friendship to share with others of their kind. There is food enough for all.' He addressed the ringleader by name, and every other man among that poor company, recognising and giving each his hand in greeting, unmindful of the grime of coal dust upon theirs. There was a confused shuffling of boots, then a shamed silence, as they glanced at each other with unease, seeking some lead as to how best to respond. Those upon the green were frozen into silence, the children bewildered, the womenfolk shocked and fearful, the men tensing themselves to defend their families and themselves.

There was a muted, indeterminate argument among the intruders, then the strident tones of one who would have spurred them to violence, but his bluster faltered and died away, unsupported. They stood there, awkward and unsure, eyes downcast. It would have needed the merest sign of triumph or animosity from those upon the green, Peter Morrish knew, to once again inflame their anger. He sought, despairingly, for some way to make them feel accepted and to ease their humiliation before the many who had witnessed it. Even as he pondered, Eynon came stumbling unsteadily across the green, with Saranne, her head held high, clutching little Henrietta in her arms. All eyes were upon the boy as he tottered determinedly to Peter Morrish's side, his childish face set hard with concentration. With a sigh, he clutched the curate's hand, steadying himself and beaming triumphantly for the sheer joy of achievement. Then he half ran, half stumbled to John Barnet's side, looking up into the blackened face and laughing with unaffected joy at this strange, wondrous spectacle. Then, clasping the handle of John Barnet's coal-grimed spade, he drew him urgently into the waiting crowd as Saranne held out a hand to welcome and greet each of the colliers.

Carne, who had stood transfixed with apprehension beside Charles as the impromptu pageant was enacted, gave a groan of relief and ran forward to pick up his son. Megan, who had released Eynon unwillingly upon Saranne's fierce instruction, felt the knot of tautness in her chest dissolving. Sara made to move to be with Peter, who was talking kindly and cheerfully to the newcomers, guiding them towards Mrs Hodges who stood nearby, waiting beside her home-baked victuals, plump face wreathed in proud smiles. Peter looked up and glanced towards his wife, and nodded almost imperceptibly. She, in turn, smiled and nodded back, eyes bright. They had travelled beyond the need for words.

564

Chapter Forty-eight

Rhys Llewellyn was not best pleased by the loss of his company's lucrative contract with the Merthyr Ironworks. Apart from the financial loss, there was the deeper blow to his personal prestige and that of the company. Someone had blundered in not being aware of the challenge from the Hartrey-Havard company and the precise details of their bid. It had happened too often of late. He had been made to look a laughing stock before his shareholders, and even those who laboured in the mines. Arrogance and self-confidence were the necessary qualities of any successful entrepreneur and Rhys Llewellyn, who was lacking in neither, looked for a convenient scapegoat to blame for his defeat. Mostyn received the full brunt of his displeasure.

'I cannot understand, Mostyn, why you allowed such a fiasco to occur!' he fumed.

'I, sir?' Mostyn's tone was cold.

'Certainly! Who else? It was your responsibility entirely.' As Mostyn made to protest, Llewellyn continued furiously, 'I am the chairman and managing director of this company, sir. I delegate such particulars to others . . . those whom I deem to be reliable. I am disappointed in you, sir! Bitterly disappointed!'

'I cannot be held accountable for the wiles of others. It is not my affair,' countered Mostyn stiffly.

'Not your affair? Not your affair, you say? Of course it is your affair, sir! I hold you responsible for the day-to-day running of the company, a task you seem singularly unfitted to undertake. I fear, Mostyn, that you have grown too

565

sanguine. You dissipate your energies upon drink and spurious chit-chat, instead of setting your mind to the business involved.'

'I did not have full knowledge of Carne's bid,' he muttered sullenly.

'Did not? Then it was your business to have probed and questioned, paid for such evidence, if need be.' He regarded Mostyn with distaste. 'Was it simply arrogance or some deeper personal motive which drove you? It has certainly cost us dear.'

'I am not my brother's keeper!'

'No, I am well aware of the fact! It seems you are quite incapable of managing your own affairs, much less those of your rivals, or the company which keeps you in luxury,' Llewellyn declared contemptuously.

'I will not stand whipping-boy for you, sir!' muttered Mostyn with ill-suppressed anger.

'Will you not, sir?' Llewellyn's voice was deceptively mild. 'Then perhaps you had best resign before it is forced upon you by circumstances. I warn you, Mostyn, that I will brook no more of your idleness and arrogance. This is my company. Litchard's influence is all but ended, and Danfield relies totally upon my advice.'

Mostyn had turned insultingly upon his heel and would have made scornful escape had not Llewellyn's fury halted him.

'Damn your insolence, Mostyn! Will you not learn?' He grasped Mostyn's shoulder and twisted him around fiercely, so that they were angrily face to face. 'All that you are is owed to me! I have made you, and can break you, you understand? One word . . . one word . . . that is all that is needed.'

Llewellyn's face was suffused with colour. A vein pulsed hard at his temple and his eyes were reddened and engorged as he strove to gain control of himself. Mostyn stared superciliously at the saliva flecking the corners of his father-in-law's mouth, then, with no attempt to conceal his amusement, calmly unloosed Llewellyn's fingers from their grasp

566

upon his coat. His voice was languid, bored even.

'I feel, sir, that your own inadequacy has marred your judgement. If I have made my own fortune, then I have made yours too, and those of the investors. Were it to come to a struggle for ascendancy, then I would be confident of matching my powers of persuasion against your own.'

As Llewellyn strove for reply, Mostyn conceded smoothly, 'But it will not come to a battle. We are realists. Our forces are better combined than wasted in conflict. Do you not agree?'

Llewellyn nodded mutely, shamefacedly wiping the wetness from his lips.

'We work towards the same end,' insisted Mostyn, 'to secure a prosperous company for Adam to inherit. That binds us more firmly than petty disagreement. Small setbacks there must inevitably be. A contract lost is of little lasting account. It will serve to spur us all to greater effort in future.'

It was not an apology, Llewellyn knew, but he took the hand which Mostyn extended to him nonetheless. Better an uneasy truce, he thought, than a Pyrrhic victory. Despite his blustering threats, Llewellyn was painfully aware that Mostyn had, indeed, made himself indispensable. 'Yes. It is to Adam's future we must look,' he agreed, swallowing his humiliation.

'Indeed, sir,' Mostyn could afford to be magnanimous. He saw a way both to redeem himself in Llewellyn's eyes, and to punish Carne for his temerity. That would give him every whit as much satisfaction as claiming the Litchard-Llewellyn Company for his own, Mostyn reflected smugly. Then, as an afterthought, and, of course, for Adam's sake too.

Mostyn drove at once to Thatched Cottage in the cabriolet, still seething inwardly at Llewellyn's scathing contempt for his failure. He knew though that, in reality, he had won the argument. He had proved himself indispensable, both to Llewellyn and to the Litchard-Llewellyn Company, and yet bitterness rankled. The triumph he should have felt was subdued by the certainty that Llewellyn, whom he had always admired, despised him. They were enemies now, in business as well as in their private concerns.

Saranne greeted Mostyn with that superficial courtesy which she had learnt to show him for Laurel's and Carne's sakes, and accompanied him to Carne's small study, leaving the brothers together. It was a relief to escape Mostyn's presence, and she returned with renewed enthusiasm to romp with Eynon and Henrietta in the nursery under Megan's indulgent rule.

Mostyn's congratulations to Carne were fulsome, his smile warm and free of malice. 'A small skirmish in the battle, Carne . . . and easily reversed. I warn you, the war goes on.'

'Then I had best prepare myself.'

They laughed companionably, awkwardness averted, each glad to be at ease in the other's company.

They engaged in desultory conversation for a while, before the real purpose of Mostyn's visit became clear.

'That useless plot of land, in some backwater, which Jane Prys was absurd enough to leave you . . .'

Carne, who had been pouring two glasses of Canary wine, delivered one into Mostyn's hand and regarded him quizzically. 'How can it be of interest to you?'

'It once belonged to Great House . . . a Havard property, in grandmother's gift.'

'Indeed. That is how Jane inherited it.' Carne waited in silence for explanation but Mostyn seemed ill-inclined to speak, fidgeting nervously, studying the rim of his glass with concentration.

'I am thinking of restoring the Havard estate,' Mostyn blurted at length, 'repurchasing those properties sold at father's death.'

'Your reverence for our inheritance, and the past, does you credit. I would not have suspected such . . . romanticism.' Carne's face was expressionless.

'Then you will sell it?' Mostyn asked stiffly.

'No.'

'Sell it, and you may name your own price,' Mostyn persists more vehemently, colour flaring beneath his skin.

'No. I have answered you. I will not sell it!'

'Then lease it to me! You have no use for it. It is an arid, worthless plot.' Mostyn strove to calm and ingratiate himself. 'I swear that Jane's poor ruin of a house shall remain upon it, untouched, if that is your objection. You have my word upon it.'

'Have I your word that it is sentiment alone which drives you? Reverence for times and people past?'

Mostyn, smarting at the irony in Carne's voice, hesitated before turning upon him in furious attack. 'Damn you, Carne! You are a selfish swine! Unfeeling! It is jealousy that holds you back, envy that it is I who own Great House, not you. Jane's hovel means nothing to you. Admit it! It is spite alone which impels you!'

'I fear, Mostyn, that I am no longer in a position to offer you the cottage, or the land,' declared Carne equably.

'Not?' Mostyn's expression was a comical mixture of incredulity and dismay. 'Why not, in God's name? Who else would offer for a mean little hovel, and such useless soil?'

'The Hartrey-Havard Mining Company.' Carne's face was blandly inscrutable. 'The deeds are already transferred and in their keeping. Had you come but an hour earlier, then you would have met our attorney, Randall Walters, and the signatories.'

Mostyn's mouth was slack with disbelief, his skin so drained of colour that Carne felt pity rise in him against his will. He watched his brother's hand grip so tightly at his glass that his knuckles gleamed white and he feared that it would shatter within Mostyn's palm. Carne turned awkwardly away, pretending absorption with some trivial task upon the desk, unwilling to be witness to such discomfiture. He felt no triumph, only a sadness of hurt, as of old.

569

'Why?' Mostyn's voice was harsh, querulous. 'Why have they bought it? It is of no use to them. They have no claim upon it! It is Havard land!'

'And a Havard has control of it still.'

'To what end?'

'You are not a fool, Mostyn. This charade need continue no longer. You are as aware of its value as I. It is the land needed to link with the drift mine we have already driven into the other face of the mountain. It will give us one common base, help us to expand, cut costs and risks in the mining.' He paused. 'But I need waste no time and effort in explaining it to you. Was it not your own hope to secure Jane's land and use it to the same purpose, as a link to your own drift, on the far side of the valley?'

Mostyn replaced his glass upon the desk and looked at Carne wryly as he said, 'You have learnt your lesson well, Carne. I congratulate you, brother.'

'As I congratulate my teacher.'

They stared at each other for a long moment in silence, Mostyn, possessed with sick rage and disgust at his failure, Carne, unwilling to further humiliate him. Then, for a fleeting second, Carne believed that he saw amusement upon his brother's face, a reluctant softening and warmth in his manner. Mostyn had actually moved forward, hand hesitantly outstretched, as if fearful of a rebuff, but at the sharp knocking upon the door of the study, his hand dropped uselessly to his side.

'I have brought Eynon and Henrietta to bid good-bye to you, Carne, for they were insistent upon doing so before leaving to spend an hour with Peter and Mama.'

Henrietta had stretched out her arms, not to Carne, but to Mostyn, crowing and chuckling, demanding to be fussed and cosseted. It was with reluctance that Saranne delivered her daughter into his arms, and only then after a sharply puzzled glance from Carne. Mostyn first adjusted his cuffs fastidiously, clearly apprehensive and ill-at-ease, but soon they were regarding each other delightedly, with Henrietta reaching out a chubbily dimpled hand to caress his face and murmur endearments in a language of her own.

'You see?' cried Mostyn, with genuine pleasure. 'Henrietta recognises me as a kinsman. She feels the bond between us. Are we not a handsome couple?'

Saranne could not reply for the resentment constricting her throat. That they did, indeed, make a handsome couple was undeniable, as was the vivid, startling resemblance between them. But for Henrietta's lustrous violet-coloured eyes, so like Saranne's own, they might have been father and daughter.

'You are the handsomest couple in Penavon and beyond,' declared Carne, struggling to suppress his laughter as Henrietta clutched so fiercely at Mostyn's hair that the tears spurted to his eyes and he was forced to unclench the tiny fist, which he did patiently and with smiling good nature.

'I fear,' he drawled, amused, 'that like many a young gentlewoman before her, and many another not so well born, she can scarce keep her hands from caressing me.' His eyes above Henrietta's prettily tumbled curls met Saranne's rigid gaze, his own challenging and filled with malicious amusement. 'You see, Saranne,' he observed conversationally, 'Henrietta is a young lady of exquisite taste and discernment, who finds my charms quite irresistible.'

Saranne all but snatched her daughter from his arms, making Henrietta cry aloud in distress at the brusqueness of her handling, and from sheer frustration.

The look Carne gave Saranne was one of bewilderment, turning to condemnation as he asked his son, in an effort to ease the abrasiveness of the exchange, 'Eynon. Will you not pay your respects to your Uncle Mostyn?'

Eynon, a sturdy replica of Carne, came forward obediently to make a bow and a greeting. He was quite remarkably assured and self-possessed, regarding Mostyn with interest and curiosity.

'Well, and do I meet with your approval, sir?' asked Mostyn, light heartedly.

'Adam says you are a devil, Uncle . . . but you are really

571

quite ordinary. Is he not, Papa? He has no horns . . . none at all!'

The childish remarks, so innocently blurted, caused Carne to stare at him in dismay, and even Saranne looked embarrassed and confused. Eynon, seeing, but not understanding, the awkwardness his words had caused, looked apprehensive and close to tears. It was Mostyn who saved the situation, his laughter ringing out, appreciative and free, as he lifted Eynon and whirled him around, dizzied and delighted, before setting him safely down. 'No, I have no horns, nephew,' he said, uncontrolled laughter thickening his voice still. 'I am sorry indeed to disappoint you . . . but devils come in the most innocent forms, do they not, Saranne? That is their power.' He turned again to Eynon. 'Perhaps,' he suggested with a smile, 'I have a forked tail and am keeping it well hid.'

Eynon looked at him assessingly, biting his lip in concentration, before declaring solemnly, 'Not by the cut of your breeches, sir.'

'Now, there, sir,' said Mostyn to Carne amidst general laughter, 'you have the makings of a wit and a dandy, and an honest observer.'

Saranne merely smiled and took the opportunity to shepherd the children gently without.

'Is Uncle Mostyn really and truly a devil, Mama, as cousin Adam swears?'

'What an idea!' chided Saranne, cleverly putting an end to his speculation.

Despite Mostyn's leaving Thatched Cottage in good humour, by the time he returned to Great House, the old resentment and sense of injustice had resurfaced to lay his feelings raw.

Adam had, of late, learnt to dread his father's coming, for the anger he unwittingly aroused in him, and for the hurt caused to his mother. He was a sensitive, intelligent boy, protective towards Henrietta as to all small, dependent creatures. That morning, upon his walk, he had chanced

572

upon a wounded bird and had carried it home tenderly, despite his nurse's protestations, and had cared for it until it died. His nurse had summoned a servant to see that it was decently disposed of and was attempting to comfort Adam when Mostyn returned.

Adam wept so fiercely in making explanation that Mostyn took him viciously to task, berating him for such girlish weakness and calling him a milksop and a fool. There was venom and spite in Mostyn which owed nothing to what had occurred, and Adam was its victim. Yet, surprisingly, the boy faced up to Mostyn calmly, his tears undried upon his cheeks, to declare with spirit, 'I loved him, Papa. He had done no-one any hurt.'

'That is not the point, Adam! Such grief is a weakness, excessive, and to be deplored. Worse, it is effeminate!'

As Adam made no reply, he declared pettishly, irritation rising, 'It was naught but a common bird, a creature without value or feelings, and of no account! You make yourself foolish before others, a laughing stock!'

Laurel had come into the nursery and schoolroom unobserved, to see the antagonists facing each other warily, then to hear Mostyn repeat scornfully, 'A laughing stock! Does not that shame and humiliate you?'

'No, Papa.' There was no insolence in Adam's reply, only honesty. 'They may laugh at me, if they choose. It makes no matter.' He looked at Mostyn in genuine puzzlement to ask ingenuously, 'Why is it right, Papa, for people to laugh at me, but wrong for me to cry for a dead bird? Is it better to be cruel than to be kind?'

Mostyn ignored the question and, in his impatience, gripped Adam by the shoulder of his coat to exclaim in exasperation, 'You are rude and impudent, sir, and aim to mock me. I warn you, do not try me too far!'

Seeing the fear and bewilderment upon Adam's childish face, Laurel stepped forward with deliberation to make her presence known, and Mostyn released him guiltily. His face was flushed, but whether with shame or anger, Laurel did not know.

'I have come to take you for a ride in the carriage, Adam, as I promised,' she said smoothly, before ordering him, 'Hurry, my love, for I have already delayed too long. Tell Nurse to wash your face and put on your outdoor clothing.'

'I am able to wash myself, Mama,' he reminded reproachfully, but he hastened to do her bidding. At the door he turned to ask expectantly, 'Where shall we go, Mama? To Eynon's and Henrietta's house in the village?'

'Yes, my dear, if you choose.'

Adam's face was bright with pleasure as he said with simple sincerity, 'I like it there best of all . . . best of anywhere.'

'Better than Great House?' Mostyn's voice was cutting in its scorn, but Adam stood his ground, and did not flinch as his father declared contemptuously, 'It is nothing more than a workman's cottage! A commonplace labourer's dwelling, without merit!' He turned angrily upon Laurel to accuse scathingly, 'You see where your wilful interference is leading? The child has neither taste nor discrimination! You make a philistine of him.'

Adam stood uncertainly, fingering the doorknob, before blurting defensively, 'But it is a kind house, Papa, and Megan is always glad to see me. Is she not, Mama?'

'Megan!' The iciness in Mostyn's voice frightened him as he demanded incredulously of Laurel, 'He makes friends of scullions? Illiterates? Is this your care for him?' Adam's mother signalled urgently that he go and he scurried away gratefully to stand without the door, heart beating painfully. 'You will stop these ridiculous jaunts to Thatched Cottage,' Mostyn commanded coldly, 'or go alone! I will not have the boy mixing with riff-raff . . . nonentities. Is that understood?' He moved forward threateningly and took her by the wrist.

'Let go of me.' There was a venom and disgust in her tone as she delivered a fierce blow to his face, wrenching herself free. 'I warn you, do not raise a hand to me, Mostyn for, if you do, I shall scream aloud and alert my father and all the household.'

He tugged at his cuffs, pretending indifference, seeking to gain control of himself, and of her. 'You are foolish, ma'am,' he said languidly, 'and bore me with your fantasies. It is you who have maltreated me. Now, if you will excuse me.'

'No!' The harsh denial halted him and he waited irritably, fingering the weal upon his cheek. 'Well?' he demanded. 'You have more to add?'

'Only that the people at Thatched Cottage, your kinsfolk, are decent, honourable people, who accept your son and accept me for what we are . . . and not what we pretend to be. I would hesitate to allow our son to glimpse that filth and depravity which attend you – the scum you are pleased to call "friends". They would corrupt and destroy him, as they have destroyed you!'

The supercilious smile had died upon Mostyn's lips and he walked towards her, jaw clenched, fist upraised to strike her.

Laurel's voice was calm but filled with loathing as she said with certainty, 'You cannot deny it, because it is but the simple truth. So you seek to bully me into submission, to terrify me, as you terrified your son.'

Mostyn stood irresolute and beaten, then he turned brusquely upon his heel, yet Laurel's voice was quiet and inescapable.

'If you ever again raise your hand against me, Mostyn, I shall see you publicly disgraced. But if you ever raise your hand against Adam, then I shall kill you!'

He could not doubt that she meant it.

Chapter Forty-nine

Carne's time was increasingly taken up with his new work at Hillbrook and the expansion of those mines already in existence, as well as the transporting of coal by river, road and canal. The new contracts had meant the building of new loading bays and wharves, and also subsidiary waggon-ways to help them to compete more successfully with the coal fields along the coast, which had natural advantages in supplying coal direct to the ports. Charles, too, was working harder and longer to negotiate new sales and to increase investment in the company, and Saranne complained that she and the children rarely saw them. If they actually deigned to put in a brief appearance, they were too tired to make sensible conversation. Her criticisms had been made light-heartedly, yet not without an edge of sharpness, for she saw how overstretched and irritable both men had grown, and feared for their health.

Laurel invited them to dine at Great House, the party to include Sara and Peter and their guest, Bishop Copleston. Danfield, too, had been invited, but it was feared that Rhys Llewellyn, whose business affairs had taken him to London, might not have returned. Carne had shown as little enthusiasm for the excursion as Charles, and had demanded to know who else was to be present. Saranne had not dared to disclose that Laurel had confided that it was some unknown business contact of Mostyn's. 'His name escapes me, for I have met him but the once. He is as dull-witted as a sheep, and on a par for conversation . . . Come, Saranne, do!' Laurel had implored, 'otherwise we shall all die of yawning through boredom.'

'Who else is to be present?' Carne's question, repeated, recalled Saranne guiltily.

'No-one that I know of,' Saranne had replied innocently, assuring herself that if she had prevaricated, then she had not actually lied.

If the two gentlemen's surrender had been less than enthusiastic, then they compensated for it by escorting her in Charles's new, handsomely appointed carriage in admirable style. So it was that, in rare good spirits, they confidently entered Great House.

Carne, upon being introduced to Mostyn's guest, paled and grew tense, his acknowledgement so stiff and uncivil that Clarissa glanced at him in alarm, believing him to be ill. Carne, seeing the expression of sly triumph upon Mostyn's face, managed to compose himself enough to murmur a few words, and to move on to converse with Laurel and Danfield.

'Damn Mostyn! Damn his arrogance and stupidity!' Danfield exclaimed impassionedly. 'That jackanapes would have been shown the door, were Llewellyn here! Whatever can have possessed you, Laurel?'

Laurel, bewildered, looked towards Carne for enlightenment, but Carne merely murmured, 'It was none of Laurel's doing, nor Mrs Llewellyn's, and my leaving would serve only to humiliate them, and to please Mostyn.'

Danfield looked at him hard, then nodded, as Sara, Peter and his godfather arrived, and attention was diverted towards them.

Sir Robert Crandon, owner of the *Bristol Maid*, had travelled from London for the sole purpose of persuading the Litchard-Llewellyn Company to use his shipping line to transport coal to ports within the British Isles and beyond that, to the continent. The contract had yet to be signed, for Llewellyn was absent, and Crandon was ill-disposed to linger in what he considered a 'God-forsaken hole' with boring provincials, unworthy of his attention. He made no effort to hide his irritation.

The gathering, although small and intimate, was, consequently, less than convivial. Even Clarissa's skill and tact as a hostess could not rescue it from dullness. The guests individually exerted themselves zealously to add humour and lightness to the conversation. Bishop Copleston, a gentleman of wit and scholarship, struggled manfully indeed with an almost saintly devotion to keep the exchanges alive. Yet even his fervour availed him nothing. An added blight upon the assembly was the unfortunate presence of Penry Vaughan, although, to his credit, he was less odious than expected. It was the grossness and disinterest of the guest of honour, the ship owner, Sir Robert Crandon, which defeated all, rendering the occasion sterile. It was during the meal, when his boorishness to her guests had already deeply offended Clarissa, that the company was revenged.

'I believe, Mr Havard,' Crandon addressed Carne with studied insolence, 'that you have a small local mine.'

'That is so. We are beginning to diversify, to make progress,' Carne replied civilly, unwilling to answer him in kind.

'Indeed?' Crandon's smile was supercilious. 'Your brother informs me that your partner, Hartrey, was a labourer . . . a farmer of sorts?' He did not wait for a reply, but surveyed his glass morosely before declaring dismissively, 'Such a small concern can scarcely be expected to compete. Indeed, I have never heard it discussed, nor even mentioned, elsewhere. I own, I had no prior knowledge of it!'

'Oh, but I have heard of your concerns, sir,' Carne replied.

Crandon merely nodded.

'In fact, it was my . . . unforgettable privilege to sail as a deckhand upon one of your vessels.'

Crandon, alerted by the cold venom in Carne's tone, put down his glass, to ask abrasively, 'And where did this privilege take you, sir?'

'To hell and back, sir . . . like many another aboard!'

578

There was a shocked, disbelieving silence as Carne continued expressionlessly, 'It was on the *Bristol Maid*, Sir Robert, that I sailed. Do you recall the name? I ask, for it is burned into my mind as fiercely as the shackles burnt into the flesh of those slaves we took aboard.'

'That is infamous, sir!' Crandon's already florid face was engorged with blood, his words slurred with outrage. 'It is the vilest slander.' He appealed vainly to Mostyn, declaring, 'Am I to be spoken to thus? I am a guest, sir, at your table!'

'It is the simple truth.' Carne's voice held certainty.

'This is an outrage! I will not be insulted by such calumny!' Crandon scraped his chair back, seething with fury, to accuse, 'You forget yourself, sir! The tribunal called to investigate the matter exonerated me completely. I had neither knowledge nor complicity in the affair. You will retract before all, or lay yourself open to a charge of slander. Be warned!'

'I will face it willingly.' Carne's tone was clipped, incisive. 'For it might serve to draw attention, once more, to the stinking corruption of slavery; the selling of human flesh and souls for gain. The stench of it fills my nostrils still – I cannot be rid of it, nor, yet, of the cries of those suffering the torments of the damned. They were fearful of death, yet more fearful to survive.'

Mostyn had risen, pale-faced, to take Carne's arm and make awkward apology to Sir Robert Crandon before demanding, with icy persistence, that Carne retract his accusation.

'If I have offended any uninvolved in this company, then I regret it,' he said stiffly, 'but I have made no accusation . . . I have spoken of my own past, and the grief of what I witnessed. I asked Sir Robert a simple question, and one no innocent man would cavil at.'

Carne and Crandon stared at each other balefully, locked, it seemed, in some private battle of wills, neither willing to cede until Crandon said harshly, 'I will accept your apology, Havard, as you will accept the court's declared finding of

579

my innocence.' He scraped his chair forward to the table with noisy deliberation and, with a defiant glance at the rest of the company, continued with his interrupted meal. Mostyn, face still drained of colour, watched Carne seat himself, then returned coldly to his place at the head of the table.

'It is a damnable and filthy trade . . . a trade in human misery,' the bishop exclaimed feelingly, 'and one cannot but share Havard's disgust at its continued existence. I do not wonder he speaks so forcefully after the horror of witnessing it! One can only echo his pity and shame.'

'Indeed, your Grace . . . a most vicious and reprehensible trade,' agreed Penry Vaughan. 'It shames and degrades all it touches.'

Mostyn's voice came coolly and with languid disdain, 'Quite so, Cousin. Even those innocents like Sir Robert. Even you and I, sir, whose fortunes are, most unfortunately, invested in the shipping line concerned.'

'Vaughan?' The bishop's surprise and disgust were evident.

'I did not know, your Grace . . . I confess that I leave such transactions to Mostyn, my cousin, looking to him for financial support and advice. It was without my knowledge . . . I mean, sir,' he declared frigidly to Crandon, 'that I do not doubt your involvement . . . No . . . innocence, I mean! Any more than my own.' Dear Heaven, he prayed silently, let the bishop believe me, else I shall not be elected canon of Llandaff cathedral, and that much at least, is owed to me. It was but a matter of time. Vaughan smiled ingratiatingly at Crandon, and with sickening unctuousness at the bishop, but neither made return.

'I believe,' declared Clarissa with praiseworthy diplomacy, 'that the gentlemen will have matters of import to discuss. Shall we adjourn to the drawing room, ladies, and leave them to relax amicably over their port?'

Sir Robert Crandon, to his disgust, had profited not at all from his ill-advised foray beyond the civilising frontiers of the capital. God knows, he thought, he had suffered enough by subjecting himself to the boredom and savagery of such a cultural wilderness as Penavon. Yet, to return with the contract unsigned had added insult to those indignities already endured. He was grateful to shake the coal dust of Penavon from his elegantly buckled shoes.

'Damnation, Mostyn. Will you not take telling!' Rhys Llewellyn had exploded irascibly upon his return when he heard the full story. 'There is no question of our signing such an agreement! Would you have us tarred with the same brush? Have us known publicly as supporting slavery? Have you no sense?'

'Sense enough to know that the terms were advantageous,' declared Mostyn fretfully. 'I cannot, for the life of me, see what is altered! You knew of the tribunal, and the verdict. Crandon was cleared.'

'Are you deliberately obtuse, or merely foolish, sir?' demanded Llewellyn.

'I believe that I am the only one involved who is clear-sighted enough to see that the partnership is to our advantage,' returned Mostyn, looking to Danfield for support, but finding none.

'Clear-sighted? I beg to question it, sir! You are wilfully blind, or lacking in basic intelligence, if you cannot see that, far from earning money from it, we would lose more from the goodwill sacrificed from others. Danfield? Are you with me on this?'

'I am indeed, sir.' Danfield's reply was immediate. 'It would serve no purpose, save to inflame public opinion and to further inflate the ego of that pompous, ill-mannered parvenu, an upstart, without brains or breeding.'

'His manners are no concern to me!' Mostyn flung at him. 'Our aim is to make money . . . to compete, and win.'

'His manners, or lack of them, most certainly concern me, sir,' Danfield rebuked quietly. 'The man is a boor and, I do not doubt, unscrupulous. I have no reason to doubt your brother's words, for I know him and Charles Hartrey to be men of the highest integrity, who would not lay false

581

accusation. Havard would willingly have taken the matter to court and aired it publicly, if need arose.'

Llewellyn nodded affirmation, demanding of Mostyn, 'Where, sir, would that leave us? I will answer for you. It would leave us as guilty as he, and as shunned and ostracised. Would you bankrupt us? There are other shipping lines which would be eager for our custom.'

'It is cant, hypocrisy!' Mostyn fumed.

'Then you had best deplore it privately, and accept it publicly,' declared Llewellyn unrepentantly, 'for Danfield and I are the major shareholders, and we are agreed.'

'As we are agreed that Crandon's open contempt for Llewellyn's family and guests might well reflect his contempt for us . . . and, given opportunity, he might treat us in the same cavalier fashion. Come, Mostyn,' Danfield urged, 'concede that it is for the best. You have no option.'

But Mostyn was not to be mollified, saying, 'Only a fool would judge a man's worth by his manners.'

Danfield smiled, shrugging, and admitted languidly, 'Perhaps . . . but it would be a greater fool who would discount them altogether.'

Llewellyn nodded and looked steadily at Mostyn before gathering up his books and papers, and saying without malice, 'In business, one must learn to tell the real from the counterfeit if one is to succeed. I believe, with Danfield, that it is your brother who told the real story.'

Mostyn, his ill-humour carefully under control, smiled and said disarmingly, 'One would expect no less of a Havard. On that, gentlemen, as upon all else, you compel my agreement.'

The two great rival mining companies expanded and prospered, barely able to supply all that was demanded of them by the ironmasters, the newly developing factories and mills, and the fierce demand for coal both in Britain and overseas. Competition sharpened their appetite for development and innovation and they vied with each other in opening new drift mines as well as exploring new levels in those already in existence. They built new waggonways to link them with the network of canals already established by the ironmasters. They bought fleets of barges. They created their own shipping lines.

The Litchard-Llewellyn and the Hartrey-Havard mining companies *were* Penavon. Peter Morrish sometimes feared that they had bought not only Penavon, but the people. They owned them as surely as they owned their dwellings; the shops which supplied their needs, the taverns and meeting places; the land and all which lay beneath. As the unusable waste from the mine workings grew, cramped into the hollows of the encroaching mountains, so did the fortunes of the owners. So, too, did the accidents, the respiratory diseases from blackdamp and dust, the burns from firedamp, and the crippling rheumatic afflictions from crawling in the wet, airless levels.

Yet it was the fly-by-night companies which did the crueller harm, those shoddy speculators whose sole object was to rape the countryside of its mineral riches to satisfy their greed. They threw up cheap, insanitary dwellings; rabbit warrens with rooms into which they crowded as many workers as could be housed. Even these insalubrious hovels were shared between those who worked by day or laboured by night. They slept as many as eight or nine to a cell-like room, sharing a bed with others, or sleeping rough upon the boards. They washed themselves in a nearby stream, which acted as a sewer for their bodily excretions, for drinking water, and to wash their coal-grimed clothes.

Those with wives and infants fared worse. There was no escaping the foetid rooms with the stench of unwashed flesh and the wailing cries of the babes and hungry children. Tempers grew raw and violence flared, swift and unprovoked. The women grew desperate, striving vainly to keep families fed and their infants silent, that their menfolk might sleep in peace. Those women widowed or abandoned were forced to labour in the mines, their children at the mercy of the minders, often feckless, gin-sodden creatures, unfitted to labour, who kept them quiet with laudanum.

The children, drugged and unresponsive, grew sickly, too weakened to cry, too nauseous to eat, bodies stunted, minds dulled.

Sara set up a crèche for such children in a disused byre, and with gifts of money from Clarissa, Laurel, Saranne and Charles, hired two strong dependable girls to care for them and to provide simple, nourishing fare. At Peter's insistence, she charged the mothers a halfpenny a day for each child, to save their pride, for many were averse to accepting charity. Yet she could have filled the cribs within the byre a hundred times over, and still have turned the needy away.

Saranne's visit to the crèche developed in her mind a confusion of half-formed ideas and plans of how she too could improve the lot of the women and children. She tried to explain them to Carne as he drove her one day in the gig to see Laurel at Great House. Unfortunately, tiredness made her sound carping and critical, and he, in turn, was angrily defensive.

'What would you have me do?' Carne demanded irritably of Saranne when they passed a group of young children trudging their way along the highway to Penavon, their faces grimed with coal dust and their working clothes ragged and filthy. They shuffled rather than walked, bowed down perhaps with weariness, each one clutching his precious candle and a box that had earlier held his daily bread. There was none of the jostling and careless chatter of Saranne's own children and they seemed to her like sober, hard-burdened old men. They stepped aside to let the carriage pass, eyes and teeth gleaming appreciatively at so rare a sight, and they dutifully bowed their heads and mumbled greeting, then resumed their shuffling march.

'What would you have me do?' he repeated scathingly. 'Would you have me dismiss them? Abandon them? To what, Saranne? Penury? They are fairly paid for their labour. We observe every rule for their safety. They have hope of advancement to other work, responsibility. They would rather be fed than dead!'

The callousness of the remark chilled her and distressed

him, for he had not meant to speak so.

'Is that to be all the choice they have in life? To be fed or dead? Dear God, Carne, what have you become?' The tears started to Saranne's eyes as she exclaimed furiously, 'I swear I no longer know you! You are changed.'

'Of course I am changed!' Remorse and the injustice of her attack incensed him. 'So you are changed, and our lives! The carriage you sit in, your home, your food and clothing, all you possess are owed to mining! You scorn me for providing them, but you do not reject them!'

'What would you have me do?' she cried, brushing her tears away angrily with her fists. 'Would you have me walk barefoot, go naked, or wear sackcloth and ashes to atone for your sins?'

For a moment the absurdity of it softened him and made him smile and he would have halted the carriage, taken her in his arms to soothe her and confessed his own regret.

'Well?' she demanded irately before he could speak. 'Would it please you to have your own children labouring like animals? Crawling in filth and water, in terror of darkness?'

'No more than it pleased me that you slaved as a pauper child, with none to ease your hunger or bring you solace!' Carne's voice was cold. 'My efforts have spared our children want and suffering, but it seems that you are more obsessed with the fate of others, holding me accountable!'

'Damn you!' she exclaimed despairingly. 'You twist what I say! You will not listen, nor understand!'

'I understand that there is but one choice. They may work in the mines, endure the hardship such labour brings and thus remain at home with those they care for, and who care for them – or they may choose paupery. If so, they will know hunger, separation from all they hold dear, and work as fiercely in the mines, the factories, or upon the land, but for others, who hold them valueless. Is that your solution?' He whipped the horse into swifter movement and turned his back towards the road, anger a cold knot within him.

'Damnation, Carne! You are no better than a slave-master yourself!' she accused. 'You have no thought save for power and money; the flesh that can be bought!' Her voice rose despairingly. 'I felt pride when you railed so fiercely at Robert Crandon. Yet there is nothing to choose between you! Power is your god! I feel nothing but disgust for you . . .' She faltered, terrified at the enormity of what she had said, and bitterly aware of his ashen face and the pain she was powerless to undo. She tentatively stretched out a conciliatory hand, too wracked with tears and guilt to speak and beg his forgiveness.

'If you are so concerned with the evils I spawn, and my selfishness, perhaps it were better that we remained apart awhile.'

'Perhaps . . .' Her voice was stiff, unforgiving.

'Perhaps you will devote your efforts, since prosperity buys you time for the luxury of idleness, to setting right the wrongs you so despise.'

'Yes. I shall most certainly do that!'

'Then I wish you well in your efforts! They will, at least, spare me uninformed and spurious criticism! Yes, I most assuredly wish you well, and offer you use of that money which you affect to so despise.'

'My own efforts will suffice,' she declared disdainfully. 'I have no need to buy goodwill or favour!'

'As you choose,' he replied dismissively.

It was the first time that they had quarrelled so coldly and with such intensity of feeling, each knowing that his outburst had been unreasonable, but unwilling to make apology. It was the same pity, the same discontent, which had driven them to hurtful anger, but there was no easy way to repair the rift between them.

Carne spent the night in his small dressing room upon an improvised bed, pretending some urgent business meeting which had kept him too late to risk disturbing her. Saranne, in a torment of concern and remorse which only served to fuel her annoyance with him, pretended indifference. For days they treated each other with frosty courtesy, punctili-

586

ous in their correctness. Their conversation was that of strangers, remote and disinterested. They were careful to offer neither praise not criticism, and spoke only of those things which were uncontentious and essential for the smooth functioning of the household.

Henrietta and Eynon were bewildered and clung to Megan childishly, as of old, sensing, but not fully understanding why the atmosphere of Thatched Cottage had changed. Megan was tight-lipped and, inwardly, censorious, but made no open acknowledgement of their stubborn disagreement. Carne and Saranne were acutely unhappy but too foolishly proud to admit it. Finally, one night, when Carne had gone to his bed in the dressing room, she arose determinedly to discuss the matter with him. She would murmur stiff apology and so help to break the deadlock – abase herself, if need be, for it was her firm conviction that she had been more seriously at fault. Carne, impelled by the same thought, met her upon the passageway to their room and their surprise melted into laughter. There was a return to their marriage bed and a passionate avowal from each that such foolishness would never again occur. Carne's declaration that he was entirely culpable was met by Saranne's denial and the avowal that she, alone, was the offender. Their forgiveness was as swift and passionate as their lovemaking, but the argument remained unresolved.

Upon the following day, Saranne paid her usual visit to the poorhouse. Yet now she came as the wife of Carne Havard, a son of its original founder, and not as a pauper. She arrived elegantly dressed, in a fine carriage, and was greeted with a deference bordering upon unctuousness. A beautiful, assured woman, successful, and to be admired. Yet, as she stepped over the stone threshold and saw how little it had changed, her hands within the delicate suede gloves were shaking and she was once more four years old, and afraid. Her kinship with those within was as powerful as her kinship without its imprisoning walls. She was no longer Saranne Havard, but Anne-without-a-name, as valueless as the rest.

Saranne had made many such visits to the poorhouse, trying to ease the lot of those within, comforting the aged and impotent, the women suckling babes, the sick, and the children. Yet always she felt a barrier of reserve between herself and those she hoped to serve. She was no longer one of them, distanced by time and circumstance, changed, as Carne had predicted, by an affluence they could not share, or trust.

She glimpsed Rice Mostyn Havard almost at once.

The boy had been so engrossed in watching a robin feed upon the few spare crumbs tossed from his pocket that he did not, at first, hear the carriage approach. Saranne, seeing with pity the rawness of his hands clasped awkwardly around the handle of a besom, and the mottled blueness of his feet upon the frozen turf, felt an ache of pity. When he turned to face her, shock drove the colour from her face and she was forced to steady herself against the door of the carriage. The coachman roughly pushed the child aside, fearful that Saranne might fall, then hurried to aid her descent, but she scarcely saw him or his steadying hand. Her eyes were upon the child, whose fair hair and features against the tattered poverty of his clothes were unmistakably Mostyn's. The boy had turned away, too nervous to stare, and was engrossed upon sweeping the leaves and worm casts from the grass with furious concentration, head bent upon his task.

'Boy! You there!' Her voice sounded abrupt, querulous in her own ears, but she could think of no other way to address him. 'Come here,' she commanded.

He turned and came obediently to her side, dragging the too-large besom awkwardly behind him.

'What is your name?'

He stared at her gravely, eyes clear and intelligent under the pale brows, but made no response. Then he returned to his sweeping, strokes rhythmic and steady upon the frozen grass.

'Did you not hear me? Has the cat got your tongue?' she asked.

The workmaster, a gaunt, acidulous man had hurried out to greet her. He took the boy roughly by the shoulder and shook him fiercely, demanding impatiently, 'Are you deaf, boy? Or merely insolent? Tell the lady your name!'

The besom had been shaken from the boy's grip but his hands, numbed by the cold, stayed curled as if he still held it.

In her pity for having caused him harm, she would have dismissed him, but the workmaster, still holding the collar of the boy's coat, jerked him around cruelly to face her, declaring, 'Answer, I say, else it will be the worse for you!'

The boy looked at her in mute appeal and licked his lips before blurting, face crimson with defiance and shame, 'It is the same as yours, ma'am. Havard. That is why I did not tell you, for I am mocked and beaten for it by the others . . . I am Rice Mostyn Havard.'

She saw his lower lip jut and tremble, then the glint of tears upon his lashes as he said with pathetic dignity, 'It is my name, ma'am, and I cannot help it, for it was given to me. I would change it if I were able, for I know we cannot be kin, and I have never claimed to be so.'

The workmaster, incensed by such gross over-familiarity, clouted the boy savagely about the ear and ordered him curtly within, but Saranne said commandingly, 'I would have him stay!'

The workmaster looked nonplussed, then stubbornly mutinous, but did not dare overrule her, declaring, 'I think, ma'am, he would be better employed elsewhere. He is a stubborn, disagreeable child, hostile, and without friends. Moreover, he is idle, although punishment is serving to curb the worst of his excesses.'

'I do not believe him to be idle, sir. He was gainfully employed at sweeping when I arrived, and stopped only at my command.'

'Indeed? Then it is to the credit of my training,' declared the workmaster unabashed, 'for, by nature, he is given to slothfulness and deceit.'

'Yet he does not claim kinship with me, nor renounce

589

his given name,' countered Saranne sharply. 'That argues, not deceit, but honesty, even at risk of punishment. I will take him with me.'

'Take him with you, Mrs Havard? Where, ma'am? He is to be apprenticed to the chimney sweep in the village . . . it is all arranged,' he spluttered helplessly. 'I cannot countenance it.'

'Can you not, Mr Grimthorpe?' Saranne's voice was deceptively mild. 'Then I must ask you . . . no, command you to reconsider. If my credentials are to be questioned, perhaps you would wish my husband, Carne Havard, my brother, Charles Hartrey, or Sir Peter Danfield to vouch for me? I assure you that they will willingly support me, should you require proof of my integrity. Shall I say that you have requested proof of it? Doubt it, perhaps?'

'No, certainly not, ma'am. An intolerable imposition,' he mumbled. 'I had no such thought in mind. You misunderstood me.'

'You will arrange to see to the necessary formalities then, and send for my carriage, that I may take Rice Havard with me?'

'At once, Mrs Havard.'

She took the boy's hand firmly in hers and clasped it tightly, but the workmaster made no move, saying agitatedly, 'You will find him useless as a yard boy, ma'am. There are others, better fitted, more intelligent. I do not rightly know if it is wise to take him.'

'I do not need a yard boy!' Saranne's tone was dismissive. 'Nor a servant of any kind. He comes into my home as a child, and companion for my own children. He shall be treated no differently. Now, if you will order my carriage . . . or must I search for it myself?'

The child's cold hand had relaxed within her gloved one as she squeezed it reassuringly. When the carriage arrived, she made no explanation to her coachman but lifted Rice Mostyn calmly within. Dear Lord! What have I done? she wondered as she looked at the boy's set, bewildered face, so strangely familiar. What will Carne say? How will I explain it to Laurel? I shall lose her friendship, and Adam will be forbidden the house. Yet, looking at Rice Mostyn, she could not be sad, nor afraid. It was owed to him, for a child should not inherit the sins of his father, but had a right to inherit his name and make of it what he might. She took Rice Mostyn's thin hand in hers, to comfort both him and herself. She would not let him go.

Chapter Fifty

Carne was tired and filled with remorse and grief. A boy of eight, while pulling a loaded coal tram, had fallen beneath its wheels, his leg severed by the impact. Dr Tobin had done what little he could but the child's fear and stifled sobs amidst the sickening bloodiness had ripped Carne through with rage and guilt. The surgery had been vicious, crude, and so agonising that Carne, helping Jack Hollis to hold and soothe the boy, had all but vomited.

Carne drove the boy home, ashen faced and weak from shock and loss of blood. His mother, a widow with two younger children at her skirts, carried him within, stoical and tearless. She neither railed at Carne nor screamed abuse, but set herself to making the boy comfortable and hushing his fears. There was a pathos and dignity in her which wrenched at his heart and he saw, frozen upon Jack Hollis's face, a reflection of his own grief.

'I beg, ma'am, that you will allow me to settle Dr Tobin's bill and to provide what necessities and small comforts . . .' He broke off, ashamed lest she think he believed her son's injuries a debt so easily repaid.

'I thank you kindly, sir, for your concern . . . and you shall pay the doctor's bill, for I have no way to meet it else.' She glanced protectively towards the boy. 'It is true that times are hard and that Huw is become our only breadwinner, but we will manage somehow.' As Carne moved to make protest, she said, without self-pity, 'There is a place of Mrs Morrish's in the village where infants may be taken to be cared for, if need arise. I shall work in

Huw's stead, if you will allow it, and if no room for the others be found, then he shall care for them here, when he is able. He is a good, reliable boy, and will take telling.'

'No!' His sharp denial halted her and made one of the infants cry. She gathered the child up instinctively, cradling it to her. 'He will be paid his full wage, ma'am,' Carne declared gruffly, 'now, and for as long as he is unfitted to work. Then, after, when he is able, he must come to me, and I shall find him employment at some other task, but his earnings will not suffer.'

Without the dwelling, Jack Hollis said flatly, 'It was a kind gesture, Mr Havard, sir, but I fear you will not convince those in authority. It is laid down by the company that, following accident, half wages be paid for six weeks. It is a rule, sir.'

'Hell and damnation to the rule!' Carne declared savagely. 'I will pay from my own pocket, and none shall know of it. You will speak of it to no-one, you understand?'

Jack Hollis nodded, 'I shall not speak of it.'

I offered to pay for small comforts and necessities, Carne thought helplessly, as if comfort, like bread, is something to be bought. Dear God! What could comfort me if it were Eynon crippled in his stead? I should throw the money back, and curse its giver.

He walked into Thatched Cottage burning to tell Saranne of the horrors of the day but unable to speak of them, for his feelings were too raw. Saranne rushed to him, blurting news of bringing Rice Mostyn home, and he stared at her in silence. Then the rage and fury of the day, so carefully suppressed, rose chokingly within him. 'You have done what?' he shouted furiously, his anger spilling over upon her. 'Are you mad, Saranne?'

She retreated, terrified, from the viciousness upon his face, then stood and held her ground, fearful for a moment that he would actually strike her.

'You have brought Mostyn's bastard here? Into my house? What madness and cruelty has possessed you? Have

593

you no thought for Laurel and Adam? Must your own selfishness always be served?'

She tried to speak, but could not for the thickness which closed her throat. She could not control the hateful weakness of tears.

'Cry!' he declared savagely. 'Cry, if you will . . . Wallow in your own righteousness and self-pity!' He thudded a hand fiercely into his palm, saying brutally, 'I have just come from a woman who had reason to weep, yet did not, for she had a strength and courage which you lack!'

'You must let me explain,' she cried, frightened by his cold contempt. 'It was for him, the boy. I beg you, Carne, do not judge me until I have made explanation.'

'What is there to explain? You have satisfied your own selfishness yet again. You have ridden roughshod over the feelings of others, indifferent to their hurt. Does that not explain it all?'

She would not deny it, for rage had taken him beyond all reasoning, but she insisted passionately, 'He will stay here. I will not have the boy moved!'

'Will you not? I assure you that *I* will remove him. You may try to stop me, if you have a mind to do so.'

'The child stays!' She faced him squarely.

'Damn you, Saranne! He goes! I will not have Mostyn angered and Laurel humiliated. That is an end to it.'

'No, it is not an end to it! If he goes, then I go too. I swear, Carne, that I will leave, for I will not have him rejected and humiliated more. It is Mostyn's crime, and the child who is paying.'

The argument raged on and Rice Mostyn, awakened from his bed and peering through the balustrade, thought with desolation, It is I who am at fault. They fight over me. I will not be able to stay, although they were kind to me at first. He felt terror and panic stifle him. It was dark without, and they would set him down in a strange place. What could he do? His mind was confused and, for a time, he was unable to think or make movement, for the hopelessness within him. He could not return to the poorhouse, for they would know he was at fault. They did not want him here. He was a failure and would be punished, and all would mock and sneer. He would find his way to the village, and beg the chimney sweep to take him in, for fear some other boy would go seeking work. He rose unsteadily and made his way dispiritedly to his room, gripping the smooth stone within his pocket tight, as if it might give him courage to act. They had burnt his clothes, so he must dress in those he had been given, but he would return them, for he wanted none of their charity. Quietly, his heart beating so hard that it was a violence at his breast and throat, he crept quietly down the stairs, across the deserted hall, and into the kitchen. Then, unseen, and too dejected to weep, he made his way out of the house and across the yard, half running, through the all-enveloping darkness. He ran until his breath was raw and there was a fierce pain in his side. The grotesque shapes of trees loomed menacingly about him and the harsh screech of a barn owl jarred the cold air, but still he ran on blindly and without direction. His new stockings and shoes hurt his feet and he felt tears burning upon the frosted coldness of his cheeks. When he could run no more, he sank down upon a crispness of drifted leaves and slept where he lay.

Carne, his vicious rage spent, was shamed by his unreasoning anger, eager to explain himself to Saranne and make amends. She listened stiffly at first, reluctant to understand or forgive, until the tragedy of what Carne had seen and endured broke her resolve. Yet there was still a painful reserve between them because what had been spoken in heat and anguish could not be denied, even in reconciliation.

'I should have spoken to you of the boy . . . discussed it with you. It was reckless of me, Carne. Yet I could not let him suffer more.'

'No,' Carne admitted heavily. 'You did right in bringing him, Saranne. I cannot doubt that I would have felt impelled to do the same.'

'Despite what might ensue?'

He hesitated only fractionally before replying firmly,

'Despite what might ensue.' Yet he felt no real conviction as he offered, 'Shall we not go and see the boy? I had best learn to recognise our new son.'

Saranne put an arm gratefully through Carne's, aware of the effort it had taken to speak those conciliatory words. She dropped a grateful kiss upon his cheek as she led him up the stairway and towards Rice Mostyn's room.

Saranne's bewilderment at finding the child's bed empty made her rush distractedly from room to room, her panic equalled only by Carne's remorse lest the boy had overheard their quarrelling and fled into the darkness, fearing yet another rejection. When the nursery maid who slept in the small bedchamber adjoining Henrietta's room was awakened, her consternation was as great as theirs. Yet, their combined searching yielding no trace of him, Carne ran immediately to the stables and awakened the coachman and the stable lad in his loft above the stalls, giving them urgent instructions to take lanterns and search the countryside about. The child was young and in the darkness could not have wandered far. The coachman must take the gig and keep to the highway, while he and the stable lad would take a horse apiece and ride out, separately, into the quieter byways, searching hedgerows and ditches, byres and barns, lest the boy had crept within for shelter and warmth.

It was Carne who found him, huddled asleep where he had fallen, exhausted, upon the bed of dead leaves. Rice Mostyn opened wide his eyes, started, and cried out in the piercing lantern light, then cowered like a small terrified animal, as if he would burrow from sight beneath the drifted mound of leaves. His face was streaked still with traces of rubbed tears, and his thinness, and likeness to Mostyn, tore Carne with pity and grief. He lifted the boy into his arms and said roughly, his voice unsteady with hurt, 'I am taking you home, Rice.'

'To the poorhouse, sir?' There was a resignation in his voice, a dulled acceptance.

'To your . . . your family at Thatched Cottage.' Carne touched his cheek with tenderness against Rice's cold one, then rubbed his numbed hands to warmth and feeling within his own.

'And will I be sent away tomorrow, sir, when it is light?' he blurted anxiously. 'I tried to find the chimney sweep, but could not, and grew tired. I had best go to him, sir, for fear he finds another boy.' He tried to struggle from Carne's arms, but cold and fatigue defeated him and he began to weep helplessly.

Dear God, thought Carne, what has life done to him, and we, in our callousness? He lifted him gently into the saddle, saying, 'Keep your arms firmly clasped about the mare's neck. Lean against me, and I will support you. You need have no fear that you will fall, for I will not let you go.'

Rice Mostyn's eyes were heavy-lidded with sleep as Carne stripped off his thick coat and wrapped it carefully about the small figure. The boy smiled, then closed his eyes, secure within the encircling arms and ready for sleep. The horse's hooves stirred the dead leaves, its breath gentle upon the frosted air and, beneath the thickness of his coat, Carne felt the frailness of the sleeping child's bones and his vulnerability.

I did not answer his question, he thought regretfully, and now he will awaken still fearful that tomorrow he will be sent away. Then memory of his words came clearly to him. He had made a promise and a vow. 'Lean against me, and I will support you. You need have no fear that you will fall, for I will not let you go.' Carne hoped his words had brought the boy comfort. He knew that whatever the future held, whatever must be endured, his own life and his nephew's were inseparably bound.

Success had at last brought Mostyn the power and riches which he had so long craved, and he was no longer raked by that restless urge to prove himself. Success was his by right: he had earned it by his own efforts. Business still excited him and he could bargain as keenly and feel as fierce a triumph in the winning. Yet, as with his search for diversion and pleasure, it no longer ruled his life. Llewellyn believed that he had matured and grown calmer and more dependable. He spent more time now in Adam's company, joining him at his games and riding lessons, praising him for his perseverance and lessons well done. To Laurel's delight, a closeness had developed naturally between father and son and Adam seemed no longer in awe of him, but rather to seek out his company. Mostyn spent less time too at the gaming tables, seeming to have outgrown his compulsive need to compete and his need for the stimulus of risk.

Laurel had mellowed towards him and once, when they were alone, in a rare demonstration of gentleness, he took Laurel's hand and laid it against his cheek. Then tenderly kissed her palm before closing her fingers with his own. She did not withdraw or show displeasure but was touched by his genuine emotion and need for contact. Yet as swiftly as he had made the gesture he turned and walked abruptly from the room, leaving her confused and unsure of herself. He had known little affection in his childhood and could not be blamed, she thought, for being unwilling or unable to bare his true emotions before others, fearful always of rejection. Yet, if she helped him by showing him undemanding loyalty and affection, might they not, in time, grow close, past hurts forgotten?

That night, Mostyn came quietly into her room and stood uncertainly at the foot of her bed. His face, childlike, and without its customary arrogance, seemed to her as defenceless as Adam's in sleep. He knelt, unspeaking, beside the bed, eyes grave and awkward with pleading, lest she send him away. He seemed so timid and unsure as he lay his head upon the bedcover that Laurel reached out involuntarily to touch the clustered curls at his nape. It grieved her to see him so abject and cast down, and her touch strengthened to a caress. Then he stood for a moment, awkward and undecided, and she held out her arms in pity and reassurance. Their loving was, for the first time, of a depth and wholeness she could never have dreamed, and she surren-

598

dered herself willingly to the new tenderness and passion born in them both. He stayed in her bed until morning and awoke to smile at her with surprise and delighted recognition. All that day, and every moment they were apart, she was as aware of him as she had been in the early days of her loving. Only now, Laurel was sure, Mostyn loved her as deeply as she loved him.

Saranne's clumsy confession that she had taken Mostyn's son, Rice, into Thatched Cottage as her ward, had reopened the old wound. Laurel had believed it to be healed and scarred over, but she knew now that it had been but a surface crust. One careless blow had laid it bare again, and, try as she might, she could not escape its pain.

'Saranne has done this deliberately to drive us apart!' Mostyn raged, consumed with angry resentment. 'She has thrown your friendship in your face! Demeaning and insulting you before all.'

'No.' Laurel's voice was tired and low. 'I cannot defend her, Mostyn, but there were few in Penavon I could name as friends, and with Saranne, Sara and Megan gone . . . there is none.'

'Then you are better served without her.'

'What she did was from caring,' said Laurel dully. 'She would not see your . . . the pauper child suffer as she. No, it is you, Mostyn, who demeaned and insulted me.' It was said without anger or accusation, and guilt made Mostyn's anger the fiercer.

'I have paid for it, Laurel, God knows,' he exclaimed, 'and had thought it over and done. I could not know I would be paying for it for the rest of my life.'

Laurel might have spoken then but indifference had given place to a jealousy which tore her with the roots of pain. She strove only to wound and punish him. 'Are you entirely selfish?' she raged, incensed. 'Have you no thought for the boy? He is your own child, a creature of flesh and blood, not an inconvenience to throw aside like a burden. Will you not go to Carne and beg that the child be sent away to some school or institution where he will be cared for and his future assured?'

'I'll be damned if I will!' His refusal was vehement but, when he saw how angered and hurt she was, he forced himself to submit, saying, although his every instinct was against it, 'If that is what you truly want, Laurel, I shall go. I shall entreat and beg, humiliate myself before my brother, if need be. I shall do whatever is needed.'

Laurel nodded and carefully skirted the place where he stood, unwilling to touch him even accidentally in passing. There must be no contact between them, no surrender of flesh, until it was done and the boy beyond her sight and reach. Mostyn begged her to forgive and, in time, when the pain had dulled and become bearable, yes, she might forgive . . . but she would never forget.

Later that evening, Laurel heard Mostyn appealing to her despairingly at her door and was almost moved to unlock it and let him enter but she shut her mind and heart to him, that he might feel the anguish he had heaped upon her. She heard the clattering of Mostyn's horse upon the cobbles and then the thud of its hoofbeats muffled by the grass, then his wild cry as he entered upon the highway, urging his mount on.

What violence have I wrought? she asked herself numbly. What viciousness drives me to reject him? She waited until daybreak beside the window for his return. Yet, even with morning, he had not come. Dry-eyed and weary, she took her place at the breakfast table and forced herself to eat and drink, but she tasted nothing except her own hurt. She had driven Mostyn away. It was she, after all, who bore the heavier guilt.

Mostyn did as he intended, riding determinedly from gaming den to gaming den, gambling recklessly and with little real interest in whether he won or lost. Those who owned such places, without exception, greeted him obsequiously, knowing him to be a man of substance, well able to pay any debts he might incur. Acquaintances and

600

fellow gamesters merely nodded, their attention all upon the tables and the fall of cards or dice. Some played nervously and with little pleasure, like automatons. Others remained expressionless, their faces masks to hide their fear, elation or cupidity. Mostyn's alone showed boredom. He tried to rouse himself to interest but could not. Hell and damnation, he thought irritably, what am I doing here? What ails me? He rose, yet again, and without a word left the tables, pushing past others, his manner taciturn and surly. Yet, wherever he rode, he was aware of a sameness, a lack of excitement. Glancing about him at the faces of his companions, he saw in them his own disillusionment. Were they all, as he, seeking escape from others or from themselves, he wondered disconsolately. He could tell them that there was no escaping.

He set out for the taverns he knew best, thinking to numb his senses and find release. Yet, strangely, he became, not confused, but more clear-minded, the pain within him keener. When he could drink no more, he mounted his horse and rode out to a bawdy house, where he was known, and his tastes and preferences voluptuously catered for. Yet, once again, he was filled, not with eroticism and excitement, but self-disgust. He found the drabs coarse and sluttish, their attempts at seduction gross. Shamed by his impotent fumblings, he threw his money down and, pretending drunkenness, left the place. Then he rode wildly and without purpose until fatigue forced him to rest within a small copse of alders. In a stupor, he slept heavily and undisturbed until nearly noon. Then, dry-mouthed and unshaven, he untied the horse from the branch where it had been tethered and rode, heavy-eyed and sullen, to Great House. He stabled his horse and entered the house and his bedchamber unseen, lying unwashed upon his bed and dozing in his boots and clothing.

He heard the comings and goings of servants and the call to dinner below but made no effort to rise and groom himself and put on fresh linen. Then, when he was sure that Laurel and her parents were occupied at their meal, he arose and took some coins from the drawer in the table beside his bed and quietly made his way to the stables. Let Laurel fret and worry at his absence, he thought vengefully, for she had denied him comfort or solace. She would be fearful ere long that some misfortune had overtaken him, an accident or deeper tragedy for which she alone was culpable. He would return to the gaming houses and bide his time until she was fully repentant. Yet the prospect of humbling her, as of gaming, failed to appease. Perhaps, after all, it would be more satisfying to bathe and dress himself and await Laurel's return to her room, letting remorse drive her willingly into his arms. Then he would accept her surrender with splendid magnanimity.

For a moment he stood undecided but, finding the stable lad to be absent, surreptitiously saddled his horse and led it away as quietly as he was able so that none would know of it. Already it grew dark but he rode through Penavon village towards the gaming house without benefit of a lantern. Then, inexplicably, he slowed the mare, turned her about and, with a swift urgency, set her upon the road to Thatched Cottage.

Mostyn did not know what had suddenly impelled him to turn and ride to Carne's house. He could not admit that in times of trouble it was to Carne that he had gone, tearful and apprehensive, but confident that his childhood world would be set to rights and his grief eased. Yet, now, Mostyn whipped himself to anger and self-pity as relentlessly as he whipped his horse to effort. Carne had always demeaned and belittled him, giving him no credit for what he had achieved. It was jealousy which motivated him; jealousy that although he was heir to Great House and Penavon estates, it was Mostyn who had secured them for his own. His resentment showed in his every word and action. Had he not developed the Hartrey-Havard mines, fearful that Mostyn, through marriage and his own business acumen, had grown powerful and rich? Had he not connived with his scheming pauper of a wife to influence Laurel against him, pretending friendship, then publicly humiliating her?

Worse, had they not evilly poisoned Laurel's mind against him, raking over the ashes of a dead affair? He had bitterly atoned for it, so long denied her affection and her bed. And now, when all was resolved between them, and Adam's affection won, they sought to ruin him! Anger seethed within him and his grip upon the reins tightened with pain. He would not allow this upstart, this bastard child, to come between them! The affair was dead; ended before it had begun. A coupling without affection. An aberration, no more. He would be damned before he would allow it to destroy all that he had fought so fiercely to achieve.

By the time his horse had borne him into the cobbled yard of Thatched Cottage, it was in a lather of sweat and foam, its breathing raw and Mostyn's discomfort as acute. The issue must be resolved, here and now. He would stand no more interference, no lies or prevarication. The child was his by right, to dispose of, or to command. He, and no other, would order the boy's future. He was determined upon it. Let Carne rant and rage, or threaten him with public scandal or the law! He would stand his ground and do as Laurel asked. She would like him the better for it and, if it came to a fight with Carne, then he did not doubt that at the final reckoning his brother would face defeat. What Mostyn could not achieve by brute force, others would be paid to continue.

Carne, seeing Mostyn's choler and his fierce trembling as he thrust aside the servant to enter the hallway of Thatched Cottage, was more concerned for his brother than alarmed. Mostyn's face was puffy and unshaven, his clothing dishevelled, as though he had slept in it. He could not doubt that it was drink as well as rage which had driven him so disgustingly to neglect himself. Mostyn was the most fastidious of men and would never venture abroad so filthily disordered unless he was befuddled beyond all self-respect and reason. Carne took his brother's arm and tried to lead him into the study but Mostyn angrily shook off his grip, declaring contemptuously, 'Do not lay your hands upon me! I am not incapable, nor needful of your support!'

Carne motioned him to a seat, saying, in an effort to calm him, 'Whatever is to be said, nothing is to be gained by childish anger or accusation. Let us discuss it soberly.'

'Dear God, Carne, your bloody arrogance astounds me!' Mostyn exclaimed, forbearing to be seated. 'You call my anger childish? Childish, you say, when you have all but ruined me! It is you, sir, who is childish, in your puerile efforts to get the better of me!' Rage had made him almost incoherent.

'I do not know what it is that you accuse me of, Mostyn!'

'Do not add lying to your viciousness!' Mostyn said scornfully. 'You are a damnable hypocrite and cannot deny it! I have beaten you fairly in business, so jealousy drives you to take revenge. You seek to destroy me, parading my by-blow to humiliate me before Laurel, and to make me a laughing stock before others.'

'What you are, you have made yourself!' exclaimed Carne, stung to sharpness. 'Your vanity and indiscretions need no aid from others! If it is your son, Rice Mostyn, of whom you speak, then, yes, I have taken him into my house, not from revenge, but charity, offering him that which your parsimony denied him.'

'Do not patronise me, nor parade your virtues,' declared Mostyn, 'for I know full well that it was Saranne who planned it from perversity and to turn Laurel and Adam against me. She has always been vindictive and I have borne her spitefulness too long, refusing to let her come between us as brothers.'

Carne hesitated, eager to refute it, but knowing that there was indeed some deep-felt animosity between Mostyn and Saranne. 'Saranne brought Rice Mostyn to Thatched Cottage simply to offer him shelter, and to spare him hurt,' said Carne defensively. 'It was done from pity and her knowledge of paupery.'

Mostyn, unconvinced, took refuge in blustering, whipping his anger against Saranne into lashing accusation. 'She hates me, and has deceived Laurel bitterly. Saranne

604

betrayed her callously, and to serve her own ends. You cannot deny it, Carne! It is plain that she strove, not merely to help the boy, but to sow mistrust between Laurel and me. He is as much a pawn in this wretched game as Laurel and Adam, to be moved and ordered at will!'

There was a sound of disturbance from the landing above the staircase and some murmured words and confusion. Mostyn broke off his tirade, face flushed, to accuse with cold anger, 'Do you hope to conceal the boy? Spirit him away perhaps, lest I find him? By God, Carne, you are as deceitful as all the rest!'

Before Carne could bar his way, Mostyn had thrown open the door and was ascending the stairs, leaping them in his haste to prevent the collusion he suspected. Carne, although swift moving, could not reach him and, before he could act, Mostyn had hurled aside the nursery maid guarding the door to Rice's bedchamber and had entered irately within. Saranne, who had awakened the boy from sleep and had wrapped a bedcover about him, was feverishly trying to hustle him without to safety. At seeing Mostyn, the child stared, frozen with fear and uncertainty, as Saranne turned to put her arms about him protectively to shield him from the stranger's wrath. Too late. Mostyn, now incensed beyond all reasoning, grasped her wrist and tore her angrily away, then hurled her brutally to the floor where she lay useless. Then Mostyn took the boy roughly to force him outside.

Carne, fearful of what revenge Mostyn might take upon the boy in his blind fury, stood squarely in the doorway, defying Mostyn to pass. The whole air was charged with violence, like the atmosphere of savage inevitability preceding a storm.

'Let me pass, Carne! Else, I swear, I shall kill you!' Mostyn's face was twisted with anguish. 'He is mine, and you shall not interfere!'

Carne shook his head obdurately, 'Then you must do as you threaten . . . I shall not let you take him.'

Mostyn raised his fist and brought it crashing against

Carne's jaw to send him reeling and stumbling, trying desperately to regain his balance.

Rice Mostyn, abruptly released, had watched the assault, too terrified to run without to the nursemaid's arms or even to move away from the fury of the conflict. Pale faced, and huddling awkwardly in his blanket, Rice heard Saranne call out to him in agitation and, startled, made to turn, stumbling upon the trailing cloth and sprawling clumsily. He reached out instinctively for support, dragging upon Mostyn's sleeve, and Mostyn, in fending off his grasp, twisted clumsily off balance. The movement was so quick and confused that Carne could only watch helplessly as Mostyn struck his forehead a glancing blow against the corner of the linen chest. The crack of the impact sounded harshly as Mostyn, blood pouring from the wound, tried vainly to rise from his knees. Carne reached out a hand to help him but Mostyn thrust it fiercely aside, dragging himself to his feet, eyes glazed and unfocusing. Then, without a word or a glance at the terrified boy who was helplessly weeping in Saranne's arms, he pushed past Carne and the nursery maid and stumbled down the stairs and out into the yard.

Carne hesitated, filled with pity for the boy, and might have gone to him had not Saranne shaken her head and gestured that he follow Mostyn, lest he come to harm. Rice, almost beside himself with guilt and fear, had buried his face against Saranne's bodice as if to shut out the reality of what he had done. His shoulders were shaking and Saranne felt the wetness of his tears as he gulped and sobbed apology.

'Hush, now, my love. 'Tis not your doing,' she soothed, but he would not be consoled, knowing the stranger's anger had been all for him, although he did not know why. It had begun long before he had blundered against the man, causing the gash to his brow.

'You will send me away now . . . or to the justices, for I am wicked and idle, as they say?' He sniffed hard and wiped a hand across his nose.

'Indeed we will not! We will forget he ever came,' said Saranne crisply.

'But if he dies, Mama . . . they will send me to the gallows?'

'No, never!' she assured him. 'It was an accident . . . nothing but a bad dream and, when you awaken tomorrow, you will know it to be so, and forget, I promise.'

'I do not think I will forget,' he said doubtfully, 'he would have taken me away. I do not know what I did to make him angry.'

'No,' declared Saranne truthfully, 'no more do I.' Save, perhaps, in being born, she amended silently.

Carne had hurried down the staircase, filled with irritation and concern for Mostyn. Despite the years, he still felt the old, familiar tug of responsibility and pity for him, as he had felt in childhood. He could not, in all conscience, allow his brother to leave physically and mentally scarred, believing himself to be unloved and unlovable. It was a belief which had crippled Mostyn from infancy and dominated all that he did or thought. Carne must seek him out and beg him to return within, that a doctor might be summoned to tend the gash upon his forehead. Such a blow might well cause confusion, or lack of concentration and giddiness, and set his safety at risk.

'Mostyn . . .' he called out in agitation. 'Stop! Return with me, that we may discuss things calmly, brother to brother.'

Mostyn turned. In the downfall of lantern light from above the stables his face was pallid and blood-smeared, his shirt front stained crimson. 'There is nothing to be said!' Savagely, he wiped away the blood oozing from his forehead and dripping from his mouth and chin. 'We are not brothers! We are strangers!' Despite his whipped-up anger, his voice broke uncertainly.

Carne took a step towards him, urging, 'Let me at least send for a physician to see to your wound.'

'No! Go back within.' Mostyn's voice was contemptuous.

'You have betrayed me and sought to humiliate me. I am less to you than . . . a bastard child! I am nothing.'

Carne reached out to take his arm and urge him within but Mostyn broke away fiercely, crying, 'Damn you! Damn you to hell, Carne! You are the one person on earth I could always rely on and turn to for help, and you have failed me. You are no different from all the rest!' He turned upon his heel and, as the stable boy emerged from the stables with his mount and made ready, Mostyn set his foot in the stirrup and hauled himself up into the saddle, snatching the lighted lantern from the boy's hand. In a second he had urged forward the horse and was away, almost trampling Carne beneath his horse's flailing hooves.

'Mostyn . . .' Carne's pleading voice died away unheard, but his brother's words came back with cold clarity upon the darkened air.

'I shall never come to you again . . . It is ended . . . All ended!'

Chapter Fifty-one

Danfield, who had been dining informally at the house of his uncle, a magistrate, arrived at Great House in the greatest of lathers, his usual languidness forgotten. He demanded to see Mr Llewellyn or Mr Havard upon the instant, stressing the urgency of his mission to the footman. Rhys Llewellyn hurried out without delay to receive the news, fearing that it must be some accident or misfortune at the mine which had brought Danfield in such haste.

'Mostyn? Is Mostyn here, sir?'

'No. He has been absent all day,' admitted Llewellyn, adding sharply, 'the news you bring concerns him, Danfield?'

'I fear so.' Danfield's manner was nervous, his face troubled, as he blurted, 'It is on account of Evan Lloyd, sir, your former clerk.'

'Lloyd?' repeated Llewellyn testily. 'What has he to do with Mostyn? He is immured in Cardiff gaol, convicted for embezzlement.'

'No, sir. He has escaped.'

'When?'

'Some two days since.' Danfield looked uncomfortable. 'I heard the news not half an hour ago and rode here as soon as I was able.'

Llewellyn's face showed nothing but puzzlement as he confessed, 'I fail to see, Danfield, how this concerns either Mostyn or me. Unless the authorities would have me persuade others to deny him shelter and bid him return?'

'No, sir. It is Mostyn he seeks . . . threatening to revenge himself and swearing that Mostyn lied at his trial.'

'But that is palpable nonsense!' Llewellyn declared angrily. 'The fellow is unbalanced, a convicted felon!'

'Then all the more dangerous,' declared Danfield quietly. 'I had best ride out and warn Mostyn. You know where he is dining? Where he is most likely to be at this hour?'

Llewellyn's face flamed with colour as he hesitated, then said awkwardly, 'I know not. He has left neither message nor address where he may be reached.' He added stiffly, 'You will know best those taverns and gaming houses he frequents.'

Danfield nodded curtly, plainly reluctant to be upon his way.

'There is something more . . . something you are concealing from me?' Llewellyn said heavily. 'I beg you will tell me all, Danfield, for this concerns Laurel and Adam too. It had best be told.'

'You are right, sir, in supposing Lloyd to be unbalanced. It is suspected that he had help to escape, and upon the road . . . he struck his gaoler a vicious blow with the iron shackles at his wrists, splitting the man's skull. It is therefore not only an escaped fugitive, but a murderer, they now seek.'

'But he is shackled, and surely cannot go far? He will be captured and returned.' Llewellyn's gaze faltered, his voice dying uneasily. 'Lloyd *is* shackled, is he not?' he appealed anxiously.

'No, sir. That is why they fear others aided his escape, those beyond the prison. His shackles were found abandoned in undergrowth, some three miles from the gaol, and severed cleanly, as at a blacksmith's hands. It is believed that he was smuggled away upon a farm waggon or cart.'

'He has been seen since?' Llewellyn demanded.

'Once, sir, and travelling alone, beyond Golden Grove. It seems he had sheltered overnight in a byre and a farmer had rashly challenged him, bidding him be upon his way.'

'And?' demanded Llewellyn irritably.

'And received a poorly aimed pistol shot in warning.'

'I will ride with you,' Llewellyn said, 'and summon as many of the household servants and those in the yard as can be spared. Some must remain on guard, lest he comes to Great House searching.'

There was a confusion of noise and voices raised in argument at the servants' door, and Bowles, the footman, came almost running in, the coachman beside him in a state of shock.

'It is the stable lad, sir, Gibbs. I had but a moment turned my back upon him and was set upon another task . . .'twas not my fault, for I could not be forever watching . . .' He was gabbling incoherently in his distress until the coldness of Llewellyn's voice served to sober him.

'What of the stable lad? There has been an accident?'

'No accident, sir. He has been struck most viciously and, for a while, was bleeding and senseless. I all but took him for dead.'

'He is conscious now, and knows his attacker?' demanded Danfield.

'Yes, sir . . . for the fellow spoke to him roughly and with threats of violence, demanding that a horse be saddled. But Gibbs would not, and tried to call out for my aid, but was beaten to the ground with a pistol.'

'The man?' demanded Llewellyn tersely.

'Evan Lloyd, sir . . . from Penavon.'

'Gibbs is sure of this?'

'He is indeed, sir, for Evan Lloyd is his own cousin.'

Mostyn, when he rode out from Great House, did not see the frail, malnourished figure at the gate. Lloyd had been waiting silently in the concealing shadows of a pillar, feeling neither coldness nor the discomfort of his aching limbs. Yet Mostyn was as absorbed in his thoughts of Laurel's rejection of him, and Saranne's spite, as was Lloyd in his thoughts of vengeance. For the first time in his life, Mostyn felt loving and yearning for another, beyond that dependence he felt upon Carne and his protectiveness towards Adam. Saranne had maliciously tried to rob him of his wife's new feelings for him, and to make him suffer for a childish prank, a moment of thoughtlessness.

Evan Lloyd watched Mostyn ride out and would have levelled his pistol at him and shot him down but Mostyn's swift urging on of his mount, and Lloyd's nervousness and hesitancy, prevented him. He would creep within the stables of Great House and steal a horse, that he might follow his prey. He had killed once, and would kill Havard too, as relentlessly as any other who stood in his way. There was nothing now to lose. Mostyn Havard had robbed him of all that mattered in life: his good name, his self-respect, his freedom. His brother, who had aided his escape, had begged him to flee to safety in another place, where he was unknown, and might begin anew. When the shackles which bound him were broken apart, he had known terror, weeping, not from the joy of freedom, as they supposed, but lest he fail in what must be done. He had promised that they would see him no more, and they had set him handsomely upon his way with fresh clothing, money, victuals and a pistol, lest some footpad or rogue harass him upon the road.

When Mostyn urged his horse out of the yard of Thatched Cottage, the lantern clutched against the reins and setting a pool of light about the mare's forelegs, he saw nothing, for his eyes were blinded with the flow of blood and with tears. He damned his weakness and those who had caused it, unmindful that it lay within himself. He could not believe that Carne had treated him so cruelly, when it was his brother who had always calmed and comforted him, believing the tie of blood to be deeper than any other. He felt a deep weariness, and did not know if it sprang from loss of blood or a deeper, more destructive, hurt. Cold and unseeing, he let the mare take him where she would.

'Havard!'

He turned instinctively at the sound of his name.

'Here!' the voice commanded thickly. 'This is owed to you.'

An explosion of shot tore at his sleeve and, although he felt no pain, he was aware of the warm stickiness of blood. Hell and damnation! Danger raked him alert and, almost without thought, he urged the mare across the byway and up the hilly slope to the mountains. The lantern shed little light but he had no need of it; he was familiar with every inch of the place, every pathway and quarry, every last gully and stream. Were he blind, he could have found his way unerringly, and the horse he rode was as confident and sure. He did not know what rogue or madman followed, intent upon crippling him or causing his death. The death would be the fool's own. Unarmed and, despite the hurt to his brow and the flesh wound numbing his arm, he would set him a chase to remember and regret! Higher and higher Mostyn rode, the blood surging in his veins, lending excitement to the race and filling him with a wild exhilaration. Here he was free of sadness and of hurt, god-like, set apart. None could touch him for fleetness and beauty of flight. He was at one with Nature and the earth, part of the sky and warm air. Soaring. Invincible.

Evan Lloyd, too, knew every turn and twist of the track, every stone, crevice and blade of grass. His childhood had been spent upon the wildness of the mountain, gleaning kindling and bracken, trapping wild creatures to stave off hunger in order to survive. He had learnt cunning, and far greater than Mostyn's will to survive was his fury to hunt him down and kill. He followed insistently, relentlessly, sure that his time for triumph must come. The bobbing and weaving of Mostyn's lantern gave him direction. Once he had gained ground enough to aim a shot but, in his haste and nervousness, it had gone wide. When Mostyn hesitated, then took the path which skirted the old quarry where the wise woman had died, Evan Lloyd knew that the time was right. The sweat was running from his hairline and fusing his clothes to his flesh, and his heart thudded with the rhythm of the horse's hoofbeats. His mouth tugged into a rictus, the muscles stretched tight in fear as he took the way through bracken and gorse, the stream, and the narrow schism in the rock.

Mostyn, proud and elated on the mountain path, had lost sight and sound of his pursuer and dismounted, laughing aloud for the sheer triumph of his victory. He had won. None could match or subdue him. The blood had congealed and crusted upon his brow but he paid no heed to it, glancing towards his shattered sleeve to see what damage had been caused to his flesh.

The beam of the lantern spilled light upon the gaunt, cadaverous face of Evan Lloyd, a cold death's head, his pistol cocked and ready. Lloyd's finger was upon the trigger, yet, for a second, he hesitated, shocked by the bloodiness of Mostyn's face; his terrified, pleading gaze, the eyes of an animal held in a trap. Evan Lloyd's finger tightened . . . Mostyn sprang with a cry of violence and fury . . . The gun exploded against his breast and he felt the fierceness of it in a blow that sent him falling to his knees. The lantern, released, lay amidst the bracken, its light upon his startled, disbelieving face. There was a bubbling of blood in his throat, and some escaping the corners of his mouth, but Evan Lloyd felt no triumph, only pity and remorse for what he had become, another executioner. He hurled the pistol away and fell to the grass beside Mostyn, sobbing and begging God's forgiveness, trying to cradle Mostyn's head and bring him ease.

Mostyn felt a great lethargy and knew it to be the beginning of death. He could hear the rasping of his own breath and Evan Lloyd's tears, but all as a play, acted by others whom one might study without sharing their emotions or pain. I cannot die here, he thought foolishly.

Suddenly, Mostyn felt a great surge of awareness, an energy born, perhaps, of realisation and despair, or the clarity of death. With a fierceness of anger, he hurled Evan Lloyd away and struggled to his feet, swaying and staggering hopelessly at the quarry's edge. Evan Lloyd ran with arms outstretched to support him and, weeping and smiling, clutching him in remorseless embrace, Mostyn dragged him over the quarry's edge. Now he was flying, soaring, weightless, through the rushing air. There was a redness before his eyes, a misted blood, then blackness that offered no terror, only a promised peace.

Carne never spoke of the grief of finding Mostyn's body, and that of Evan Lloyd, locked in a struggle or embrace that had lasted unto death. Peter, too, remained reticent, disclosing only that he allowed Carne, first, to descend alone, and then struggled awkwardly down the quarry face to give what little comfort he might. Then, slowly, and sick at heart, they made the journey to Penavon that Rhys Llewellyn might send out men to bear the body to Great House, as custom decreed. Laurel, watching from the window of her room, saw Carne and Peter Morrish ride in through the pillared gateway and knew from their bowed heads and the rigidity of their stance that Mostyn was dead. Dry-eyed and resolute, she left her room and, without knocking or hesitating at the door, entered the library where her father would have received them.

He turned, looking from Carne to Morrish helplessly, and Peter hurried to take her arm and lead her to a chair. She moved as if trapped in some dream, aware of it, and waiting only to return to reality. She supposed she spoke, for voices answered her, but they, too, had no meaning. It is I who am dead, not Mostyn, she thought numbly. If I were alive, there would be too much pain to bear. I am empty of life and feeling, flesh grown useless. It is no more than I deserve and I shall be paying for it all the rest of my days. There will be no ending to it. She rose and looked at them as if they were strangers all.

'I thank you for coming. It was kind. You will excuse me now . . .' Her voice was slurred, her gait unsteady and, at the door, she stumbled and almost fell.

Clarissa, glancing into the room and seeing the three men standing mute and shocked, and Laurel's desolate face, ran to support her. 'Oh, my dear, my dear. I did not know, could not have guessed,' Clarissa cried desperately. 'Lean

615

upon me, my dear. I shall take you to your bed.'

'No, Mama.' There was all of grief in Laurel's denial as the tears came and, with them, the pain of loss. 'I closed the door, Mama.'

She repeated the words over and over helplessly until Clarissa feared that shock had robbed her of reason. Then, when Laurel was settled in her bedchamber and Dr Tobin had provided her a sleeping draught, Clarissa sat beside her, holding Laurel's hand as when she was a child.

'I closed the door, Mama . . . I should not have done it. I closed the door upon Mostyn, and he never returned.'

Then Clarissa understood, but could give no easy comfort.

The people of Penavon were shocked and bewildered. There is a pathos in the knowledge of a life brutally cut short and, when the victim is handsome, successful and loved, then it is all the more cruel. Mostyn was all of these things and his youth had been denied the bright promise of a future. What might he not have accomplished, had he lived?

The inquest was brief, the coroner sympathetic. The young stable lad had no recollection of Mr Havard riding out, for the blow to his head had rendered him insensible. Yet he had recognised Lloyd and named him his attacker. Llewellyn's coachman insisted that Mr Havard was a most courageous gentleman and a fine rider, and he could not doubt that he had been waylaid by Evan Lloyd. Instead of fleeing he must have pursued him to his death, despite the pistol wound.

The coroner was swift to concur. The sympathy of all would be with Mr Havard's widow and young son, denied a helpmate and father. Of the murderer, it was fitting that a man given to deceit and violence, who had tried to besmirch an honest man, then kill him in an insane rage, should meet his death by his victim's hand.

At the funeral, Laurel seemed courageous and beautiful and Mostyn's young son, Adam, brave, although clearly filled with grief. People wept openly and Carne Havard appeared the most distressed of all, unable to hide his tears. His wife, walking beside him in her mourning weeds, was compassionate towards him, although her eyes were dry.

Saranne, consumed as deeply as the others with guilt and remorse at her part in Mostyn's dying, tried several times to see Laurel and explain her actions. Her visits to Great House met with the same answer, to the embarrassment of the servants and her own distress: 'Mrs Mostyn Havard is not receiving, in view of her recent bereavement. She asks that you leave your card.'

After a while, she tried no more and accepted that she could do nothing to redeem herself in Laurel's eyes. The invitations to Great House were never resumed. The old intimacy which had brought Clarissa and Sara so much pleasure died with Mostyn, never to be resurrected. Six months from the day of the tragedy, Rhys Llewellyn and his family removed from Penavon to Berkshire, to a country seat which had become Clarissa's by inheritance. The rift between Saranne and Laurel remained unhealed. Carne, already burdened with sorrow at his brother's death, felt deeper regret that he was to be denied sight of Mostyn's son, who would reach manhood unknown to him.

Rice Mostyn Havard was the one remaining link with all that had been between Mostyn and Carne. Saranne determined that the child would never know the identity of the stranger who had tried to abduct him and bring him harm. All she could give the boy, for now, was the assurance that his father, like Adam's, had been a courageous man, brave and fearless in death. There would come a day when he would demand to know more and then Carne would be obliged to tell him. Already the episode which had so terrified him had softened and grown less vivid in his mind, and he never now spoke of it. Saranne prayed that he would forget, or if he did not, that he would never make connection between Mostyn and the man who had assaulted him so callously. She prayed, too, that one day her remembrance of Mostyn might be as shadowed and unreal as Rice, his son's. And that Carne would cease to blame her.

Seven months after Mostyn's death, Carne Havard became the new owner of Great House. Despite a painful stirring of memories, and the poignancy of Mostyn's death, he could not help but feel a quiet elation as he took possession of his old home. It was, he supposed, the natural relief and gratitude of one who, after long journeying, has returned at the last to his roots.

Saranne was resentful that he had taken such a decision without consulting her but she had known from the beginning that to possess Great House was the culmination of his dream. Carne Havard was now a stranger to her and guilt at Mostyn's death kept her silent. She only wished that there had been no rift between the two brothers. Mostyn was dead and Carne already held more power, more property, more money than could be spent in a lifetime. His children would inherit. What now was his goad, the compulsion which drove him so passionately? He was not seeking to build a future, but to recreate a past.

She knew she could, with effort, create a present for herself and her children within Great House and brave the ghosts of those whose shades still dwelt in this place. She set about the task of making Great House a home but, while doing so, she had never felt so remote from Carne, and as little valued. She could see no way to regain what had been lost between them with Mostyn's death, nor how it could end.

When news came from Charles that their bid to buy the Litchard-Llewellyn mines had failed, she could not find it in her heart to be sorry, or to offer Carne honest consolation. Nor had he turned to her. The mines had been sold to the Sir Robert Crandon Company and Penry Vaughan had become an unwitting shareholder. She knew that it seemed to Carne that all he had laboured to achieve, and all he possessed, counted for nothing.

Chapter Fifty-two

It was thirteen months from the date of Mostyn's death that Saranne received a brief letter in Laurel's hand. It stated simply: '. . . Danfield and I have been wed, modestly, as befits a widow, at the village church in Berkshire to which I and my family have removed. Lord Litchard, who spends a great deal of time in London, has made us a gift of his country house and estate, and will remove himself to the dower house, declaring it to be more comfortable and convenient . . . Adam is well and happy. Danfield and Lord Litchard treat him with the greatest affection and kindness. I shall keep remembrance of his father alive always in Adam's mind, for he was a hero at the last, and deserving of it . . . I do not think we shall ever return to Penavon. It holds too much sadness. Danfield has thoughts of selling Litchard House. I trust I will remain, although absent, your friend, Laurel.'

Saranne wrote back in the warmest of terms, sending her felicitations at the marriage and a thoughtfully chosen gift to mark the occasion. She pleaded with Laurel to send occasional news of herself and of Adam, whom she and the children still missed sorely. Thus a hesitant and sporadic correspondence began which, in time, softened into the old amity. It pleased Saranne that Carne would now have news of his nephew, for the boy's leaving so soon after Mostyn's death had grieved him deeply.

There was one who was never mentioned in Saranne's letters, nor enquired after by Laurel. Rice Mostyn was too vital a reminder of what had gone before, and whatever could not be spoken of openly, with charity, between friends, was best ignored. That was the tacit understanding. Yet his living was as firmly in the thoughts of both as Mostyn's death.

To everyone's surprise, Charles Hartrey bought Litchard House from Danfield and pleaded with Sara and Peter to live with him there. However, Peter refused, confessing that its grandeur might keep away those parishioners whom he most sought to help. They would find it intimidating perhaps, and believe him to be equally unapproachable. Charles did not try to change his mind but went to live at Litchard House alone. Saranne feared that it was morbidity which drove him but Sara knew that he felt closer there to Henrietta. Her joyous young spirit pervaded the house as surely as it pervaded his memory of her. Unlike Carne, it was remembrance, not forgetfulness, which Charles now sought.

The shadow of Mostyn's violent death still lay heavily over Carne and Saranne and they were unable to speak of him with the honesty and compassionate understanding of old. Saranne felt that Carne held her entirely to blame for the tragedy, in bringing Rice Mostyn into their lives. Carne, who had grown to love the boy, was reminded of Mostyn in every expression, every small gesture, every word, as he was reminded of his own guilt. He was wracked with pity and remorse but could not speak of it openly for he knew that Saranne had despised his brother. He believed that Saranne's coldness forced them apart, while she believed that he no longer had need of her. Great House and the drift mines seemed more real to him than flesh and blood. They lived and cohabited physically within the same walls, yet in emotional isolation, neither able to reach out to the other.

To add to this discontent, the Sir Robert Crandon Mining Company had quickly established itself in Penavon, taking over the Litchard-Llewellyn mines and with them its workforce. Carne and Charles, denied opportunity to add the drift mines to their own, kept determinedly apart from the

newcomers. Carne thought it inconceivable tha
and Danfield would willingly have approved the sale to
Crandon, whom they affected to despise. Llewellyn, too,
had refused to have dealings with him in the past. What,
then, had finally persuaded them? Surely it was not a question of money alone? Charles never revealed to Carne what
Danfield had shamefacedly confided to him. It was
Llewellyn's decision. Lord Litchard had taken no part in
the transaction and Danfield had supported Llewellyn for
Laurel's and Adam's sake. The simple truth was that
Llewellyn held Saranne accountable for his family's humiliation and Mostyn's death. He had openly declared that he
would deal with a slave-master before a murderer; a murderer of his own kin.

It surprised no-one that there was rumoured unrest in
the Crandon mines, with grumbling and disaffection among
the workforce. The new company was ignorant of mining,
its only motive immediate profit. The colliers' complaint
was that they were forced to work in the cruellest, most
hazardous, conditions, in seams so narrow and inaccessible
that coal could only be cut when lying down, often in
stagnant water, with the ever-present threat of chokedamp.
They were cursed and abused by Swerdlow, the manager,
and accused of idleness. Their wages were cut to near-
starvation level. So embittered and incensed did the colliers
become that they threatened to withhold their labour. The
manager, in turn, threatened to evict them from their
homes and close the company's food shops, should they
strike, believing that the prospect of unemployment and
starvation would halt them. Instead, they silently walked
out of the drift mines, every man, woman and child.
Swerdlow's carriage was stoned and the houses of the mine
officials picketed by torchlight, their windows smashed. In
the end, the docked wages were grudgingly repaid and the
flames of rebellion doused. Yet resentment smouldered and
none could doubt that were it to be fanned by callousness,
it would flame into a blaze beyond control.

Carne and Charles had watched the confrontation with

... or vindictiveness, grateful only that it
... without bloodshed. They believed that,
... Fox and Jack Hollis in daily contact with their
... workforce, and in authority over them, such grievances
... ould not be allowed to fester and deepen. Yet it had been
a salutary lesson. Hardship and ill-treatment had moulded
the men into a community, aware of its latent power. It
was a power which the mine owners would ignore at their
peril.

The new Sir Robert Crandon Deep Shaft Mine, the first in
Penavon, was sunk amidst firm predictions of failure and
harsh reservations from Edward Levis and others about the
dangers to the colliers working below. The hazards of poor
ventilation, inadequate drainage, the threat of explosive
gases and roof falls so deep underground were almost insur-
mountable. Levis actually halted Swerdlow's carriage upon
the highway to offer practical advice upon the safety of the
men but was curtly rebuffed and told not to interfere in
matters which did not concern him.

'We are running a business, sir, and not a charity!'
Swerdlow blustered. 'Since you are so under-occupied at
the Hartrey-Havard mines, I suggest you offer your services
at the poorhouse!' He whipped up the horses and scornfully
drove on. Thereafter, upon his orders, Levis was barred
from the mine and guards set upon it.

Peter Morrish also tried to reason with Swerdlow, in
vain. He boasted proudly that he had managed to contain
costs by lining the shaft with dry bricks, cutting both time
and the expense of using mortar. Moreover, dry bricks
might more easily be used again, should the shaft be abandoned. He had, he confided with satisfaction, further econo-
mised by sinking only one shaft instead of the usual two.

Morrish, disturbed and sick at heart, demanded, 'But is
that not a dangerous practice? Will it not set the miners at
risk?'

'It will set our venture at risk, sir, if we squander our
capital on useless refinements. That is the simple answer!

The investors demand returns, not promises! Now, sir, if you will excuse me . . . I bid you good-day. My time is fully occupied with the work I am paid to do.'

'As is mine,' Morrish declared stiffly.

'You are free, sir, to attend to the spiritual welfare of those employed here.'

'I am concerned with the whole man, woman or child,' Morrish rebuked coldly.

Swerdlow smiled wryly. 'I do not doubt your good intentions, sir. You may preach and succour them without hindrance from the pulpit as often as you choose, but in their own time and yours. They are contracted to the Sir Robert Crandon Mining Company for twelve hours of every day. In that time, we own them, lock, stock and barrel.'

'But they are not guns, sir, inanimate objects to be owned and bartered, they are people, human flesh!'

'Human flesh, starving, may be converted for a crust of bread,' declared Swerdlow, turning dismissively upon his heel.

Carne, with Charles beside him, had ridden out on horseback to meet Edward Levis at their newly enlarged drift mine to discuss the purchase of a water balance windlass, their thoughts upon the advantages it might bring. Suddenly, there was a wild thunderous roar, an explosion of sound which seemed to vibrate the air so fiercely that there was a physical pain in their ears. Carne's horse reared wildly, hooves raking the air, as Charles cried aloud in an agony of shock and fear, feeling that the pressure upon his eardrums must force them to rupture. Carne's first thought, as he steadied the terrified horse, was that it was an earthquake, for the earth still shuddered, and no other power could create such elemental force.

'My God!' His voice was raw with horrified recognition. 'Oh, my God, Charles! The deep mine! An explosion in Crandon's deep mine!' He turned his horse abruptly and, as Charles made to follow him, cried out harshly, 'No! Get to the drift mine. Tell them to bring out the men, with all the tools and equipment they can muster.'

Charles, riding his mare more fiercely than ever in his life before, was aware only of the need to do as Carne bade. He rode swiftly, frenziedly, the mare in a lather of sweat and foam and possessed of the same urgent excitement.

Carne, too, spared neither his mount nor himself in his fury to reach the stricken mine and the disaster, for that is what it assuredly must be. There was no excitement within him, only fear. The image in his mind rose clear, a torment even after he closed his eyes despairingly to banish it. He saw the ravaged face of the penitent, skin charred and peeling into blackened strips, as obscene as the burnt rags fused to flesh. There would be many such deaths today and a few who would weep for the ease of death, unable to bear the pain of survival. He did not know if he could bear the full horror of what he might find.

Saranne, riding to the village with Megan and the children in the carriage, heard a long, distant rumbling, as of thunder, and turned to look at Megan questioningly. There was a strange sound borne upon the air which neither could give name to; then the sound of the church bells, agitated, clanging alarm.

'The mine, Megan! Carne's mine! Quickly! Turn the carriage!'

She could barely form the words for the terror which gripped her.

Megan, seeing the anguish upon her face and the tremors which invaded her, turned the horses. Eynon and Rice sat rigid and pale-faced, clinging grimly to the sides of the carriage, while Henrietta cried with distress. It was Megan who raised her voice to calm them and Rice who held Henrietta close and dried her tears. Saranne's mind was upon Carne and no other. Should he be injured, or dead, then life, and all else, would mean nothing.

Megan had no need to ask where the disaster had occurred for it seemed as if the whole community was moving in the same direction. It was at Crandon's deep mine. All along the way were young women with infants in their arms, or toddlers clutching tearfully at their skirts, hurrying singly, or in small silent groups, faces set and fearful. They stood aside as the carriage passed by, holding the children close, then continued on their way, eyes downcast. There were makeshift waggons too, upon which were huddled the old and those too crippled or weakened to walk. Saranne, hugging her own grief, was unaware of them or their desolate faces, but Megan felt their wretchedness as if it were her own.

Carne found Swerdlow amidst the thronging crowd at the pit head but could wrest no sense from him, for he was incoherent with shock and despair. He seemed to have shrunk, grown suddenly old and confused, assailed by guilt and fear of the carnage below.

It was the overman who took command, at Carne's bidding, and answered his urgent questioning. There were fifty below in all, forty men and the rest women and children, the oldest a lad of thirteen, the youngest an air-door boy, no more than five years old.

'I have been below, Mr Havard, sir,' said the overman, 'but there was little I could do alone, for part of the shaft had collapsed. Although I tore at the bricks with my bare hands, I could not get through.'

'You heard cries? Shouts for help?' he demanded sharply.

'Yes, sir. A few, and weak, but whether real or imagined, God alone knows! Although I cried out in return, they were not repeated.'

The tears were coursing through the coal dust on the overman's face and his hands, held stiffly before him, were skinned and bloodied, Carne saw, by his earlier frantic attempts to tear at the rubble.

'I was afraid, sir, to use naked light so I laboured in darkness.'

'There will be help from my men, and soon, for they are already alerted, and will bring safety lamps and whatever tools and equipment are needed. You may depend upon it!'

'It was the firedamp, sir!' the overman blurted. 'There will be none surviving that blast. The fire would have raged fiercer than all hell itself. 'Tis swift as a wind rushing, and we may thank God it is so.'

'But the voices?' Carne persisted stubbornly.

'Had they survived the blast, however briefly, they would fall victim to chokedamp, and suffocate.'

'You know where the men were working?'

'Yes. The upper four-foot seam. 'Twas known to be fiery, sir, and I had made complaint, but . . .' He glanced towards Swerdlow, adding bitterly, ''Tis money that talks more persuasively!' He broke off, trembling with agitation, to declare, 'I will go back below, now, sir. Even if all are dead, it is owed to them. I am overman! They are my responsibility!'

'No!' Carne's denial was harsh. 'If you will set two experienced men to take turn at the winding, to guide the horses upon the whim-gin, you will better serve! We will need to rely upon the shaft rope for safe descent, and to bring up those who survive.'

The overman looked at him bleakly, hesitating uncertainly, then he nodded, 'You may rely upon that rope, sir. It was changed but two days ago, and upon my orders. Mr Swerdlow had set chains for the descent, claiming them cheaper and longer lasting, but the men would not use them. They were afeared, do you see, for chains may snap at any time, unnoticed. That rope is strong hemp and, even with over-use, its fraying would give fair warning.' He faltered. 'I will find reliable men for the whim-gin, sir, from the loaders and surface hauliers. We are few, I fear, since it is between shifts and our numbers so harshly reduced. But every man would risk himself willingly for those trapped below, alive or dead.'

As Carne nodded acknowledgement, there was the urgent sound of waggons and carriages arriving, with men on horseback rapidly dismounting to unload the tools and equipment piled high. Carne, seeing Charles, hurried towards him. Beyond, Levis was already efficiently ordering the men for action, with Captain Fox handing them safety lamps and implements. Jack Hollis and Benjamin, Carne saw, were already beside the overman at the whim-gin, testing its safety and instructing the hauliers in the turning of the harnessed horses upon the gin arm. They must descend, Levis decreed, five men at a time, to be relieved by others each quarter hour, for no more could safely be accommodated.

The overman at the mine was the first to be lowered, despite the rawness of his hands. He was determined upon it and none could persuade him otherwise. Carne rode the shaft with him upon the rope, glimpsing, beyond the pit head, the anguished arrival of Peter Morrish and Sara upon a cart. As he descended into the darkness, terror rose in Carne's throat and all but choked him. He would suffocate, he thought, panic-stricken, like those poor dead wretches below. The safety lamp, clamped to his waist-belt, gave out an eerie light which served to darken the shadows about him, its glow pale upon the ragged, dry-brick walls and the cavernous blackness about him. Then, with eyes closed against the nausea and terror which threatened to over-whelm him, he found himself upon the pit bottom amidst the rubble of fallen bricks, rock and coal. From amongst those about him, whey-faced and anguished as he, the over-man's blue-white eyes shone luminous against the grimed skin, his smile a rictus, so that Carne could believe it to be a skeleton, trapped in the light. Then the bloodied hands began their fierce thrusting away of brick and stone, stead-ily, remorselessly, fearful of what they might find, and as fearful of what they might not.

It was a long, arduous fight through to the men beyond, for every obstacle had to be cleared by hand, painstakingly, lest a spark from pick or shovel serve to ignite gas and cause further explosion and roof falls. The buckets from the whim-gin were carefully loaded and hauled to the sur-face, each ascent and change-over by the men more hazardous and likely to cause disturbance to the crumbling walls of the shaft.

Above ground there was an air of pessimism lying over all, deepened and broken by the ponderous creaking of the whim-gin, with the plodding tread of the horses upon their circling walk, the lighter tread of the hauliers, and the snorting and fidgeting of the horses at the carriages and carts.

When Carne and the overman, and those who had laboured with them, were winched to the surface, grimy and defeated, it was to see Megan driving in on the carriage, with Saranne and the children. Fear for them made Carne flare in uncontrollable anger, his gaze upon Saranne.

'What, in God's name, has brought you here? Are you mad? You should have had more thought! . . . It is not some outing, to be enjoyed, but a battlefield; a scene of carnage!'

'What has brought us here is you, Carne . . . Our fears for your safety.' Saranne's voice was low, controlled, but two spots of fierce colour burned high in her cheeks. Carne, shamefaced, began to murmur awkward apology, but Saranne leapt from the carriage to face him. Instead of the rejection he feared, she was looking at him with all the old tenderness and understanding. A naked love. She put a compassionate hand to his sleeve and he nodded, then turned wordlessly away, his eyes raw with treacherous tears.

'We will return at once to Great House, my dear,' she promised quietly, 'and I shall see that victuals and drink are brought for all who labour here, and for those who must wait.' She saw the anxiously huddled groups of women and children, and those upon the carts, and her throat constricted with pity. 'I will send blankets and sheets enough for bandaging . . . should . . . should any survive.' The fear lay unspoken between them and Carne glanced towards the carriage, trying to smile reassurance at Rice, Eynon and Henrietta, but the smile was a grimace in his blackened face and Henrietta, bewildered and fearful, began to weep anew.

Before he could go to her, Dr Tobin was beside him, calling out urgently to Megan, 'Miss Griffin, ma'am . . . I do not know how many, if any, will survive this holocaust, but . . .'

'But if they do, you would have someone tend them and ride beside them upon the carts?' she asked.

'The injured will be taken into Litchard House, at Mr Hartrey's orders . . . and the dead to Penavon church. Mrs Morrish is there. She will not leave lest there be need for her,' he replied.

'Then I will remain,' declared Megan firmly. She surrendered the reins to Eynon and scrambled down as Saranne moved to take her place.

'Miss Griffin . . .' Dr Tobin's voice was low. 'You cannot know the reality of it . . . what you must face. The wounds and burns will be bloody and agonising . . . the men savage with hurt . . . It will be sickening beyond belief . . . I do not know if you are prepared.'

'I am as prepared as any other,' Megan said quietly, 'since none will have known such tragedy before. It will be harsher to bear for their wives and children . . . and for those who survive.'

When Megan had returned to Great House, it was just before midnight, and Carne came shortly after. Saranne, who had anxiously awaited their coming, had no need to ask the outcome. It was there in their ravaged, grief-stricken faces. Megan had wept until she could weep no more.

'How many survivors, Megan?' Carne's voice was bleak.

'We rescued five all told . . . although some were . . .' His voice faltered and died away.

'Two only . . .'

'That child . . . the little air-door boy?'

There was a silence in the room so intense that it seemed that no-one breathed or moved, as if their own lives, as well as the child's, were somehow dependent upon the answer given.

'No . . .' It was scarcely more than a whisper. 'Two women . . . that is what Dr Tobin said . . . he made no mention of a child.'

Carne let out a sigh. His face was expressionless, but within he was ripped through with such a fury of pain and rage that he thought he must die with the violence of it. 'There is little more to be done tonight.' His voice was unsteady. 'We had best take what rest we may. There will be work tomorrow aplenty . . . and grief, I do not doubt.'

They made their way, reluctant and exhausted, to their beds. None could speak of the horrors seen, nor hope for sleep, although fatigue drove them to the edges of despair. Carne crawled upon his bed unwashed and unable even to undress himself, and Saranne lay beside him, taking him gently in her arms, cradling him to her breast, hearing the roughness of sobs shaking his body, the bruised flesh of his hands too raw and broken to hold her in return. Her tears mingled with his, for him and the dead child, and all who would never again feel the comfort of warm and loving flesh, only the coldness of earth and a darkness that was absolute. Carne, although he closed his tired eyelids, could not sleep. He had no fear of the nightmares which might come to him, for none could equal what he had seen that day. Awake or sleeping, it would return to haunt him. There were things he could speak of to no-one, and it were best to keep hidden. He prayed soundlessly for the salvation of those who no longer had need of it and, as helplessly, for his own.

There were, at the last, forty-nine dead at the deep pit and only one female survivor, a second woman having died of burns and shock but twenty-four hours after the blast. Of the five who had been trapped between the shaft fall and the roof collapse, none lived for more than a short while once they had been brought out. The air-door boy had been lifted by Peter Morrish, unscathed it seemed, his flesh as innocent of hurt as if he had fallen quietly asleep at his labours. Morrish had taken him to the surface, clutched in his arms, unwilling to let him go, even to the

630

woman who ran from the silent crowd to claim him, taking him jealously into her arms. She refused to surrender him to the charred bodies which were being covered and gently lifted upon the waggons and carts. She rode with him in her arms, dry-eyed and white-faced, staring before her with eyes as sightless as his own.

Carne would never forget the pathos of those disfigured corpses, and those who came forward in terror or resignation to claim them. No more would he forget the stench of burnt flesh and the smell of decay. It hung upon the air as heavily as the palls of smoke and grief. He would always remember how, beyond the second fall, and in the four-foot level where the fiery seam ran, the safety lamps had spluttered and all but died, and how he had had to order back the rescuers although the overman fought with Jack Hollis, beating at him unmercifully, all but crazed in his fury to reach the dead men. Then, when his passion was spent, he had wept like a child, making meaningless apology, and Hollis had taken his arm, weeping with him, and leading him without. The mine, Hollis had already known, would never be worked again. It was unsafe, and none would return to it. It would be sealed and left. A tomb for those who had perished within. A harsh, black dust, and paid for with blood and bone, and the grief of many.

Peter Morrish and Sara had been assisting those with the harrowing task of identifying their dead, and loading the remains upon the carts and waggons. Appalled and sickened by the waste, Morrish found it hard to bring comfort to those who grieved, for he was in sore need of spiritual and emotional comfort himself, drained by the twin horrors below the earth and above. Swerdlow roused himself to stand beside Peter Morrish as the rows of charred and broken flesh increased. In the lantern light the manager's face was pallid and glistening with sweat; a drowned man's face, seen through a film of water. Morrish uttered no word of comfort to the man. He felt no pity within himself, no forgiveness. Memory of the dead child he had held in his arms was too recent and Swerdlow's arrogant insensitivity still too raw.

'A tragic accident! . . . a tragic accident! . . .' Swerdlow kept repeating, 'for which none can be held to blame.'

'You have been below, sir?' Morrish's voice was hard.

'No . . . my duty is here, sir . . . to direct others to best advantage . . . to take responsibility overall.'

'Yes!' Peter Morrish's tone was cold, lacking all charity. 'It is clear that you, alone, must bear full responsibility.'

Swerdlow hesitated, mopping his face agitatedly with his kerchief and licking his dry lips, unable to still the trembling of his limbs as he blurted clumsily to Dr Tobin, 'You are brave, sir, very brave, and you, Mr Morrish. I do not deny that much is owed to you both. The company will not forget it.'

Tobin was too disgusted to speak, but Peter Morrish declared contemptuously, 'No, sir! The bravery is not ours, but lies in the dead you see about you, and those barely living! Those who pursued their labours sedulously, day by day, for such reward. It lies too in those now widowed, or fatherless, or mourning the death of a woman or child. It is to them that the company owes a debt!' His tone was scathing as he ordered, 'Look about you, sir! I do not say, Remember it, but forget it if you can! That is your only salvation . . . I pray, sir, that memory of it will linger with you as long as with those your arrogance has so brutally touched.' They were the first such words that Morrish had spoken in all of his life and he would not withdraw them, although he mourned his failure as fiercely as Swerdlow's.

Upon the day of the burials, the early morning mist lay upon the river and the hills, vaporous and thick. It shrouded and veiled the sun, as if its brightness were an affront to those who mourned, an indelicacy to be ignored, lest it cause offence. Those who grieved their dead had kept quiet vigil by night beside the coffins. Those unknown, and buried uncoffined and in winding sheets in a mass grave, were mourned by all.

632

Even as the first hymn rose, to the carven roof of Penavon church, and echoed from its walls and seeped through the stained-glass windows, the mist rose, and the sun shone bright. The voices joined, soaring, lifting, raised in pity and love, too fierce to be spoken.

Carne gazed around him, so burdened with sorrow and regret that his voice faltered and cracked upon the notes. How dear this place was, and the people within. Memories shifted and stirred, dark and swift-changing as the motes of dust trapped in the light-beams from the high windows, and as elusive. Those whom he would see no more, taken in death: Rice Havard, the father he had loved, and Rhianon before him. Jane and Hywel Prys, Mostyn . . . Mostyn. A pain wrenched at Carne's heart, fierce as a knife-thrust. He had loved him, and tried to believe that Mostyn had understood and had redeemed himself at the end. There were other faces, other lives; Marged Howell, Jethro, Henrietta Danfield, Ruth Bessant . . . poor, wretched William Oates, but seventeen years of age, and Septimus Fortune, companion and friend, his death an unhealed wound.

He glanced up to see Penry Vaughan's eyes upon him with undisguised hatred and, for a moment, he was that child again, within the library of Great House, feeling the terror and bewilderment of one dispossessed and losing all in life that had meaning. Saranne's hand slipped understandingly into Carne's and he thought wryly, No, I do not hate him, for without Penry Vaughan's betrayal, I would never have found the true meaning of my life. Saranne, Eynon, Henrietta, Rice, and those whose loyalty and friendship enriched my life. He glanced towards Sara, her eyes proudly fixed upon Peter Morrish, then towards Megan seated beside her, and felt a great richness of love and humility. It spilled over to embrace Randall Walters, all but blind now, and listening with the intentness of those deprived of one sense and relying more profoundly upon another. These are my people, Carne thought, as Rice Havard had thought before him, and generations before, lost and unknown. I will help the families of those injured and dead, financially and in kind, to survive the horror of their tragedy. Money, although it can bring only comfort of the flesh, is all I can offer. Yet Peter Morrish, with so few worldly goods, has been of more spiritual service to these people than I. I have brought them only death.

Within the church, Peter Morrish's quietly spoken words fell sorrowfully upon the rows of coffins and the grieving; a passing, a promise. Carne's eyes, blurred with tears, lifted towards the fox-red hills. For a moment he could believe that they alone remained unchanged, his comfort and help as in childhood. The stained glass held not the redness of ferns, but of blood . . . and the hills beyond were of blackened ash. He had tried to save a people and killed a valley. Now he had killed his people too. Oh God forgive me! he wept inwardly. He could never forgive himself.